LUCKBORN VOLUME 1: TEARS OF THE MOON GOD

D. A. HOLLEY

First print edition 24 October 2024

ISBN: 978-1-7369854-4-1

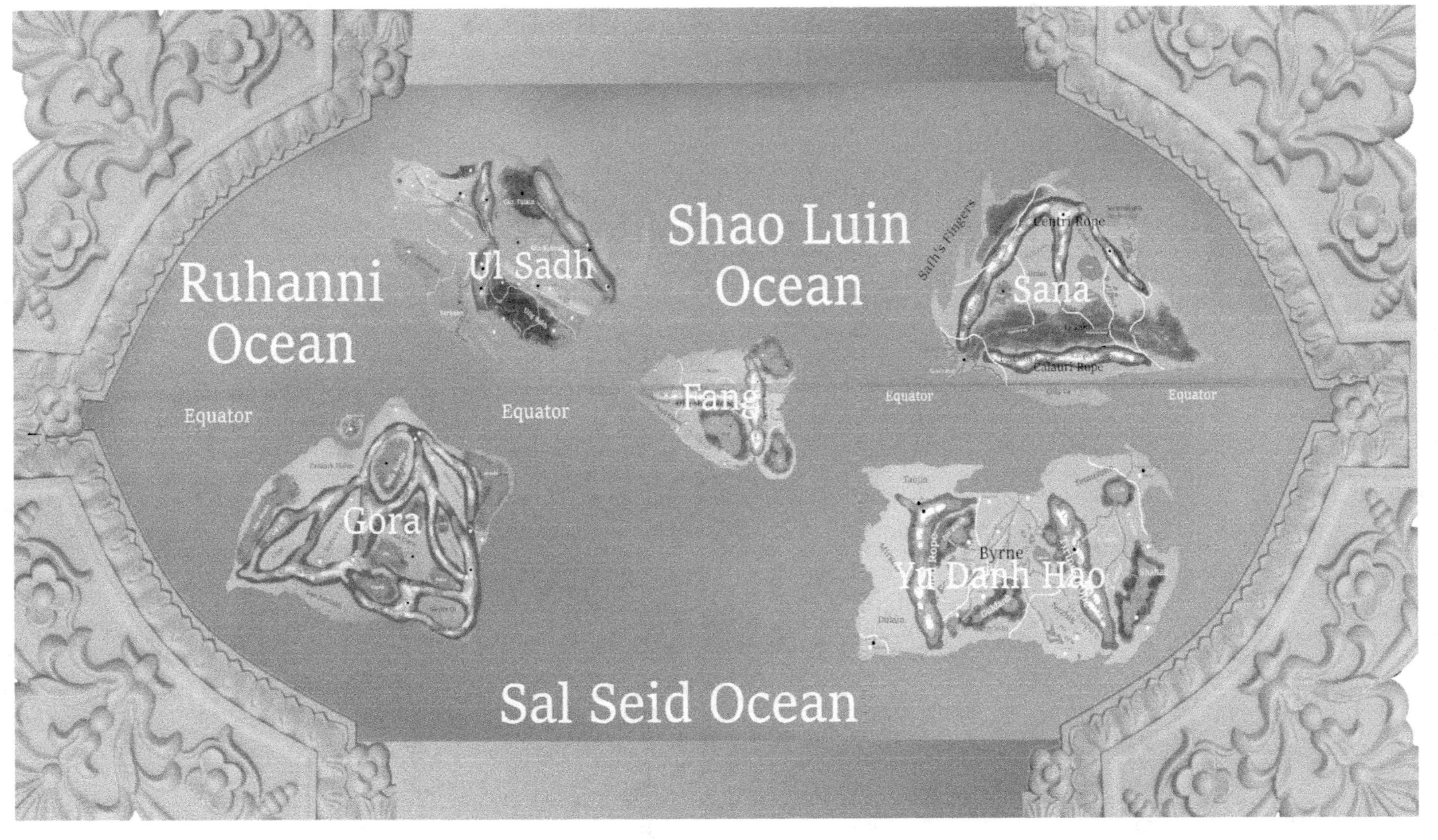

Ruhanni Ocean
Shao Luin Ocean
Ul Sadh
Sana
Sath's fingers
Centri Rope
Calauri Rope
Fang
Gora
Equator
Equator
Equator
Equator
Yu Danh Hao
Byrne
Sal Seid Ocean

Dramatis Personae

Katuwiti

Lura - a Katuwiti forager
Katuwan - a Katuwiti hunter
Xirakura - a Katuwiti spirit caller
Zanwakahat - his brother
Janeira - zanwakahat's wife
Hanwari - a Katuwiti tribesman
Kitwati - a Katuwiti hunter

Magura and Uari

Dakaraluta - a jailer at Ouran Goul pass
Luken - a jailer at Ouran Goul pass
Hurin - the mayor of Ouran Goul pass

Gil Garo

Dupec Safar - a Cloud Man
Ungol Safar - chief of the Dumas Gil Garo
Shaelein Safar - his wife
Coltang Krul - chief of the Tipik Gil Garo
Tanta Krul - his wife
Chakta Krul - their daughter
Arrak Sarr - Chief of the Kachin Gil Garo
Daera Sarr - his wife
Tamlin Sarr - their son
Tursa Hawkeye - chief of the Hakka Gil Garo
Kuuda - his first born (son)
Alaar - his second born (daughter)
Shaede - his third born (daughter)
Karse - her husband
Tulukh - their son
Boen - his fourth born (daughter)

Arrada - his youngest (son)
Gulang - chief of the Kirche Gil Garo
Saerin - his wife
Gaulakh - his first born (son)
Saafha - his second born (son)
Karsa - his third born (son)
Sircha - his fourth born (daughter)
Kachukh - his youngest (son)
Sarri - chief of the Cuu Gil Garo
Shaki - his son
Sauman - chief of the Chikata Gil Garo
Shira - a Cuu youth
Krisna - a Cuu youth
Bora - a Cuu youth
Dangal - a Dumas tribesman

Nixians

Kiresh Njack - a midwife
Syrj Njack - a scarab
Jinga Njack - an engineer
Dinei Njack - a priestess of Ul Sharak

Wanderers

Shulraki Alran - a Sun Man
Xi Didura - a Cloud Man
Ank the Sanark - a Sun Man
Hanuman the Elder - a Cloud Man
Sao Njack - a Sun Man

Uelfin

Saijin - a fortuneteller
Hakka - a matchmaker

Goths

Wu Bane - a pathfinder
Rhul - a Shard

Samil Bane - Wu's half brother
Liudao Bane - their father
Mistress Bane - his wife

Raukha Cartel

Gaul No Eyes - a hand of Raukha
Jaunz Faedrin - a graemein sanark
Garam - a lamb
Hiram - a lamb

Sarkahni

Lisandra Almaine - an old woman
Lisk - a villager in the Fingers
Dane Laebram - a miner

Sangar

Delores - an old woman
Delbert - an innkeeper
Alaster Crouch - an armorer

Pathfinders
Timin - a pathfinder
Suli - a pathfinder

Moonkin

Ibrim Alghoul - a Tulakka prince
Lufir al Suen - a Tului deserter
Faez A'doelle - an escaped slave
Jule the Red - the left hand of Ao Nii
Ordien the White - the right hand of Ao Nii

Tulakka

Abellard II Alghoul - a Tulakka king
Nerus I - A Tulakka king
Ezekus I Alghoul - a Tulakka king
Abellard III Alghoul - a Tulakka prince

Hassan Alghoul - a Tulakka prince
Samara Alghoul - a Tulakka princess
Namira Alghoul - a Tulakka princess

Gods

Lanfin - God of Music
Mu - God of Darkness
Ao Nii - God of the Moon
Gorgus - God of the Sun
Liandal - Goddess of Fate
Tirulain - God of Games
Uldal - God of Ways and Paths
Hou Rok - God of Smiths
Shakh - God of Hunters
Ji Hara - The Rat Goddess
Shah Jagat - Elder God of Death
Fang Ilra - Elder Goddess of Discord
Zara Uyat - Elder Goddess of Order
Mahan Mahain - Elder God of the Mind and Madness
Katcya - Elder God of Luck

Spirits

Echo the Rope - a mountain spirit
Chanwat - a creek spirit
Ho'o - The North Wind
Astair - The East Wind
Salein - a lake spirit
Duijus Kanh - a cave spirit
Syrk the Barren - a creek spirit
Syrk the Bountiful - his sister
Taojin La - a swamp spirit
Rein - a mountain spirit
Hod the Rope - a mountain spirit
Ul Sharak - a river spirit
Gora - a great king
Ban the Rope - his lover
Yu Danh Hao - a great king
Harkanh - a great king
Tao Shein - a plains lord

Gonsai the Wall - a canyon spirit
Sufa Salein - a forest spirit
Pantham Kris - a defunct plains lord
Lafol the Fish - a creek spirit
Gandes Fae - a cave spirit

Prologue

Sonorous song in the voice of a god flooded the Halls of Time. The deep, invasive melody dredged up old hurts and a long simmering anger from deep places within Hanuman the Elder. He heard the edge of fear in that song, the echoes of it came on stronger in the voices of countless inconsequential beings, God Lanfin's direct descendants, who joined him. Deceitful players in the grand games of the gods—the fights they waged with mortal lives—those unholy beings lent their strength to their father, sanctioned his designs for their futures. For all mortal futures.

He closed hooded eyes. His planar cheeks lay slack and ran into a heart-shaped jawline that burned youth into cherubic features under the crazed array of silver lines running across his muted, brown skin, a shatter pattern much like his father's. He sat, and waited as the song threatened the world beyond with instability, as it enticed the River of Time away from its bed, onto a new track carved shallow and wide into the bedrock of the world outside, to dig in deeper with each passing generation, until time again was made stable.

A rumble took the earth. Soft vibrations traveled across his legs, into his belly and chest, out through rattling teeth and shaking fingers. This shift would bring forth new opportunities, explorations into a time not his. A new life seized, its actions recalled, a man would be immured here and forgotten. His birth undone and death denied him, he was coming.

It has been too little time since the last one. He thought.

The intervals between reclamations had been thinning. The interval between seizures, between him and the next man to be taken, amounted to thousands of years. Tens of thousands. A day in this place felt so much like a year without sight of the sun and moon to guide it, without the interplay of darkness and light. Above him was a veil of gray clouds drifting aimlessly, promising rains it never delivered.

How long since Shulraki died for the last time?

Tears for the Moon God

He sifted through memories that did not belong to him, memories which were nonetheless a part of the Elder's identity now, which had shaped him.

He could not identify those splinters of the pathfinder's soul by any direct means. He had been unsuccessful in finding those memories, and perhaps they were not contained here at all, but there had been accounts in other places, outside of the man and the scattered pieces of his soul. Accounts from others who remembered them.

A disgraced gate guard in the employ of a rebel faction in the bush. A counselor who believed too much resemblance lingered in his bald peer for the man he had helped slay, and both counselors in the cabinet of a politically savvy but nonetheless arrogant queen. A trader in the employ of one of Shulraki's rivals. All of them had been strategically placed to see their task done. All of them were remembered by someone, and yet the man himself, the Core of their shared soul, remembered none of them.

He had seen into those memories, too, had seen how they ended with the death of Shulraki Alran, his arrival in the Empress's Land of the Dead.

One hundred years or so, certainly.

A gate guard—a scar running across his cheek which was self-inflicted, who was clad in light armor and poppy red velvet, had been the last to go. The last glimpses of a queen deposed accompanied their downfalls as seen through the eyes of that errant counselor so suspicious of his peer.

Execution. Unceremonious execution on the throne room floor. First for the queen. Then for the conspirators who murdered her.

He wondered what accounts he might find of the aftermath hidden in these new divisions within the halls, the avenues chaining this newcomer to the Halls of Time, to Shulraki's domain, and then to Ank the Sanark's, to Xi Didura's and then to Hanuman's. Five reclamations in all of the time this world had lived beyond Time's touch.

Only five, now.

He wondered what this newcomer had done. What he had done to warrant this punishment. To live out his days in hell.

A sword in its scabbard rested across Xi Didura's knees, and his eyes were trained on it. Such swords were crafted by one maker, were of exquisite quality...every one of them a unique weapon imbued with power to imitate what lay in nature or in the godly form, and bound to one, mortal soul. He sensed the echo of the maker's will inside a song rising from some place east of him, some place outside these labyrinthine halls where time moved and lives played out, and the contributions of each individual fed like tributaries into generational streams, defining whole eras.

He recognized that echo, saw in his minds eye an island concealed within a tower, a verdant hill, a vacant dais and a cherry tree rising from its heart. He wondered at why that weapon had been given, whose soul had been bound to the herm, why he had been reclaimed.

This was no place for blissful souls or those with honorable intentions. It was a hell set forth by the gods for those who had committed the worst kinds of sins. It was strange, then, to think his master would make the same mistake twice.

"No, that's not quite right, is it?" he mumbled as the rush of white-capped

Prologue

waves drove hard across dry halls, promising the formation of new avenues with this newcomer's arrival.

Rein will never take on another acolyte. He promised that much.

But here was a mortal man, a man touched by an Elder God and carrying its power, or he would not have been seized by the God of Music, would not have been sentenced to this state of un-being, this erasure. Here was a katcyakin of unknown origin, his deeds stripped from the record, being purged from the annals of history as he sat there watching Wrath, feeling its pulse quickening behind hammered steel as it called to its cousin.

So fast coming behind Shulraki Alran. Are we so much more a threat in these waxing days?

Between Hanuman and him had been tens of thousands of years. Before Ank's reclamation, the interval had been nearly as wide. But something had changed with the Sanark's taking, and the interval that preceded Shulraki's taking had been less, fractionally attuned to the precedent set by those who came before him.

In the years since his claiming, a century could not have gone by, and yet here was another. Perhaps the last for some time yet. And God Lanfin was enraged by this claiming.

Why was he so enraged?

He turned his head away from his sword. Shadows played against the planar ridges and valleys defining wide and high cheekbones, sharply tapered eyes forested with thick eyelashes. A blacksmith's build made a rock of Xi Didura as he sat and played his fingers over the lacquered, wood scabbard. His skin was crossed over with wavy, honey lines like those crossing disturbed water, the surrounding skin a deeper shade of amber.

He watched as faint mists picked a path across the distant horizon, mists to call forth a coming flood. The River of Time could only take so much pushing before it flooded its banks, drowned all of these halls in murky waters. He had almost escaped the last time it happened...the only time.

He watched those mists pick up under the washed out gray ceiling—the Goddess of Storms held back and yet honor bound to block sun and moon alike from setting eyes on those imprisoned here—and wondered what this newcomer had done. How close he had come to spitting in the eyes of the Waxing World gods. How close he had come to inviting the attention of the Great Arbiter onto them.

He must have done something truly foul to be taken so soon.

He climbed onto his feet, fastened his scabbard to his hip, and set off to meet this newcomer. To offer condolences if the need should arise, but mostly to say hello.

Great waves rose over the heights of the labyrinth's cyclopean walls. Lanfin's song suffused the halls, joined by countless thousands of others. Ank held himself back, listened to the fury threaded harmonies, the cascade of voices joining their ancient father's theme. He held himself back, for to join that song would be to invite unwanted attention to him, would alert the god to how deep the well of his great deceit went. How much was there that the gods wished was not? He was not ready to make his play just yet, would not be for some time.

A white crest formed at the height of the wave as the Great River climbed, leaving its banks behind for brighter pastures. The river followed where Lanfin

Tears for the Moon God

guided it, off and to the east, toward a break in the clouds where a dazzling sun pressed rays of golden light into this domain, a rare showing of his power in this place without change.

He delighted at seeing those rays of light, and knew the others must be so entertained by this showing. At least, that Xi and Shulraki would be. It was no secret to him that the Elder hated the Sun God, Gorgus, but that was his business. It was of no concern to the Sanark what the others had done to anger the gods—who they hated most within the pantheon and why. He had chosen to go to this place of his own will. He did not regret his choice.

Still, the river slipped its banks and promised the formation of new halls built from the clastic sediments and stones within its former bed, and the arrival of a newcomer with them. Endless pools would be left in the wake of this reclaiming, pools containing the arcs of so many lives as the man had touched, as had been affected by his actions through proxies, through others who had come in contact with him, lived with him...or under him.

He did not wonder why the god was so angered. In the song was a window into a past reclaimed, and he saw quite clearly what transpired there. He had seen what transpired in the life of Shulraki when he was reclaimed. Did not have need of those pools in the way Hanuman did, nor was he over fond of the idea of losing some of himself to them. The Elder had gone quite mad before the arrival of the first of them after him, had most likely not realized it then.

He pitied that man, but knew too there must always be a first. The explorer on his expedition across the new frontier must inevitably make mistakes in his enterprises, and the mistakes made by that man had been grievous. Had cost him much of his sanity in those years of loneliness, visiting in on other people's lives, their memories, becoming them for precious hours across the unending day.

He listened, and saw the old, squat shack on its hill, the house of the Luck God, and knew the newcomer had made his wish...had received his blessing. And he closed the new chapter in the long history of the Wanderers there. He needed no more from the god, nothing more from the newcomer. Nothing in those visions would change his life in any gainful way, after all.

Hell is eternal.

He touched his cheek. White paint covered every inch of exposed skin from the top of his bald head to his toes. His palms and the bottoms of his feet were covered in red ochre, and even streaks of the same pigment connecting his under eyes to his chin, like tear tracks, crawled up to what would be his hairline. The Sanarks of his homeland all wore this paint, but his served a different purpose than theirs, an extra purpose beyond the ceremonial calling to the body's purpose, the twin souls it housed.

Behind that paint was skin the color of polished gold, the mark of a katcyakin, a Sun Man. He wondered which breed this newcomer would be.

Sun Man or Cloud Man? Will he break the trend, or will he set it?

The wave rolled across open lands, carried the body of the river behind it. In its wake, the first halls would be forming, rocks piling on rocks, gravel filling in gaps like mortar. He sensed a building pressure as elder power rose to guide them, as discordant energies laid out paths those walls would close in, as mad power hemmed in pools and isolated memories, as the lives of countless mortals were snatched up, and they were given a new lease on life. A chance to start over.

Prologue

Shulraki marched after the river. Rare was the moment when a Wanderer saw it with his own eyes. Ank would have been the last to have such an opportunity, would have seen this towering wave carry on ahead of him with Shulraki's own reclamation. It was a beautiful thing, this vast wave, this monumental wall rolling ever onward toward whatever avenue the God of Music had set forth for it, and yet the sight of it saddened him.

Within that wall of water were countless lives, hundreds of millions or maybe billions gathered up and hauled off to live again in this wide, new world. There were opportunities inside that band, to live in absence of whatever ills had plagued them. The great tragedy of it all was that they must forget all they had done in those reclaimed lives, the ones they had lived in the shadow of this newly arrived usurper.

He could be nothing less than that. The gods did not see fit to seize just any katcyakin. They were not all held equal under the laws of those ancient creatures. There were cloud men whose throats were cut when they were moments out of the womb, sun men who had brought prosperity to their people the world over. There were those who had done services to the gods in their time, and had been given over to Shah Jagat when their climb into old age had ended, and the fight went out of them, and they could finally be at peace.

No, this was not a final resting place for good people, katcyakin or others. It was a place for those who had flown too close to the sun and had their wings clipped. Though he wished he could remember what he had done to warrant seizure, he nonetheless knew the gods had made no mistake in taking him. It was no secret to him Fate wanted something from Saodein, that the nation was a means to her ends. Whatever he had done had thrown her plans for the nation into disarray.

He smiled.

Thinking about those perilous days never failed to bring him joy. If there was one thing he could take away from them, it was that being immured here was a proportionate punishment to the crimes he had committed across seven lives. Joy, then, was for knowing what he had done was worth it. That the taste of revenge was sweet.

He shambled after the wave as new walls were built ahead of him, as the corridors were filled with scattered ponds all choked with reeds, with carp and slender eels swimming in their depths, all there to twist the stomach into knots, all eternally out of reach.

Lordosis twisted his spine, carved a prominent hump into his back, and a shroud of black silk covered his hobbled figure. Long arms pumped back and forth as his feet beat an uneven cadence over chipped tiles and sandy soil. He dodged those pools as they emerged, the strips of land between them becoming narrower as he pressed on. Tapered, mono-lidded eyes fixed on the wall of water, watched as carp and eels drifted through them, as disturbances in the wave gave way to vivid scenes taken from lives lived within the river's embrace. Thick, white hair swung around his shoulders and spread across his back, and beneath a crooked nose, a coin imprint bearing the bust of his former queen had been seared into his lips, where it remained to remind him of the first time he had died. The only time he remembered dying.

Tears for the Moon God

The images that came back to him were all births and deaths, with no connective tissue to tell him if a mortal born in one scene was the same who died in another. The images rose up and collapsed shut again in mere seconds, giving him just enough time to latch onto them. Violence took some of those down—battles fought in contested lands, from tall ships on wide seas, murders in houses and streets played out in quick flashes. But not all of those ends were met with violence. As many eyes slipped closed against blissful faces in dim lit rooms, as many of those lay peacefully in bed with loved ones crowded around them.

The pools formed up so close together now the footing became treacherous. To fall to one side or the other would be to take the forbidden plunge, and come away less than he was.

Waters cast across his path blocked his way forward, and the wave rolled on, leaving a lake sprawling across a wide open lane and the waters crawling back toward him. He wondered briefly if this was the bank of the new river bed, wondered if he had found the way out of this place at last.

Cyclopean, stone and gravel walls continued to emerge as the lake spread wider, and the cresting wave had not yet toppled. He held himself back from it, unwilling to take the plunge for fear this broader body of water held its own secrets, concealed in plain sight. If this was part of the greater design of the Halls of Time, or if it was something else. Something new. Something the gods themselves had not predicted might be.

He held back as the waters were set, the walls rising up around them, and watched that wave make pace away from him. Watched as it rolled toward a new bed, and a far bank materialized barely within sight of him. Watched as new walls rose up to close in the far shore, to close it off so that he could not see it. And this expanse of the Halls was fixed, the true and last barrier between his stable domain and the new territory defined by the life of this new prisoner. Where all the lives reclaimed were those he had touched, and all of those memories were stripped away, leaving each of their owners a second chance.

To live again. To live better. If they could only resist the temptation to live out the same lives.

The wave collapsed. Its leading edge carved a path downward. Its white capped fringe rolled over, formed a barrel. Spiraling waters reflected images taken from countless lives back at Sao Njack, a dazzling array of events he had lived fed back to him through the eyes of so many others.

There were people he knew in those scenes. People he had come to call friends. Allies in wars he had waged against kingdoms and nations spanning half a continent. Enemies pulled down by his hand or the hands of his regents, and others. There was his shield maiden, the wicked old crone who had helped in his time of need despite everything he had done to her people. There was Xirakura, a shaman from a guardian tribe who had been so kind as to heal his father once. There was the royal family of Tulakh, who he had deposed in what would come to be his greatest regret in this life. Countless images all dancing in and out of focus called to battles across all of the lands of Ul Sadh. Battles he had fought and won. Battles he had lost. His empire consuming more and more territory until he was met with the man who would become his lover, who even now birthed an ache in his chest beneath the clavicle. An ache that had nothing and everything to do with love.

Prologue

Kaleidoscopic images cascaded across the barrel wave as it rolled forth, carrying him on and on, down and down toward landfall. Kaleidoscopic images gave way to singular truths, singular visions. First, the dilapidated house he had gone to within the Echo Rope, the place where he had made his last requests of the Luck God, to whom he owed everything. Then to a forbidden place surrounded by dunes. A shrine which was really a tomb; a tomb which was really a prison. To see the one he loved in stark relief against barren earth which spanned to the horizon, to touch on distant mountain ranges to the east and west, Echo's ancient rope, and Rasheik's younger towers.

His lover was uncommonly tall, broad shouldered and thickly muscled. He had inherited his father's blunt jaw and planar features, his mother's softer eyes and lips. His skin was a muted shade of brown and crossed over with lighter traceries as all Cloud Men were, and he dressed in the way of the Dumas Gil Garo, his tribe. Grouse and crow feathers danced in his hair, which fell in a curtain down his back; a thick, beaded braid slung over his shoulder. A gold armlet encircled his bicep on the same side, one forged to resemble a suspended flame. War paint greased his torso, arms and legs, and a double handprint made to look like the spread wings of a crow dressed the lower half of his face. He was everything Sao Njack had ever wanted, the only man who had ever truly made him feel human.

And he would never see him again.

The barrel collapsed. Waters rolled over his back, forced him under. He was drowning. His lungs seized around inhaled water. Whole schools of carp and eels swam around him.

The current pummeled him. Beat him down, threatened him with broken limbs and bruised muscles.

It raked him over broken tiles and coarse sand. Left him in its wake as the wave spilled forth toward its new bank.

He hacked, vomited musky water onto the tiles. A crater welled up before him, and two fish flopped around madly inside it. A carp and an eel, just those two.

He hacked up water, and the crater drew it into itself. Sweat oozed from his pores, water bled from every one of his orifices. The stream swam away from him, leaving him bleary eyed and exhausted, and the crater was filled. Filled with the essence of him.

His memories.

His life.

His eyes drifted closed. At the edge of the new formed pool containing the essence of his life, of him, he passed out

Part 1:

Wanderers

Figures in Shadow

Mahan Mahain crossed Ba Gora Plain. The East Wind chased after them, a gusty whisper tickling the back of their neck. Six personalities were housed in the Elder God, and each vied for dominance over all the rest, a constant shifting seen in the way shadows played across their figure, highlighting and obscuring features, making new beings of them by making use of the available qualities.

Ba Gora remained sleeping, oblivious to the Elder God's passing and the spirit tailing them. A single strike, a brief but pointed display of their power, might shake their shadow loose, grant Mahan Mahain their privacy, but that would never do. It was better, now, to be seen. Better to invite attention from her betters and her peers. They would not be returning to this place once their errand was done, after all. Who better to ensure their work was not undone than the spirits who rode the four winds, and their master.

Sha Kron was no fool. He remembered the first days, when spirits and gods waged war on each other, the old alliances broken and the gods made usurpers. It had been him who helped set the balance of powers in place in the Waxing World and beyond. He would not have forgotten the dangers housed within this shrine, this place beyond the sanctioning of even the God of Ways, where no true road traveled.

Other gods than them had plans for this world, and the consequences of their intervention would be devastating. Not just to Mahan Mahain, but to the host of spirits they sought to aid. And they were far too ignorant to weather this cataclysm.

The East Wind, Astair, followed; her touch soft against their neck, brazen for that she made contact at all. The spirits, all but a few they could count on two hands, were seldom so brave. She made her presence known. Her voice among the reeds, her touch on their back. She knew the danger in confronting an Elder God, yet she did not hide.

They paused in their approach.

This spirit, so bold as to touch them, to reach for the God of Mind and Madness, wanted to be known. Wanted them aware of her. And they saw in her a use.

Figures in Shadow

Perhaps—they dare not get their hopes up, for this was a world for madness—an ally.

They waited there amid the grasses. The mountainous horizon a distant shade, a wraith whose own lord had been free of the subservient order a Rope might enforce for too long. A judgment was soon in coming, they suspected, but it could not be unveiled by the mountains alone, could not be enforced without a master's influence.

They knew which master might assert order on this chaotic, unbalanced world, which would do the least harm to those short-lived creatures who infested their hides, burrowed deep under their skin, walked like lice across their scalps where dense forests grew like hair, providing them shelter.

The winds may not like it, but this conspiracy, this meeting of old enemies, would save them even as it broke them. The time of the Arbiter was coming to a close. Too many voices were risen in dissent, too few valued the great separation— its consequences, its promises.

Mahan Mahain turned to The East Wind, a corporeal entity at last.

An unwitting mortal confronted with Astair would see her as a diminutive child—an unassuming girl, her hair the color of wet straw and hanging lank over a round face. Her eyes were bright and discerning, but the gaze she set upon the god belonged to something ancient. A gaze filled with wonder and worry, for what was done here would have far reaching consequences, echoes spanning far across this world.

She watched the shadows play over their features, hunting for distinct faces, to identify who would speak—which voice, which personality would emerge to confront her.

Would the voice be that of a sympathizer, someone she may reason with? She did not know.

They did not, either. The six personalities who shared the name Mahan Mahain were in flux.

The War Lord kept his focus on the ever watchful moon, a creature he disdained, for the madness which would be soon in taking the Lesser God conflicted with his own desire for logic and reason. Bloodshed he understood, but Ao Nii was too often indiscriminate about which lives he took. Too often, the moon god could not be reasoned with. And so, the Neutral Mind would not abide him.

The Hag watched the mountains, where she could wrest control from the others, for it was them who would suffer most should this plot bear the intended fruit. Too long with no Rope to guide them, yes, too long left under the impression the old times were dead, a bitter memory. The Fouled Mind could not abide them.

The East Wind might fear those two. They were cunning in a way their mad counterparts were not, and too stubborn for her silver tongue to be of much use.

The shadows ranged over the planes of Mahan Mahain's face, crossing through four other domains as each of their remaining personalities observed and passed their judgment on the cherubic spirit. It was not in the nature of the god to be of one mind in matters such as these, yet a consensus of sorts could be achieved.

The majority coalesced, and a speaker was chosen.

The shadows played with their features, highlighting the hollows of their cheeks, drawing a narrower profile. A madness entered silver eyes, a disordered melancholy which lived in the god, which called to their regrets. The shadows

Tears for the Moon God

danced across their robed figure, forcing the silhouette to shift, become slight, somewhat feminine, though the visage was still decidedly male, or perhaps closer to man than woman. The body, as it appeared in that moment, was angular and slim. The shoulders were not overly broad. The limbs flowed in a way that spoke of natural grace.

Ordered madness, the Sage, emerged. A youthfulness born in grief—not for any lost love, not for any victim of Shah Jagat, but for all who lived, for all who were afflicted with the condition of suffering—defined him.

The East Wind was not mollified.

"Walk with me, spirit." he said, his voice smooth like ice, of middling tenor.

He gestured along the path he had been traveling, a path undefined. The Gods of Ways and Hunters avoided this place, for the roads, the inlet paths, would not yield to them. Such passages inspired fear in them, for their ways home were in constant flux, unreliable and thereby unwelcoming to those whose natures lay in tracking and navigation.

The spirit obliged. Her hunched posture, the way her gaze shifted at the slightest sign of movement, spoke to her anxiety. A burrowing owl burst into the air in a flurry of plumage. Mice scurried across the roots of tall grasses, but they would not come close enough to see the Elder God. Only to know they were there. Only that. Their mother was not here to protect them.

"What do you know of poisons?" the Sage asked.

"Very little, sir." she said. "Why should the wind care if man succumbs to a snake bite? Healing is for the rivers and the streams."

"Ul Sharak does not heal."

"Death is its own form of healing."

"And the winds do not cull?"

She shook her head. "Our way is not to enforce a judgment on those creatures."

They were close now. Close to their destination.

Ba Gora forgive me. One day, you will come to understand.

"A poison has taken this land." They said. "The balm against it is chained."

She flinched, and they knew their intent was plain.

They pressed on. "There are plans within plans associated with these lands, but they are not all ours. Our children seek what they have always sought, but they are closer to attaining it now than they have ever been. This requires our...intervention.

"It is with great sadness we witness your clashes, you understand. Yet, we recognize a necessity for greed, a lust for power. Their power has been uncontested for too long."

"Uncontested?" Astair protested, a hot flush blooming in her cheeks.

They understood her anger. It changed nothing.

The entrance of a cave, flush with bare earth and situated such that the grasses swallowed all notion of it until a traveler was nearly upon it, emerged before them. Hot, persistent breath was exuded from its mouth.

The East Wind knew what this place was. The roads the gods might take would not lead within a day's journey of it, but she was not so bound. No road took root in open air, for the skies provided no footholds, and the Spirit of Breath would allow them no glimpse of the shrine.

Mahan Mahain remembered.

Figures in Shadow

This chaining had been no easy task. It had tested the ancient alliance almost to its breaking, tested the spirits and the Elder Gods alike.

"You would sunder this peace." The East Wind asked. "To what end? The Lesser Gods are tested. Daily, they are. There are spirits in these lands they fear--"

"Who fear them in turn. Or who treat them with indifference, as the Rope Lord, Echo, and his woman. They are not without adversaries. On this we are in agreement. But they have reached a stalemate, and this we cannot abide."

She paused. They kept walking. She watched their back, wondered at their intent, the meaning of this...violation.

"Why?" She called after them. "Why now?"

"Because they have grown to understand what I have just expressed. There is advantage in indifference. They have decided to exploit it, and thereby threaten this tenuous balance."

"And you will correct this imbalance? By freeing...*him*?"

"I have no such power." he assured her. I am merely here to apply pressure where it may set the wheel to the track, where momentum may be built."

"Toward what conclusion?" desperation had entered her tone. Still, she did not follow.

A private smile touched their lips. "Reprisal. The opening, if you will, of the third act."

The East Wind was silent. She turned her back on them.

Not an ally, then. Not yet. The Sage thought.

Not ever. The Warlord intoned. *Not now.*

A messenger, to awaken those monsters of the old times. The Harlot drawled. *To bring Tak the Fire to violence, if he can be swayed.*

The Warlord laughed. It was a sound cold as iron and mirthless.

Mahan Mahain passed into the mouth of the nondescript cave. That its inhabitant had been so long without sunlight was its own sin. That he lived where the gods could not see, one more. But the worst sin, the greatest cruelty, the weakness they sought to exploit was other than those trivialities.

The Great King had a lover. A spirit and a man. And they alone could reunite them. If not in body, then in mind. For theirs was the domain of thought and its consequences, and the Rope once loved by the Great King of this land, owner of its first empire, was claimed by the Sage's own voice. A madness born in grief, which he alone could resolve.

Which he alone could cure.

As the healer drew poison from the vein, so would his promised balm be applied to the lover's spirit.

The shrine's entrance was unremarkable. A jagged-walled tunnel carved by wind and water into the bedrock, which descended at a shallow angle for a quarter mile before taking a steeper turn. This close, the Great King's power could be felt like thick rust on the edge of a knife. An even flow, interrupted by pits and valleys but steady, grating against Mahan Mahain's skin.

The Harlot's malice was palpable. Chaotic energy rippled through her, compounding with every step Mahan Mahain took forward.

What made the Harlot excited should give them all pause. The Hag had never been a beacon of moral superiority, but she was nervous now. She did not like this,

Tears for the Moon God

any of it. That they should be in this place, where they had not walked in millennia...was this needed? Could there be another way?

But no, that ship had sailed. The Warlord knew. The Sage, too, understood the need for this errand. The time was long past that something be done to reassert order. There was this, and there was tipping the Scales. To bring the Arbiter into it would be to invite madness into the mortal coil.

No, this way is better. The gods would quail in the face of him, to know his wrath so...summarily.

They would follow this path for it was the lesser evil. They would follow it to its end, and the gods of the Waxing World be damned. Their enablers would not sit idly by while these events unfolded, that was true, yet still this was the proper path. The most egalitarian. The least complicated.

The tunnel closed on an open pit flush with its base, the floor a disc of obsidian lacking any obvious flaws. A fire burned eternal from within a brazier like a manger, all of iron and black with old soot around its edges, and beyond it rested their quarry.

Chains pinned the Great King to the smooth wall behind him. Each link was inscribed with glyphs of a language long fallen out of use, whose origins predated humanity's migration into these lands, their infestation.

They remembered the first inhabitants of the land. A hard people. Theirs had been a bitter world—war torn, in constant flux—but from those bitter times came the workings of greater forms, of greater purposes.

Within those chains were locked the stories of twelve lands, twelve mountain ranges. A promise of an end to their trials. There also were ancient prayers to the gods they worshipped. Some lesser, confined to the Waxing World. Some, like Mahan Mahain, greater, beyond mortal comprehension.

In the chaining of the Great King was a history, yet the hands that carved those glyphs belonged to no mortal, no common man. Salt still powdered the ridges where the carving had grown crude, scarred the iron in places, muddying the faint, ember glow which emanated from them.

The figure chained there was slim, square shouldered, and toned. His onyx hair hung loose about his shoulders, except for twin braids at his ears which were decorated with stone beads and bands of gold. A gilded cuff clung to his right wrist, and on the left a bangle from which many feathers dangled. Another pair of bangles circled his bicep, and a beaded necklace held secure a gold chip inscribed with similar glyphs to those binding him over his chest. The pendant was not of the same making, the name etched into it a token of remembrance. He was otherwise naked.

The Great King watched Mahan Mahain approach the brazier in silence, watched through cold, silver eyes which shone out of a bronze, boyish face—hollow cheeked, the nose sharp and slightly down turned.

They recalled the depictions the Katuwiti attributed to him. Brutal likenesses, which envisioned him a broad-chested brute, tall and domineering. It was in the nature of legends to confuse details with increasing frequency as time flowed along its unerring path. For the tribes of his lands, a fusing of identities, a convergence, had blended the figures and faces of the king and his lover.

Mahan Mahain regarded him, the shadows swirling about him, drawing out hard planes and sharp ridges, highlighting shoulders, diminishing hips. The man that emerged was unemotional, calculating. The last of the six to take part in this errand, the Mask.

"No time for small talk, then, old friend?" the Great King said coldly.

"We were never friends, but perhaps we can be allies for a time."

"A hard sell." The Great King lifted his arm, the chain links clattering against each other, adding their own emphasis to the truth he had not spoken.

"In this, there are those who might sympathize." The Mask said. "Katcya, for one. Shah Jagat."

"Gods as likely to betray you as I." The king spat. "Luck and Death, such tenuous things, so quick to claim the innocent."

"You would claim--"

"What claims I once possessed to this world are long passed into new hands. Your brood ensured it would happen, did you not...when I had lived beyond my use."

"Enough, Gora." Mahan Mahain's tone was a blade in the dark. "Of all of the kings we warred with, you were the most indifferent to mortal occupation. This and this alone is why I seek to aid you. Were your goal of domination achieved, the world would suffer little. Better you, then, than Ul Sadh, or Fang, or Harkahn."

Gora's eyebrow twitched. "Strange for a god to view me as anything but an obstacle to his own success. I am humbled. You approve my conquest?"

"Hardly." Mahan Mahain said. "Your time will come, Gora Soft Touch. When it does, I hope you remember who opened the path for you."

They turned to leave, to return the Great King to his eternal isolation, that he might think. He was sorely out of practice in that.

"What's in it for you?" Gora called after him.

Mahan Mahain smirked, and said nothing.

Let him chew on that, too. What could I gain from cutting you loose, Gora?

He paused then, and almost as an afterthought, gave voice to the last of his truths, the only one—at this moment, in this place—that truly mattered. "They say Ban has gone mad in your absence. His screams are heard across Sufa Salein's forest. He cries out to you, yet you do not hear him. A last cruelty from the Tetract and my kin for him. Though, of course, you could not have known.

"I was thinking. Perhaps, I will pay him a visit. For all that he is mad, there is still value in convening with such a tyrant."

He stepped up the sloping path, and left this time in truth.

Gora contemplated Mahan Mahain's words long after he had left. Visitors among the gods had ceased to flow into his shrine long years into the past. The exhilaration of gloating before a once conqueror—thorn in their side, struck down not by their hand, but by those they would come to call enemies—had lost its appeal it seemed. Or, perhaps, the edge his memory instilled in them had been blunted.

Ban had never been as flexible as him, as adaptable. It was his steadfast refusal to tolerate the schemes and politicking of lesser spirits that made him so useful, yet that hardness, that brutality was his undoing.

Alone among the Rope Lords, he had been selected for imprisonment. Too loyal to a Great King to be trusted with his freedom, he alone among his kind would see the Wandering Period ended. They sought stability, and brought it forth from wrong places. Trusted too much in their own power, too little in Gora's ideal.

There could be peace made between the kings, those with the proper

Tears for the Moon God

temperament, if those who ruled could be convinced of the merits of joint lordship, of becoming not king but steward over their vast territories.

Yu Danh Hao had understood that; though like Gora he was not prepared to capitulate to another throne. Too long and too fierce had been their conflict, but perhaps the fires of their old rivalries had cooled, perhaps a treaty could be drawn out of the ashes.

The Elder God, for all they were prone to these forays into unknown territory, was unaware of the echoes of their choice, the ramifications a lone, free king would sew into this world. Did he seek the breaking of the Scales, a reunification of what had long been separate, or was the Great King to be used and cast aside, to bring down those who would see that very task done.

There were loyalists and dissenters among that order. Those who would see their father resurrected. Those who would see the Master of the Scales usurped in favor of their own agendas, to sit where he now sat, and become arbiter between Waxing and Waning worlds themselves.

There were the third kind, in those days. Those whose ambitions lay elsewhere. Those we called friend in the days after the child that should not have been was slain. But those were different times. Before Sal Fier was poisoned, the seas he ruled left in chaos. A mistake I would not have allowed to pass had I known what Ban intended.

Ban, the vengeful fool. There were reasons for his imprisonment. The Tetract had been greatly disabused of notions of peace between their kind and his. Lines drawn in the sand, communications cut, old bargains abandoned.

Dark times, indeed.

He considered what shape the war renewed might take. Ul Sadh would have to be dealt with. And Sana. Both had been tyrants in their time of freedom, both savage and bloodthirsty rulers. They had not understood the nature of their...infestations. The gods did not fear the spirits, no. They never had. The spirits were an adversary their greed would bring them into conflict with one day. They had simply decided the day had come, in the aftermath of that unholy war, when the Great Kings were weakened. No fear there for him. No fear to keep the God of Mind and Madness back.

It was not the spirits they feared, but humans, the mortal races. Those who had sprung up in defiance of all their predecessors had known, from the silt heavy depths of a great river, who possessed in them a gift beyond comprehension.

It was with them he now placed his faith. The uelfin, the graemeins, the Katuwiti, countless tribes and peoples all bound to that ever turning wheel called evolution. The gift of growth and change, of innovation.

He reached down, the chains taut, cuff grinding into the joint of his wrist, and pressed a slender finger to the obsidian plate beneath him. With a trickle of power, all that the chains would permit him, he traced out a series of glyphs. Glyphs of binding, drawing on a power not entirely his own.

Not power enough to break free of his chains, perhaps, but enough to influence, to guide.

He focused on a forest both distant and close. A patch as intimately linked to him as the thin strands of hair along his forearm and yet removed, so far removed from this hole where his heart had once been.

In that forest was the sister shrine, the last resting place of his lover—the only man he had ever loved. There would be people of power there. There had been

Figures in Shadow

those who left that sheltered forest before, those of the guardian tribe.

One among them had ranged close to power in a life now recalled, and he latched onto him. He held that mortal soul in his hands, a malleable figure inviting his touch. He embraced the mortal soul, the Katuwiti Spirit Caller's being, and imbued it with his essence. He carved out his seal, a series of glyphs arranged just so. He seized the mortal soul, bound it to his pulse as so many spirits after him had done with countless mortals, and did so by force.

There would be no drawing on his power for this Spirit Caller, but the power would be within him. He would seek healing, but to no avail. What spirit possessed enough power to challenge a Great King? Which spirit would be such a fool?

He bit into the meat of his thumb, drawing blood, and dragged a streak of it across the sketchy lines of that image. A forgotten seal with which he claimed the Spirit Caller's soul, a channel through which his power could one day be expressed. When the time was right. At the place of his choosing.

As his cursed mark etched itself into his chosen acolyte, he felt the echo of his pulse within him, and knew he had been successful.

Let the first play of hands in this great game unfold. We will see who comes out the victor, and who is left reeling from the clash.

Shield Maiden

The pain of loss was slow in coming where a life was abruptly taken, but it lasted far longer. A loved one fallen ill, the grief of that loss was a dimmer light the hopeful child, the elder, the cousin or friend clung to. Despair, so protracted, climbed ever toward acceptance. Though the truth that the one who would be lost must be claimed, that no mortal could live forever, was brutal in its provision of clarity, before the disease ran its course; a cold acceptance could be obtained. The necessity of an end to the suffering, both for the dying and those who survived, became a gift. In ending, the family was left with their grief, a sharp outpouring of emotion, but it was expected. Had been for some time.

Sudden death was far crueler. In its wake, Lisk was left with a hollow carved out where his mother, all that she was, had been. He had not known how much space she had taken up within him, how much he would feel her presence in her absence. Within that hollow, there was nothing. Grief, sorrow, anger...those emotions lingered somewhere outside of him, and he was left to feel nothing. To believe what plagued his sight was illusion, the God of Mirrors come to play a cruel trick on him. That he should feel...something, anything, became an accusation. A curse lingered in the shadow of his mother's corpse, promising a time would come when he was not compelled by some force to feel so indifferent, so uncertain.

Lisk watched as Lisandra Almaine drew a silk shroud the same light blue as the sky over the face of his mother. Identical shrouds covered dozens of other bodies, those that could be recovered after the most recent of Saodein's assaults on their lands, the Fingers.

The sun watched from its noonday height as still more bodies were pulled from the ruins of his village, as their bearers lay them along the line, extending it along the slope of rocky beach before the breakwater. Smoke drifted from burnt wreckage where homes, his own among so many others, had been razed. Discarded valuables were scattered across bare earth where countless, booted feet had crossed on the march inland.

The soldiers were gone, but the damage they had done could never be forgotten. Screams in the night. The earth trembling behind concussive explosions. Plumes of dust and soot, shattered wood, raining down on innocents whose lives were swiftly taken.

He knelt before his mother's shrouded corpse, bowed his head, prayed to the spirits. Ul Sharak. Shao Luin. Those other spirits in the Empress's menagerie.

Lisandra's light touch on his shoulder brought him up short, drew his gaze compulsively to meet her crystal-blue eyes. Hard, unyielding eyes which hid her own grief.

She had known his mother well. Had known those countless others. As he looked into the pale moon of her face, he saw what these decades of war had taken from her. There, in the soft set of her jaw, in the hard lines creasing her forehead, the way she seemed to lean into herself. There, in her, was grim determination. Her grieving would be done in private. Her people, the survivors, needed a rock. The stalwart support of a wall against which to lean.

"Do not pray to the spirits to bless your mother's passing." she said. "They will lay hands on our enemies, too; for it is not their way to choose sides. Removed as they are from the pain we must endure, having lost nothing, incapable of losing anything...they are no saviors to us."

"Then to whom?" the question refused him. A dam had emerged, forcing him back into silence as he lay his burden on her shoulders, unable to stop himself.

"Pray instead to the elders, my dear. To the god who first took life from us. He is even more removed than them. And his motives are far more pure."

"Shah Jagat?" he whispered. "Merciless--"

"He is not the source of this cruelty." she said. "That is a mortal thing."

Her gaze roved over the sky, the shallows of Shao Luin's sea, the spar of rock jutting out across that sea, defining the neighboring peninsula from which the Fingers derived their name.

"What now?" she whispered. It was all she would grant him to define her own grief, that it lived inside her, a hollow she would fill with purpose.

He understood, then, how she had survived so many horrors, how she could still press on. Her grief had harrowed her like an arrowhead, the shaft angled in one direction, a singular focus steeling her against the eroding of self, the slow action of grief's waters against her stone. War had hardened her, inoculated her against this poison. Within it, she had found purpose, a driving force to fill the hollow.

She moved down the line, leaving him to his grief, these last moments to be in solitude with his mother, to find his acceptance.

he heard her mumbling to herself as she walked that line, walked away from him.

"To put an end to this time of darkness, an end to occupation. Who might shield us from the contempt of our neighbors? Which spirit...."

He lost the last of her ruminations. Though he did not know, would not come to understand until the night arrived and his mind wandered in confused half sleep, he was hearing her last words. The last he would hear for many years.

Lisandra was leaving, a pilgrimage taken in earnest. Her people were dead, or in the throes of such grief they could do little else but weep. She would see an end to this. An end to Saodein. But to see her ends met, she needed power. A power she could not attain in these lands.

It was not grief but rage that gripped Lisandra's heart. The opening moves in this war had been made long years before her birth. There had been attempts at

Tears for the Moon God

diplomacy, then. Saodein, still reeling after a godly intervention in their lands, the shape of which no record of history could identify with any certainty, had been seeking new ground from which to draw fresh resources, then. Men to conscript into their forces, grain and other food crops to feed a starving people, a means of rebuilding.

In her father's time, the shape of conquest had come in the offer of gifts, the sending of emissaries loyal to the crown. There had been factions within the nation, then, who themselves were at war with each other, a battle for the heart and soul of the people, for succession. It had been a confusion fit for exploitation among the Sarkahni of the Fingers. Saodeini expatriates, refugees, crossed the vast sea to resettle in quiet villages, were taken in with open arms. They brought with them strange customs, rituals, matters of culture which brought with it a reshaping of the unincorporated lands, a blossoming within which the Fingers was reborn. Reborn again.

Sarkahn's Fingers had enjoyed a brief renaissance in those days, coming from a place of greater power in the politics of a broken realm. And all that had been built was torn down before her twentieth summer.

She reflected on that first shaping, the one that had taken her father from her. Her mother. Countless relatives, friends. The attack had been sudden and brutal. The rebels and the various princes of their rival nation had, it was said, forged an alliance, signed accords of peace against the promise of equal shares in governance, yet as the old empire rose anew, the gods turned their gazes elsewhere, left Sarkahn to defend against these invaders alone.

There had been grief then. A breaking of her spirit, a shattering of an innocent, a young woman left to wander alone in desolation on the heals of mass murder.

Decades of drawn out skirmishes, small scale assaults, raising crude standards across the countryside as the occupation line shifted back and forth, like lolling waves under the moon's guiding hand. Decades of pain, destruction, revolution, rebuilding. Each new unveiling of power, each shift in the landscape of her life, hardened her, until grief became an abstract thing, its purpose to carve out a space to be filled with something else.

Grief, to make room for something stonier, unyielding—to drive away every soft edge, every piece of her that had been...sensitive...that saw the colors in the world bleeding into each other. And now, as she turned her gaze away from that ever growing row of corpses to set eyes on the home she had kept for all of these years— a smoldering pile of wreckage—she could not bring forth enough feeling to care. She had lost everything that mattered to her a long time ago. What were a few more memories? A few more broken things?

Cold anger held her in its grip, chained her to a bitter resolve. She walked among the corpses, aware the eyes that followed her hunted for sign and symbol that she felt the same pain they did, that she was capable of those emotions still.

She passed the last of those bodies, the widow weeping over the shrouded figure of a husband taken before he'd reached middle age, her belly swollen with child. That child would know his father's heroism, his story, but he would never know the man. He would have an incomplete picture, an imaginary reflection informed by his limited capacity to give form to the figure, not even enough to identify him in truth. Sorrow for the boy was for his mother to give. Sorrow, with every look she set upon him, for the image of the man she loved would be drawn out of him with age's climb into manhood, and she could not help but be reminded of what she had lost.

No kind words passed from Lisandra to the widow as she ambled by. No lingering over the husk that had once housed a soul.

Shah Jagat, if you have any mercy, guide me to power. To protect my people. I will give you all you desire, everything within my reach. Let us know peace.

She passed them by, the expecting mother, the corpse. Passed by those laying fresh bodies, some mangled almost beyond recognition, who they identified by known markings, old scars, trinkets they wore. Out of the ruined village. Away from the destruction.

In her ancient bones, she felt renewed weight. She prayed, and the gods answered, guiding her steps as she walked. A path opened before her. She knew not where it led, but she followed. Shah Jagat, it seemed, walked in her shadow, promising revenge—the icy hand of judgment, a tipping of the Scales. He walked in her shadow, and the promise of death drove her on.

Shah Jagat watched the one called Lisandra Almaine depart. With her left the last great hope for an organized resistance in the Fingers, the abandonment of her home to the slaughter which would follow.

She knew what sacrifice she was making, that with her passing, the people Sarkahn so jealously guarded would cease their prayers to the river and the ocean who had, for so long, stood in opposition to him. The landscape of a mortal mind was a mercurial thing, which shifted with the touch of the subtlest breeze. She knew, then, that her passing left them exposed to occupation by their enemy, and knew such a vulnerability could only be temporary, for an Elder God walked with her.

Maggot flesh slithered around a wide smile, creasing the God of Death's gaunt cheeks. He watched through a veil of fine chains suspended from his silken cowl, watched and waited.

The souls of those fallen in the one sided battle of the night before stood at his back, a row of several score mortals bearing the wounds they had suffered in life. Blood dripped, pattered onto smoothed stone which was darker than sin, adding a percussive, soft music to the scene unfolding before him.

The bluff to the west of the waterfront village provided them a last look upon their homes, the survivors who mourned them. They would not approach, for this was no curse of Gur Tulain, to be dangled as bait as the decrepit spirit pursued new acolytes. Their closure must come at a distance, for now.

A golden-complected man materialized at his side. His skin was traced over with lines, like the spangled surface of a pool, and he was naked, as was his custom. Loose, blond curls dressed his head, and his eyes were silver flecked with gemstone shades of green, and red, and blue.

"What do you want, Katcya?" Shah Jagat asked, his voice light as a desert breeze, lacking inflection.

The God of Luck grinned, a most unpleasant gesture. Where Katcya smiled on mortal kind, chaos soon flourished.

"Strange, aren't they? These creatures?" he said. "To fight pointless wars in perpetuity, seeing nothing of the great picture unfolding about them."

"A means to an end at least some of our children believe us blind to."

Tears for the Moon God

Katcya nodded. "How's the son?"

"Do you truly care?"

"No, I suppose I don't. He's kind of a downer, that one.

"It seems a cult has formed in your honor. They would freely give their souls to you, even so close to Ul Sharak's band. Might it be they discover their own vulnerability? That she would have an army to bring against our bastard children. Do you think, perhaps, these simple-minded people awakened to some variation of the truth?"

"Doubtful." Shah Jagat eyed him. He was suspicious of his counterpart. Alliances had risen between them before, when need drove them together, yet they had often soured. As did all the pacts the Elder Gods made amongst themselves eventually. Though he suspected this was Katcya's intent, he saw little reason to trust in him.

Katcya possessed but one unshakable loyalty, one pursuit too noble to be subverted, and it was not to any god, elder or lesser. Nor was he over fond of the spirits of the land, sea and sky.

"A visitor attended me at my house recently. It seems Lanfin took note, for he has since been immured within Time's Labyrinth, as so many of my kin eventually are."

"You granted a wish."

A malicious glint entered his steady gaze as he found Lisandra, watched her walk from her home into untamed lands.

"A peculiar dream, the Sun Man had. So few seek me out these days. Most are satisfied with Ho'o's explanations of our...relationship."

"Your point?"

"He asked for progeny, to establish true bloodlines. His desire was to create a self-sustaining people of the katcyakin."

Shah Jagat turned now to face the smiling god. His pallid flesh was marred by a blush rising in his cheeks, a flush of anger. "You granted his wish?" His cheeks were bunched tight around an answering grin, and there was a strain in his voice.

Katcya shrugged. "Of course I didn't."

Shah Jagat returned to his observation of Lisandra.

"Now, unfortunately for all of us, I did set the terms of a certain deal with my brood long ago. Children can be quite the pain, wouldn't you say?" Katcya patted him on the shoulder. "In making good on my promise, I took his petition to some rather reluctant others, whose role in fertility is far more direct than my own. And to my surprise, they said yes!"

Shah Jagat seized him by the shoulders. Baring his teeth, he shook the other god. "Are there bloodlines now in truth? Answer me!"

Katcya swatted his hands away. "There are. And that is why I have come. I taste change on the air, a coming disaster. *The* disaster. As such..." he cast up his hands, emulating tipping scales.

"You would have me leave them alone? Knowing how much damage a host of them might cause. That the Arbiter may seek to tip the Scales in the other direction...preemptively."

"He may not be around much longer. If my kin are to be killed. Or culled."

"This is about *them*."

"As you say. Lanfin cannot hold them. Cannot now we have need of their skills."

Shield Maiden

"We?"

"If you will work with me. Be warned, however, Mahan Mahain effects his own plans. To our benefit, perhaps, but perhaps not."

"I will think on it, Katcya. Though I do not like it."

Katcya giggled. "You never do

God Uldal

There was silence inside the God House of Ways. Rare was the day pathfinders were called to the hilltop, and though he hid it behind a stony exterior, Dupec Safar was nervous. He had only recently been risen as a full acolyte under his god. The others had tenure, experience and power he sorely lacked. They had been outside, had walked along the shifting paths whose gaping maws even now sifted in and out of focus, at the hill's broad base.

Mountain crags and spires, lichen and scrubby moss rose and were replaced by an arid waste; and then lush jungle. One gate gave way to the next, and twenty other portals winked open alongside them, closed, shifted from one scene to the next. Unmolested wilderness was replaced by open highway. Highway was replaced by the bustling chaos of a city thoroughfare, the quiet of a dark alley, a village lawn, horse tracks cut into a sea of amber grain and amaranth, the vastness of an ocean as seen from the deck of a trader's ship, and then the band of a river alongside which tile roofed towers rose, and waterwheels pulled from the river's depths.

He glanced at Wu Bane, sitting alongside him. Among the acolytes and initiates under the God of Ways, he liked him best. He had been taken as a child, just as Dupec had, though for different reasons. Beyond that portal was a home that couldn't feel anything like home. A place intrinsically linked to who he was, and he wanted badly to go there.

From the corner of his eye, he met Dupec's gaze. A dark mop of curly hair crested his wide head. His bone structure was delicate and refined. Epicanthic folds at the corners of his eyes, together with his round face and diminutive stature called back to his heritage as a Goth.

The Goths were a powerful force among the byrnese peoples, but they enjoyed little influence in the city where he was born. There, another power claimed dominance. The uelfin, descendants of the river spirit, Oe, and God Lanfin. His father was one of the few who escaped serfdom in that city, and it was him who he wanted to see most.

Many, quiet conversations had passed between them in the waxing hours of the night, when the moon was not yet full and the hunt was still a long way off. Pillow talk, giving voice to dreams that might one day come true. That might come true at last, on this day, if they played their cards right.

Wu's path winked out and was replaced. Dupec forced himself to look away, to

God Uldal

set his gaze on the god who had raised him.

Uldal's chin was hidden behind a heavy beard which fell to his sternum. Brown hair shot through with gray covered his legs, and his knees were prominently bent—tapering from powerful, hairy thighs into cloven hooves. Stag antlers erupted from the sides of his head, and black talons dressed long fingers. His torso and arms were full and muscled, a runner's build that, with the wild cast to his dark green eyes, made something feral, one with nature, of him.

The God of Ways sat cross-legged, and his acolytes were arrayed around him, sitting and waiting for him to perform the commencement for this meeting. He observed them, quick flashes under a heavy, furrowed brow.

Jaunz Faedrin, his second, had come from Sana's Horn, where a piece of him remained. He was of similar height and build to Dupec, which was no surprise. Jaunz had been his mentor in his youth, had put him through a ruthless battery of exercises to mold him into the man he was today. His skin was painted white, with red ochre covering his palms and the flats of his feet, and finger width lines of the same pigment drawn across his face, running over his eyes and down from his bald head to his chin. This was the customary aesthetic of the Sanarks, warrior priests among his people.

Which soul did you leave behind, old man? Dupec wondered. It would be better for them if Jaunz Earth Souled inhabited the body he permitted to come here. His Sky Soul was erratic, too easily distracted by petty things. It was this soul he usually sent to the God House of Ways, allowing his Earth Soul to remain on the Horn, to keep watch.

Another contender for Jaunz' place should he one day step aside, Timin was Magura—dark-skinned, lithe and tall. He had proven capable with the spear more than once in contests between these three, yet he lacked the Graemein's advantage. He had never trained under a spirit, was possessed only of the powers imbued in him by his training under the God of Ways. He and Suli were both made weaker for this oversight, and Dupec did not value following in their footsteps. Like his mentor, he would one day claim a place under a spirit of the lands, skies or seas. The lone question was which one?

Suli sat on Timin's other side. She maintained a tense posture. Their last skirmish had left her bloodied and her ego hurting, but the hurt was temporary. They would pick up the old argument again before long, and maybe she would come out the better for it. The two were an even match, though their styles of fighting were wildly different. Suli favored short swords, like the Nixians who raised her. Her swords, like Timin's staff and that odd switch Jaunz carried, were absent now. A show of respect for their god.

Though she was not born to their tribe, she dressed like a Nixian. Supple leather jerkin, elbow length, fingerless gloves and thigh high boots were layered over a hooded, one piece coverall the color of unpolished stone. The better to blend in with the shadows in the forests to the south of Gonsai Wall, with the grasses near its height, and the dunes in Sha Ruhhad's desert to the north. But where the Nixians had tilted eyes and brown complexions, she was pale, her hair dark and thin, her eyes wider and set over blunt features that made her look somehow plain, unassuming.

God Uldal turned his gaze from Dupec to Wu, was met with an even stare, yielding no emotion, as the others sat back. He cast his gaze to the sky, where dusk was fast yielding to night and the first stars peered back at him.

Tears for the Moon God

"Darkness watches, yet he dares not call the hunt this night. The moon slumbers." He said, invoking the three gods with whom he shared close bonds.

His gaze shifted to Jaunz Faedrin. "Why does the Horn shake with laughter?"

"The shrine remains uncompromised. Sana remains sealed. However, echoes of this laughter have been felt throughout the world. The Raukhas give answer from Crow. There is silence on the Ba Gora plain, but a visitor has been seen there. An Elder God."

"Which god?"

He shrugged. "They suspect The East Wind knows. They felt her pass in the wake of this trespass, but she will not speak of it."

A grim set to his lips, he turned to Suli. "Anything to add?"

"The guardian tribes are feeling the weight of recent disturbances in their lands, confirmation of what Jaunz has reported." She looked to her counterpart, who nodded. "The uelfin of Cratom claim a change has come over God Lanfin's song. They recall a moment in the past. They say this is a refrain."

"Yes, he did recall someone some twenty years ago as we assess things. There will be echoes of it at critical moments in that man's life." He snatched a glance at Dupec. "When he seeks to ease time's flow away from the events that transpired then. Delicate work." He stroked his beard thoughtfully, his gaze unfocused as he turned introspective. "Keeping it all from crashing down around us. We must hope he knows what he's doing."

"The uelfin are nonetheless confused. They say this most recent taking is dissimilar to those that came before, and in particular that of Shulraki Alran."

Uldal spat in the dirt. "Leave his name out of this. He has been forgotten in the world beyond. He will be forgotten here, too."

Dupec's gaze snapped away from his master. He was not alone.

The God of Music seldom sought to recall a life. There must be immense pressure on him to do so, pressure from the Elder Gods. Uldal had not welcomed the scrutiny he came under in the wake of his acolyte's reprisal. Many a god's plans had been cast into disarray because of him, and they had not forgotten. Such chaos invited into the world by one of his acolytes was a dark mark on his legacy. One he now shared with God Mu, Rein, and Echo before him.

Shulraki's story was told to every new acolyte to come into God Uldal's glade seeking mentorship. A tale spoken to them but once as initiates, to warn them off from exploring the gifts they would receive to their limits. Shulraki had stumbled onto a secret he should never have known, which had been a mystery even to their god before his rise and fall from grace. Death was no bar to a pathfinder. At least, they could cheat it for a time, if they were clever. But to do so would set the pantheon on fire, and they would inevitably be pulled from the flow of time for their indiscretions, if they could not be removed from play in the Greatest Game by more mundane means.

Their deaths would not be pleasant. Would not be quick, either. The gods were vengeful creatures.

His gaze shifted to Timin.

Timin cleared his throat. "Shah Jagat has been sighted on Ul Sadh. Together with God Katcya. It seems they have set eyes on one player in a recent escalation between the Fingers and Saodein, though the nature of their interest remains a mystery."

God Uldal

"Then they would act against their children. Liandal will have a hand in this. So, too, Tirulain.

"Watch this player, but do not let him know you follow. Find out what they are after. Why they have chosen to meddle here."

Finally, his gaze rested on Dupec. The silence that followed was deafening. he had not realized how difficult it would be to speak in the presence of these people, whose tasks seemed so incomprehensibly vast, so deeply complicated.

"You have a proposition?" his bushy eyebrows twitched upward. His gaze flicked to Wu. "Both of you do, no doubt."

"I would like to go home, God Uldal." Dupec said. "To Gil Garo. To winter there."

"Why?"

"To...to meet my parents."

"Strange, how time aligns along the same, predictable lines. Always the same patterns. One year forfeit. Another arisen in its place. Still, the same cycle. "

Dupec ground his teeth, anticipating rejection. Tao Shein Steppe offered more than just family to him. There were powerful spirits there, spirits who had contended with the gods in more unstable times. Spirits who had won those contests. If he could find a place under one of them, he would be as Jaunz Faedrin was. He might well rise to replace him one day.

His ambitions were not all that drove him to seek Gil Garo. He had yearned to see his parents, to meet his family, throughout all of the years of his life. A confused memory lingered in the back of his mind, something placed there by an unnatural force. Children so young were not capable of object permanence. They remembered nothing from the first few years of their lives, yet he remembered. Remembered something from the night of his birth.

His family had wanted him to return. He would like to see them. To know them. In knowing them, perhaps he could fill that hole inside of him that never seemed to close. He could feel complete then.

"Stopping you would be an inconvenience for me, but go with this warning. Stay well away from Duijus Kanh. If you must seek power, look elsewhere. His path can only lead to destruction."

"I will heed your warning." Dupec bowed low. His heart was thundering in his chest, his nerves riddled with static. *I can go home. I can see them in the flesh!*

"You?" Uldal said, turning his attention to Wu.

"I want to return to Cratom. There is a spirit there I'd like to court. If I can't convince him of my merits..." he spread his hands. "...there are others who might be amenable to me."

Dupec kept his gaze forward, his hands to himself. He wanted to reach out, to rub Wu's back, give him that small measure of reassurance.

This pursuit, this line of reasoning, was an excuse. Easy enough to see through. It was a lie to cover his truth, which he may come to regret if their god caught wise. But the gods were not omnipotent. God Uldal could not see what lay in Wu's mind, could not know his thoughts.

Hubris may well cover his deception. It helped that Jaunz knew what he was after, too. What was driving him back to Cratom.

"The spirit?"

"Sorry."

"Who do you wish to...court?"

Tears for the Moon God

Wu flinched. "Hod. Hod the Rope."

Uldal reeled back and cackled. "A fool's errand, boy, but a noble pursuit nonetheless.

"Should you pull it off, my very misguided, young acolyte, I'll see fit to give you a boon. But failure in Hod's rope often means death. Even for those who I claim."

"I'll do my best, God Uldal."

"Your best will hardly be good enough." He thrust a finger in Jaunz Faedrin's direction. "Do his best."

The expression Jaunz set upon him was unreadable. "Let me give him something for his trouble."

"What is this? You want to pass him a handicap?"

"Cratom is not kind to the Goths. I intend to give him a token that might see him through the city safely."

Jaunz rummaged in his pants pocket. He produced a gold trinket. A shepherd's hook with a tiny hand wrapped around its stem. He stood, approached Wu and passed the trinket to him.

"Look for an inn called the Black Lamb. But be careful. There is no one in that place worthy of your trust. It is nonetheless the safest place for you."

Wu accepted the token, bowing where he sat.

Jaunz returned to his place under the watchful eye of God Uldal.

"You know what you're doing to him?" the god asked.

"I do."

"Your requests are granted." the god said. "But do not test my patience. I will expect you both to return here by the time of the spring thaw."

"Now go! All of you."

The five acolytes rose, and departed. Each approached a different path, intent on a different destination. Dupec and Wu would return to the long house where the initiates slept, a house without a roof or beds, a place one with nature. They would have those moments to obtain their effects before their journeys, and then it would be to arrive in the world. To arrive at home, where Dupec hoped to find himself in good company, and Wu hoped to find absolution. Something that would look to anyone with eyes and their wits about him like murder.

That lone, confused memory came to the fore of Dupec's mind. He peered out through infantile eyes at a sky bright with the light of thousands of stars. The band of the northern lights shown green and wavering in the darkness, and the snows were cast in gray and lavender hues. Two faces, each of them bearing resemblance to him but missing the mark by several degrees, loomed over him. There were tears in their eyes, falling onto his swaddling as the man set him on the roadside, his thumb pressed to his forehead.

His mother spoke. "You're name is Dupec. Hope." she said, her voice weak, warbling. "I am Shaelein. Your mother, and...your father is Ungol. Ungol Safar...of the Dumas...Gil Garo." she took a shuddering breath. "Come back to us. We love you."

She smiled.

A man in his twenty-second year, he found an echo of that smile crossing his lips. *We'll be together soon, mother. We'll make up for everything we've lost, then.*

The glade beyond God Uldal's hill was bathed in moonlight. The moon, a white

God Uldal

orb nearing full, peered out from behind a scattering of thin clouds, all traveling at a clip on slip stream winds whose echoes brought soft breezes to the God House.

The breezes came from the east, soft and exploratory. Astair's curiosity was depthless, and she had ample reason to show interest in the dealings of the God of Ways and his kin. It was here, in a timeline recalled, a life never lived, that the first steps toward cataclysm were taken. Here, before God Lanfin drew the Great River free of its banks, where a tyrant was made.

And he was born again. Risen. An adult in his twenty-second year, just as he had been then, he was here in the flesh, and the one man who could have stopped him was absent. Was recalled in his stead.

Nothing good can come of this. She thought, observing the bulky, naked man where he lay against a bed of soft mosses. A bed grown out of raw earth.

Next to him, a slender man of an age with him, who traced his lineage to the Gotha Kingdom, half a world away. A place that was—even as these two lingered in the silence, wakeful and breathing in deep, tired gasps, their bodies covered in oily sweat and the smell of recent sex lingering in the air—without moonlight. A place under watch from the sun and sky, from Gorgus and Shirad, their gods. Gods who waited for a change to come, to proclaim to them that this wolf was vulnerable, divorced from his god, his mentor, the first of the lovers he had taken in that life recalled.

She sensed the tension in the air. That Mahan Mahain had seen fit to visit on a Great King, on Gora Soft Touch, galled, but there was something in knowing the Elder God sought to work with the spirit. Something she found discomforting, and yet more pleasing than what she had witnessed since then.

Dupec had been one of three of his kind in the world when first he lived. There was that one recalled, yes, and the other, the Apostate of Flame far removed from them, who had never met this man, had, for much of her life believed herself alone in the world, the only one of her kind.

What plans does Katcya have for her? She wondered.

His prior conspiracies had been a miserable failure. Whatever play he had intended in the Greatest Game had been thoroughly diffused with the reclamation of his best pieces, the resetting of the clock as it were.

But a curiosity had risen in his stead. Something she had not expected.

No longer were the katcyakin just three in this world. She had seen them, scattered about, rising up in places where the Elder God of Luck was not, where she had not sensed his presence. And perhaps he could escape her notice. By some convention of his power, perhaps he had simply arrived where she was not, leaving his mark behind with those varied tribes.

But she did not think so.

Something was amiss in this world. Far and away beyond Mahan Mahain's involvement with Gora Soft Touch, God Katcya's recent travels, the ones she had noted, established deviations from the usual patterns. The God of Luck was making his own play in the games the Lesser Gods played, and she wanted to know why.

The East Wind passed, leaving sweat cooling in the night air against Dupec's back as he gazed into Wu's eyes. Their fingers twined together in the space between moss beds, neither spoke as they caught their breath.

His muscles ached, his hips felt heavy and his loins drained. This had not been a brief encounter. He had relished those last moments with his lover, had wanted to linger with him, in his embrace, as long as he could. It would be some time before they saw each other again. If they both made it back in one piece.

"I'm going to miss you." He whispered.

Wu nodded. "It's for the best, though, isn't it?"

"You aren't sure?"

He shook his head. "Not since Jaunz passed that seal to me."

"He's only trying to help—"

"I know. But...what does he expect I'll find in Cratom?"

Dupec shrugged. "He's been all over the world. Are you surprised he knows a little about your hometown?"

"No, not that. Just...why tell me to...I suppose it doesn't matter. What about you? Do you think your people will accept you back?'

"I think they'll see me as an outsider. But my parents...I have to meet them."

Wu shied away from Dupec, his gaze drifting to their hands, following his muscled arm to his shoulder, lingering there.

"You'll be okay." Dupec said. "You're strong. And she's a coward."

"She's cunning enough to have replaced my mother. I don't know how she did it. She couldn't be strong enough to have killed her. It must have been blackmail of some kind."

"She removed you once, too." Dupec pointed out.

Wu hissed through his teeth.

"I'm sorry. I shouldn't have—"

"It's okay, Dupec." Wu said. "We'll see each other when its over, okay. But we should get some sleep."

He twisted around, putting his back to Dupec, leaving the space between them to remind him that not all was well in the life of Wu Bane. That there were still those things he could provide no comfort against.

He lay his cheek against the mosses, pawed at the narrow strip of soil between them. Sleep was not swift in coming, and it was broken too soon. As night fled from the glade and the long house, new shadows pooled against ancient columns and the sun climbed over the high walls, a terrible, burning eye come to watch over them. A call to the old times when the gods had been at war, for it was this aspect of the Sun God's power that kept the peace between those Lesser Gods, a means of keeping the master of roads neutral. Always neutral. And his acolytes under control.

He crawled over to where Wu slept, and lay a kiss on his cheek. He left him to sleep as he ventured off to gather his effects, all that he would bring with him into the Tao Shein steppe, and set off for the hilltop, and the long road home.

An echo of Dupec's parting kiss burned against Wu's cheek. He waited until his lover was well clear of the long house, the last of his heavy footfalls trailing off into the distance. He had never been good at goodbyes. Throughout all of those times Suli had been called into the world, all of the times she had gone home to Nixir to speak with her elders or visit in upon what family remained to her, he had never learned to part with the ones he cared about gracefully.

It's better this way.

He would have liked one last look at Dupec, but that last parting glance would have felt too much like a tragedy. Too much like...*don't think about that right now.*

There would be time for reflections on his former life soon enough, without

God Uldal

letting intrusive thoughts spoil this last moment of peace. Time enough, while he was planning for the coming reunion.

Still, he would have liked to see Dupec's smiling face looming over him. Would have liked to hear him telling him one more time that it would all be okay. He would have liked the chance to promise him one last time they would see each other on the other end of their journeys, that this separation was only temporary, but even that would feel so much like a lie.

He might come back in one piece. He *might*. But he was not certain he would. Not certain enough to make the promise sound true in his ears.

Dupec arrived with his effects at the hilltop. He remembered his first approach, when he had graduated from the first stages of his training, had passed the first milestones in the conditioning of his soul and had been allowed to move onto more difficult fare. Passing the doors was a selfless act. It demanded the abandonment of self for a time.

For an unaccomplished novice, the stitching together of two disparate roads in far flung places was delicate work. Years of practice made it as easy as breathing.

He was dressed in a deerskin coat that was somewhat uncomfortable for how tight it clung to his torso, and the traditional, linen riding skirts the Gil Garo favored. Insulated, deerskin pants hugged his legs under the length of green fabric, a practical addition to the traditional attire for the steppe in winter would be a harsh place, resembling little the glade where God Uldal kept his house. A pair of broad scimitars were sheathed at his hips, and a pack containing hardtack, flatbread, a tinder box, a skinning knife and twine, was fastened to his hip behind one of them.

All roads led to Uldal, and all of those sanctioned by him were open to his acolytes to travel. There was no such thing as a long journey for a pathfinder. The doors must yield, and they did.

He fixed the correct path in his mind, drawing from memory, and let go of himself. Who he was, human ideas of place and time, of fixed positions and all they entailed. The door before him fell open on a stable path. A horse track carved into deep snows, a track teaming with activity as tribesmen made haste for their winter camp. Tribesmen who looked very like him.

He hesitated at the precipice, thinking again of those two who had left him on the roadside, the memory burned into his infantile mind, never to leave.

He stepped forth, and through

Cloud Man

The North Wind roared across the steppe. It whipped up powder snows to wash over the wide track the Dumas caravan followed. Dupec walked with them, blending in among some twenty-thousand nomads, but keeping his distance from them.

He thanked Ho'o for providing him cover among the drifts. Though they drove a deep chill into his bones, the howling winds stole snow from the mounds, a precious cover to keep unwanted eyes off of him. His curse would be noted among the Gil Garo. In returning, those driving winds, the dancing, powder snows, were a gift. A means of making his return unremarkable, until he again reunited with his family.

The caravan wound through the first encampments, those on the vulnerable fringes where the late coming sects were forced to settle. Sentries watched the open plains, their gaze fixed unwavering on the horizons.

The caravan passed among yurts made from buffalo hide stretched over long, arched poles, which crawled toward the icy band of Shan Lao's river, on his way to join with Galadir in the lands to the south. In the distance, the snow capped peaks of Shar Lau's range, and the Fang, Fan Ryu, looming over its neighbors. The mountains clawed at the skies, the last of their foothills leagues off from where the Gil Garo made their winter camp.

Tribesmen clad in hide and furs drew water from the river, visited upon makeshift granaries and smoking pits where camp cooks and stock keepers passed bowls and sacks of raw produce and meat to those of their sect who needed them.

Over top of the yurts, he saw the bowed roof of a more permanent structure. The lodge towered over the surrounding dwellings—a long, blocky shaft fronted by twin columns carved from thick timbers and preserved with thin washes of wax.

At last, the caravan came into view of a patch of land along the river itself, a prime place set aside for the chief who was last of his line, and his people. Already, yurts were being erected, plugging the gap, and the earliest arrivals to the insular patch—deep within the shifting city and well protected—were pulling rugs and camp beds from horse carts, pulling them through the sloped entrances of their winter homes.

Cloud Man

With winter, the Gil Garo returned to their city, a city that would only remain until the spring thaw forced them away. The Dumas would remain here for all of those months; and he suspected he would remain, at last, as well.

He approached a middle-aged couple as they fussed over the contents of their cart. The husband's cheeks were wind burned, and thin cracks ran across the bridge of his nose. His wife was sinewy and hard from her years on the road, and her cheeks had begun to sag around a narrow jaw.

Dupec approached the husband, keeping enough distance that his markings would not be immediately obvious.

"Sir, where does Clan Chief Ungol sleep?" he asked.

The man shrugged. "He beds down by the river. Maybe four hundred steps."

His wife set a glare on Dupec. "Who's asking. You look like a Dumas, but I've never seen you."

"I have not walked with the tribe in many years." Dupec said.

"An exile." She spat. "You'd seek a judgment from him, but you'd be met with silence. Exiles don't--"

"Quiet now." Her husband said. "Let the boy speak."

She glared up at him, then turned that hostile gaze on Dupec. Her husband's gaze roved over him, taking in missed details. The details he so badly wanted to go unnoticed.

"On second thought...he'll see you, I think." he said.

His wife followed his gaze, took Dupec's measure, took in what she had missed on her first pass.

He was discomforted by the way she looked at him, and that discomfort redoubled as her eyes widened with something like recognition, and then narrowed.

"Fah!" she seized a rolled carpet and hauled it into the yurt.

"Don't mind Cudla." the man said of his wife. "She never believed you would survive. The others haven't. You look like him, you know. But you'll see that for yourself soon enough. Come. I'll take you to your pa."

He gestured toward the river, and Dupec followed.

"You know who I am?"

"Who you were." the man said. "Less than that. The very night you were born, the midwives left a knife at your mother's bedside. We had a rash of cursed births around that time. They weren't taking any chances. Your parents might have done it. Plenty of people wished they had, but they were given a choice same as everyone else. Be honest with you, I think they set the precedent. Too many people might have seen fit to keep their own cloud men if they'd seen the chief doing it, but we couldn't take care of them. They're shifty, those—

"I'm sorry. I don't mean to offend."

"It's okay. I don't harbor any ill will toward our people for the choice my parents made."

He snorted. "I suppose that's good, then. Here. This is the place."

They drew up to a lone yurt whose entrance flap was distinguished by a wooden crest suspended from a beaded, hemp chain. It was the only mark to differentiate it from those surrounding it. A pair of horses were tethered to stakes at its side, with slack enough that they could wander to the river to drink if they so chose, and the cart next to them lay empty except for a bale of hay from which one of them fed.

"I'll leave you to it." he said. "But if you'd like a listening ear or a cup of something to warm you, don't be a stranger. You learned control, didn't you?"

"You have nothing to fear from me." Dupec said.

"Good. I'm Dangal, by the way. Good luck with your reunion." He hastened off to his own yurt, to finish the unpacking.

Dupec waved to him as he trudged off. He stood outside the yurt for several moments, willing himself to step through. He had waited a long time for this, and yet, now the moment was here, he was unsure of himself.

What do I say? he wondered. *How does someone greet the parents he never knew? How will they think of me?*

He dawdled there, an expanding list of worries freezing him in place. He might have remained longer, but a snort from one of the horses startled him, cutting him away from the host of his fears.

Before they could crowd in again, he stepped forward.

He pushed back the flap, and walked into the warmer interior of the yurt.

His father had aged greatly in their time apart. Steely streaks ran through his umber hair, and crows feet forested his dark eyes. His attention was not on Dupec for the moment, instead fixed on fire glow radiating through the iron door of a small camp stove.

His mother sat on scattered cushions opposite the entrance, a needle and thread in one hand as she studied a small tear in a forest green, linen skirt.

She saw him before his father did. Her eyes grew wide, and she dropped her stitching.

"Ungol." she breathed. "He's back."

"Shaki?" he asked. "You'll have word from your--"

His gaze found Dupec as he turned from the stove. For several moments, a suffocating silence lingered in the yurt.

Dupec took a backward step toward the door, not thinking, and almost knocked over a gilded statuette of a spirit he had never seen. From a low manger in the shadows the other side of the hearth, an infant wailed.

A sibling? He wondered. *A recent birth, too. I wonder how many children they've had. Some of them must be close to my age.*

Renewed excitement rushed through him at the thought of it. He might have siblings to bond with. What was more, those children implied his parents had gotten on with their lives, had found some way to be happy.

Without me. His momentary excitement ebbed away. A strange mix of emotions fell over him. Happiness for them was mingled with a selfish anger, or maybe it was a smaller kind of sadness stealing over him. He had hoped their lives had been happy, even as he could not be part of them, but seeing the evidence of that joy made him feel so...*alone.*

His father rushed to the manger. He made cooing noises as he reached to stroke the baby's head.

"Now, now. It's okay. No need to be angry." he said, Dupec forgotten for the moment.

"Ungol, now is not the time." Shaelein hissed. "Our son is here. Your Chain can wait."

"I'm sorry, son. This must be awkward." Ungol said without turning from the fussing infant. "I'll explain when the time is right."

The infant stopped its fussing, and Ungol stood. He crossed the yurt's single

Cloud Man

room and embraced Dupec.

A surge of emotions passed between them. Hot tears ran over Dupec's cheeks, but he could not remember when he'd started crying.

He returned his father's embrace, as his mother joined them. Ungol let him go, let his mother have her moment with him.

Shaelein touched his cheek. She couldn't quite believe he was there with her, not a ghost but alive, warm and breathing.

"You've grown so much." she whispered. "You were so small when last I saw you, and now...you look so much like your father."

"Stronger in the cheeks. He gets that from you." Ungol said to her.

She nodded earnestly "He does, doesn't he. But you...you're a man! We've missed so much. So much we can never get back."

"I'm here now." he said, the words sounding awkward in his ears. "Let's not dwell on what was lost. I would hear the story of your lives these last twenty years. And I'm sure you'll want to know mine."

"Sit, sit." Shaelein said, arranging cushions for him.

He took the offered seat, and his parents seated themselves near him.

"I...have a sibling?" he asked, his eyes on the manger.

Ungol laughed. "No, no. A misunderstanding. What lay in that cradle is not human. Such creatures are bound to the soul, a link in the chain between man and spirit.

"It is my link to Gandes Fae."

Dupec arched an eyebrow. "A spirit of memory. Is this how you left me your gift."

"I'm glad you see it as such." he said. "We weren't sure how you'd take it. You might have seen the memory of us as a curse, having no way back to meet us. We couldn't be certain the god that found you would allow you to come back."

"The god who found me is...agreeable enough, I suppose. Though I'll not say my childhood in his glade was always comfortable."

"Who was it, then?" Shaelein asked. "We thought, perhaps, the Gods of Ways or Hunters. There was also the possibility Ho'o took you. He takes orphans, but he usually demands a toy."

"It was as you expected then. I was taken by an acolyte, taken to God Uldal. I will have to return to him...at times. But he has granted me the winter for my purposes."

"Then at least one god is merciful." Ungol declared. "They are not all so kind.

Xirakura

A sudden, sharp pain surged across Xirakura's chest. A scream welled up in his throat as he gnashed his teeth together. The pain—like molten glass being dragged over him—carved tracks across smooth, sunkissed skin. Slick blood weltered over lacerations, hot and oily and thin.

Beside him, to either side, figures rose, pressed soft hands against him. Man and woman, they embraced him, each wearing an expression of concern as they looked their husband over.

Tears streamed down his cheeks, dampening the mattress beneath him, glossing the sides of his long neck. His body convulsed under his spouses' touch. His wife flinched back. His husband helped him sit, sending fresh waves of pain to sail through his limbs.

"What is wrong with him?" his wife, Lura, whispered.

"His chest." his husband, Katuwan, hissed back. "Look at his chest."

Xirakura clawed at the source of this agony, the place where blazing pain raged white hot along his sternum, across his ribs. A whimpering breath welled past his lips, the pain subsiding, retracing the avenues of his nerves to settle, cold, in the pit of his stomach. To flow against his copper skin, crawl back into the brand and settle in duller relief.

His frantic clawing subsided, his abdomen unclenching, mind clearing. For a time, he could make out only darkness in his bedchamber, the soft dampness of the soiled quilt underneath him.

Katuwan's arms snaked under his back, his thighs. He lifted him from the bed, corded muscles bunching under his weight. Wordlessly, his wife went to strip away the modest bedding, remove it to a wooden bucket at the swollen chamber's side, near to the sloping, age-ringed wall.

In night, the walls of their home were impregnated with water drawn from deep within the earth. The tree it was grown into drank until it was full, passed vital nutrients to its branches, to support a dense canopy.

Katuwan drew him from the chamber, hustled down a too narrow corridor. Painted images lining those walls were distorted by the swelling, the whole channel made almost unnavigable for how much fluid pulsed behind the wood.

He dipped into an adjoining room. Lura followed him.

Xirakura

Flint struck stone. Sparks drifted through darkness. Hearth fire blossomed beneath a kettle and she retreated.

Katuwan set him before it, drew down a wooden spout. Fresh water flowed into the kettle as fire built under it, providing comforting warmth as the bathwater began to steam.

By firelight, he was finally able to find calm enough to look his spouses in their faces. Lura's was a snowy sheet against the darker pallor of her body. Her round eyes were wide still, but her breathing was even. Beads laced into her hair recalled him to the time of their meeting. He had chosen her first, but she had been reluctant, had courted another suitor, remained in waiting for the month approaching the new moon.

The message had been clear enough. One love could not hold her heart. He could not hold to her alone, either. She ran delicate fingers over the length of her forearm, where tattoos traced the likeness of the braided flowers he had thrown onto her doorstep. His gaze traveled to her shoulder and down, where still more flowers were drawn in sepia tones, them calling to Katuwan's own bridal wreath.

Katuwan regarded her beside him.

"You are okay?" he asked.

She nodded rapidly. She was shaking.

He turned to Xirakura, then, and Xirakura to him. His gaze was steady. He hid his fear well, though Xirakura had known him too long not to see the tells. A grim downturn to his full lips, the balling of jaw muscles deepening the hollows of his cheeks.

He was close to panic. As Xirakura had not chosen him, not forthright in haste, he had been first to lay his bridal wreath at the slighter, younger man's feet, a gesture of sincerity in his intent. To love him.

Time made the bond mutual, but Katuwan did not mistake Xirakura's hesitation. He had taken on a labor in convincing him this thing could work, that something beautiful could be kindled between them. Now, the old uncertainty entered into his amber eyes, into his posture. The tattoos crossing his shoulder were of the flowers hard won from Xirakura, placed in that position of dominance to signify the depth of his commitment.

Xirakura reached for him, touched the flowers. A gentle caress, to remove that mercurial poison, which he had long thought abated.

"Easy, my love." he said. "I am fine."

"I hear you, but you have not seen." Katuwan said. "Let that decision come when you have witnessed."

"What does it mean?" Lura whispered.

Katuwan joined her at the hearth. He helped her up, and together, they hauled the kettle to a basin carved into the hardwood floor, which was sealed with fired clay to keep the tree from absorbing water. They poured its contents into the wash basin, and then Katuwan was helping Xirakura to his feet, into the steaming water.

He took up a sponge and pressed it to Xirakura's skin. Xirakura snatched the sponge from him.

"It's fine." he said, meeting his husband's eye. "I can handle washing myself."

He started with his chest, where the stinging was born anew under the abrasive foam. He hissed, and Katuwan reached out to take the sponge away. Xirakura warded him off. He needed to do this himself, if just to prove these strange happenings had not made a child out of him.

"This is...." Lura's gaze fell to Xirakura's chest.

"Yes, he has been claimed."

"But...why? Why now? What spirit or god would have reason to mark him like this? Without warning, too." she said. "What purpose does it serve?"

Katuwan reached out, not for the sponge this time, but for the raised markings spanning the middle of Xirakura's chest. He touched one pattern, high up, near the joint between Xirakura's clavicles.

"These are written in their language." He said. "The one the spirits taught to the first tribe. I can't read them."

"Try."

He shook his head. "All I can make out is chains. There is a hawk, and chains."

Xirakura froze, sponge pressed against his chest. Soap foam ran down to pool against his naval. The implications contained within those words were incomprehensibly vast. The Chaining was a legend known to every Katuwiti tribesman, told at bedside from father to son, mother to daughter. A story long lost to the other tribes, of times impossibly bloody, when the spirits clashed with the gods and the beating of war drums was unceasing. When whole lands were lain to waste, their spirits broken and destroyed, and usurped by new and harsher spirits only when the echoes of those deaths were finally and totally silenced.

He resumed his scrubbing, the work a distraction from his thoughts.

Two pairs of eyes remained fixed on him, both knowing the omen could not be ignored, the call could not go unanswered, and knowing, too, they would not leave him to walk this path alone.

"Chains? Not him, it couldn't be!" Her gaze touched on Xirakura's eyes, then Katuwan's. Xirakura saw his fear reflected in both of their faces.

"No. No, it couldn't be him." Katuwan said. "He is too far gone. Too compromised by madness."

"Not Ban the Rope, then." Xirakura sighed. He could take some relief from that. It was his tribe's duty to defend the shrine of Ban the Rope against trespassers, to ensure the spirit remained sealed. But he was not the only one in these lands who was bound in chains, imprisoned in a shrine held away from people, and spirits, and gods.

Xirakura shook his head, unbelieving even as the evidence was burned into his flesh. "The hand is Gora's. It must be."

"How can it be? He is under constant watch. The Tetract spirits would know a violation of this magnitude had transpired. They would seek to unbind what he has done before any damage could occur.." Katuwan said.

"Whatever the case, it seems I am to betray our people as his regent." Xirakura said. "Ban walks in the king's shadow. They were lovers, were they not. In all of our stories, they were. If the object of Gora's desire is liberation, it will not just be for him. He will want his lover unchained, too.

"I cannot allow it."

"Is there no way to stop this?" Lura said.

"Sufa Salein, maybe." Katuwan breathed. "He is old enough to remember the Chained One's time of freedom. He might help us."

"Maybe." Katuwan said. "But he was not powerful enough then to stop him. Will he be now?"

Xirakura

"Chained as he is, he cannot command that much power." Xirakura said, getting back to his cleaning. He tried to pick out glyphs within the markings, but his knowledge of the language of the first tribe was less than Katuwan's. It was not a commonly studied thing among the Katuwiti people.

"If not him, then Tak the Fire is our answer."

"No one knows where he is."

"Some do."

"What do you know, Katuwan?"

"There are those who lay down arms, who repent for slaughter and violence. Those who seek a sheltering hand, repentance. They can help us find him."

"The Rahad?" Lura said. "The Rahad is answer enough. We will go to them."

"And die with them. When the gods set eyes on me, and seek to take my life." Xirakura said. "Let us get through today. I am needed by my people. Healings must be performed. Blessings ahead of the new moon for those who have not yet accepted their betrothal offerings."

Lura chuckled at that.

He met her gaze, tried on a smile. It did not feel right on his face, but it lightened his mood some.

She had been one of those. In the early days, when they had all come of age and began to show interest in each other, he had laid his bridal wreath on her doorstep, to find Katuwan had done the same. Had things worked out differently, they would not now be wedded to each other, but Katuwan had proven to be a consistent partner. He had been right to take a chance on him. On love.

"Let us get through tomorrow. Remedying this may be as simple as leaving it alone. There have been others who did in the past, haven't there?"

"Maybe." Lura said.

"How many have been marked that we know?"

"At least one." Xirakura said. "A handful probably. If they are not in our stories, they must not have been much remarked."

"We will see if you are right, then. But I think we should seek Sufa Salein anyway." Katuwan said.

"I will think on it. But he is prickly. Calling to him would be a risk."

Katuwan nodded. "I understand."

Through the sheer curtain suspended in the entrance, he could see the silhouettes of figures moving among the swollen boles of great trees. What light penetrated this deep below Sufa Salein's high canopy speckled the fabric, a greater dimness suffusing everything, robbing the forest beyond the threshold of detail.

Outside, hunters were already gathering, belting thin cords of waxed hide around their midriffs, strapping short bows around their shoulders, and quivers filled with bronze-tipped arrows. Craftsmen were toiling at kilns, or dipping threads of soft wood into pots of clean water for weaving. Upon the looms, the weavers spun flax and used it in the making of blankets and carpets for those who had a need. Everyone had their place, their purpose. A Spirit Caller's place was to provide healing to the people, a gateway through which they could convene with the spirits of this jungle. He could not ignore his purpose much longer. He was needed.

But to venture outside was to make his last night's suffering known, to shape it

Tears for the Moon God

into something tangible. What rumors might have risen up in the morning hours would be abated, but what rose up in their place might be worse. Something as simple as a snake bite in the middle of the night would evolve with evidence to contradict those mundane theories writ plain across his chest and belly. In the presence of spectators lay a brutal awakening. That Gora's touch was real. That his newfound scars must be noted...by others.

He laced a cord around his midriff, folded his genitals under it. He secured a gourd to the strap, a warty, bone-white thing carved over with geometric designs. They were all the effects he took with him. The Katuwiti valued utilitarian dress. They did not see reason to layer heavy fabrics over themselves as outsiders did. But this was one time in which he would have liked something more covering. Something that might obscure the fast healing lacerations across his torso.

He must see this wound opened so that it could be healed, see the infection of the mind drawn out before it could fester.

Yet still, he hesitated.

The naked shadows of men and women passed in fitful streams across his home's veiled entrance, and he knew they could see his own shadow painted across it, waiting to be received into the world as he had never before been reluctant to.

the rumors would swirl about them in his absence. A spirit caller fallen ill in the night. His spouses grieving over his compromised condition.

The old crones would go on until every other villager was convinced of a rumor spoken with conviction, and the truth tasted like a lie.

Lura had already gone, off to forage across the forest floor for what food stuff Sufa Salein might part with. The spirit abided no lasting harm to his lands. Stories told of early attempts to grow crops in the loamy soil, the retaliation that followed in the wake of a tree's felling. No, the spirit would not abide the insult, but he did provide. In his own way, on his own time.

Lura had gone, to distract herself with such labor as suited her, as was her habit in uncertain times, but Katuwan remained, an ally, an escort and a friend, to see him through these first, tender steps, into a new beginning.

He rose from the cushion he had been occupying, but the cook fire where flames lapped at open air, pushing smoke into a floo grown into the tree itself, which funneled it into still, humid air. He crossed to where Xirakura stood.

"You are sure you do not wish to rest? No one will miss you. Not for a single day." Katuwan said, his calloused fingers traveling Xirakura's flank.

"I am sure." Xirakura said with more confidence than he possessed. If Katuwan pressed him, he might back down, might return to the bed chamber, sequester himself, test his resolve again tomorrow.

But Katuwan saw the resolve in him, saw what he needed to see. Tomorrow might stretch into another day, and another, until he was no longer certain he could leave. Until he convinced himself that this omen would become no more than a burden to his people. That he would become their burden.

He had the resolve to confront this bitter truth now. He did not need to be coddled, doted on by a concerned lover. He needed support, and Katuwan provided.

His husband laced his fingers into Xirakura's. He faced the doorway.

"When you're ready."

Xirakura took a deep breath, renewing the pain in those tight cuts as his chest expanded. The cuts had already dulled in color from angry red to a softer pink. It

Xirakura

seemed the healing would be a rapid affair, the recovery brief.

He stepped forward. Katuwan drew back the veil and they stepped onto the dirt avenue outside.

A woman's gaze fixed onto Xirakura. He recognized her as Napura, whose grandchildren were only a handful of years his junior. A motherly smile was twisted into something far less pleasing as her gaze snapped to his chest.

"You are wounded." she said. Her eyes widened as the meaning of those lines came to bear. She dropped the wicker basket she had been carrying, scampered up the avenue and away.

"This is going well." Katuwan said. The chuckle that followed sounded forced.

"We press on." Xirakura said. "While my nerve still holds."

There was work to be done. Work he needed to do himself, if only to take his mind off the fast healing scars and their meaning. "You might be needed--"

"I am yours today." Katuwan said. "The hunters will bring in enough food for our hearths without me, I am sure. Even the lads are capable enough."

"You saw to that." Xirakura said.

"Not alone." Katuwan's chuckle was genuine this time. "Many a man might have lost patience at this new crop. I nearly lost mine."

They crossed the village, the grown homes of other families, other couples and more flowing from their mouths to see the day begun. The soft knock of hammer on chisel, the crack of splitting wood, filled the air as they passed a team of youths busy with the work of breaking down dead wood for hearth fires. A pair of fishermen hauled a large catfish between them, while two others carried in the dugout canoe they had taken for their expedition in the dark hours of the night.

Some families milled about in the earthen patches between trees. Children clad in swaddling playing at games of shadow or pantomiming the busy work their parents were about, pretending to be about raising their own children. A pair of elders chattered in the deeper shade of a yet undisturbed tree, its rough bark unbroken, the trunk uniform save for a small boil near the roots.

Someone is expecting. But surely if they were that far along, I would know of it.

He noticed a gaggle of old women seated on quilts a short distance off with their heads together. Every village had its gossips. That fist-sized lump would give them fodder for weeks, as it grew with the help of the expecting parents, slowly beginning to take on the appearance of a Katuwiti house as it was shaped under their guiding hands.

A middle-aged man, a potter called Qetuala, waved greeting. His smile faltered, his hand stilling in air as he settled on the scars. The disturbance drew the old women out of their conversation, to watch the exchange at hand.

Qetuala approached. With no consideration for Xirakura's boundaries, he ran his thumb over some of those markings.

"I mistook this for a wound, lad." His gaze darted from the scar to Xirakura's face, then to Katuwan. His suspicion was evident as he settled on Katuwan, but abated quickly.

He shook his head. "Marked by who? Or is it a secret. You've been chosen as sure as I breathe clean air. Why, I wonder?"

Xirakura shook his head. "I badly wish I knew."

"I see here...chains." Qetuala tapped his finger against Xirakura's sternum, causing him to wince. "Sorry, lad. Didn't mean to cause pain. It's all I can make out,

Tears for the Moon God

only...chains. Not old Ban. Couldn't be. Half mad, that one. Barely recalls his own name these days, they say.

"You seek out Sufa Salein yet?" his gaze flicked between them. He satisfied himself that they hadn't. "If anyone can read that, it's him. Old, old spirit, but then you know that. Or you wouldn't be much of a spirit caller, would you be? Beats going outside, doesn't it? Those people, the Uari and the Magura...they're not like us. Strange customs, and that. Uncommonly cruel, those people."

He shook himself at the thought of them, and shambled away.

The couple moved on.

"He has a point." Katuwan said. "Sufa Salein was chosen to guard the Rope Lord's shrine, a distinction the Tetract would not impart lightly. He may well know something of use."

"I confess I considered that, too. But he is not prone to sitting still for long. He will be far away from here, out of reach."

"If you call him?"

"He may come. He is fickle, prone to fits of obstinacy. Not at all like his kin among the mountains and the streams."

"If there is a chance, it is worth the effort."

"Tonight, then. Outside the village."

A field mouse broke out of a pile of rotted leaves, then darted for fresh cover. Xirakura set himself in its path, crushed it underfoot. Bones cracked against his heel. Gore greased the skin there, and he dragged his foot across soft earth to rid himself of it.

"Even here the Rat Goddess sends watchers. She would stake that much risk on knowing what has happened here." he lamented.

"This is not a new occurrence. They have been in abundance, lately. The hunters say they've seen seven in ten days. There will have been more they did not see."

"God Lanfin's hand is in this."

"Where the rat crawls, the snake slithers. He is always a presence within her schemes."

"There are other hands in this, then. There must be, or why send so many of her eyes to watch us?"

Katuwan shrugged. "To that, I have no answer."

"Your touch is unwelcome." Hanuwik said.

He sat across from Xirakura, the hearth in the sitting room of his home between them. No fire burned there, yet his eldest children, themselves scant years from casting down their own bridal wreaths--worked over the makings of supper. His son, his complexion uncommonly fair, his features sharp and angular like his father's, butchered trout while his daughter skinned and cut wild potatoes for boiling.

"You would choose this suffering?" Xirakura asked. "Your wife ails, Hanuwik. She needs treatment."

"I will call to another village." Hanuwik insisted. "It is not that I wish to offend, but such markings are suffused with energy, which will taint whatever work you perform."

"You don't know that. There is no reason to think--"

"Which spirit claims you?" he demanded. "You do not know. You do not know because the spirit is either newly risen or old beyond our reckoning. In either case, your healing may prove more harmful than the affliction itself. I will not risk it."

Hanuwik had been the third to propose this possibility to him, upon seeing the mark against his chest. A choosing, where it could be clearly identified, might prove a blessing. In most cases it did, though it was an uncommon thing. Of those who had been so marked, there were only four in the Katuwiti histories. Were there more, they had fallen out of memory and lore, leaving their legacies to be forgotten.

The reasoning was sound, but it left the villagers in a difficult position. Spirit Callers of Xirakura's ability were a rarity, and he was one of only two of his kind still young enough to hold anything of use in his village. One man could not heal every ailment that befell the villagers alone, yet he would have to. For the rest, other villages might provide, but they must meet the needs of their own people. What little they could give could not be enough.

Katuwan chatted quietly with the children, joined them at their work. He had been amenable to providing these distractions in other homes, as well, giving Xirakura space to converse with his kin as those conversations inevitably soured.

He said his goodbyes to them, and joined Xirakura at the entrance, the conversation having ended on tense but respectful terms.

They departed. Dejected, Xirakura chose the straightest path home.

"Was he the last?" Katuwan asked.

A curt nod. "He is now. There is little point maintaining the illusion that our people will allow me to provide for them."

"You're angry."

"I am frustrated." Xirakura's sigh was heavy. "A Spirit Caller who cannot call on spirits. Not for lack of ability, but for lack of support. Half of them won't look at me, Katuwan. Even you struggle."

Katuwan shook his head. "You misread concern for your wellbeing as something distasteful. Tonight, we will call on Sufa Salein. He will answer."

"What can he do?" Xirakura sulked. "You said it yourself last night. There is only one who can fix this, and he won't answer."

"I never said--"

"Tak does not take on acolytes. For all he lends his hand to shelter, there are limits to his mercy. He will not fix this. And Sufa Salein cannot fix it."

"You cannot know that." Katuwan said. He gestured expansively toward the forest. "The spirits provide, do they not. They have no obligation to us, yet through their mercy, we are sustained. This once great king is shackled, restricted. That mark was born with but a trickle of his power. I correct my past self, if you will listen. Sufa Salein is free, the chosen guard against the Rope's shrine, while this chained one is shackled and powerless. He will heal you. He will know how to if he cannot."

"Maybe." Xirakura said flatly, glaring at the ground. He did not want to speak of this any longer. He saw that Katuwan, in this small victory, was mollified, and left it there. There was little point in making his true feelings known. Let him feel a measure of reassurance, even if the man himself couldn't share in it.

They ambled on as their peers craned their necks to catch sight of the mark that was stirring up all the rumors. It seemed he had failed to abate them, too.

Ung Tsang and Ung Tsong

"It seems a long time coming, but you must feel everything is happening so abruptly." Ungol said.

He led Dupec through the Shifting City, along paths increasingly congested with people of the various sects. Ungol had been diligent in informing his son of the warriors customs and adornments he could use to identify them. The teepees they passed belonged to the Tipik. Their chief was a close friend, though loud and abrasive in a way the rest of his people were most often not. Most of the men were shaved bald or near enough, their beards braided into thick ropes that hung over their chests. They favored turquoise jewelry, which he saw in earrings and fetishes.

The Cuu worshiped the four winds before any mountain or stream. Their horses were fastest among the sects, but they tended to be cautious, preferring ambush tactics in their raiding. Thin bars, a ritual scarification, were carved in even rows beneath their right eyes. The right to wear them was given after their first raids, the untested among them were given first choice from the stores of bangles and jewelry the robbed trading caravans possessed.

"Gulang rarely pays a kind word to anyone, but he is well respected among the chiefs." Ungol was saying as they neared the wooden structure he had first seen on his approach the evening prior. His sect is the fiercest among our people. So *he* claims. I suppose the evidence is there in his strangle hold on the Ung Tsang title these last years. His sons, you see. They've been in the habit of winning the tournament. Year over year, since they began coming of age."

"I'm sorry, which sect is this?"

"Kachin. This isn't too much to take in?"

Dupec shook his head. "There was time enough to read in Uldal's keeping, though I am grateful to have names to put to these leaders. Records, even well kept as Uldal's are, often miss details. Or ignore what the people they describe view as important."

"You've been humoring me, then. Haven't been idle these long years."

"Not humoring." Dupec said. "Listening. What knowledge I came into was never as complete as what I might have gained were I here."

His father looked stung.

Ung Tsang and Ung Tsong

"I didn't mean--"

"It's okay. Some wounds must close in their own time, and your mother and I...we've lived with ours a long time. I should not have presumed."

"The Kachin, then. They win the tournament every year."

"When they have a son to bring forward. Though this year it will be the twins, daughter and son. They'll have a hard time of taking both titles with Chakta their rival.

"Chief Coltang's daughter. She'll represent the Tipik.

"To your other question. There is Ung Tsang and Ung Tsong. Both victors are given over to Duijus Kanh cave to carve their names into the wall, but this custom is largely ceremonial. Legends speak of a pact between an ancient chief and the spirit, but they are just that. Legends.

The true benefit of holding the titles is political. The chief to whom Ung Tsong belongs has first choice in raiding lands for the next year. Ung Tsang's chief is given the deciding vote in council matters."

"So Gulang has power to decide what will be done with me?"

"There is some latitude in that for us to take advantage of. Gulang has decision power in instances of a tied vote, and that power will only reside with him if his youngest son is victor of this year's tournament, which will be held in three days time. He has real competition to contend with from the Cuu and Hakka sects. Their chiefs are friendly to the Dumas."

They came within the shadow of the towering lodge, and Dupec noted a pair of horse statues carved from the same, sturdy wood as the rest flanking the main entrance. They reared on hind legs, their faces carved in frozen screams, eyes rolling. Behind them, a frieze was carved into the forward wall, depicting a pack of wolves on the hunt.

Ungol followed his gaze to the wolves.

"Duijus Kanh and his Swans hold much favor among the wolves. It's said Meichekh, his favorite concubine, can control them, but many would argue their obedience is for the cave spirit alone, a kind of mutually beneficial agreement, as both wolves and the spirit loathe the moon god."

"Uldal is favored by Ao Nii." Dupec said. "Though I would not account them friends. Among the gods, such bonds are tenuous."

Ungol patted his broad shoulder. "We respect the God of Ways here. Just as we respect the God of Hunters. Whatever bonds they share with Ao Nii, they have not earned our disdain."

"Then I have little to fear for being bound to him."

"Come. The chiefs await us." He guided Dupec toward the entrance.

"Before we...." Dupec said, drawing his father up short. "The tournament. It might do more harm than good, but were I to participate...."

His father's expression rose to a momentary, profound joy. Pride was etched into his features, there in his posture.

"You would make me too proud." his face fell. "But the decision is not mine. You wonder rightly if the chiefs would allow it. If they would not see you as a foreigner even knowing why you were kept away. I have no answer, my son, but that is not a reason to fret."

"We can't know their hearts." Dupec agreed. "They've not met me yet."

"Time we fixed that." Ungol pushed open the wide door, and they passed into a dim chamber, its only source of light a low burning fire in the recessed center, which was ringed by benches. Most of them were occupied.

He recognized the chiefs by the descriptions Ungol had given him.

Coltang loomed, tall and broad, over all the others. He joked with a man almost as big as him who was growling a steady stream of curses under his breath, trying and failing to ignore him. By the shorter man's fire-orange skirts and the tiger's eye disks in his ears, the way his wiry beard hung loose around his chin, he must be Gulang.

Across from them sat a gnarled, sinewy man whose long, braided hair was beginning to thin at the crest. He bore no visible scars, a departure from the rest of them, and his gaze was akin to a bird of prey as it settled on Dupec. He was the oldest man among them. If Dupec did not miss guess, this was Chief Tursa, of the Kirche.

He was having difficulty finding the qualities in the old man that made him so popular among his people. Even before any words were spoken, he seemed brutal, unempathetic.

Next to him sat Arrak Sarr of the Hakka. He was compact, nearly Ungol's age, with hooded eyes and a sag to his cheeks that was beginning to soften a strong jawline.

On Arrak's other side sat a man half the age of the next youngest chief, who was newly raised to represent the Chikata. He presented himself with an unbecoming serenity Dupec suspected was grudging acknowledgment of his unfamiliarity with the station, a misguided pursuit of acceptance within the established hierarchy.

Last, then, was the chief of the Cuu, an unassuming man whose expression was unreadable. His eyes were a startling shade of blue, icy and discerning. He, too, was of similar age to Ungol, perhaps a handful of years younger. Laugh lines framed his thin lips, and though he was easily the shortest man in the room, there was no mistaking a certain grace within him. A self assuredness that belonged to a seasoned fighter.

Ungol led Dupec to an open bench, waited until he had seated himself and then ventured off to join his contemporaries across the fire, sitting with Sarri, the Cuu chief.

"This is the son!" Coltang bellowed jovially. "He looks enough like you. Broader in the chest, but the same blunt jaw and tepid affect."

"Don't be an ass, Coltang." Gulang snapped. "His status as a chief's son is meaningless. He was banished, for good reason. Were he to reenter our society, the question we must answer is one of safety."

"Then ask the question." Coltang said. "Better yet." His expression lost its former levity, replaced by something far more severe. "Can you control your curse, Cloud Man?"

"I have learned that control." Dupec said, nodding.

"There you have it!"

"A few words hardly demonstrate proof." Sauman said, his tone verging on belligerent. "I would like a demonstration."

Several pairs of eyes turned to regard him.

"A demonstration for all of us here. We cannot abide admonitions of utility where no evidence is present."

"A demonstration, young Sauman, would risk death to one of us here." Tursa said coldly. "Who would you volunteer for this fool's errand?"

"Likely himself." Sarri sniped. "Doing us all the favor of shutting him up for a moment so the grown ups can speak."

"Your concern is well placed, Chiefs Tursa and Sarri." Dupec cut in. "But you are riding on a poor assessment of my...abilities. Katcyakin alter probabilities. Sun men work their gifts unto themselves, often without thought. Their working of this gift increases the likelihood they will be met with good fortune, and decreases the likelihood of misfortune befalling them. Some may never know the taste of failure. Most will never experience severe injury.

"Cloud men, by contrast, project that gift outward, increasing the likelihood of misfortune in their surroundings. Uncontrolled, as is often the case, this can lead to tragic accidents or unexplained illnesses for the people around them, but a living person, or a person in general, is not a necessary focus for that power.

"As an example."

Dupec trained his gaze on the fire in its pit. It guttered and died, leaving the chamber in darkness.

"Spit in the eye of a god." Tursa mumbled.

Flint struck stone, sparks cascading into the now cold pit. The logs refused the effort, having no energy to give.

"Wood!" he said. "Sauman, now would be the time!"

The Chikata chief hurried over to a pile somewhere distant, found it with his knee.

"Ouch!"

He hustled back, delivered fresh logs to the pit. The patter of a clod of horse dung falling over the fresh stacked wood. Sparks danced anew. The dried dung caught. Tongues of flame rolled across it, and under Tursa's delicate coaxing, the fresh wood caught.

As the fire came to illuminate the faces of the chiefs, Dupec found his father, noted the approval with which Ungol favored him.

"An acolyte of any common air spirit could do as much." Sarri said. "Some clarity is in order, young man. Who was it that found you when your parents left you on the road?"

"The woman's name was Suli, an acolyte of God Uldal of Ways and Paths. He placed me in the keeping of a Graemein Sanark, Jaunz Faedrin, who had power enough to suppress my curse. Between Jaunz and God Uldal, I was able to master my innate ability, and learn a form of soulbinding. I can demonstrate that as well, if you wish. Though I would rather not do so here."

Gulang belted out a laugh. "Your boy's got balls, Ungol. I see your play, but you'll not take my mantle up so easily."

"What is this about mantles?" Sauman inquired. He was not the only one who looked confused.

"You're likely too young to understand. Tursa has as likely forgotten. It seems the boy wants a shot at Ung Tsang. Though it is worth asking...to what end?"

"It is the best means, I think, of garnering acceptance from my people. For my return."

"We are voting on two things, then." Sarri said. "Whether to accept Dupec Safar back into the tribe, and then whether he may contend for a chance at Ung Tsang."

"Ung Kanh Dui, you mean." Tursa said under his breath.

Tears for the Moon God

Coltang chuckled. "A bullshit title. He doesn't strike me as the type to pretend at airs. And look at him. He has no idea what you're talking about."

"No, I am not." Dupec said. "Though now you have me curious. What is this title? What latitude does it grant among our people."

"Our people." Gulang grumbled. "He certainly does like to put the cart before the horse, doesn't he?"

"Ung Kanh Dui is an ancient title bereft of all meaning. It is the distinction given to a steward of Duijus Kanh himself, his own acolyte. But no such acolyte has existed outside of legend, and there is little point in focusing on those." Coltang explained. "If you win the right to be called Ung Tsang, you and my daughter will walk within his cave and carve your names among the countless others already written there. That is our custom. Should you venture deep enough, legend has the Swans will escort you personally to him. Rest assured, it has never happened. Not in our memory. But that is the tradition we hold to."

"Better to be safe than sorry, isn't it? After all, they do like to steal away infirms." Arrak agreed. "Food for their master."

"A grisly practice." Tursa said. "barbaric even by the standards of spirits."

Gulang clapped his hands together. "How would you vote on the first matter?"

"In the affirmative." Arrak said.

The other clan chiefs voiced agreement.

A weight lifted from Dupec's shoulders. He hadn't realized how much of a burden the uncertainty in that looming decision had become.

"For the second matter, I ask for closed debate." Sarri said. "No clear headed decision can be reached with him present. This is, after all, a matter of cultural significance. Our people will meet an affirmative decision as a matter of controversy."

"I understand your concerns." Dupec said. "And agree with your sentiment. However, I would say to all of you that I adhere to tribal custom. I am of precise age to participate in this trial, and had I grown in your keeping, I would be expected to participate as the son of a chief.

"That is all I will say." he rose. "I give you the floor."

He walked away toward the entrance.

Behind him, Arrak said to Sauman: "See that? That's how you win respect from your equals."

"But he is not our equal." Sauman protested.

"He will be." Gulang said.

The door fell shut before the Kachin chief could say more.

He passed the Cuu camp on his way from the compound. By custom, the camps chose grounds according to who had arrived first, taking up residence in defensible positions first and then fanning out from there. The Tipik and the Kachin had been among the last to arrive.

The Hakka, under Arrak Sarr must have been first. Had secured advantageous holdings for the Dumas, who held a weak position in clan politics as their chief had no present children.

He wondered how the sects decided who might lead at council, how to divide raiding lands, in years when no chief could produce a son or daughter. Uldal's records had been silent on the matter, but there were other records in other god

Ung Tsang and Ung Tsong

houses which might offer greater insight. The Rat Goddess was said to have the most complete histories the world had ever known, transcribed, as it were, by her acolytes into every known language in the Waxing World. So, too, her frequent ally, God Lanfin, possessed vast stores of knowledge as a byproduct of his travels through time. And then there was the Goddess Liandal's collection of diaries, but he dared not invite her attention.

The Goddess of Fate was never satisfied with watching time and all of its tidings pass, and she hated the man who would claim to be Dupec's father. Katcya was not much loved by the Waxing World gods, but there were those who treated him with indifference, those like Uldal who rarely played hands in the Greatest Game. Liandal was unlike them. Her diaries, a secret to no one, yet of secret construct, were filled with people like him. Those blessed with rare gifts, born into powerful households. He had avoided her attention for most of his life, but she would take note of him sooner or later. She could not afford to leave him alone.

An itch formed between his shoulder blades. The sun god was watching from his throne in a sky unmolested by clouds. The North Wind had ebbed in the night, but lingered as a breeze, his attention focused on Tao Shein's steppe, on the Gil Garo and their sprawling, temporary city. Something was brewing on the horizon. Ho'o seldom lingered for long, yet he would not move off for some time, if Dupec's hunch was correct. For now, his acolytes carried the wind southward across Ul Sadh, across the Shao Luin ocean, to Yu Danh Hao and then Harkanh where the winds reunited to argue among themselves, the momentary distraction opening the way for he Goddess of Storms to do her work.

He passed from Cuu territory into Hakka, circumventing the Dumas camp on his way toward the jagged belt of the distant Shar Lau range. A Fang thrust high over the rest of those peaks, and he felt the attention of yet another spirit, young in comparison to those who enjoyed his company but more powerful than any of them, and stubborn. Notoriously so.

Fan Ryu's attention was not for him.

He must have an acolyte among the contestants.

So, too, The North Wind's claim was contested. The day was warmer than the previous evening. The South Wind, Thera, was coming, but she had not arrived yet to drive her brother from the city.

There was an omen in that.

He wondered what shape this contest would take. The records in Uldal's archive had been less than informative on that prospect, as well. The chroniclers who gathered around him were seldom interested in such trivialities as coming of age rituals. They favored broader scale structures. Diplomatic relations exploited, the rise and fall of dynasties.

Blunt force shook him from his thoughts, wheeling him around as a body collided with him. He spun on the Dupec, the gold armlet encircling his bicep and the feathers laced into his hair. A young man, of an age with him and of the Hakka. He was a mass of compact muscle, pretty in an almost feminine way. His lips full, his cheeks wide and planar over a narrow, hairless jaw.

"Watch where you're going!" he snapped, color rising in his cheeks as he lifted himself from the ground.

Behind him stood a Cuu youth, tall and whip slender, his skirts the color of the sky, embellished with a braided belt heavy with agate beads, the kind shot through with streaks of blue.

He was laughing.

"Shut up, Shaki." the Hakka man said. "The insolence, to knock a chief's son onto his knees."

Dupec held out a hand to help him. "I'm sorry to have been an impediment, young lord. But perhaps you have mistaken the order of events."

Shaki's laughter redoubled as his friend swatted Dupec's hand away.

"Who do you think you are." he growled.

"Dupec Safar." he said. "Newly returned after a long absence."

Shaki's laughter died in his throat. His dark eyed gaze roved over Dupec, noting the cloud lines.

"Tamlin. He isn't kidding. You remember what your father said. Chief Ungol...he had a son. A cursed son. He could make us sick. Or cause us to fall off a horse!"

"Do you see a horse under me?" Tamlin groused, studying Dupec. "You might be right. A Cloud Man...but--"

"You're Chief Arrak's son." Dupec cut in. "My father believes you might seize Ung Tsang from Gulang's family."

"What do you know. You've been among us for what? A few hours? A day?"

"Don't worry." Shaki said. "He's always like this, but he means no offense. Will you join us? We're about to scope out the competition. The fighting pen is back in my father's camp."

"You're Sarri's son, then." Dupec said. "I'm afraid I might not be welcome there."

"Nonsense!" Shaki smiled broadly. "You'll be participating, won't you? You're about the right age, yes?"

"That is why I may not be welcome. The chiefs are debating that very prospect. It would not do to give the wrong impression where it concerns my intent."

"You've been gone a long time." Shaki pressed on, ignoring his expropriations. "They'll want to see if you can hang, you know. This contest is serious business. If you win, Ungol will never let old Gulang live it down!"

"Who are you bound to?" Tamlin asked, betraying his haughty disposition for a moment's curious probing.

"Now, now, no cheating." Shaki waggled a finger in warning. "You know the rules."

"He doesn't." Tamlin noted.

"We'll have to fill him in then. On the way."

Sudden as a gust of wind, Shaki was on him, a hand pressed to his back, turning him round.

"Spirit calling or soulbinding, both are permitted only in the last round. The chiefs and those who wish to become chiefs offer their kids in contest, so there are always a few wild cards in play. You won't be the only one.

"And no lethal force. One year a boy accidentally crushed his opponent's windpipe, and he died before a healer could get to him. The boy was exiled. I've heard the Swans fed him to Duijus Kanh."

"A vicious rumor." Tamlin intoned. "We saw him near Ruc's border. He's living on the outskirts of a village. They'll let him no closer."

"I like my version better."

Ung Tsang and Ung Tsong

Shaki proved to be an animated and talkative companion as he led Dupec and Tamlin to their destination. In some ways, he reminded him of Wu, so full of laughter, when he could be enticed to forget about the dark marks in his past.

He was off in Cratom now, seeking his pound of flesh. If their god discovered his deception, he would have him whipped until every inch of him was coated in blood, until he could not move without feeling raw pain lance through him. But he needed this. At the end of his errand, when he had finished what was begun all those years ago, maybe the cloud would lift away from him, and he would be free. Free to be as this man was. Unburdened by what had been, and able to meet his future with a smile on his face. With no more darkness lingering in his soul..

He suspected, as they returned to Cuu grounds, that he had found his first friend among the sects of the Gil Garo, and wondered if Tamlin, too, could be so called. So far, he seemed disinclined to accept a bond with him, but time might change his mind.

The arena was little more than an expanse of frozen mud. A ring of fire pits framed it on all sides, and a series of bleachers formed a half moon at the back, leaving it exposed to the wide road on the other side.

Within the arena itself, men and women, all of an age with Dupec, sparred or ran through forms. Many among them did so with an unnecessary finesse that belied attempts at intimidation, but among the serious contenders, the posturing was met with ambivalence. Fewer women than men occupied the space, but the men, those not engaged in their practice, ventured over to them with an alarming frequency, favoring one in particular who seemed annoyed at the constant interruptions as she practiced her forms.

Tamlin followed Dupec's gaze to the diminutive, well muscled woman. Her dark hair was cropped short, and there was a hard cast to her blunt features. Binding tape was wrapped around her chest, poking out underneath the collar of a restrictive tunic. While the other women had chosen to embellish themselves with jewelry and paint their faces, she went completely unadorned. She was not here to invite the gaze of potential suitors, she was here to practice, to work her forms, cut out any weakness that might hinder her in the upcoming tournament. She was not for them.

Dupec found himself respecting her dedication, even as she battered away attempts from some of those men to court her. He could see those brief but frequent interruptions were wearing on her. Her patience was quickly dwindling.

Tamlin sneered. "That's Chakta. You'd have better luck hitting on an overturned bucket. She rejects everyone."

"Likely because she's uninterested in men." Dupec said, seeing the truth of his words in the details of her dress, the way her gaze avoided even the men who did not approach her.

"You think?" Tamlin said. "It would explain why she rejected me."

"He doesn't take rejection well." Shaki whispered in Dupec's ear. "Thinks he's too pretty for it."

Tamlin ignored him. "You'd have to be brave to hit on her, anyway. Her father is Coltang, and he's very protective of her."

Dupec thought of the giant among the chiefs. A man he suspected knew how to fight, whose own forms his daughter had likely adopted.

Tears for the Moon God

She swept in low at a would be suitor's knees, jabbed out with the broad side of her arm, knocking him flat.

"Leave me alone." She growled. "You can see I'm busy. That goes for you, too."

The men around her scattered like rats at her dark scowl, their hopes of courting her dashed.

He suspected it would not be long before they were back, and knew there could be no success for their efforts.

"Coltang's going to have a good year." Shaki said.

Dupec privately agreed.

A wave of unfamiliar sensation washed over him, then. The most peculiar feeling this had happened before, that he had stood in this spot with these men, watching this very moment play out.

We have our paths before us. Where yours takes you, I cannot follow. But walk with me, for they cannot unwrite my history. The thought came with the alien sense that he had heard someone speak it to him before. There was the edge of song lingering, barely perceptible, behind it, too. The feeling this had happened before, that he had been standing here, thinking this very thing, at another time in his life. If he could only remember when it was, who had spoken those words to him.

As the sensation ebbed away, he walked into the yard, made for Chakta.

"You don't want to do that." Shaki said. "She's already angry."

Shaki hadn't moved. Tamlin remained back, but Dupec's intentions were pure.

He positioned himself where she could see, waited.

"Did you not hear me?" she demanded, not looking at him. She ran through her forms. He spotted weaknesses the others had missed. Jaunz had been insistent in teaching him to cover his weaknesses, had at times been brutal, but the training had yielded a second sense, the ability to see through stances and attacks, to find his rival's weak points and exploit them.

"I'm not here to ask for your company." he said. "Only to offer myself up as a sparring partner."

"Your loss. Most of the men have already learned better."

"I am not most of them." he said.

She took a better look at him. "You're that Cloud Man my father was talking about. Ungol's son, right?"

He nodded.

"No funny business, then. No altering my luck to suit you." she took a stance.

He positioned himself across form her, arms raised, noting the bend to her knees, the way she kept her legs spread wide.

An unstable base makes an easy target. Jaunz' voice echoed in his mind, deep and harsh.

"I'll referee." Another woman said, approaching.

She was half a head taller than Chakta, slender and somewhat boxy, and a secretive smile turned up the corners of her lips. By her pigtail braids and the painted circles on her cheeks, she was Cuu.

She had seen these contests before. Had seen the results. He suspected she thought herself witness to one more defeat among many, a suitor's misguided attempt to court Chakta, which would end in bruises. Not least to his ego.

"Begin." Her hand chopped down.

Chakta surged forward blindingly fast. A feint to Dupec's chest obscured a

Ung Tsang and Ung Tsong

thrust at his right leg. He stepped back and her fist sailed through open air, unbalancing her.

He spun to her left, chopped down on her trailing leg, knocking her off balance. An open hand blow to her back sent her keening forward to land chest first on hard earth.

She gasped.

Shaki whooped. He clapped his hand over his mouth, looked to Tamlin.

Tamlin folded his arms over his chest, muscles bulging. He scoffed.

"You got lucky." Chakta righted herself.

"That's a Sun Man's gift." he smiled. "I've never been so blessed."

She took up a stance, exposing the same weakness.

The other girl called the fight, and again Chakta was the aggressor. Dupec slapped her uppercut away, swept her lead leg out with a well aimed kick. the sudden widening of her stance caused her to grimace as dull pain ran through the tendons in her groin.

He knocked her over.

They resumed their stances.

"Begin!"

She took a defensives stance this time, leaning back in wait for his attack.

Bad mistake.

He thrust his fist toward her chin, a feint disguising an open hand blow to her chest.

The blow knocked her off balance, forcing her again to widen her stance, providing him the only opening he needed.

He ducked low and swept both legs from under her with a backward sweep of his arm. She landed hard on her back.

"How did you do that?" she demanded, righting herself.

He shrugged. "My master thought I would find hand to hand fighting useful."

"That wasn't my question."

"I observed. You lack nothing for raw power and you pay attention to your opponent's movements. Those are admirable qualities in a warrior. But you attack from a weak base. Your stances are too wide and clumsy, and that weakness leaves you open to a counter. When pressed.

"I had the same problem, but my master was quick to correct it. Keep your legs closer together and isolate your movements, and you'll not have much to worry about from your competition."

He held out a hand to help her up. She accepted it.

"Where have you been?" she asked. "To pick up skills like that?"

"Wandering a path with no end."

She looked into his face, her expression hardening. But he sensed the confusion lingering behind that rigidity, and thought he understood something in it. Something more than she was letting on. "Find me later?"

She stalked off, out of the arena and then down the road toward the Tipik camp.

Shaki and Tamlin closed on him, then.

"That was incredible!" Shaki said.

"It was okay." the girl who had been refereeing said.

"Oh come on, Bora." Shaki said. "You've never seen someone beat her three times. In a row! He's got mettle, that one."

He clapped Dupec on the back.

"I tend to agree." Gulang called.

He emerged from the shadow of the bleachers, trailing the other chiefs, Ungol among them.

"It has been decided that Dupec Safar will be allowed to participate in the Ung Tsang tournament, provided he does not use his luck altering powers to advantage him."

"Clearly, that will not be a problem." Tursa said.

Ungol hung back as Sauman approached.

"One last thing." he said as he closed on them. "Your father will not be in contact with you until the morning of the contest. Our tradition is to isolate the contestants from their kin ahead of the tournament. To prevent cheating.

"I've been selected to ensure no cheating occurs. As such, you and all the other contestants will remain in the Chikata camp until the morning of. A yurt has been provided for you there.

"Now please, all of you, come."

Ungol waved to his son. "I'll see you in two days time."

Dupec tipped his chin at him. Together with the other contestants, he followed Sauman away

Grief

Shaelein sat with her husband. The low camp bed they occupied was new, fashioned on the road in the summer months to replace the old, compressed mattress they'd agreed to get rid of, but its frame had weathered many seasons. Wood worn smooth from incessant polishing had long lost that peculiar odor of old forest, but it was the very same one she had given birth to their son on decades past. The small, round table on which a fat candle burned had been in her keeping in those days, as well.

It was there that the midwives had left the knife with which they had severed the umbilicus, and with it, hope of any true bond forming between mother and child.

There, wiped clean of blood and gris. There for her use, to deliver death to her god cursed boy.

They had sat in silence for hours, it must have been. Hours of spare eye contact, with neither able to be the support the other needed. They had known, then, what their choices were. They had known there could be no chance at happiness. No celebration for a birth which must necessarily be followed by a burial.

All those years of avoiding the subject.

She had kept the outfit she'd intended for him to wear when first she presented him to the world. A one-piece thing fashioned out of a fawn's soft, dappled hide, the feet encased and padded with rabbit fur. A hood she could snug around his chubby cheeks. It had become a habit, when the silence became unbearable, to take it from its place at the bottom of its chest. Just to feel it in her hands, to have reassurance that it had not all been for nothing. That she had been happy once.

She should be happy. Dupec was home, wasn't he? But she had missed so much of his life. His absence haunted her in his presence. Who was he? Who was she to him?

Not his mother. Not really.

Ungol stripped off his clothes, his bare back to her as he resumed a silent staring. Her baby clothes may serve no purpose to her son now he was grown, but her husband's relics still had utility. The things he had kept, he had retained out of hope. An armlet passed from father to son for generations, gold, wide, with a dancing flame rising from its crown. Feathers of the grouse and crow. He had purchased pots of paint from a Hakka tribesman who was known for his skill with pigments, and the wells rested to either side of the adornments, like incense at an altar.

She supposed this was an altar of a kind, to ply the spirit he was sworn to.

His familiar was silent for the moment, sleeping soundly. The morning of the tournament was on the horizon, and the ugly creature would be left to walk in the open in the lead up to it, a matter of ceremony she would rather he ignored. The Dumas did not hide their disdain for the creature, what it meant. Many of the others, of other sects, would not either.

"Gandes Fae warned me." he said. "When I visited him in his caves. I brought a goat with me from the hillside, alive but hobbled. A goat and ten men from a hill tribe I'd run across in my travels."

"You don't need to--"

"I do." he cut in, a hard edge creeping into his voice. "Mol Fae were everywhere, buried in the loose sands, down in the bedrock. They made the appearance of a graveyard, where every body belonged to an abandoned infant. I was horrified. Even when they attacked I could only freeze while the hills men frightened them off with torches and clubs.

"I would never have reached the spirit without them, and what did they earn for it?

"Death. Their blood mixed together in a wooden bowl from which he drank. He warned me even before I took their lives."

He held up three fingers. Three questions in exchange for the goat. Each of his faces would answer only one, and they are of wildly different temperament. the first spoke softly, kept things short but nonetheless pointed. the second was much more confident, and long winded. The third met me with open hostility, but I trusted in its honesty.

"Three questions. How long would I live. Would I marry. Would I have a son?"

She watched him watch his altar, listened as he told the story. She had never heard this tale before. He spoke to no one of his pilgrimage to Gandes Fae. She had always assumed it was because the taking of dark spirits was not a well met thing among the Gil Garo, even as they claimed allegiance to Duijus Kanh. But this was a lie she told herself. Underneath it was a bitter truth. He had witnessed a trauma there, which kept him still. And she could not make herself compel him to relive it.

"Will I have a son?" his chuckle lacked warmth. "To be young and stupid again. So many better things to ask, but he was forthcoming in his answer, and even now it haunts me.

"A son you will have if you set forth on this path, who will not be raised by you or any mortal. One to make the spirits cower, to spread waste in fruitful lands and lay slaughter at your feet. And he will spit in the eye of a god, but pray he finds no lover. Alone, he is dangerous. In kind the one who steals his heart will steal away all you love in him, and he will be left hollow."

"He cursed our child." she whispered after a time.

"He may dip his fingers into the river, but he does not guide God Katcya's hand. Nor can he influence any mortal birth." Ungol said. "He spoke of what he saw, but futures are not fixed. In my hubris, I chose his path, thinking I could change it.

"Gandes Fae did not curse our child." he looked into her eyes, and she saw his grief. For as much as their reunion with Dupec had brought him renewed joy, and pride, it had also stirred awake a sleeping darkness. "I did."

The Lake

The corridor Shulraki shambled down was so densely populated with memory pools, he was forced to navigate past them along the fringes. One foot in front of the other, heel to toe, heel to toe, until he was well clear of the worst obstructions.

There were pieces of his story he was missing, pieces he did not know whether it was wise to confront. He had given his last orders to his Shards and then died, had allowed for his execution to take place; the charges—conspiracy, fraud, evasion of taxes, robbery all the way to treachery against the crown—fictitious nonsense crafted by his enemies to see him pulled down, his trade empire dismantled and the pieces redistributed among them. He might revel in the memories of his queen's last moments, as seen from a safe distance, but those very memories spoke to deficits inside him, in his mind, where though he had been given this second chance at life, the memories ended with his death—a blank slate where the deeds of his Shards should be.

Death had not made him whole again.

What was contained in those pools? Somewhere in this labyrinth, the pieces of his soul must have their own ponds, their own isolated pools filled with all of those things his soul had forgotten.

What would that mean for me? That they have claimed their own identities? That they are not me any longer?

He kept on, not knowing where he was going but knowing well enough where he was. There were zones of overlap, like brackish estuaries where great rivers met oceans, where the people who had lived in one time and another were kept. Broken things, their memories, lacking rationality. In those places, the pools ran over, ran into each other, and as they converged identity was lost in places, the floodwaters running so deep the motes they formed became impassible except to walk through them, and hope he wasn't dragged down.

Along the borders between his and the late emperor's domains, those floods were thickest, quagmires where histories converged, where one people and another collided, and were lost in discordant conflagrations where the river had been pushed aside once, and then again.

He thought of ruins.

As the waters began to merge into single entities, pools joining hands over land

Tears for the Moon God

bridges ahead of the creeks and streams they would form down in those interstitial zones. He thought of ruined palaces and shrines, ancient road markers all eroded and covered in moss. Broken walls, ash stained and overgrown with creeping vines and pitcher flowers. All the ruins of mortal innovation and decay. All the ruins of civilizations fallen. The ruins of mortal life.

He knelt at the edge of a wide lake, a body of water which spanned this corridor, the next, who knew how many after that. The lake must contain the lives of tens of thousands, hundreds of thousands of lives, every one robbed of identity and individuality.

Do they come back? After the push.

He disturbed the waters with a finger. They clarified, and from them founted forth kaleidoscopic visions, windows into countless lives all playing out one after another, growing more frenzied and more chaotic as the ripples drifted away, until the entire lake was alive with crazed imagery. A woman nursed a baby, her hair a wild tangle barely kept under a bonnet. An old man played a lute and sang to passersby on a dusty street. A young couple rode a gondola down a wider river—the luminous riverfront districts of a sprawling city to one side of them, dark, dense forest to the other. A large man polished off a bottle of spirits and then ran after his wife, grabbed her by the hair and spun her round for a beating. A group of thugs robbed and then killed a youth in an alley choked with shadows. A horse was dragged down in a Gil Garo raid gone wrong, and its rider stabbed to death as its broken legs kicked and scraped, its eyes rolling as it flailed. And a woman gave birth in the shelter of her home, the new father pushing stringy hair out of her face, holding strong as she clamped down on his hand.

Everywhere, scenes of mortal hope and fear, anger, betrayal, grief and joy played out across the endless waters. Their borders were indistinct. The colors ran, the scenes blended together, leaving behind nonsense displays, echoes of fate and history so distorted they lost their narrative purpose, bowed under the weight of loss and wounding.

Those windows into other lives collapsed. One after another, in tens and twenties, in hundreds, and thousands, they crashed in on themselves and returned to murky obscurity. And in those murky depths, fat carp and pan fish drifted unconcerned.

He leaned back against the dry bank, in a patch between pools just large enough for him to sit, and let himself drift.

Is this what the river is like? Meaningless, nonsense collisions. Lives weaving in and out of focus, a great tapestry all of random threads and each thread the twisting of so many lives into the fabric of existence. Is this what it's like for them. To see everything from far off, through a lens we can't access. Is this how the gods see us?

But then...how similar to the view from God Uldal's hilltop. All those doors flitting in and out of focus, promising grand adventures in far flung places, mesmerizing views and all of the tastes and sensations of belonging where you don't belong at all. As if you were born to be everywhere at once, and yet nowhere at all.

No. There is hope on the paths in his sanctuary. This? There is no hope in these waters. Only grief. Loss. Destruction. Only calamity and discord.

If he was pulled down into those waters, would he be drawn into a lost world? Its features, its borders, defined and finite, such a world must belong to fate. It could not but hope to be driven by predetermined futures, even broken as it was.

The Lake

Could there be comfort in such a world? If such a place could exist at all, would it be comfortable? Would it be stable? Would it have room for someone like him?

If he could not have death, perhaps he could have something in its place. Life after death, but a life with some meaning.

He inched toward the lake, edged back. There were promises in those waters, but he was not sure yet they were what he wanted. If he must emerge on this bank again, what might happen? He did not like not knowing. He had seen Hanuman the Elder, understood well the consequences of messing around in other people's memories. So many at once might break him, break his mind, but was it worse than an eternity in these halls?

He edged back further, not trusting himself to abstain from doing something reckless.

I should find the kid. A nice chat with a friend. To take the edge off.

He need only cross it. He knew where Sao Njack would be. The poor thing never left the side of his pool. Never had stopped grieving. He would be there. They could talk. And Shulraki wouldn't think about the lake for a while.

It would have to be enough. It would have to be. He was running out of reasons to stay away.

They were etched into the body, the vestiges of life. A faint pulse beating behind cooling flesh, the stiff carotid palpitating just at the edge of notice. Though the eyes were glassy and dull, there was a spark behind those vermilion lenses, a spark of awareness. The skin was pale, had begun to show obvious signs of rot—a breakdown of collagen fibers, a sagging around hollowed cavities.

It was not for Ank to judge the others too harshly for missing the signs. When every fiber of their being was so singularly concerned with escape, what were these little details but insignificant ventures off the beaten path, momentary distractions from more meaningful pursuits.

This uelfin was locked in a state of perpetual decay, but the soul did not flee from its flesh. He had seen far worse than this one. Gangrenous bodies, their bellies swollen with noxious gases, their eyes dried until they resembled hard tack and seeping gelatinous ooze.

And still, their souls did not flee. Could not flee. Death did not walk the Halls of Time. So bound to the ceaseless flow of the river, it seemed to him the god, the spirits, those who concerned themselves with finality must remain within its currents, ever reaping from the mortal coil, never stepping onto the river bank.

He seated himself beside the rotting body, the abandoned child of God Lanfin and Oe, and took her head in his hands. He twisted her body around, settled that heavy head into his lap, and passed gentle fingers through a shock of hair the color of the sea. Her unwavering gaze found the cloudy sky, that endless, sprawling gray, and a granular aura washed over him, traveled down the shafts of his forearms, across his hands to envelop her.

A pathway opened between them. One soul and the other, twin pulses in the close, cyclopean hall. In that pathway, the promise of release.

"I will free you from this flesh, but I cannot free you from these halls." He said. "My offering is not free, you understand. I will need your help when the time comes. You will know when it has come."

He watched the last spark of life leave her eyes, a last exhale escape her lungs

Tears for the Moon God

as all activity ceased. At last, the soul was free to wander, to wander with the rest of them, in spirit.

He watched as blue smoke drifted away from him, the contours of a slender, naked body coalescing within the cloud. The entity turned corner and faded, leaving nothing of her memory behind save a thin ether to distort the air for a few moments longer, before it too faded away.

He found Sao where he had expected to. He had been the first of the Wanderers to make contact, but then it only made sense he would be. The others might venture far from their origination points, but proximity had a way of helping things along. Had it not been for a certain measure of ambivalence, Shulraki had no doubt Ank would have been the first to find him when he was immured. As it was, Xi had found him before Hanuman, and he had quickly decided who he liked more between them.

Would I call Xi Didura a friend?

He decided he would. It was no secret to him the sword maker was working with Hanuman, though which of them was the mastermind behind their schemes remained a mystery. Hanman lacked nothing in the way of intellect, but he had lost so much of his mind in his years of isolation, and then more with each new Wanderer introduced to these hallowed halls.

And Xi?

He had his merits, but Shulraki doubted very much he had been overly concerned with tactics or strategy. He was not a soldier, or a man of noble birth. He was a tradesman. A skilled one, but nonetheless.

Still, he has his integrity. He is far more unified in his identity than Hanuman. It counts for something.

Sao was sitting pensive by the pool. In his taking, he was given back his youth, he must have been. The number of lives he had affected, millions scattered across this lone reach of the maze, implied he had traveled far in his life. That the passages around him were so vast, and intricate made the argument. But more than that, what could be glimpsed in those pools implied Sao Njack had built a sprawling empire, one greater than any ever seen on Ul Sadh, a feat that must have taken decades of near constant expansion to pull off.

Yet the man seated before him was not a middle-aged tyrant, emperor of the vast holdings of four or five already large and powerful nation. Here was a boy barely into his twenties, his features taut and unlined, soft, almost feminine. The Nixians were a beautiful people, with defined cheekbones and soft jaw lines, a sun kissed glow about them and those gracefully tapered eyes forested with thick, dark eyelashes—all features well suited to idolization even without the Sun Man's ethereal, golden pallor.

Sao could have been a statue. It was not hard to understand why so many had followed him. He must have been seen almost as a god to his people, to the common rabble of the southern kingdoms—Tulakh, and Sanguhr, and Saodein. A coming deity to free them from their oppressors, a giver of hope immortalized in their arts and in their histories.

But not anymore.

All of that...most of it anyway...would be gone now. Isolated to these puddles and ponds, as it were. Still, he could not help but wonder what life under the

The Lake

Nixian's rule must have been like. What it could be like, if they ever escaped this place.

He sat beside him, at the edge of the pool, and watched carp flit about in its depths.

"It's been a while." Sao said without inflection. His gaze was fixed on the pool.

"It has." He agreed.

"Have you come to ask about my lover?"

Shulraki snorted. "What good would that do?"

"It's all anyone else seems to care about." Sao leaned forward. He dug his fingertips into damp, sandy soil at the pool's edge. "But I don't like reliving those memories. Too much hurt. Too many regrets."

"I well understand." Shulraki said. "But no, I don't intend to bring you down with painful memories. Memories you should cherish, I might add. If I could remember all that befell me, I would be happier than I am."

"You seem plenty happy." Sao drew away from the pool, set curious eyes on him. His fingers played in the dirt still, but at least Shulraki had his attention now. At least he had that.

"Yes, well..." Shulraki smiled. "Easy enough to hide your truth when you've spent your entire life in court politics."

"I...I understand." His gaze shied away, and he rested his chin against his knees. "What's bothering you?"

"Aside from what bothers all of us?"

"You'd be used to that by now."

"You haven't left this pool since you arrived."

"Being close to it is comforting."

"It isn't good for you."

"I agree."

"Then why remain?"

He chuckled. "What will happen if I leave? Someone will discover I'm gone, and take a dip. Maybe it'll be someone with pure intentions, but then maybe not. If I leave, I make myself vulnerable. Much in the same way that a wrong move in a game of kugi leaves the player exposed."

"That game is about deception, isn't it?"

Sao nodded.

"Are you playing such a game?"

"Isn't everyone?"

"No. Not all of us. Not me."

"No, I suppose not. But you accomplished what you set out to do, didn't you?" Shulraki grinned. "With lasting effects."

"I did wonder why the sudden upheaval in Saodein. The monarch there was strong, intelligent...she had a mind for strategy—"

"All true enough, but she was also prone to double dealing, playing factions against each other. Moves of that kind may feel intelligent, but each is a gamble taken against your own life, your own stability. You make many enemies that way."

A mirthless grin spread across Sao's cheeks. "I know that better than most."

"You understand we're not enemies. Even Hanuman does not wish to see you harmed."

"Hanuman wants what all tyrants want." Sao growled. "He won't be satisfied unless he has a means of controlling me, to keep me under his thumb."

"He's done a poor job of it then. He has nothing on any of us."

"He has your memories. He has pieces of you housed within him which he can use to his advantage."

"He is also quite mad."

"Which makes him more dangerous, not less. My lover was the same. If I could right one wrong, it would be healing him of that madness. I may never have been recalled had I succeeded."

His fingers grazed the edge of the pool. A breathtaking scene exploded across its surface. A line of horse archers arranged across the vastness of a plain, a railroad track running at angle to them and a line of strange machines near it. The army stood against a line with no soldiers, at least none visible. Behind the archers, an army like had never existed in his time falling out of sight behind towering siege engines, monstrosities in metal.

At the heart of the line, a picturesque Cloud Man who went unarmored, his chest bare, inviting arrows to find homes in soft places, welcoming the possibility of death. Grouse and crow feathers formed a crescent wing in his hair, and a band like a static flame encircled his bicep.

His expression was grim as his horse trotted forward, the lines of soldiers shifting restlessly behind him. He raised a broad-bladed sword over his head and loosed a silent cry, and the scene fell again to obscurity.

"You have no idea how much I miss him." Sao said, his fingers retreating from the pool to paw at the sand once more. "And he doesn't remember me at all."

"How cruel."

"And yet well earned. I might even believe we deserved it, but I've come to a different conclusion recently."

"Which is?"

"The gods could grace us with mercy in the form of their gifts. The ones who refuse to are the same ones with most ability to do so. What we chose resulted in hurts suffered by one of them. Just one. And they brought down wrath and fury on us for it. But in the aftermath, we discovered just how much they had, how much *one* of them horded away and denied us.

"If they should guard their gifts so jealously, when they could spread them across the world, when in doing so, they might bring prosperity to all peoples, then we were not wrong for our deeds. What we did was right for our people. They only saw it as a great wrong because we had become a threat to their power. Their insular, uncomplicated way of life. And I think, now, if given the choice, I would not pull back when they came for their pound of flesh. I would instead take off their heads and leave them flailing. Such is the injustice of it all."

"You hold the gods as your enemy?"

Sao reached out and patted his knee, smiling knowingly into his face. "Not all of them, but most."

"Tell me. If you could have those memories stolen away, locked behind a closed door where they cannot plague you, would you leave them there?"

"In doing so, I would lose memory of who I was, and who I needed to be. I would not be myself, then. Not with any sense of clarity. And if those memories were locked away, I would search for them constantly, knowing something was wrong. I couldn't live like that, my friend. It would kill me not knowing."

The Lake

"There is a lake between your domain and mine, where the people who lived in my time and yours are kept. There are many there, and no distinction is made between them. I've thought about joining them."

"Why?"

"Because that locked door is within me. In death, I didn't have to confront what my Shards did after me. I knew what I asked of them and it was enough."

"But not anymore."

"Not anymore." Shulraki agreed.

"I might be able to help you."

"How?"

"My first master was a lake spirit called Salein. His power relates to memory."

"Ironic." Shulraki glanced at the pool.

"Memories have echoes in the soul, Shulraki. If you want to open that door—"

"I don't. Not..." he swallowed around a lump in his throat. "Not now."

"I leave the offer open to you." Sao said. "If that lake is on your mind again, find me. I'll do what I can for you."

"You are a man of many mysteries." Shulraki chuckled. "One day, perhaps."

"Anything for a friend."

The Valley

Moon beams painted the valley floor. Rein mountain rose, a jagged, gray monstrosity glaring down at Helein Four Eyes' party, the camp they had staked out in the lowlands; glaring from behind a wall of shorter peaks all capped at their heights in stark white and washes of gray. A belt line of exposed rock bifurcated the mountain, a no man's land dividing its quieter roots from the blood-stained snows higher up.

He wondered how many corpses were buried under the drifts. How many people's climbs had been ended before they saw the summit. The entrance to a shrine was situated somewhere near the mountain's base, where Rein's dominion ended and the Taojin siblings ruled. He lingered on the thought of them. Taojin La, whose pulse through the earth, even from this distance, beat a lively and vibrant rhythm. Her brother was sleeping. *He will stay that way, won't he? Until she's had enough.*

Swamps were so much different than anything else he had encountered over land. There were places within the tidal zones of the oceans that bore some resemblance to them, where two spirits shared power. In the oceans, there were places where many spirits worked in cooperation with each other, where no single one would claim to have power over the others. Among terrestrial spirits, such cooperation was rare—isolated to the swamps and the marshes. There was little need for joint stewardship over other lands, and the spirits who dominated them were too jealous besides. To share power was to accept an inferior place in their hierarchies. Those at the apexes would never abide such cooperation. They would perceive it as weakness.

The forests and the mountains had their hierarchies. Rein pledged himself to Hod the Rope, like any other mountain, and cooperated with Suiseth and Dam Bao, the Range Lords who embraced him, though both held on loosely. It was unwise to challenge a Fang, even for such powerful spirits, and among those few high peaks, Rein was the tallest and the strongest.

He tested the gourd at his hip, wondered how long his body would last if the mountain chose to ride him. How Rein compared to Sufa Salein, or Ouran the Giant, or Zanzark. Was he greater than them, with all of their vast holdings, or were they

The Valley

stronger? More to the point, would a foreign spirit so many orders of magnitude stronger than him, who was able to subvert his will on a whim, know to flee from his body before he died?

There is always that risk, isn't there?

Well within the valley was a floodplain and a river. The band, black in the moonlight, glittered to reflect the stars. He sat on an outcrop near enough to it, a pockmarked boulder at his back, its shadow a shield to keep him comfortably distant, and prevent prying eyes from seeing him. On those heights, the moderate temperatures he was coming to enjoy here would be a memory, and him left to grapple with a dry flowering of ice on the wind. A cold to make him savor these moments, remember fondly and longingly these last touches of true warmth, and the freedom they brought with them.

He had foregone his clothes. The skin around his elbows and his knees had become ashy, with none of the butters and oils he needed for grooming. Wool against his joints bred a fire in them he hoped the waters down below would drive back, but he was not ready to make the descent.

Someone else had claimed this stretch of river. Another man stood in the shallows, tossed water over his lithe body, scored away several days hard travel— salt and dirt, sweat and oil.

That other man's clothes were strewn across so many sticks. A pile of leathers were mounded atop a rock, leaving a loose-fitting, hooded coverall, briefs and stockings suspended and drying.

Nixians were a peculiar people. Their patriarch said they lived in caves and dark tunnels, and only came out to collect water and trade with people in their southlands. But that wasn't entirely accurate. It couldn't be. There had been times, in Xirakura's memory, when the Nixians had sent envoys to Sufa Salein, routine expeditions taken with the help of pathfinders for the purpose of ceremony, to reassert a solidarity between tribes.

A diplomatic people, then.

But he did not know what to think of them. He did not trust the youngest one. He was hiding something. They all were. He kept his hood up, wore a mask sometimes, and when he did, he would not be bothered to take it off for a day and a night if he could help it. He had taken to wearing that mask more and more as they marched into Suiseth Range. He supposed it might keep the wind off his face on the high passes, but in the lowlands? And the others, his father and his cousin, did not wear them.

Here he was, naked as the day he was born, washing the dirt off his skin and believing all the while he was alone.

They are not the only ones hiding things, are they? He could see it plainly enough in the way those Raukhas sometimes joined their heads together, in secret meetings where they discussed unknowable truths. Helein was always present in those meetings, one of a few ever constant faces.

To look at her was not to see an elite in Gaul No Eyes hierarchy. She was as plain as wet plaster, and was just as charismatic. Her complexion was pallid, her eyes a murky shade of brown set under bushy eyebrows. Her lips were painfully thin, he had noted that on first seeing her. A difference he had not noted in other cultures, which was quite common of the people of Qin Loc—and, perhaps, of the Byrnese people more generally.

Tears for the Moon God

He had noted flashes of silver at her hips, across her ankles now and again as she ambled along, her pants legs riding up just enough that the sun caught on the hidden knives there. Plain, unassuming, but he suspected all of this was calculated. She was a Raukha, which meant she was a crook. She served a Hand of Raukha, which meant she was likely a killer, as well.

And Sao Njack? His kin? They knew too little of their benefactors; knew less than he did, and he knew next to nothing. The object of their travels was obvious. There was only one reason to climb to the summit of Rein Mountain, and that was to obtain a sword. But what purpose did the Nixians serve? Jinga was just an engineer. His son was the acolyte of a lake spirit. A healer, maybe; but if so, he was not a particularly good one. He held his own with those long knives he carried, but then they all did. And his cousin was a better shot with a bow.

There is another mystery in need of solving. Both Sao and his cousin practiced a form of spirit calling...something they referred to by that name, but it was nothing like what Xirakura did. They could not draw in the spirits they called to, and maintained conscious control over themselves when they did. Distance had no bearing on their abilities. They did not have to make use of the spirits who dwelt in relative proximity to them. And that was curious, wasn't it? They could not draw on any spirit they chose. They had their one, each of them, and only that one.

And he did not know who either of them was beholden to. Perhaps these men were hiding something in plain sight, an ability which would make them formidable enough to challenge the mountain and succeed, but he doubted it. To that end, they had shown no exemplary skills.

Down within the river's wide and shallow band, Sao Njack trekked to shore. He tested his garments, and his shoulders slumped. He found a stone blockier than the rest, and seated himself atop it, ruffling his hair, shaking out the excess moisture.

Xirakura did not want to disturb the other man, but it was late, and he would have liked to get some sleep before they struck out in the morning. He decided to leave the comfort of his rock and its shadow, get done with what needed doing despite Sao Njack's presence.

He marched down to the river, his clothing bundled under his arm. When he was halfway, he broke into a run. He cast the bundled clothes onto the river bank, pelted into the waters, and dove.

Icy cold stole his breath away. Within the current, he heard the voice of the spirit, a tinkling laugh playing against his eardrums. He breeched the surface, cast his head back, threads of thick, straight hair whipping in a wide arc. He leaned back, floated, and the current drifted around him, keeping him in place.

Sao bolted upright. He looked ready to run, but froze instead. There were his clothes, waiting for him, his travel pack leaning against the rock his leathers rested on top of.

What a strange, strange man.

A surge of raw energy flowed into him, and Xirakura heard a voice within it, a spirit speaking to the Nixian, though it sounded from far away.

"Don't!" the spirit said, and the power ebbed away.

"How did you—"

"I'm sorry. Had I known you would respond—"

"No, it's...you won't tell anyone about this." Sao said. "Will you?"

A darker flush had bloomed across Sao's cheeks. In the moonlight, he looked lighter than he did in daylight, but then he was not normally so exposed. Still, without that hot, dark flush, his face and neck were still lighter than they ought to be. *Maybe the moon is playing tricks on me.*

"Tell them what?" Xirakura asked.

"That I'm..." Sao cocked his head to the side. "How are you doing that?"

Xirakura looked about himself. He supposed it must look odd that he was able to stay largely in one place with a swift current flowing all around him.

"This?" he chuckled. "This isn't me?"

Sao cast about wildly, hunting for other trespassers intent on this intimate moment.

Xirakura wondered at that, too. "Would you calm down, please?" He said. "No one else is here. It's just us."

"Then who is keeping you stable?"

"That's an odd question."

Sao reached for his small clothes.

"Are you sure you want to do that?"

"This is getting uncomfortable."

Xirakura chuckled. "I can see that." He played his hands through the waters, enjoying the feeling of the river's current flowing between his fingers. "There's no need to be so prudish, you know. My people only wear swaddling until we've been taught not to void ourselves wherever we're standing."

"That isn't why." Sao snapped.

"Then what is it?"

"It's just...you know exactly what it is."

"I promise you I don't." Xirakura assured him. "You do look ridiculous holding up that wet scrap of cloth, though."

Sao set it back down. "You promise you won't tell?"

"Tell what?"

"Don't play dumb. *Please.* If this gets out, they'll—"

Xirakura took a closer look at him. His skin *was* lighter than it ought to be, that was true. Even in the moonlight it was obvious. It held a burnished cast, caught the light in an unnatural way. He had never seen someone so complected.

"Ah." He said. "You're golden."

"Y-yes. That would be what I'd rather not have made public to these...these Raukhas."

"Why?"

A vexed expression stole over Sao's features. *So whatever this strange condition is, it is common knowledge to his people. He must think I am a fool.*

"You want money? Some other favor?"

"You misunderstand. I do not know what having golden skin *means.* Why should it be a big deal if our employers know?"

"Because...you really don't know?"

"No more than you seem to know why I'm not drowning in this river. Call it a cultural difference." Xirakura righted himself. He planted his feet in the silts, marched ashore.

Close up, the cast of Sao's skin was even more apparent. As he closed the distance, a westerly breeze spilled into the valley.

"You're a long way from home." The West Wind, Zephos, said gruffly.

Tears for the Moon God

"I suppose I am." Xirakura shrugged. "Familiar company is well appreciated, old friend. Will you stay for a time? I'd like to catch up, if you will humor me."

"Who are you talking to?" Sao asked.

He shook his head. He had often felt disappointment in the people around him since leaving home. His gift was far from universal, but his people at least knew enough to treat his conversations with the spirits as immaterial. Until they had concluded, anyway. Then, they might ask their questions, ask after what news the winds might carry. What the mountain wanted. Why the forest needed his ear.

"Why is golden skin noteworthy?" Xirakura asked.

Zephos cackled. "Poor man. I suppose your people have never seen a katcyakin before."

"What is a katcyakin? A child of the Luck God?"

"Close enough. This one is uncommonly lucky." Zephos explained. "Sun men are like that. They set out to do something and the chips all land in the right order. They rarely fail."

"Ah. I see. Why is he so nervous, then?"

"Something is wrong with you." Sao said.

Xirakura gestured for his silence. His mouth snapped shut behind a frustrated snarl. But then, he could not be blamed. No one he had met in the time since leaving Sufa Salein forest still remembered the old way. He had thought these folk from another guardian tribe might remember, and knew in this moment he had been hoping for something that could never be.

Still, he could not judge too harshly. He was just as ignorant of the Nixian way.

"He is afraid of being used is my guess. People have a way of seeing katcyakin less as people than as tools for their use. At least, they see sun men this way. For cloud men, their birthright is usually marked by death soon after they are born, unfortunate though that is. One was born not far from where he hails from, you know. I suppose it is noteworthy that two would be born in the same lands, within so many months of each other.

"Now, I must be going. I have a date on Harkahn, and I'd rather not be late."

"The old argument?" Xirakura chuckled.

"That one exactly."

"Could you do me a favor before you go?"

"Depends."

"Could you dry the poor man's clothes?"

Zephos cackled.

A gust of wind lifted Sao's small clothes, his stockings, and his coverall into the air. With a flourish and a wet snap, water peppered the ground, and his clothes drifted into a tidy pile atop his leathers.

He watched with a vexed expression as the clothes folded themselves and settled, all in the same motion. "Really, how are you doing that?"

"I am a spirit caller."

"So am I, but I can't do anything like that."

Xirakura shook his head. "You misunderstand. I am a *spirit caller*. I was born one. I speak with the spirits, and they speak with me. And if I am willing to, I can house them within me for a time. That way, they can act through me. Speak through me. You see?

"The spirit of the river is Daelus. She finds me amusing, I think, so she helped me to float while I washed myself. The West Wind, Zephos, is who handled your clothes."

"Huh." Sao said, for lack of anything else. "How do you come into an ability like that?"

"By being nice, Sao Njack." He smiled. "I won't tell them what you are, don't worry. I think, maybe, I can trust you now."

He brushed past him, marched toward his bundle of clothes. He'd have liked to ask Zephos to help him with the drying, but the moment was passed. He had given up a boon to the Nixian, a matter he felt fine about.

Besides, without Zephos around, he had a reason not to put on those itchy things for a bit longer. He didn't think he would ever get used to them.

"You didn't trust me?" Sao called after him.

"No." He responded, taking his washing to the river. "And you did not trust me, either. Probably still don't."

When Sao said nothing more, he looked over his shoulder. He found him fully dressed, seated on the rock with his travel pack open, dabbing makeup onto his neck.

That's why he looks different. I should have known.

Hanuman lay spread eagle across the flagstones. Each time he entered a memory, he came away from it feeling like a drowned rat. In some ways, he supposed he was.

There was nothing wholesome about invading another mortal's memories, occupying their skin in some forgotten trencher the great river had abandoned. It was unbecoming, but a necessity. He had seen through too many windows, looked into countless lives. With each plunge, it became harder to hold himself together. He had been falling apart for a long time. That shedding of pieces of him, the accumulation of other pieces, stop gaps to fill in the voids left behind, memories of other lives infecting him, had become his normal for a time. It was only when Xi arrived he began to suspect something was wrong with him, that those memories did not belong.

There were places within him so discordant he could not piece together enough of any one life to know what belonged to who. There were other places, deeper places, where he believed his life--that strange fiction he had lived in the flesh, which was stricken from the record and forgotten—was almost whole, where the arc of his life made sense for a time, and the gaps between memories were not so easy to notice.

He lay sprawled across the floor tiles, one, sandaled foot still underwater; heaved air into burning lungs, waiting for the ache in his head to pass, for the ring like auras, the dark shield against his sight, to dwindle, and the labyrinth to return to normal around him.

"Splashing around in other men's memories, I see."

"Quiet, Shulraki." He snapped.

Delicate hands dug under his flank. Shulraki rolled him over.

"You really shouldn't do that." He said.

"I've long passed the point at which such travels can harm me."

"As you say." He heard the mocking in Shulraki's voice. Those powdered nobles of ages long after his were prone to it. He was convinced they couldn't help it.

Tears for the Moon God

There had been no kings in his time, no rulers among men. There had been few enough of them in those days, and too many enemies surrounding them for such petty squabbles as who had the right to govern. In those days, they had barely discovered the art of taming livestock, had only just become an agrarian society, and all of it possible for the secrets his father kept.

"Well, as you insist on playing around in the mud, perhaps you can tell me who this puddle belongs to?"

The dark was beginning to fade, leaving a gray mist where the curtain had parted. Spots and streams fluttered into focus, fled to the corners of his eyes as soon as he found them.

The confusion was beginning to set in. He did not think much of Shulraki. The Sun Man seamed content to remain here, trapped in Lanfin's Labyrinth, with no reasonable pathway to escape.

He gave up before he ever arrived here. Almost as if he knew he would end up here. As if it was unavoidable from the beginning.

"A man named Xirakura." He said. "One of my closer descendants, it seems. A Katuwiti."

"Never heard of them." Shulraki said.

A flash of white, bushy hair swam across the edge of his vision. Shulraki had seated himself uncomfortably close to where he lay.

"A tribe who still practices the old way. They are not well known."

"Something you gleaned from your other wanderings, no doubt."

"Yes."

"What have you learned from him?"

"Not enough."

"Oh?"

Hanuman tried to sigh. Fire blossomed in his lungs. Mucosal, harsh coughs racked him. It was several moments before he had gathered himself enough to speak on.

"Very little about the nature of his life is relevant to me. Some months spent in the employ of a Raukha of middling rank—"

"Well that's interesting, now isn't it. The Raukhas were quite useful to me in my own time."

"He was not using them." Hanuman growled. "They were using him. Wasting his talents, too. They wanted him for a guide. They could have invoked their target through him, had they understood his power."

"A guide to where?"

"You ask too many questions."

"I am a naturally inquisitive person. Is that so wrong?"

"It hardly matters where. His time with my quarry was brief. At least, there is not as much there as I would have liked. Or, I suppose, he may have endured an absence, wherein their paths split. I do not know."

"Well you'll just have to dive back in, then, won't you." Shulraki patted his leg. "I think I've heard enough, in any case. Though, I would caution you to pursue this path at your own risk. You may well be better off simply asking our newcomer how he ended up here."

"I have found asking is not always the most reliable route. Men of our kind tend to lie, or obfuscate the details of their lives which embarrass them. None of it will help us."

"Right."

Hanuman's could just make out the hazy outline of Shulraki's hunched figure as he rose. A bulky silhouette, the man's posture stooped, his robes swaying as he shambled off. Though he spoke in a loose, inviting manner, there was seldom substance behind his words. His truths may well have been the hardest to uncover.

If not for the Sanark, that is. He corrected himself. He had never found Ank's memories, nor the memories of the Sanarks who served with him. He had begun to think they had been purged in some way, but who would have done such a thing.

Why would anyone wish to conceal his memories in *this* place? Where there was no hope of escape, and all of the labyrinth's inhabitants had committed heinous acts in their time of freedom? What might he have done to earn such a punishment. That even the possibility of another Wanderer stumbling onto the secret was too much a gamble to be risked.

In a world in which all pasts were mysteries in need of plumbing, in which each man held onto his own truths and shared little, Ank the Sanark remained an enigma. Why ought he have secrets even Hanuman the Elder could not uncover? With all of his knowledge of the lay of these lands, the rules and conventions they were bound to, even the gods who were involved in the creation of these Halls of Time.

He suspected there was something within the absence of Ank's memories, a critical detail he had missed. Maybe he had some knowledge of a way out, but then...why would he remain? What incentive could there be for staying in this isolation?

No, it must be something else. Something the gods themselves don't want known. If not a way out, then perhaps a way to fight them. Some truth about them.

Pursuing that end had proven a fruitless effort.

Too many moving parts in this scheme. Everything riding on a razor's edge, and me sitting here worrying over these mysteries like a dog a marrow bone.

What knowledge have I gleaned from these wanderings? Nothing of consequence. Nothing worth inviting more madness into me.

Onto the next pool I suppose. Then into the memories of another. Perhaps the next account will be worth the price I must

In the Dark of the Night

The yurt Sauman left them in was less a hut than a compound. Within the slab-sided construction was a central room framed by various private chambers which the contestants laid claim to almost as soon as they were left alone.

He was surprised to see Shaki chose to room with Bora. He had assumed they disliked each other. It hadn't occurred to him they might be lovers.

Tamlin spared no time immersing himself within the sparse knot of women when they were all gathered. None of the contenders had brought any effects with them, but Sauman had assured them their belongings would be soon in coming, once they had been checked over.

Shaki disappeared with his girlfriend, and as he sat alone near the largest of several wood stoves, atop a series of cushions placed there for their comfort, he heard their laughter from their room.

Small figurines of carved wood set up on daises formed a ring around the room; were interrupted by the entrances to short halls and outlying chambers. He suspected they told the tale of the gathered powers here.

Fan Ryu—a broad shouldered man with a blue-painted dragon looming behind him—drew his attention. Thera, too, was represented as a human figure. Her skin was white as porcelain, her eyes painted a fierce, virulent blue. Painted twigs emulated lightning fanning around her like a snake's hood.

He saw an age-stained rendering of God Katcya. Fittingly, the gold paint covering it was chipped, giving the impression of cloud lines without meaning to. The figurine had been added hastily with the decision regarding Dupec's admission.

There were surprises among those statuettes, too. The mud worm, Galadir, represented coiled about himself, ready to spring forward at the slightest provocation.

He noted a willowy figure in silhouette, positioned atop a kugi board. It could only represent the God of Games, but an acolyte of his would pose problems well beyond this tournament. As much as Goddess Liandal, he would prefer to avoid drawing God Tirulain's eye.

Chakta approached him. It seemed she was still intent on finishing their conversation from earlier.

"You don't appear to want company, but you'll have mine."

In the Dark of the Night

"Given the choice, I would rather you than some of these others."

Chuckling lightly, she sat next to him.

"I thought you were trying to get in my pants when you approached. That's all any of these fools want from me." She rolled her eyes. "But you aren't interested in me are you?"

"Not just you."

"You don't like women?"

He smirked. "And you only like women."

"Takes one to know one, I guess." She said. "We could be friends."

"I could use more of those."

They exchanged warm smiles. Noticing their enthusiasm, Tamlin stuck up his nose and stalked off. Chakta snickered.

"You don't like him much do you?" Dupec said.

"It's not all that deep. He likes strong women. Always has. But I've told him a million times I'm not interested and he won't let it go. He's going to hate you now, you know."

"Would I be wrong to assume he thinks you're interested in me. Now he's seen us laughing together?"

"You would not be. But I have this theory, see. I don't know how much truth there is to it, but it seems right enough."

"I see."

"When we were kids, he would follow the older boys around. He would make this face, and his cheeks would get all rosy like he was embarrassed. I always thought...well maybe...." She shrugged. "Maybe there was something to that."

"But then we got older and every winter I would see him surrounded by all these pretty girls with great tits and cute smiles—"

"You're really showing off your priorities."

"What can I say?"

He snorted. "So you think he's gay, too."

She pursed her lips and nodded. "Bisexual. Probably."

His gaze drifted down the corridor Tamlin had just left. "I don't know about that."

"You wouldn't, though, would you? You only just met him."

Thin clouds chased each other across a dark, night sky. They bared down, bringing with them a wet chill which drove into Ibrim's bones. He watched them pass the full moon, watched as its bloody aura stained the edges of those that drifted too close. He had waited long for this night, had tracked the moon's movements for months, and he was not alone.

Nervous men and women cast sharp glances at each other. They checked over weapons, unbound them from harnesses. Some made a show of stretching, tensing muscles, practicing forms he suspected would be useless when the time came for fighting. Few among them were true warriors. Few had held a weapon for any great length of time. These were the desperate, the huddled masses, who Tulakh's royal family had failed.

He held some responsibility for them, for their arrival on this desperate plane amid fields where Ung Sakh's roots had been pushed back, fields which supplied the capital—with food, with comfort.

Tears for the Moon God

They knew as he did that this night would be bloody. The nights when the moon was full, when Ao Nii was at his strongest, always were. Even as they waited in the shadows, harsh, white light painting their faces, drawing in shadows to pool around pitted eyes, playing against angular cheeks, sharp, long noses, touching on padded shoulders and armored chests. Ao Nii was in the world somewhere, waging violence against a spirit or a god, his most loyal acolytes trying in their desperation to push him back, compel him into the sky, back into his keep.

It was a hopeless endeavor. No mortal, no matter how strong, how long standing in the moon god's light, could stand against him. Not this night.

His gaze flicked over hard faces, taking in cursory details. Months of watching, pouring over lunar charts, identifying constellations the moon had passed. For most, the exercise would be for nothing. Most would know death's embrace this night, a trail of corpses to mark the passage of these foolish people across the skies.

No advantage for a prince. None for a soldier. *We are all equal under his gaze.*

The thought embittered him. He would never be king, that was true, but he would have this power. It was his right. His father would see him, know him for his worth. In this act, he demanded it from him.

The moon broke through the clouds, casting off thin haze, revealing its serenely smiling face to him, to them.

He teased the broadsword at his hip loose of its scabbard, a soft push with the thumb, the snick of metal against tanned leather.

The moon's rays slashed through clouds, and The West Wind clawed them away, lowing behind a rapidly expanding gap through which the stars could watch unobstructed, could look down upon the Tulakka warriors, merchants, thieves, assassins, the third prince himself.

And weep.

Stars fell, stabbed the earth in pairs, one and then another, twin flashes, their streams lingering after them for far too long.

The last of them smashed aground fifty paces from the gathered mob. As if by instinct, they scattered, putting as much space as they could between themselves without risking being left behind.

In the moon's shadow, crystal spires resolved in slow turns. Parapets, forward walls, a city sprawling out from the feet of a vast palace that made the pristine domes and towers of his home look rough, unfinished. They drank in moon beams, a red cast marring their edges, promising fury and death even as the structures loomed, a beacon of peace and serenity, on high. From a crenellated gate, its doors flung open, a stairway materialized, its steps glittering like precious gems, spangled light pulsing within them. One step, then the next, each born as the last grew stable, mist edging toward them, coalescing, becoming something of substance, alien and yet familiar.

The steps broke against earth, the tails of meteors rising columns to frame those ghostly stairs, the path to the god house, Ao Nii's keep.

Ibrim's sword flashed out of its scabbard. He bared his teeth charged the steps, roaring to silence his fear. The screamed challenges of his people, his competition, followed him, echoing into the night.

Dozens of booted feet chased after him. Bodies overtook him, sailed by as his feet touched steps and he climbed.

A bonfire glow filled the gate in the sky—vast, crimson, brutal. A roar of rage without purpose, the call of madmen frenzied by Ao Nii's violent touch against them, against their souls, tore from hundreds of throats. Acolytes clad in that violent light poured through the gap, thundered down the steps to meet them, to raze whatever they came across when they inevitably reached land.

Too fast they were upon the Tulakka.

Blood sprayed from deep wounds, yet the moon kin carried no weapons, raised no swords. A touch proved enough to maim. Proximity, the attention of those mad moonkin enough to wound as red auras and blade-sharp air currents found weaknesses in armor, laid open flesh.

Knives flashed at an acolyte's throat and the man they belonged to was cut down. the acolyte fell on the fallen figure. Teeth clamped down on a Tulakka throat, tore. Cartilage and flesh dangled from his jaw. Vacant, silver eyes peered down the staircase, into night's darkness.

Where was God Mu, to save this creatures? Where was God Uldal to guide his path? Were those gods not honor bound to keep Ao Nii at bay, to hold him in place until his rage subsided. The spirits ought to be converging on the base of this staircase, and yet to his ears all was silent.

The ravages of this battle, wanton destruction, carnage—his brain refused to process any of it, drove him forward, pushed him to let go of panic, to ignore the plight of the people around him. There would be time for reflection later. Time in which to grieve. Now, he must survive. Only that. Survive, and climb.

His sword arced through cold air, took the distracted acolyte's head from his shoulders. Too late for the soldier, but his climb was not ended.

He fell back.

A pair of women pushed past him. He watched as long swords danced and flickered, as the stream of acolytes tore through them, ending a short lived assault with their annihilation.

He took his advantage, rushed through the gap they opened. Bodies pressed in on every side, and he was alone within the tide of madmen.

He picked his targets, heart thundering in his chest, thought held at a distance. He rode instinct, delivering killing blows to the backs of skulls, hamstringing acolytes, mortals overwhelmed by their god's embrace, taking off limbs.

More bodies fell. More Tulakka. More acolytes.

Gore spattered his hauberk, made treacherous footing of the steps he crossed.

He held to the middle as still more bodies fell, plummeted over the sides of the steep rise, into slow currents, to drift earthward. If they were not dead on slipping, the fall would kill them.

They had known the risks, or thought they did. He had been a fool to think he knew anything of the climb at all, to think any record of it could prepare him.

The sour smell of iron filled his lungs. Blood flecked his lips.

An acolyte hurtled toward him. He threw himself out of her path.

The acolyte reached out as if to embrace a thief who held his knives at chest height, ready for violence. He reached out, latched onto the thief's cheeks, twisted.

He lost her to the hordes, the ever more desperate climb.

His thighs burned. His back ached from the exertion. The acolytes were advantaged by the high ground. He was forced to bear the pain they did not.

The gates yawned before him, too far distant to make out details. Still more bodies fell. The push of fresh bodies through the gates was ceaseless. An army

Tears for the Moon God

passed through that hellish portal and he knew those that reached his lands would savage all they found there, until in daylight sleep finally took them; knew, too, that if his climb did not end soon, he would die like any of those who had fallen at lower altitudes. If he did not make it, if dawn came for him, if the sun god rose against the moon, he would fall, and the journey would be fruitless.

Life. To continue living. He clung to this one need, poured his soul into the task of staying alive.

His pace slowed. His arms tired under the labor of holding his sword upright, and his swings became sluggish, pathetic things.

His climb, now, was decided by the indifference of those who passed him, and with slow recognition he saw they did not pursue him, did not look upon him.

Madness lingered in their stares, but it was colder. Control was tenuous, but these were not commanded by the all consuming lust for death.

He slowed to a crawl, down on hands and knees. He was less than a dog. Foggy tile spanned the field of his vision, vitreous columns, crystal domes and spires on the height of a matte, white cliff. Those streets were devoid of life. Even the cold eyed acolytes he had seen come past were a memory, and the ghost city of the moon god, the God House of Ao Nii, was enshrouded in that maddening, red glow.

He crawled, closing on his salvation, dragging himself across those final steps. Pain with every intake of breath, slow fire in his every muscle...he was dying. He was certain of it. He would never make it to the threshold, not past the gates to certain safety.

He slithered on his belly, reached for a last step, looked behind him, looked to the carnage. Blood oozed over the steps, dripped earthward. Bodies sprawled across the staircase, falling into obscurity. Those who passed him marched beyond them, paying them no attention, treating them as if they belonged there, were a part of the staircase itself, unremarkable.

Dozens of lives were reduced to land features, objects not worth grace, or grief. He dragged himself across the step, his sword rasping against its edge, rolled onto cobbles.

Well below him, the acolytes of the Moon God were spilling into his lands. His father's guard would be meeting them, holding Tulaen against the destruction they would reap. What care the king for the people who lived outside, who would not heed the evacuation order. They had known what was coming. Some would survive this night. Most would not. But he had his taste of success. What care should he have if the people he would represent were dying. He had won his place. He could build his legacy, and finally, his father would see him.

Villages burned, smoke billowing into the sky. Light and the echoes of sorcerous clashes drifted from them. He lay on his back, turned his gaze to the sky. The moon smiled down on him, too close and yet far removed from where he lay. He drank in cool air, felt it fill his lungs, push away the sharper pains of recent exertion and replace them with something dull, something distant.

He closed his eyes, listened to the rushing wind, her calls of judgment for the armies of Ao Nii's chosen kin. The wind came from the east, and he cracked his lips around a smile.

What would you have me do, Astair? Saodein expands. They will not stop at the Fingers. And my house is too weak to oppose them. But you know my heart, or would claim to. That this pursuit is taken in selfishness. A desire to be seen as useful, to be

In the Dark of the Night

a son to a man who cannot love. Who cannot afford to.

The gods have their games, cast their stones, lend to that kingdom their blessing. Is it wrong, spirit, to seek an answer to their press? Is it wrong to walk this path?

Hands took him under his shoulders. His body was dragged over stones. Deep shadows pooled over his face, and he met oblivion. The greatest darkness. A dreamless slumber.

A low fire burned at the heart of a circle of polished stones, each of them the size of a man's head and pulled from a creek, the edges polished smooth. The stones reflected startling hues back at the three gathered there, and a second ring hemmed them in, echoing the glimmering shades of that inner sanctum from behind. Agate and tiger's eye predominated, lending added warmth to a cool, dark night.

Monkeys ran along high branches within the forest's canopy, their screeching calls echoing eerily. The high yowl of a wild cat in heat was answered by the lower-pitched call of a suitor. There, too, the boar snuffling and snorting, the clatter of disturbed stones cast away from hooves and the sandy slide of something heavy being dragged into a den.

Katuwan and Lura cast about nervously for the sources of those sounds. Any moment, some predator might break into their humble circle of fire glow. Any moment, some brazen animal might attack them. But Xirakura was not afraid. An intimate familiarity with this forest and its spirits gave him reassurance that he was safe. He had consorted with the spirits of the streams and springs, those who guided the breezes, who guarded deep caves and sat vigil atop high hills. There was nothing to fear for him from this forest. Nothing he could not fend off.

The one exception was Sufa Salein. For him alone, he was nervous.

Night's deeper darkness changed the spirit. He became volatile, aggressive. In daylight, he was a guardian, a protector of the people. At night, he was a hunter, a predator. It was this penchant for aggression that would be needed if he could be enticed to challenge a Chained One.

Xirakura sat within the ring of stones. He felt the fire's embrace against his skin, its essence echoing in his blood. Katuwan and Lura sat with him, forming a triangle with him, a barrier for his protection as the ritual commenced. They held their right hands to the flames, the palms of their left hands slashed open and pressed firm against raw earth for the land to drink.

His hands, both palms slashed open, were pressed against their thighs. Slick blood greased their legs, forming a seal between his fingers and their skin as it dried.

The calling of a spirit rarely required such sacrifice, but Sufa Salein was a different breed. He was much older than most of those spirits who inhabited these lands, required more from the shamanic entities who sought to summon him. Life, the chance at it, was not enough. The Spirit Caller who sought him must hold fast against his will. He would not come for just anyone.

Yes, the spirit of the forest was a protector to the Katuwiti people, but his ways were not theirs. His whims informed by different values, other sensibilities.

The carved gourd rested in Xirakura's lap, its slender tip touching his naval, a narrow hole pierced through it forming a dark tunnel from soft, unblemished flesh into its hollow.

Within the thrumming, the pulsing of steps—rhythmic like heartbeats—of the

Tears for the Moon God

spirit. Tree trunks shifted. Whispers passed through the canopy, compelling the creatures of the night to a reverent silence. The boles groaned, drawing sharp glances from Lura and Katuwan beyond the edge of the circle. Neither had witnessed a ritual of this magnitude, a calling with this much weight.

As the spirit neared, Xirakura's heartbeat quickened. His jaw clenched. He had done this before. He was one of the very few living who had, yet he could not deny the gooseflesh spreading across his arms, the tightness in his chest. There had been dangers in that calling. Those dangers persisted.

Footsteps rolled across the ring of stones, and a host of lesser spirits watched, their presences felt like shades among the trees. They hid, but they could not avoid his sight. They yearned for him, but he refused them. Unseen hands pawed hard earth where Katuwan and Lura sat. The spirit tasted the blood seeping into his roots, warm and liquid.

More footsteps, closing in on Xirakura. He closed his eyes, willed his mind to silence. Like water, his soul slipped from his body, followed the path from naval into gourd, making space. Sufa Salein slipped into him, rode on raging channels into the spaces Xirakura's fleeing soul evacuated.

Energy suffused the air. The earth vibrated with it, a low thrum he heard in his spirit. It drew the spirit of the forest close, promised him a rare succor.

Dwell in my body. Live in my skin.

The thrall of being at the spirit's mercy, the anticipation of it, gripped him. A sudden burst of anxiety was crushed under the greater weight of responsibility, of discipline. The spirit had as much to gain from this exchange as he did, as much to lose.

Ecstasy.

Riding him gave to Sufa Salein the opportunity to experience the heart-pounding sensation of living a mortal life, the vulnerability, the eminence of death. That it must come for the mortal vessel in time. That he could not live forever. A spirit of such power riding his soul came with risk for both of them, but it was this risk that drew the spirit into him. Risk became a token. That surge of adrenaline—so short lived, so sweet—pulled with a magnetic force, pulled on other spirits lesser than the lord of the forest, but they were not invited.

The hollow within the gourd was filled. His consciousness slid away, leaving behind a partial awareness, a calming hand to aid his body in accepting the greater presence of Sufa Salein.

He felt the pulse of the trees, water rising and falling within their boles, the clatter of one leaf against another, thousands of small movements compounding, creating a music within him. And there, too, was a terrible pain, like fire washing across him, knives gouging into the gaps between muscle and bone, flaying him open from the inside.

The spirit settled within the hollow he had opened. His eyes fluttered open, sap green and luminous in a way they had been but once before. His arms lifted. Muscle grated against bone, but the pain was for Xirakura alone to bear, a transition into a greater symbiosis. If he died under the strain of holding Sufa Salein's vastness, the spirit would die also, the lands made barren, the Katuwiti compelled into the mountains where other spirits might provide. And Ban the Rope would be left unguarded. If Xirakura died, his way of life died with him.

"Speak, children." The spirit's voice boomed through Xirakura's lips. "I cannot be long. Perhaps a score more years, this creature might hold me and witness no pain. He cannot but bear it in silence now.

"Why have I been summoned? Why have I been called?"

"He is chosen." Lura said softly. "For a terrible purpose. See the mark he has been given. See who possesses his chain?"

She gestured at Xirakura's chest. The spirit followed her gaze.

He flinched. "There will be an answer!" he snapped. "Tenfold, an answer!"

"You can remove this poison?" Katuwan asked. "Can't you?"

"The touch of a Great King? Perhaps. But not him."

"Then--"

"Silence." The spirit's tone was cold. "Few have been our victories over such entities. Even the Tetract struggled to seal them. The Elder Gods were required. Too many lost among us. Too many wastes opened, wounds delivered.

"I cannot push back against Gora, for the ripples that press against him, the echoes of our argument, would have far reaching consequences. But take this lesser peace. He was never the worst of his kind. Far more terrible were his rivals...for you."

"What does he want with...with us?" Lura whispered.

Sap green eyes latched onto her. He took her measure, his jaw working as if chewing, a tick Xirakura had never possessed. He weighed her, hunted for some mettle within her.

Did pathos guide her? Would it lead her down paths best left untraveled? Or would cold logic prevail? Could she crush hope's embers within her long enough to see sense?

He decided on a half measure. A piece of the truth.

"He pursues a binding, as he has never done before. With my host, he has succeeded in shaping a beginning."

His gaze drifted to Katuwan. In like manner, Katuwan was weighed and measured.

"He will run from you, to preserve your honor. He will think of it as a gift, that you not be burdened with his fate. You must follow where he runs."

Katuwan bowed his head. "It will be done, old one."

"You know what all fel creatures seek, child." Sufa Salein intoned. There was hidden meaning in his words, the shape of which Katuwan understood.

Sufa Salein's gaze shifted to the darkness. He was reluctant to leave Xirakura's body, but to remain risked causing lasting harm. He drew away from the Spirit Caller in slow increments, savoring those last tastes of mortality, the terrifying, wondrous knowledge that he rode a razor's edge upon which his own near eternal life could be ended. Swiftly. Unremarked in the moment, but the consequences marked in the minds of mortal, spirit and god alike.

There was power in humanity. Power in their unpredictability, for they existed outside creation. Theirs had not been a divine inception, a fountaining forth from the mind of a lonely god or the blossoming of a seed in the immortal womb. They had been weak in the beginning, but even in those early days, they had grown swiftly, had become dangerous.

He savored those last moments as his essence poured out of Xirakura, leaving ample space the spirit caller's own soul quickly filled. He savored them, for he knew one day these mortals would know their power, and would usurp the gods and spirits alike. He yearned to understand them, as so many others did, yet they remained a mystery.

Xirakura's eyes fluttered, the luminous green replaced by amber as he returned to full command of himself. He looked on the haunted faces of his spouses, saw all he needed to see reflected there.

There had been no healing. Sufa Salein had failed him.

"Help me, please, both of you. Walking will be difficult for a time." he said.

They exchanged a look which he ignored. Pity or concern, it did not matter. There was no help to be had from the spirit. He was left with one option, then, a realization that pained him less than he had assumed it would.

They converged on him, helped him to his feet. He kicked earth onto the fire, his legs weakened by the press of the forest spirit against his body. The fire died, leaving darkness to fill the space it had carved out for them.

They walked away in silence, Xirakura placing the brunt of his weight on their shoulders. A weight that was the least of their burdens, and, if he succeeded in leaving them behind, the last of them.

Saijin's Song

It was not in the nature of the Crystal River to abide man's innovations long, not where those contrivances of wood and metal would hamper the free flow of her waters. But she made exceptions for her kin, the uelfin. Water wheels and grain mills stretched along her banks, ferries freighted passengers from the forested north shore into Cratom. She abided those structures for the sake of her children. Only them. And they prospered.

The streets of Cratom were choked with horse carts carrying tourists and would be acolytes to her shores. Along her sandy banks, towering brothels, matchmakers' houses and institutes where lay people could have their futures read cut across the horizon. The sun's attention was fixed on her glittering band, watching the swift current edge around low, stone walls, push wheels which pulled water and let if fall in misty sprays back into her depths. His attention, so rarely fixed on any one thing for long, had remained for all of the months of summer, denying the goddess of storms her right to bring rains from which the spirit might drink.

From the window of one such tower, Saijin watched the crystal sky, watched thin clouds drift by riding the slip stream breezes the Spirit of Breath provided. It seemed he, too, was unusually focused on the river and the sprawling settlement at its southern shore. On the north side, untamed forest drew close to the waters, yet that spirit remained ambivalent.

In the low chambers of the tower, visiting patrons awaited readings from fortunetellers with no gift for scrying, paid coin for useless pandering conducted by con artists and defunct actors, players in a game they had no business dabbling in. They were not uelfin. They held no blessing from God Lanfin. They had no gift for reading futures, but if they could convince those ignorant tourists of the lie, they might make a life for themselves. The uelfin's blessings were many and varied, and not all of them were offered selflessly.

Few knew the true nature of the river spirit. Few understood it was not with her but with her children the unraveling of possibilities could be done. In their ignorance, Saijin had cut his teeth, made his fortune on the backs of undisciplined minds while his ancestor turned a blind eye.

Yet now, he was troubled. The song his ancestor sang had struck a discordant rhythm, a melody of taking, taking back what once had been free of him. The song suffused the air, penetrating all that was embraced by time while other, older beings stole away memories of what had come to pass.

A mortal was taken, yes, and his deeds undone. But who? Why?

At few times had the crimes of a lone mortal proved great enough to warrant recalling him. The mortal still lived. No birth could be undone, for those were the domain a god who loathed Lanfin, loathed the God of Music for his cooperation with those she would call enemy. Yet the event of this birth was sealed, a stream within time's labyrinth dammed off, and the mortal trapped beyond time.

The melody shifted then, providing a window through which he might see. He reached for it gingerly, for such windows could be dangerous, such revelations as they contained guided by a god with no love for his descendants, those who had abandoned him for his once lover.

Oe shield me. He prayed.

With the contact, his fingers slipped through shimmering air. A vision materialized.

He saw himself, skin the light gray of predawn looming under a shock of violently green hair. A crosshatch tattoo enmeshing his right eye. His eyes a startling shade of red, glossy, almost fish-like. He was clad in the raiment of a foreigner, deer hide embellished with beads and gold chains, and with him were two others. A human, and a spirit in chains.

The chains, he realized, were broken. The discordant melody enmeshed them, yet the spirit was freed. Above and outside, the horizon was painted a bloody red. A gaping, dark wound interrupted the horizon, and from it spilled...bodies. Dozens. Death embracing them even as they fell, an army of mortals there to catch them.

He turned to the human, saw in the planes of his face, the feathers laced into his braided hair, the bow-legged way he stood as if accustomed to riding, sign and symbol of a people who had never been tamed, who had never, to his knowledge, known a single ruler. He saw there, too, that the man's skin was a muted brown, almost gray; that it was traced over with lines that intimated the spangled surface of water.

Katcyakin. Cloud Man.

A Great King cut loose. The pantheon of the gods shaken to its foundations by the coming of their father. What *justification*, Lanfin? Why ride this dangerous current?

He retreated from the vision. His father's intent was made plain, though there were truths hidden within time's stream he would not reveal, missing pieces.

The Lesser Gods made a choice, it seemed. They would bury their elders in favor of the master of those unfathomably ancient beings, whose power knew depth in a way their children could barely conceive of. In their greed, they would usurp them.

What purpose will taking the mortal serve? he wondered, yet he thought he knew. The removal of an obstacle. God Lanfin would have him believe the katcyakin was who caused this flight into oblivion, that he was responsible for the Allfather's liberation. His mistake lay in showing Saijin the other, the adversary.

Saijin drank in breath. He tested his voice, found the clarity of note he needed. It was taboo to cross the songs of Lanfin with melodies that ran counter to it. The uelfin who did would be pursued by that god, destroyed. But this was no fate mortals would weather. They would be crushed in that conflict.

Which may well be the point.

Saijin's Song

He sang, shaping a melody with the power to unwind, to loosen his ancestral father's hold on time's vast stream. He would need to act quickly, if he was to evade God Lanfin's grasp. There would be need of an acolyte of Ways, or of Darkness. Someone with the power to take him from this city, to a place of safety. The only place of safety.

With his song, a gap was opened. A gap through which, for precious moments, the taking might be reversed.

Within Time's Labyrinth, his song echoed fiercely, clashing with that of his father, his ancestor, the god who sired his people.

The song was suffused with his mother's power, for with her was love found, were mortals united. He hoped he did not misjudge what lay at the heart of this taking.

In love's embrace, a window opened. A grieving man might travel it, might find what he had lost. He shaped the song, waging war on a god who now knew him, who saw into his soul and was enraged. God Lanfin's full attention was on him now, leaving the Wanderers, lost in his labyrinth, precious moments to act. To force time's flow in a new direction, which might see this vision and all it entailed undone, a new future embraced.

Taojin La sat cross-legged on a patch of loamy soil. Pools of murky water choked with reeds flowed from the base of the low, wide hill, stretching for miles. She felt the pulse of the swamp, her home, her domain, felt it as twin heartbeats— one belonging to her, carried through waters where fish wandered and crawdads dug out homes. The other belonged to her brother, a pulse buried in soft earth, slow and rhythmic with sleep.

Were he awake, he might have joined her in her silent vigil, might have listened to the song on the breeze. This song was not like the whispered verses the winds were wont to carry. It lived beneath the rushing of tall grasses, the creak and sway of cattails, the clatter of leaves along the branches of scrubby, wraith-thin trees. This was a song of yearning, spoken in two voices. The lead, a familiar voice which belonged to a god for whom time yielded, to whom it must yield for he was its lord.

The second voice belonged to a stranger. It was no less beautiful to her ears, it rang no less clean, yet the rhythm it set ran in counter tune, earnest, almost harsh. She sensed...*defiance*. A resistance to the vision the god set forth, which he presupposed was just, the only valid path. The stranger's cadence held open a window, and she lingered in its embrace.

His child rebels. But why?

The window through which this uelfin had glanced must have revealed something. Something unacceptable. Desperate need ran through every note, a refrain inspired by fear, predicated on what he viewed as a necessary rebuke, rebellion against a power whom, with his promise of peace demanded a path of destruction, an era marked by usurpation and violence.

What do you seek, young one? What have you seen in your father's chosen future?

She set her gaze against the mountains, against the towering, snow-capped peak called Rein, whose ruling spirit had given mortal kind sword craft so long ago, who so regretted having given them anything at all.

She followed his slope to its roots, to the foothills crawling ever toward the swamp she shared with her brother. There, a dark crater was bored into the earth, a passage into a shrine which had existed before her birth, which, she suspected, would remain long after she died. The waters dried up, the reeds made brittle and dead. The path into the mountain cared nothing for what lay at its feet, but she did.

A rumble shook the earth, creeping through bedrock, disturbing her pools into a frothing madness. She shifted her position, rode the vibrations like a warrior rode the horse. The song became an argument, the forsaken son stubbornly throwing his voice against the father in his fury. The one meddled where he should not. The other attempted to assert his authority, to crush the will of the one who defied him.

The rumble grew in intensity, and still she remained. Remained as cold laughter cut into the song sung in two voices, called her attention away from their argument to something more immediate, which was filled with promises of vengeance. For her. For her brother?

No.

For the gods themselves.

The halls of Lanfin's Labyrinth were suffused with soft music. It echoed in stagnant pools, through still air where black flies swarmed over the carcasses of those who had fallen there. The bodies were an infrequent but powerful reminder to Shulraki Alran that life went on beyond those winding, narrow lanes. Somewhere, there were people who could gaze upon open lands and skies, their view unobstructed by the gray brick of walls erected to keep them in place, isolated but never alone.

The song was joined by others. It often was in the night's following the claiming of a new prisoner for the labyrinth. The accompanying melodies were usually in step with the main theme, enriching it with the agreements of countless uelfin, who wrote the makings of mortal fates with raised voices, opened paths in keeping with their father's designs.

A Wanderer could only listen, glean what could be comprehended from the patterns that defined an age.

He listened, heard the resistance in one melody, the opening of a window with the winter fugue. The counter melody was insistent, demanding validation. The lone resistor was met with a chorus which sought to drown it, yet it remained.

An uelfin had broken the taboo, was even now guiding the future in a direction his father railed against. Two voices raised in opposition, an argument which weakened God Lanfin's hold on the passage of time, eroded barriers which had for so long held the merchant lord back.

He sat with the body of the fallen uelfin at his back, a pool of murky, sour-smelling water before him, watched his wavering reflection, the carp and the water snakes wending through its depths. The pool clarified, silts receding toward its edges, leaving a mirror in its place through which he saw himself.

Wild, white hair tumbled over broad shoulders. His crystal eyes held none of the light they once possessed. He should have been dead. For a time, he had thought he was, that this was the punishment Shao Luin had chosen for him, to wander these corridors until his feet bled, walk until to continue would carve tracks into muscle, leave him crippled as time pressed on, and what little was keeping him sane was stolen away from him.

He was dressed in the robes he had been buried in, black silks of divine quality, the scar from a red-hot coin pressed against his lips which had since been removed, leaving the image of the late queen of Saodein forever etched into the skin.

The burial rite had been done in keeping with tradition, but there had been no love lost with his passing, no kind words spoken from the mouths of his betrayers.

The mirror fell away, a memory rising from its depths to replace it. There was the gloom of deep jungle, a lone fire burning in a cleared patch of earth. He focused on that place, the shacks rising around it, staked to the boles of ancient trees as a defense against predators.

He wondered if Shao Luin had been denied her claim to his queen as she had her claim to him. If God Lanfin's fury had snatched her out of death's grip, placed her back on her throne to lord over the oligarchs she had sanctioned to murder him.

He touched the pool. Delicate, golden fingers scattered the image. Water welled over the pool's edges, passed around him, wove him into the song. He was seized, thrown away into a world and a time well removed from the labyrinth and its maddening promise of stability. Was cast into the Waxing World or a reflection of it, to live again for a time. To feel once more what it was to live.

He sat in the village square, the fire's warmth firming his cheeks and forehead. A boar roasted above it, skinned and impaled on a naked timber. The occasional hiss of fat dropping into the pyre drew him away from his contemplation of the song and its counter melody.

He sat, enjoying the aroma of pork on the air, and waited.

A woman emerged from the forest. She was foreign, Sarkahni if he did not miss his guess. A woman too old to be traveling, yet hardened by the memory of a youth spent in conflict. He saw that in the scars crossing her forearms, the way she carried herself.

She had seen many fights in her day. A trail of saodeini corpses must lay in her shadow, a shadow which stretched all the way back to her home. Whichever backwater village that might be.

There was a wrongness about her. A departure from the fashions of his time was the most obvious sign. Her dress, though threadbare and roughly patched in places, was not the thing of voluminous skirts and tight bodices favored by saodeini women, and neither was it the more conventional attire of a Sarkahni fish wife.

The uelfin sang, and in singing had opened a window into this place, but it was not a place from his memories. No place he had ever visited. A remote village in Saodein, to be sure, deep in Ung Sakh's jungle. Had one of his Shards visited this village?

But no, that doesn't make sense, either. I would have some sense that I had been here if it were that, even if I did not remember specifics. A sense of being grounded, at least.

He chewed on that a moment longer, working through the incongruities.

The uelfin sings in counter time. Not to open a window through which we might reflect on our pasts, but through which his present is laid bare for us to influence. To direct time's flow against his father's wishes.

But why?

She sat with him by the fire, and he noted that though she had been recently washed, her clothes bore signs of hard travel. Dirt stains, rips in their sleeves and skirts she had no time to mend. Her shoes were cloth, the soles rubber yet not made for the road.

Tears for the Moon God

She had left in a hurry. He wondered what compelled her away from her village in such haste. Suspected he knew the answer.

"You're a long way from home." he said.

She snorted. "Home? What's that? A pile of rubble. A few burning roofs."

"Have you come to resettle, then?"

"Just passing through."

It was clear by her tone she had no desire to talk about what had befallen her. In truth, he did not, either. Lanfin's hold remained on him, and the uelfin could resist only so long. There was not time for remembrances of past traumas. Not space for his pity, or her sorrow."

"The queen...is she alive?" he asked.

Thin lips spread in a sneer. "She's been dead almost a century. Her children and their children, most of them, were casualties of the succession war." she took his measure. "I should think you'd know that. Even this isolated, magistrates must come to collect taxes. Your father might have told you the story, yeah? Summed up the whole history in a few words."

"This is not my present, love." he said. "Mine was a time when Saodein's interests in the Fingers were little more than ideas. Dreams of a conquest which interested the crown little."

"You couldn't be more than fifty." she said flatly. "Besides, none but the spirits and the gods were alive when that happened. The mortals who witnessed it are all dead. Most from old age."

"Then Shulraki Alran never raised his hand against the throne?"

She shrugged. "The name doesn't sound familiar."

"You're pursuing something I understand all too well, but your errand is doomed to fail. the gods stand with Saodein. They did in my time. They will in yours, as well."

"You know nothing." She said.

He sensed the offense lingering behind her words, though her tone was even. He pressed on cautiously.

"There are spirits whose power they fear, who might help you. But follow this path, lass, and they will come for you. The Halls of Time are no place for the vengeful. A lesson I have learned too well."

"Halls of Time." she scoffed. "A tomb for--"

She looked him over. "You're a Sun Man."

He saw the pieces clicking together in her expression, the renewed tension in her posture.

"Now, you are beginning to understand." he smiled serenely. "An uelfin sings in counter time to the god he would call father. It seems he disdains the design his father would set in motion. He opens this window through which Wanderers might travel, but it is closing. I know not how much time I have.

"Turn your gaze away from Saodein. I confess, I am pleased to hear that back stabbing witch is dead, but your purpose must be greater than raining blood on these lands. The answer lies in the Echo Rope. An oasis called Akkad which is never in one place long. Find it, and you will find Kushein, whose power expressed through you will be a shield against gods and spirits alike."

"Why her? What do you want from me?"

His grin broadened. "What I want matters little, for I will never have it in truth.

Saijin's Song

The Wanderers are lost and will remain that way, our actions bearing little consequence, our histories erased.

"Sarkahn...you grew up there. That is your home. To defend it, you will need a shield. She is the best you can find."

"You still have not answered me."

"A shield for two purposes then. First, to protect your kin. And then to defend those the gods have laid in your path. Your destiny is being written, my dear. But who holds the pen?"

The counter tune died in the singer's throat. Water rushed around the fire pit. She shuffled back, cursing. The waters rose up around him, crashed inward, and he was gone.

Lisandra cast about for signs of other witnesses, anyone who could verify the stranger had been there. The soil was damp, her shoes waterlogged. She had seen those waters seize him, had seen them pull him bodily into the earth, yet she could not believe he had been there, that just moments ago she had been speaking to him.

Her breath came in short, choppy inhales, the hairs on the backs of her arms standing on end.

That man was dead. It was there in the details. Even gold-skinned, the cast of his pallor was muted, the skin almost waxy. His eyes held no light of their own but took in the light of the flames in a way that seemed, in retrospect, unnatural. And then there was the coin imprint, seared into his lips.

She was familiar with the practice, had seen the way saodeini dressed their dead. A coin to buy passage along the Ul Sharak band, an offering against a price she had never asked for, from any mortal.

Dead, and speaking to me as if he'd never known the spirit's embrace. Had known none of Shah Jagat's mercy, either.

Was this the shape of Lanfin's fury. That this man should be denied death and yet forced to live in corpse flesh.

Who was he, this Shulraki Alran? She couldn't help but wonder. The crime he committed must have been terrible to invite the anger of the gods, but those very gods had forsaken her. Even now, they aided her enemies in the fall of her civilization, the slow but certain erasure of an entire culture, its way of life.

Too many questions. Too few answers.

There was merit in the idea of pursuing Kushein. Every culture across Ul Sadh was availed of stories of her. Kushein, who was wife to the Rope Lord, Echo, who traveled the ranges within his cordillera atop the back of the oasis spirit, Akkad—a gift from the Iron Spirit to her husband.

It was said Kushein could withstand the assault of an Elder God, that she had done so unflinchingly in the old times. It was said the gods all feared what may come from violating Echo's Peace, that to go against these three spirits would be their undoing.

There could be no greater shield for her people, no greater means of defending them, yet she hedged. What did she know of the Wanderers? Should she trust a dead man's advice?

One story, told to her at bedside when she was just a girl, came unbidden to her mind. Memory had a way of breaking things into pieces, and cobbling them together as if they were whole, even as critical details remained out of reach, but she

Tears for the Moon God

thought she remembered the important parts.

There was a conflict, wasn't there? Something to do with these Wanderers. Or was it just the sun and cloud men of the time?

She couldn't remember. There was something there. A confluence of events which seemed relevant, as if the tale bore some weight in what unfolded before her now. She was certain Echo the Rope played a role in that tale. That Kushein had something to do with it, too.

The people of Saodein had their own myths with regard to where Echo's Peace had come from, and why the gods, elder and lesser, left those spirits alone. She suspected every culture did. It was the way with old, important stories that the details of their tellings should become murky as time went on, but they should nonetheless persist in whatever way they did.

If only she could remember the version her parents had been so keen to tell her, or barring that, the details of another telling. One of those that came up later.

Hunting for those details felt like scaling a wall with no grooves or vines, no footholds. A wall covered in slick oil. A headache was pressing against her temples, and she let it go.

She turned from the fire, the roasting pig, as a saodeini villager came to rotate it. She hurried to the lodgings she shared with a local family, intent on shutting herself in her room, to remain there until she must leave. The road called, and she feared where it might lead.

Who could know him? All witnesses to his time are dead.

There was one, she knew. A spirit of memory. She did not value the idea of meeting him, but the temptation remained, ash on her tongue. An old spirit, and one whose hold was close, but he did not love mortals. Cared nothing for them.

Still, there would be answers with him. Three questions, the price written in blood.

She pushed the idea away, but she could not deny its pull. No more than could she deny the draw of Kushein's power, the sudden yearning to wear it in her spirit.

A shield for her people. An end to Saodein's provocations.

A detour into the mountains. I can make a decision after that. Just a jot across the hills. Echo's Rope is a long way from me. It wouldn't do to go in blind, not knowing whether the spirit would accept me, what offering she might ask for.

Her justifications rang hollow as she closed on the house, its windows a-light with candle glow. And she knew, just as certainly as she knew her briefly met companion was a dead man, that she would walk that path. Pay the price. Get her answers.

She climbed the rope ladder to the home's trap door, shoved it open. The memory of the Sun Man lingered with her, but she would bear it in isolation. Bear it on the road as she fled from this place and the secret power it held over her.

That a man could escape Time's Labyrinth, even for a handful of moments. That of all the people in this world, he would choose to speak with her.

Why?

The uelfin's song came as a shock to Xi Didura, yet he knew where he would go before the first, defiant stanza closed. There would be no love for him from the spirit he sought. His history had died with his imprisonment, but signs of him remained.

Saijin's Song

It was a secret forgotten by the time Shulraki Alran or Sao Njack walked the world, that the first of their kind were born before the god Lanfin emerged. Before a god's hand guided the flow of time, before the uelfin arose from his trysts with the river, Oe, katcyakin had lived. Hanuman among them, they had lived among those first humans, settled among them. They were, he had come to believe, God Katcya's gift to his chosen people—cloud men and sun men alike. A gift to feed his endless curiosity.

Their histories might be purged, their grand acts undone, but something of them lingered, twisting time's flow, the God of Music's song, like stones thrown into the current, disrupting its flow.

He climbed toward the peak of a mountain, the weight of the sword at his hip hard felt, the empty scabbard the other side of him doubly so. Snow ranged down the slopes for leagues before it broke against grassy valleys and the boles of withered trees. No clouds in the sky to shade his passing.

The Spirit of Breath would know him. The sun would mark his passing. But this was not his time, a curiosity he would like answers for.

The Elder will know of this. Half mad or not, he has his moments.

He saw, in the near distance, the elaborate temple his once master kept.

The lands themselves had lived long before the first mortals crawled from the mud, had seen all that passed since those tumultuous days, when fire ran wild across their forests, and the oceans quaked in fear of Great Kings risen from mountains and plains. They remembered. Remembered all that God Lanfin and his kin would have them forget.

He approached the temple. There, before its entrance, sat a pair of figures. he recognized them both, found the calm he had been missing in the presence of the one who was not his master.

A warm expression alighted on Hod's weathered face, as Rein's was shadowed with anger. The wounds suffered between them—Cloud Man, Fang and Rope—ran deep, but it had not been Hod's trust he betrayed.

He remembered with mingled joy and sorrow the moment he had won his place in their keeping, when he had earned Rein's respect.

A fight. Blades blurring, whooping as they sliced wind. Blood on the snow, the cuts shallow. A gash to Rein's cheek barely registered, a hiss and a gout of steam spurred on by the spirit's preternatural healing.

More blows. The broadside strike of a blade. A few minutes turned into hours. Gone, the obligation to continue. They fought for the joy of fighting, the moment to moment play of sword strokes unfolding, parries met, feints detected.

A man without his gift would have succumbed to the mountain spirit within moments.

Feints that should have pressed him, blows that should have connected instead met open air, drove plumes of snow into the sky, provided cover for his own rebuttal.

Play and counter play. For all that Rein now hated him, he still felt kinship with his mentor.

Rein climbed to his feet. The tallest mountain in the Waxing World should have a spirit of like stature its master. Rein was that and more. A giant standing eight feet and broad. He had a blacksmith's build, arms accustomed to swinging thick hammers, a wide neck, startlingly fierce eyes the color of ice peering out from a rigid, sun-darkened face.

In his every detail was the master Xi remembered. His hair bound in a severe bun, onyx and sleekly glimmering in the sun's cold light. He wore no embellishments, but presented himself in the garb of a blacksmith. Sensible tunic, padded leggings, a well-worn leather belt.

Hod was everything he was not. His black hair flowed out of a sloppy bun to swim around his shoulders. Thick mustaches wove into a beard which fell to his chest. He was diminutive next to the Tower, his friend, a few inches shorter than Xi himself, and dressed in military relief's. The pants coal gray, the jacket crimson and finely worked.

A pair of swords leaned against a post under the temple's eaves, both in lacquered scabbards embellished with floral designs which were integral to the wood itself. The one was slimmer than the other, made for swift movements, for sharp maneuvering. Hod's style was wild, flexible, contrasting Rein's curt, unflattering, yet brutally efficient forms. There was an economy of motion about Rein's swordsmanship, an attention to detail that allowed him to pick out the patterns his sparring partners tried so hard to hide. There could be no winning against either of them without deception, and it was in deceiving them, in playing to their ignorance, that he had won his contest against the Fang, had won his place under him, as his only apprentice.

He tipped his chin toward the two spirits, sat in the snow, feeling the bite of cold against his padded legs and ignoring it as he did the brisk weather.

"Some nerve." Rein growled. "To come to the one place I might find you. Lanfin may hold your soul, but he will not stop me taking your head from your shoulders."

"He would view that as a mercy." Hod said, his voice light, airy and soft. "It is good to see you, Lord Didura. Though, I imagine you have little time. Lanfin will assert order again soon."

Xi nodded. "First, an apology."

Rein snorted derisively. He crossed his arms over his barrel chest, his bulging muscles making him look even broader.

"Greed was my vice. You would have been right in granting me that sword, for it led me down a path of self-destruction. I should never have whored my skills out to those who offered their coin."

"A pathetic apology from an insolent bastard." Rein spat.

"The other matter?" Hod prompted.

"No tea today." Xi murmured, noting the absence of the usual cups and kettle. "Some things do change."

"Some do, but not for lack of investment. I heard the song, Xi. I knew you would come here when you realized." Hod said. "No time, then, to honor tradition. But speak." He gestured for Xi to say his piece. "Your time is running thin, I think."

"There is the matter of the sword you took from me." Xi said. "I need it passed on. I am asking you to remove the binding. Place it where someone might find it."

"For what reason?"

"This song bears meaning. A challenge to the gods. You know what the object of this game they play is. The Wanderers will be needed in our collective defense against them."

"The Wanderers will have no bearing on the--"

Hod gestured for his silence. It was all that was needed. "Take with you this truth. The Great Kings are stirring. At least three Elder Gods have been sighted in our world. On Gora, and on Ul Sadh. A Katuwiti spirit caller leaves his house in pursuit of Tak the Fire, but I suspect his path will take him to Ul Sadh eventually. These happenings assume a conflict between the elder and Lesser Gods, a thing unprecedented."

"Then the old powers are at the heart of this." Xi said, scratching his neck, where stubble had begun to grow in after a recent shave. He met Rein's eyes. "The sword, Rein. If the Wanderers are freed, I can do the binding myself. Not to any lord, but to the Wolf of the West. When the time comes, he will lead us. As he leads all of the katcyakin."

"A handful of spoiled children." Rein scoffed.

"No longer. His lover is among us. He is reclusive. I think it's depression. A common ailment inside the Halls. He is not altogether talkative, but then that isn't out of the ordinary either. We have spoken in the past. Those conversations have been revealing.

"There was a meeting at Katcya's God House, an act that can never be undone. The one they once called Dragon of the East was chosen for a task."

"The emperor who incited the last cataclysm." Hod said. "He would be involved in this mess."

"He was tasked with establishing bloodlines, forging out of the katcyakin a true race. Dupec will lead them."

The Rope and the Fang met eyes. An uneasy silence descended over the mountain top.

"Give him Spite." Xi said. "I'll make sure it's bound to him. I don't want a repeat of last time."

"I'll think on it." Rein said. "But that sword is dangerous."

"*He* is dangerous without that sword." Hod said.

"You've said yourselves the katcyakin will be needed in whatever's coming. He may be the best hope we have of throwing off the yolk the gods set onto us. Your kind and mine."

Water rose around him. It crashed over him, and he was taken away. Back into the Halls of Time, to wait.

The Elder knew what the song meant. He had heard its likeness before, a building pressure, a mortal reaching toward a conclusion the shape of which he could not know. Each time the singing came, a lone voice or countless clashing with God Lanfin, the shape of that future was changed. One step taken in a direction he was once averse to, which seemed now the only answer worth hearing, worth taking the time to contemplate, to plan for.

His had been an age of unity. Or unity of a kind. Before the Scales were hewn from the bones of fallen spirits, the blood of maimed gods. When the Great Kings walked free, waged their petty wars for domination. He had lived, then, in the shadows of creatures greater and more terrible than the Wanderers who came after him, there with those mortals fresh sprung from the mud, to wage war in the name of his own father.

Time is coming. He recalled his brother, a corpse by the time Lanfin claimed his place in the Waxing World's pantheon. Heiman had been spared this fate by happenstance. Whatever shape his existence took on after death must be more

Tears for the Moon God

peaceful than this.

How he missed him. However unstable he might be, however compromised he might become, Heiman the Younger remained an anchor. These thousands of years did not draw those old wounds closed. Hanuman remembered his brother fondly, and tortured himself with thoughts of what could have been. Balance was in knowing what he could not change, in knowing what had transpired in those early years could not be reversed, not truly; and knowing, too, that within grief was memory. As long as he clung to the one, he would not lose the other. He could not.

The others thought he was mad. Even now Ank the Sanark, willowy and tall, watched in silence from a safe distance. He wore the paint of a graemein with distinction, and there the old mystery reared its ugly head. Perhaps it was one more cruelty in a life overflowing with them that he should be seen for his gift and not his vision.

Waterlines traced the contours of his muscles, climbing over subtle hills, descending into shallow valleys. Muted, brown skin interrupted by lighter veins, a likeness explored in shaggy curls, the wide set of his nose, eyes the color of polished silver and shot through with narrow veins and specks of crystal red, green and blue.

Ank remained. Feet fast. Unwilling to take this gift. To see the deed done, the necessary plans set in motion. To see himself free, absent his history and able to make anew what he had forged in the waters of Graemlin's river thousands of years before this child of Lanfin emerged from the womb.

The Elder reached toward the still, mirror-like pool before him, smiled at Ank, and touched it.

He was in a shack with one, lone room. A god house which should not have been, the god who owned it elder, from a world not his own.

The god house stank of dust and mold, of stagnant water from a well at its heart. A bucket loomed over the void at the well's heart. It was rotted and filled with holes.

He sat before the watering hole and waited. Wind and rain had rotted the wood—were it not imbued with godly power, the whole structure would have come down long ago. Motes of dust swirled and spiraled in streams of light which pierced through pin holes and cracks in the walls and roof; and in the space between, shadows wavered, coalesced and shifted. They danced in disarray, casting the images of countless men in silhouette, and no two quite the same.

God Katcya played with him, flitting through the various shapes he had taken throughout the long arc of mortal history, painted the walls with their forms.

He latched onto one that resembled him, fixed his gaze onto it.

"I see you, father." he said. "The truth of you."

Katcya emerged from that shadow. He was naked, his skin gold and traced with cloud lines.

He climbed the lip of the well, dangled small feet over darkness. His gaze was fixed on Hanuman, cool and unbothered. He thought he detected a hint of satisfaction in his father, a knowing glint in his eyes.

"You were expecting me?" he said.

His father gestured airily. "Consequence of a plan well laid. Of course, I have had help. There would have been no success in this endeavor if I had chosen to act alone."

"What is the shape of this plan?"

"Funny thing to ask after so long away." Katcya chuckled. "Maybe how have you been? Have I given you any brothers or sisters. No, I suppose that would be obvious. You've been in the keeping of some of them. For quite some time, no?"

"There is no time for that, father."

"No, I suppose not." Katcya rubbed his cheek. "Not now, at any rate. Your mother would be proud, you know. So long spent in isolation, yet you are still as sharp as ever. Mostly."

He winced at the mention of his mother. He had seen her die, when the gods came to claim their pound of flesh. Had seen many die. His village—among the first human settlements, a secret kept as mankind spread across the backs of the great powers of the world—razed as the wrath and the fury of those ancient beasts, those unfathomably powerful creatures, came to bear.

We did find, in those days, that the gods were not of one mind, didn't we? That some, however few, did not see our coming as a violation. Our birth as a theft.

How does Ao Nii fare. Knowing what he knows, having felt that betrayal himself.

His father seemed to know his mind, for he changed the subject abruptly, legs swinging in and out of focus as he leaned against the well.

"The Wanderers are in the world. Creatures of habit, all of you. Too predictable by half. I've sent them gifts, guided the right hands to the places they will be most of use. Obsession is a vice, but it has its utility.

"Right, well, I'd like it if you got close to Sao Njack. Use whatever means you think best, but do know the arc of his life touched many, many more than those others. Excepting Ank, of course."

"Do you care to inform me of why he was immured?" Hanuman growled.

"I'm sure he'll tell you when he's ready." Katcya said evasively. "But his business is his business. Ours concerns the late emperor. His lover set out on a path I might like him to repeat...with caveats. They stumbled onto the right answer, you see, but the way they went about it was too obvious. Too dangerous, too. I'd like to see that corrected. The path they chose...well it was the wrong way to reach the right destination."

"They chose no path." The Elder said. "You know that better than anyone."

"Liandal will not be a problem. She can scribble away in her diary all of the adolescent if she chooses, but the one she would command is beyond her power to control."

"Mahan Mahain is involved in this. You cannot trust them."

"And they cannot trust me." Katcya said too confidently. "What better alliance could there be than one between two narcissistic gods with far too many balls in the air to spare a hand helping each other?"

The Elder sighed, squeezed the bridge of his nose. All the years spent in absence of his father had done nothing to make him more bearable.

"The point is the various actors Sao collected were together able to do what no one before them could, but they did not have the benefit of his legacy. The first wave of kiddos will have recently come of age. Lisandra is even now on her way to Echo's rope, to find Akkad and seek Kushein's acceptance. Xirakura has left his village in pursuit of Tak the Fire. A complication, I confess, I did not see coming, but one which I believe will prove valuable.

Tears for the Moon God

"Ibrim is with your brother's man. Some irony, a Sun Man choosing to bind himself to the moon. I always thought it odd. Which leaves Dupec Safar, and a plan is underway for him as we speak. Sao will be critical in shaping him, of course."

"From afar, as it were." The Elder said. "Of course, Liandal and Tirulain will see fit to intervene. They well remember Fang Ilra's intervention. They will seek to mollify her, even as their own plan takes shape."

"Which is why I've involved Sha Kron. Though he will be reluctant to play their game. He is ever the hesitant one."

The Elder watched his father, his frustration barely contained. Sha Kron would prove a complication they could not afford. He need only steal the breath of one party in this engagement to bring their plans to ruin."

"I'm afraid your time is up." Katcya cocked his head, listening to the song as it came to its conclusion, as Lanfin reasserted order, compelling his defier to silence. "I love you. Always have and always will. Now go find Sao Njack. Your part in this will be passive, yes, but perhaps more critical than any of the other moving pieces comprehend."

"Before that." The elder raised a hand, to stop his father's rambling. "Who will it be. Not Ul Sadh certainly."

Katcya shook his head. "The obvious choice. Though, I fear, his claim will be contested.

"Goodbye, my cherished son. Say hello to the others for me."

He waggled his fingers at Hanuman.

Water crashed over him, drawn not from the well but the river. White spray stole the image of his father, and he was again within the windswept Halls of Time.

Ank watched him return. He turned, and walked away.

Dupec lingered in the dark, sleep evading him. After years of sleeping on a bed of moss under the light of the stars, the bed chamber felt cramped, isolating. The camp bed he was provided was lumpy, stiff and unyielding. Scrub moss was so much softer, was buoyant and fit to his form. This bed was a dead thing, he realized, incapable of repairing itself, stuffed with cotton debris, the fabric lifeless and coarse.

He wondered how much of his discomfort was locked into physical changes, immersion in this world, which had only existed in books before he arrived among his people. How much was in the alienating knowledge that books and pictures were dead things, too. That records of culture, of distant plains and the life their inhabitants led was fixed in time, incapable of change once the ink was set, yet attempting to define a people constantly changing. A people whose every secret could not be witnessed by an outsider, for which some things were taken for granted, so banal in the eyes of the native that they did not need mentioning.

Fact was a superficial thing, but the philosophy which informed it was sometimes too complex to be captured in simple words. The historian chased after the why behind the what, but the people were not always forthcoming, not always aware there was an answer to give. Or thought the answer not worth giving.

Ung Tsang filled his thoughts as he tossed and turned in this bed. *What if I lose? Is this a victory worth taking?*

He thought of God Uldal, his warning to stay away from that cave. A cave he had never seen, which was surrounded by hills of gold fineries, a season's taking

Saijin's Song

from the other peoples of the steppe.

Why did that place pull on his soul as it did? Why did it call to him so? He could win this tournament, he knew he could, but what would be lost in entering that cave? What might he find waiting for him there?

And if I lose? Will I give into that pull? Will I go into that cave anyway, without the protection of the treaty?

He had seen the mounds of gold and fine pottery, trinkets and jewelry, chalices and bowls and tools. Mounds placed at the edge of the city, near enough Duijus Kanh's dark maw to entice the Swans from their secret hold, to take their tithe against the people's protection, for the dark spirit's protection was not free. He was not generous. He gave them what he did for a price, and if Dupec Safar entered that cave without his victory, he would demand a price of him, too.

He felt their eyes on his back, felt the watch the gods and spirits alike kept on the Shifting City. Much rode on this trial, and yet he could only discern its edges. The gods had plans for the Gil Garo, but did they include him? Was he to thrive in their embrace, or would they smite him?

New weight depressed the edge of his bed, down by his feet. The person who came to visit him worked with flint and stone, sparks cascading over a lantern they had drawn to their ankles. They had made no sound upon entering, had not announced themselves until their weight rippled through the mattress, to alert him to their presence.

"Chakta?" he whispered.

"No." The voice belonged to a man, but it was not deep enough to be Tamlin's, lacked the nervous energy that defined Shaki.

He considered it might be another pathfinder sent by God Uldal; but if it was, it was an acolyte who walked in the world, which he had not met before.

He eased up against the headboard, dragging himself on his elbows, watched the stranger at the edge of his bed.

The sparks danced, caught on an oil soaked wick. Flame guttered, sputtered to life. Soft light spilled out from behind the glass, illuminating the stranger.

The first thing Dupec noticed about him was the odd cast to his skin. Neck, face and chest, and fingertips. All that was exposed beneath leather and linen was the color of polished gold. The man was dressed in the same light armor Suli favored, but his eyes were narrow and tapered, dark even against the light cast by the lantern. Thick, straight hair shadowed his forehead. His cheekbones were high and defined; soft, pink lips full and pouty.

There was melancholy in his expression, in the set of his slender shoulders.

A Nixian, and a Sun Man.

Dupec drew on his birthright gift, that innate ability which altered probability to the detriment of others. He reached for a knife snugged under his pillow, lashed out.

Steel rang against steel. The Nixian's blade a blur meeting his.

He slashed again, carving a sweeping arc from the other direction. The Nixian reached out. Fingers closed around his wrist, the touch surprisingly gentle.

"I hoped you would remember...something of me." The Nixian shook his head. "A fool's hope, I suppose. So much has been stolen from us.

"Please drop your weapon. I am not your enemy, nor do I wish to spend what little time we have together fighting with you, Dupec."

Tears for the Moon God

The knife fell out of Dupec's hand at the mention of his name.

Who is this man? A lingering sense of familiarity battled with his desire to protect himself—a tug on his senses, on his spirit.

The other gods would not be complacent. They may well have sent an assassin, yet he did not think this was one of theirs. Did not feel the presence of another of those entities guiding the Sun Man's hand.

"You should be dead." he whispered.

A joyless smile spread across the Nixian's lips. The gaze he set on him was brimming with emotion. There was the melancholy of a man who had lost a great deal, but there was also...*love.* It was the same expression his mother had set upon him when first she saw him, which felt incongruous coming from a stranger. As if he missed something critical about them. Not him, not the stranger, but them together. Two men who did not know each other, but *should.*

"Who are you...to *me?*" he asked.

"Time's stream is not fixed." The Nixian said, looking away from him, to the stable flame in its chamber. "We found that out the hard way, didn't we? When you attempted to set Ul Sadh free.

"You were out of your mind by then. We argued. I believed what you were demanding would ruin us. All that we had built would come crashing down in a conflagration. You were inviting cataclysm. At the time, I thought I could prevent the gods coming for us, if only I convinced you to leave them to their game, but that, too, was foolish. We had gone too far even before you became that person to go back to life in any way peacefully."

"My father isn't dead." Dupec said. "I would never seek to free a...a great...just who are you?"

"As you are now, you wouldn't. But you were...*different*...then. The loss of your father broke you. I didn't intend for it to happen. It was a mistake. My fault he died, yes, but the circumstances were...I didn't know what I was doing. Liandal guided our hands in all we did, then, but she can't touch you now. You have a protector against her."

"Who are you?" Dupec demanded. An ache was forming in his temples. The Nixian spoke of a past that never was, which spoke to a future that could not be.

"I am the Dragon of the East, Sao Njack. The first and last emperor of the Nixian people. With you, I conquered all of the lands of Ul Sadh, united them under our banners. Dragon and Wolf. But that is not important right now.

"The gods have taken an interest in your people. You can feel it, can't you? It has nothing to do with their traditions and everything to do with you.

"Tuluis Fel will attack your people, and you will be faced with a decision. You may ignore their raid or seek to avenge those whose lives they stole. This was the crucible in your eventual rise to power, which saw you set on the path of the conqueror."

He reached out. Dupec flinched back as he caressed his cheek, those eyes drunk with love and longing, the touch warm and inviting, and alien and confusing because it was those things. His soul throbbed in its cage, squirmed under the light pressure of those fingers as they traced vibrating lines across the contours of his cheek and jaw.

"I need you to be my wolf again, Dupec. I need you to answer Tuluis Fel when they come, and free them from the tyranny they have endured for so long."

Saijin's Song

"I am not your conqueror. Your...wolf." Dupec protested, brushing his fingers away. As the gap opened between them, he realized he missed that touch. Wanted it back, and yet he denied himself his desire, his *need*. "And you are a stranger. What right do you have to make any demand of me?"

The Nixian sighed, chest collapsing, shoulders arching forward. He set his elbows against his knees, and looked into Dupec's eyes.

"I wanted to feel human." he said. "All my life, it was my only true desire. Every step I took was in service of that truth. That I could not be harmed, would never suffer a broken bone, a loss in combat, any grievous wound.

"The other children in my city shunned me because I always won their games. The elders treated me like their own son, because the feats I would rise to one day would bring an era of prosperity to Nixir. I was celebrated, for what I am, but few people knew the man I was, that I was dying inside.

"And then I met you. In Gur Tulain, after our mothers died. Under the Heart Tree. I saw you reaching for the forest lord's fruit, and I tried to stop you. The fruit is cursed, but you didn't know that. You saw an enemy where I saw a friend, an ignorant stranger. It's strange how time leaves echoes of us behind. Here I see a friend in you, and you see a stranger in me. I yearn for you. I suspect you yearn for me, too, but you can't let yourself admit it yet. Because the person who knew me is dead, and the person you are now does not know what we shared. Thirty years made meaningless because that bitch wrote some words in her diary." His expression darkened, and he pulled back the neckline of his reliefs, revealing a puckered scar just below his collarbone. The darkness faded, was replaced by something harder to define. Something complicated. "Meeting you under the Heart Tree was the first time I felt human. Only ever in your embrace could I feel that way.

"Stranger still, I fell in love with the only man who ever managed to stab me."

His gaze turned unfocused. He listened for something Dupec could not hear.

"My time is nearly over." he said. "I've left you a gift. Sanctioned by God Katcya. Our people will be a people in truth, now. Bloodlines. The eldest of them will be about your age. Excepting Rori and that Hand of Raukha. They'll be older, but they won't come to you yet. If they do at all.

"They will need you to lead them, to protect them. You will need them, too, if you are to do what I need you to. Find me where the river of time stops flowing. If some part of you still loves me, find me."

A trickling sound filled Dupec's ears. He cried out as water thrashed over the figure, and pulled him away, into some unknowable place where he could not follow.

Chakta and Shaki rushed into his room. The lantern still burned. The edge of his bed was drenched in water which smelled of silt and scum.

"What happened?" Chakta asked, casting wild glances around the room.

"I don't...I don't know." Dupec gasped.

Every muscle in his body was taut. A miasma of discordant energy swirled around him, threatening misfortune to anyone who came too close.

"Stay back." he held up his hand. "For a moment."

He schooled his mind to stillness, following a path through the chaos of his thoughts to a space where sweet nothing bloomed, pushed out the white noise.

The miasma retreated, was contained within him.

Tears for the Moon God

"There." he said.

She rushed over to him, placed hands on his arm and forehead, a motherly gesture. "No fever. No disturbance in the spirit, either. Was it a nightmare?"

"There's water on the ground." Shaki knelt next to a muddy patch on the earthen floor. "But there's no well here. The river won't expand this far until well into spring, either.

"Someone was here." Chakta's gaze latched onto the ground either side of the lantern. There are boot prints. Fine work, but not ours."

Shaki approached the lantern. He traced the grooves where the soles had pressed in. "Something about this feels wrong."

"Of course it does!" Chakta snapped. "We need to find Sauman. Get him to bring the chiefs together. They'll know what to do."

"Who the hell visit's a man at this hour, anyway?"

"Shaki!" Chakta growled.

"Never mind." Dupec said. "What does it matter. He was probably half mad, anyway."

Chakta raised an eyebrow. "A friend of yours?"

Dupec started to shake his head. "I don't know. But telling Sauman is the right thing to do. He can alert our fathers."

"You suspect an attack?"

He nodded. "I can't say for certain, but I know one thing if I know anything at all. When foreign warriors come calling in dark hours, violence usually follows. My god can only protect us so much. Others have been watching. It seems they have plans for us."

Chakta scoffed. "They're always watching. It's what they....she cut off at the hard look he set against her. "...do."

"I'll find Sauman." Shaki ambled back into the hall outside. Chakta squeezed Dupec's arm. Wordlessly, she followed.

Part 2:

The Greatest Game

Leaving Home

His home was filled with the soft sounds of slumber, broken here and there by rustling linens as one or the other of his spouses shifted in their sleep. The village outside was similarly quiet. Gone were the howls and grunts of hunting night beasts. In the predawn dark, birds sang from their branches, heralding the return of the ever watchful sun.

He twisted to face the short hall, the grain of living wood telling the tree's age as it drew water up into its bows. Languid ripples waxed and waned through sloping walls as the tree drank from a reservoir deep under ground. Faintly, he heard a spirit's whisper. Shahalanak's domain spanned beyond Sufa Salein, ran under the mountains and into other fastnesses. He contemplated asking after those outside lands, what those other peoples were like, but what insight she might provide would be stilted. As much as any Katuwiti village, she thrived in isolation, and all the creeks and springs she fed left her to it.

In the embrace of darkness, his two loves lay in each other's embrace, ignorant to his absence.

If it could be any other way.

He took in his surroundings, the home they had built together. Memories were breathed into the wood, etched into a throw Lura had attempted to weave, which the elder women had taken from her when their patience reached its limit. Slips in the weave made a lumpy ruin of one edge.

Katuwan's first hunting spear was hung from the ceiling. It dangled from two, thin ropes; was half the length of the spear he carried into the wood each morning on the hunt for wild boar and deer to bring back for the butchers. The spear had been made for him when he was eleven years old, before a growth spurt that would make a towering man out of him. There had been those awkward days when he was still getting used to his body, then. And Xirakura had been quick to tease him. His own sudden rise into adulthood had come a few months later. Memories of those fledgling days when he and his lovers were still finding themselves came back bittersweet. He did not know when next he would see them, was terrified by the prospect they might never be reunited.

He ran his fingers along its shaft. A wild snatch of feathers dangled from its

Leaving Home

broad, flint head, and hand prints in yellow ochre traveled down its length. With this spear, Katuwan had been declared a man, and placed in the company of more seasoned hunters.

Xirakura shouldered a rucksack, threaded an unstrung longbow through leather bands and fixed it to the top. A quiver filled with arrows hung from the cord belted around his hips, and a skinning knife was secured behind the gourd opposite.

Across the walls were painted images of animals and spirits. The faces of important ancestors climbed a wide post of petrified wood that glittered like so many precious stones; and there around it, sheltered within its shrine at the back of the chamber, were stories written in ancient glyphs, one for each of their families. The Katuwiti were not often concerned with putting things down in writing, carving them into the living wood of their homes, but these were the most important stories to their families. Stories worth preserving.

Time and all of its histories had a way of passing through cycles, and so those tales formed wheels and spirals across the walls. He fixed his gaze on the story he had taken for himself, of another Spirit Caller, an ancestor, chosen for a purpose by the spirit of the mountain, Ouran the Giant in this telling, though the details were never fixed. One telling spoke the name of a Range Lord, the next a Fang, and then a spirit of the sea. With each telling, the story was reshaped, new details added and others forgotten. In that way, a living history was manifest, the original story was lost, and each variation was accepted as valid in its absence.

Time had a way of passing through cycles. Be it Gora Soft Touch or Ouran the Giant, or Empress Shao Luin of the Dead Lands, time had chosen him for a purpose, and with him, a loop begun with that forgotten ancestor was closed.

His gaze fell to the floor. Katuwan and Lura...they would not understand. He had lived with them for so many years, had loved them for so long, but he could not be with them. Not until this curse was lifted. Perhaps not ever again.

The markings across his chest had healed, and now presented themselves as raised scars, clean lines, a lighter tone than his skin but no longer pink in the way of fresh healing.

He contemplated going to them, whispering a last goodbye, but knew it was a risk he could not take. If they awoke, there would be no leaving them behind. What trust lived between them would sour, and they would watch, avidly, for signs he might attempt this once more.

He turned from his home, drew the thin flap wide, and stepped out into a humid darkness, leaving them behind.

It's for their own good. He told himself, but the words sounded hollow. What was to be an act of altruism disguised a selfish urge to bear this burden alone. It was not what they wanted. It was what was needed. To keep them safe.

Dawn's dim light crept into the front room of their house. From their bedchamber, he could see the shift playing out on the tarp, pushing in around its edges. Xirakura's leaving might have surprised him six or seven years ago when their relationship was still fresh, but not now. He left because he believed what he was doing would keep them out of harm's way, that it was for the best he take on this journey alone. He was a fool to think they would let this go without a fight. He had earned himself a few hours lead, but he was not skilled in the bush. Even with the spirits on his side, they would close the gap eventually. They had to.

Tears for the Moon God

His husband would seek to expand his lead on them, but the advantage was theirs. Katuwan and Lura alike spent more time in the forests than he did, more time picking over land, tracking the movements of game. Xirakura was not a hunter. He had no need for the skill, no reason to learn the ways of disguising his steps, of moving in silence across broken ground, where dry foliage and fallen twigs made a chaotic maze, and sound footing was hard to come by.

He shook Lura gently by the shoulder, waking her.

Lura yawned. He had not been the only one to drift off too soon. Had Xirakura dozed off before them, they might have the advantage now. They had both let their guards down.

"He's gone."

"How long?" she asked.

"A few hours, maybe. The trail is not cold yet, but we need to leave."

"You have an idea where he's going?"

He nodded. "The Rahad congregate in cities. If he's seeking them, he'll go south. The elders say there is a city of good size on the coast."

"Not Sufir, then?"

He shook his head. "Landlocked. Unless he finds a pathfinder or a darkling there, he will have no way of getting off Gora. He'll go to Faed City."

"Then we should take Ouran Goul Pass."

"Yes." He nodded. "Yes, Ouran Goul is the way."

She rolled out of bed, snatched a pack from its hiding place behind a nightstand.

He navigated to the washroom while she gathered her things, and belted a leather cord around his hips. He took up his own pack from behind the basin—one already prepared and waiting for him. He snatched his longbow and his spear from their resting place near the hearth, secured the bow to the rucksack, then went for his arrows.

He met Lura in the hall. "Ready?"

She had belted a leather cord around her breasts, and the ratty, old quilt she'd taken a shot at knitting all those years ago when the village women taught her weaving was strapped to its height. A skinning knife was fastened to her hips with a separate cord, one which would need sharpening.

"Ready."

They ventured outside.

Few of their people were out of their homes, but those who were noted the travel packs with raised eyebrows. Katuwan and Lura gave them no pause to ask probing questions as they hurried into the jungle.

Katuwan caught sight of a fellow hunter, blunt featured and missing teeth from a fall that had bashed his face against a rock. His nose was crooked from a break associated with the same incident, and his back was bowed with late waking, the morning's lethargy leaving in waves, not entirely gone for the moment.

"Take care of our home, Kitwati." he shouted to him as they passed.

"Where are you going?" the hunter asked, suddenly alert.

"Husband hunting!" Lura called.

"We'll be gone a while, maybe. Depending on how far he gets before we catch him." he added.

"Where?"

But they were already passing the edge of the village. The hunt was begun, and

Leaving Home

they set themselves to the task.

"Whatever he thinks to gain...." Lura said.

"Less a gain, I think, than preventing a loss. He thinks we can't handle this. Better leave us behind than let us become entwined in what is coming."

"He said this to you?"

"In so many words." Katuwan shrugged. "He may try to hide things from me, but I know his tells."

"You aren't regretting this? Choosing me?"

"Because you came with him? Lura, we are past this, aren't we?" he took her by the shoulders, touched his forehead to hers. "Marriage is work sometimes, but I did not just choose *you*. I love him. I will do anything to make sure he is safe."

A feeble smile crossed her lips. One day, he would convince her. If it took another seven years, he would.

He pulled away from her. "There is no need for concern. I would not have laid a wreath at his door if I believed we couldn't love each other, do you understand? I am not lying to you."

"It just seems that maybe...maybe I dragged you into something—"

"Quiet, now, please." He said. "We need to catch up with him. We're wasting time."

"Liandal guide our hands." Lura said, making a warding sign.

"You think its a good idea to involve her?" he asked.

"I think if he has the spirits on his side, we have no choice but to call to the gods." She explained. "But the goddess will provide. She will see an advantage in us I think. Who would you call on?"

"Maybe you're right..." he said after a moment. "...but I would not choose her if I could help it. The moon has always favored us. Luck is also fond of humans.

Her lips firmed. He knew what she was thinking. A grief stricken god made volatile by madness, and a trickster. Neither was particularly stable.

But Goddess Liandal was cruel. Mortals were her pawns in the endless games she played, and she cared nothing for them.

It was the risk that decided him. Lura was not as short sighted as their husband. She was never quick to decide anything. Always, she was the influence that tempered them, the one whom in pensive silence revealed truths hidden in plain sight.

He looked to the trees and the litter strewn earth for signs of Xirakura's passing. The spirits of the mountains and the streams, the plains, and lakes, and winds, might side with them, but one at least was with them.

Sufa Salein provided. In his own way, and at his own time, he always provided. In this, he would see them to him, reveal the path he followed so they could be reunited once more.

The Black Lamb

The ferry drifted through thin mists on its way across Oe's band. Ivy dripped from lattices framing the deck on three sides, leaving a viewing window at the fore through which tourists could obtain their first looks at Cratom. The other patrons aboard the wide vessel wore serene smiles and cradled each other in their arms. Most who came to the city were couples seeking a blessing from the river spirit for a happy marriage, though there were always those others who came for the city's more lecherous services.

Oe was a vain spirit. This city flourished with her blessing, but her mercy was not for the Goths. Alone among the cities across the Gotha Kingdom, reaching into the southern nations who occupied Byrne Plain, Cratom was a stronghold for her descendants, and they alone were permitted to obstruct her band. Mills powered by her swift currents ground millet and wheat for their pastries, white smoke lifted from the forge houses. The mountains loomed in the background, untamed forest rising toward snowy peaks where Pongyin made treacherous passes for miners coming along the only safe road from their villages, a road which passed through Cratom—bringing trade in iron, silver, and lead.

Hod resided high among those peaks, but it was not for him Wu Bane came. An elaborate lie to secure God Uldal's blessing could be shed now, and his true intentions explored. He had unfinished business here. Before he left, and returned home to the hilltop in a glade which was never in one place long, he would see his business concluded.

God Uldal would have him yoked to a cart bearing stones to break a mule's back if he discovered the deception, but the gods were not omniscient. Most could see little in the minds of mortals. Wu benefited from his ignorance, from the silence of his peers, his mentors. Suli knew little of the nature of his errand, of course, but she would not have understood. Dupec and Jaunz knew his need. They had lost things themselves, whole lives ripped away from them when duty called, or a curse drove a wedge between them and their people. They understood purpose, if they did not believe in revenge. Revenge must be his purpose for now. He would find something to fill the space it left behind when he was done.

His coming to the God House of Ways had been the result of a mother's cruelty.

The Black Lamb

One who would dote on him until the time arrived to supplant him, and then leave him lost and alone, hoping he would never be found. Returning was the first step in righting a grievous wrong.

This is justice.

The city's serene skyline provided the illusion of peace, but that was all it was. A lie its residents told, all of them, to travelers seeking their blessings, their readings of futures that might never be all wrapped up in vague language, begging a patron's imagination to fill in the gaps.

There was a tension here he intended to exploit. A shadowed hand pressed against the city he sought to use. His stepmother was somewhere among those hills, secure in the family estates she had stolen from him; content in the belief that she had done away with the true heir of House Bane. Satisfied that she was safe, and he was dead.

The ferry brooked against a long dock. Workers, all of them Goths, bound ropes to its posts, drew it flush with the dock, mounted a low ramp against its edge. Tourists disembarked across the ramp, marched off and divided along the lanes with their cargo in the hands of strong men who lumbered into the streets after them. New lovers and those soon to be wed would seek matchmakers, acolytes of Oe, to cast offerings into her waters against the health of their relationship, not knowing Oe's gift had little to do with love. Others came with offerings nestled into wicker baskets to float within her band, to seek promises of lovers to be found who would be theirs and only theirs, who would emerge out of ether to court them. And if their prayers were answered, it would be by sleight of hand, in the office of a well paid matchmaker. An uelfin, if they could afford one. A Goth, if they could not.

Still others checked purses to ensure their coin had not been compromised. Those would seek out uelfin soothsayers for a reading of the songs. They would look to the future for guidance, and be met with the harsh realization that nothing beyond the change they sought to make was certain. That they may be guided into a future which did not benefit them, but which played a part in a god's designs. The uelfin were not allowed to resist the whims of their ancestor. Singing in counter-tune to the God of Music was taboo. What lay in an uelfin's words could only be trusted so far, for none would dare to cross their Father. No one was that much a fool.

Almost worse than Goddess Liandal. He thought as he slung his pack over his shoulders. He dismounted the ramp. *Fate and Music. Both soulless, conniving monsters.*

The games of the gods favored no mortal. He suspected their eyes would be upon him sooner or later, but time was just another path. A path that could be traveled could also be locked, those who followed in a Wanderer's wake left directionless, and the Wanderer unseen. His presence unfelt and unnoticed by any but the most tenacious hunter. And God Lanfin was no hunter.

He pulled on the binding in his soul which God Uldal had spent so long developing within him, a power that could not be denied him even by the hand of his god. His essence spread across the dock before and behind him, shifting waters unseen by all others, a patina to prevent the eyes of gods and acolytes from settling on him.

He marched within the flow, up the hill road, away from the bank, down narrow corridors in search of an inn which Jaunz had recommended with a gift and a warning.

Don't trust anyone you meet in this place. He thought to himself. Though what would have drawn a Sanark to a place like that, he could not say. Jaunz had never given him the impression of a cut throat or a thief. He had always seemed a pillar of morality.

He touched the long knives at his hips, fingers grazing iron handles wrapped in rough leather, the better to accept his grip.

He pressed on, turned onto a broadway lit from above by lanterns suspended from wires which crisscrossed overhead. Hawkers called to travelers, shook arm loads of useless pendants and charms. Card readers enticed would be patrons to have their fortunes told, a gift no Goth had ever possessed.

Throngs of drunken tourists and traders filtered into brothels and pubs. There was a sense in this district of abandon, of unrestrained opulence and carousal to make the God of Revelry weep.

Yes, he remembered these streets. He had visited them often with his father when he was too young to comprehend the full weight of what transpired here, of what drew men like flocks of birds to these wooden towers and their secret promises. He passed several inns before he found the one he needed. The sign was in disrepair, weathered by driving rains, but if he squinted, he could make out the impression of a sheep. There was no name written below or above it, but he did not need one. The color of that emblem was enough. This was, if he was not terribly mistaken, The Black Lamb.

He passed the threshold, shoving in the door, and entered on sure feet with his back straight and his chin tipped upward. He did not want to appear weak in front of Cratom's most distinguished bastards.

The dissolution of the image of Jaunz Faedrin—Graemein Sanark, proud and stable and just—came in steps. He was known to this place, and it was known to him. There were truths in that his young student would not have believed had the evidence not been in front of him.

The front room was a claustrophobia inducing space. Narrow channels formed a complex maze between round tables with splintered faces. Dust pooled in the corners of the room, seeming to have been swept into them for the aesthetic, and cobwebs hung heavy from the eaves. The whole place smelled of stale sweat and sour beer, and as he crossed to the bar he was met with quick flashes from ragged urchins of a sweeter, more acrid aroma. To a one, the gutter spawn were glassy eyed and slumped over their tables, most with untouched beers clutched loosely between their fingers.

In the far corner, a small group of men quibbled over the details of some agreement between them. Nearer the center was a man who looked somewhat like Timin, who leered at a posh, young gentleman who was seated across the parlor from him. The dark-skinned, maybe Magura man was dressed in a black tunic, and trousers held up by crimson suspenders. A pair of black-handled knives lay on the table in front of him. He sipped his beer, eyes trained on the youth, who looked pointedly in every direction he was not in.

All around were thieves and strong men, vagrants and murderers—people whose presence transformed the image of Jaunz Faedrin into something far colder and crueler than the man he believed he knew.

He approached the bar, waited for the gnarled, slab-armed barkeep to come to

The Black Lamb

him.

"What do you want?" the barkeep asked. His mouth was stuffed with cotton, and his jaw was swollen on one side. One of his eyes was hemmed in by angry, purple flesh and his nose was splinted into place.

He polished a glass with a snow-white towel, the cleanest item in this place, looked Wu up and down.

"Well?"

"Sorry. I need a room."

"We're full."

"I'm sure you have space for—"

"Look, kid. When I say we're full, we're full. It's nothing personal. You just look like...well, you look like a narc."

Remembering Jaunz's token, he rummaged in his pocket. "Maybe this will change your mind." He set the trinket—a hand wrapped around a shepherd's hook, the third digit dressed with a ruby fragment—on the bar, and stepped back.

The barkeeper's eyebrows twitched. He winced as the flesh around his eye tensed, and shoved the trinket away from him far too delicately.

A pall of silence had descended over the room. It was broken by the dark-skinned fellow's laughter.

Clapping, he said: "This is rich. If you could see your face, Donny." He was taken by mad laughter again.

"Shut your fucking mouth, Garam!" the barkeeper said without looking at him. "There's a room for you upstairs. And uh...let's leave the Hand out of this, eh. I didn't mean anything by it."

Wu nodded. "Okay."

"Second floor, fourth door." He said.

Wu replaced the trinket in his pocket, and left.

The room wasn't any better than the common room. An inn should supply some comforts, though if he was being honest with himself, he would not have enjoyed any of them after so long spent sleeping on moss beds by starlight. Except for a sliver seen through a dirty window, he could not see the sky, and even that glimpse was marred by reflections. An oil lamp provided the only light, and situated next to that grimy window, it stole the pulse of the city from him, robbed it of detail, concealed that sky he had grown so accustomed to seeing in its full glory.

A pampered, noble child lost in the woods, he had never thought he would grow accustomed to sleeping in wild country. The sounds—animal growls and screams, padding footsteps, twigs snapping and horns grinding into tree trunks—all came on too close for comfort, and too far away to make sense of them. How long had he spent struggling against his binds, shouting for help until his throat was raw. All he could manage were insubstantial rasps, gravelly, desperate croaking, tender sobs.

He had been convinced, then, that he would die alone. That no one was coming for him. That he was too far away from anyone to be heard, let alone found. It had been God Uldal's mercy that saved him, yes, but in those early days his sanctuary had been a frightful place, removed as it was from everything he had ever known. And the god himself was a monster out of his nightmares—not the kind benefactor he wanted, but the stern father he needed. There was mercy in the god's embrace. Mercy in that he need fight no longer, need grapple with deep hunger, cracked lips,

Tears for the Moon God

the incessant needs of mortal flesh not at all.

What was he doing here? In this ramshackle inn so deep in the corridors of a hometown that had long lost its comforts, where strongmen and murderers and thieves congregated and did business.

He could go back. He could claim his mission to discover Hod had been foolish, that he could not have done it because the spirit did not want him, but that would be to accept this reality as immutable. It would be to let *her* win.

He needed to meet with someone, and he intended to do it tonight, before the man became aware of his presence. There were questions he needed answers to, and who better to fill in the gaps in his knowledge, provide context that may help him succeed in his errand here, than a matchmaker.

There was the matter of those men downstairs to consider, as well. That Garam...he knew more than he was letting on. He had recognized Jaunz' seal. He was a Raukha, that much was clear, but who did he serve? Who did he report to?

He would need to watch the man, keep him off his trial until he had a better grasp of the situation. The others had been reluctant to comment on what transpired between the barkeeper and him, which implied Garam was more important than them, of a higher status.

He could become a problem for me. He thought to himself as he squared off in front of the lone bed with its ratty, pilled up quilt and sweat-stained pillows. An end table was positioned before a window looking out into a narrow alley. The alley was hemmed in by tall buildings on the other side, and what windows faced inward were dark. The rooms might be empty or the patrons asleep, but he doubted anyone of importance was staying in them. Who would go running to report on the patrons who stayed in this place, anyway. All of the eyes he did not want on him were in this inn. Most were still in the common room, nursing drinks and going about their night's business.

He drew on his soulbinding, that particular flavor God Uldal had been so tenacious in teaching. He would never get used to the sensation of splitting off a Shard. That strange knitting of flesh, the pulling apart of skin, the painless flaying of muscle and emergence of fresh bone from the existing stock. The vibrations that almost tickled along his ribs as the Shard soul split away from his own, leaving him less whole, hollow in a way that would not be righted again until that fragment rejoined with the rest.

The Shard worked its way free of him. Its torso emerged from his back, arms jerking and twitching as they were wrenched clear of his shoulders. Thighs, and then knees, and then calves and ankles emerged from his hips, and the Shard stepped free, crawled over a lumpy mattress, used thick bedposts for support as it twisted around and sat next to him—clothed as he was, identical in its every detail.

The Shard turned to him. He had found in naming these things he granted them some autonomy, and spared himself the sense that they were truly human, that this Shard was in some way equal to him. In naming it, he became its superior.

"You will be Rhul." he said. "You will sit here, move around a bit. When I have gone, you will behave as if you are the Core Soul, you understand?"

"You are being followed." Rhul said. "Or you suspect you will be. I am to alibi you?"

"You are to provide me with a smoke screen, Rhul. Keep those eyes engaged, fixed on you. I have delicate business to attend to in the city. I need you here,

The Black Lamb

holding the watcher's attention, so that I can attend to it."

"Haffa." Rhul gripped the ratty bedspread in tight fists. "I hate that man."

"Try not to think of him too much." He said. "I would suggest some light reading as a distraction. Or you might practice with your knives. I do need you awake until I am well gone, though. Give me an hour. If I'm not back by then, you may retire."

Rhul grinned. "Constructive activities for your personal benefit. Is that it? Read, so you may learn. Practice, so your muscles know new forms. Sleep so you are rested. Can I eat, at least? You were hungry when you cast me out. I might be inclined to have a drink, as well."

"You may eat, but take your food up to the room. And no drinking. I need a clear head."

"You're no fun."

Wu moved to the window. He unlocked it, slid it up. "You have your instructions. I'm leaving now."

He climbed over the sill, masking his presence before his leading leg was over it.

"Do you ever wonder if a Shard could lead a normal life. Independent of its maker, that is." Rhul asked.

He hesitated.

The Shard was a part of him, body and soul, but he never knew how much autonomy it really had. He knew it could not ignore his orders, that the power of his will would compel it to do as he asked, or in absence of any spoken orders, fulfill his intent as it stood upon his summons. But this was not the first time a Shard had spoken to him as if it wanted independence. It was not the first time it had philosophized about its own humanity.

But this question had already been answered. The strongest of Uldal's acolytes lived within the Halls of Time. That much was known. All record of his existence was erased, yet still he lived on. Shulraki Alran—who had split off six Shards and then died. Shulraki Alran, whose Shards succeeded him for seven years, to carry out a plot to end the life of his queen, and throw her court into chaos.

He had explored the limits of what a Shard could do, and what it could be. Seven years for six Shards. But Wu sometimes wondered...if he had placed as much energy into one Shard...if it was possible to do so...could that Shard have lived a long life? Could it have grown old? It would always be subordinate to him, that much was evident. Even after his core had been slain, the Shards lived on.

Can you live a full life independent of me? That's what you want to know. But the concept of independence cannot apply to you, because in everything, I am your master. You can't deny me. Would you, then, try to run from me? I would compel you to come back, to be drawn into my soul so that I could become whole again. This feeling of emptiness...it isn't pleasant.

But then, if you lived that life far away from me, would it be filled with happiness? Is it that you are the same creature each time I summon you, with the same history, the same personality, the same values and wants and needs? Or is it that you are a different person each time I summon you, a rejection of some energy of mine, but not the same? Never the same.

"Perhaps you could live beyond me or independent of me for a time, but that time would be fleeting. You would live with uncertainty for all of it, and you would

Tears for the Moon God

die far sooner than you might like to believe."

Rhul's searching look would haunt him for weeks. A piece of his soul he may be, but he had feelings. He may be identical in form, but he was not in content. None of them ever were.

What was personhood, then, except a summation of traits and characteristics, elements fostered by nurturing others or dismissed and thus buried. If he shaped this Shard, if he let him remain corporeal longer than the task at hand demanded, what might he become? Yet the risks were too great. As long as a Shard remained outside of him, he was vulnerable. He was weaker for having pushed that piece of himself out, and he could not abide that weakness longer than was necessary.

"I'm leaving now." he said. "Try not to think too much about this, okay."

He swung his other leg over the windowsill, and slipped out.

The Hunt

He peered out from behind his father. He clung to Liudao Bane's pants leg, snatching glances at the uelfin when he thought he wasn't looking.

The matchmaker's chambers were suffused with the aroma of lilies. They stood proud and elegant, rose out of porcelain vases chased with chaotic lines and swirls of cobalt glaze, in styles that dated back centuries to a time when the Goths had been in control of the river city, before God Lanfin spurned the spirit, Oe.

The grieving period was over. A man of Liudao's stature was expected to take on a suitable bride in the wake of his late wife's disappearance. There were rumors in the streets of foul play, and though they spoke them in whispers, Cratom's citizens could not hide their perceptions from him. A child of his blooding was expected to distance himself from the politicking of his father, to understand little of what transpired between Lord Bane and the uelfin, but he was not naïve.

He understood the need to keep appearances. He did not grieve for his mother, had not accepted what the Goths and the uelfin said was true. His mother was still alive somewhere, and though he hated what she had done, he could not bring himself to accept the pretender his father would court soon after this meeting, either.

He watched the uelfin matchmaker as he scribbled notes onto a document's margins, listened to the interchange of questions asked and answers given between his father and him.

The matchmaker met his gaze. He stepped back behind his father, clinging tighter to the seam of his pants. The matchmaker scared him, not just because his presence promised the coming of a new mother to replace the one he had known and loved, but because in the low light of his chamber he was monstrous.

Wide eyes drank in the light. Dusty, blue hair shot through with threads of green played over his porcelain pale forehead. He reminded Wu of a carp. His features were wide set and full in a way that seemed inorganic, and though he exuded a kind of poise, it was the softness, the self-assuredness of a snake waiting to strike.

Like his ancient father, his ancestor. A monster whose melodious voice spoke of mortal doom and glory, two sides of the same coin.

Tears for the Moon God

"What of you, young man." the matchmaker asked. "What did you like about your mother?"

"I don't want to talk about her!" he flinched back behind his father.

"Now, son." Liduao reached behind him, pushed Wu out of his hiding place, into the open where the matchmaker's cold gaze could find him. "This is important. Haffa has asked a question of you. You will answer him politely."

Haffa waved him off. A gentle smile alighted on his lips. "I take no offense. The loss of a parent is hard on a child. Perhaps we've brought him into this too soon."

"No." Liudao said. "He'll cooperate. Won't you?"

The look he set upon Wu told him there was no other option. He would cooperate or he would be punished when they were away from prying eyes.

"Fine." Wu said.

"Why don't we try a different path." Haffa set his pen aside, steepled his fingers. He leaned forward in his chair. "I knew your mother. I performed the matchmaking service which saw your parents wed. Do you think I made a mistake with them?"

"No." Wu said uncertainly. He didn't like where this was going, not least because he couldn't see where it was going.

"She was headstrong. Independent. She was perfectly fine with the idea of being alone. Preferred it to the idea of being with a man she could not love. Very fatalistic, that one." he glanced at Liudao. "Your father, on the other hand, was enamored by the idea of an easy relationship. He wanted someone meek, even reserved. Uncomplicated, you might say.

"But, as these things go, what a man or a woman dreams of is seldom what they need. Rare is it that the imagined coupling is meaningful enough to last, and other factors may arise that bring their romance to an end."

"Like my mom running away."

"Like that, yes." he agreed, though his tone was somewhat strained. "I cannot mend what transpired between your parents, but I can assure you they loved each other."

Much to his disdain, Riverwalk House was still standing, though at this time of night a spare trickle of foot traffic filtered into it. It was bad luck and bad manners to solicit a matchmaker after sunset, and he suspected the superstitions swirling about those covetous pimps and madams were not matters of coincidence. Often haughty, arrogant and short on patience, even the honest ones were prone to making statements. He remembered very clearly, Haffa, master of this house, demanding that his apprentices cram so many poppies into his office the place began to look like a garden shed. That had not been for his father, though there had been some lack of understanding which, when the felt insult was made known, needed smoothing over rather quickly. The uelfin may see themselves as superior in Goth peasantry, but it did not do to imply the king's voice in Cratom was a whore.

He tucked that memory away, a spiteful plot half formed in his head, pinned for later use. There had been no time to fuss over preparations for this reunion. Go to a flower shop, and he would have been noted. He had not met him, but he suspected his younger brother shared some of his features. Enough, at any rate, that someone in either of the better ones would have recognized him.

Besides, he's probably long forgotten that incident. What's the point in being petty if the old fool doesn't remember?

His mother had hardly been gone a month when his father had taken a new woman to be his wife. His father's second marriage might have been a political necessity. Such things were, in the way of noble courts, often seen as such. But for all the years that had passed since Wu's parting with his family, he could see no advantage in that monster's blooding. She was neither nobility nor royalty. She was not a power broker in the Gotha Kingdom or neighboring Nu Empire, or anywhere else of importance for that matter. She had been a lowly maid at some nondescript inn in one of the city's less popular districts. By his accounting, she was a peasant woman whom, in her vain pursuit of a better life, had clawed her way into a soulless marriage with the most powerful Goth lord this side of Oe's band.

What he could not comprehend was how Haffa, who was known for his seeming addiction to professionalism, could have let it happen. Could have encouraged that marriage, set Liudao Bane on a collision course with the help.

If every man has his price, what was yours, Haffa?

Riverwalk House had changed in subtle ways since his last coming. The bones were the same. It remained a structure in the uelfin style, a prominent tower, its base level river stones cemented together with a light gray mortar; the next three levels wood plank laid vertically, and the windows long and crossed with slender, wooden bars. Some of those windows had curtains drawn behind them, and he suspected this was for some ambiance. Haffa did not keep whores in his house when Wu was young. If Haffa could shed some of his integrity once, he could do so again.

The bones were the same, but the paint had been redone. No longer were those high walls crimson. Instead, they had been done up in a powdery shade of blue, too muted to be a true pastel, and the window frames were done a blinding white. To one side of the tower was a grain mill, and this too was owned by uelfin. Oe would abide no impediment to her river's progression from its head waters to its basin save those constructed by her descendants. In that way, the uelfin's special status was preserved. The caste system was made sacred. The Goths must struggle while the uelfin grew fat, must work the trades but may never own the means of production for any one commodity.

A grain mill, so simple a thing. The wheel dug into the river, dredged up buckets of crystal water and hauled them over and again to be returned to that band. The wheel turned, and gears and shafts bit into each other, worked stones hidden within the wide, rocky, barrel shaft to grind wheat into flour—the germ separated from the powder and set aside, the refined product sold at a premium.

He watched the wheel rotate once, twice, and again. The baskets rose almost to a height with the third floor ceiling of Haffa's tower, before crashing toward the river again, showering the avenue's end in dense mist.

He crossed the street, the weight of Jaunz's scepter heavier in one pocket than the sack of coin in the other, though the coin undoubtedly weighed more. Soliciting Haffa's attention with the scepter would bring expediency to this matter, but it would leave him exposed. The seal had gained him undue attention once already. It may not be wise to reveal it again. He did not know who in this tower might comprehend what it was or what it meant, and the wrong eyes could just as well find his father or the bitch he'd let steal his mother's place.

He passed the threshold, entered a clean foyer and then sitting room within

Tears for the Moon God

which few waited. He suspected none of these were here to see the master of the house. None of them had the appearance of being moneyed. They wore clothes of sturdy make, but their adornments were unfussy, died in cheap colors and without embroidery. The buttons on one man's shirt were lacquered wood, pretty for the contrast they provided to the white fabric, but easy to come by, even to make himself if he had access to a button press and sand paper.

The man regarded him as he approached the clerk's desk. The desk attendant, a madam, peaked out of a room down the hall, saw him and glided up to the podium.

"How can I help you?" she asked.

He hesitated. *Scepter or coin?* He elected to use the more mundane method. He fished the sack of coin out of his pocket and set it on the table.

"I need a matchmaker. Your best Goth. I don't trust the uelfin way, you understand."

"Tomorrow will suit you better. You know the omens?"

He sniffed. "Superstitions and folklore. All in the name of preserving a fragile ego. I will take my chances."

"You're certain of this?" A match made by moonlight is--"

"A match made to fail." he cut in. "Insofar as the maker of the match feels cheated. I am willing and able to pay more than the service is worth to see this thing done and done properly."

"Price is no object?"

"None."

She lifted the sack between forefinger and thumb, lacquered nails glittering in the soft light. They looked almost black in that light, but a discerning eye picked up a subtle, reddish tint, matching her eye shadow.

Her appearance, in its every calculated detail, was a test and a trap. No self-respecting matchmaker would entertain an unserious individual long, and so the woman fronting his operation must be a seductress, a tease, inviting attention but granting no favors.

Her dress was opaque silk, cut modestly at the neck but hugging her curves. The print was a sweeping array of flowers, bright bursts of color on a dark background. Loose curls cascaded over one shoulder, her edges clean and precisely laid, and gloss and paint gave her lips the depth and color of a glistening apple.

He kept his gaze trained on her face, her eyes, as she dipped at the shoulders, hair sliding over her breast, and tested the weight of the sack.

"No object indeed." She smiled up at him. "You're sure you wouldn't rather wait for the master?"

"Is he in?" he asked.

"In, yes. Available, no. He is uelfin, though. You do not trust their ways."

His expression soured. He wondered if she saw through him. If he was selling this act.

She shrugged. "Suit yourself. Come with me. I'll take you to our premier matchmaker. The *Goth*, that is."

Amusement fluttered across her face--a quirk of the lips, a scrunching of the nose.

She led him down the hall to a staircase. They climbed to the second, the third floor, passed through a gilded grate behind which a wide-chested guard stood watch. She led him down that hall and again down an adjacent corridor, at the end

The Hunt

of which they climbed to the fourth floor.

She opened a door close to the height of the steps. It was, for the moment, quite empty, and he allowed her to guide him to a vacant seat at a desk within. The desk was loaded down with thick barreled candles, and incense suffused the air with the aroma of cinnamon and clove, and something earthier.

She pulled out the chair, and he seated himself "Lady Yeuh will be with you shortly."

She left him, closing the door behind her.

Every matchmaker claimed to be a master of their art, and each had a host of methods they swore by. He was not at all sure whether this one kept him waiting because she was offended by his late coming, or if she watched unseen for him to reveal his secret self.

She gave him time, and he used it to make observations of her chambers.

Her chambers were by no means lavish. Nonetheless, he could see the effort she put into it. Wealth gained, the woman must have funneled a hefty sum into furnishing and decorating the cramped quarters, giving to them a closeness, an intimacy. White curtains fell from ceiling to floor, obscuring walls and making the entire expanse look open, welcoming, grander than it had a right to be. Flowers were a matchmaker's best weapon, and she had taken the time to exchange them just for him. Yellow tulips, and baby's breath. The baby's breath was fresh, the tulips desiccated husks. She was angry with him. He must have caught her as she was readying to return home.

Home was still a long way off for her. Her children, if she had any, would have to cope with her absence a little longer. Her husband, or her lover, would have to look after himself. He did not intend to keep her long, but what would her modest if unexpected absence be if not karma. She did not *need* to keep him waiting. She did not *have* to drag this out.

Her desk was clean. Wrought iron feet and elegantly carved legs climbed toward a thin, planar surface of soft wood, some kind of pine maybe—and if it was so, local.

He schooled his features to stillness, giving away nothing substantial. It hardly mattered what kind of temperament the matchmaker believed him to have. She was just an obstacle, a prop he would use to evince a sense of normalcy, to alibi him, perhaps, if things turned ugly. *God, I hope things don't get ugly.*

He had plenty of reason to hate Haffa, but whatever the reason for his hatred, it did not rise to the cold rage he felt for his stepmother. It did not justify murder.

The matchmaker emerged from a shadowed gap in her drapes. She was more than a head shorter than him, and plump. Her lips were wide and thin, and she had the wrinkled prune character of a Goth in her twilight years, when any day may bring death.

If she was the best the house could offer, she had earned her reputation. No one worked into their last years who was not desperately poor, or who did not love what they did. Need should have ceased to be a motivation long ago. No, she would be the latter sort.

She climbed onto the seat behind the desk, folded her hands together. No papers here, for her way was not Haffa's. Were this a casual meeting—an interview, as it was intended to be—she might commit all she gleaned to secret notes or simpler memory, but he had no intention of giving her the choice.

Tears for the Moon God

She opened her mouth to address him. He pulled on his soulbinding power, a static rush filling him, and launched himself at her.

The scrape of chair legs against tile.

A shrill cry cut off by his hand. A channel opened between them, a path cutting her off from whatever sorcery she might possess.

This was dangerous. Old as she was, if she possessed a relationship with a spirit, the connection would be deep. It would be worse if she was acolyte to a god. This method of restriction was not intended to circumvent soulbinding. The gods were not prone to hanging themselves from their own ropes.

He clapped one hand to her mouth, coming behind it with a fresh pulled dagger, which he set against her throat.

"Do not struggle, and I'll leave you breathing. My fight is not with you." he said.

He withdrew the dagger, eased back against the desk. He abdicated his seat and crossed to the wall of white curtains. Working quickly, he cut one down, then cut a series of long strips from it. He returned to her, several of them draped over his arm.

"You don't have to—"

"I do."

"But you said you're fight was not—"

"You know quite well why I can't leave you free."

She hissed, launched herself at him. He sidestepped her and her swiping claws, wrapped a length of velvet around her wrists, looped it around both of her arms. He pulled hard on the remaining length. The cloth snapped tight, stopping her short of crashing aground.

She shrieked.

In a series of swift motions, he bound her wrists, then gagged her. He finished with her legs, then ran a final piece of cloth from her ankles to her wrists behind her back, leaving enough slack that she could lay comfortably, but giving her no chance for escape.

He felt her testing the path between them, approached her. "Better for both of us if you went to sleep."

His fingers traveled the sides of her neck, found artery and vein, and pressed. He watched her eyes droop, flutter, and close. He did not release until he was sure she slept. She would wake too soon—he knew that—but he needed only time to leave; and he did.

Into the hall and down. He might have opened a new path, entered Haffa's office by a different channel, but to do so would leave an impression.

He found the entrance where he remembered, and hesitated outside. Haffa may be in there and he may not be. He may have seen his arrival in Cratom on some stream of Lanfin's song, telling him he should run, or that something would be asked of him he did not wish to answer. The uelfin had their windows. Lanfin's one mercy for them. As many became soothsayers as matchmakers, but such a boon was dangerous. See the future with perfect clarity and he may seek to change it, but beyond the point of change, he could not know what was to come. How long must he be blind? How long before he faltered?

Strange how something as simple as a doorway could have so strong an effect on him. There was nothing conspicuous about it. Wood grain gave it some character

The Hunt

behind a heavy, dark gloss. The surrounding corridor was dimly lit, yes, but there was an appropriate sense of calm in those cream tone walls, in the soft carpets muffling his steps, reminding him of grass and moss and uneven ground with the way they pressed against his boots, the way the balls and arches of his feet responded to them. A door as entirely ordinary as anything else about the matchmaker's house, this elitist floor, where so much coin could be traded away against a bride or a husband meant to last a lifetime.

He wondered whether, in his pursuits, Haffa factored in happiness. If enjoyment was a principle concern in his final decision, or if it was of little consequence to him. If the marriage lasted, it must be happy. Or, at least, man and woman, man and man, lover and lover, were content in some restrictive sense of companionship.

He let that train of thought go. It came too close to an uncomfortable truth. His father may well be happy with this woman, his second wife. He may have wanted her, all that she was. And if that was true, he was not the man his child had revered. He might be just as monstrous, just as conniving, as her.

He twisted the handle, pushed in the door.

Haffa sat behind a writing desk. Pots filled with lilies of various kinds were scattered across his expansive quarters. A terracotta vase sat at the foot of a chaise lounge in the triumphant Goth style of fifty or so years ago, all foiled in gold leaf and deep ebony where the wood was exposed. A pair of bi-fold screens lay open, exposing a half moon balcony and the edge of the grain mill's water wheel. It hauled trenchers filled with water upward from this vantage, promising a fated return to the river. He could hear the rhythmic *splash, splash* of their liberated contents returning home, a soothing sound for a man plagued by uncertainty.

Haffa had not aged a day in nearly twenty years. There was gray at his temples, and streaked through a shock of blue hair. Lines creased his wide forehead and wrinkles covered the backs of his hands. He had not been young when Wu had known him, yet it was as if time had forgotten him. He still possessed that unnerving composure, a calm which ought to be yielding to panic in the face of who approached him; yet he did not look up from the notes he scratched onto blank pages within a leather bound book.

He used red ink, detailing negative traits in some suitor he had recently seen. Another two pens, both silver chased and fitted with sleek cartridges, rested against the surface of the wiry, writing desk. They would be in black and violet. Both difficult pigments to come by so far from the sea. The man himself was clad in a tunic of simple cut, of a fine, satin silk. He had never been for gaudy prints or showy frills, but he knew his station, the significance of it. He was not averse to putting it on display. In modesty was power. In simplicity, radiance.

Bright, discerning eyes peered out from wide sockets, and the cast of his skin was like unfired porcelain. He set his gaze on Wu, inviting him to sit in the unoccupied chair the other side of his desk with a gesture.

Wu made no move toward it, but shut the door behind him.

"You look very like your brother." Haffa said. "Though I suppose he has more of his father in him. A blessing, wouldn't you say?"

"You knew I was coming."

"Haffa grinned. "In a manner of speaking. I did not expect you so soon, but given the nature of your disappearance." he spread his hands. "You have questions?"

Wu stared at him for several seconds, searching for what to say, what to ask first.

"Yes, well, that is to be expected." Haffa returned to his papers. "You have stormed the keep, finding nothing you could not handle in the halls and along the avenues between you and I. Now that I am cornered and, quite frankly, helplessly at your mercy, what is left behind is a different kind of space."

He waved all of that away. "Humor me, if you will, but I suspect what you most want to know is...*why?* Why I paired your father and your mother--"

"Don't call her that!"

"Mistress Bane, then.

"You'll have to understand I had little choice in the matter. There were, and are, powers at work in this city who are better left alone. If I believed you would listen, I would tell you to flee before they catch wind of you. My own motivations hardly matter in this, but you must know the results were inherently political."

"What happened to my mother." Wu asked. He was not ready to address the matter of most concern. More, he needed to know. To know why she left. Why she left *him.* "Where is she?"

"I suspect she is dead." Haffa's perfect calm remained unbroken as he fixed his gaze on Wu. Wu flinched away from him, opening that alien space Haffa spoke of again.

The fate of his mother, the first Mistress Bane, meant nothing to Haffa. Why should it? She was but one more Goth in the city, an arm of a king the uelfin deigned to tolerate. What was she to him?

Yet there, too, was the silver lining. His mother's death confirmed she had not simply abandoned him, that all of what had befallen him was not predicated on a choice. But there was finality and not closure. She was just one more person who had been taken from him, ripped away in that woman's schemes.

He wanted to hit something. Instead he clamped his teeth together, balled his fists at his sides. There would be tears this night, when the rage yielded, but he would not spill them here.

"Where is she?" he demanded.

"You already know the answer to that." Haffa set down his pen, folded his hands in his lap.

"She's a Raukha, isn't she?"

His cheek twitched.

Wu came close to reaching for his knives, hidden away as they were under his trousers, the hilts just higher than his wrists. He could see himself pressing the edge of one blade to the matchmaker's neck, demanding to know everything he knew. "You should know I intend to kill her. Raukha or not."

"Then alerting her spies would be unwise."

Wu's gaze flicked to him. "You work for her?"

He gave no answer.

You work for the Raukha Cartel?"

"You might call me a victim of their exploits. Compliant with their demands, when such demands are made of me, out of a sense of self preservation. You will find there are many in this city who share my plight. However, there are limits.

"Again, I must advise you to leave the city before they catch wind of you and

The Hunt

your schemes. As penance for my crimes against you, the innocent you once were, I will not alert them to your presence. I will not debase myself by robbing you of a chance at salvation. But you must leave. You cannot handle them. Not on your own."

"There is no salvation in leaving that bitch alive. You are a coward, Haffa. You were then, and you are now. You capitulated to a predator and a murderer. You are responsible for my past, my present and my future. And nothing you do now, nothing you have seen or will see will change that.

"You're just like all of your kind."

"The Goth woman you bound earlier will have alerted my guards of your presence by now, young Lord Bane. I believe it is past time you were going."

Wu cast a glance behind him. Shadows crossed the threshold.

Cussing, he pulled his knives, rounded the desk, placing Haffa between him and the guards as they stormed his chambers with weapons drawn.

Briefly, he contemplated taking Haffa hostage, but the gap was too narrow, the guards were already closing the distance.

The water wheel spilled its contents into the river, drawing his attention to the folding doors. He spun on his heels, pelted toward them, onto the balcony. He grabbed the marble rail, vaulted over it, slammed into the wheel.

He latched onto its cross beams and swung himself around to the side as a knife whistled past his ear. The wheel carried him up. Another knife whizzed past.

Up and over, and down. Water spilled from the trencher above him, dousing him in cold mist. Pushing his bangs out of his face, he searched through heavy mist for the road down below.

There!

Cobblestones. The barrel side of the mill. Wooden steps descending toward a long dock, where grain boats were tethered and waiting in the night gloom. He focused on the first of the dock's planks, and in his mind's eyes summoned forth the image of his rooms, the entrance to them, open and waiting. A surge of power flowed through him, and out. He touched the plank with his spirit, stitched those disparate places together. The door was cast open.

He leapt off the wheel, rolled across the steps and through.

Rhul sat on the edge of the bed where he had left him. His gaze was fixed on the opposite wall, and Wu followed it in time to see the knife sailing toward him. The Raukha, Garam, boiling out of the wall and rushing him, knives wending through still air.

In quick flashes, he took in the details he had missed. Blood splashed across the floor. An overturned chair pressed against Rhul's back. Ropes holding him against it. His wrists were cut crossways. The cuts were clean but shallow. He was losing blood but not quickly. Not so much that he could not be saved; if only Wu could touch him.

"You thought you were being clever, shaking me off your trail." Garam snorted.

A flurry of blows was met with a rapid succession of parries. Steel rang against steel.

"What are you after, pathfinder?" he demanded. "Why are you here in Cratom?"

Wu pressed him, launching into an offensive. Suli's teaching was carved into his flesh, in his bones. He would not fall here. Not in a knife fight. Not to this man.

Tears for the Moon God

"What does he want? Why is he interfering?"

Garam forced him back onto the defensive. He slashed for his ribs, a feint meant to disguise a low cut to the inside of his knee which he stepped free of. The back step forced his legs wide, and he was forced to move away from Rhul to close.

A series of blows, a cut to his elbow severing the tendon there. A back end blow to his chin. Garam kneed him in the stomach, just under his ribs, and he collapsed.

That quickly.

He was not prepared to die. If this was the caliber of that woman's hands, if this was the extent of her power...

Garam loomed over him. He took his right arm in a firm grip, laced his free arm under his shoulder. He kept his black-bladed dagger angled at Wu's neck.

"Why is Jaunz interfering in Cratom?" He demanded.

"Interfering?"

"Make this easy on me, will you? What does the Hand want?"

"I don't know."

"Talk! What does he want with Adam Five Eyes?"

"Who is Adam Five Eyes?"

He withdrew his blade, then lifted him onto the bed, onto Rhul's lap. "Take him back."

"There is no need for hostility." he said. "We have a misunderstanding. Just...take your Shard in before it dies. Please?"

He did as Garam asked. Not for his sake. Rhul's death would leave his soul damaged. There was no means of repairing it. If he died, that piece of Wu left with him.

"I'm sorry, Wu." Rhul whispered. "He caught me—"

"It's okay." He said.

He focused on himself, the integrity of his soul. He envisioned it as one mass, and Rhul as a part of the whole, absolved of identity. Of individuality.

Garam's observation of them was unwelcome, discomfortingly quizzical.

"Did you think a Shard was merely a doll?" He asked defensively.

Rhul's flesh gave way to him, and he dropped the intervening distance onto the bed, his back leaning against the chair. The ropes hung loose, pressing against him, and his arm was healed of the severed tendon there, a benefit of having so much of his energy within a corporeal form. There was healing to be had for both Shard and core.

He tensed his wrist, feeling the ache where Rhul had been cut, an echo of the damage healed. "A misunderstanding?"

"I was tasked with finding an adequate guard to transport my master out of the city. He is being hunted. You seemed like a good candidate to help us, until you revealed yourself as a Rauhka."

"I'm not."

"Why are you carrying a Scepter of the Hand, then? You must be working for one of them."

"I assure you, I have no idea what you're talking about."

"The seal you passed over to Donny when you came in. It belongs to Jaunz Faedrin. I'd recognize that thing anywhere."

"Ah. That." His eyebrow twitched upward. "I'm a pathfinder. Jaunz is one of my superiors in the God House of Ways. I didn't know he was a Raukha until tonight."

The Hunt

"And he directed you to this place. Without even the courtesy to tell you what you were walking into."

"So this person you're trying to protect. Are they the ones chasing him?"

Garam shook his head. "But they do not want conflict with who does. I think they understand that is a contest they can't win."

"Must be some scary people if even the Raukha Cartel doesn't want conflict with them."

"You could say that." Garam agreed. "What about this person you want to kill? Who is it?"

Wu's lips parted around a sneer. "I only tell that to my friends.

"You need a pathfinder. I suppose that makes your guy's destination obvious. It'll be dangerous getting him there, and I have my own needs. Maybe we can make a deal. A death for a life."

"I'm listening."

"I'll help you get him to Ur, if you help me kill this person I so badly want to see dead."

"That would be a rather straight forward use of my abilities."

"You know I can't get you all the way there? We'll need the cooperation of the Nixians once we get past Gonsai Wall."

"I do, but you'll take us at least that far. I can handle the rest from there if need be."

Wu held out his hand. "We have a deal then?

"A death for a life? I think so, yes." Garam reached out and shook it. "Now, who are you trying to kill?"

A fury rose in Wu at the thought of her. A flash of memory played across his mind. Her back to him as she walked away. His hands bound together around the bole of a fir tree, head twisted around, tears blurring his vision as she left him for dead. Color rose in his cheeks, an immense heat flooding him. "The Mistress of House Bane. My father's second wife."

Garam's gaze fell on him. He saw the severity of the lost Lord Bane's conviction there. He reeled back and cackled, a guttural sound filled with wicked mirth.

"Oh, baby boy." he said. "You precious imbecile. You haven't come to take a woman's head. You've come to start a war."

Initiation

"Wake up." A hard shove into Ibrim's shoulder.

He reached out, his body reacting before his mind caught up, slapped the arm away.

The acolyte retreated a step, his boots thudding heavily against stone.

Ibrim opened his eyes, set his gaze on the man as his memory returned to him. The vitreous walls let in moonlight, a perpetual glow. He had not seen more than the blush of sunrise since arriving in the God House, and then just its first, fierce touch crawling over the world below.

The sun was always in pursuit, it seemed, threading its way across the sky with the moon ever ahead of it, flagging at times, at other times opening the gulf between them wider, so that even that first flush of anger was driven into obscurity.

"Get dressed." The acolyte commanded.

"A moment." Ibrim said.

He remembered the previous night. He had been marshaled down the hall beyond his room's lone door along with a troupe of other acolytes who had come into the city at the height of other full moons, from nations and cities so far removed from his own that their accents and markings and customs were unknown to him. There had been a graemein among them, tall and stout, and covered head to toe in muted red paint. Which color the graemein wore had something to do with which soul inhabited the body, but the Sanarks he had seen depicted in old books all wore both. This was the first time he had seen a man of the people clad in just one color.

I wonder why that is.

There had been others, a kaleidoscopic array of peoples from disparate cultures, who haled from other kingdoms and even continents. He had seen some of those peoples in the flesh, when they made port in Tulakh, or walking the streets of Tulaen. Most he did not know except by reputation, or artist renderings. The Graemein was like that. So was a Tak moran woman ahead of him.

He had recognized her by her stout, broad shouldered build, the bald pate exposing a tattoo of a single flame, not unlike those worn on the robes of the Rahad,

Initiation

at the join where her skull met the back of her neck.

All in a line, they had been escorted under guard to their rooms within a barracks which let in moonlight and views of a sprawling city through solid walls enchanted to appear vitreous from this side. In these halls and chambers, every room was made to look as if it had a direct view of every horizon.

The effect was disorienting. God Ao Nii gave clarity to all things, it seemed, yet Ibrim had found none for himself. No longer a prince, nor a soldier. What was he in the grand scheme of the god's stronghold. Where did he fit into its hierarchy?

The acolyte seized him by the midriff, unceremoniously tossed him onto the floor, where stone collided painfully with his knees and elbows.

"You will do as is commanded of you, initiate. Until such time as you are deemed worthy."

The acolyte held out his hands, then. White sleeves obscured everything above the wrist, yet both hands were branded, the markings of a slave or a prisoner.

The gall, to speak to a prince like this. The nerve! A slave should know his place.

The acolyte sneered. "Dress. Now. There is much ahead of you which you may find unpleasant. Today, however, is a day for learning. A first step toward comprehension. Of us, and of yourself."

Ibrim allowed the slave to help him to his feet. He bit down on his anger and crossed to a wardrobe where he took up an unadorned, floor-length, white robe and dressed himself.

The acolyte moved to the door, opened it, gestured him into the hall where dozens of others were already gathering.

Other acolytes stood in lock step with the new initiates, one for each of them. They stood in militant lines— their backs straight, silver-chased boots with upturned toes facing forward.

Their charges fidgeted, cast nervous glances about themselves. Some few stood with the same careful grace as their handlers, eyes forward, ignoring all others.

He sensed a hardness in them. In the graemein and the tak moran woman he had seen the night past. In the red-eyed Tului behind him, who looked close to death even as he stood unmoving, unyielding, obedient.

He wondered at the Tului man's presence as he joined the line, as his own handler assumed the precise posture of his peers next to him.

Myth, and rumor with the flavor of myth, spoke of those people; granting only the impression of pale skin and red eyes, a penchant for violence. All else was shrouded in mystery.

They had a king, so it was said, that no one had ever seen. A king old beyond reckoning, or perhaps of a dynasty in which generation after generation assumed the same name, shrouded themselves in secrecy so absolute none, perhaps even of their own people, could say what they looked like, where their locus of power was, which god or spirit they worshipped or from whom they derived their power, their...dominance.

Wordlessly, the acolytes began marching. The initiates fell into step with them.

They marched down the hall, joining others along a principle thoroughfare which spiraled downward within the embrace of a darkness which only suffused this corridor, this hole within the barracks they all occupied.

Dozens of initiates marched down the corkscrew passage—open darkness to their left, the pathway broad enough to accommodate the double file procession,

Tears for the Moon God

but only just. They descended onto a bridge which let out into the city proper, under a star strewn sky and down, down roads populated with acolytes who had proven themselves in the eyes of the moon god. Past children unburdened by the knowledge that their society was built upon slaughter, that their mothers and fathers had committed heinous acts even before they arrived at the height of the stairway. At the gates.

Would they be permitted to remain when they came of age? Did the moon god demand their avowal, that they should share in the burden of knowing madness, of being overrun by it?

He wondered how many of those children would survive into adulthood. How many were without mothers or fathers. Who had lost brothers or sisters to the blooding witnessed in the world below?

Had he taken their kin on the climb?

The procession arrived at a broad spar of crystal, the palace rising in its opulence from the plateau, elegant and splendorous and terrible.

And terrible because of its legacy. All that existed here was built on blood and death.

But so is every great kingdom. Every palace is a graveyard for the destitute. Every king's bed sits on its builder's legacy, the last place his life held meaning.

A set of doors as tall as three men standing foot on shoulders yawned open. Cold light poured from within, blinding Ibrim as he passed through with the rest of the procession.

The acolytes broke into rows, formed a grid with their charges within the cavernous expanse beyond. They turned in unison to face the far wall, where a fresco mural depicting the god, Ao Nii seated atop a scarlet pillow—his back bowed, face down-turned, ink-black hair falling over naked knees, fanned across an expanse of otherwise unrelieved white—was sealed into the wall.

Before it was a plaque of gray stone, large and set within a crater, so that the mural made it small even as the files of initiates and acolytes were left entirely in its shadow.

Seated with his back to it was the first acolyte Ibrim had seen, the one who had come for him in the wake of his flight, his trial.

The acolyte was clad in a wine-red robe, a black stole fringed with gold tassels draped over his shoulders. He rose, a scarlet miasma emanating from him, washing over the gathered others, driving back the purer light the chamber had known until then.

Ibrim watched the plaque behind him. The slab grew darker, darker, until it resembled obsidian. The glyphs etched into its surface burned like fire, wavered and spangled and flowed.

The acolyte spoke, his voice like thunder in the chamber. "Our god is broken! Madness afflicts him. In accepting him into us, we accept madness. Each of you...all of you...will succumb to that madness by month's end. Your time is come. The great cull must commence, for there is no stopping the tides of melancholy, of rage. The ebb and flow of emotion, an outpouring from our god into us, and through us into others. With us is grief conveyed, one person to another, from our god to his people, from his people to all peoples. For his loss is great!"

The glyphs writhed, cast ghost projections, smoky exhalations to drift between bodies, filling spaces with languages long dead, which might well be the first words

Initiation

ever spoken. By the spirits. By the gods.

Ibrim recoiled as a series of glyphs streamed past, afraid they would cling to him should they make contact, suffuse him with a magic of binding the limits of which would not be made apparent until too late.

"From love was born defiance. Our god railed against his enemies, against their agents. From love were born alliances when our god, Ao Nii, was whole. Our order possesses sympathizers. We are not alone."

The glyphs pulsed, gathered and pooled in the spaces between acolytes and initiates.

"What is this?" he hissed.

His handler glared at him, and he descended into silence. *One day, I'll knock this one senseless. He'll understand the way of things then.*

"Man rose from clay basins, weak as cracked porcelain. He was flawed. She rose and breathed and took life. But man was a mistake, an accident. His flowering from the earth was unsanctioned. He was anomaly, a mystery to all who had come before him. Not inspired by the mind of a tyrant, yet that was the way. It must be. Not bound by his design. The gods were confounded. They had known life given. Now, they saw life *seized*."

The glyphs formed columns, rose through red haze, climbed toward the high, domed ceiling where intricate frescos depicted other gods, opulent scenes, paint ground into plaster-filled holes in intricate molding, windows into an improbable sky. There was Mu, maggot pale like his father, stag antlers thrust from his skull and that unrelenting sadness in his dark eyes. There was a femininity in his features, a vulnerability which was reflected, too, in the depiction of God Ao Nii behind the acolyte stumping for his god. There was feral Uldal, gazing sternly past thick eyebrows from atop his legendary hill. And Shakh, God of Hunters, a goliath beast obscured by shadows, his only clear feature a glowing, yellow eye.

The glyphs danced across those images, flowed in concentric rings as they climbed, and avoided the fifth, at the dome's very height, completely. Within the carve out, where they would not touch, was a Sun Man. Cold, blonde curls hung loose about his head, and unblemished, gold skin covered him from his hairline to his feet. Liquid silver eyes shot through with threads and flecks of gemstone blues, reds and greens peered out of a cherubic face; and he was slender, tall, clad in a deerskin jerkin and breeches that cut off along his thighs. He leered down at them, the point at which his gaze was fixed indistinct, seeming to take in everything at once, and each person individually.

"A life given. A life seized. What difference could there be between us. Mortals and gods, ought we be divided? The gods remembered the spirits. They remembered the weakness they displayed as they themselves rose into the world, the indifference with which the gods treated them. They recounted their mistakes, and some among them sought to destroy us. End us for good. For mortal kind, *humanity*, was abomination.

"The gods found themselves divided. And some believed us worthy of life, of growth. And those others thought us fit for extermination. But we persisted, not by ourselves but because those sympathetic gods, and the spirits those gods chose to ignore too long, came to our aid in our time of weakness. God Katcya descended onto the mountain where first man sprang forth, and found love among those humans. And he took upon himself a wife, and with her fostered two children."

Tears for the Moon God

The acolyte gestured to the Sun Man. "So, too, our god fell in love with God Katcya's second son. And he taught him his ways, and birthed in a human soul the gift of power. And the elder was taken by the mountain, and the mountain taught him his ways, and he too was gifted power. But the gods, those beings so plagued by greed and power lust, discovered this plight, and they ignored those gods and the people they wished to protect no longer. There was war then.

"The Elder gave his freedom." Red haze emanated from the glyphs, descended across the dome, sparing the fresco depicting the Sun Man. "The mountain gave his peace."

The glyphs crashed earthward, an avalanche of words in a language long forgotten, carrying with them the will of a broken god.

Ibrim ducked, threw his hands over his head, a useless shield.

"The Younger gave his life." the acolyte intoned harshly. That scarlet miasma closed on the floor, bathing the auditorium in bloody light. "And our god gave his sanity."

Glyphs crashed into him, into all of those gathered around him, sparing no one. He saw red—walls and crashing waves, smoke spilling forth as heat traced the paths of his veins and nerves, crawled into bones and organ meat, pushing ever inward until it was integral to him, inseparable.

Ibrim found himself on the floor, his throat ragged from screaming. His hands were still clasped around his head as he cowered away from that energy, unable to escape it.

Silent tears dripped from his chin, and it was some time before he could summon the strength to open his eyes, to leave behind the ebbing waves of crimson, scarlet and vermillion, the countless other shades of red and black, red and black, rising and falling at the edges of his vision.

"The first time is the hardest." his handler said.

I'm going to have to endure this again? This...grief.

"Come." the acolyte offered him his hands. The aggression he had displayed earlier was gone now. In its place was sympathy. "Stand. Walk with me."

Kneeling, he took Ibrim's weight onto him and helped him to his feet. They walked from the chamber.

There were bodies scattered across the floor, some bleeding, though from his vantage he could see no obvious wounds. Some acolytes remained among them, moving among the rank and file, pushing eyes closed, delivering blessings.

They walked through a dark portal, Ibrim and his handler, and up heavily eroded steps.

They entered a room. A bed was situated in a low-ceilinged cubby at the back. A table and two chairs were arranged in the intermittent space between the bed and them. Atop the table were a pewter pitcher and matching cups, a heel of bread in a whicker basket, a bottle of dark, red wine. There, too, was a lone, fat candle which was giving off too much light. Its sides were carved over with glyphs akin to those Ibrim had seen in the auditorium, those which lived within him now.

The acolyte gestured at the far chair. "Please sit."

Ibrim did as he was told, remembering the last time he had disobeyed. Whatever newfound kindness this acolyte chose to put on display, he did not intend to test his patience just yet. Did not want to earn his wrath.

"What...happened?" he asked.

Initiation

The acolyte assumed the other chair, pushed the basket his way. "Eat."

"I'm not..." Ibrim took the bread, bit into it. In truth, his stomach was violently upset and he was not at all certain the bread would stay down. But it was not worth the argument.

The acolyte poured a cup of water for him and passed it across the table. He ignored the wine, which Ibrim badly wanted, if only to calm his nerves.

Ibrim took a long draught from the glass, washing the cloying wad down.

"You were afflicted by a small taste of God Ao Nii's grief. Over the next weeks, you will daily incur doses of that power, a little more each time, until you are ready."

"And...and then...will I become--"

"Yes." he said. "It will be worse for you than most, I'm afraid. If you can tolerate that power, if you endure the trial to come, then you will be allowed to learn our arts. As you heard from God Ao Nii's Left Hand, it was not always this way. God Ao Nii's crime was in courting a human, forming a bond with him the Elder Gods, some of them, viewed as pathological. The same is true of God Katcya, but God Katcya possessed then and now significant power God Ao Nii does not, and did not, have access to. He took his fight to the gods, and they struck him down. They killed God Katcya's younger son, and imprisoned his elder in a labyrinth beyond time.

"So, God Ao Nii grieves, and we must endure his grief. That grief is overwhelming to most humans, but we must endure. We *must persist*, because we are one arm of defense against godly interference in human lives."

He poured more water for Ibrim. "You'll want that."

Ibrim took the offering, drank it down.

"I've said my piece. Do you have any questions for me?"

"A few."

He gestured for him to speak.

"What happens to the kids? They're all over the city."

"Their parents either came here from the world below or grew up here and became acolytes of God Ao Nii. They will be sheltered for as long as they remain children. We have safe places for them, which are well defended by the strongest of us. They have never been overrun."

"And when they come of age?"

"They make their choice. Most choose to become acolytes. For some, it's a matter of following in their parents' footsteps. For others, it is a refusal to give up the way of life they have always known. The world beyond one's home is scary, even when the choice to venture into it is freely made. For those who choose another path, they are released onto the staircase."

"Where they will die?"

"You saw that not all of us who descended the staircase were out of control. Those of us who remain secure within ourselves act as escort. You likely passed out from the exertion long before you saw the first of them, but there were those among us who were not beholden to the Moon God's power, and they will be finding homes in your homeland by now. Anything else?"

"Just one thing, I guess. Why should my trial be worse than most?"

The acolyte chuckled. He turned up his hands, the brands clearly displayed across his wrists.

Tears for the Moon God

"I found my path in Dol Shakar."

"I'm not familiar--"

"It's a mine. Seems a world away now. I was a slave there, oh, thirty years ago now. There was a faction there who might have helped me get free, if I could contact them, but in those days they weren't in the habit of making themselves easy to find."

He smiled at Ibrim's obvious confusion. "Tale for another time. The point is I found myself in a slave camp, with no hope of escape, and while there was a pathway out, of a kind, I couldn't find it. I wasn't all that bright in those days.

"The day of my escape, the crystal stair descended early. It was nearly the day's height, and here this staircase touched down almost at my feet, as if it was begging me to climb it. I thought it was God Gorgus smiling down on me, but then a shadow crossed the land, and a flood of moonkin started pouring across the camp, murdering everyone they came in contact with. The slavers were there faster than I'd ever seen them respond to any common riot. They might have been trying to shore up their losses. That's what I believe. It couldn't be out of any sense of compassion for us.

"Someone seized me around the chest and started dragging me away up the staircase, and the next I knew, I was here. To tell you the truth, I think he might have been the only one with a claim to this place who was still clinging to a shred of his sanity. Or...if there were others, they were busy dragging their own prizes out of the camp."

"Prizes."

His expression changed then, a darkness building behind his eyes. "That kind of madness leaves marks. When the moon moves to eclipse the sun, the madness takes hold of nearly everyone. There's no running from it. Our strongest people, God Ao Nii's chosen disciples, can barely keep themselves in check. If they drag off someone on the ground, so be it. In the moment, we're just possessions to them. They should be keeping God Ao Nii contained, but how can they? In those moments, our god's own madness has taken command so completely he is willing to throw his might against the sun. He is done running. The rest of us can only hope our instincts tell us to run far away from that fight, and then that we survive it.

"H-how often do these things happen?"

The acolyte shrugged. "How often does our god find reason to fight back? He has been showing signs of renewed vigor lately. Or perhaps it is better to say his madness is growing more profoundly. He is becoming more erratic. It may well be that it does not reach its tipping point by the time of the next full moon. It may be that he is calmed before any such point can be reached, but I do not hold much hope in that outcome.

"To answer the question that brought us here, your trial may be more difficult than most and it may not be. But if it is, it will be because the eclipse came before the blood moon. Because God Ao Nii chose to attack God Gorgus in his domain, where daylight touches the land. It will be a moment of clarity that does it, but do not judge him too harshly. God Ao Nii behaves in the way he does because someone precious to him was ripped away. His madness comes from his love of mortals. That is why we follow him."

He rapped his knuckles against the table. "Now, time to get you to your rooms. You'll need sleep after that dosing." His chair screeched against stone as he pushed it out and stood. Ibrim followed him from the room.

Ung Tsang

A wide tent had been erected outside the dirt pit where the contest would be held. Through thin, tarp walls, he heard the rabble of the crowds, conversations shouted over each other, the excited fervor of spectators from all of the sects ready to see how their representatives faired. Criers placed odds and took wagers. A few of them took odds against Sarri's potential upset, demanding to know who thought the other Cuu contenders might force Shaki out of the tournament.

He spared a glance for the other man. It could not feel good to hear so clearly how much the downfall of his own father was worth to his people. How much of the year's horde they were willing to part with to see him cast down.

Who would come out victorious? Who would fall out before the first round closed? The bets continued to pour in as the fathers of the contestants entered the tent.

Sauman had taken on the burden of explaining the rules to the contestants. He did so without inflection, disseminating this information to a group who had seen countless, identical trials, who were barely paying attention to him.

There were to be two contests. The men and women would enter the pit separately, the fighting conducted along gendered lines. In years in which a two spirit was competing, that person would fight with the group they identified with most strongly. It had been seven years since such a contest had occurred. In years when a chief had no child to offer, another child from his extended family could be offered up in his place. In years when the chief's seat was contested, those who sought to depose him would provide champions of their own. So on and so forth, he explained, though none of those scenarios had any bearing on this fight. He was met with glassy-eyed stares throughout most of it.

There was to be no use of magic in the first of the two rounds. Soulbinding and spirit calling were forbidden. This was true for Ung Tsong and Ung Tsang. The last five standing would move on to the second round, in which both forms of magic were permitted. He did not mention Dupec's innate ability to alter probabilities—he did not have to—but this lack of acknowledgment seemed to rankle some of his peers.

There would be no mortal injury delivered by any party in either contest, regardless of the use of magic, and no intentional maiming, either.

Dupec thought this odd. None of the sects were without at least a handful of competent enough healers to mend whatever damage was done. *Maybe this is a matter of honor.*

He recalled his time in the God House of Ways. No such distinction was ever made among God Uldal's acolytes. Not once they had learned to cast off a Shard.

He concluded his speech and dismissed them. They scattered along the tent walls to wait for their fathers and mothers. Dupec took up a place near the entrance as their loved ones marched in.

His father carried a hide pack shut fast with a drawstring. He approached him, set it on the ground, and unbound it.

He pulled clay pots from the pack, gold adornments. He handled them delicately, his hands shaking as he withdrew an armlet in the shape of a suspended flame.

He turned it over in his hands, stood up, and looked Dupec in the eyes.

"My father passed this to me for my own trial, as his father passed it to him. From father to son, we have welcomed each new generation with the passage of this heirloom for generations.

"A flame burns in the heart of every man. Uncontained, it consumes him, leaving behind only rage and the desolation it brings. But contained, it can be guided. A source of passion and compassion, a force of purification and renewal. In one hand, the flame destroys. In the other, it brings clarity, a sweeping away of dead things, giving nutrients to the soil to bring strength to what comes in its place.

"Fire grows the grasses of the mind. It brings new life to old lands. Guidance, yes, and purpose. Wear it now, as a reminder."

He held up the band. Dupec held out his arm, and he slid it over his bicep, where it hugged his muted skin gently.

"Thank you." Dupec said, for lack of knowing what to say.

Ungol looked away from him then, a shadow of unease twisting his features. He reached for the pots, opened the lids.

He dipped his fingers into one of them, coming away with a thick glob of black grease paint. He spread it over his hands.

"The Dumas are guided by the crow. Our enemies among the Ruc'an, Loqui, and Jahhar see only death in her wings, but she is wise. She sees through every hole in our defenses and theirs, both on the field of battle and in the mind. From her, we draw insight. Wear her image on your skin."

He reached up and cupped his hands over Dupec's cheeks, palms pressed against his lips. The grease left an imprint like fanning, predawn wings after his retreating fingers, and the pigment was cold and wet against his skin. An uncomfortable feeling he accepted without complaint. He did not want to offend his father, when so much of their relationship was so new.

This was important to Ungol, important to *him* if not for the same reasons. To Ungol, it was a last rite of passage he could share with his son, which he felt he did not deserve but which he performed because he must. For Dupec, it was a moment in which vulnerability could be shared, a weight lifted even as new weight was added. Expectation arrived to replace the less palatable conflict that had been his relationship with his father. What was meant as a mercy had been a kind of curse, even beyond what God Katcya gave to him.

Tears for the Moon God

There, too, was the drive to forget. The Dragon of the East rode on his shoulders, promising an unraveling of ideals, a night which might see violence, if the stranger spoke true. He needed a distraction. His heart ached for this stranger, yet he could not understand why. He should fear the apparition, but he felt no such emotion. Or felt it as a byproduct of something harder to describe.

This was his distraction, a place in which he could lose himself in the drive to make his father proud.

Ungol washed his hands of the grease with a bladder of cool water, dried them on a rag prized from his bag. He took red paint from another, wheat yellow from the last. He traced lines across Dupec's chest, arms, legs...speaking all the while of the symbolism. For this contest, Dupec was allowed only a loincloth and the feathers in his hair, and the cold was biting even within the walls and before the stove at its heart. But God Uldal had long driven the emotions from him in this. He took in the cold without judgment, reached into himself and buried the urge to shiver, to chatter his teeth, to show that it bothered him.

The drying paint pulled in the chill, amplified it, but still he would not bow to it.

"From the grouse, we draw strength. Strength comes in the ability to yield. It is utilitarian. Directionless, it yields to nothing, and so a man is made brittle. Resourceful is the grouse, driven by purpose. Its purpose is survival. We are aligned in that. So, the grouse teaches us to bend our will to the task of surviving, to give strength to purpose, and become flexible, adaptable, from growth.

"With these markings, you are made a man. You come before your father a child and leave a man. In youth, you are uninitiated, and must be tested. I'll see your mettle, and you will know I see it. This test is not yours alone, but belongs to your tribe, to know the strength, born in wisdom and growth, of the Dumas. In you are us all represented, my son. With you, we are honored."

He finished his painting, gathered his supplies and stepped back. His eyes watered with unshed tears, and he smiled. "You will do well, win or lose, son. But know that I will always be proud of you."

He clapped him on the shoulder, and took his leave, joining Coltang and Sarri on their way from the tent.

Tamlin approached him, then. Scowling, he looked him over—head to toe, back along the same axis to settle on his face. A stony regard fixed on him, all of the chief's son's disgust was made plain. This was not a man who would come around easily. Not one who viewed Dupec as anything but an invader and a pretender. And the words that came from him stung, because some part of Dupec Safar saw the truth in them.

"You mock our traditions by being here, wearing your war paint." He said. "No matter what your father thinks. No matter what he says. You will never be one of us.

"Go back to your god."

He marched off.

Dupec watched white dots like a fawn's coat dance across the backs of his legs and buttocks as he joined the cluster of others the other side of the tent. His father had given him a thick choker of gold, and matching bracers for his wrists. Collar and bracers were both covered, every inch, with eroded glyphs in a style that did not belong to the Gil Garo, or any tribe he knew in these lands. They must have been pilfered from the hoard of some well traveled dignitary, a Jahhar horse trader who tracked far to the south perhaps, or a visitor from the outlands who had come to Tao Shein Steppe to beseech the lords of the western kingdoms.

He wondered why Tamlin Sarr hated him. They had exchanged so few words, yet none had been pleasant.

An itch climbed the length of his spine, spread across his shoulder blades. A most peculiar sensation washed over him, as if this had all happened before. This exact exchange, in precisely this place and at this moment. He could almost convince himself he knew what would happen next.

Perhaps this was some magic his nighttime visitor had left him with, a sense for goings on in near futures, but he thought not. What power could a man so thoroughly trapped beyond time have? What influence could he impress onto the world beyond his prison's walls.

He came to me. Is that not enough?

He paused, his gaze fixed on Tamlin, and wondered what might happen if he went against his gut. What might change about this whole ordeal if he chose a path that did not seem quite right. That did not fit into the designs foisted upon him—by the gods, by that stranger who claimed to be his lover.

Sauman returned as the last few parents filtered out to take their seats in the stands opposite the pit from the tent. He positioned himself in the entrance, folded his arms behind his back. He was not an imposing figure, but his gaze was stern as he panned over them.

"Contestants for Ung Tsong, please gather before me." he said. "As is custom, you will go forth first for the culling."

The women in the tent all gathered. In total, there were just eight. Among them, Dupec found Chakta, and Sircha, Gulang's daughter. He smiled at Chakta, roved past her to Bora. Shaki hugged her tight, whispered something into her ear. She blushed, slapped his arm playfully.

He released her and watched her go, joining Dupec as Sauman took the women away.

"What was that about?" Dupec asked.

"Nothing, nothing." Shaki said, but he was blushing fiercely. He rubbed the place where she hit him, his gaze on the open entrance and the pit, where the women had begun their battle. They took up positions, none approaching each other, while the crowds hissed and cheered.

A fresh round of bets were placed, occasional screamed numbers breaking through the roar.

"Your woman seems like she's hiding some talent. "Dupec said, eying him sidelong. "What's her story?"

Shaki shrugged. "Her mother is a hard woman. They say she fought a pack of wolves and beat every one into unconsciousness. Just a story, but she scares me anyway."

"And you chose to risk her?"

Shaki nodded. "Bora's much nicer. But she'll make it past the first round fine. She's got an eye for strategy, so if she's as wise as I think, she'll wait for her opening and take out who she thinks will be a problem for her later...when their back is turned."

"Cowardly." Tamlin spat, hearing their conversation. He did not look at Dupec.

Tears for the Moon God

Shaki shrugged. "When faced with bad odds, you do what you have to do or you get beat. If this was a raid, she'd be the one coming out with the greatest horde and the fewest wounds."

"Dangerous if true." Dupec murmured. "Some gods play their games in the same way. Distract with one hand, strike with the other. If a distraction exists, exploit it."

Shaki raised an eyebrow. "You've had strange bedfellows. Did you meet many gods in your time away?"

"One or two." Dupec said. "My god doesn't often invite others into his house. Most are like him in that way. Need drives them together, but they hesitate to form close bonds. Certainly, he has no great love of his kin. He loathes most of them."

"Which ones did you meet?"

"Hunting for rumors?"

Shaki winced. "Just curious. Our people rarely seek out the gods. We favor spirits. they tend to be better to us."

"Out of curiosity, then." Dupec said. 'What would happen if one of you became Ung Kanh Dui?"

"A stupid question." Tamlin said. Others among the gathered men were paying close attention. The smarter ones did not broadcast it, but he knew they listened for clues as to what they might be up against, which they might use to their advantage. No one has taken the title in generations."

"But its possible someone could?" Dupec intoned.

"It will never be you." Tamlin scoffed.

Shaki snorted. "You love birds. Get a room for all our sakes."

Tamlin's scowl was for both of them, though his glare was for Shaki alone. "It would depend on the spirit, but most of us would forfeit our ties to our masters whether we wanted to or not. The spirits don't always care what we want. If Duijus Kanh is as powerful as they say, maybe Tao Shein or Rasheik could withstand him." He placed an odd emphasis on those names. "But others...he would shatter those bonds. He wouldn't think twice about it."

"And if the one who found him was bound to a god?"

"Same scenario. Which god? Ao Nii? He'd shatter your skull before he ever let you near him. They hate each other. I suppose he couldn't do much about your..." a hostile glare from askance fell on Dupec. "...disease. If that's what you're worried about."

Dupec grimaced.

"No need to be nervous, friend." Shaki patted him on the shoulder. "Whether you enter his cave or not, you won't find him. No one ever does. Even the ones who say they have seen the Swans can't prove it. So take it from me." He smiled. "You're better off not thinking about him. Someone will go into that cave. Someone will carve their name into his wall. But whoever it is will walk back out having seen nothing but stone fangs and smelling of mold and dust. Same as every year."

Sauman returned with the women. The first three to enter were unconscious and nursing bruises. They were helped into the tent by old healers from Sauman's tribe, who set them against carpets and set about assessing the damage. Behind them came the victors, among them all of the expected contenders. Bora breathed heavily, clutching her ribs but walking on two feet without aid. Chakta and Sircha barely bore a mark, but both were slick with sweat and neither would look at the other.

Their contest must have ended on an unsatisfying note. *They'll pick it up in the second round, more fiercely than before.*

Sauman called the men together. They assembled.

"I'll remind you, no maiming is to occur. No matter how much bad blood is between you." He looked pointedly at Tamlin, then at Dupec. "Come."

They followed him from the tent, into the roaring crowds and onto their arena. Ungol sat with the other chiefs in the first line of bleachers. All of them wore stern expressions, giving away nothing.

"Take your places!" Sauman commanded.

The men fanned out. They settled into fighting poses, their gazes flicking from one rival to the next.

Dupec stood alone, taking no stance. Various bets were made against him that he could hear, many naming who they thought would take him down.

He looked to the sky, watching fat clouds pass under the sun. A soft breeze came down from the north, bringing winter's chill with it, tightening his skin, stiffening joints. He kicked his legs, flexed his fingers, shaking Ho'o's unwanted attention off, bringing flexibility back into his tendons.

"Begin!" Sauman's hand chopped down. The betting ceased. In its place rose raucous calls, shouting and booing and cheering all mixed together, a dull roar to drive up tension inside the arena.

Hungry, aren't they? he thought.

Kachukh rushed him from his right. Tamlin came from his other side. He twisted around Kachukh, arm crashing into Gulang's diminutive son's belly, knocking the wind out of him.

Tamlin fell back in time to dodge a leg sweep. He whirled around Kachukh, bringing a savage elbow down on his back, intentionally avoiding the other man's kidneys and spine.

"Urhng!" Kachukh grunted, striking the mud. An open palm strike from Dupec to the side of his head knocked him unconscious.

Silence. Lasting several seconds.

The upset had been swift, merciless. The crowds near enough to see held their breath. A renewed sense of caution took the other participants. With three strikes, he had convinced them their suppositions had been in error. In three, concise strikes, he had upset the balance.

Gulang would no longer be chief of chiefs. His son's hubris had ended a years long rein. Someone else would take up the title, and no one could say who it would be.

The era of Kachin dominance was ended, and all certainty was gone.

Gulang cussed, vaulting to his feet, his hands balled into white knuckled fists at his sides.

"Get up!" he bellowed. "He didn't hit you that hard! Get up for your sect, Kachukh!"

But Kachukh couldn't hear him.

Sauman emerged then, patted Kachukh's cheek. He gestured with two fingers, and a healer came to collect the unconscious man. She pressed her palm to his forehead, closed her eyes and nodded.

"A clean hit." She pronounced over the commotion.

Tears for the Moon God

She removed her hand, and Sauman helped her carry him out of the pit. The fight resumed.

The other contenders put more space between themselves and him. Even Tamlin stepped lighter, his prior hubris taking a back seat to a renewed sense of caution. Taking on Dupec would not be the one-sided beating he had assumed. He would have to choose his opening wisely, if he didn't simply wait until he had the advantage of his spirit calling on his side.

Working in step, Shira and Krisna moved on Tamlin. Their attacks worked in concert, but Tamlin stepped out of their path, his eyes all for Dupec as he rammed his fist into Krisna's flank, leapt around an attack from Shira meant for his ribs.

On the other side of the pit, Shaki ducked and wove around a man whose name escaped Dupec, wearing him down as his father, red-faced, shouted at him to fight like a man from his place in the stands.

"I didn't raise a coward, did I?" Sarri roared, the tendons in his neck bulging under hot flesh.

A barrage of blows, missed connections, left the attacker winded, moving too slow. Shaki smiled at him, approached, scrubbed his knuckles hard against the cocky bastard's cheek. His attacker hit the ground.

Tamlin did away with Shira shortly after, bringing the first round of the contest to a close with five left standing, four of whom appeared completely unbothered.

Dupec glanced around at the others as Sauman called the match. The healers took their charges into the tent, carrying one each between two.

Tamlin and Shaki, he had expected to make it through the round. Though Shaki was often nervous, and careless with his words and actions, he was a chief's son, and his father was a hard man besides. Arrak, though mild mannered, had raised a formidable fighter of his own, which was to be expected for there was advantage to be had in winning this contest for him personally. Quiet ambition was far more dangerous than the belligerent kind, but were this one to succeed, the chief's leadership would be a benefit to the tribe. Among the chiefs in contest this year, he seemed the most well received and, perhaps, the most discerning. Though Ungol would be a patient leader, compassionate, who knew when it was better to yield than to fight.

Despite his previous bungle, Krisna had fared better than expected, leaving Sarri's hold on the Cuu tenuous, an open question for Shaki to answer.

Sauman stood aside to let them pass into the tent. The last of them to make it through this preliminary round was an unknown to Dupec, certainly, but also to the others.

He bore some resemblance to Sauman, but was younger by at least ten years. They may have been related, or the resemblance might be incidental. He was not dressed the way the Chikata were. The turquoise jewelry in particular should have marked him as Tipik, one of Coltang's, but his embellishments missed the mark, were not donned in the same way or with the same comfort a true Tipik felt.

"Who is he?" If he had been in the yurt they shared in the lead up to this day, he had not made his presence known. Had not left his private chamber, in fact. Was he a cousin, born of a marriage between a sister and a man of the Chikata? It seemed likely, but then Sauman might acknowledge him.

As it stood, the two did not look at each other. Sauman barely seemed to register his existence.

Ung Tsang

A disgraced relative, then. Maybe even a bastard.

The man had not engaged in fighting in the first round, had hung back unnoticed by the others as they sought to eliminate the greater threats. He advanced, yes, but as a consequence of indifference. Why bother at all, if in the next round he would face them armed with magic.

Who is his master? Which spirit? He wondered.

With the men settled and the healers doing their work, Sauman called the women forward once more. They passed from the tent to begin their last fight. At the end of it, one would come back as Ung Tsong, and he had no illusions about which it would be.

Coltang will be so proud. He grinned.

Shaki took note.

"It's customary for the men to watch, you know." he said. "Bora will be expecting me to, of course, and I'm sure your little girlfriend would be happy to see you, too."

"You have it wrong if you--"

"I'm kidding. I'm kidding." Shaki clapped him on the back. "Lighten up. It's almost over."

Dupec's gaze settled on the mysterious fifth contender, who sat alone in a shadowed corner of the tent.

The resemblance to Sauman was, he supposed, incidental. What few features they shared could be explained by a shared heritage which extended no further than a few generations. A divergence more recent than existed between sects, coming not closer to kinship. He was uncommonly pale, that was true. Where the Gil Garo were mostly rich shades of brown, his skin tone rose almost to cream.

His gaze shifted to Tamlin, who was also watching the other. He made the decision to approach. Whatever the other man's grudge, he might still be able to glean something from a short conversation with him.

The visitor's warning still lingered in the back of his mind. Perhaps they would make it through this day without anything noteworthy happening, but he could not shake the feeling that stranger had been telling him the truth. He could not shake the feeling this newcomer, this stranger, was part of it.

"Did anyone come for him?" he asked. "A father?"

"Why do you care?"

"He didn't fight. You don't think that's odd?"

Tamlin shrugged. "He's probably not confident in his fists."

"He wears the paint, but the style is...off."

"You would know that how exactly? You've been here less than a week."

"I take your point." Dupec let it go.

He could well have grown up outside the Gil Garo sects, knowing of their culture only what he could glean from books.

The paint climbed from his collarbones, across is neck, over his lips and cheeks, formed a jagged web. The angles did not flow like they should. The lines were finger thick and branching, like veins. He wore no feathers in his hair. The turquoise beads around his neck hugged too tightly, and the disk-like earrings dangled from his lobes instead of being housed within them.

He dressed like the Tipik, but his dress missed the mark by small increments. The resemblance, though close, was just not quite there. The paint looked nothing

Tears for the Moon God

like Chakta's. If they were of the same sect, should they not bear at least a customary resemblance to each other.

He stepped toward the entrance, rejoining Shaki just within it. There was nothing else to be gained here. Nothing else he could learn about the Tipik pretender. They passed through, Tamlin and Krisna following in their wake, and sat on hard, uneven ground at the fighting pit's side.

The fight had already begun.

Bora hung back as the first sorcerous clashes came on. Chakta and Sircha had already done away with the contenders Dupec did not know by the time she made her move.

Bora rushed Sircha, came not for her body but the shadow it cast. Sircha danced out of reach, her shadow chasing after her.

Bora pivoted, coming for Chakta instead.

Seeing her opening, Sircha raised her arms, a sharp gesture. Water rushed to her, snows melting, lending her icy streams which she wielded like whips, lashing out at both women viciously.

Bora slid for Chakta, touching her shadow on the way past.

Chakta's smiling face collapsed into itself, her face losing its coloring, becoming mud and falling apart. Her body crumpled. Chunks of dirt and clouds of dusty soil showered the hard, earthen floor.

She was behind Bora. She lashed out with a well aimed palm strike to Bora's neck. The echo of the blow reverberated too forcefully across the pit.

Bora collapsed in a misshapen heap.

A water whip sliced through Chakta. More mud collapsed. She was on Sircha in the time it took Dupec to exhale. One more palm thrust. Sircha ducked low, spun.

The water pooled together, a shield plate between them.

Chakta planted her feet.

The shield blasted forward. Swirling water crashed into her. She reached through the maelstrom, grasped Sircha's wrist.

Sometimes the strongest defense against an attack was to lean into it. A lesson hammered into Dupec by his master.

Sircha crumpled, her body twisted into a painful position, her head and the balls of her feet almost touching, belly thrust into the air over straight legs, arms dangling.

"Match!" Sauman called over the roaring of the crowds.

He crossed to Chakta, took her hand and raised it high over her head. "Chakta of the Tipik! This year's Ung Tsong! Chief Coltang wins first pick of raiding lands!"

The Tipik among the crowd raved. Some wept openly. With spring's arrival, they would find themselves in a new era of prosperity. Their sect would not go hungry, and the horde they took would be vast.

Sauman released Chakta as Coltang rushed to receive her.

He took her in a bone crushing hug, lifted her off her feet and set her down.

He turned to the crowds, shaking his fist and yelling. "Pride to the Tipik! Pride to my daughter!"

Sauman ushered him back to his seat.

Privately, Dupec wondered if his own father would show so much spirit. But he was already decided. There would be no chance of that. Though he would like to bring his father as much honor, he had come to an understanding. God Uldal and not Ungol's sensibilities informed his choice now. His father's honor was a politically unstable reality. Advantage for them both lay elsewhere. In someone else.

But there was an art to games of politics. An art in deception and provocation.

Yes, his father would be made proud, but not for the reasons he wanted. He would see, today, the shape of bravery.

Duijus Kanh would be approached, but not as he had always been, and not now. There was time, yet, for that which must occur, but first was the establishment of something like trust. Faith for the people in a stranger.

The stranger emerged from the tent as Chakta joined her father in the stands.

Sauman called them into the pit. They took up stances around the circle, and he called the match.

"Begin!"

Dupec wasted no time. His assault was swift and merciless. A vanishing act, and in the same step a splitting off of two Shards.

Fury crossed the stranger's face as the Shards converged on him, a rage he had not expected.

A collective intake of breath. The watchers had not expected this display to begin on such an aggressive note. Neither, it seemed, had the contestants.

Ice flowered, a column thrust from mud for one Shard's chest while the stranger's shadow pantomimed a punch the man had not thrown. It connected with a Shard's shadow's chin. The Shard's chin was thrust upward, dull pain lacing through his jaw.

Dupec joined the fray as the other contenders commenced their own fights.

Let them finish each other off. It was to everyone's benefit to see these monsters done. They might weaken each other, at least. Make the task of taking down the victor easier.

Shaki's sudden surge of power startled the audience and contenders alike. Thin tracers of electricity danced around him.

So, he's Thera's acolyte. Dupec thought, glancing in that direction to mark him.

He charged Tamlin, fast beyond seeing, electricity trailing in his wake and...

Passed through him.

Dupec smirked. *I'd have been wrong about you, though.*

He drew on his soulbinding powers. Three palms lashed out. Three strikes. Two to the stranger. One to the chest, the other the back, the third to his writhing shadow. The magic the stranger wielded was unknown to him, but the effect was instant. Soulbinding sorcery bled into him, closing one path and opening another within him.

His tether to the spirit he consorted with was thrown into disarray. The path between spirit and acolyte was muddied, leaving him vulnerable for precious moments.

Three fists. Three blows. One to the cheek, one to the gut, the last to the back of the knee.

The stranger crumpled, unconscious.

Dupec turned on the others. His Shards scattered.

Tamlin met Shaki's fast flying fists with stony indifference, each blow passing through him as if he were a ghost.

He reached out, grabbed Shaki by the scruff of the neck, and rammed him into the ground. The force with which Shaki struck was greater than his slender body should allow by several degrees of magnitude. He struck the ground and stayed fast, the cheek that faced the sky depressed as if some invisible force crushed it.

"Ah." Dupec said, comprehension dawning. *Rasheik. He must have spent some years in the Rope to find him.*

Krisna's breath hissed past his teeth. He raised his fists, daring either of them to attack, and Dupec understood this, too.

Yes, Fan Ryu, I see you watching. He saw the spirit reflected in the man. Krisna was patient, then, and discerning. Enough to see past the creek spirit, Furuk's tricks, to find the Fang himself.

Dupec ignored him, and Tamlin did away with him with little effort. A man impervious to damage was not more than a living statue. Tamlin did not need to move him, but simply make him bow.

As Dupec walked past, he laid a hand on Krisna's shoulder, muddling the connection between the mountain and him. Tamlin's magic did the rest, crushing the poor lad under his own weight. A weight suddenly far more immense than he had any right to.

"Mass density." Dupec said, locking eyes with him. "Manipulation thereof. The well traveled in your master's service are capable of more, but you are too young."

The crowds were silent. Some strained to hear his words. He saw that. Saw that this had not gone at all how they expected.

Dupec closed the distance. He recalled one Shard into his body, the double backpedaling into him as he moved forward, his back rippling sinuously as the twin conjoined and was absorbed.

"Three years to find him. Then one more in training. But I've been in the keeping of a god almost since the moment of my first breath."

He lashed out, a feint. Tamlin countered, rendering himself intangible.

Dupec reached into him and held. He closed a path, and one opened in its place, throwing one more tether into disarray.

The effect was temporary, lasting just long enough to pull Tamlin into corporeal form, for him to recognize the wrongness within him.

Dupec retracted his hand before it could get caught in solid flesh. His Shard eased Tamlin onto his knees.

He turned to Sauman, then, who looked ready to call the match.

In the stands, Ungol watched his son's conquest with rapt attention. He sat so far forward on his seat he was barely on it, and he was not alone. Among the chiefs, Gulang alone lacked apparent investment in these happenings. Gulang, who sulked for his loss and the apparent rise of a staunch rival, whose son had materialized by chance.

Dupec crouched, tapped the ground thrice. "I surrender."

A sharp intake of breath. A hiss from Tamlin. Boos and curses from the watchers, denied their clean victory, what all of this had been building toward.

"Let this be a lesson, Tamlin." he said. "Your grudge is meaningless. Your father is in command of the Gil Garo, but the favor was mine. This is the shape of humility. There was never any winning for me, but I could not have you questioning my heart any longer."

His Shard circled Tamlin, whose anger had given way to colder shock. The Shard joined Dupec's flesh, climbing into him, to be absorbed. A piece of his soul

Ung Tsang

rejoining the whole.

He helped Tamlin to his feet. To refuse the gesture would break too far from decorum, would cause tension between sects that had, for all he could tell, walked in step for many years.

Sauman passed Dupec, a questing glance spared for him as he took Tamlin's hand in his, raised it over his head.

"Victor! Tamlin of the Hakka sect. I declare you..." another glance at Dupec, a hesitance to called the match. A glance spared for Ungol, who wore an expression almost of grief, his shoulders slumped but an understanding half smile touching his lips. "Ung Tsang!"

Still no cheering. An array of light clapping. All here knew Tamlin could not have won except in this way. They would feel cheated by this victory, cheated in the way Arrak's son was cheated. No clean victory. The father's leadership would be questioned, but advantage was his. Gulang would have undermined Ungol at every turn, but he would support Arrak. Ungol would support Arrak. They all would.

And Arrak would know he needed their support. That his rule, however brief, was given to him by an ally's wayward son, who he had abandoned, a gift wrapped in sacrifice.

Dupec left for the tent. The healers were already ferrying unconscious men into it. He passed by the watching women. Bora and Sircha, both awakened with smelling salts and sitting where he had been sitting.

Perhaps, he would have taken his clean victory. Perhaps in this other life with the Dragon of the East, the enigma who said he loved him, who he thought he might have loved, he had done just that. But that very enigma had spoken of an attack, of bloodshed looming like an axe blade over the Gil Garo.

He needed them united. Needed them to survive.

Trickles of Memory

A soft whistle passed through Ank's lips. He loomed over the corpse of an uelfin, a manic glint like a bare, live wire driving back the usual cold detachment that so defined him. "What have we *here?*"

He squatted next to it, tapped its sunken cheek. "You could be dead. It would be a mercy. Do you want to die?"

He grabbed it by the chin, forced a stiff neck into motion, forced the head to nod.

"Yes, sir. I'd like that very much." He said, pitching his voice high.

"Well rest assured, I'm happy to oblige. The only problem is I don't have the right skill set and the one who does is tired. You see, he already let one of you off today, and there's that prickly matter of...well, I suppose its none of your business.

"Would it inconvenience you to wait just one more day, so he can build up his strength?"

He fingered its lips, fluttered them open to emulate speaking. Mossy teeth flashed as he pulled the lower lip back, and disappeared as it snapped rigorously forward.

"It would. It really would." He said in that high pitched voice. "I've been laying about like a fat sack of lard for....for...for I don't even know how long. I need to stretch my legs, sir. I really, really need to."

"Well have I ever got news for you." He tapped the uelfin's strangely flat nose, a nose which blurred the lines between ape and reptile. "I may not be able to push that lovely soul out of your body, but I *can* give you a change of scenery. Do you cast a shadow? You *don't?* Well, we'll have to fix that."

He reached over his head and pulled as if wrenching open blinds. A lone ray of sunlight broke through the clouds, touching on the uelfin corpse.

"Funny, isn't it?" He grinned down at the corpse. "They put so much effort into the decor, fashion a whole host of rules and conventions with the seaming hope that all the little mysteries will remain just that, and yet..." he looked up to the sky and chuckled, enjoying the subtle warmth of the sunlight on his face. "And yet they take it for granted that for every rule they enact, every convention or sensible precaution they cobble together, there must always be gaps in their defenses.

Trickles of Memory

"A little order in all of that chaos, and what not. You get it!"

He pulled on the helpless corpse's flank. "Well, I suppose it can't be helped. Oh, look at that! Look at *that*. A shadow, dearest me! A shadow! We can use that, now can't we?"

He rolled the uelfin onto its side, away from the labyrinth wall toward its center, where the sunlight was strongest. The uelfin's body cast a strong shadow, black as ink, and he focused on it, drawing forth from a well of maligned, erratic energy within his soul. He reached for the corpse and the shadow. The shadow quivered under his touch and spread, climbing the flank of the uelfin, gobbling it up in coruscating waves until it was entirely consumed in pitch blackness, abyssal energy as cold and empty as any void could be. The darkness boiled away, ribbons and orbs floating into the still, close air, and took the body with it, off to where his Earth Soul lingered, in a reach of this labyrinth where it would never be found, to await its exorcism.

"Kindness has a price, my friend." He mumbled as he watched the last few bubbles pop and vanish. "But I promise, it'll be worth it in the end."

Hanuman inhabited Ibrim's flesh, and through him witnessed the events of his life unfold. What remained of his mind was pared back, leaving a thin thread of consciousness, a rope he might climb when he chose to return to the Halls of Time, to inhabit his own body once again. For how, he was Ibrim Alghoul, and he was uncomfortable.

Through Ibrim's eyes, he saw a domed, stained-glass ceiling high overhead. Soft rasping suffused the throne room, the play of gloved hands over a rawhide drum. He could no more peel his back off the floor than if his limbs had been bound in chains. He could not lift his head, could not shift his gaze in the direction of his brothers, or his father. All because of that blasted drum.

Hassan's delicate fingers lay limp against his palm. The foreigner had given him at least that comfort. Simple though it was, he could almost believe it a mercy. Small comfort in having his brother so close, to have him known to him. The foreigner could not have known how close he was to Hassan. Closer than he had ever felt toward his sisters, Nimira or Samara; closer still than he had ever felt toward the first prince, his eldest brother, Abellard III.

The mosaic above depicted the first king of Tulakh, Nerus I, seated valiantly atop an armored horse. Sun rays burst from him. Like the sun dominated the sky, as it pushed back the darkness, gave warmth and life to the people and kept them hale; so too, King Nerus I gave life to the Tulakka, shielded them from hurt, pushed back the darkness of uncertainty, and shined. Like the sun, King Nerus I became the center of his people's world, and from him was Tulakh born.

His father had fashioned himself another Nerus I, but Abellard II of House Alghoul, High King of Tulakh, had none of his character. He had been weaker than his father, Ezekus I, and vain. His children reflected his vanity. None more than Abellard III. Hassan alone was humble, and he supposed it was this rare humility that drove Ibrim to like him.

What could Hassan have done as king? But that was not his purpose.

Abellard should have been born second. Hassan ought to have been first prince. He would have seen them through the foreigner's invasion, denied him conquest. Vanity had been their undoing. His father's motives had been shortsighted. Pitting influential houses against each other, manufacturing conflict between them to dilute their power. He had created fertile ground for backstabbing in his time of rule, left Tulakh exposed to occupation, the throne prepared to be usurped.

Were his father dead, Abellard in place of Hassan as First Captain of Arms, and Hassan king, they would not now be laying in a line, prone against the floor, listening to that accursed drum as blood pounded in his temples. His rage at how useless he was, how inconsequential in the grand scheme. Sao Njack would never have risen this high, would not now be sitting in his father's throne—that blocky, marble thing King Abellard II embellished with so many cushions, which the Dragon of the East refused.

"Stand, your highness." Sao's voice was soft, of middling pitch. He spoke in the tone of someone completely assured of his own victory.

Sao punctuated his command with a few drumbeats. To Ibrim's other side, his father rose, and was briefly framed in all of his glory at the edge of his vision. Clad in flowing purple robes, a silver, silk overcoat hanging to his shins. The edge of his crown, a flowing, steel-gray beard, were just visible if he strained to see it. Abellard swayed on his feet. He laced his hands behind his back, and Ibrim was not at all sure if he did so by Sao's command or his own.

"Bow." A double beat. "On your knees."

Abellard II dropped to his knees on the flagstones. He turned his face a few degrees in Ibrim's direction, met his third son's eye. There was a warning there—unnecessary given Ibrim's detainment, his complete inability to break free.

Hooked nose, pitted eyes, his cheeks hollow where thick hair retreated and was replaced by days old stubble. His father was gaunt, sickly. The days leading up to the occupation had worn him down, made him older than his years. He was defeated, yet still there was that spark of defiance in his gaze. He had been made to bow, but he was not yet broken.

He believes he can negotiate. Ibrim thought to himself. He wished he could look the foreigner in the face, that he could make his hatred of him known, pierce straight to the bone. *What hope is there, father. He will have his way. He has broken our spine. There is nothing left to throw at him except useless curses.*

"Now, this does not have to be painful." Sao Njack said.

His father scoffed.

"You may find my terms amenable enough, if you keep an open mind. Grant that you will not be able to retain control over your military. They will be assumed into the armies of the Nixian Empire. Your officers will be assigned to new companies, and those companies will be mixed, so that no one faction raises a challenge to my rule in your name, do you understand. The officers will be scattered across Sanguhr and Nixir. The best among your strategists will be needed for the Saodein offensive, though I assure you they will not be treated as any less than equal to their foreign partners.

"You will retain control over domestic issues. You will retain appointing power for your cabinet. Your day to day life will change only negligibly. A portion of your tax revenue will go to the Nixian Empire to be redistributed, but rest assured it will not be wasted. I am a believer in educating the commonry, ensuring they have a means of rising in both power and privilege. I do not; however, believe in hereditary rule. As such, you will be the last true king of Tulakh. Your sons will have their opportunity to rule, but blood will not grant them any guarantee. Not any longer. If they are to have power, their right to it will be decided by common people. Yes, the very ones you look down your nose at every day. They will choose who leads them."

"In the same way your right to rule is validated?" Abellard II growled.

"I suppose it seems somewhat hypocritical on my part, doesn't it? I have conquered your lands. And not just yours. To date, I hold three thrones and even now intend to revive a fourth, for me and me alone. Of course it must seem to cheapen my legacy that I will not stump for the people. That I place myself so far above them.

"But did you know, King Abellard II Alghoul, that katcyakin, yes all of us, are sterile. We do not possess the ability to sire children. My kind can never be a people. In that way I suppose we are a bit like mules. With me, my line ends, but in my death, for I cannot live forever, there is hope for people like you. This empire must have a supreme ruler, or it will fall apart. Someone must rise in my stead. If you can win the hearts of your people, it could be you.

"It will be left to the rulers of your various fiefdoms to decide who rules in my stead. Perhaps a Nixian will take up my legacy, but then, perhaps one of your own will have risen in popularity by then. It is far from impossible that a ruler of Tulakh could rise to assume my seat."

"And I need only bow to you?"

Sao chuckled.

A flurry of drumbeats. A door opened somewhere in the distance to Ibrim's left.

"You may be seated, my princes."

Ibrim felt the muscles in his back and legs tense. He was lifted into a sitting pose, able now to turn his head. His new vantage gave him his first clear look at the Nixian conqueror.

He was shorter than he would have believed, and almost every inch of his skin was covered. A pouchy, stone-gray coverall hugged his body under a leather jerkin. Fingerless gloves climbed most of the length of his arms, and matching boots crawled past his knees. The hood of the coverall was thrown back, revealing red-brown hair sweeping over a golden brow. He had forgone the mask the Tulakka generals reported he wore in battle, and that accursed drum—the barrel s shallow cylinder covered in desiccated muscle tissue and fragments of bone; tanned, lance tiger skin stretched over the head—lay in his lap, supported by his shin where it crossed the other knee. His eyes were tapered and dark, his lips pouty and his cheekbones prominent. He was the perfect vessel for a cult to rally around, a man made to look like a statue. Someone who's gold forged busts would look almost lifelike next to him, because his birthright demanded it. Because an Elder God saw fit to smile down on him, and he chose to use that blessing to destroy everything Ibrim held dear.

His sisters stumbled away from the servant's entrance. They were both bound, heavy shackles chaining their wrists together behind their backs. Their feet were left free, but neither resisted the guiding hands of the servants that saw them into the heart of the throne room.

Marble pillars cast shadows on the distant walls. The throne room was a broad disk rising toward that glass ceiling, the sconces to either side shallow and unlit.

The conqueror's gaze traveled across Ibrim's brothers, lingered a hair longer on him.

Tears for the Moon God

"You need only declare yourselves my subjects. You may see this as a violation, even a betrayal of your people, but know that life for the common man does not change overmuch when one ruler usurps another. They live under the same taxes, enjoy the same freedoms to a large degree. In every way the change in their lives is negligible...until it isn't. You will not have betrayed them by capitulating to me. Tulakh will go from a nation to a province within my empire, yet the change will be meaningless to them. In fact, they stand to gain a great deal. No more tariffs from Sanguhr or Nixir. No restrictions on their ability to travel from one province to another. They will, I think, be quite happy."

"I would sooner die." King Abellard said.

Don't be a fool, father. If we declare our surrender here, we might still come out of this okay. He said himself he can't live forever. He said that. He is mortal like any of us. If we capitulate now, we can plot against him later. We can kill him and take back our kingdom. But you have to keep yourself together.

"I thought you might say that." Sao Njack said. "Unfortunately, I have no interest in whether you live or die. Shall we go down the line? Would any of your sons like to declare their fealty to me?"

Hassan spoke up, surprising him. "I would."

Ibrim turned sharply toward him.

Hassan took after their mother more than their father. More than any of them, in fact. The hard lines and pinched features bred into them by their father were absent in him. His face was wide and round, his nose only slightly protuberant, his cheekbones flat.

He looked like he had eaten something sour, and there was a strain in his voice, but he had said the words. Had done what was inconceivable for their father, and betrayed the old man in kind.

"Would the first prince or the third, perhaps, like to accede." Sao's gaze traveled over them.

Neither spoke at first. Then Prince Abellard cleared his throat.

"You are a disgrace, emperor. You are worse than any common dog. I hope one day you are struck down and brought low. I hope your people have you drawn and quartered, and the pieces of you are dragged through the streets for all to see. Look upon this mangy dog and see that he is just human! Look and see how he was slaughtered. I hope, for all of the people you have hurt, that you face such cruelty."

Sao's expression soured. "And you, third prince?" there was an edge in his voice. Something in Prince Abellard's tirade had rankled him, yet his voice remained soft, devoid of real cruelty.

"I wish to abstain." Ibrim said.

"I cannot permit that."

"Then I will accept exile."

"I cannot accept that, either. You would only raise an army in the countryside to challenge me later. Would you not at least like to see what life is like under my rule? Are you not at all curious?"

Ibrim did not answer.

"Just give him what he wants." Hassan said under his breath. "You all are being foolish."

"For my friends, I am more than fair. For my foes, however...your sisters were given the same choice as you. They chose loyalty to their father over what was best for your people. I wish I was not met with such disappointment, but it cannot be helped."

He whipped up a rhythm against the drum. Hassan stood wordlessly and left, his steps mechanical, taking him away from the throne room.

"For your civility, I will award you with absence. You will not have to see what transpires here, *Steward* Hassan."

If there is one good thing to have come from this, it will be that.

He did not miss the impending anguish washing over his brother's face. A door fell open, and he passed through it.

The rhythm became frenzied, a flurry of beats pounded against the drum head. A pair of servants stripped Samara and Nimira of their clothes, took up the piles and stepped back. The rhythm changed, and Nimira stepped toward Samara. As she closed the distance, and to Ibrim's horror, Samara's ribs splayed open. Raw bone punched through flesh. Muscle fibers tore into ribbons, raw meat parting to reveal heart and lungs in grizzly detail. They spread wider, forcing her shoulders back. Her arms bent at odd angles. Her elbows popped and shattered, her hands climbing shakily toward her shoulders, where skin and muscle parted to admit them.

Nimira's breast shattered, ribs flayed apart like wings. The flesh across the nape of her neck splayed apart. Blood oozed around her exposed trachea as it detached from her head, adding a hollow, rasping music to join the drumbeats as air continued to pass in and out of her lungs. Neither woman cried out as their bodies betrayed them, as ribs joined in a morbid embrace, forming a cavity between them which was filled in swiftly with sinew and flesh. Their organs shifted to fill in vacant spaces. Nimira's arms twisting around, her shoulders crackling with the force as her back bent, her hands pressed backward against the ground, her legs twisting. The knees were now backwards, and her facing the floor. Samara's arms twisted upward. Ribs broke and joined the remains. The skin of her back merged with them, forming wings of brown flesh which closed swiftly around the beastly prominences. Bat wings, sinuous and small and inelegant. Her head slid toward her sister's, chin merging with cranium, flesh pooling around the joins as some twisted healing was done on both sisters, joining them as one entity.

Ibrim vomited into his lap. He squeezed his eyes shut, unable to see more, unable to process what had happened to his sisters, how cruel this monster could be. He had never accounted himself kind, but there were limits to his cruelty. He could never have done what this Sun Man did. He could not have forced a family to watch as he mutilated their siblings, their daughters. How could someone be so devoid of feelings, so beyond empathy, as to justify this *savagery*.

Tears leaked from his eyes, traveled over sharp cheeks, down the edge of his jaw, and dripped. His stomach roiled, threatening him with more violence as another sickly crackle punctuated the air.

A wet pattering. Footsteps coming closer. The creature uttered a guttural, animal wale.

He squeezed his eyes shut harder.

"Third Prince Ibrim." Sao's voice was as devoid of emotion as when he had first spoken. "I have changed my mind. You *will* be permitted exile. You may not remain in these lands. In any lands I control now, nor the lands I acquire later. You are left with the mercy and the security of Ur. I will not pursue you there. But if I should encounter you again, I will see to it that you are joined to this beast."

Tears for the Moon God

"As for you two, King and Prince Abellard, I leave you to take care of your kin. She will live as long as any mortal, provided she is well fed and watered. You will have no servants. You will not be permitted seats in this castle. I will see to it you are provided with lodging and an allowance to cover your expenses, and you will see to her for as long as she lives. That is my judgment."

Ibrim kept his eyes shut. Another guttural wale escaped his sisters' throat. Chains rattled. Awkward footsteps carried her away. Servants swooped in and whisked his brother and his father away after her. They took Ibrim under his arms, and dragged him from the throne room, to be evicted from the palace now and forever.

He was empty. Emptier than he had ever been. All the sickness had gone from him, together with all of his fighting spirit. He would never see home again. He knew that. Hassan would not come for him, would not seek to raise arms against this emperor. His father and Abellard III would never know peace. Their task may well lead to their own deaths, a surrender of its own kind, and he would live out his days in Ur, a useless, ineffectual nobody, scrubbed of his identity and broken. He would have to find satisfaction in that. Anonymity might grant him the ability to forget. He hoped it would. And by the same token, he knew he could never scour that image from his brain.

Like cattle. He bent them to his will like cattle. Their bodies. Their minds. Nimira, so sharp witted and now a mass of gore and broken bones with her face. Samara, oh poor Samara.

He shuddered, his feet dragging behind him. He could not even summon up the strength to walk within the embrace of those servants. Could not help wondering if they were just as frightened of that monster as he was, or if they saw what he had done as justice. If even now, as they dragged him through halls and down corridors in pursuit of the gates and the city beyond, they believed his family had paid their due, had, in fact, deserved this.

Night stole away his senses, compelled him into a crimson haze of rage and grief. Chained to a rock, Lisandra's influence restricting the flow of power from the moon into him, from within him outward, Ibrim Alghoul was helpless, and yet it was better this way. There were those who could contain themselves when the full moon rose, but he had not joined them. Had not climbed into the embrace of that sacred order of warrior-priests, Ao Nii's inner circle.

Tight shackles grated against the bones in his wrists, chafed at his skin as he struggled. Dried blood stained the backs of his hands, drip patterns running across them and down his fingers, to pool against his nail beds.

He had not seen a wash in two days, long enough the oils caked into the creases in his joints became uncomfortable, yet not so long that he ceased to recognize the reek of his own body. Curry, pork and onions, the flavors of his homeland were twisted into something foul, an aura which might have drawn in flies and biting insects if the raw power exuded from him did not drive them back. If that crimson cloud did not threaten death upon anything that got too close.

"Let me die." He muttered weakly, but the toad seated just within the tree line at this clearing's edge would only watch. She would not permit release of any kind, as it was not the will of her master. Lisandra Almaine had been a worshiper of death before she found her shield. She might still be, it was hard to say. Some irony, then, that she would deny him another soldier, another pet to add to his menagerie.

"Just let me die, please. It was a mistake, inviting this curse. A mistake I would undo. Please, please, let me die."

The toad, a creature the size of a large dog, stared through unfeeling, amber eyes—its pupils square, the ridges across its wide muzzle dotted with pronounced warts and fissures. It almost succeeded at blending in with the shadows and the stones, except for a prominent, red stripe against its throat, which swelled and retracted as it breathed.

The dry clatter of autumn leaves scattered by swift moving feet; the snap and crackle of underbrush pronounced the arrival of her master.

Lisandra, all sinew and bone, sharp-nosed and hard-eyed and all of the stern matron, emerged from the forest.

She was not alone.

In her wake walked a hunched figure, a wide hood drawn up over his head. At the sight of him, rage welled up in Ibrim. From the depths of his soul came a memory of tragedy, of disfiguration, abomination.

The entity resolved. Fingerless, leather gloves climbed past his elbows. Boots of the same material crawled across his thighs. Stone-gray underclothes, a leather jerkin...he wore a drum at one hip, a sword strapped to his back which he had not had with him the last time Ibrim had seen him.

"You swore!" he screamed. "You swore you would leave me here! Leave me alone forever!"

"I have done a great many wrongs in my life." Sao Njack said. "What I did to your sisters, Ibrim, was unforgivable."

"You know each other?" Lisandra arched an eyebrow.

"We do." Sao said. "I conquered his kingdom. I exiled him."

"YOU DESTROYED THEM! VIOLATED THEM!"

"You did what now?" Lisandra turned on him, then, unchecked fury painted across her pinched features.

"I assure you, he does not mean—"

"SAVAGE! MURDERER! MONSTER IN THE SKIN OF A MAN!"

"Be easy, Ibrim. I am not here to harm you." He turned his gaze to Lisandra, his shoulders hunched, everything about him uncertain. "This was a mistake."

"Whatever you did in your past, you'll have to pay for it eventually. Now sit." She gestured curtly toward the clearing, well within range of Ibrim's influence.

A sudden, sharp hunger overtook him. *Yes. Get close to me. I'll see you die. It will all be okay then. I'll see you die and it will all be okay.*

"You'll keep up your defense until—"

"Until I am gone, yes." She said. "It will be just you and him then. You'll have to keep him contained. Rest assured, it is no easy task keeping him under control. He'll lash out whatever you do. It will remain this way until the full moon passes."

"I can handle it." He said.

"Prove to me you can, and I might be inclined to help you. If what you ask of me is reasonable."

"It isn't." He said. "But I believe you'll align with my way of thinking."

She chuckled. "We'll see about that."

She ambled away. "Come along, Agnes." The toad lurched after her.

Tears for the Moon God

As they faded from sight, Sao unslung his scabbard. It was painted white and covered with tiny blossoms and vines which looked to have been pressed directly into the wood under the lacquer. The blade he drew from it was as black as coal, shot through with traces of a lighter material, rose gold perhaps. The weapon was broad and double edged, the cross guard and hilt of simple design and wrapped in pink leather.

Ibrim watched him plant the longsword tip first into the loam, drive it firmly into the ground so that it stood on its own. A red stain on the air retracted into him, and the madness, rage and grief leaked away as it faded. He was, he realized, coming to his senses. The moon was just beginning to rise in the eastern sky, the last beams of the sun retreating over the mountainside, and he was sane.

He eyed the sword with suspicion, looked past it to its wielder. "H-how did you do that?"

"My life has been filled with complications...betrayals." Sao said absently. "It's no excuse for the way I treated you."

"You promised you would not hunt me." He whispered. "You swore to it."

"I promised I would kill you if I ever saw you again, too." He said. "Sometimes, you have a change of heart. Though, I did not expect to find you here. I never suspected you would heed my warning. I thought I'd have to put you down, see to it that you died."

"As you say, sometimes you have a change of heart."

"The God House of the Moon." Sao's gaze drifted skyward, to where the moon heralded the coming of night, and a last few shades of violet were edging out of the sky. "You thought you'd use God Ao Nii's power to kill me? I doubt he would have sanctioned it."

"He has no say in the matter."

"You still want to kill me?"

"More than anything."

"It won't bring your family back."

"No, I suppose it won't. But it'll make me feel better."

They lingered in silence for a time.

"What did she mean? She'd help you...if what you asked for wasn't unreasonable. Whatever she said." He asked.

Sao shrugged. "Just what she said. I'm to look after you. Make sure you don't break those chains and rampage across the hillside. In exchange, she'll help me with something I, quite frankly, wish I didn't have to do."

"And that is?"

Sao smirked. His gaze still fixed on the moon, he looked as though he was only half here, the other half drifting along to some other place where things were less complicated.

"Fate has a way of tossing what you want right in front of you, doesn't it."

"Making you question if her schemes will be your undoing."

"Oh, rest assured, they will be. The Goddess cares nothing for me, but as it stands, I believe I am her best means to achieve whatever ends she desires. Our goals align, though I would have it any other way. Otherwise, why would she place you in my path, Prince Ibrim? Why cast three people who hate me into my path, each of whom possesses an ability I might find useful."

"Which might also end you?" Ibrim added.

"Indeed."

"God Ao Nii had a lover, you know." Ibrim said. "Long ago, he fell in love with a mortal. A Sun Man. Heiman the Younger."

"What happened to him?"

"He died. By another god's hand. God Ao Nii never recovered. So, with each passing full moon, he grieves. And we are all forced to share his grief. It is the source of our power."

Sao's head dipped low, the hood drawn down to shadow his face. "Ironic, isn't it? A Sun Man dies, and a god is stricken with grief. Katcya falls for a mortal woman, and the world as we know it is brought to its knees."

"You made that possible."

Sao met his gaze, then. A chill ran down Ibrim's spine at that look. A look of dark longing, of regret. In that moment, Sao looked very much like God Ao Nii, the god's own grief reflected in a mortal man, the two of them of a kind, bonded in some inexplicable way.

"Do you know how it started?" he asked. "I lost my mother. I was not even on this continent at the time. I was on Yu Danh Hao, climbing Rein Mountain." He gestured at the broadsword. "This sword came from a contest there. A story for another time.

"Once finished with the mountain, and I'd very much prefer never to return there, I set sail to return to my homeland, together with my father, my cousin, and a pair of others not of these lands, my closest friends. We left them at the edge of Gur Tulain forest. It was no place for them, two spirit callers of an uncontacted tribe half a world away. They had no business in that forest, but the time of reprieve had not ended, yet, and my father and I needed to pay our respects, needed closure.

"Dupec had lost his mother around the same time, in a campaign in Tuluis Fel. It was fate, I think, that brought us together there. Under the Heart Tree, where the spirit dwells, I saw him reach for a fruit among the branches. He was hungry, and far removed from his father and the supplies they had taken with them. The forest is akin to a maze, difficult to navigate. I saw him reaching for it, that glimmer of desperate hunger in his gaze, and I swatted his arm away.

"He did not speak any language I knew at that time. In our lands, it is the saodeini language we use when all others fail, but across Rasheik's rope, that nation has no influence. Their culture has never found roots there.

"He did not speak my language, and I did not speak his. But he saw me, and I saw him, and I knew he was katcyakin, that he was a Cloud Man, my opposite."

Sao unbound his jerkin. He removed it, slipped his arms free of the underclothes and let them fall away, revealing a puckered scar two inches beneath his collarbone, a nasty gash which had healed poorly.

"He stabbed me." He said. "It was the first grievous wound I had ever suffered. Until then, I had believed it impossible for me to be wounded to the degree that I was. It was the first time in my life I felt human. I longed to have that feeling, to know that kind of vulnerability again, but I couldn't find him."

"You fell in love with a man who tried to kill you?" Ibrim cackled. "You are as sick as I always believed. A disgusting wreck of a man."

"I will not deny that." Sao said. "But consider my point of view. I had been a kind of idol, no better than a statuette people came to pray over in a shrine to one

Tears for the Moon God

of the gods, to everyone I knew except for my mother and my father, and a few others, I suppose. I was to herald the beginning of an era of prosperity for my people. I was to bring water from the depths as no one else had in generations, and keep my people well fed and nourished, without need for them to struggle, or send their children to die in pursuit of apprenticeship to Ul Sharak.

"I was the golden son. An object. You cannot imagine how it killed me inside to be seen not as a person, but as a means to an end."

"You did not have to kill my sisters."

"I didn't—"

"You did!" He snapped. "After what you did, they were not human anymore. They were not themselves. What would you call it...what you did? Twisting them to your whims, leaving them hobbled and broken, unable to think except to dip their heads to a bowl of food or water. You made animals of them, and they behaved like animals. They could not even speak after what you did.

"I received a letter from Hassan two years after you cast me into exile, to tell me Abellard III took his own life. A year later, my father followed him. Hassan could not bear to visit them. Could not bear to see the horror my sisters endured. Nothing in your past could justify what you did to them. You were worse than any tyrant. More a monster than anything you created."

"I am truly sorry, Ibrim." Sao said. "Nothing I can do will ever relieve you of the pain I caused, nor make up for my sins. But know that I will do anything I can to make it right."

"You can die." Ibrim said coldly.

Sao met his gaze, held it this time. He peered into Ibrim's soul, so he believed in that moment. The bastard looked past the walls, the constructs he had placed between himself and his unending grief, and saw the truth of him.

"You can take my life." Sao said. "When my business is finished, you can have it. The right to kill me."

Ibrim scoffed. "Your word is meaningless."

"My word is iron clad. I'm going to kill my lover, Ibrim. I'm going to put an end to him once and for all. He intends to do something unforgivable. I'll stop him at any cost. Though it pains me, I will drive this blade into his heart, and kill him."

Ibrim stared at him, unable to find words.

"When it is done, I will pass that very sword into your hands. I will kneel before you. I will not resist. As he dies, with the taint of his curse in the air, mingling with my own, rendering my good fortune null, I will kneel before you, and let you kill me. It may not make up for what I did to your sisters, but it is all I can give you. And I will do so freely."

A rushing wave crashed through the trees. A great river, frothed into frenzied rapids, collapsed around Ibrim, divorced Hanuman the Elder's mind from his body, this reflection of the man who now lived, in absence of these bitter memories. Hanuman was propelled from the memory, and collapsed against cold tiles, at the edge of the pool containing Ibrim Alghouls's life.

He regurgitated water, a torrent propelled from his lungs to spatter tiles and earth. Claws dug into stone, feet found purchase against waterlogged silts. He clambered to his feet, crawled toward a nearby wall, pushed his back against it.

Panting, his chest aching, limbs weak and limp, he recounted the details of

Trickles of Memory

those memories, forced them into a corner of his mind, to be packaged together under the banner of *someone else's life,* not to be mingled with his own, to muddy the waters of who he was, how he had come to be. What was him and what was the other must be separate, even as the life of that other was vivid in the forefront of his mind.

There were dangers in delving other people's memories. He had made his peace with that. A necessary sacrifice in pursuit of his eventual escape, the prospect of true freedom.

He recalled the throne room, the darkness in Sao he had not seen in the man laying so often next to that pool containing the arc of his own life, so jealously guarding it that the Elder could not himself wander into it, and see from the man's own perspective what had befallen him.

Ibrim spoke to a beast within Sao, a monster lurking beneath the surface, one who saw opportunity, who saw too that everything came with a price. There was his pragmatism, his sense for the truth of things. It was a sense Hanuman the Elder well understood.

There, too, in that clearing on the side of the mountain—a place that pawed at something deep in Hanuman's memories, those that originated with him, which had become so eroded after his many adventures he could not quite place it—a willingness to make the necessary sacrifices, to see what was needed done at any cost, to include surrendering his own life.

Was it just talk? Was he truly willing to throw away his life for that cause?

There was the possibility he was manipulating Ibrim, taking advantage of a lingering undertone of madness, of desperate longing in order to exploit him for personal gain. Would he really have allowed Ibrim Alghoul to slay him once he saw Dupec dead? What was this monstrous act his wolf intended to see done? What could bring a monster around to the idea of atonement, divorce him from his hunger for power so soundly as to throw it all away, an empire and all that came with it, for a chance at the life of a man he loved?

Twin Streams

Ung Sakh was not a forest with one voice, but mistress of many. A wild boar drank from a stream down current from where Lisandra crossed. The boles of great trees noted her passing, whispered with the voices of minor spirits. Her forest was alive with cotton-backed fairies, who drifted among the branches toting seeds toward hordes they would soon forget how to find. Seeds to give life to new fairy trees.

One alighted on shadow-strewn earth almost at her feet as she made the far bank, letting her skirts fall over damp ankles.

She dropped her shoes on the ground, a column of ants shifting their path to avoid them as the fairy set aside the seed, dug a small hole with tiny hands to plant it. She picked up the seed, placed it in the hole. The fairy smiled up at her, and buried it.

A breeze gusted through the wood. The fairy's back bristled, and the current carried her upward, into the bows of the canopy and out of sight.

Lisandra pressed on. Saodein did not deserve this peace and tranquility. They did not deserve Ung Sakh's blessings, the abundance of fairies, the calm in these deep reaches of the jungle.

The boar lumbered back into the bush, leaving her to forage for food among the low shrubs.

In its wake, the stream's waters boiled, and a figure like a child climbed out onto the bank to join her. It watched her through lambent eyes, shining sap green like precious stones in sunlight. The young spirit watched as she slipped into her shoes, watched and waited.

"Where do you go?" It asked, its voice warbling like the current. "With your heart so darkened. What is this stain on you?"

She met its gaze, held it for a long moment.

Where, indeed. The road to Echo's Rope passed through the gap in Gonsai Wall. No travel could be had for her except with a Nixian escort, and she had nothing to pay them with. There was the matter of finding supplies, too.

Ung Sakh provided plenty of opportunity for foraging. She had no trouble finding mushrooms and berries, knew how to fashion traps for fish with river stones, how to snare small game. But illnesses she had no immunity to might find her, and she could not go long without fresh clothes, suitable boots for travel.

The nearest village could be days away. She had no way of knowing where the saodeini settled, which way a proper town might be. How she might come into money with which to purchase medicine, clothing, or a tinderbox for fire making. She tired of twisting sticks against logs, of watching thin tendrils of smoke waft into the air as her arms grew tired.

"Your stream is visited by mortals, right?" she asked. "Where do they live?"

The spirit shrugged. "They come from all over, though few care to stay long. They pray. Then they leave. None ask after me."

"The content of these prayers?"

"Requests for healthy children, mostly. Sometimes they ask me to see their dead safe. The ones they lose."

"You're a spirit of fertility?"

"Of exchange. Better they don't ask this of me. I am only so strong."

She winced. "Your way must not make you many friends."

He shook his head. "Alas, no. They ask for the wrong thing. I provide, but it costs too much."

"What's the right question, spirit?"

"Bring me fruit from the fairy trees." he said. "And I will tell you."

She scoffed. "I have enough trouble getting food for myself without pissing off the fae."

She marched away.

"I know where there is a village. My sister walks past it nightly."

She paused.

I can help you in other ways, too. If you'll help me. Now, where is it you're going?"

"Up hill."

The spirit chuckled, a belly laugh, too knowing.

"No, that way is bad. Bad men live there. More, there is a spirit who hates them."

She stiffened against her will. The spirit took note.

"Bring me that fruit, mistress. And then let's talk of how I might help you. If you seek *him* out, you will need my blessing anyway."

She cussed under her breath. "As you wish."

She followed the trail of fairies to a warty, squat tree alone in its clearing. Fairies crawled across its branches, down its trunk—like lice in its high canopy, an infestation. She wondered if the tree welcomed them, or simply tolerated them.

Bark cracked around a yawning mouth, startling her.

She stepped back as two knots above the seam quivered, as the tree trunk blinked away sleep.

Its hollow-eyed gaze settled on her. "What do you want?"

"Fruit from your branches, friend." she dropped into a curtsy. It paid to show respect to a spirit, however lowly.

"All the trees and shrubs about, and you come to the one who does not yield." he grumbled. "Not for me, but for a spirit."

"Little boy? Bald as an egg? Bright, green eyes?"

It screwed up its face, a look of disgust. "Still owes me a debt after the last

Tears for the Moon God

harvest. I'm not an orchard tree to be picked over. Of course, he'll not have told you any of this. Stubborn lump, he is. Half as bright as he appears."

"One of your fruit. That's all I ask."

"What did he promise you, now? Out with it, lass."

She hesitated. "A blessing. For a woman a long way from home."

"Knowing nothing of our customs, likely. You watch your back with him. He'll not leave you till he's got what he wants, and he'll not tell you what it is he wants neither."

A golden fruit the size of her fist, translucent like some berries she had seen, dropped from a branch and rolled to her.

"He's not a powerful one, but he can turn nasty if he wants what you can't give. All those stillbirths..."

She took the fruit and thanked it.

She returned to the creek. The spirit waited for her there, received the fruit when she offered it.

"The nearest village sits where my stream and my sister's join. Just follow her band a bit northwest and you'll come to it. The foothills of old man Ergol's range are just beyond it, but be warned. He doesn't abide strangers. Especially who seek him out."

"And the blessing?"

"Step into my current." he said.

She did, though reluctantly. The fairy tree's warning was still on her.

"The question they never ask." she said. "What is your name, spirit?"

He beamed. "It's Syrk. Glad to make your acquaintance. And you are?"

"Lisandra."

"Well, Lisandra, my creek is always muddy up stream. The people up there like to dump their refuse into it. Seem to think I enjoy polishing it off and taking it down to join the tides of mother Herka's river. They want healthy births, strong babies, but they'll not have them as long as they make me spend all my energy cleaning up their messes.

"Anyway, you ask for a blessing. I'll grant it. But I have a request."

She found her feet sucked in by the mud, realized she couldn't tug them free.

"As I'm at your mercy." she said politely, though she wanted to smack the smug grin off his face.

"Yes, well, could you return their debris to them? You needn't make it obvious. Just dump it off at the edge of the village, opposite the join in my sister's stream with mine. That should get the point across."

"Fine." she said through gritted teeth.

"Great!" he approached her, placed his fingers around her abdomen. "In a younger woman, my blessing would leave noticeable changes, but you'll not have to endure them."

Warmth bled into her belly, settled there. Truth, my sister confers healthy births with ease, but not everyone knows which band is hers. There." he removed his fingers. The mud pressed against the soles of her shoes, lifting her onto firmer ground. "Gandes Fae is who you're after. You'll need a goat to sacrifice. He'll not answer your questions otherwise."

"What is the nature of your blessing?"

"Makes you unpalatable to his children. They'll smell an odor on you they don't

Twin Streams

like. You'll pass right by no problem. Some describe the odor as boiled eggs, but it lasts just a month. Bathe in the moonlight and it will be gone far sooner." he said.

"If your sister confers healthy births, what do you do?" she asked, and climbed out of the stream.

"As I said, the energy has to come from somewhere. For every woman who prays over her stream, one or two find mine instead. Ask my blessing, I'll make you barren. Ask for a healthy birth, and, well, you're probably already with child, right? I give what is asked of me. It's not always misguided. Plenty come to me for my services, wanting what I can give them for whatever reason. It's only hard to tell the difference because well...." he lifted his hands.

"You don't make the distinction. Or they don't."

"I'm sure you understand."

"I don't." she said. "but I'll clear your stream."

His expression brightened again. "I thank you, mistress Lisandra. And I'm sorry."

"For what?" *Right. The blessing.*

She laughed. *Barren. As if that ship didn't sail years ago.*

She marched off along the creek, heading west.

The join between Syrk's stream and his sister's arrived before her within an hour. She had expected a longer trek before reaching it, but knew gratitude for Syrk the Barren had not lied. The spirits cared nothing for mortal virtues of morality or fairness. Their own ethics were alien to her, had been for all of her life.

Still, she had never met one who would rob a woman of her fertility. They may not always think to warn their patrons of the curses that came with their blessings, but this seemed less a mistake than the original intent. If Syrk the Barren spoke true and he needed raw energy to provide to his sister stream, then it made a kind of sense he would withhold such information, but did the means justify the method?

They could simply do it the old fashioned way, these people. Leave it all to chance.

Regardless, the nature of these spirits was unkind. Their ideas of reciprocity were unjust.

She followed the band of the sister river northwestward, followed it for miles as the gloom deepened, and evening approached. Woodsmen would be coming back to their homes, hunters with their kills. Their wives would be there to greet them, many with children hanging from their skirts or babes cradled in their arms, ready to begin the work of making the night's meal, then setting the children to the petty work of sweeping floors with witch brooms and dusting off counters and embellishments, the things that made a house a home.

She neared the edge of the village. The homes were raised several feet off the ground, sporting rope ladders, their roofs peaked to drive heavy rains past. They were pegged fast into the boles of trees, with stilts to provide extra support. Dense mosses and pitcher flowers dangled from the eaves of older homes, and fresh herbs grew in shallow boxes fixed to window sills.

Men and women brought in a harvest of fat papayas, durians and citrus fruits in wicker baskets. They fastened the baskets to tow ropes, and elder children lifted them through trap doors.

She crouched by the creek, spoke low so the saodeini villagers would not hear.

Tears for the Moon God

"Your brother has a task for me. Where is this refuse dump? And can it wait until I've purchased a fresh change?"

"Your pockets are empty." the sister said, her round face emerging among the soft churning foam where water passed over stones. "How will you purchase anything from these people?"

"Never you mind." Lisandra snapped. "There are always opportunities to barter in isolated places. Work to do, stories to tell against the prospect of a hot meal."

"There are men of the capitol on their way to collect taxes." She said. "They take them against fruit and rice. Extra yield grants coin in gold, but their wagons are always full of it.

"You could steal some."

"You're as deplorable as your brother."

She blinked.

"I've no love for these people, but I've no fight with them, either. They're not soldiers, that is clear. They'll only suffer if the coffers come up short."

"They'll come up short anyway. The collectors will fix their books to reflect less than they took, and none the wiser."

"You don't like these people, do you?"

Tiny hands emerged from the waters, spread in a gesture of indifference. "They ask too much, and leave their garbage in my brother's band. Humans are wont to do as they please. Revenge is not in my nature. I see it in yours."

Lisandra grimaced. *This insipid little...* "Not for common folk. They're victims the same as me. Once, they came to my shores seeking refuge, telling tales of meaningless death, executions and that."

"Mother says their queen is dead."

"You know a fair bit about these people for a lowly tributary."

Water tinkled like so many bells around a shrug. "You need money. Probably food and...that rag you wear needs mending or replacing. The soles of your shoes are coming loose, too."

Her gaze dropped to Lisandra's feet. "I feel it in the mud. They've got days at best before they're worn all the way through."

"Rude little shit." Lisandra stood upright. She hiked up her skirts and stepped across the band. These spirits made her miss the more mild mannered creeks and streams about her homeland. They had been nothing but unpleasant since she met them.

"Make him wait at your peril. You'll not endear him to you by ignoring your obligation."

"It'll be done, don't you worry."

"The bend is south of the village, but barely. Just beyond the tree line."

"Then why did he tell me to follow your band?"

"You'd have gotten lost if you went that way. The village isn't visible from the other side."

She waved without turning, and marched off, skirting the village to the south. The bend in Syrk's band came on just shy of its outskirts, beyond a thicket heavy with bushes and vines which did the service of blocking her view of the village from her, and her from it.

Her breath caught as she laid eyes on what the spirits had called trash. She had not known what to expect, but it was not what greeted her.

Twin Streams

Dead eyes, glassy and dull. Round faces. Plump, bloated bodies. Grey skin. Some of them were deformed, too bulbous or conspicuously flat. Some others were missing chunks of skin where the water had already rotted it away, and wisps of black blood and ooze drifted away from the piles, downstream to spread sickness to other villages. Worse, every one of those corpses belonged to an infant.

Stillborn, he said. They've been dumping their young in his creek. "Oh, but this stinks of retaliation."

The village hated the spirits of these creeks. They made that abundantly clear. They had seen to it that others were warned against making deals with this spirit, that no mistake could be made about his purpose. But it was shortsighted, this endeavor. It was selfish.

They'll have spread disease to other peoples for their own gratification, poisoning the headwaters like this. Just when I think I have comprehended the depths of saodeini arrogance. There is no bottom to these people!

She hissed through her teeth. She had seen many horrors throughout her life but this...this enraged her. Bodies fallen in battle—barring a river's flow—she could understand, but this was...it was maniacal.

Suddenly the thought of robbing them seemed more palatable. They had, after all, robbed who knew how many others of health. Maybe of life.

She knelt by the river, removed the first, infantile corpse, set it delicately against the bank. Flesh sagged between her fingers. Her stomach roiled.

The odor was potent, her actions, shifting corpses around, releasing stronger waves of rot as she pulled one and then another from the waters.

In all, she removed eight corpses from the band, its flow becoming more uniform, more powerful, with each infant corpse dragged free.

All of them retrieved and set aside, it flowed anew, waters ahead of the dam drawing back into the banks to flow unimpeded until he joined hands with his sister again.

He emerged from the waters grinning. "You can leave them there. The point will be made."

"How far have these people fallen." she muttered. "To stopper the flow of a creek with rotting flesh. The sickness--"

"Is theirs. Of the mind and spirit. A plague of ego which tells them this is right, that no toll should be required from us for our blessings. We should grant a gift where none is earned, you understand. But what do we care if they demand our services free of charge? They know hubris, and meet us with anger when we point it out to them."

"Go." she said, waving her hands around her head, her eyes closed. "Just please go away. I've had enough of you."

He dipped back below the current, and she turned back to the village, scrubbing putrid flesh from her hands in the dirt.

"The sooner I am gone from this country the better." She growled. "Poisoning a creek out of spite! Gods help us!"

Ouran Goul

The beginnings of Ouran's foothills were marked by a subtle rise in the slope of the land. Sufa Salein sprawled across his roots, climbed high onto his slopes, an expression of inequity. The mountain could not but bend its knee to the forest, so vast was the distance between them, the disparity in their power.

Xirakura climbed—the ancient, untamed jungle thinning as he neared the high passes where the forest lord's influence waned, and the range lord's strength was most potent. He climbed, and dappled sun became strong beams scattered across clearings, pushing back ferns and other shrubs which preferred shade and cooler temperatures.

The odors of rock dust and moss suffused the air, the freshness of the forest forgotten with the last, wide boles of Sufa Salein's trees. He wondered if Ouran maintained friendly relations with his cousin. Rare was the need to call on the spirits of his mountains—the lesser plains skirting higher slopes, populated with lush grasses that yielded, eventually, to stiff lichen; the glacial brooks and streams near his heights. There were mysteries contained in his embrace, secrets for the Katuwiti, a hesitance to elaborate on events of the outside world which he suspected came of a greater allegiance to those peoples, or a need to dissuade his people from leaving their vigil over Ban the Rope.

Whatever the designs of the spirit, he found his way unimpeded. As he mounted a road carved out of the slope—leveled and cut into a ridge hanging over the inside lane, so that the outside track was touched by sunlight—he was struck by the eclectic array of other travelers making way along the pass. They led horses by their reins—tall palominos, work horses burdened with carts and open-topped coaches—came down from the mountains, up from the plains.

None bore any resemblance to his tribe. There were those more pallid than him who wore heavy leathers and furs. Their faces were narrow and long, their eyes wide set and positioned at slight angles to either side of their noses. Caravan guards marched alongside trader's wagons and sporting chain hauberks and skirts, defenses for a guard accustomed to contested marches. They would provide a roadside defense against thieves in the high passes.

The others were dark-skinned. Some so much so they seemed to repel light, cast it off in gray and blue shades. Their garb was of spun flax or wool, thin and loose, and died in vibrant colors, or crisp white to rival the snows. He noticed ritual scars across the bridges of the men's noses, the women's cheeks. Wondered at their significance. Were these markings intended to differentiate between adults and children? Were they betrothal scars? Were they worn by warriors or medicine men. They did not all possess them, but most did. The patterning of dot scars and slashes was different on every face, some pinpoint thin, some longer and wider in circumference. They looked to be made at needle point, or with the tip of a thin dagger.

They eyed him with suspicion as he passed, and none stopped to speak to him. Was it the weapons he carried or the unfamiliar cast to his skin. Perhaps it was the tribal adornments he wore, the tattoos climbing his right arm from wrist to shoulder.

He thought of Lura, then. She would be fascinated by these people, would espouse endless theories about what it all meant. And Katuwan would put an end to her ruminations and conspiracies, wielding his courage and affable nature on the way to ask blunt questions of those people.

His heart sank thinking of them, their pursuit of him. He was not fool enough to think they would accept his choice, that they would simply settle for a life in absence of him. But how far would they pursue him when his trail ran cold.

His destination, as far as he could go in this land, was obvious. He did not know how far distant Gora's other ports were removed from Sufa Salein. Could not guarantee his safe arrival at them. Faed City, then, was the only place he might go, the only port he could seek. But would they follow him that far? Would uncertainty, the perils of lands they did not understand, whose ways they did not know, drive them back?

Give up, my loves. Turn back. There is nothing but pain on this path, can't you see?

The road bent around the mountain, and beyond the bend lay a town, an outpost marked at its borders by wooden watch towers. The gates spread between them lay open, permitting free entry to those who approached.

He immersed himself in the crowd gathered before it, passed unimpeded onto the main avenue through.

Wooden homes with flat roofs, windows fitted with vitreous glass sheets climbed the slopes, following carved streets connected by ramps and staircases both dusted with gravel and sand. The residents were an eclectic mix of peoples, settlers—most of them—who wore the leathers and furs of the mountain peoples, a practicality adopted by most of those lowland dwellers for the passes were colder than their native lands. The inns were teeming with patrons. Hawkers lined the avenue—traded in amulets of protection against the perils of hard travel, hardtack and dried fruit, or spirits disguised as elixirs for every ailment one could think of, from malaria to impotence.

Grifters taking advantage of ignorance. He turned up his nose at them.

A woman, seeing him, clapped her hands over her child's eyes. A number of others pointed, their faces contorted in anger or disgust. One shouted up the street at a man in a peculiar uniform, a silver badge dangling from a thin chain over his chest. Coins riding his right shoulder. He sported chain mail, a heavy stick the length of his forearm at one hip, a short sword scabbarded at the other.

Tears for the Moon God

He gestured at two others dressed in the same attire, and they converged on him.

He noticed other parents shielding their children's eyes as one of the officers unlimbered his club and another produced a pair of rope cuffs.

"Come with us, sir." the first said. Thin scars rode the contours of his neck around his voice box "You're under arrest."

"Arrest?" Xirakura furrowed his brow, hunting after some analog to the word which might help explain it. There was no such concept among his people.

"Detainment? You're going to jail, sir. For public indecency."

"Sorry?"

The officer looked him up and down, raised an eyebrow precipitously.

"You left home with what? A strap to hold your bits up. Think of the children...*for the love of*...I can see your penis. It's *lewd!*"

"I believe we have a misunderstanding." Xirakura reasoned. "In my culture, it is seen as impractical--"

"What culture is that? Both the Magura and the Uari wear clothes. No preoccupations with shit customs or the exhibitionist--"

"Exhibitionist?" Color rose in Xirakura's cheeks.

"Look at his chest, Luken." the second officer intoned. He was dark like those lowlanders, but lacked the dot scars they favored, and he spoke with the same accent as the first. His gaze had settled on the scars covering Xirakura's torso.

"This a Magura thing?" the first asked. The third took Xirakura's arms and forced them together behind him.

The second shook his head. "Might be a Saph thing. Some in Crow have markings on their chest. Not this elaborate, though."

"Old man Hurin will want to ask some questions, then." the first, Luken, said.

The third bound Xirakura's wrists. He pointed him in the direction of the slope.

The second touched the gourd at his hip, cupped it in his palm and drew it close.

Xirakura hissed. "Don't touch that."

"Must be some kind of witch. The ones who consort with dark spirits among the Magura sometimes keep gourds like this. Say they're means of trapping devils."

Xirakura's breath caught as the Magura officer, for he could be nothing else, yanked the gourd free.

"I'm confiscating this." he met Xirakura's eye. "Gods only know what you've trapped in it, but I'll not have you unleashing it here."

"There is nothing in my vessel—"

"Then you admit it is for trapping devils."

"That's not what I—"

"You're coming with us. We'll add a charge for consorting with fel creatures to your ledger, as well. You'll have a chance to explain yourself when Hurin gets to you. For now, you should shut your mouth. For your own sake, that is. We make use of tribunals here, sir. Like civilized people."

Xirakura scowled at him. *Civilized, huh?* He knew what the officer meant.

He clamped his mouth shut, and resisted no further as they ushered him up the ramp.

The town officers handed him off to the jailors with little ceremony, and the jailors proceeded with as little decorum to throw him into a barred cell. The jail was, as best he could tell, otherwise empty. At least, he did not see any other prisoners in the cells he had passed.

The restraints on his wrists were removed, his weapons and the pack containing his supplies removed to a heavy table on the other side of the room, where the guards proceeded to dump his possessions onto its surface. They picked through them carelessly, earning occasional winces and growled curses from him as the contents of his life were met with all the care a child showed to his toys.

He watched, livid, as they scattered everything he had taken on the journey, shook out his pack, touched each item with greedy fingers.

"Dakara was right." one of them said. "To think Hurin would want to see this thing. It stinks of foul sorcery."

"He said it was empty, yeah?" said the other.

"He said he suspects it's empty. Could be there's a nasty surprise in there and we just got lucky."

"There's a map." the first held up the unrolled vellum. "It's outdated. Doesn't name any city on Liu Seid."

"He must not be a Raukha, then."

"One less thing to worry about. At least we don't have to piss off that bitch, Katein."

"Quiet. You don't know who's listening."

The guard sniffed. "Fine, then."

The door warbled open, and a broad shadow fell before Xirakura's cell, preceding the man it belonged to.

"Hurin." the guards bowed.

"We've a strange one." A jailor said.

"Raukha?" Hurin scrubbed thick fingers through a beard that hung over his chest. Black wool pressed against the contours of a thick belly, and several rings of fine make stood out against his fingers. His knuckles on that hand were thick and uneven, consequence of a poorly set breakage. A proper healer would have had no issue mending such a wound.

He thought of those fake elixirs he had seen a hawker trying to dispense with when he arrived. *Would a village like this have one?*

Dark eyes, forested in wrinkles, peered out past a beak-like nose to regard Xirakura, a passing glance on the way to the contents of his pack, and the objects he had worn on the strap now laying against the table top.

Hurin's gaze returned to him, navigated the contours of his chest, the glyphs carved into the flesh across his torso.

"Not Magura. Not Uari." he grumbled. "Only one tribe he could belong to, then. Take him out of that cell, will you? And remove his restraints. You've offended him enough for one day."

"But sir, he has an implement of witchcraft. Dakara said he uses it to consort with demons." one guard protested.

"Fah!" Hurin swatted the accusation away. "Maybe the Magura use something similar in that way, but not him. He's not theirs, is he?"

"W-what is he?" the other guard screwed up his face.

"Katuwiti. You'd do well not to put your ugly fingers on that gourd of his." he looked pointedly at the first guard, who was holding up the instrument to examine it.

Tears for the Moon God

The guard dropped it.

Xirakura winced. So did Hurin.

"Just get him out here and leave us, you fat fingered shit."

The guards scrambled to unlock the barred door, bring Xirakura around and set him in a chair. They marched out of the room, leaving Hurin alone with him.

Hurin rubbed his neck. "I'm sorry for them. A Katuwiti hasn't been seen at our outpost in more time than they've been alive."

"My gratitude." Xirakura said. "For seeing sense where your people refuse to."

He lifted himself out of his seat, belted the rawhide cord around his hips, tucked himself into it.

Hurin glanced at Xirakura's belly. He met his gaze and held it, ignoring his charge's relative nudity. He gestured at Xirakura's chest. "I don't recall seeing markings like those on the last of your kind to come through this pass. What brings you out of the forest."

"I've been chosen for a task." It was not a lie, but it tasted like one. "By a spirit of consequence."

"A journey befitting a Spirit Caller, I suppose." Hurin said. "I'm sure it comes with its own dangers."

Xirakura nodded.

"I have a proposition for you. My daughter has been afflicted with a curse. Drank from the wrong stream, it seems. What healers we have are too weak to rid her of it, but your kind...well, you might well undo what they could not."

"If you know which spirit."

"I do." Hurin dipped his chin in acknowledgment. "A nasty customer. I've told her too often not to play near his creek." he sighed, rubbed his forehead. "She's a spirited one. Disobedient at times, but a father cannot but love his daughter even as she heeds none of his warnings.

"Heal her, and I'll provision you with supplies, and proper attire. Your people may not put much stock in our ways, but you'll find the going much easier if you take a few precautions."

"My duty is ensuring the health and safety of my people." Xirakura smiled warmly.

He could not help but feel some relief at the prospect. His own people might deny him his right to perform his duties for them, but in this man was a blessing made in ignorance. An acknowledgment he did not know the significance of, which he greatly appreciated.

"I suppose I can extend my services to yours."

Relief washed over Hurin. He held out his hand, another unfamiliar gesture.

Xirakura hesitated, and took it. Hurin clamped down on his hand with all the force of a caiman snapping its jaws shut. "Thank you, tribesman."

"You may call me Xirakura." he said, as Hurin released his grip.

"Come, then. My home is not far."

Xirakura gathered his belongings, shouldered his pack and secured his gourd to its customary place at his hip. He followed Hurin out of the jail, ignored the gawking onlookers as they climbed higher into the town.

Lafol the Fish

Hurin's home was a sprawling manor low on the rise of Ouran Goul Pass. Within was a maze of hallways rising into a second, and then a third level, a fitting challenge to any of the town's inns.

His daughter's room was removed from the entrance to the third floor, leaving it isolated. A family portrait hung on the wall by her door depicted Hurin, his wife and three children; two sons and his daughter—whose softer features must have come from her mother's side, but who sported her father's thick, raven hair. It seemed out of place in a hall otherwise bare of paintings, too large to have a place in the corridor in truth, and he suspected it had been recently moved there, perhaps when the daughter's condition had taken a turn for the worse.

Hurin held the door for him, allowed him to pass.

The girl lying in a four poster bed, the down coverlet snugged to her chin, was a ghost of the girl in the picture. Her mother, a willowy woman, light of hair and eye, sat in a high backed chair at her bedside, pressed a steaming towel to her forehead, dabbing away sweat from high fever.

The girl's cheeks were gaunt, bones protruding over hollow pockets where the fat had retreated. She lay in sleep which was, at times, interrupted by harsh, dry coughs. Each time she made a sound, her mother squeezed the delicate hand she was holding.

Her mother's regard fell on him. There were the telltale signs she hadn't been sleeping. The dark, puffy circles under her eyes, the way she ground her teeth together, willing herself to keep her eyes open as eyelids fluttered at the edge of falling, threatened to take her away from the daughter in her time of greatest need. When the woman was less than useless except as a shoulder to cry on, a familiar, comforting face. She set that gaze on Hurin, curiosity giving way to a question she couldn't ask, a hope she dared not put words to.

"A healer, my dear." he said. "Come from the forest down slope. He consorts with spirits."

"May I?" Xirakura approached the girl. Her mother edged back against her seat to allow him room. He laid a hand on the girl's forehead, checked her pulse. It was weak. The curse was in her blood, it seemed. The spirit was not so strong as to push it far into her soul, or perhaps the contact had been brief.

"The spirit?" he asked.

"Lafol the Fish." Hurin answered. "A spirit of purification. He prefers isolation."

"Her offense was breeching his shelter, then." Xirakura said knowingly. "Likely, he cares little what transpires downstream, as long as his chosen home is not compromised."

Hurin nodded. "He purges the water of impurities. We take from his stream, but not at the headwaters."

"I'll call on him. He will come, but he will not heal her. Not now."

"Then what is the point?" his wife demanded. "We speak with him and get nothing?"

"You will ask of him what he requires of you to make up for your daughters transgression. He will be more amenable to you in my presence, but there is always a price for a spirit's cooperation. His will not be much of a burden. He is not a spirit of great consequence."

"If we pay this price?"

"He will remove his poison. She will recover."

Both parents looked as if a weight had been lifted from them.

Without preamble, he seated himself on the floor, placed his gourd between his legs so that the tip touched his naval.

He closed his eyes, and spoke the name of the spirit.

"Lafol the creek spirit, who makes waters run clean, I call on you." he said.

A presence loomed over his shoulders, its touch light but cold. The spirit's mother was a lake in the earth, who—in grinding at earth with water under pressure—gave birth to a spring and then a shallow stream. He was not particularly old, this spirit; was born to one of those recent generations, but he had been around long enough to develop an understanding of the mortals around him, to attain the comprehension necessary to prioritize his own interests. These people would always prioritize themselves; so it became the spirit's first duty to protect his own body, his own health.

He felt the underground lake's waters flowing through him, like blood through mortal veins. Too young still to draw power into himself—to call tributaries to him and supplement his own power with theirs—he must sustain himself on her essence for now. Take what she was willing to give, and hope the rains came to feed him. He was not a powerful spirit, but it took little strength to curse a child into sickness. A trickle of power to tear this family apart.

"Take me as your vessel." he whispered. "I offer myself freely."

The spirit poured into him, occupying space left behind as his own soul flowed into the gourd.

His eyes opened, ice blue to match the color of the spirit's stream, the light which played across its rocky bed.

"Ah, the daughter." it said. "But this isn't right. The body screams. The flesh scarred. What afflicts this vessel!"

Xirakura's face contorted in agony. "What fights me so? State your cause and hurry. I cannot hold. I cannot...retreat!"

Lafol gasped through Xirakura's teeth.

"We ask your price for our daughter's health, spirit." Hurin said, his confusion

Lafol the Fish

evident on his face.

"You would use a cursed vessel for this?" Lafol snapped. "He will kill me. The chains! So restricting. They clench, cut off...my breath."

"We did not mean...we didn't *know!*" the mother gasped.

"Gold...in the amount...of two pounds. One for the taint I must endure. One for your daughter's indiscretion. Just...let me go!"

The agony ripped through Xirakura's body. He sensed the wrongness pouring into the vessel, trying to touch his soul. He retreated from it, and came close to costing himself a way back as Lafol coward inside his body. He climbed, fought waves of nausea as he forced the spirit out of his flesh, resumed occupancy in his stead. Lafol was forced from his body, was shoved bluntly away. Back to his creek's headwaters, to nurse his wounds in the shelter of his mother's spring.

He blinked rapidly, the color of his irises shifting from ice blue to amber once more.

He heaved a great breath to still the roiling in his stomach.

"You'll have your provisions as we agreed." Hurin said. The scowl on his face told Xirakura the rite of calling had been compromised. The spirit angered.

He did not have to venture far to comprehend why. The scars on his chest burned. Sufa Salein had been reluctant to ride him long, though he had not believed, a the time, it was for any other reason than to keep them both alive. He had not believed these marks, this choosing, would act as a poison against the spirits around him. It seemed he would not be able to call on weaker spirits, would have to consort with the old and the powerful or risk killing the land, and the people who relied on it.

My people were right to refuse me.

"You'll have that for the answer you granted us. But you'll leave our post before nightfall. Whatever curse afflicts you, I won't allow it to spread to my people."

Xirakura nodded reluctantly. "I am sorry our parting must be tainted by this affliction."

"Lafol said he could not leave you of his own will." Hurin said. "That he was chained to you."

Xirakura's expression was one of sorrow. "It is the greatest gamble for a spirit to ride someone with my gifts. They risk dying if they remain too long, if it is too taxing on my body to house them. *He* was dying, but it confuses me. A weak spirit like him is not difficult for me to house. I have been in the presence of creeks and small streams for hours at a time without succumbing, even coming close. Yet...if I had not pushed him out, we both would have died. Your creek would have dried up. What fairies dwell in your trees may have died away, too, and the trees would not have fruited then.

"This marking has proved more malicious than I suspected."

"You humble me, Xirakura." Hurin said. "But you must leave now. The sooner you are gone, the better for us.

Gil Garo

It was inside his yurt provided to him that Dupec found Ungol. A sparsely decorated, single chamber greeted him, having been newly erected for his use while he remained in the Chikata camp with the other contestants. Fine rugs and pillows were spread across the earthen floor, and a wood stove prized from the Dumas reserves occupied the center. A figurine in the shape of his god rested on a low table in the far corner. A figure hoofed and horned, wild haired and bearded, and otherwise human.

His mother had taken him as far as the entrance, but she stood outside, giving the men a moment's privacy. She had not been particularly upset by his surrender. It seemed she had expected it.

Not so for Ungol.

He had attached his hopes to the newly returned son, rekindled some ambition once lost to him, and the expression he wore when he looked into Dupec's face reflected those confused emotions—melancholy and betrayal, brutalized hopes and emerging insecurity. He could not understand his son's decision, would not accept it.

Difficult conversations did not become easier by waiting. His father needed assurance, that this decision—for it was that and neither man would call it other than it was—had been right.

He sat with his father before the hearth. Outside, Shaelein's steps retreated, taking her away to a warmer place, where she might invite conversation among friends. They had, after all, had plenty of time to talk on the way here. What good would it do to wait in the wings when all within the yurt seemed still.

"What I can't understand is why." Ungol said. "He was *defeated*. Chief Sauman would have called it for you in that moment, knowing nothing of what you did. Right there!" he smacked his fist against his palm.

"What *did* you do, by the way?"

"All paths lead to Uldal." Dupec tapped is father's chest, over his heart. "Even those in here."

"You locked his powers?"

"A tether provides a path between spirit and man. Not so between man and god.

Gil Garo

What I did could have killed me, were I not fighting men so young and inexperienced. In place of their tether to the spirits, I opened a path between my soul and theirs, a bond they couldn't use. Because I'm not bound to a spirit, there is nothing to act *through me*, so there is nothing for them to use." he explained. "But there was never any winning for me in that tournament. If I had not conceded to Tamlin, my victory would have created tensions between the Hakka and the Dumas. Had I let him have an easy win, it would have left him with his own suppositions about me validated.

"I chose to lose in the way that I did because in doing so, power between the Gil Garo sects would be balanced, with Arrak's choices as leader dependent on support from both you and Gulang. And it seemed to me there was that chance, a narrow chance but still one worth taking, that in making Tamlin see I could have beaten him easily, and refusing to do it, he might let go of some of his anger toward me, too.

"If I had accepted victory, the chiefs would have questioned whether or not I used my katcyakin powers. There would be tensions among you. Arrak now needs your support and Gulang's to secure his hold on his new title. You are friends, right? You'll support him?"

Ungol sighed. "It seems you have learned something of the games the gods play in your time with God Uldal. I saw a child I had lost and found again in you. I should have seen a man."

"Those things do not exclude each other." Dupec met his eye, noted the fire reflected in that gaze. "Are you angry with me?"

Ungol shook his head. "What anger I had has faded. I am saddened by your choice. That is true. But I cannot help being proud."

"Proud?"

Ungol nodded. "You show the qualities of a good leader at a young age. To sacrifice your own desires for the well being of our people. It is in the recognition of this need I see the making of a chief. Perhaps, one day, you will lead the Dumas in my stead. How can I not be proud of that."

Dupec nodded, solemn, not smiling. "There was someone in the contest who struck me as odd. The pale one with the Tipik jewelry."

"He may well be. The sect is quite large. I don't know many of them."

"Did he seem odd to you?"

"He did. The paint stuck out to me. The way he wore his earrings. But some among the tribe have taken outlander wives or husbands. They are rare, but they exist. Possible the boy was one of those, whose father came from Ruc or Ao Lein, or the Jahhad Empire, and did not embrace our customs. It would follow that his father did not come to paint his son's face because he would not have been seen as one of us."

Ungol laid a light hand on his shoulder. "Put him out of your mind." he smiled knowingly. "Or would you have him place this burden on your shoulders. To know one not so different from him viewed him as other and enemy, where he ought to accept him as kin."

"I'll think on it." Dupec said. But his late night visitor's warning was still on his mind. No attack at the height of the tournament, but the day was not over. Night loomed like a shadow in the east, promising darkness in the coming hour. Chakta and Tamlin would be entering Duijus Kanh's cave soon, but what would they find?

Tears for the Moon God

Duijus Kanh's mouth yawned before Chakta. Tamlin was a stone beside her. Neither was foreign to the idea of hard won loyalty. But theirs were not masters of darkness, not creatures for which cruelty was a shroud worn in indifference, for whom even murder could be justified for its own sake.

She noticed he did not step closer to the entrance, knew he was thinking the same thing she was

The swans are in there somewhere. Will they really leave us alone?

She had not wanted to enter this cave with him. Among those who had entered in the past, more than a few had gone on to wed and bear children. She had no desire for either, had hoped her companion on the path would be someone who understood that. Someone like Shaki, or Dupec. She may not know much about Chief Ungol's son, but she knew enough. He was just like her. In one way, he was. It would have been so much more comfortable to enter this cave with him.

Tamlin was not always the haughty, dispossessed, petulant asshole he pretended to be. He hadn't always been this person. Beauty in a man who knew he was beautiful had a way of cutting out the soft parts of him, leaving behind a being with no depth—a sense of place so shallow it consumed all that he could be. Her lack of interest frustrated him. His refusal to see her for herself aggravated her. It was hypocritical.

She had known others like him. Had seen it time and again in the way they stared, longingly, at people who shared their features, their bodies, their feelings. There was ever that state of denial, that preamble to accepting their truth. She hoped he found the courage to accept his.

Maybe this walk will help. Then again, she had never been sure of him. He was always surrounded by women, but there were those four years he had been gone from the tribe, seeking out a spirit with the hope of becoming his acolyte. That would have been time to become himself, to be who he was when the expectations of the tribe were left behind. It may have been that coming back had changed him. That whatever life he had lived when away had bolstered him, and he was simply not ready for his family, and his tribe, to know.

Arrak had gone into the snow scattered field, but he watched from a distance, gave them space enough to speak openly, but remained to verify they entered.

The ancient treaty between Ung Kanh Dui and Duijus Kanh was lost, but the traditions were not forgotten.

Arrak cleared his throat. It was almost time. He recited the opening statement, the last words he would speak to them before they emerged once again from the cave.

"Send your strongest and bravest into my cave, and I will guard you." He said. "The moon cannot touch what the wolves watch. No harm will come to you, so long as your kin enter, and carve their names into the rock. From you I draw power, and with that power I vow to defend you. And from the bravest among you, I will take my acolyte, to become my voice in all matters concerning your people. If they may pass my test.

"So spoke Duijus Kanh to the first Ung Kanh Dui. Be brave, Ung Tsang. Be brave, Ung Tsong. Honor his legacy with your courage."

Chakta stepped forward.

Tamlin's gaze snapped to her. He was not ready. She could see that plainly

Gil Garo

enough. But before his father, he could not keep back. Could not let her be the braver of them.

He cussed under his breath, and followed her forward. "What's your hurry. We have all night."

"It's okay to be afraid, Tamlin." She whispered.

"What is there to be afraid of? The Swans? They only eat sick people."

"Are you sure you didn't catch something from one of those girls you're always flirting with?"

His cheeks reddened. "I'm not...no of course not!"

"Well then you have nothing to worry about. Besides, they only take people who are too weak to last the winter."

"You don't know that for sure."

"Your own father walked this path." She said more confidently than she felt. "So did mine. Both of them came out fine."

She stepped down onto the debris strewn slope inside the mouth of the cave. He fidgeted at the entrance, glanced over his shoulder at the moonstruck silhouette of his father.

"Are you coming or not?" she said.

Seeing no other choice, he followed. His father would not leave until both of them had returned. As was his newfound duty, as Chief of Chiefs.

Tamlin might have hedged at the entrance all night had it been anyone else presiding over this rite of passage. Had it been Chief Ungol, or Chief Gulang, there would have been far less pressure on him to show he could be strong.

She could not help but be glad that it had been Chief Arrak who watched over them. There was nothing to fear from this cave, she must tell herself that, but she did not value going it alone, even if her companion was no one she wanted to be alone with.

Standing with Chakta before Duijus Kanh's yawning mouth dredged up the old itch again. A new Chief of Chiefs, his father stood well back from them, amid powder snow dunes, a silhouette wreathed in moonlight to remind him he must be brave. If it were anyone else watching over them, he might have stood here all night, gone just far enough inside to satisfy the old agreement. But he could not look weak in front of his father. He could not bring him that shame. The chief had been down this path, hadn't he? He never talked about it—none of those who had stood where he was standing did. But he had come out again untouched.

He came out fine. Why shouldn't I?

He was not brave. Not like Chakta. He was a coward. He had believed, in his long trek through the Shar Lau range, down into Sildein and then Gaspar, that the lord of the cordillera, Rasheik the Rope, must value bravery, strength, and tenacity above all else. He had been wrong, then. Though he pretended otherwise, those qualities did not live inside him. They did not define him as they did his father. Nor did he believe it was any penchant for honesty that decided Rasheik on him.

It was those features he hid away, the ones he buried. His compassion, the way he so often set his wants aside for the sake of others. They were not qualities that would help him here.

Duijus Kanh was not kind or generous. The Swans did not aid the Gil Garo out of any sense for kinship, and their protection was certainly not charity. These were spirits for whom even murder could be justified for its own sake.

He noticed Chakta did not step closer to the entrance, and wondered if her thoughts aligned with his. This was a task which was too big for them.

They're waiting for us. Will they leave us alone?

He knew he was not her first choice, that if it was up to her, she would have that newcomer, Dupec, by her side.

There is a man who is brave. He was not sure of that one, not sure why he had done what he'd done. He had been on the precipice of victory. It was his right to be here, to walk this path. He had earned it. But even as he acknowledged the right of Ungol's lost son to be here, to pursue Ung Kanh Dui—be it a fictitious status or something real and true—a weight settled in his gut. Dupec Safar was not Gil Garo, not really. Why *should* an outsider stand where he now stood? What gave him the right to call himself one of theirs when he had lived and grown into who he was in their absence, from the day of his birth until now.

He understands that, doesn't he? That's why he threw the match. He knew I couldn't accept it.

Chakta might have preferred him. He understood well enough why. He had not made things easy for her, but what choice did he have. Any of those women who flocked to him would have expectations he did not want to entertain. They would inevitably want families, and all the preamble that led to them. Things he would rather not....

No, that's not quite right, is it?

Behind them, his father cleared his throat, and he recoiled.

He had been gone from the tribe four years, almost five. He had been free to be who he was then. And when he returned, there had been that moment when he thought he would say it, speak his truth out loud and live the way he had when he was away. When he was allowed to. And then he had set eyes on his father.

Those half-formed plans died that day.

He was a coward. A coward did not belong here.

"Send your strongest and bravest into my cave, and I will guard you." Arrak said. "Let them carve their names into the rock. From you I draw power, and with that power I vow to defend you. And from the bravest among you, I will take an acolyte, to become my voice in all matters concerning your people. If they may pass my test.

"So spoke Duijus Kanh to the first Ung Kanh Dui. Ung Tsang, be brave. Ung Tsong, be brave. Honor his legacy with your courage.

Chakta stepped forward.

Tamlin's gaze snapped to her. He was not ready. She could see that plainly enough. But before his father, he could not keep back. Could not let her be the braver of them.

He cussed under his breath, and followed her forward. "What's your hurry. We have all night."

"It's okay to be afraid, Tamlin." She whispered.

"What is there to be afraid of? The Swans? They only eat sick people."

"Are you sure you didn't catch something from one of those girls you're always flirting with?"

His cheeks reddened. "I'm not...no of course not!"

"Well then you have nothing to worry about. Besides, they only take people who

Gil Garo

are too weak to last the winter."

"You don't know that for sure."

"Your own father walked this path." She said with confidence. "So did mine. Both of them came out fine."

She stepped down onto the debris strewn slope inside the mouth of the cave. He fidgeted at the entrance, glanced over his shoulder at the moonstruck silhouette of his father.

"Are you coming or not?" she said.

Seeing no other choice, he followed. His father would not leave until both of them had returned. As was his newfound duty, as Chief of Chiefs.

He might have hedged at the entrance all night had it been anyone else presiding over this rite of passage. Had it been Chief Ungol or Chief Gulang, there would have been far less pressure on him to show he could be strong.

There was nothing to fear from this cave, he must tell himself that, but he did not value the idea of being left behind. Even more than disappointing his father, being left alone in the dark with the Swans to take watch was frightening. There was comfort in having a companion, even if she hated him. At least she was a familiar face, a calming voice in these uncertain times.

If the Lord of Wolves loathed the moon, he did not extend that hatred to the God of Darkness. Duijus Kanh yielded to God Mu, or perhaps they could be called friends, for it did not take long for the moonlight bathing his mouth to recede, shadows to pool, coalesce, and then become absolute.

Within the embrace of that darkness, the winter chill was pushed back, and though Chakta would not have called this place warm, she could almost convince herself that in this lessened cold, a carpet of a kind had been rolled out for them.

"Why didn't they give us torches?" Tamlin groused. "It's creepy how dark it is in here. The least they could've—"

"Are you going to complain the whole time?" She said.

"Would you blame me if I did? I didn't even want to be here."

She paused. "You didn't?"

"Chakta, we've known each other since we were kids. In all that time, did I ever give you the indication I wanted this?"

"You've been an arrogant prick since you came back from pilgrimage, so yes. I'd say you did."

He sighed. "Fine. I guess I got a little hung up trying to impress everyone."

"Everyone being all those women who follow you everywhere like lost dogs?"

Silence from him, a welcome relief. He had it right. She would not have chosen to spend her time with him be it here or anywhere. He was a hypocrite and a coward, and she had no trouble seeing through him. She had never understood why no one else could.

As the silence opened between them, other sounds came to her. Water trickling over stone, droplets beating an uneven cadence against the ground. A breeze from the south whistled through the cave, and just behind it, footsteps.

"Woah!" Tamlin said. "You feel that?"

"Feel what?"

Fingers probed her shoulder, danced along her arm and then firmed around her wrist. Tamlin's grip was gentle as he guided her hand to the side, and her fingers

Tears for the Moon God

made contact with the wall.

There were lines there, unnatural patterns carved into the stone. Some of them were so eroded she couldn't make sense of them, but there were newer carvings among them—letters spelling out words in their language, the names of those who had been here before her.

She followed the contours of those letters, sounding out the names in her head.

"Oh." She said as her fingers finished a circuit over a name she recognized. "Oh, that bitch."

"What?"

"Berni Vakh. You ever meet her?"

"She's that Cuu lady who followed Chief Sarri out to sea, right?"

"The one they call an honorary Swan."

"You recognize any other names?"

She shook her head. "No."

"I think...Safar...something Safar. Raguhl, maybe."

"No idea."

"Chief Ungol's father had a name like that, didn't he?"

"Maybe." She said. "Hey! Come here. Feel right here." She guided his hand over another name.

"That's my dad!"

"Arrak Sarr." She chuckled. "He didn't make it very far, did he?"

"Makes me wonder if the other chiefs did."

"We can look for them."

"That means going deeper."

"Don't be a puss, Tamlin." She marched onward. Hurried footsteps pursued her.

As she traveled, she continued to run her fingers across the walls, and paused where she landed on a name she recognized.

"Ungol Safar." Tamlin said. "And there's Shaelein. I guess she made it farther than he did." He chuckled.

Sounds like history is going to repeat itself. She thought to herself, and snorted.

He seemed to take that as encouragement.

They traveled on this way until the names began to dwindle in volume. What comfort she took in their presence was displaced by a growing anxiety. The names this deep down were not ancient, but none of them belonged to anyone she knew either. Be it from stories or other sources. She recognized surnames among them, was surprised to find another Krul this deep down. One who would have been long dead before her father set foot in this place.

"We should turn back." She said.

"Just...wait." Tamlin said. "This doesn't make sense."

"What doesn't?"

"Come here. Feel this. Tell me I'm crazy." He said.

She approached where he was standing, reached up, let him guide her hand across a name.

She flinched back. "It must be a coincidence, right. There's no way he's been here. When would he have—"

"Why is his name here, then?"

"Dupec is a common enough name." She protested. The idea that Chief Ungol's son had somehow evaded Sauman's watch and entered this cave, that he had penetrated this deep before turning back, didn't sit right with her. It implied he was not the honorable person she believed, that he was the kind who would stop at nothing, break whatever rule, ignore whatever tradition he needed to in order to get what he wanted.

Besides, it doesn't make sense. If he had come this far, he would have been claimed right? He wouldn't even have been at the tournament. Why would he need to be?

"Didn't you say he had a visitor the other night?"

"That's different."

"Maybe they're connected. That...and...and this."

"Can we turn back now?" she demanded. The joy she had experienced up until now was rapidly giving way to paranoia. How far from the entrance were they? How long would it take to get back.

"Okay." He said.

"She tramped back up the sprawling corridor. *No way that's his signature. It must be an ancestor. It has to be.*

But that signature wasn't eroded like the ones around it. The lines were crisp, as if they had just been carved into the stone. She thought of the visitor, the overturned lamp, damp earth and fresh boot prints. Hadn't he given Dupec a warning? Was that not why he had come to him?

Rustling in the dark. The whisper of steel sliding against leather, padding feet making haste toward...*something.*

These were not sounds that boded well in the night gloom spread across the thin walls of Coltang's tent. A shadow, painted across the tarp wall, two and then three, all moving on their own but fixed to the same pair of feet. He rose—silent, light footed. The spy or the scout could not have belonged to the Gil Garo tribe. None of them would be so brash in the skinny months, not so bold as to harrow the flank of their cousin, to deal in killing for the sake of blood feud when winter's grip was on them.

The Swans?

Duijus Kanh's concubines were not unknown to him. The Tipik camp was close enough to their cave to invite them, but why would they come so close to him. No one in his camp had fallen ill that he knew. No child had been stillborn. None had suffered an accident and spoken of it, to healers or friends. He would have heard.

Were it them, they would come up hungry, a pointless pursuit driven not by need but hubris. Then again, the shadows painted across the tarp were not unhuman. They bore no obvious signs of disfigurement, and they were male.

Whoever this was, they were aware of the Gil Garo culture. Three shadows, for Duijus Kanh was mated to three women. Three, but spoiled in that the assailant could not hide his feet, the place where those shadows stood together.

One cocked his head as if hearing something. The other two froze in place, waiting. Three together, they rushed away. Shadows drew earthward, and left no impression that they had ever been.

He crossed to a chest on top of which were two hammers, long-handled, their heads wide and square and bound in gold. The handles were of one piece with the heads, bound in ivory. The weapons had been made for a prince, whose caravan the Tipik had robbed on its way to a state visit with the Jahhar royal family. It had been as nothing to take them from that coddled boy with the powdered face, shadowed eyes. Perhaps the assailant belonged to his kin, a mercenary or a soldier sent on behalf of Jahhad's emperor to pay a debt.

He would not have passed unnoticed. Would not abide the vengeful shedding of his people's blood, not tonight.

No time, then, to do more than take the hammers, to pass through the entrance flap of his home clad in small clothes, feet bare.

"What is it?" his wife hissed.

"Stay here, Tanta." he said. "Just a suspicion. A presence on the wind."

"A Swan?"

"No." he grimaced. "No, I think not."

He passed into the Tipik camp, following the path of the assailant through wide lanes, tall teepees to either side arranged in neat rows, his people sound asleep.

Shadows played on the edge of one a hundred or so steps ahead of him. The assailant turned a corner.

He adjusted his grips on the hammers, laid chase.

The assailant's path took him away from the Tipik camp, toward the yurts which marked first the Cuu and then the Dumas encampments. He traveled toward the river, avoiding lanes where people gathered, using cart shadows and the lesser light of the moon to his advantage.

He quickened his steps, closing the distance. An itch formed between his shoulder blades.

There were those among the Dumas who might be targeted by an assassin. Ungol, for one. He was not well received by all the Gil Garo, but then he was far from alone in that. No reason to attempt assassination. There was the matter of how he had come by his compact with Gandes Fae. If those of the village whose sons he had slaughtered found him....

But that was more than twenty years ago.

And there was his son. A Cloud Man might bring rise to superstitious preoccupations. Suspicions about his history, his loyalties, what danger might be inherent in his presence. He could have enemies none of them knew about. Enemies gained in his time within the God House of Ways, or enemies of God Uldal himself.

He closed on the assailant, who slowed ahead of a yurt not far from Ungol's. Closed, and saw him clearly for the first time. Moonlight made him pallid, though he was already too pale to be Gil Garo. At least, too pale to be *only* Gil Garo.

The man was of average height and slender, dressed like a Tipik but missing the mark by degrees. His earrings were small and dangled from his lobes. His hair was short cropped, yes, but he wore no beard. And though he went bare chested, turquoise beads rattling along threads across his chest, he wore pants in a style unfamiliar. Black, hugging tight to his legs. No skirt to cover them, the material thicker, padded leather.

Coltang rounded the nearest yurt, taking cover as the assailant closed on his apparent quarry. He hunted for a pulse, called to his spirit master for the power he had won so many years ago.

Sildein answered, driving a force to humble mountains into him. It bled into his limbs, pressed into the backs of his eyes and spread, adding weight to his muscles, enervating him with unnatural vigor, to enhance his speed and strength, harden his skin.

Gil Garo

He whipped a hammer across the intervening distance between the assailant and him.

CRASH!

The earth exploded under the assailant's feet as he brought up his blade to meet the hammer. Force that should have shattered the long knife instead rebounded. A shadow lashed out, caught its cast shadow, and it froze in midair.

Coltang reached for it, calling it back. He met resistance, a tug of war with neither him nor the assailant touching the weapon.

He whipped the other hammer, imbuing it with the energy of Sildein's right hand.

White fire surged around it. A second shadow reached, a second knife came up to meet it. The fire drove the shadows into the assailant's feet, to hug him close.

A look of surprise.

Ice Shards stabbed out of still air.

What lord do you follow, killer?

The magic was familiar, but it was nothing like he had seen from the Gil Garo. Hadn't that kid in the pit with no name used similar arts.

The assailant ripped the beads from his neck. Hidden among the turquoise stones was a slim vial filled with dark liquid. The assailant pushed it between his teeth, crunched.

Violent red climbed across his veins, illuminating him in the dark. His eyes glowed like embers.

Coltang called his hammers back, compelling them with savage magnetic force. They snapped into his waiting palms.

The assailant charged.

A yipping call tore from Coltang's throat.

Figures broke from yurts. Lamps were lit. He noticed Dupec passing through the entrance of the yurt the assailant had targeted.

Dupec's gaze passed him, settled on the one who would be his assassin.

"Of course." he said.

Dupec's stony expression, his seeming lack of surprise at the attack, sent a chill rippling down Coltang's spine.

Another yipping call answered his.

More lanterns. More light to make the shadows dance.

Dupec rushed the assailant.

Coltang whipped his hammer. The assailant twisted around it and into Dupec's thrust out blade, broad and in the style of Dumas weapons, the edge serrated.

Gore washed his face and chest, the assailant's head nearly taken off. The assailant crumpled as Dupec drew back a step.

The hammer sailed around and back into Coltang's waiting hand.

Dupec reached for a snow drift, ripped a chunk free and washed the blood from his skin.

"Don't let them cut you!" Dupec called.

Some comprehension donned on Coltang. He nodded. *Blood Lords.*

Dupec ran for his father's yurt; Coltang for his camp. The sounds of fighting were everywhere along the river.

The Tipik had been infiltrated. His people were in danger.

He rushed back the way he had come. The Dumas could take care of themselves.

Tears for the Moon God

His daughter and his wife were out there, vulnerable. His family, his sect, needed him.

Ice crawled across the floor of Ungol's yurt. He readied himself for the coming attack, while Shaelein pulled at the expanding sheet, breaking it down, water coalescing about her arms and torso.

They had made a mistake coming here, whoever these assailants were. Had not predicted their presence would be so swiftly noted, met with such robust defense, but the Gil Garo were accustomed to watching their flanks, reading in the night's stillness the patterns of passing armies.

One sect on its own might be taken by a great enough force, but all of them together?

"They must be insane. To think..." Shaelein cussed.

"The design of the assault is intelligent enough. Organized. They'll have brought an army. Not some ragtag rebel faction." Ungol said.

"Too organized." She agreed. "First, the chiefs, yes? Then anyone who might have influenced enough to form a strategy against them."

Shadows played in the entrance, shifting independent of each other.

The assailant rushed the space, leaving no time for thought.

Ungol hefted his sword. His mol fae familiar climbed the wall behind the attacker, pounced. Curled fangs closed around the assailant's neck, took head from shoulders in a savage clamping of mandibles.

Breath gusted from its spiracles. An infantile wail distorted the slack, child's face on its hairy back into a mask of pain and anger. Blood sprayed from the stump of the man's neck as Ungol reached to yank up the head by its hair.

The man's features resembled his own, but he was several shades too pale to be Gil Garo, his eyes too round and his nose narrow and sharp. He looked to be of an age with Dupec, but lines creased his face even as Ungol held it up to examine it, a preternatural advancing of age, leaving him a husk of who he had been when he was alive.

"Strange magic." he said, tossing the head away. He made an observation of the body lying prone against the floor. The mol fae would not touch it. It preened its mandibles, pausing now and again to wail and spit blood and mucus.

"Why does it not eat?" Shaelein asked, watching as it spat dusky blood onto the ice.

"Tainted blood." he shrugged. "She doesn't like the taste. It's bitter."

"Will it kill her?"

The mol fae paused to glare at her.

"No." he said. "She warns us not to let the blood touch us. Not if we are wounded. To wash it off before the opportunity arrives for infection."

"W-why?"

"The magic is in the blood. These are men from Tuluis Fel."

"The forbidden kingdom?"

His nod was curt. "They must have traveled far for this."

"We have no quarrel with them."

"We do now."

He stepped past the body, into the field outside. Lantern light threw shadows

Gil Garo

across packed snows. In the distance, the river was awash with glittering spray as soldiers of Tuluis Fel stormed the Dumas camp. Yipping calls announced the new attacks in the Cuu and Hakka camps, of fighting closer by. Iron rang against iron. He saw his own men swinging swords and pole arms, locked in battle with enemies whose shadows flickered and danced with them, attacking in the way that Tipik pretender had when the tournament reached its final round.

A second assailant, a third, rushed him. Shadows reached with shadowed blades to strike where he stepped. He moved out of their path as Shaelein lashed out with water, slicing through the first's throat, across the second's chest.

Dadang's magic was wielded expertly by her as she dove into a crowd of oncoming soldiers clad all in black, whipping blades of clear water around her, taking down six in quick succession, not letting their shadows touch her.

Blades of ice crashed down around Ungol. Deftly, he wove around them, carved a line across the intervening distance. One hand reached for his assailant. His palm pressed against the soldier's forehead and a dark pulse rippled through the shaft of his arm, into the other man's head.

The mol fae lashed out at another attacker intent on cutting him down from behind as the first soldier's gaze became unfocused, as tears leaked from his eyes and his shadows withered and quaked underfoot.

Ungol's blade parted his ribs, sank through flesh into heart muscle. The fight was over before his blade ever made contact. Locked in his worst memories, his self-styled killer could do nothing except drink up all his sorrows.

The mol fae surged into the coming horde, crawled over bodies, gnashed sharp jaws around throats and limbs. Blood sprayed, gushed from still pumping hearts.

Shaelein's waters washed over the wailing creature, who held her husband's Chain, washed them of the tainted blood as it sought to performed its terrible work, protecting her husband's back as she joined in this dance of shadows, seized on ice and converted it into a torrent for her use, fed it into the liquid flows at her command.

So bound, the Blood Lord saw through the eyes of his subordinates, saw them felled by the chief and his wife. He saw the Tipik chief running for his own encampment, to organize his forces behind him.

We can't have that, now, can we.

He commanded his troops to follow, a squad of fifteen to remove him before the Tipik could have their commander.

Do not kill if it can be avoided. he commanded, the missive a whisper across many minds. *Better to possess him. Control benefits us more than elimination.*

The Tipik had been most accommodating hosts. So ignorant to the enemies among them, who arrived with them to the Shifting City, relayed their ways, their weak points, so diligently.

The problem arose not with Coltang the Anvil, but with the other insurgent. No love between Tuluis Fel and God Uldal; yet he must have known something of their intent. Why else send his acolyte?

A Cloud Man at that.

A directive whispered across his mind, come from his superior officer. The Crow their lord had chosen to lead this campaign.

Do not engage with Dupec Safar. Your task lies elsewhere. Within the cave.

Tears for the Moon God

That task is beyond us. We should await reinforcements. He responded.
None are coming. It is now or never. The Crow pressed. *He is distracted.*

He passed wordlessly from his observation of the Dumas chief, Ungol, to execute his order, knowing he would likely die with the spirit's claim to this land uncontested.

Dupec saw the officer as he passed. His dark leathers were embellished with strips of scarlet cloth, a gold sigil pinned to a sash crossing his chest, which hung over his sword belt, interrupting access to the scabbard. A multitude of shadows writhed beneath his feet, covering all points of attack, lashing out at any Dumas who came too close.

He saw his mother fighting together with his father and a creature whose eerie shape struck him with a palpable terror.

Is that the shape of my father's magic?

His mother washed its segmented body clean each time it took life, lashed out with frothing whips of water from behind it, adding more bodies to the toll.

He split off a Shard, and the doppelganger ran in their direction.

He rushed after the officer.

A wise warrior sought the head of command before he dealt with common soldiers. Eliminate him and the command structure was thrown into chaos.

Blood soaked earth made his footing treacherous, but he did not slow.

Horses screamed. Still more charged across the lane ahead, mounted riders laying into the enemy forces with swords, firing arrows at others more distant.

He lashed out at an oncoming assailant with his sword. It tasted blood, and the assailant went down.

He drew on his magic, a sorcerous burst which shortened the path ahead of him, placing him in reach of the officer's shadows as they felled three Dumas warriors, knee capped a horse, and sent it skidding then rolling to pin its rider.

He lashed out. The strike played against a waiting blade in the hand of a shadow, stopping the thrust short with the officer having done nothing, even to turn to face him.

The shadow latched onto his, and pushed.

He hit the ground hard, the blow knocking the breath from his lungs.

A horse warrior galloped across his path. He rolled in time to avoid being trampled.

The officer was clear of him, heading not for the long house where the chiefs convened, but toward the outlying camps of the Kirche and Tipik.

He loosed a yipping call, imitating the battle cry of his people. A horse warrior looked over to him in time to see his sharp gesture toward the officer.

"Take their commander!"

An arrow knocked, loosed. The shaft flying on still air.

The arrow was cut down before it struck home, the officer running. Running toward the Tipik camp, then northwest.

To the cave. he realized.

He hauled himself to his feet, drew on the power of his soulbinding, opening a path. The cave mouth loomed before him, yawned in the moonlight amid snows made gray by the gloom, a world cast in indigo shades.

More enemies poured into its mouth, a force to match what had come for the

Gil Garo

Dumas. Their approach was being contested at the flanks. Tipik and Kirche riders charged. He sighted Tursa atop a dun stallion among them, hanging back, shouting orders at his warriors.

Arrows fell into the horde of infantrymen, taking them in the chest and throat. Horses fell under preternatural blows, broken legs, blooded flanks.

Blood flashed. Gore soaked the land.

A wounded rider rose amid the chaos of clashing bodies, the cut to his ribs mending too swiftly, his eyes glowing coals as the assailant who had attempted to kill Dupec earlier in the night had been.

He loosed a cry and charged at the Tipik soldiers he'd been fighting alongside moments earlier.

Kirche riders loosed arrows. His body bristled with them.

He fell. Dying, his body shriveled, aging years in heartbeats. The corpse that hit the ground was not a young man but an elder, wrinkled and broken and gnarled. He looked *dry*. As if life drained out of him with his blood, leaving a crude, leather sack behind.

Dupec watched, horrified, the battle forgotten for several heartbeats as the weight of Tuluis Fel's magic settled into his mind, the scope of that power made evident.

This fight...end it quickly. End it now!

He roared, rushed into the hordes, carved a path among the bodies. Infantrymen fell on Tipik and Kirche corpses, pressing lips to open wounds, tasting blood. Their eyes glowed with the poison in their blood.

Dead or dying tribesmen rose, stumbled away from them, charged their friends, their kin.

He turned his efforts against them, those who came too close, those distracted by their feeding. Sliced into Tului flesh, delivered killing blow after killing blow.

He severed another Shard, another, left them to aid in the slaughter of the fiends as he pushed for the entrance, dancing to avoid striking shadows, meeting blades in the hands of foes familiar and foreign.

The cave swallowed him.

More fighting. The clangor of blades. Stones crashing. The earth shaking underfoot. Light painted the walls in bursts, illuminating countless names carved into them, some so old they were no longer legible, others fresh and undamaged. Light flashed. Thunder echoed from deep in the cave. Pale figures flashed into being and faded.

The sounds of screams played with the thunder.

Lightning surged. Water rolled almost to his feet and fell back again. Bodies stiff with the rigor of an electric storm flaying nerves, burning flesh.

He followed the current, his screams lost in the chaos.

Shaki. Arrak Sarr.

He recognized them, saw that they were the source of the assault. Thera's magic rippled across Shaki's skin. His eyes glowed a cold blue in the darkness.

A Tului officer danced with them, sinuous in his movements, attacking their flanks, blade whipping out to touch flesh.

Shaki backed away from a well-placed thrust as Arrak raised a wall of water between them.

The wall crashed over the officer. Electricity ripped across it.

Tears for the Moon God

The officer fell. A score more soldiers toppled with him.

More officers charged past him. He noted one in particular among them, his rank marked out with a cuff around his bicep, and several medals pinned to his scarlet sash.

The officers surged forth as Arrak sent a fresh flow of water past, taking another several soldiers into its grip but avoiding Dupec entirely, leaving him on a dry patch of rock.

A way forward opened for him. Bodies stiffened and fell as Shaki's assault was renewed.

Ice crawled over the walls, around the rushing waters, walled them in, walled them off. The dykes remained as Arrak fought to thwart them.

The officer's leering face was illuminated, painted in gray shades as he turned to run into the depths.

Near to Arrak but too distant for him to reach, Chakta raised a barrier of water, made weaker than his by inexperience. The wall froze instantly.

Tamlin fought alongside her. A blow to his head passed through. He reached out toward the officer who had attacked him, grasped.

The officer's shadow lashed out.

Dupec's roared warning came too late.

He fell, unconscious.

The officer's blade came for him.

Dupec was on him, then, blade meeting blade, palm thrust for his chest.

He whipped his scimitar around as his palm made contact, felt the sickness touching his soul as he opened a path between them—he was gambling with his life, and he knew it—and cut the officer off from his spirit as his blade sank into the side of that soldier's neck.

Blood flew.

Dupec twisted from its path, into fresh summoned water.

Chakta screamed. She lost control. The waters crashed, taking Dupec with them.

A roar to drown out the chaos. The demented caricatures of three women streamed among the officers, past them into the mass of infantry. Their passing removed all but the high officer, who wounded the tallest of the three as she passed him.

Black blood fanned across rock, was washed away on the current.

Several dozen soldiers fell writhing on the ground, were displaced by Arrak's torrent.

Quiet.

Except for the thunder of Dupec's heart against his ears, his chest.

Blood.

The cave illuminated. Wolves howling in the distance.

A blow to his chest. He toppled. Darkness swallowed him. He didn't have time to register the second blow to his head before unconsciousness took him.

Tamlin blinked water from his eyes. Chakta was helping him to his feet. Dupec lay prone nearby. The Swans had left a trail of corpses in their wake.

He saw them in the flesh, the stories painted across their features, them traveling amid the names of countless Gil Garo men and women, at least some of whom had thought them more than scavengers of the diseased and dying. They

Gil Garo

lashed out barehanded, snapping throats, breaking off limbs to spray gore across their naked, moon-pale bodies.

Black eyes.

Duichekh, long necked and tall, but thin as a wraith. Meichekh, almost human in appearance, her beautiful, round face marred by scaling around the eyes. Kachekh, small and stout, ugly as a mossy stone.

The last officer left standing raised his blade against Dupec, raised it over his neck in two hands.

The blade thrust down.

A gnarled, wide hand wrapped around it. Amber eyes enlivened by hate struck terror in Tamlin even as he came to his aid, to *Dupec's* aid.

The officer broke from the creature's grip, twisting his blade free as shadows lashed out beneath his feet.

Spears of ice thrust from stony earth, crashed into the towering figure, broke on impact. A wolf's pelt swayed from the figure's shoulders as he came for the high officer, raking clawed fingers across his path. His topknot wavered back and forth as he dipped low, launched off all fours, filed teeth bared.

Silver plate armor gleamed in the electric light across his chest, a chain tunic clattering as arms reached out, claws dug into legs.

The up thrust from the spirit vivisected the officer.

Beyond him, what remained of his army crumpled, writhing, aging unnaturally fast. Their screams broke through dying throats.

The Swans rose from their assault on the soldiers. They turned in unison to their master, their lover.

Duijus Kanh.

Tamlin backpedaled until he struck the wall, sank against it, not trusting himself to speak. Not certain what these next moments would bring.

Duijus Kanh looked to Dupec, then. The Swans followed his gaze.

"Returned, have you?" his voice was deep, rasping, a growl to match the wolves he consorted with—who alone among the spirits they would listen to. "The gods couldn't keep you away. Not even after they took everything else you cared for."

His gaze flicked to Tamlin, to Shaki and Arrak, to Chakta. All of them watched him with the same terror he felt.

He settled again on Tamlin. "You were his friend."

He shook his head. "No, that time is locked to us now. Once, maybe, but you are wounded by jealousy. You were then, too.

"Take them away."

The words were not for the Gil Garo, but for the Swans. Take them to their people.

Chakta reached for Dupec, to collect him. He swatted her hands away.

She yelped, cowered away from him.

"He, you will not have. Not yet." he reached under Dupec's arms, hauled him onto his back.

"My cousin will pay for this. You will give answer for his crime." Duijus Kanh's gaze was fixed on the distant mouth of his cave. "Wait for him. Wait for Ung Kanh Dui."

Tears for the Moon God

He looked to the Swans. They converged on Arrak and Shaki.

Kachekh made for Tamlin and Chakta. The sweet, motherly smile she favored them with did nothing to make her more alluring.

"Come now, you'll need healing." she took Chakta by the shoulders, helped her up. Tamlin rose, his distrust for her warring with a deeper urge not to earn her anger.

"Good little ones." she said. "Follow me. Come now. the treaty holds, though there will be no carving of names for you this night. We've too much to do. Walls to wash. Floors to scrub. The blood runs deep in our little home, doesn't it? You'll see your friend soon enough, trust."

She bundled them off. Tamlin twisted to look back at Duijus Kanh, to see him stalking off into the cave's depths with Dupec hanging over one shoulder.

"I'm in your debt." he whispered.

Kachekh turned to him, glanced under his shoulder to look at Dupec. "Not for the first time, I am sure. But as my dear love pointed out, that time is past.

"I suppose it makes sense, doesn't it? The Wolf of the West was ever a thorn in that lot's side. But then, he is defanged in absence of his Dragon. The one those Nixians were so fond of.

"It's tragic, really." She led them toward the mouth of the cave. "The only man old Dupec ever loved, taken because he wouldn't listen to good wisdom.

"Attack a god in his home, he did. A pyrrhic victory if there ever was one. Brief lived and hard met with treason. He'll not much love the poor boy if he knows.

Part 3:

Hindsight

A Spirit's Gift

The quilt had been stitched by Lura in the first year of their marriage, a crude attempt at mastering a skill she was ill equipped for. It had been this fact, the shoddy quality of the weaving, rough stitching that caused the thick, knotty fabric to dimple in odd places, that had decided her on taking it with them. Leave the good quilts for when they returned. There would be comfort, then, in those familiar, forgotten remnants of the life they had left behind.

But how long will we be away? Months? It must be. She ran the rough fabric across her fingers, feeling the dimples as they passed over rough calluses.

Katuwan fussed over bowstrings in the gloom. The forest canopy she had known all her life retreated along a ridge a spare handful of paces from where they squatted. Carriages and caravans passed on their way up and down the wide lane there, but for their position relative to the ridge, she could only see the heads of man and beast, and the tops of their wagons.

Oxen blared disgruntled notes, their crooked horns weaving as they wagged their heads, and the sun watched on from behind swift drifting clouds. The west baring breeze was not strong. By the time it was well past them, it would have lost its power, been blocked completely by Sufa Salein's great trees before it ever reached the village they'd left to itself.

Tak the Fire, their answer, could be anywhere at all. He could as well be in the next pass, buried in the next valley. Maybe beyond the mountains to the east, or the west, or the north was a valley perpetually engulfed in flame. Maybe the spirit opened a channel for only those who had pledged themselves to his pacifism.

The Rahad would know. They must. But there was no guarantee they would find them in Faed City, if their journey took them that far.

Does he hide from other spirits, too? We should have asked Sufa Salein.

It was strange that such a powerful spirit would swear not to commit violence. Stranger still, for his very nature was destruction. Pluck a flower from the vine and it would die, but let it catch flame and it ceased. The vine was consumed. The tree it clung to was scorched. The flame consumed until it was snuffed out or doused, yet this was to be their healer. His nature destruction, how could he heal anything.

She carved a path through the weave with Katuwan's skinning knife. The weave parted.

She dragged the knife across it a second time to sever stubborn threads, and then repeated the process midway down the larger of the two cut sections. *There go our memories.*

Katuwan selected a piece of gut string and cut it down the middle, thinning the thread he intended to use to make clothing of the quilt. He took up a cruel needle he'd carved from a green stick before he set to this work, and threaded the gut through what passed for an eye. Leather could be tied off and remain in tact for the most part. The cord would hold well enough. The simple garment it produced was practical, but the people following that road would not abide the Katuwiti way. She had seen that much when she scouted ahead, slithering up the slope on elbows and knees until she could see over that ridge, to see there pale-skinned people clad in dense leathers and furs from their necks to their toes, and dark skinned people wearing tunics and skirts that hung loose over their bodies, hiding their flesh behind layers of fabric from at least the knee upward. For the women, most did not even let their hair fall free.

It did not take much thought to conclude there was a reason they were so heavily clothed. That her nudity would cause problems for them, to say nothing for Katuwan.

She had considered it may be wise to go around this pass, but if they were caught circumventing whatever civilization thrived at this choke point, they may well be jailed, and Xirakura had too much of a lead on them as it was. And then there was their need of supplies. She could forage effectively in the forest, but she knew those lands. She knew which plants were edible and which were poisonous, which counteracted each other's poisons and which could be used for other purposes. There was not much need for herbs and ointments with a Spirit Caller husband, but those herbs came in handy for minor ills and injuries, and the other households, other families, having them was as much a boon to Xirakura as he could ask for. He did not have to come to them for every thing, then. They had their means of handling the little things, leaving him free to manage bigger, more taxing problems.

But out there? Beyond this pass were lands she had never ventured into. She would have to pay attention to the way those other people interacted with their world, pray to the local spirits and give offerings, and hope they gave answer to her pleas for their attention. It was better to take this risk, see it done. The outsiders used money, so the elders said—coin and sometimes paper notes which held value because those people agreed they did. The entire system was ridiculous. What value did a flimsy piece of paper have that the jackfruit did not? What was the use of a gold or silver disk that was not outdone by flint or shale?

They would need some of that, too. *It won't be easy. We'll have to steal it.*

She grimaced.

Katuwan paused to look at her. In one hand, a wide strip of quilt which he had folded around his waist. In the other, the threaded needle, the other end knotted and the length dangling from where he had pierced it through the weave. He looked ridiculous. She supposed she would, too, soon enough.

Tears for the Moon God

"Something wrong?"

"I was just thinking." she said.

He returned to his work, looping the needle back around and testing it against the weave, looking for an obvious gap. "About what?"

"How we get supplies? Food stock that will not spoil. More gut for your bow. Money."

"No need to worry about gut." he said. "Easy enough to come by that on the road. Fletching, though? Arrowheads?" he shrugged. "Maybe those are more difficult."

"Maybe." she agreed.

"Food, too. We can hunt on the road. There is always game. You just have to be smarter than it."

"Money, then? We'll need proper clothes. These won't work forever."

He grimaced. "I see your point. We'll have to steal it, won't we?"

"Not a nice thought."

"No, but how else do we get by? Beg? Who will give us money? Even if they are generous, how long will it take?

"No, we'll have to steal it. Take it from someone who isn't paying enough attention. Or maybe...what kind of dwellings do these people have?"

She shrugged. "What do the elders say?"

He chuckled. "Many things and nothing. You know how they are."

He pushed the needle through the fabric, tied it off on the other end. Three stitches. Enough to hold the garment together around his waist and prevent it coming apart at its height. The skirt hung to his knees, not covering them. She wondered if it was enough to keep those strangers happy. If they found something lewd or dishonest about exposed knees, or chests. He had done nothing about covering his torso.

Then again, there had been men—laborers, maybe slaves—she could not tell, but knew there were societies out there that did not see such things as owning other people in the same light as the Katuwiti. Ownership was for possessions. People could not be owned. Or should not be--men who went bare chested, who whipped oxen into motion, or drove the wagons. The heat was harsher out in the open than it was on the forest floor. Gorgus was not sympathetic. It was his anger she felt on her cheeks and shoulders. It must be.

"Come. Your turn. We'll make something for your chest first."

She stood up and reached for the cord there, holding her breasts in place. He shook his head. "The gut might break. Better if you leave it."

So she did.

He wrapped the fabric around her back, and she lifted her arms so that he could pull it under. He drew it tight, and began stitching. Before he was halfway through, she reached under the fabric, tried to adjust its placement, make it roomier.

He drew it tight again as soon as she pulled her hand away.

"I need you to be still." he said.

"It itches."

"Mine doesn't?"

"I never thought it itched when it was just a quilt."

"It was never this tight on you."

She rolled her eyes. "This is going to be a long road."

A Spirit's Gift

"Of course." he finished stitching the band in place, cut the thread and tied it off. He cast aside the remaining length and laced the other half of his bow string into the needle, then clamped the needle between his teeth. He took the last piece of fabric, wrapped it around her waist, and knelt before her. She stroked his shaggy head as he set about stitching the skirt into place.

"They won't care about your hair?" he asked.

"It's only the dark ones that cover it."

"Probably."

"This thing itches worse than the first one."

"I went to a meeting of the elders with Xirakura once. Zanwakahat was there with Janeira."

She scoffed.

Katuwan ignored her. He always did.

Xirakura's brother was fine. She even liked him. But the woman he'd chosen for a wife had done nothing to endear herself to her. Janeira was a shameless gossip and a teller of tall tales, and she could not see how she had negotiated herself into the lifelong affections of such a pleasant man. She had not been overly sad when the elders called for Zanwakahat to be Spirit Caller for a neighboring village. She missed him sometimes, but his absence meant Janeira must bother another village's women, and be far away while she did it.

"They were meeting an outsider. You remember? You had decided to stay away because...well."

The needle grazed her leg. She hissed. "Be careful with that."

He pushed the needle through the fabric. To his merit, he did not touch her with it again. "They were to meet an envoy from another land. A guardian tribe on another continent. It was to be the first time meeting them for Xirakura and Zanwakahat both. I watched as the world opened onto some other place. A hole in the trees, into a city with stone buildings all mounted on the walls of a big cave. It was like nothing that exists here.

"And the elders stepped aside as the strangers came through. They were wearing as many clothes as those pale people up there." he gestured toward the ridge with the needle. "The way you describe them. But their leathers were tight over flowing underclothes. Layers on layers. I didn't understand. One of them was very young, and he took one look at us standing there. His eyes raked up and down each of us. I am not kidding." She was giggling. His eyes had gone wide with such seriousness she had rarely seen in him, and she was sure he was sincere. "He gasped, and clapped his hands over his eyes. I have never seen someone so red before or since. His whole face was like a sweet berry.

"Hold still."

"With you making me laugh like that?" she took a deep breath, willing the shudders in her chest and belly to cease. "Oh, these poor outsiders. It must be hard to be so uncomfortable all the time. Waiting for something to make them quiver with anxiety every second of the day."

He was chuckling now, too. The needle jittered as it passed through cloth, but missed her leg. It was a closer call than she would have liked. He pulled the thread tight, cut it and tied it off. Her skirt was no more a defense against whatever minor reveal would set the outsiders off than his was, but it would have to suffice until they could find something more permanent. Something which was hopefully not so

Tears for the Moon God

itchy.

"What's the plan?" he asked.

"You don't have one?"

"Do I ever?"

She smiled down at him, and drew him up by his chin.

He stood, wrapped her in his arms and kissed her forehead. "Thank you for putting up with me."

"Always." she whispered. She let herself be drawn into his embrace, corded muscle holding her to his wide chest, and snuggled her head under his chin. "We're going to find him. At the first settlement, if he hasn't moved on by then. If he has, we know where he'll go."

"He's an idiot sometimes."

She chuckled. "He cares."

"What are we going to do about money?"

"I thought about that. These people don't look like they'll hand over whatever they use to barter with easily."

"So we rob someone—"

She shook her head. "No violence. We'd put a target on our backs. We don't look like them. If they catch wise, they'll know exactly who to look for."

"So we do what?"

"Cut their bag free." she said. "They must keep their coin in something. And it would be something easy to access. So we go into the village or city or whatever this pass is, and then we look for people who don't seem to be paying attention. I'll need one of your knives, though. Unless you want to sharpen mine."

"Keep the skinning knife. Until we're past this place, anyway. I can sharpen yours when we settle down for the night."

"No violence." She pressed her forehead to his chest.

He stroked the back of her head. His chin passed over her crown, hunting for a clear view of the ridge and its passersby.

"No violence." he agreed.

Katuwan's first sighting of Ouran Goul stole his breath. The city, for it must be that, was defended by tall, boxy towers. From within them, archers panned over the road. He wondered if they worked in tandem with Spirit Callers, or what those outsiders called Spirit Callers. Wondered, too, which gods and spirits protected these people, or if their monstrous constructs offended the spirits in these mountains, along this pass.

What spirit of the land would allow a people to give rise to these dead structures, these loosely woven lanes meandering around houses and inns and places of commerce all made of dead things and stone? Yet there was artistry in the designs of those buildings. A fat, multistory estate loomed high atop a hill, looking down its nose at the common rabble in the lower reaches of the city, and their own homes were painted to match the sky, in shades of blue with white trim, or the clastic gravel their streets were composed of. Earthy shades, stone taken from the surrounding hills. Did Ouran sanction this construction, this pilfering of his resources? Did Safreit, or Shaudein. If the Range Lords were permissive, what about the mountains they governed?

He saw the vestiges of wells dug into the earth, themselves barrel shafts

A Spirit's Gift

mounted with stone and scattered hither thither throughout the city, in yards where lush grasses grew tall along pathways carved across them. Trees struggled for purchase within this city, finding places to take root where mortal man allowed. But there was no forest here, and those trees bore the blossoms of late spring, early summer. As he passed under one such tree at the edge of the road, he noticed one of those blossoms fluttering against the current of the others. The petals flicked back, a pointed chin and heart-shaped face peering at him. The fairy's cherubic body showed signs of starvation—a swollen belly, dull eyes, its ribs thrust up against skin which clung too tightly.

He shook his head. "This is not a good place."

Lura followed his gaze to the fairy, and winced. "What can we do? The tree won't survive without its guardian—"

"One guardian." Katuwan lamented. "Where are the rest?"

He approached the tree, pulled down a branch. Petals cascaded over his arm, stuck in the rough weave of his skirt. The bow gave no resistance. Dark splotches along its length revealed a pattern of blight. The trunk was not yet severely impacted, but it would be.

No wonder there is but one. One fairy clinging to his mother, who has grieved the loss of too many brothers and sisters already, but knows nothing else, and so stays. What a terrible life for such a short lived creature.

The fairy would die alone if left to its own devices, having lingered too long in a tree that could not bear fruit, which would produce no seed from which to grow new offspring. The tree's line would be ended, then, a thought he could not abide.

He bent to the earth, rummaged through scrub grass and plucked wildflowers from among them. He fashioned these into a hasty bouquet, and held it out for the fairy to see. With the gift, he offered his hand, and the fairy climbed into it, its eyes wide jewels fixed on the tiny flowers, bursts of color which drew it down the length of his arm, to climb into the flowers and lay there as if it had found a soft bed. It rubbed its cheek against a blue trumpet. Taking care not to jostle the bundle too much, he tucked it into his waist, and returned to Lura's side.

She smiled.

The tree would not survive beyond harvest season. Not beyond the dry season. But its line would be preserved. If only they could find a tree in better health, to unite him with a new family, so he might court a maiden, find new prosperity in rearing his own young.

They passed between the sentry posts, under the eyes of the archers, and into the sprawling city beyond. Though many entered the city and left it, the press of bodies was not so thick the journey along the main artery was uncomfortably close. Wide spaces opened between clusters of people, both those who came from the mountains and those who came from the plains beyond Ouran's feet. Most gave them a wide birth, but there were no few eyes on them. They did not look like these outsiders, did not dress like them. Their skin was copper hued—not midnight dark like the lowland people, nor nearly white like the mountain tribes. They traveled lighter than those others, shared few features with them. He suspected he looked uncomfortable. He certainly felt so.

Those staring eyes gave him pause as he kept pace with Lura, moved along that main thoroughfare, wondering all the while what she was looking for.

"It appears we've been noted." he said.

Tears for the Moon God

"Yes, this might be harder than we expected." she mumbled. "We'll have to be cautious."

His gaze passed over travelers and denizens of the city, flicked from cross street to cross street, hunted for narrower corridors, places where shadows pooled and he might be lost to prying eyes. Surely, if he could find a place to hide, he could hunt for an unassuming somebody. Then maybe he could dart in, take what he needed, and fade away without being noticed.

But there were too many watching him. Too many who looked on him with hate.

"I'm inclined to think they don't like us, Lura." he said.

"They've never seen us." she countered. "What do they have to dislike?"

He contemplated that. Something was off about them. It was as if they anticipated a poor interaction, as if they knew he and Lura had intentions for them they would not like. But then how could they? Certainly, they had done nothing but walk a straight line.

"Xirakura." he whispered. "He must have offended them."

"In what way? He sometimes lacks foresight, but he is not rude, or arrogant, or otherwise unkind. Who could hate him?"

"They hate us."

"You don't know that."

"Why else do they glare at us? He did something to offend them, and they now see us as the same."

"Are they wrong?" Lura grumbled. Her shoulders sagged. She turned onto a cross street mounting the hillside, and they marched. "At least we can lose some of their eyes. There will be fewer the further we get from their main road."

"Maybe we should find their elders." he suggested.

"If they have any. Those other tribes, the ones who send visitors...they aren't all governed by a circle, are they?"

"Some aren't governed at all." he said. "At least it looks that way. The Nixians have elders. The graemeins have something else, but it looks much the same. The Tak moran have chiefs. Who can say for the other tribes. We don't know them well. The Hanwari haven't sent anyone to us in generations."

"We have sent our people to them, haven't we?"

He shook his head. "I don't know. That's the business of Spirit Callers. Maybe Xirakura knows."

"Maybe."

They took another branching street. As Lura had predicted, the crowds had begun to thin on these higher slopes, leaving mostly locals behind. One woman, upon seeing them, took her young son by the shoulders and led him into their home. All the while she pushed him across their quaint lawn, she shot rude glances over her shoulder, directing them mostly at Katuwan.

"I don't like these people." he said.

"Then it will be easier to do what needs to be done." she said. "The sooner we are done with our business, the sooner we can get away from here."

They climbed higher on the slope, until they came almost to the city limits. It was not a long hike, but to arrive at this place from the road, they would have had to cross their village and return several times. These people took up far more space than they did, leaving behind little for their modest infrastructure, and even less for the natural world to encroach on their territory.

The fairy tired of the subtly rocking bouquet, and climbed his torso to a more stable perch on his shoulder. It rested its back against the side of his neck, closed its eyes, and went to sleep.

Ahead, he sighted another tree of the kind the fairy had come from. Pink irises peaked out from the hearts of white flowers, and dusty, yellow stamen poked out from their concave cores. He took helm, and guided Lura toward it.

The tree was situated within a circle of golden slabs. As they neared, he saw inscriptions across them in the same ancient tongue as had been burned across his husband's torso. Glyphs that climbed down each slab from its height to its foot, where broken ground obscured the bottom most portions. Winding through them on its way down from a well hidden spring within a craggy outcrop some way in the distance was a narrow stream. It wove between two of the unnatural structures before carving a path down toward the village.

He approached one of the constructs, examined it. It tapered toward a rounded tip, and the edges were corrugated, made to look like a feather. The others were of the same construction. Each made to look distinct from the other, but sharing in common the same motif. They rested at odd angles, as if they had been tussled out of order by a strong wind, but they were frozen in stasis.

The tree at their heart was hale and free of blight, and many fairies socialized among its branches. Babes yet to gain their petals peaked out from nests made of woven grass. In the lowest of those nests he spotted polished stones, probably taken from the narrow banks of the creek. He patted the fairy riding his shoulder on the leg, rousing him.

The fairy climbed to the edge of his its perch on hands and knees, dropped down to the crook of his elbow and swung round to get a better look at the tree and its tribe. Excitement flourished in those dulled, jewel eyes—eyes gone wide with palpable wonder. Katuwan came near to the tree. He snugged the bouquet into the crook of a branch, and pressed his free hand to the trunk. The fairy crawled down the length of his arm and clambered toward the bouquet, where a number of other fairies were amassing to take in the vibrant display, nuzzle the blooms and drink their nectar.

They laughed and chattered among themselves, some of them flashing appreciative looks at the newcomer.

Lura laced her arm around the small of his back and pulled him close.

"You've done well, husband." she said. "He is already so popular."

Behind them, the creek waters trickled. A loud rushing noise preceded a large fish breaking the surface.

Katuwan spun round to face it. Its mouth was wide set and its head flat. Its dorsal fin was a mass of rigid spines webbed together with kaleidoscopic flesh that seemed to shift its colors with every minute motion of its body. It reminded him of a catfish for its mud-brown body, the whiskers extruded from its flat face, but it was smaller than the catfish in Sufa Salein's forest, and no such creature bore such colorful fins.

"To see three of your kind in one day." he said, his voice guttural and deep. "You must be related." His gaze flitted from Katuwan past Lura to the tree, to the bouquet and the half dozen fairies gathered around it. "What kindness. The other was just so, too. Cursed, but not unpleasant. He followed the forms."

Tears for the Moon God

"It is our way." Katuwan said. "Where did he go?"

The fish contemplated him. "Away. In what direction, I do not know. Only that the lord of the city below cast him out. I cannot blame him. The spirit caller is tainted. Such curses sometimes spread, and his daughter was sick."

"He tried to heal someone?" Lura met Katuwan's gaze.

The spirit grunted. "He succeeded. For I was who made her sick, for toying in my headwaters. The penance was paid, and she is hale, but the father was not happy with your friend. He must be that, yes? And he sent him away."

"He is our husband." Lura said.

"Ah ha ha." the fish laughed. "A husband you hunt. He has abandoned you?"

"For our own benefit, so he believes." Katuwan said. "Thank you, spirit. You have set our hearts at ease."

"If only I believed you." the spirit said. "But here. Take this as payment for giving your wayward fairy a home. You have likely saved his life."

The waters parted. White froth churned against the creek's bank, and a pile of gold rose from the silts. The coins spilled over the bank, and the fish retreated. "For your kindness. It may not make up for your husband's affliction, but it is helpful, no?"

"Thank you." Katuwan said. "Your mercy is appreciated. May your waters always run clear."

"Ah, but that is precisely the problem, isn't it?" the spirit slid under the surface. "The waters must be murky at times, else they may never find clarity."

Its voice faded with it, and when it was gone, they knelt by his creek and collected his boon.

"No need to steal from them." Lura said. "When the spirits grant us their favor."

"Perhaps your prayer to Liandal guided us onto this path." Katuwan agreed.

"A mercy from the goddess, but I would rather she sent a tracker." she scraped the last of those coins out of the mud.

The Price of Healing

A psychosomatic itch crawled across Faez A'doelle's wrists. God Ao Nii awaited, and he did not value the sight of him. His condition was worsening by the day. The whispers spoke of a deepening rage smoldering in him, erratic behavior they hadn't seen in over a decade.

He rubbed at the numbers branded into them, identification for a slave that had escaped, a missing number in the grand procession of captured peoples in the mines at Dol Shakar.

He had done right in telling the Tulakka acolyte of the impending threat from Ao Nii against the world, but like all of those who had come to the god house in the last few years, he was woefully unprepared.

Am I ready?

Vitreous walls looked out on a star strewn sky, the moon a massive globe following the city across night darkness as God Gorgus lay chase from just over the horizon.

How long until he turns around? How long before we are all thrown into madness?

He remembered the last time. The South of Fang, Cham Emirate and the desert across its border were no place for kind people, but he had been his own man then. The slavers had faired worse than the Apostates of Flame, that was true, but no one had walked away from that conflict without their scars. The body could be healed, but the mind remembered every hurt it suffered, played those moments out on an endless loop to torment all of those who had witnessed the violence, the spilling forth of frenzied mobs from a staircase that should never have been there.

Even the children who had passed from the god house were not immune to that rage. Even those who had never claimed to be his acolyte. Just living in his presence for a time was enough. Just being in this place, this city in the sky, was enough kindling to light the bonfire in their souls.

Sweat slicked his palms, and he stuck them into the pockets of his robes, grinding salty fluid into fabric held tight in balled fists.

The children will have to be bound. Wood between the teeth to keep them biting off their tongues.

Tears for the Moon God

We should be calling on God Shakh to hide them, and God Uldal to take them away.

Will they answer if we ask for them? Will they even come to contest our god's descent?

He hoped they would. They were honor bound to save him from himself, weren't they? They had been there in the first days, when the great war was fought. They had known him before the madness, as no living mortal had.

He turned a corner, and came upon a vast, open doorway. Scarlet light emanated from it so thickly it was hard to make out what was beyond it. And he must go there, to witness himself how bad his god's condition had gotten. To witness, and hope he could still be dissuaded from this course. That it was not too late. Nothing good ever came from challenging God Gorgus. In this time of waxing, the sun god's power was potent, and God Ao Nii was waning. He hated to think what a contest between them would look like if the Great Arbiter moved against them, if he put his thumb on the scales, denied God Gorgus his power, denied all of those gods who were waxing in power in this world that was drunk with it.

Standing before that cavernous arch and to either side were the highest among their order.

Jule was clad in violently red robes, the color so much like fresh blood. The skirts, darkening as they traveled across his shins, swirled about his feet and across the tiled floor. He wore his stole, and a lace cap obscured his eyes and nose. Twin, silver chains hung from his hip, and he clutched a gaudy, ornamental halberd in his dominant hand.

Jule would lead the charge into the lands below. It was his duty as the Left Hand of Ao Nii.

Ordein was similarly robed, yet the lace trailing his cap was pinned in intricate folds so that his aquiline face was visible. Burn scars ran across his neck and the left half of his face, a mutilated eye socket looking into a dark void where a firemane cub had attacked him when he was young. The customs of the Tak moran had long struck Faez as barbaric. They yearned for Tak's flames, strove to command them, and were denied their great wish by the lord they would claim to serve. It was said the Apostates of the Flame originated with them, in defiance of the Rahad, calling back to legends of a spirit of fire who had reveled in the act of destruction, treated annihilation as an art. Their version of Tak the Fire was an abomination, and yet the very structure of their beliefs was what made Ordein an anomaly. Alone, it seemed, among his people, he embraced the Rahad message of peace, embraced a legend of the moon which spoke of a healer, a friend to mortals, and embraced a pacifism no one living across countless generations had known from their god.

When the night came, when God Uldal called his hunt and God Mu ended his watch over this city, the creature that dwelt just past that brutally red portal, the lace would come down. He would shield his face, stay back, and lead the effort to keep the children safe, to fend off any acolyte of their god who dared attack the keep.

Many would die, then.

Perhaps, Ordein's pacifism was not what it seemed. Perhaps pacifism was not even the right word for what he must do.

What is pacifism to a moonkin? When your leash is cut, Ordein, what does your

The Price of Healing

madness look like? Is it the suicidal abandon of the fallen ones, all clad in shrouds of gray mist and melancholy? Or do you lash out like the soldiers in Jule's camp?

More importantly, will you stand aside when our god rises to madness, or will you stand against him?

He paused outside the doorway, and bowed to each of them. "Highest."

"He is waiting." Jule boomed.

"How far has he fallen?" Faez directed his question at Ordein. One did not speak to the veiled while on his feet. Were Ordein elsewhere, he would have prostrated himself before Jule, would have crawled across the floor on hands and knees if he was not granted leave to stand.

"He endures." Ordein answered, his voice soft and lilting. "For now."

Faez bowed to him again. He marched past, and into the embrace of that red haze.

God Ao Nii was splayed across the floor tiles. Straight, obsidian locks which would be carried in the hands of two initiates were he to walk forth into the city were fanned about his crumpled form, and white robes which emanated their own, gray light were spread in the opposite direction. Wide sleeves were pushed up over thin, porcelain pale arms. Slender fingers played with a crystal chalice, pushing it this way and that as the god's black eyed gaze followed it despondently.

The god was a beautiful creature, pristine flesh containing a monstrous spirit. The red glow refused to alight on him, the color bleeding from him into everything it touched, making the walls sweat acrid tar.

He tried not to look at those walls, the way they seemed to melt, the way energy buffeted them, rending cracks and pockmarks into the crystal, compelling it to leak black carbon.

Only a god could exude such power as to make that crystal weep. Soon enough, his taint would spread beyond these walls, into the palace and then the city. When the day of judgment came, it would follow him into the world, to chew on the structures the poor, unsuspecting peoples in whatever land must host him had built.

He marched until he was inches from his god, until his heart might give out from sheer terror. And he sat.

And he waited.

"Bear into me the essence of your grief." The moon god said, stealing the words from him. "But I do not want to. In grief, there is memory. It is all I have left of him."

He pushed the chalice away. It was the only thing in the room not sweating tar.

"Have you known love, dear acolyte? Have you known the taste of it?"

"She is dead, master." Faez said.

"Then you know grief."

"I do."

"Has it left you?"

"No."

"I've forgotten his touch, yet the sound of his voice still haunts me. Were I to see his father, I would know one who understands. Were Echo to let me into his oasis, I would see again my friend."

"I know, master. I know."

"You do not." Ao Nii seethed.

Tears for the Moon God

"Give me your grief, master. Press it into my soul."

"So you can pass it to others. So they can know a pain they do not want. A pain they never asked for."

"Yes."

"Why?"

"It is my place."

"It is not." He pulled the chalice toward him.

"Tell me of him, then."

He pushed it away again. "What does this cup contain? Do you know?"

"I do not."

From the edge of his vision, he saw movement in the hall. An uncomfortable shift in the stances of both Ordein and Jule.

A chill ran through him, then. They knew what was in that chalice, didn't they? They had been gifted that knowledge. *How many others can say the same?*

He should be honored, yet he could only pity this unfathomable creature. This enigma, whose memory spanned so many generations, who had lived so long in this state.

"It was a gift, I think." Ao Nii said. "Though I cannot see it as such. Water from the River of Time, a gift from Lanfin. He made an offer of peace, after he took Hanuman the Elder. After my love was stolen from me."

He pushed the chalice toward him then, his gaze lifting from it to settle on Faez A'doelle's face. Fathomless, black eyes bored into his soul, and he held that gaze, wishing not to offend the god by shying away from him.

"Water once of the river, which settled into a pool the first time Lanfin pushed against it.

"To drink it would be to witness a great unfolding of the self, to invite into me part of the man it belonged to, and feel his embrace once more. But to drink it would leave me less than I am, some part of me torn away to make room for those pieces of him which linger there.

"And if I could find the pool. If I could wade into its waters, I would find myself in his presence, to live out memories of us once more, and I would come away with those memories, but still more of me would be lost. I would not be myself then. I would be something different. Something changed. Memory, my dear acolyte, is a poison. Even gods are not immune."

His god nudged it closer to him, into the crook between his folded legs.

Jule and Ordein emerged in the doorway, then, but at a warning look from Ao Nii, they halted.

They watched on from their vantage, and Jule had unveiled his face.

"You were taken when I challenged my great enemy. Soon, you must live through a second. But take this as my gift to you, Priest Faez A'doelle. Touch the water in this glass. With the tip of your finger, and only that."

Faez reached forth with his left hand, his dominant hand. Ao Nii turned pensive, but he made no move to stop him.

He reached forth, finger extended, beyond the rim of the chalice.

Behind him, Jule hefted his halberd, and Ordein knelt down in prayer.

He touched the water in the cup.

Laughter. He heard it in many voices. There was music, there, too, which was played on drums and pan flutes, a music without the cadence he associated with

The Price of Healing

song. It was crude, experimental, driven by emotion. The laughter became a part of it. He tasted something green and fresh on his tongue, smelled mountain air and tall grasses, and river water.

"What in..." he whispered.

Heat baked into his face and neck as if he was awash with fire. The laughter morphed into harsh screams, the music tumbling away into chaos. He flinched back, nearly knocking the chalice over.

God Ao Nii caught it around the stem. He dragged it back toward him.

"Lanfin does not give us gifts, warrior priest. He saw in me a weakness he would exploit. In those days, we divided ourselves into factions. He aligned with Gorgus and those other gods who wished for your destruction, and the Greatest Game, *our* game, was born.

"It is the concept of a war without fighting." Ao Nii said softly, for Faez alone to hear. "Waged through mortal proxies, the manipulation of spirits of the land, air and sea."

"But not fire?" Faez said absently. The chalice transfixed him. He could not look away from it.

Ao Nii shook his head. "No, never him. That argument is ended. Too much would be lost in betraying him."

A silence descended between them, then; and Faez turned his regard on the god. Fear gave way to curiosity. Pity to something rising toward understanding. His comprehension of the god was limited by his mortal perception of the world, the way it worked, but he thought he understood what drove God Ao Nii to turn on God Gorgus. A part of it, at least.

Take with you not my grief, for it is warm in that it is familiar."

"Then what would you give me in its place?"

Ao Nii offered him his left hand. Jule marched into the room then, and Ordein bowed his head.

Faez took the offered hand, pressed his fingers into the god's open palm. The tip of his index finger was still wet with time's waters.

"Know instead my fear."

The screams made sleeping difficult. They came from the next room over, where the Tului man slept. It was, he reflected, some irony that he ought to be holding up better than his neighbor. He had led a coddled life, largely sequestered within the royal palace at Tulaen. Even on the rare occasion he had been allowed an outing into the city with his brothers and sisters, they had been under guard, the streets cleared of ruffians and urchins before they were permitted to step free of their palanquins.

This city's beauty eclipsed that of his home, but it came as no comfort that it must. Where every room within this barracks came with expansive views seen through illusory, quartzite crystal, there was no scarcity with which to delineate the castes. He shared his view with the lowliest of paupers, and he suspected the halls within those houses and towers scattered across the city beyond were much the same. Where every view was magnificent, each became mundane. There was nothing to be possessed here which did not belong to everyone else, nothing which differentiated him from the rabble.

Is this Ao Nii's design? Are we meant to be eternally equal in his eyes?

Tears for the Moon God

No, I think not. If we must be so, why bother with classes of soldiers, with ranks among his charges? Why bother differentiating between acolyte and initiate. If we are all deemed equal, what point is there in that? The best of us would be treated like anyone else, wouldn't we? But I've seen no evidence of this. Nothing at all to indicate his God House is a place without royalty.

The screams persisted. He was growing tired of them. The palace at Tulaen was no stranger to humanity's impulses. Always, there was chatter in the halls, even in the waning hours, when night wound down in impending darkness, awaiting the dawn. Always, there was work to be done. Servants poured into the palace under the charge of their masters and mistresses, spread across the halls, infested vacant rooms armed with wash buckets, mops and sponges. Yes, there was ambient noise within the palace. There was laughter, singing, conversation to be had, but the walls between rooms were of stone, the antechambers of important apartments set behind heavy doors which restricted the noise to their confines, the bedchambers far enough removed as to be shrouded always in silence.

In all of his years, he had never considered how noisy those common dwellings, inns and houses, must be. How little defense they truly had against the human voice, the bray and low of livestock, the clack of wheels against flagstones.

He could deal with those cries throughout the night, and for however many nights until they ceased. He could cope, but he did not want to. And he was not in the habit of allowing others to dictate to him what he must endure, whether explicitly or accidentally.

He climbed out of his bed. Cold tiles pressed against bare feet as he pranced more than walked to the door. He kept the sheet wrapped around his shoulders, secured around his waist. It would not do to be near naked in the presence of this foreign commoner, but he would not do more to dress himself, lest he lose some of what remained of his lethargy, struggle after this needed confrontation to return to sleep.

He twisted the knob. Much to his surprise, it was unlocked. He passed into the hall, veered left and tried the knob of the next room. It gave, just as his had.

That's appalling. If anyone with a mind to could open this man's door, the same must be true of his. A confrontation may well be forthcoming if he did not act promptly, find a satisfactory means of barring his door. He would need to wake earlier, to remove it before his handler arrived to retrieve him, but wouldn't that show some strength of character? Would it not be wise to present himself as if he was ready for him, dressed and alert and waiting, when he arrived?

He passed into the room, found it a mirror of his chambers. The bed was situated against the opposite wall. A wardrobe peered out of a shadow near the far wall, and there was a stunning view of the city to match his.

Truly, where there is no scarcity, there can be no artistry. What kind of god would allow such an oversight?

The Tului's back was arched, his shoulders and thighs pressed into the mattress beneath him. The sheets were a twisted mass enshrining his legs, leaving his chest and arms exposed, and the duvet was a rumpled mass cast onto the floor near his feet. He wore a rictus of pain, and aggressive, scarlet light flickered in his dark eyes.

He cried out as Ibrim approached him. He gnashed his teeth together, and Ibrim shook him by his shoulder.

The Price of Healing

"Hey! Could you keep it down? I'm trying to sleep."

Scarlet eyes fixed on him, welling with unspilled tears. The rictus yielded, yet his teeth remained gnashed together, cheeks bulging with the effort of fighting off what had afflicted him. He fixed that scarlet eyed gaze on Ibrim, exhaled through his nose, unclamped his jaw. It looked as if it took some effort.

"Leave." he whispered.

"I'm sorry?" Ibrim said, but he released his grip on the man's shoulder, took a step back.

"You shouldn't be here."

"I would be inclined to agree, but as it were, you are being quite loud and I must insist you try to find a solution to that...well, that problem. It's annoying."

The Tului's teeth came together, then, catching the edge of his lip, drawing blood. A scream welled up in his throat.

"You see, that really is rude. I must insist you—"

"AAAAAAH!" Tears weltered over his cheeks then, spilling forth from eyes wide with bewilderment. Whatever battle he fought, it seemed he was losing. And in losing, he denied Ibrim whatever peace he might have gained from this errand, had it gone another way.

It would come to this.

He approached the bed again, seated himself at its edge. He took the poor man's head in his hands, fingers caressing his cheek, pushing onyx locks out of his face. The Tului looked up at him, a startled doe, and he met that gaze with a compassion he did not feel. There were times when a ruler must feign sympathy, even as he saw no reason it should be needed. They had both been subjected to the poison of Ao Nii's madness, had they not? And this man, with his harder life, with whatever lay in his past, ought to be made out of stronger stuff than this. Why was he wallowing? Why was he not able to contain himself?

There again is that irony. If I can weather this, should he not be able to?

"There, there now. I'm sorry, friend. I truly am. I had assumed...well, it doesn't matter now, does it? You are in pain. I see that. Is there anything I can—"

The Tului's mouth opened. His head twisted into Ibrim's wrist, teeth clamping down on his forearm.

"OUCH!" Ibrim smacked him. "Are you *insane!*" He beat at him, shook his arm, trying to free it of the Tului's jaws, but the bastard held on, and sucked.

Seconds ran by with the Tului clinging to his forearm, seconds of him beating him over his head, across his body, wrenching his arm away with increasing force.

The Tului released him. He tumbled backward. His back slammed against the far wall, knocking the wind from his lungs. For what seemed like too long, he was left there, the drumbeat of his heart filling his ears, blood leaking from the bite wound on his forearm.

And then the Tului was on him, caressing him, teasing his limp arm away from his lap where it rested. He examined the wound, traced lines with his fore and middle fingers across it, and the wound closed.

"I'm sorry. I didn't mean...it doesn't matter what I meant, it's done. But don't worry, okay. You're not going to turn into...well, you have God Ao Nii's protection. My king can't affect you."

"Wh-what did you *do* to me? What did you do to me?" Ibrim demanded. He shut his mouth before anything more could come out.

Tears for the Moon God

Sitting there against the wall of a room he had no business being in, yelling at a man who had moments before been in the throes of a pain he could not comprehend; he sounded like a crazy person. Had sounded raving mad even before the man bit him, and could he have expected any different? The man was compromised. What defense did he really have at his disposal except to bite him?

He had known he was the aggressor in this situation even before he had left his own rooms, but he had been that before. Had been that with his own charges more times than he could count, but no one had ever had the nerve...no, the *gaul* to attack him!

The outrage! To attack a sitting prince of Tulakh!

But the look in that man's eyes—regret, shame, something very like fear—left a sour taste in his mouth. The Tului placed on display all of the compassion he had been denied, and did so without any need for cajoling.

Guilt thrashed through Ibrim. He pressed himself against the wall, hoping irrationally that he might simply fuse with it and vanish from this appallingly indecent scene. And all that it implied.

"I really am sorry. I never wanted this. I guess...I guess that's why I'm here, isn't it? People like me...we don't leave Tuluis Fel much. For the protection of others, really. And I suppose because there are no roads. The king doesn't much like the God of Ways, you see...well, I suppose that's neither here nor there. I didn't want to leave, but I had to. Because...because I knew if I could find this place I'd be cured."

"C-cured? What plague have you infested me with?" Ibrim suddenly felt nauseous. In his mind's eye were the impressions of disease, and he ran through a litany of illnesses known to him because of it. Only some of them had ever impacted the Tulakka people.

The Tului arched an eyebrow. "You don't listen well, do you? You won't be afflicted by the poison I carry. Ao Nii's influence will have seen to that. But it's not as easy for me. I've been in Tuluis Fel's embrace too long. I've been afflicted by this curse very nearly since I was born. Escaping it has taken months, and may well take months beyond this night. Do you understand?" His gaze flicked to the vitreous wall and its view of the city, of the perpetual night sky. "Of course not. You've probably never even heard of a Blood Lord...let alone a Scarlet Baron."

Weakly, Ibrim shook his head. "If you'll allow it, I'd like to return to my room. This talk of curses and illnesses is bad for my constitution."

The Tului grimaced. "You must be nobility. Nobody but that sort ever talks about their constitution. I suppose nobody other than them would think it appropriate to barge into someone else's sleeping chambers."

"Royalty, actually."

"Indeed." his lips formed a thin line, his gaze growing detached. "Thank you for feeding me. I was starving. Now, best you were off to bed, don't you think? I'm feeling much better now. We should both take this as a positive, in particular as I was able to stop myself from bleeding you dry."

"I-I'm sorry, wh-what did you say?"

"It doesn't matter now. You need sleep. A bite to eat in the morning. You'll need your strength before this is over. But before you go...for my peace of mind...what is your name?"

Ibrim hesitated. What harm could there be, truly, in revealing his name to this

The Price of Healing

man? He had already done all the harm he was going to do, both physically and psychologically. What else could he truly do to him? But he was reluctant nonetheless. To give him his name was to establish a sense of familiarity. And with that familiarity, it was quite likely this creature would accost him again, when he was once more vulnerable. He could hardly allow that, could he?

He relented.

"It's Ibrim. Ibrim Alghoul." he said, and added as if it were an afterthought, even as it was delivered mechanically after all of those years of reminding people of his own station, power and influence, whether they asked for it or not. "Third prince of Tulakh. Fifth in line for the throne. If my sisters get their affairs in order, that is."

Were he not so terrified of this creature, he might have smiled. He usually did with the delivery of that last line.

Oh, Hassan or Abbelard might take the throne, but Samara? Nimira? They had no interest. Or if they did, they lacked any of the power their elder brothers exuded, and much of the influence besides. Yes, Samara was an exquisite combatant and Nimira was better read than any of them, but both well knew their father did not view them as contenders for the throne, any more than he viewed Ibrim, the youngest of his siblings, as a prospect.

Nonetheless, it paid when playing games of politics with stubborn nobles to remind them of his station. To insist on it.

But here, in the God House of the Moon, in Ao Nii's God House, such titles were meaningless. Such games may well be pointless, insofar as he did not know their rules. Why did he insist on approaching this man, with all of his sorrow, his compassion, his good nature, with such pomposity, this vapid disregard for their shared status? In a month's time, they would both go mad, and it would be a madness uncharacteristic of the moon god, which would drive even his most accomplished acolytes into a frenzy. Against that, what was it to be a prince? Did his title, his blooding, matter? He was only human.

So, too, the man before him was just human.

The Tului chuckled lightheartedly. "Do you always insist on your own importance this much?"

He did not answer.

The Tului shrugged. "My name is Lufir al Suen. You can call me Suen. Listen, come back any day, but never at night. You understand? The moon's pull on a Tului breeds in us a thirst, and I'd rather you not tempt me. I am in weaning. It isn't as bad in the day, when everyone is active, but then God Ao Nii sleeps. Now...well, in the future, it's really best if you just bear it, even if it is a nuisance. I don't mean to bother you, Mr. Alghoul, but it really can't be helped.

"Speaking of which..."

He drew away from Ibrim, moved on his wardrobe and prized open the doors. From inside, he liberated something, a bulb of some kind which looked midnight black in the gloom. He bit into it.

"What is that?" Ibrim asked, his curiosity winning out over his anxiety.

"Hibiscus. A calyx. The flowers don't work as well." He noticed Ibrim's confusion and elaborated. "They're outlawed in Tuluis Fel. It's part of the weaning. I guess you could call it an antidote of sorts, but it doesn't work right away. My handler managed to get some from the Rahad some time ago, and he's been trading

Tears for the Moon God

with them every full moon since then.”

“H-how many?”

“How many have I been through?” Seun munched on the calyx, looking askance at the ceiling. “Four. No, five. They say it’ll be another seven before I’m fully healed.”

“A year to escape your curse. And here I am believing my pursuit is noble.” Ibrim breathed.

He climbed to his feet, approached the exit. It was still ajar from when he arrived, certain sign there were no guards present in these halls. Perhaps they believed a culling of sorts would take place among them, that the strong or the savvy would survive while all others were purged, as the madness, the grief they were compelled to experience grew, and grew, until the full moon...*the eclipse, damn you*...arrived.

“You’ll come back, won’t you? I promise I won’t bite you again.”

“I-I’ll think about it.” he hurried past the door, back to his rooms. He climbed into his bed but sleep evaded him. Suen remained on his mind, taunting him with his good candor, his cursed hunger.

Duijus Kanh

"What happened in that cave?" Sarri asked.

Tamlin sat near the flames at the heart of the Chief's Pavillion. Present with him was Chakta, wrapped to the chin as he was in a buffalo skin blanket. Her gaze fell on the flame. She had been there as he had, had seen what he had. Countless monsters surging forth, choking off light at the end of the cave. Flows of thinned blood clouding Arrak's waters, thunderous crashes, the sizzle and flash of lightning coruscating on waves, flickering out to strike down enemies one after another, and yet still they came. Shaki could not hold them back. Neither could his father. Neither could Tamlin or Chakta, and the clan chiefs, the others, were not coming for them.

They might have died there. *We could have died there. Should have, but he saved us.*

He recalled the behemoth figure come forth with his Swans. A figure half in shadow, the skin of a wolf or a bear draped over his back. He recalled those cold eyes, eyes that had never known warmth, winter's bite held in amber pools. Eyes that settled on him and then moved off. Recalled the naked forms of three women, not quite human, savaging the rank and file of their assailants, their adversaries.

We should have died.

He looked up into his father's eyes. Arrak's jaw was set, but there was that piece of him hiding behind the stalwart facade, the piece which grieved. They had lost so much so quickly, so much they could never get back. He had almost lost his son this night.

Tamlin had come out of that cave a man or something like one. His transition should have been something to celebrate, yet it was a tainted victory, something which had seen him exposed to such horrors as the old man would not have inflicted so soon upon his son. Blood shed in raiding season was a different animal, its own monster but one expected, which the Gil Garo must come to know eventually.

But he had seen his own horrors in the night, before the last of the Tului fled. His kin cut down, to revive themselves, to fight for the enemy against their blood. One could not witness such a nightmare and remain the same. He had come out of

Tears for the Moon God

the night changed, knew that his son was the same, and saw it in him.

Tamlin saw in that steady gaze, in the hard set of his father's jaw, the grief driven down deep into him, saw defiance in his father. This was what a true leader was, one who held his burden close to his chest, explored its contours when he could finally be alone. He must exude strength, even here, even among those who had lost so much.

And his loss was not small. A wife. For Tamlin himself, a mother. Gone, and the hollow left in her absence not yet filled. He was not sure how to feel about his mother's passing. He was not sure how to feel anything at all.

Gulang was a stone, but he had lost his middle son in the night. When night fell again, he would, together with his wife and remaining children, dig a grave for Karsa. They would do their grieving then, but not now. Not while duty held he must be strong.

He was close to breaking.

These stories were whispered across the camps, had been spoken to Tamlin by the very man who now interrogated him, and did so because it was the necessary thing to do. The chiefs must know what happened in that cave, to inform their plans for the future. Was it safe to remain in Gil Garo for the winter? Must they strike camp and move? Would Duijus Kanh protect them now the forbidden kingdom was involved?

But he *had* protected them. Together with his Swans. Had surfaced in that cave, come out of his hiding place in the bowels of the earth and defended them.

And he had been furious.

"That rage." Tamlin whispered. His gaze shifted away from Chakta, found Ungol Safar by accident. He flinched away.

Ungol had lost his own son. Twice now, he had lost that son. What must it have been like to have his most secret hope, his most sacred dream realized...to have his heart broken again.

"Who's rage?" Coltang asked.

Tamlin found the chief's gaze, yet it was Ungol who remained on his mind. He had been wrong about Dupec Safar, had been wrong to call him an outsider, to disparage him the way he did. That he was allowed to enter the cave of Duijus Kanh had been purely the consequence of Dupec throwing their fight. He had been entirely at the other man's mercy, his every defense ripped away, defanged and declawed and bound and stolen away from his magic as he had been. There had been no path to victory for him except by Dupec's forfeiture, and he felt like a fraud. Even as he grieved for his fallen kin, even as he remained there for far too long in silence, he knew himself for a fraud, and a coward.

He had been afraid when the Tului came for them. Had been ready to run. He would not have stood and fought against them if not for Chakta, would have folded, succumbed to their poison. Would have done so well before Arrak had arrived to relieve them.

"Who, Tamlin!"

"Duijus...Duijus Kanh." Chakta said. "He came...with his Swans. They drove the enemy back. Laid slaughter." Tamlin's gaze fell on her as she grappled with the words, the hard truths hidden within them. "His rage was...palpable. Anger for Tuluis Fel. He called him..." she swallowed hard. "...called him his cousin. And then he stole Dupec from us, and carried him back into the cave. And the Swans left with him."

"Was he alive?" Ungol interjected, meeting first Chakta's, and then Tamlin's eyes.

An answer passed in silence between them.

He nodded. "Thank you."

"Dupec Safar lives?" Coltang said.

"He was their target." Gulang said. "Who else could be? We have no fight with Tuluis Fel. Never have. Then he arrives and they are on our doorstep, shedding our blood, stabbing us in the back!"

"For them to do so would imply we were allies to them. We were not." Sauman said.

"Careful now, Sauman. You're starting to make sense." Sarri grumbled. "They have made an enemy of us. What they have done is tantamount to a declaration of war. The question we must answer is how do we proceed?"

"There is the matter of Dupec Safar to consider, as well."

"He had a visitor in the night. He would not say who." Chakta said. "Before the tournament. There was water on the floor of his rooms, a lantern. He said...said someone was going to attack us. He didn't say how he knew. Not exactly. But there was someone there. Someone who must have told him something and if we would have listened...oh, spirits, if we would have just listened to him."

"Who else knows about this?" Gulang asked.

"Watch your tone, Gulang." Coltang spat, all of his daughter's protector.

Gulang ignored him.

"Shaki. He was the only other one who was there. And Sauman. We told him something had happened."

The other chiefs looked to Sauman, who shrugged. "They told me there had been an intruder. That is all they said. When I went to look in on Dupec, what they had described was gone. The boot prints had been scored away, if they ever were. The lantern was back in its customary place. The bed was not wet, either. I told them it had been handled, and sent them back to bed."

Chakta nodded at this. "He did that. We obeyed."

"Retrieve my son, Sauman." Sarri said without looking at him.

"Do not presume to--"

"You were warned of a disturbance and you failed to act. What worth is a leader who treads without caution in the face of such adversity. You should have informed the rest of us of this."

"There was nothing there to support their claims!"

"Be that as it may, we would have known. Such losses of life as we have endured may not have been necessary, if you had stepped out of our way."

Sauman vaulted to his feet. He marched on Sarri.

A casual flick of the wrist from Coltang. Sauman crashed to his knees, the effort of staying upright an obvious burden.

"Whatever insult you perceive, Sauman, you will not bring violence into this chamber." He said. "We handle our disagreements with words. We do not fight among ourselves, lest our clans engender blood feud."

"Fuck you!" Sauman hissed.

Another languid flick of the wrist from him. "Find his son. I am sure I'm not the only one who would have a word with him."

Tears for the Moon God

Sauman rose. Glaring at Sarri, he marched from the pavilion.

"Whether we were informed of it or not, the attack has happened." Gulang intoned when he had gone. "Tuluis Fel has made clear they see in us an enemy worth exterminating. We cannot allow them to succeed. If the question of Dupec Safar remains up for discussion, we must make a decision concerning him now."

"As well a decision about how to engage with the Tului." Arrak stroked his chin, his gaze for Chakta. "You said Duijus Kanh referred to Tuluis Fel as he and not it, implying he perceives the name to fit a person, and not a place. But we have only ever known Tuluis Fel, the nation."

"In the annals, our oldest records of history, are references to Tuluis Fel which refer to him and them interchangeably. Those of us who have studied them believed this to be a quirk of our language, since withdrawn from the lexicon we use in modern times." Ungol explained.

"Has Gandes Fae any knowledge of this?" Gulang asked.

Ungol closed his eyes. In the gloom behind him, his mol fae whined. The infantile cry made ice of Tamlin's blood. As a child, he had been terrified of that creature. He had never completely grown past it.

His eyes sprang open, and they were onyx black to their corners, matte, as if he had no eyes at all.

"Dark spirits abound." Ungol's voice was hoarse and deep, guttural in a way it never was. Sarri scooted away from him on the bench, and it did not seem the action was entirely conscious.

"What is he--"

"Quiet." Arrak gestured for his silence. Coltang regarded his daughter, pressed a finger to his lips.

"What sacrifice might you make?" Ungol demanded in that glottal baritone. "Pursuant to the answers you seek?"

Knives drawn by Coltang, Gulang, Sarri, and Arrak. Sauman returned with Shaki in his shadow, in time to see all five remaining chiefs with blades drawn and ready. He froze in the doorway, the tarp draped over his forearm.

"Come, Sauman. It's time you earned your keep." Sarri said.

"You three, as well." Gulang added. "Truth, we would not normally engender Gandes Fae, but we will abide his toll in this. You will be needed."

The mol fae shook away its swaddling in a dull rumple of cloth. It climbed over the bench, into the no man's land between Ungol in his trance, and the fire.

Blades flashed. Coltang and Arrak approached the beast, blood running thick across their forearms from thin cuts to the flesh. They held their wrists to the beast, allowed it to drink, and retracted their arms when it had taken what they were comfortable with giving. They busied themselves wrapping the wounds in strips of cloth taken from a bin behind one of those benches, staunched the flow of blood, and then approached their children. Sarri emulated them, gave the mol fae the blood which was Gandes Fae's price. He intercepted Shaki, who flinched away from him.

"What's going on?" he asked, his voice quavering.

"Do you trust me, son?" Sarri reached out, took his son around the forearm and drew him toward the mol fae. A flash of steel as they approached, and Sarri held his son's arm out for the mol fae to drink. A line of hot fire thrashed against Tamlin's flesh, and then Arrak was drawing him to the creature, and its hairy mandibles

Duijus Kanh

closed on his arm, tickling him as it fed.

His father drew his arm away. He traced the contours of the wound with cold fingers, drawing on his mentor's power, and the wound knit itself shut.

Sauman gave his token last, and reluctantly. "What is the meaning of this." he said, a knife poised in one hand, the blood not yet flowing.

"The spirit Gandes Fae has answers to all manner of questions. His memory is as long as his life, and he was among the first spirits to walk this world. Chief Ungol is his acolyte, and capable of inviting his spirit into him, as he does now. Gandes Fae has asked blood price against the answers we seek, and that demand encompasses all of us." Sarri explained. "Grant him your blood, or leave. He will not be heard by someone who will not pay the price."

Sauman growled something under his breath. He slashed open his wrist, and fed the beast, his gaze set against the flaccid, child's face—its eyes and mouth misshapen voids set in maggot pale skin. He retracted his arm sharply, and the creature subsided into a mollified crooning, preening its mandibles with grizzly forelegs.

"The toll is paid, spirit." Gulang intoned.

"You wish to know of my cousin?" Ungol said.

"Your cousin?" Gulang asked.

"We are all cousins, all born of the same blood, child of the river." Ungol said. "Tuluis Fel, who would have you believe he is not a creature but a place. He is a spirit, like Duijus Kanh with whom your people consort, like myself. An old hand in the games of our adversaries, and he does not act alone.

"Ungol was warned. Take up this path, and he will have his son, but that son will bring about a doom upon your people, upon all of those who inhabit the land. So, too, he did once, and will again. Tuluis Fel is the beginning. Heed me, do not bring your war to them. It can only end in your ruin."

"Why, Lord Gandes Fae?" Gulang demanded. "They have attacked us. We cannot do nothing."

"You must! The Elders have a hand in your affairs. To go to this enemy is to play into the hands of the unseen enemy. Do not rise to the bait."

An uncomfortable silence fell over the chiefs as they contemplated the spirit's warning.

"A last question, Gandes Fae."

"The toll demands as much."

"How do we proceed?"

Depthless, black eyes regarded Tamlin, Chakta, Shaki. "Leave them to await him. March on Tuluis Fel if you must, but do not enter their lands until the blood moon has risen. Then, you will know a path to victory, and only then. But Dupec Safar must not join you. He will be needed elsewhere."

"Where?"

"He will know. He has always known." Ungol's eyes slid closed. They fluttered back open, the depthless black gone and replaced with a more human umber, which retreated into his irises, and remained there.

"What did he say?" Ungol asked.

"We march on Tuluis Fel. Whatever the spirit may believe, it is imperative they answer for what they have done. We need only wait for the blood moon. Then the way will be clear." Arrak explained.

Tears for the Moon God

"A bad omen." Gulang added. "No good can come of being out in the open on a blood moon night. Ao Nii's madness will infest the lands, as will his acolytes."

"There will be a fight, then, before the steps, should they appear in those lands. Blood shed all around." Sarri agreed.

"He insisted we leave our children behind. These three. To await the return of your son."

Ungol's relief was apparent. "Then Dupec will be okay. He will return to us."

"He will do that, but we cannot invite him into the conflict to come, lest we doom ourselves. So says your master." Gulang said.

Melancholy was etched into Ungol's features. "It will be done. We will abide the warning. We must."

"You want us to stay here...alone?" Shaki demanded of them, suddenly fearful. "Here! Where the Swans could kill us at any moment?"

"Fah!" Coltang waved away his words like a bad odor. "The Swans won't kill you. They only take the sick and those too old to survive the harsh winters here. They won't be bothered with three young people in perfect health."

"What if one of us falls ill?"

"Chakta can heal. What sickness might you have that she can't do away with?"

"We'll be alone, then? Through the winter?" Chakta asked.

"I think, yes." Coltang replied solemnly. "We will leave you with this pavilion for shelter, food to last and plenty of wood to burn. You will be fine, daughter. You are strong enough."

"Then it's settled. We bring word to our people on the morrow, and march in three days."

"When is the next blood moon?" Sauman asked.

It was Tursa who replied. "In twenty-two days."

"A hard march through snow, then." Sauman said.

"There are those among our tribes who can clear the path. Our horses will not break their ankles for our carelessness." Gulang responded.

"We are agreed?" Sarri asked.

Several nods.

Gulang looked to the three children. "We break camp in three days. You three are dismissed."

"Hold!" Ungol raised his hand in protest. "There is one more matter to address before all of that."

"Ah, your son's visitor." Gulang said.

"Indeed." Ungol agreed. "About that. Did Dupec tell you anything about him? What he said to him, perhaps. Or what he looked like."

"He didn't tell me anything, no." Shaki avoided the clan chief's eyes, rubbed the back of his neck. His grimace almost resembled a smile, but that was his way. Ever to meet nerves with laughter, to make light of what he knew to be serious. "He did seem put off, though. You could see it in his eyes. Almost like whoever visited him was a long lost friend, but there was something off about the whole thing. Maybe it was a friend who visited him, but if that was the case, it was almost like he didn't know him. Does that make sense?"

"No, it doesn't." Gulang said.

But Ungol had turned pensive. "Time's river has many branches. So, too, death's embrace does not belong to one creature. It is the domain of many spirits, and one

Duijus Kanh

god. It could be he was visited by a ghost of some kind. God Shah Jagat is said to, at times, allow the dead to visit upon the living. In some cultures, this is the common held belief."

"You think a ghost visited your son?" Shaki asked, oblivious to the temperature in the room.

Tamlin was shaking his head. "Ghosts have no need of boots. Chakta said there were footprints left behind."

"There are matters we all must attend to with our people. Time we got on with it." Gulang clapped his hands together. He was the first to rise.

"Go now, children. And prepare yourselves for a long winter. You will be each other's comfort in our absence."

Tamlin, Shaki and Chakta rose, and removed themselves from the pavilion.

With them gone, Gulang spread his regard for the other chiefs. "You all heard that bit about the gods interfering in our affairs."

Ungol shook his head. "Bad omens everywhere."

"Indeed." Arrak agreed.

Dupec awoke, a harsh ache ripping through his head, making his vision blur and waver. He blinked the distortion away, pushed himself upright.

The cave loomed around him, lit by the light of a lone lantern which left its walls in obscurity. It was warmer than the outside world, devoid of the touch of the winds and the freeze the Goddess of Storms bled into it. The warmth did not rise to the level of true comfort, but it was there, a consistent lightening of the winter's chill, ambivalent to the passing of the seasons.

A horde of treasures climbed from the lantern's feet up one wall, a hill of gold and silver atop which a beast or a man who resembled one lounged. Three, pallid women sat in plain sight near enough its base, all of them naked. They were of disparate height, their features nearly human but missing the mark by degrees. The tallest looked to have been extruded from softened wax, pulled into shape so that her limbs and neck were elongated, her hands and face wide, feet long and wrinkled. The middle sister was the most human. A moon round face, buxom figure; she might have been called beautiful if not for the reptilian scales surrounding her eyes, crossing her cheekbones. The shortest was toad-like in her proportions, wrinkled. Her mouth had a wide set to it, thin-lipped where her sister's were full and pouty.

The beast atop the mound stirred, sat upright, and they turned adoring gazes onto him.

The Swans, they could only be that, watched him resettle himself, and Dupec took their measure, and his.

"He awakes." Meichekh said. "Dearest, won't you look at him?"

"As innocent and pretty as the day we first met him, don't you think?" Duichekh added, turning her wide eyes on him.

"To have that boy again. Living flesh and bone as if he was not near thirty years the senior last we laid eyes on him." Kachekh said.

"Oh, but he was mad then, wasn't he?" Meichekh smiled. "Ready to dash the gods all of them with a bludgeon until they bled, and no one could talk him out of it."

"What is all of this talk about?" Dupec said. "I've never met any of you. How did

Tears for the Moon God

I get here?"

"In time. All in good time." Kachekh waved his comment away.

"You come before me with none of the protections my compact with your people entitle you to." Duijus Kanh growled. "Come not for my tutelage, but to save your kin. No name etched into my wall, and no need. For it was done once already, and there is no fear in your heart."

"None for a spirit. Nor for any god." Kachekh said.

His gaze on her was withering. She shut her mouth, and returned an impatient glare.

"This life is not the first you've lived, but you know that, don't you?" Meichekh said. "The uelfin's song was heard by many, but you were visited in the flesh by him who knew you.

"To what end, do you suppose?"

"I know to what end." Dupec said, but his words rang hollow to him.

Bloodlines for me to lead. Kin to set free, or so that stranger would have it. But why? Why choose me at all, when the world is so vast and others might suit this cause better? Why pursue this course, when it can only lead to my death.

Duijus Kanh nodded, then, seeing what Dupec would hide. His uncertainty. His confusion. The longing he had felt in that stranger's presence.

"He is not the first of his kind." Duijus Kanh went on, gesturing airily. "Though, to have it his way, he would be the last. To you, he was both lover and betrayer, but in his pursuit, he would have finished you. As you were, the world could only have benefited from your annihilation. As you are now, perhaps there is hope."

"He was my betrayer?"

Duijus Kanh held up two fingers. "Twice. First by accident, the offence the killing of your father. A sword whose power breaks bonds, which broke that which existed between Ungol Safar and Gandes Fae." he put one finger down. "The second was far more intentional. To stop you from doing what could never be undone, he took from the city of Ur a handful of powerful acolytes and sought to murder you in the night."

"He loved you." Meichekh said. "Perhaps he stayed his hand for that reason alone. He loved you, but hated the man you had become. To be perfectly clear, I had come to hate that man, too."

"Then you are telling me I deserved to die? If so, why do I still live? Why is he dead and I alive?"

The swans all shook their heads.

"He is not dead." Duichekh said. "To kill him would leave your legacies intact. He is immured, his history erased from the principle flow of time's stream, and your lives reset." She tapped her temple. "But we remember, for we are older than him. Older than the God of Music, and he has no bearing on our souls."

"You were not taken because his sin was greater than yours, dear boy." Kachekh said. "Yes, you turned your wrath upon the gods, but you are not the first mortal to have done, nor are you the most successful."

"There was that boy Rein took on, wasn't there?" Duichekh said.

"Yes, and there was the one Katcya raised." Meichekh added.

"Brothers, weren't they?" Duichekh said. "One murdered by a god. Oh, who did him in? Fang Ilra? Or maybe...maybe Shemin Sein. Ever mercurial, those elders."

"Kachekh waved her off. "The point is Sao succeeded in doing what they could

Duijus Kanh

not. The others were either too short sighted or too burdened by other, worldly desires to be much use. You were spared, because the gods saw use in you, the shape of which is known only to them. Sao Njack was taken because he dared to create a true race of the katcyakin, and no god nor any spirit has power enough to change it."

"He is trapped within the Halls of Time because his actions made of mortal kind a force equal to the power of the gods. Of this realm, anyway. And should they begin to wane, it will be that for the first time in many thousands of years, they are met with a true challenge to their power."

"And you want this?" Dupec said.

"I am undecided." Duijus Kanh answered. "A threat to them is a threat to us, but your kind and ours have formed a...symbiosis of sorts. What is known is that your life as my wolf began with the attack of Tuluis Fel, in this life and the old one. With Tuluis Fel you were forged into something the spirits and the gods alike treated with caution, and with Tuluis Fel, you will come to draw their attention once more.

"Do you lead the Gil Garo against them?"

"My people barely accept me. They would never follow me into war." Dupec said. "Besides, I have no desire to be thrust under the gazes of a host of maligned gods."

"What they have done before, they can again." Duijus Kanh said. "They will wait for you. You'll see."

"I see the questions within you," Duichekh intoned, leaning forward to get a better look at him. Her black eyes widened, eyebrows rising precipitously. "You believe our claims false. Some of them.

"Perhaps it is that Rein never took on an acolyte? But I would say to this, not in your time. In another, since walled off, time's current forced to follow a branching stream, he did."

"Came to regret it, too." Kachekh cut in.

"The evidence of him remains, even as the man himself was expunged. It is in the presence of counterfeit swords, made with near the same quality the mountain spirit himself imbues into his famed weapons. There is evidence of him in this world." Duichekh continued. "Perhaps, it is the claim that Katcya raised a child. The very existence of those hallowed halls, Lanfin's own labyrinth, is evidence enough of that. Brothers, the younger taken—"

"Enough." Duijus Kanh growled. "I will not have you call to the moon in my presence. Not even for this boy's sake. If he must know the story of Heiman the Younger, it will not be where I can hear."

The Swans flinched.

"As you say, love. I am sorry." Duichekh said.

"Whether my doubts remain with me is of no concern to you." Dupec said. "What matters now is where we go from here. You wish to teach me your ways, that I may become your sword against a hated enemy. My question is this. What do I get in return?"

Duijus Kanh's laugh was a poison. There was, at the same time, a genuine sense of bemusement in his booming cackle, and the hint that something darker lay beneath, waiting to claw its way to the surface.

"What is it you desire?" he asked.

"We can discuss that later." Dupec said.

Tears for the Moon God

"That we will." amber eyes flicked to Kachekh, who stood at the base of the mountain of gold.

She approached him. "You'll be mine first, then. A strong defense is key to your survival." She took him by the wrist, helped him to his feet. There was a surprising strength in her grip as she lifted him, an ease with which she handled his weight. He suspected that if it came to it, she could have dragged him from this cave without effort.

He followed her away.

Departures

Kuuda looked upon his father. He remembered him as he had been when he was a younger man. In those days, the attackers come in the night would not have bested him, would never have dragged him off his horse. His father had been a proud man then, quick to anger. He seemed so at peace now, wrapped in the rabbit fur blanket Alaar had provided.

His sister had always been the better of the two at caring for others, at nurturing them. She had taken after their father, much more than he ever had. He saw Tursa Hawkeye in the bluntness of her features as she reclined against a scattering of pillows the far side of this mud hut. Saw, too, the same tiredness, the same melancholy he felt. Their father was a survivor, but he could not survive this. Not and be whole.

He pressed the back of his hand against his father's brow. It was warm with fever, but that, at least, was beginning to ebb. It was not the blazing thing of days prior. He was healing—not as fast as he might have when he was in his forties, or his fifties, but the strength of every mortal must wane eventually. Death's embrace was slow in coming, but it must always come for them. One day, Tursa would die, but it would not be this day. One day soon perhaps, when the blood poison was finished with him, when it had robbed him of all the strength remaining to him, but not today.

The hide entrance flap was pushed back, letting in a gust of winter air that chilled the back of his neck. He turned to see his younger siblings step through. Shaede, bony and thin and as hard as their mother, hid her grief at their father's condition better than the others. She would pretend to be the rock in the stream, damming off her own emotions and shouldering the rest of their burdens, but inside she was breaking.

Boen wore her emotions on her sleeve. The tears had not stopped coming since finding daughters among the dead. The deaths of her daughters added to the toll he

Tears for the Moon God

felt in the presence of Tursa Hawkeye. How much more could afflict their family before it was too much. Before the burden on their shoulders pulled them under, and shattered them.

The wounds in his father's shoulders, and his chest, pulsated, contracted. Some of them were nearly shut now, but their closures were only superficial. There were still the arrow shaft tunnels through his flesh behind them, the true damage immeasurable. The tribe's healers had been assigned elsewhere, to heal all those others who had been injured among their sect. Those that could be healed. In every skirmish the Kirche had encountered in their years of raiding under his father, this had always been their way. Tend to the tribe before the chief.

"How is he?" Boen asked.

Behind her came Arrada. The tent flap collapsed behind him, and the cold ebbed away with its falling. Puffs of smoke pushed through the carved out flue in the wooden ceiling, carrying away the pungent aroma of rosemary and honeycomb, healing herbs to help their father along. In Arrada's hands was a wicker basket filled with yet more herbs, features of a desperate attempt to advance their father's healing.

He gripped that basket in tight fists, his knuckles standing out prominently, and in his eyes—eyes like ice, a rarity among the Gil Garo—was the sight same melancholy that gripped them all. A tension yet unwilling to be released.

Kuuda shrugged. "He sleeps. His wounds close. Beyond that, I don't know."

Boen knelt beside him.

Arrada hustled toward the camp stove. He wadded up his deer skin tunic in one hand, and wrenched open the pig iron door. "He'll be okay. He's always okay."

"Full of piss and vinegar." Alaar said. "I'll stake this years entire hoard on him insisting on mounting a horse as soon as his eyes open."

"You'll be disappointed when he tells us all to quit behaving like lost children, then." Shaede's grin lit her eyes with mischief.

"You'll take my wager, then?"

Shaede sniffed. "Shit odds. No."

"Be serious, both of you." Arrada snapped. "Our father is on his death bed. This is no time to be joking at his expense."

"Oh, don't be such a puss." Alaar said. "We're all worried, but what good does it do any of us to sit here wallowing over the old man. He'll bear the insult in his bones for the rest of his life if he wakes to find us all weeping over him, won't he."

"What do you know." Arrada said under his breath. He scooped herbs from his basket and tossed them into the hearth. "Pa has a sensitive side, too. He just rarely shows it."

"Never, you mean." Boen said. She watched their father sleep, her gaze set against him but distant, as if she wasn't really seeing him. "He once told me to save my every tear for the man I would choose to wed. I was eleven."

"You were crying in front of him." Shaede said. "What did you expect. He *hates* that."

"Would you...all stop talking about me...like I'm not here!" Tursa growled, his eyes still closed. His fists clenched into balls and relaxed. And with that he slipped into unconsciousness.

Kuuda stood then and made for the exit. "Where are you going?" Alaar demanded.

Departures

"To check on something." he said.

He brushed past the flap, out into the winter cold.

All around him his people busied themselves tearing down yurts and loading their worldly effects onto carts. They dug up food stock they had buried against the harshest months of winter, hauled casks off to be filled in Shan Lao's river, saddled horses and secured those wagons to their harnesses.

It was all happening too suddenly. They should have been here for months yet, waiting for the ices to melt, the spring floods to drive them away from the river and into the grasslands, where their dry season raids would begin anew.

All was forsaken in the face of this coming war, and he could find no solace in any of it. This choice on the part of the chiefs felt too much like the pursuit of some petty revenge, a counter blow in answer to the attack on their people. There was no point in it, nothing to be gained except for more bloodshed. They were to send a warning to the Tului, yet within that warning was an invitation to battle, to the slaughter of thousands of men and women. Children orphaned as their parents were buried in mass graves with countless others, never to be identified. The lands razed and reshaped by clashing sorceries. He only hoped whatever victory came to them justified all that was lost in pursuit of it.

He looked around the yurt, dusted snow away from bowed stalks of wheat, and amaranth, and milo. Dead stalks, as he had suspected. Blackened near the root. The berries were desiccated. They would not yield new life in the spring. He raked his fingers through the dirt, found it sandy, depleted.

He dusted his hand against his skirt. The linen provided little protection against biting air, and he did not value being exposed to the elements longer. He returned to the hut, to his siblings and their father.

"Did you find what you were looking for?" Alaar asked.

He nodded.

"What was it?"

"He's been drawing on Shi'an's power." he said, returning to his seat at Tursa's side. "When he is lucid enough. He's taking strength from the land, using it to push back the poison."

Shaede grinned. "Clever bastard."

"He'll be okay, then?" Arrada asked.

"I...I think so." Kuuda said, not meeting his eye. "We know so little about these people and their magic. It could be he beats the poison. At the same time, it could be he only extends the duration of the sickness. One day, he might succumb to it, and then...."

"And then we put him down." Alaar said grimly.

Shaede flinched.

Alaar met her eye. Wisely, she chose to say nothing. Shaede's pain was her own to bear. What happened to her son was hers to deal with.

One day soon, she'll have to kill him. But she knows that. I'll lose a nephew that day, but it will be a mercy, won't it? Then again, if I was standing in her shoes, could I do it? Could I look my own son in the eyes as I cut his throat?

He thought of Chief Ungol. The reasons had been different for him, but they were not unique to him. There had been others. Other cloud men from other lines, other families, other sects. The midwives would not take the lives of those children, but the children could not stay, live and grow among the Gil Garo. This diseased

Tears for the Moon God

child could not be allowed to live in their keeping, lest the plague of his unfortunate curse spread.

Was it wise to leave a blood cursed boy alive, even bound as he was? How were the other sects handling it? Cloud Man or...whatever these people were now, it hardly mattered. He doubted he could have made the decision Ungol did, to abandon his son to exposure, to die alone on the road, or be found by some unassuming passerby. To doom his own child to death. At the same time, one life was not worth the countless others he risked destroying. If this infection spread among the Kirche, if Shaede's son broke free, the decision may well be taken out of her hands. He may have to end it.

"Shh-shh-shh, honey, don't fret now. It's your mother. See?" Shaede's in-laws watched in silence as she attempted inanely to mollify her son.

Tulukh thrashed against his binds. Screams gouted from his lungs, frustrated noises muffled by a gag one of them had forced into his mouth while she was gone.

He had been sleeping when she left his side. The camp bed's legs had been removed, the grate and mattress strapped against the wagon bed with thick bands of leather. More bands bound her son under a series of quilts beneath which he was clad in his smallclothes. She had tried to get something warmer on him that morning, but the effort had proven disastrous. He had come close to infecting his father, then. Karse had just managed to get clear before poor Tulukh's teeth could clamp together around his forearm. It had taken three men together to restrain him long enough to get those blankets and the binds in place. Getting the gag in his mouth had been more troubling, as every effort to force the strap between his teeth risked a bite to the fingers.

He thrashed against the boards—the *thump-thump-thump* of his elbows, the balls of his feet striking the thin mattress—a staccato beat pronouncing to those too near that something was very wrong in this wagon.

There were others. Other families afflicted with the same choices as had fallen into her lap. Some of them, at least, must have come to the same conclusion. Every poison must have an antidote. Every affliction must have a cure. If there was a means of reversing what had been done to her son, it lay with the Tului, she was sure of it. They need only find it among the monsters, find it and disseminate it among the ill, and all would be well again. She would have her son back. Tulukh would be himself again.

Wide eyes flickered scarlet, unnatural light leaking from around him. She curled up her fist, closed her eyes, and struck him. He went limp.

When she opened her eyes again, it was to find Karse's mother looking on her approvingly. She had missed the blunt rod the woman cradled in her wrinkled hands. This had not been the first time the boy had been knocked unconscious. If she did not find a better means of keeping him incapacitated, it would not be the last.

Arrada will have something for this. Something to keep him comfortable.

The burial mound was covered in dried flowers. The Hakka kept them for just these occasions. The winter months saw their share of deaths. The Swans took away corpses in the night, leaving nothing to remember the fallen by. Infirms, the terminally ill, the elderly unable to make it through the winter...they culled, and the

Departures

Hakka moved on. But there were those the Swans did not take, which Duijus Kanh did not consume. Those who fell to death's embrace before ever they arrived to whisk them away into the night.

Those, the Hakka buried. In shallow graves, scattered with seeds and dead flowers, offerings to take into the afterlife with them, blessings of safe travels. They prayed that the spirits would allow them the chance to see their loved ones one last time in the forest gloom of Gur Tulain, before they must pass on.

The burial mound belonged to Daera Sarr, late wife of Chief Arrak, and he stood with their son before it. His own offering of daffodils, her favorite, lay prominently across her chest. For Tamlin, it was a bangle she had given him when he was a boy, to wear over his bicep, which he had swiftly outgrown and begun wearing around his wrist again as a man. The bangle lay where the mound joined the grasslands, where soft dirt gave way to earth frozen hard.

This was to be her final resting place, just beyond their camp's borders, amid a row of other burial mounds belonging to too many of their kin. There were other families among those mounds, others wandering the field in pursuit of the huts they would dismantle, the wagons waiting with their horses. Others who had taken those precious moments to give their blessings to their dead before they must provision themselves for the march, before they said goodbye for another season to the Shifting City, Gil Garo.

The winter would be harsh. The march would be treacherous. They would lose still others on the path to Tuluis Fel. Arrak had already lost too much, and yet he could not turn away from this path. Could not but hope that he saw his son again when the dust had settled, that he would not lose him, too.

"I'm sorry for this," he said.

"You couldn't have stopped this. None of us could." Tamlin responded in a hush.

"I'm sorry, because you have been robbed of your mother. She cannot be there for you any longer, and I am not cut out to be a shoulder for you to lean against. I was never the compassionate one."

Silence between them. Arrak searched for something to say, to help his son heal. He could think of nothing. He could think of little else beyond his own loss. His son had lost his mother, but he had lost his wife, who he had been with far longer. The one soul in all the world who knew every part of him, all of his stories, who he would permit to be his keeper. He needed her, and she was gone.

What am I to do with you gone, Daera? Our son needs me, but I am not you. I don't have your strength. I never did.

"I'm sorry." he said again. It was all he could say.

"Mother told me how you met." Tamlin said. "You were casting nets into the river. It was early spring. The ice flows were coming apart, then, but the thaw was not far along enough for our people to leave this place yet. She was watching you, but you didn't know it. She'd been watching you struggle with that net for days. Fasten the bate to it all wrong.

"She was fascinated by all the ways you could lose your bate to the fish, and succeed at catching not a single one."

Arrak snorted. "She would tell it that way."

"She told me one day she'd had enough. She'd been watching you fail so long she just couldn't continue. So she stomped right up to you, snatched the net out of your hands, and set about correcting all your knots, securing the bate in place."

Tears for the Moon God

"She thought she was so good. She jabbed a bunch of sticks into the muck in the shallows, caught frostbite standing in there bare legged up to the knee. She managed to get the net in place between all of those sticks, but I ended up having my way.

"You see, she didn't know I had seen her watching me. How do you win a woman like her over? How do you win her heart?" Arrak was smiling. He remembered those days clearly. His wife's version was accurate enough, but she liked to paint him as the bumbling oaf, didn't she? Liked to make herself out to be the champion, saving him with her wisdom. "You pretend to be a fool. I didn't expect it to take so long before she finally came to sort it all out. Days, mind. Days I spent going to the river at the same time, whether my family needed the fish or not, just so I could see her watching me with that incredulous expression on her face. It's rarely beauty by itself that entices one person to be enamored with another, Tamlin. Remember that. One day, you'll find your own lover. Beauty is fleeting. What is on the inside." he tapped his chest over his heart. "That's what matters."

Tamlin scoffed. "I'll believe you when I find that person. Just know it won't be who you expect."

Arrak raised an eyebrow. "I suppose we'll cross that bridge when it arrives. I must leave you, and I do not want to. You've lost as much as I have in losing your mother, and I would not have you without me, if there was any other choice."

"Is there not? I can come on this campaign. I can help—"

"No, son. You must stay here. It is out of my hands. Dupec Safar will need you when he emerges from Duijus Kanh's cave."

"Dupec again." Tamlin grumbled. "Why are we even entertaining him. He cannot be Ung Kanh Dui. He is not one of us."

"He chose us, son. When he let you have a victory you did not earn."

Tamlin's breath caught. His stomach twisted into a hard knot. He did not understand what motivated Dupec...why he had come to help them—two perfect strangers—when those soldiers arrived in Duijus Kanh's cave. He did not understand what the spirit had seen in him which drove him to break the covenant set in place between him and their people, and to choose an outsider as his acolyte. In his confusion lay a framework for accepting Dupec Safar as, if not quite Gil Garo in truth, then at least someone who cared for his people. But he found he did not like him, or perhaps he was simply blaming him for things out of his control. It was because Dupec remained in Duijus Kanh's care or custody that he must remain here to grieve his loss alone. It was because Dupec brought an unknown enemy down on his people that his mother lay in the ground, dead, and leaving him to survive her.

That isn't fair, is it? He couldn't have known this would happen. And if he did, how could he have stopped it?

Anger simmered inside, and he could not let it go. Time might heal this wound he must bear, but what lay at the end of it? Who would he be when Dupec climbed out of that cave? His ally? His friend?

"Dupec Safar did not have a choice in how he was raised, or where. He was abandoned by Ungol and Shaelein, left on the roadside. This is the nature of their strength. That when they were faced with the decision, they chose mercy over cruelty, selflessness over selfishness.

"So Dupec was raised by God Uldal and his acolytes. He has had a hard life." Arrak looked into Tamlin's eyes then, squeezed his shoulder. "He has also returned to us, with knowledge of our customs no less. You might teach him all that books could not, instead of fretting over whether he deserves to be among us.”

Tamlin deflated. “I suppose you have a point. But father, I don’t like him.”

“Be that as it may, he will need you.”

Tamlin’s gaze fell onto the mound where his mother was buried. “When will we see each other again?”

“No later than three months from this day.”

“Gur Tulain.” Tamlin said knowingly. His gaze tracked east and north, in the direction of those hallowed grounds. “You’ll find me there?”

“We’ll find your mother there. Do this thing properly.”

Tamlin kicked at a clod of snow. “You promise?”

“I promise.”

“Then don’t do anything stupid. If you die—”

“You will still find me.”

“But if you die—”

Arrak clapped him on the shoulder. “I’m not ready to die just yet, son. Besides, how could I live with myself if I left you alone before you could find a proper wife.”

Tamlin grimaced.

He chuckled. “Or do you have your eye on someone?”

“No! Nothing like that.” Tamlin tried to step away from him, but he firmed his grip on his shoulder, pulled him into a hug.

“I’m going to miss you, son.” He released him.

Tamlin’s jaw worked around something to say. Arrak simply smiled, and stepped away. “Gur Tulain” he called over his shoulder. “Three month’s time.”

He stalked off in search of his horse. It was time they got on the road. Though it cut at is heart to leave his son behind, it must be done. A sacrifice made against the good of the people. Tamlin would be fine. Duijus Kanh would protect him. As for himself...well, he was not so sure.

A pile of Shaki’s belongings lay in the bed of his father’s wagon. Sequestered in one corner, his effects amounted to an iron-banded trunk filled with raiment, pilfered adornments of gold and silver, and a pouch full of coins. Sarri had secreted away a band of throwing knives, a Ruc’an crossbow and a dozen quarrels beneath his son’s few changes of clothes, and his spare medicine kit.

Shaki was not the most practical of men, but he would not succumb to something as trivial as an infected wound if he could stop it. The medicine kit, a second pack filled with foodstuffs, fishing nets, a buck knife and wet stone...he was determined not to see his son dead for lack of preparedness. Shaki may well have arrived at the conclusion he would need those effects himself, given enough time, but time was not on his side. The Cuu were nearly all packed up, and the leading elements were already mounted and waiting to march. Arrak’s Hakka were already on the move, and Ungol’s Dumas were readying to join them. Soon, all of Gil Garo would be emptied, leaving just the chief’s pavilion to mark their passing.

Shaki sat on the raised walkway ahead of its entrance, sat there with Bora, saying his last goodbyes to her. He turned to his father, then, the pain on Bora’s face evidently too much for him.

“Why can’t she stay?” he demanded. “If Tamlin and Chakta can stay behind with me, there’s no reason she shouldn’t.”

Tears for the Moon God

Sarri pinched the bridge of his nose.

In truth, beyond the scope of Gandes Fae's proclamations, there was little reason Bora should not stay. On the surface, there was little reason. She possessed unique talents, having taken on apprenticeship under a god, rather than under any one spirit of the lands. Few like her existed across the tribe, but then the Gil Garo were suspicious of most gods. Uldal, Shakh, Mu...they found no reason to fear them, but those gods were aspected to mask presences, track targets. They were gods of the hunt, and hunting was an activity the Gil Garo were intimately familiar with, both in their raids and in pursuit of food.

But her god was not one of those. He was no one Sarri would trust. He sometimes found himself wondering why she saw fit to. To take on apprenticeship, to become an acolyte of the God of Games...she was not a fool, but her decision had been an act of supreme idiocy.

What was more, he suspected a god's hand was in all of this. The Tului had no reason to attack them. They were not so close to the forbidden kingdom's border that they made easy targets. The Tului would have had to march across the steppe to get to them, skirting Ruc entirely on their way to the Shan Lao river and the site of their winter encampment. If they sought some resource abundant in the lands south of their border, it did not make sense for them to attack a nomadic tribe. The possessions of the Gil Garo were minimal. They traveled light, moved often, settled in one place only long enough to weather the harshest months of the winter, when ice made the footing treacherous for their horses. They did not trade among themselves with gold and silver, and did not practice much in the way of farming.

If it was blood they were after, they could just as well have stopped in Loc, or Ruc. Why bother trekking so far for us unless a god's hand is in this?

No, he could not say there was no sense to be made out of this. He was not that ignorant. The attack had come on the heels of Dupec Safar's return. The two occurrences had come so close together it was impossible to think the one had nothing to do with the other. Considerations must be taken into account. Dupec had arrived in time to compete in their tournament, a meaningless custom with a nonetheless lucrative reward should he succeed in winning it. To be taught by Duijus Kanh and his Swans, to become their acolyte, meant attaining immense power, particularly across the steppe where the spirit's influence was strongest. God Uldal would have known Duijus Kanh's power, having been aligned as he was with the Moon God, Ao Nii. But legend held God Uldal's involvement in mortal affairs was minimal, that he was a neutral party in the great game of the gods.

Who, then, was pulling the strings? Was Dupec's arrival a preemptive response to the coming attack? Did Uldal seek to protect them in sending one of his acolytes to them?

Best not to invite more chaos. If Bora stays, her presence risks inviting Tirulain's intervention in whatever Uldal has planned for his acolyte. If, indeed, he has any plans for him. And if he doesn't, her presence still risks inviting Tirulain to manipulate our children. Through her he is given eyes and ears in a place where he should have neither, and we all might suffer for whatever knowledge he gleans from her. Whether he watches from nearby or far distant, there is too much risk in leaving her here.

But Shaki cannot know that. He will fight this until he can see no means of fighting it. He has every bit of my stubbornness, if he inherited none of my sense.

Departures

"The decision has been made. The chiefs—no, not just me—have agreed that it is best to stay in keeping with Gandes Fae's commands. You are to be left here, but I will ensure Bora is granted every protection I can manifest. We will ensure she is watched closely, so that no ill befalls her." *Or anyone she may come into contact with.*

"You're sure she wouldn't be better off here?"

"I know you'll miss her, but my hands are tied." he said, trying to keep his frustration out of his voice. If someone had told him his child would be born socially inept and disquietingly inquisitive, he might have chosen to be celibate. He loved his son, but there was no sense denying the boy got under his skin. "You'll barely notice she's gone. By the time we get back, it will be as if you were never apart at all."

"You're full of shit." Shaki said.

"Easy now." Bora said warningly. "No need to offend the man. It's only a few months."

"Or years! Wars are unpredictable. And I don't know what Dupec's wants will be when he finally comes out of that hole."

"Show some respect." Sarri snapped. "The spirit of *that hole* has been defending our people for *millennia!*"

"Some of our people." Shaki said. "His concubines do like to eat the old timers. And the children sometimes. And definitely the sick people."

Sarri clamped his teeth together. "This is no time for—"

Shaki kissed Bora's cheek. "I'm sorry my father is being so stubborn about this. I promise I'll come for you as soon as my obligation to Dupec is over." He hugged his father, who's entire body had gone rigid with anger. "I'd give you a peck on the cheek, too, but...well..."

He released him, stalked off toward the pavilion's entrance. "You know I'd have liked one last night with my girlfriend before you bundled her off—"

"Shaki, dammit! He's angry enough!"

"—but beggars can't be choosers, now, can they? Love you!"

Sarri watched him enter the pavilion.

"You're making the right decision." Bora said, surprising him. "You don't trust me. I don't blame you for it. I suppose your reaction is reasonable. I'd be put off balance if the subject of my distrust was telling me I was right not to trust her, too. But you and I...we're not fools. Someone is manipulating the Tului. There's no reason they should have attacked us. We don't raid in their lands. Our winter encampment isn't near enough their border to warrant marching this far for a light skirmish. They didn't take anything of value from us, either.

"Based on the nature of their attack, it would seem they're trying to goad us into chasing them back to their homeland, where they have the advantage. But who is advantaged by a protracted battle with them? Particularly in the winter months when we are likely to have difficulty attaining resources on the approach. We don't know the terrain. We barely have a conception of their powers, which spirits they call to...which gods they might worship. It would seem someone wants us severely weakened, which would imply we pose a threat insofar as we are at strength."

"I thought much the same, yes. I am, however, surprised your thinking took you so far."

"It's Ungol's son, isn't it? The common denominator. He arrives, and suddenly they attack. It's likely he was their true target. That they were trying to goad him into attacking them, and we were an obstacle in their path. They didn't anticipate Duijus Kanh's intervention, which meant they were unable to kill or capture him. So, correct me if I'm wrong, but am I to assume you wish to take me out of play and thus deny my god access to information regarding Dupec Safar's whereabouts?"

"His abilities." Sarri said. She held his gaze. There was no defiance in her expression. She had come to this conclusion a long time ago. She was just confirming her suspicions were accurate.

"Shaki doesn't need to know about this." she said.

He nodded. "No, I didn't intend for him to."

"Glad we agree. He'd only be worried." Smiling, she held out her hand to him. "Shall we?"

He helped her to her feet, and led her away toward the Cuu camp, where their horses awaited them.

The death of a man's ego was the summation of countless small cuts. Having reached the summit, that hallowed place wherein the battles were done and he may finally rest, he came to understand that there was no rest for him. There would never be. The curse of mortal kind was in that he must always endure, struggle onward until death took him. Only in death, in its finality, could any true rest be had. Maybe not even then.

Ungol raised his knife. Shaelein stood over his shoulder. He had performed this action countless times, had gone into too many homes throughout the last days, seen too many vulnerable youth, too many grief-stricken parents doting over their prone forms, tightening straps around their shoulders, their hips, their ankles, holding their limbs in place. He had heard too many cries, of rage and pain, muffled by horse bits, pieces of driftwood, muslin cloth.

Still, he must go on. It was his duty, his place to lead by example. To send a message to his people. That he may not endear those families to him, but a mercy must be extended to them, to end the suffering of their kin so that they might move on. He was aware of their resentment. Mothers pled from their knees, clawed at his shins and ankles, scratched at his arms, wrapped themselves around his torso and dragged, using their weight to anchor him, hoping to slow the progression of events from his entrance into their yurts to the moment when his judgment must be delivered, when his mercy must be granted, when this culling must be performed.

And Shaelein stood by him. She performed what healing she could, dictated to him which of their kin, which children, which husbands, which wives and mothers could be saved, in whom the infection had taken too quickly, who had time to say last goodbyes before the Tului madness took root.

Too many red eyes. Too many gaunt faces, baring teeth from behind curled lips, threatening their own families with violence should they win free. *And they will. They will eventually if we cannot find a means of curing them. And when they do...what?*

They marched on a nation of cursed creatures—blood drinkers, flesh eaters, murderers and cannibals all. They had no means by which to discover how virulent this infection was, how many were afflicted with it. Was it isolated to the soldiers? Was this plague intentionally passed, from person to person, granting power at the cost of morality.

Departures

He well understood that burden. *Which is why I am called to this culling.*

Killing the innocent was not easy. It weighed on the soul. The perpetrator, if he was not evil, lived with that weight from the moment of greatest consequence until his last breath--it must be so. He had lived with it for thirty years, and for all of those years past the burden had only deepened. Wisdom gave way to insight, not the other way around. Hindsight granted him some comprehension. Ten men's deaths had sealed his bargain with Gandes Fae, and in their deaths was a promise made between them, which the spirit had kept his end of for all of those years, which Ungol had kept less out of loyalty than fear. Fear first for his familiar. Any plot of grand betrayal would seal his own death. The mol fae would ensure it. And second, for what it must mean to betray the spirit. For the meaning it denuded that ritual act of. He could bear this burden if it granted some benefit to his people. He could bear it as long as it continued to mean something. But were that act to lose all meaning, his burden would be redoubled.

So, too, these small acts of violence, these small mercies. He could bear them only insofar as they continued to hold meaning. The Gil Garo had no antidote for this plague. They could not fight a curse they could not purge. Their exorcists, what few of them had trained under Furuk the Wyrm, were not strong enough to fend off this curse. There were too few of them besides. Too few by far to heal all of those afflicted. And they could not be easily contained. There would have to be those who could watch over them, neutralize their powers, keep them suppressed, and few among their kind possessed such power. Only Dupec displayed the ability to neutralize spirit calling entirely. He alone possessed that power among the Dumas.

The other sects were no better off. There were those who had come into contact with the Tului blood and its poison who had not succumbed. Those who, like him, had chosen strong spirits with some natural defense against whatever sorcery this curse was born of. But they, too, were few. Gandes Fae's gifts protected him, but what of those like Tursa? Still unconscious three days later, his family watching over his body, hoping soon—with his next breath, in the next hour—he would awaken. What horror would they be granted when he opened his eyes? Would he be the same man they remembered? Would he be something else?

He would take no chances in this. It was the way of the Gil Garo. Survival of the fittest.

It was in their treaty with Duijus Kanh, spoken plainly in the surviving lore, witnessed by generation after generation of Gil Garo tribesmen. Of their tribe, from their sects, were taken the elderly, the sick and the dying, the young too ill to survive the winter...all taken to feed the cave spirit and his Swans. The tribe was made stronger for these cullings. No longer were they burdened with the demands of taking care of those who would not survive the winter. They kept them comfortable—as long as they could, they did—and when their time came, they were taken. There was mercy in that, too. Their lives would have been ended before the great thaw arrived, their suffering made longer. The spirits knew mortal morality, knew its parameters, but they did not ascribe to it. Duijus Kanh culled among them because he hungered, but he took of them their sick and their dying because he possessed honor.

So, Ungol had been called to this. He was the leader of this sect. For the time being, he was. And when his people soured on them, if they did, they would know in their hearts even as they dragged him from his seat that he had done what he

Tears for the Moon God

believed was best. Had taken on this burden so they did not have to.

"Back away." he said softly.

The boy was thirteen. He had not asked for his name, but his face would be burned into his memory as were all of the others, another soul for him to carry until the day he finally found rest. The fat of childhood had not left the boy's cheeks. His face was round, his eyes hooded. He had his mother's crooked nose. His dark hair hung loose around his head, waist-length locks pressed under his back, spilled over the pillows he lay against. His parents had bundled him into a quilt and bound it tight with thick lengths of rope. They had secured a talisman around his neck, not a tradition of the Gil Garo, but something taken in a raid in the borderlands of Loc. At least, he suspected as much given the geometric patterns across its golden face. It might have been his first true prize, and taken recently.

The boy was thirteen.

This simple fact made what he must do so much worse. To kill a child was to rot the soul, and perhaps this was the intent of the Tului. Perhaps this poison was not endemic to their lands, but had risen up recently, and in their struggle against it they had begun to resent those peoples who were not afflicted by it. A closed border became an open invitation to harm those who they viewed as responsible. Or maybe their intent was to weaken their newfound enemy, to destroy him inside, erode the pillars of leadership by burdening the chiefs with guilt, a useless longing to return to some period in time when the person they were was not a monster, was not capable of imagining they might one day become this.

The boy was thirteen.

His knife came to rest against his throat. The hilt was held firm in a gloved hand. Linen was wrapped around his arms and chest, secured with lengths of rope to keep it all in place, to prevent the blood from touching him. Gandes Fae provided a measure of protection, but he was not sure how much. He had no love for taking unnecessary risks, and so the precautions were minded. Fabric and rope, hide gloves and jerkin. A scarf was wrapped around his neck and the lower half of his face, secured around his mouth, ears and nose. If he could cover his eyes without blinding himself, he would, but some risk was necessary in absence of the lenses the Ruc'an were so fond of.

The boy was thirteen.

His parents were well back now. His mother's face was buried in his father's chest. She was weeping.

The boy thrashed against his restraints. Shaelein, similarly covered, helped her husband hold him in place, kept his chest pressed flat against the ground. She sat on his legs, using her weight to limit his range of motion. He screamed into the gag they had fashioned out of a piece of wood and butcher's twine.

Ungol's knife traced a line across his throat, dug in deep. The knife bit into cartilage, slipped across his windpipe. Blood spilled from ruined veins and arteries, ran thick over his neck and shoulders, and into his hair.

A last useless thrashing. His fight was lost. Thrashing became feeble jerking. His body lay still, his arms and legs, his neck convulsing now and again, twitching long after his eyes glazed over, and he was lost to them.

"Handle the blood as little as you can. Throw out these pillows, and the quilts. Anything it touched. If you have a need, I will supply you with replacements. As much as I can."

Departures

He rose, took the boy around the head and neck. Shaelein climbed off of his legs. She took his ankles. They dragged him from the yurt.

When they were well outside, the parents of the deceased left to do their grieving in private, he looked to the west. Dupec was out there, inside Duijus Kanh cave, courting a dark spirit. He wondered if the spirit would demand of his son what Gandes Fae had of him. If he would be forced to kill innocents in exchange for his aid.

He hoped it wasn't so. Dupec had been through enough. They had all been through enough.

Flowers for his son lay in a pile at graveside. A sack filled with seed sat fat and heavy next to it. Karsa's body would be returned to the earth in the Gil Garo tradition, but Gulang could not accept his death.

To struggle is the nature of life, is it not?

His three elder sons had won their contests, had proven in skirmishes innumerable that they were up to the challenges of combat, that they were survivors. He had seen them fight. Had seen, too, that they were not too proud to flee when their positions were compromised. There was no sense in fighting a losing battle, and every one of them knew it. Even Kachukh knew better than to defend an indefensible position. Even he knew when to strike and when to stay back.

Karsa should not have died. *He should not have died!* Yet here was his body as proof. His face fixed in a rictus of pain. He had not gone easily. His death had been anything but peaceful.

Gaulakh and Saafha, his two eldest sons, had helped him dig the grave. They had done it without magic.

Kachukh was too young. Too young to shoulder the burden of these deeds, but every man must have his awakening eventually. Every man must face the stubborn truth that mortality came with the promise of death. That it was a stone's throw away at any moment, and a simple mistake might invite it.

He wanted to scream. He could not. He needed to be strong for his family. Saerin, his wife, was near breaking. He had promised on their day of avowal that he would shoulder her burdens, that he would become a surrogate for her pain, to fester within him so that she did not have to bear it alone. He would keep that promise.

Saerin's heart-shaped face was not well suited to tears. Angry, red tracks crossed high cheekbones. She had been days without a bath, and he had not commented. He knew her pain, knew overcoming it would take time. She needed him now, needed her children.

There was a space on their wagon which was cleared for her. She would not ride until she was ready. He would not force her to sit the saddle when she could barely be bothered to climb out of bed.

Glassy eyes peered up at the open sky. Clouds drifted by, but they were thin and high up, providing the illusion of coming snow, but promising none. Glassy, hazel eyes. Karsa's eyes.

So much lost potential.

His middle son had been the hardest working of his children. He struck out every day as if he had something to prove, and maybe he did. It was a mother's way

Tears for the Moon God

to spoil the youngest. Sircha and Kachukh had been coddled in ways their elder children had not. He had capitulated too much to her in their upbringing. He would not do so in the future. He could not bear the thought of losing another son. It was in the nature of the eldest to strike out, become the leader, protect his younger siblings. Gaulakh had become that for his siblings, had become their defender. And in Saafha was his rival in everything.

That Karsa so often felt overlooked had driven him to work harder, to take on greater challenges than either, and perhaps that was his downfall. But Gulang could not help looking elsewhere for reasons. Could not help hunting for some justification as to why his son had to die when so many others had survived. Why his family must suffer this pain. Why the Kachin must endure such hardships in the face of what had come.

Were they not strong? Had he not been diligent in ensuring they were capable fighters. Was he not effective enough to keep them alive?

Countless raids with hardly a casualty, and those savages struck down hundreds in the span of a single night! *How? What justification is there for this?*

His thoughts turned to Dupec. To Ungol. Dupec held some responsibility for this. He was their target. He could only be that. And if Dupec's return had incited this attack, had been at the heart of why Karsa died, then some of that blame rested with Ungol as well. For his weakness.

Ungol should have done what was needed when that cursed child was born. He should have killed him. Cut out the rot before it could destroy us!

He knew he was being unfair, but there was his son. There was Karsa's body, robbed of life, dressed in fresh raiment and lain in a hole three feet deep, and he could not summon the grace to pray for him.

Instead, he made a vow. Saerin was breaking, and he did not wish to cause her more pain, but he needed this. He needed to make it mean something. He was grieving, too.

"If we must go to battle for the crimes of these savages, let us go on our own terms. Our swords raised, horse hooves making thunder in the valleys and on the hills, our arrows singing on the air and our screams of rage and triumph lifted on the wind. Let Ho'o watch as we burn their villages, and Tao Shein laugh as he consumes their blood. Let the gods watch on as we bring Tuluis Fel to its knees, and let them know fear like they have never known. Let us spit in their eyes, and see how they like being blinded."

He felt the eyes of his children on him, and did not care. They might think him mad for making such lofty proclamations. They might agree with him and they might not, but he felt in his heart a building rage that would not be quieted until his weapons had tasted blood. Until he had taken his pound of flesh against the Tului people, and righted what had been wronged here.

The Tipik were on the march. Their strongest warriors led the charge, their horses plowing through snowy embankments, winter dunes broken by spears of wheat. Horses whinnied and snorted, the snow crunching under hoof as the sect broke camp, the stragglers coming up behind with wagons laden with all of their worldly effects. Still more warriors kept watch along the flanks, guarding against possible attack, and a greater force held back, waiting for Coltang to join them.

Yet he was not near them.

Departures

The chief's pavilion, the long house which was the only structure on the plains to remind those passersby in summer of the Gil Garo stake to this territory, loomed at his flank, and from behind its open doors he saw fire glow. At least one of the other chiefs' children was inside, perhaps with his father.

They've lost too much. Tanta gripped his arm, drawing him out of his introspection. This was going to be a hard winter on them all, but he would not be alone. The Tipik were his and he was theirs, and they would need his leadership on the road. But Chakta...his heart broke for her.

She had gone away from the sect before, that was true. Had gone to find and court Galadir, her own personal pilgrimage a long one. She would not be gone so long. She would not be absent her family for years as had been the case then. A few months at best. When the spring thaw came, she would again strike out on the road, and he would see her once more.

But he did not like this leaving. This not knowing what might befall his daughter, or Shaki or Tamlin. Arrak and Sarri could not be doing well with this. Gulang would not part with his remaining children, and rightly. After the death of Karsa, he must be breaking inside. And Ungol? He, too, had lost something. Something freshly gained. He must grieve the loss of his new returned son. He must hate himself for letting it happen.

And now Coltang sacrificed his daughter, and knew his sacrifice was not greater than his friend's. Ungol grieved the loss of what could have been, and there was no certainty in the return of his son to him. There could not be. For him, he had known his daughter all her life. Knew her every quirk and flaw. There was no sense for lost time, no frenzied desire to reclaim some part of her he had lost with her childhood abandonment. Oh, Ungol and Shaelein had done the merciful thing in sparing their son, but it had done them no services. In death was closure. In knowing death there was comfort. This not knowing, this distance, an ocean opening even now between his daughter and him, left too much to burden him. A grief of a different kind, for he must accept he may never see her again, and hope she survived this ordeal.

The steppe had been quiet these last weeks, but winter was just beginning. Soon would come the clashes between god and spirit. Soon would come those nights when the earth refused to stop shaking, when the moon's light pierced through clouds and madness took over the minds of innocents. Soon would come those nights when the mournful song of wolves came on unending until dawn's light broke across the land, when the Swans walked under open sky and hunted for food to take back to their lover.

He looked to his daughter, who was hard eyed as ever. He knew what hid behind that stony exterior. She may put on a strong front—she got that from her mother—but he saw the cracks. Fragile, hoping to make it through this parting without any shed tears. She wanted him to see her as a fighter, as strong like him, but she had not yet learned there was a difference between strength and ferocity. The fierce girl was a delicate being, capable of destructive force when called upon but denying whole chunks of who she was in service of a pretense. That she must be viewed as strong was not the same as being possessed of strength. Strength was not a matter of posturing. It did not come from intimidating those who she viewed as peers. Strength was born of wisdom, of knowing when to choose destruction, when violence became necessary. It was in knowing herself, accepting her flaws, moving forward from a place of understanding. Strength was knowing oneself, and growing

Tears for the Moon God

from a stable base.

He had seen that strength in Dupec. It was there in Shaki, too. Perhaps she could learn from them. That she did not have to be feared to be respected. That she did not need to be hard to be strong.

"I'll be okay." she said.

He nodded. "I have faith you will be, but know that—"

"I have wintered on the steppe for how many years? Enough, I think, to know what to expect."

"You will not have the protection of numbers on your side, kid." he said.

"Oh, don't be an ass, Coltang." Tanta chided. "You get one goodbye with our daughter before we leave. Could you keep it sweet?"

He glared at his wife. Their daughter had come into so much of her own by watching her mother. Had learned to be strong from her, to shoulder her burdens and march on. And to wield that strength so effortlessly against him. Her mother looked into his face with defiance now, letting him know in no uncertain terms that this was not the hill he should die on.

If you only knew how much I worried, Tanta. A full moon is imminent, and our records of his travel are incomplete. We don't know where his city will reveal itself this time. What if it touches down here? What if he brings his whole host against Duijus Kanh?

"Don't strike out alone. Whatever happens on the steppe, remember you have Shaki and Tamlin with you." he said.

"I will."

"And take this." Tanta produced a comb from her belt pouch. It was all of turquoise inlaid with bands of gold. He had given it to her as a bridal gift, and she had kept it safe in a little box, set away from her other jewelry, for all these years. She sometimes took it out when she was feeling sentimental, or when she wanted to show it off to the other women in their sect. He said nothing as she passed it to their daughter. "Something to remember us by."

"This is..." Chakta took it. There were the tears she tried so hard to hold back. Tears brimming in her eyes which she would not let fall until they were gone, if she could help it.

Coltang bent low and wrapped her in his embrace. "I'll miss you, kid."

"I...you asshole."

He let her go, cast a glance at his wife. She hugged Chakta, pointedly ignoring him as she said her last goodbyes. *She's your daughter to the bone.*

Tanta released her. "Time we were going. The rear guard can't wait any longer."

"I'll see you when the spring thaw has come." Chakta said.

"Before then, if I have any say." Coltang said.

She watched them go. One foot in the stirrup of his midnight stallion, he looked back at her, took in a last glimpse of his daughter. Her back was to him, and she was marching swiftly into the pavilion, where there was no chance of him seeing her cry.

"She's your daughter through and through." Tanta said smartly. She was already seated in her saddle, straight backed and regally posed.

"You would say so." he groused. "She called me an asshole, you know. Is that any way to say goodbye to your father?"

Departures

She snorted. "Sounds like she had the right of it. Now come. We're wasting daylight."

She tapped the reigns, and her horse trotted ahead. He watched her ride away. "You don't have to agree with her you know!"

"Hurry up. You're falling behind."

He cussed under his breath. He swung his leg over the saddle, settled himself and tapped the reins. *She'll be okay. She's as hard bitten as they come. She's just...prideful.*

It was in passing through the Tipik camp that Sauman saw the error in the ways of his kin. The elder chiefs had life experience on their sides, the makings of true wisdom, but they were, to varying degrees, too merciful. Too careless.

Their dead were piled into mass graves or mounds above ground. The Tipik had not buried their dead, had left them there to rot and fester. When the spring thaw came, disease would leak from those bodies. The rot which afflicted them would spread, perhaps even infest the young men and women they left behind to await the Cloud Man. When they returned for the winter again, they would find their lands plagued by carrion feeders grown fat on those bodies, expecting to lay teeth into a feast again now the winter had returned.

The rains may sweep some of those bodies into the river. The floods, expanding their banks, may well swallow them, take them downstream to torment villages with the sights of unexplained dead—bloated corpses drifting languidly along with the currents to choke Shan Lao's band on their way to Galadir's in the south. The spirits would be angered, then. Tao Shein may well be angered by their indifference to those corpses.

Eventualities I will not entertain.

He held a torch aloft in one hand; had ordered a tax to be paid in oil by every member of his sect. Lamp oil cast over the roots of hills, all of them made of piled bodies, fallen Tului and Gil Garo alike. The Chikata had been hit hard by the assault. He had abstained from disposing of their dead this long, to give those families a chance to identify their kin, to drag them off and give them proper burials. Few had managed. Grief stricken and weakened, many grew dejected, surrendered to the unknowing having spent hours sorting through the dead, hoping to find a familiar face, some confirmation that a loved one had died peacefully.

His grace was all used up. It was time to carry out his duty. It was his responsibility to see to it that his people remained safe, that they remained healthy. He could do neither for them with the knowledge plaguing him that those bodies had been left behind, that what they returned to may be a place plagued by angered spirits, refuse and scavengers awaiting a fresh host of corpses to sate themselves on. He refused that eventuality, and so the torch came down on the first mound. Fire took life at its base where the oil was densest. It licked at scraps of cloth, charred leather, burned skin. Flames reflected in countless lifeless eyes. He could almost imagine they were all looking at him, pleading with him to end this nightmare.

Let these flames purge you of your sins. Let the afterlife find you at peace. Let Ul Sharak not judge you too harshly, and Shao Luin shelter you until the day of your return. Be at peace, my kin. I only hope your families find you in Gur Tulain before his grace is gone.

Tears for the Moon God

He moved on the second mound, touched the torch to its feet, and delivered his prayer. He moved to the third. He bent to touch flame to its base.

A vaguely fist-shaped ball fell from somewhere higher in the mound. It bounced over corpses, rolled across trampled grass and packed snow, rolled and then spun and then stopped.

He approached it, stooped low and snatched it off the ground. Ribbed, the flesh a dark red. Someone had taken a bite out of it.

He approached the mound once more, looked over it, searching for the place where that fruit had dropped from. *Is there a survivor in there somewhere?*

From on high, a keening cry. He flinched back, raising his torch and holding it back, poised to attack. The keening ceased, faded into soft gurgling. He hunted for the source of the sound.

There.

A pallid face, jaundiced and robbed of all of its youth. The woman's eyes rolled in their sockets. Her jaw worked around white teeth. Her shoulder shook with the effort of trying to liberate an arm, and her other hand, protruding from under a series of other corpses, snatched at empty air.

Her gaze fixed on him. His blood ran cold, his hackles rising. She was Tului, not terribly dissimilar in appearance to him but missing the mark by several degrees. Again he was struck by how closely these people resembled his own.

Her gaze slid from his face, down the length of his arm, and fixed onto the fruit in his hand. Her clawing became more frantic. Her mouth worked around words he could not hear.

He set his torch to the base of the heap. *Let the fire purge you of your ills, and cleanse you of the curse in your blood.*

She sucked in breath, and finding a strength he did not suspect she had, said in plain language. "Eat! It helps!"

Her eyes glazed over then. Her jaw eased closed. She swallowed hard, her adam's apple bobbing, and her fingers stopped reaching. Her shoulder stopped twitching.

She died.

He looked down at the fruit in his hand. *Eat.* Was it some kind of antidote? He had never seen a fruit like it before. Or was it a fruit in truth? *It helps.*

Faed City

Brown plumes drifted across a highway amid open plains. Clusters of Magura ranchers slid fence posts into deep holes, packed them with loose dirt, hammered boards into place where their plank fences needed repairing.

A bull watched its herd from a short distance away, tested the air with curved horns. It grunted as Xirakura passed, its gaze steady on him. Thick hooves scraped earth, the muscles in its wide back tensing around raised hackles.

In the distance, a few cows lowed, a cattle dog coming to usher them away as a rancher on horseback swung a lasso round and round over his head.

The bull charged the cattle dog. The lasso snaked out, caught it around the neck, pulled it round.

The bull wailed angrily. The rancher slid off his horse, cracking the lead as his boots struck the earth. The lead smacked aground with unnatural force, and the bull's head bowed. It's knees shook with the effort of keeping itself upright.

The rancher closed on it, stroked its head between the horns. The cattle dog and a pair of field workers ushered the herd into a corral, and through. A ritual guiding of the unsuspecting animals through the motions, to ease their nerves before a fresh pass saw a number of them dead.

He watched the display. It was nothing like the hunts his husband described. There was no stalking among the grasses, sneaking up on prey with bows drawn, knives out, spears at the ready. There were no snares, no traps. There was no need for all of those preparations with the pen holding them in.

More curious was that those posts weren't rejected from the earth. That the ranchers weren't swallowed up by it. Zanzark, the spirit of the plains, was dormant, unconcerned with the razing of his lands for ranching, the activity of men in his fields.

This was but one field among many staked out with fences of similar make, some of them sporting razor wire along their heights. Patches of land carved out for ownership, houses and barns erected in the far distance were made of wood and not grown out of trees. And trees were a rarity in this land. He could sense the spirits of them, weak and inconsequential next to the powerful Plains Lord but there nonetheless, drawing sustenance from an aquifer, itself claimed by a spirit

Tears for the Moon God

with the nauseating aura so common to those who dwelled in the dark.

Fleeting impressions of their opinions of these men passed through him, caught and dispelled in flashes. The trees were indifferent. Annoyed by the cattle herds and the ruckus they raised, yes, but unaffected by the work of these men, and content to let them go on. There were memories in them, of a time when their brothers and sisters had been cut down to make wood for man's use, but the practice had long died, the wood collected from traders come down from far off reaches, perhaps in Mishakh or Kao Shakh forests, where timber was less jealously guarded.

Zanzark had long drawn away from the Magura's activities, favored them none yet elected not to interfere. His concerns lay elsewhere, a rivalry with the spirit of that aquifer, a quarrel many thousands of years ago that neither had forgotten. Zanzark left her waters alone, taking what sustenance he needed from the driving rains that came often to this reach of Gora's lands, but that did not stop the digging of wells by mortal hands, the pulling of water through his flesh, saturating the deep recesses of his soul with ice to sooth the aches they inflicted upon him.

Indifferent, then, but not happy. *They must leave him some offering before they drive their shovels into the dirt. Something to earn his tolerance.*

This way was alien, the degradation of these spirits pervasive. He wondered if this was what all lands throughout the wide, open world were like. *Has everyone forgotten the old ways?*

The clothing Hurin had sent him with was well enough made. Smooth linen left plenty of room for breathing. His pants were somewhat tight around the groin and bunched uncomfortably at the knees, but they were otherwise unbothersome. The tunic was of a high thread count, so he had said, and smooth against his skin. Still, the way the wrinkles pressed into his elbows, his armpits, posed the same problem as the pants. The whole ensemble was uncomfortable.

This land was uncomfortable.

He left his watch of the ranchers and their cattle, his fingers latching absently on the edge of his quiver, testing the security of the straps binding it to his belt strap. At least the pants kept the corrugated barrel from grating against his thigh.

Among the Magura in the fields, several of the ranchers went shirtless, a distinction he noted. It seemed these notions of modesty extended only so far. What was practical won out in those fields, but on the road no one was so exposed. Everyone was clad in garb like his, of different cuts and materials which seemed specific to their cultures. An unspoken agreement, then. The road was for modesty. The field was for practicality.

There were many Magura on the road with him. In fact, it seemed most of those travelers on their way to Faed City were of the tribe. The paler-skinned Uari had mostly been left in the Ouran Goul pass, having come down the mountain to trade and then returning there. Many of them road on horseback, or in carriages with wheels nearly as tall as he was, which were drawn behind teams of four and six horses, and those not the palominos he'd seen in the mountain passes but smaller breeds, more compact. Some traders wagons were drawn by mules.

In the far distance, a gate. A cue formed up ahead of it stretched back nearly a mile, as best he could tell.

Hurin had mentioned this, too. There would be a toll, smaller for him than for those in the carriages. A toll for entry into the port city.

A half-moon wall spread along its sides. The wall was wood panel braced with thicker crossbeams for reinforcement. Even from this distance he could make out wide guard towers just behind it, where archers or acolytes of the spirits or the gods or all three together would be stationed, sentries against illegal intrusions on the city.

Don't let them hustle you. Hurin had said. They'll try to shake you down, some of them, but you just plant your feet and look them in the eyes. And keep looking, until they back down.

But be careful, too. Whatever you do, you don't want to piss off the Raukhas.

The Raukha's, he had been very clear on this, were not to be approached. For any reason. Many a man sought help from them, but it was never as it seemed. They asked their price up front and then again when the errand was done. Most times, their asking price was higher than it was worth. Often, it was not paid in coin.

He chewed the inside of his cheek as he drew up to the standstill procession of caravans and travelers ahead of the gate. A breeze blew from the east, billowing under his tunic and ruffling his hair.

"Zephos?" he asked.

Yes?

"You know much of this world I have never known."

You would ask me a question?

"Who are these Raukhas?" he whispered.

Dangerous people. Smugglers, murderers, thieves. Among them are acolytes of powerful spirits and gods. You have no need of them.

"But I have need of...someone. I cannot traverse these oceans without some help."

There are better avenues. Friends to you. But you should turn back. This task is beyond you. You do not understand it.

A peculiar thing to say. He thought to himself. "What do you know of my task?"

It will end in ruin. For you. For every mortal. The Elder Gods play a game within the Greatest Game. Their rivals, the Lesser Gods. They will not stop until they see their ends met, and you are an ace in the hole.

"An ace in the hole?"

Gora seeks what he has always sought. He marks you not for himself but for a god, or several gods. They rarely play alone.

"And if I choose to follow this path. To seek out healing from Tak the Fire."

Zephos gusted about him. He caught the hint of surprise, and then relief.

Go then. That path leads away. Perhaps you will find a fitting answer to the question they pose.

"Thank you." he bowed.

A few among those cued up and waiting for entry into the city gave him queer looks. Again, he was struck by the peculiar lack of reverence these people showed to their spirits. A degradation in fact. *They remember nothing.*

The cue inched forward, wagon wheels groaning as horse teams trotted a few steps, a few more. Casual conversations had in the interim where groups of those who knew each other or didn't exchanged news and spoke of happenings in the city itself.

Cattle ranches quickly gave way to fields of maize and pole beans, scrubby coverings of lettuce, and then an orchard. There was a spirit in that orchard, too, one a bare hundred or so years old, new born and infantile and happy to deliver to the Magura all the fruits they would eat. There were fae among those trees, too, drifting like cotton down from one branch to the next, planting seeds in looser soil or munching on fallen fruits, becoming drunk from imbibing fermented sugars.

He smiled at the field, reached out with his soul to call on the spirit, if only to say hello.

The spirit shied away from him.

Ah. Not old enough to know of my kind. And cautious. Do you not ask for offerings, spirit?

Receiving no answer, he turned his attention away from her. One day, she would be a gnarled old crone demanding fresh bread or blood sacrifice for her cooperation, and then the Magura would know a terror. He wondered at how she was born, whose hand had shaped her. She may be the daughter of Zanzark and a forest or an ocean spirit, or perhaps a fairy elevated to a new status by her kin. There had been fairy queens before, whole dynasties of spirits whose lives were brief and easily forgotten, who bloomed, flourished and then died and were replaced.

If she was like them, in a generation or two there may well be a new queen in her place, a new spirit of the orchard, and the people of this land would know no different. No sacrifices, then. No offerings, and no famine. *A pleasant life, I think. If they can hold the imaginations of those fae long enough to win over their hearts.*

Frustrations simmered as the cue dragged onward toward the gates. A pair of paler-skinned Uari played cards across the driver's bench of their wagon, occasioning to drive their horses forward to fill a newly opened gap. A knot of women of origins unknown to him waved lace fans near their faces. They wore heavy makeup under heavier wigs, porcelain-toned powders, rouges, apple-red stains on their lips and heavy eye shadow. They reminded him fleetingly of a man he had once seen as a youth, convening with a Spirit Caller long since retired who hailed from a neighboring village. The man had been wearing a mask of similar design when he arrived, had been clad in stark, black linen robes. Behind the mask was a bronzed face, tight wrinkles around the eyes denoting prolonged exposure to hot and dry winds, his cheekbones high and his chin somewhat narrow.

The man was uncommonly short by the standards of the Katuwiti, head and chest taller than Xirakura, and still a head shorter than the spirit caller he had spoken with. There had been words exchanged before they had ventured off into the forest—quiet, sharp words. He had not seen that man return, would not see him again.

The elder had said he was Nixian, another guardian tribe come from a place beyond the seas.

He wondered if these women were of the same tribe, if they had crossed the seas in coming to Faed City, if they were inclined to return to their homes. Again, he was struck by how limited his knowledge of the outside world truly was.

As he approached the gate and its guards at last, he was struck again by that sense of vastness. Behind them, the drop gate was ratcheted into its house high over head, its teeth just visible dangling like so many stalactites over the wide gap the guards blocked. The carriage and its gambling drivers rolled through and onto a stony road, and away amid shacks and square houses with peaked roofs, so many dwellings he could almost not believe so many people lived in one place.

The mingled smells of baking bread and horse shit filled his nose as he came

Faed City

face to face with a Magura soldier in armor of boiled leather, a chain hauberk draped over his jerkin and an arrowhead helm obscuring wiry hair.

"State your business?" he demanded, his accent lilting.

His gaze settled on the gourd at Xirakura's hip. His mailed hand drifted to rest on the pommel of his sword, his expression giving away nothing.

"I'm here to hire a ship." Xirakura said.

"Your destination?"

"Undecided."

The guard grunted. He spat in the dirt to one side of the road. "No entry, then."

"Why not?" Xirakura demanded.

"Because you've no reason to be here." the guard said. "Seeking a ship to what end? You're running from something's my bet, and I'll not be taking responsibility for harboring a fugitive, now will I?"

"I'm not running from...I'm here for...fah!" he balled up his fists. "I'll find another way then."

"Only one gate you'll be going through and that's this one. You cooperate, and maybe I change my mind. Maybe you're not running after all, you get me?"

Xirakura raised an eyebrow. He thought back to Hurin. Hurin, who said the guards at Faed City's gates were liable to bully him for more than their take, to skim a little off the top at his expense. What their betters didn't know wasn't hurting them, was it?

He looked the guard in his eyes, held that gaze, expressionless.

"I'm in need of a ship, and I will find one. A Rahad vessel, or one transporting them."

"You don't look like one of them."

"I'm seeking them."

"Who knows whether they're even here. They migrate. Don't stay long when they do come."

"So you'll let me in?' He held that gaze, bored holes into the guard's skull. "I have fare."

"Two marks." the guard said. "For the inconvenience."

"One." Xirakura countered stiffly.

The guard belted out a laugh. "Cheeky little asshole, aren't you? Fine. But only because I don't want to know what you've got trapped in there." He tipped his chin at Xirakura's hip, the gourd no longer in sight for it was behind him.

"Your people really trap spirits?"

"Demons, friend. Lake Suane is full of them. Jaded lover and that."

Xirakura handed over a gold tile." The guard stepped aside, letting him through.

"Your people don't use those for the same stuff?" he asked before Xirakura was well past him.

"No." Xirakura said, and left it at that.

He needed to find an inn. Hurin had been clear enough about that, as well. Only vagrants slept under the stars in a proper city, and then because they could not afford better lodgings. The city infrastructure hinged on trade and negotiation, everything cost money. There could be no bargain made with any vendor, be it an innkeeper, or a farmer, or a craftsman—all of them would demand those gold and silver tiles weighing down his pockets in exchange for whatever they provided him.

Tears for the Moon God

There would be no asking for those sustaining qualities, for that was perceived as begging, would get him in trouble before long if he kept up with it.

None of these Magura were apt to help him out of kindness. Every interaction must needs be transactional, a concept alien to him and his people, who thrived in the way they did because each artisan, every hunter and forager, even Spirit Callers, offered their excesses to each other. The survival of the individual depended on the survival of the clan. The survival of the clan depended on the survival of the village. Everyone had their place, and everyone provided something in sustaining the village, and they were all equal. No one good, nor any one service, was perceived as more valuable than the other. Man needed food and clean water to sustain the flesh, healing to sustain the spirit, woven quilts for warmth, reliable shelter to keep him safe. The Katuwiti provided, for each other, and in providing for each other they thrived alongside each other.

This system, with its monetization of one good in relation to the next, with prices varying based upon which crop was to be sold, how rare the gift within a craft was…it was anathema, as much as these uncomfortable clothes, or the way the Magura treated the spirits of their lands, or the wooden shacks and houses rambling along their narrow, dusty roads. The glass in those windows was warped and filled with bubbles, translucent but never quite transparent, and shot through here and there with impurities which cast it in dishwater shades of yellow, gray and green. It had not been so in Ouran Goul Pass. The craft of blowing glass, of pulling it into shape or whatever they did to create those windowpanes, was performed by lesser hands here, who paid too little attention to detail, and yet he suspected those dingey, pocked and scarred panes were expensive, even as they would not hold against intruders.

In the tooling of the wood was where the Magura craftsmanship revealed its expertise. Boards flush with each other rose into buttresses carved over with images of animals, flowers, text in the language of these people, a sister tongue to what the Katuwiti spoke which he could barely read. Veiled porches were thrust out from their facades, and the facades were painted in bright, pastel colors, imitating a sunset sky in hues of pink, yellow, lavender, and rose.

He wondered if this was a people who worshipped the gods. If the sun god, Gorgus, ruled supreme over this ocean fastness.

It would fit.

He eyed the sunburst design etched into the height of a shop keep's porch roof. Alongside was a stylized moon, and opposite that, a sickle. The band of molding was of lacquered ebony.

Four gods, then. Must be. Moon and Sun, opposed to each other. Death Elder, and his son, Darkness. Yes, this must be the house of a mystic.

He elected to step off the road, climb onto the porch. It was custom in Sufa Salein for one Spirit Caller on pilgrimage to visit upon another when passing through his village.

He knocked on the door, and waited. It swung inward as the master of the house—a slender, dark-skinned man who was an inch or two taller than him—presented himself.

"What do you want?" he snapped. "A reading? You'll have to come back when'um open."

"You are a shaman among your people?"

Faed City

The mystic spat onto the floorboards, barely missing Xirakura's feet. "Depends who's asking." His gaze fell to Xirakura's hip.

On impulse, Xirakura shifted his gourd around and behind him.

"You consort with demons? Bad omen that. Best you get on your way; I don't want any trouble, now."

He slammed the door in Xirakura's face.

Some way to greet a friend. He panned over the road. *Might as well find that inn.* He dismounted the porch and pushed on.

The spoken language was difficult enough to parse out. It shared a root with his own, was somewhat intelligible in that sense, though the cadence was off, clipped where the Katuwiti tongue flowed, marked by odd clicking sounds held at the back of the throat, and the pronunciations of many a familiar word were different.

He had been able to understand the mystic, in the same way he had been able to understand Hurin. A common root, yes, but he need strain to hear it. The sister languages had branched far in the indeterminate time between their splitting off the mother tongue.

A pair of dancers in silhouette stood out between bands of flowing script. The building attached to it was two stories, long and sprawling, with many windows. Now and again a traveler passed its threshold, either coming or going. Some of those were obviously intoxicated, while others marched onto the street diligently, their steps even, their gazes fixed pointedly forward.

He passed that threshold, into a quiet common room. The bar at the back was populated by travelers and Magura locals, many of whom sipped at glass cups filled with a cloudy substance he suspected was the local brew. A number of round, careworn tables were similarly populated, and some of the patrons there consumed a thick stew from wooden bowls with elongated spoons, or ate a salad of grains and herbs with their fingers.

He approached the bar, where a barkeep busied himself dredging glasses through a barrel filled with water, to be set aside for later polishing. The barkeep approached him.

"What d'you want?" he asked. "Lodging? Food? A drink?"

"Lodging for now. Some food later, maybe." Xirakura said.

The barkeep raised an eyebrow. "What was that, now?"

Xirakura adjusted his pronunciation of the word, echoing the barkeep. "Lodging."

"Two silver bars for the night. That includes your meal. Daubo's a tile a cup if you want. It's the local favorite."

"Daubo?"

The barkeep wagged two fingers at a cup containing a milky substance that was conspicuously mottled. "Cow's milk. Fermented and that. Like beer."

"No thank you."

The barkeep sneered. He produced a key from under the counter while Xirakura passed him a gold mark. He took the mark, bit into it, then exchanged it for the appropriate tender.

Xirakura accounted for that exchange in his head. Five bars is one mark. The barkeep handed him three back with the key.

"Second floor, left wing." he cocked his chin in the direction of a staircase the other end of the common room.

Tears for the Moon God

"Thank you." Xirakura navigated around the tables, mounted the staircase. He found his room near the end of the second floor. The whole expanse barely accommodated a single-wide bed, a side table on which was mounted a candelabra—the taper candles melted to half height, their wicks burned black—and a wardrobe within which he stowed his rucksack, bow and quiver. The windows were framed on this side with sheer curtains, which would do nothing either to block out the light or obscure his silhouetted form when drawn. Yet another indication of this people's obsession with vanity.

He stripped off his clothes, glad to finally be rid of the oppressive raiment, and seated himself on the edge of the bed. The weave of the blanket was rough, and a gritty substance was rimed into it, like sand. *They haven't cleaned this room in some time, have they?*

He looked to the window, watched obscure, human-shaped shadows pass by on the road down below. *Where would I find the Rahad? They must congregate somewhere, those who need their gifts.*

He decided he'd ask the barkeep when he ventured downstairs again. He may not have an answer for where these Rahad might be found, but he would at least know where those impoverished in this city lived. *A callous people, to let their kin live in squalor. Leaving it to wandering others to give them what their own can provide.*

He thought back to the tolls at the gates. Wondered what that coin was used for. If it sat in a box somewhere, collected and hoarded against luxuries for a lord like Hurin, for the maintenance of his sprawling estates.

Likely as not there had been those in need at Ouran Goul pass. Likely as not, Hurin's own hoarded wealth would have aided them. And more to the point, it was quite probable Hurin himself had not bothered to extend his hand to them, give them what they needed. These outlanders did not concern themselves with the common good. It seemed he would find this plague of avarice spread throughout all of the world, and the isolated lands of the Katuwiti the last bastion of charity, of honest kinship.

He thought again of Hurin. *Did he not help me when I was in need? Perhaps they are not all bad, these people. But then…would he have lent me that aid if he did not also fear what I might bring onto his people, were I to remain?*

He touched the brands against his chest, followed the contours of those scars over his midriff. *Let me find these Rahad. Let me find Tak the Fire through them. This healing is overdue.*

Gandes Fae

From her vantage on the low slopes, Lisandra could see the forest sprawling across Ergol's roots, thin wisps of smoke lingering over volcanic peaks, threatening eruption should the spirits of those mountains be angered. Grassland formed a thin belt, breaking against jagged outcrops where the footing became treacherous.

She felt them watching her, an itch between her shoulder blades. Did they know the coins in her pockets came from a tax collector's chest, picked with a sturdy twig and the clip of a stolen earring. Did they suspect she came clad in another woman's dress? With a pack filled with supplies intended for her children, her husband?

Do they care?

The spirits of Ergol's range were notoriously hostile. Even in the Fingers, their anger was legendary. A plume of ash ejected from a distant peak drifted into the sky. Thunder rolled across the air, lightning cracked. The display promised an outpouring of molten rock, the coming of the Goddess of Storms to contest the mountain's claim of dominance, to inundate the people living in its shadow with driving rains, floods to cool the basalt.

No mercy for the mortal.

She climbed, leaning on a branch she'd stripped of bark and straightened over open flame the night prior. Twenty years younger, the climb would have been easier, but she was not the spry thing she had been in her prime years.

She labored up the steep incline at angle with the cliff's edge, careful to stay out of its shadow for fear the thrust out ledge at its height would come down on her.

She passed settlements, staying well clear of them. No telling if the residents were Saodeini or Sarkahni. The war effort would be known to them, the mines and forges working double time to yield bars of iron for weapons and shields.

Rumors had long reached the Fingers of Hou Rok's push into Sarkahn plain, a festering anger from the spirit for the god's subtle violations of their treaty. Soon enough, the land would rise up against Tao Baduhr, and the old war would begin anew.

She wondered who these miners traded with. If the gods influence had extended to this side of the range yet. How long it would be before the Range Lord was forced to answer him.

Tears for the Moon God

The old tales spoke of an alliance. Three spirits bringing their wrath against the God of Smiths, the clashes reshaping the land, driving Galadir into a new track, his old riverbed abandoned, the villages along it forced to move, abandoning whole settlements in the night as he railed against the insurgent. Mountain slopes overrun with falls of ash and molten rock, killing thousands. The plains seized by earthquakes, fissures swallowing whole armies.

She hoped she did not live to see the day that war was begun. That her life ended before the spirits faced down the god. Wars of that kind were never kind to mortals.

She pressed on, traveling by daylight, making camp in sturdy hollows, following paths higher and more treacherous each day. Rockslides blocked her path. Ash rains pushed her back down slope. Flood waters made whole valleys impassable. Weeks were made of what should take days. Still she climbed.

She stopped in one village on the valley slope the other side of a mountain the locals called Wane, for the spirit was weaker and the mountain smaller than those which surrounded it. She purchased a goat there, and the shepherd gave her a warning.

"Trust nothing he says, dear." the toothless elder said; bushy, white eyebrows twitching. "Some things are better left mysteries."

She had not told him where she was heading, but his warning told her she was close. Perhaps, the business of selling goats for slaughter was his means of survival, of taking coin from travelers; then again, perhaps his warning was genuine.

She ignored him.

The next morning, she found the cave, a narrow corridor carved by wind and water into a towering cliff, the other end of a narrow pass strewn with the remains of humans and game animals.

Seeing these skeletal remains, she considered turning back, but Syrk's blessing was with her still. She would not have his protection a second time.

She lit an oil lantern, took the goat by its leash and led it forward.

An infantile wail echoed back to her from close by.

Local custom might well demand sacrifices to the spirit, a payment in blood to keep his children idle. Still, she approached. Whatever custom these hill people abided, she could not simply let an innocent lamb be killed by whatever monster occupied this place.

The pallid child lay atop a mound of fresh turned earth. It's mouth was contorted around a scream, limbs curled in close and half buried in the dirt. She crouched, supporting herself against the walking stick, and reached to stroke its hair.

The baby wailed. It's hollow eyes flared unnaturally; and she keeled back, sat hard in the dirt.

Her goat screamed.

Earth shot into the air. Legs wrapped around her chest, pinning the arm from which the goats leash ran.

It bolted, dragging her and the mol fae with it, toward the entrance.

Wiry fur pressed against her throat, filled her mouth as the mol fae's head reeled back, mandibles spread wide.

It hissed, dislodged itself from her and ran on spindle legs to climb a wall, where it remained, hissing, watching her.

Gandes Fae

She righted herself, dug in her feet and pulled at the leash as another of the creature's came for the goat.

She pulled hard. It flopped onto its back, legs kicking as the mol fae pounced. Hooves punched into its carapace. Black blood and pale gore spattered its fur.

The mol fae curled in on itself and was still. She crawled back, dragging the terrified goat after her, gathered her lantern, her walking stick, her heart pounding.

"Trust nothing he says." she breathed. "Trust nothing in this *gods forsaken* cave!"

She wiped her hands against her dress, breathed deeply in an effort to still her pounding heart.

She closed on the goat, stroked its head, cooing to it. It calmed down enough that she could lead it, but kept close now, its flank bumping into her as she navigated the cave tunnel, steering clear each time she encountered a pale, fleshy bubble on the ground, knowing none of those children could be human.

The wailing became an eerie music as she pressed on. Now and again, silence descended, but the wails broke it within moments. Each time, she jumped, fearing another attack might come, knowing the goat held none of her protection.

Down and down she traveled, crossing paths which led into other corridors, twice being forced to choose a path where the main tunnel was blocked by bones, or by too many of those creatures to navigate safely between them.

In the cold, dank depths of the cavern, she came into a wide chamber, its ceiling high and hollow near the back, implying the beginnings of another tunnel.

Something in that dugout stirred. Spindle legs tested the stone-strewn earth. Long, oiled fangs followed, looming over a satin sleek carapace, the back bristling with dark fur. The creature had three faces. A woman's face, lips pursed, eyes narrowed in dreamy aplomb peered out from its meaty neck. A man's face, prominent brow looming over hollow cheeks, a strong jaw, was nestled into its head where a spider's eyes ought to be. The last peaked out when the head dipped low, a child's face that lacked distinct features of boy or girl.

The creature observed her through the man's eyes.

The cave walls hugged its thorax on either side, where its body fell away into obscurity within a shallow alcove. Yet still, it dominated the space with its sheer size, and she could not discern whether she hugged her goat to keep it under control, or to comfort herself in that monstrosity's presence.

The goat screamed its protests into the stillness, and in the tunnel behind her she could hear the clicking of spindly legs as they played against rock, and knew the spirits children were watching.

"Who calls on Gandes Fae?" the creatures asked, and she realized with painful clarity how much of a mistake this errand had been. "Who stinks of fouled water and indecision."

The woman's face regarded the goat. "An offering? She comes seeking answers. The questions plague her, enough to risk Ergol's anger. To risk our...appetite."

Gandes Fae kicked a stone bowl toward her. It swiveled on its base, came to land upright.

"Offer your sacrifice, then." said the child. "It's throat must be cut by your own hand, the bowl filled with life blood."

She withdrew a skinning knife from her belt with trembling fingers.

"H-how many questions--"

"Three. "One for each of my faces, answered in truth." the man said.

Tears for the Moon God

She held the goat's chin up, using her legs to keep it from backing out of her hold. She raked the knife across its neck, guided it over the bowl.

Its scream came out as a rasp. Its struggle violent and then weakening, until it could only twitch, the vitality leaking from muscles with its strength.

It died in her arms, the bowl filled, blood spilled over its edges to paint the ground.

What have I done?

She tasted bile in her throat.

"Bring it to me." the man said.

She picked up the bowl, out of fear that to disobey would earn her a swift death more than any aspirations toward clarity.

She brought the bowl before the spirit, set it there, retreated, leaving space enough between them, but keeping clear of the goat that she did not have to see it. The evidence of her own cruelty.

The spirit dipped its head, the woman's face pressed lips to the bowl and drank.

"Aah." the man gasped.

"To taste blood warm and fresh. So long denied us." the child whispered, a warbling ecstasy in its tone.

The woman drained the bowl, her eyes closed, savoring every drop which passed across her tongue.

Blood dripped from her chin as the spirit raised its head.

"Sweet succor." she wheezed. "The offering is made. The terms accepted."

"Three questions." the man said. "Three answers given freely. Ask of me the first."

"I've come a long way, you understand? Having left my home exposed. If I am to answer Saodein's aggression, push them out of the Fingers decisively, I need power." she explained. "I am told a spirit called Kushein may help me, but I have my doubts. Is a shield for the Fingers truly the best answer? If I may be frank, I would much rather a knife in the dark."

The spirit reeled back its head and cackled, the sound deep and guttural. She flinched back, her heel striking the still twitching goat.

"Oh, how Kushein's power would serve you, but it has once before. Sarkahn's fingers purged of Saodein's influence, and the plans of those gods who supported them were sundered. You will go to her without regard for our answer, as the seed has already been planted in your mind, and though Lanfin's river ever flows, he can but push its path only so far. You will go to her, because you have already, in a past he would rather you forget. And she will save your land, woman, but she cannot save you."

She stepped over the goat, putting it between herself and the spirit. No amount of distance would ever feel like a comfort as long as she remained in this cave. She suspected, should the spirit be so inclined, its attack on her would be swift. There would be no thought for escape, no time. She would be consumed, one more memory collected within the vast mind of the monster.

Its sinuous neck twisted, curled back over its meaty torso. The woman's face was revealed in perfect clarity, nestled in a scruff of wiry, black hair, a grizzly mane hanging over an underbelly which throbbed as it drew air into its spiracles.

Played out across waxy, pallid flesh, the effect was nauseating.

She gave no time for Lisandra to contemplate what the first face had said before

Gandes Fae

making her own demand. "Ask what you will, dear. Ask and I will give answer."

Thoughts raced through her mind. Kushein was the only answer, just as the dead man said. The best answer for her people. But what was this about having met her before, having inherited her power? Shulraki had mentioned the Halls of Time, hadn't he?

"Do I know someone...someone who is trapped..." she worked spit back into her mouth, tried the question again. "Do I know someone who is trapped in the Halls of Time?"

Another gout of laughter. Harsh breath hissed out of the spirit's flanks. It kicked up motes of dust, suffused the chamber with suffocating heat and the fetid odor of advanced decay. The dust obfuscated the feminine face, the serpentine neck curling down as the woman began to speak.

"We agreed, did we not? Truth in answer to the questions posed." the man's face said.

"You will invite his attention? Is it wise?

"Lanfin is but a Lesser God."

"He is not the only one with a hand in this. Recall, it was not his choice to claim that one. There were others, then, as there are others now."

"Rasheik will protect us." The child hissed. "We are too valuable to him. He will not lose us."

"Answer." the man insisted.

What the hell? Lisandra thought.

The man scowled darkly at the woman. The neck arched upward again, leaving her in plain view as the dust finally settled.

"There is one within the Halls called Sao Njack, so named the Dragon of the East at the height of his power. A Nixian, their one and only emperor, he conquered or united the various lands east of Rasheik's spine, your hated enemy included.

"But he fell. An accident of fate which stole both liberty and love from him. He ventured to Ur, where he came to meet you. You conspired with him, then, to bring about an end to his lover, with whom he had conquered your lands, united them with the rest under the banner of their growing empire. Do you understand the significance of this? I think not. No, notions of so vast an empire, so tentative a peace, the crushing weight of it can only be beyond you. But it was.

"So, too, it was your shield he needed. To stand against the gods themselves, wielding Lady Kushein's power to save him from them. All in service of bringing an end to the one called Dupec Safar, his lover, your enemy, before he brought an end to your way of life. To all of yours."

Thoughts congealed in her mind's eye, slowing as ideas of what was true and real were again broken apart and reconfigured. As Gandes Fae's answers to her questions revealed a depth beyond what little Shulraki had told her, revealed to her that she was part of some grand design. That this was no life she wanted, yet it was one she could not escape.

The gods are watching me, aren't they? And for no reason I should like.

The woman glared upward as Gande's Fae's neck stretched outward and descended. It's spider-like legs spread wider, its thorax collapsing heavily against gravel-strewn stone. The little boy's face was revealed. It fixed hollow eyes on her, its soft chin thrust toward the ceiling, forehead nestled in a snatch of fur at the base of the spirit's neck.

"Your last question, Shield Maiden."

Tears for the Moon God

She giggled. *Finally, a spirit with some manners.*

Later, she would contemplate how disquieting the experience had been that this moment must seem so absurdly...humorous. That she should know such terror that to press on being afraid meant a diffusion of tension was necessary. She needed a break of some kind, to assure her she would make it out of this hole in the ragged earth. That a break was needed, in hindsight, would bring with it some notion that the question she asked might well have been pushed out of some inane place, some over stimulated part of her brain usually cordoned off and forgotten, which spilled forth its hilarity, but only to protect her sanity.

I've lived before, have I? Some glamorous life spent hunting tyrants in the company of other tyrants. I've lived before in a world with such vicious bastards about that my aged bones were deemed too useful to ignore. And what good did it do? All washed away downstream along with the Great Snake's piss and a bunch of bad memories.

Only the truly damned go to Ur. What could I possibly have done to piss off the gods so much. The Fingers couldn't be that important to them. Could they?

She clapped her hand over her mouth, stifled the chuckles clucking past her teeth, and asked her final question. In hindsight, yes, she would come to believe she should have asked something else. Perhaps asked after the identify of Shulraki Alran, why he had come to visit her. Or she could have pressed for more information about this Nixian emperor. She might have bothered to ask after where she might find allies to defend her home, or who this Dupec Safar was, why he was so important.

But in the haze of the moment and with the furious wish to leave this place behind forever a refrain behind the more coherent thoughts rustling around in her mind, she asked instead:

"What do I do?"

As if the revelations come in answer to her first two questions were not alarming or esoteric enough, the child's answer proved to be as helpful, and more ominous than all else she had born witness to.

"What do I do?"

"You run. With darkness in your shadow, you run. Beyond Gonsai Wall, you run. To Salein's cave, to Nixir. A hated enemy come as an ally, one who has twice sought your death, awaits."

Hunter, Pathfinder, Seer

"This is a whore house." Wu said indignantly.

Garam chuckled. "The man you will be working for is a businessman before he is anything else."

"This is hardly a business."

They stood outside the brothel, a monumental structure which consumed the length of an entire block. From within open windows, he could see the merchandise striking suggestive poses, many of them pressed against the glass with nothing whatever to cover them. Night had long since fallen, and what decorum the streets demanded in daylight had gone with the moon's rise. Debauchery reigned over the streets of Cratom. Here on this cramped avenue, it was king.

Exhausted looking men filtered out of hidden exits and around corners to rejoin the crowds passing from tavern to palm reader to hawker and then tavern again. They sported dopey grins and more than one was holding up their pants by the waistband, having apparently forgotten their belts in the rush to get out before they were charged for an extra hour.

A number of madames stood just inside the entrance, waiting to take new consumers by the hand and lead them to private rooms to await the working girls of their choosing. He had never been inside one of these places, had seen glimpses of them flash across the wall of doors surrounding Uldal's hilltop but had never been brazen enough to pass through, to invade those corridors and rooms filled with odorous perfumes of sweat and shameless abandon.

Garam laced his arm into the crook of his elbow. "Come now, don't look so tart, Lord Bane. The Funhouse is here for your enjoyment."

Garam dragged him forward, and he stumbled through the entrance after him.

They entered a lounge thick with sweet smelling smoke. Off to one side was a well attended bar. Raucous laughter and shouted conversation almost drowned out the lively music a house band was playing from their low stage in the lounge's far corner. The performers swayed drunkenly around their instruments, missing notes at times to the chagrin of no one, and singing in atonal, sibilant voices raised high, as if in yelling they came closer to the tunes they were chasing after.

Garam stabbed a finger toward the back of the house. "That's for the high

Tears for the Moon God

rollers. Moneyed people." he shouted over the din.

He was pointing at a carousel. The revolving stage was populated with glass cages, all lit from below with soft, red light. Within each cage was a man or a woman, sometimes both, all as naked as the day they were born and swaying at the hips. In one cage, two women kissed passionately, their hands roving over each other's bodies, pawing at breasts, performing vanishing acts with slender fingers pressed between thick thighs. In another, a man contorted his body into improbably shapes, his cock hard and pin wheeling at the slightest provocation.

A smaller crowd had gathered at the foot of the stage. Its members waved sacks of coin over their heads. Notes of purchase passed from attendant madames to the victors in bidding wars over popular harlots. Money changed hands, was counted against a wide table off to the side. Strong men stood guard over the carousel and helped harlots out of their cages, escorted them around the stage and through a curtained entrance behind it while the madames fell on the victors, escorted them away through a second entrance and up a staircase where their rooms awaited them.

"How depraved." Wu said.

"Don't be such a prude, my lord."

"You can stop calling me that any time."

Garam ignored him. "I see you eying that hulking masterpiece."

He leaned in until they were almost cheek to cheek, looking over his shoulder in the direction of a well muscled Goth with an uncommonly strong jaw line. He had been staring, not because he wanted something from the man. Never that. He did not need to lower himself to bidding against a horde of sweaty lechers for the attention of a stranger who, if he knew anything at all of the world's oldest profession, had been intimate with several men and maybe women just in time since he arrived for his shift.

He was handsome, but he was not who Wu Bane wanted. At best, he would be a surrogate for someone he could view as a person of interest. Someone he had reason to miss when he was gone.

"Can we get on with it." he demanded.

Snickering, Garam patted his shoulder. "This way." he led him toward the entrance the madames were taking the victors through, deviated at its feet and led him to a lift instead. The lift was velvet walled and situated behind a gilded grate made to resemble a great sunburst which was framed by so many flowers. A guard looked the assassin over. He reached for the grate, and hesitated when he saw who accompanied him.

"Who's your friend?" he asked, his voice gruff and booming.

"A business prospect." Garam replied. "Saijin will be expecting us."

The guard raised an eyebrow. "Will he now?"

"As he is prone to reading what lies in those songs God Lanfin likes to sing, I suspect so."

The guard grumbled something too low to hear. He wrenched the grate open, and Garam gestured Wu through.

He stepped inside after him.

The guard closed the grate and cranked a lever in the wall beside it. The grate chugged to life, carrying them away from the lounge, and then past the next floor, to settle on the third level, where another guard was waiting to receive them.

Hunter, Pathfinder, Seer

They passed this one by as soon as the grate was open, and marched down the hall opposite until they arrived at a door which was the only one along its length.

Garam rapped his knuckles against it. A few moments passed in silence. He raised his fist to do it again, and the door sprang open, revealing lavish apartments. They were all clean lines and angles, the drapes pristine white and framing the entrance onto a veranda framed by a wrought iron rail. A chaise lounge rested near the open doors, and a trellis behind it was dripping with honeysuckle vines, all in bloom. The flowers pushed their fragrance into the air, further expanding on the impression of airy, expansive lodgings.

An uelfin lounged in that chaise, eating grapes from a silver tray atop a wiry stand next to it. His hair was a violent shade of green, and hung lank over his pale forehead. His eyes were red, and a crosshatch tattoo peeked out over a sharp cheekbone on the right side.

The uelfin reminded him of so many stereotypes associated with those people. He was posh, dressed in the finest silks all tailored to accentuate his slender frame, and his every languid gesture spoke to the feigned elegance so many powdered nobles the world over maintained. This was a man who had never known a hard day's work.

Wu instantly hated him.

"What have you brought to me now, Garam?" he took Wu's measure out of the corner of his eye.

Garam slid onto the edge of a writing desk near the apartment entrance. A cool breeze filtered in from the veranda, and the uelfin's gaze drifted languidly toward it. He bobbed his head to a rhythm neither Wu nor Garam could hear, a song to extrapolate on the present, and sought to define an uncertain future. To bring it into focus.

"Who is the fool?"

"I'm sorry." Wu said.

"Well, you must be a fool if you have agreed to help me. Any sane person would run for the hills." He flapped his wrist in the direction of the distant Pongyin range. "Just being in my presence may well put a target on your back. The gods are not merciful."

"They would risk offending God Uldal."

"You're important to him, then? He knows why you're here?"

"You seem to think you do."

The uelfin snickered. "Of course, I do. I saw your arrival before you ever touched a toe to the dock. You've come here under false pretenses, with a mission in mind, but tell me something. Is it worth what I am asking of you?"

"I believe it is, yes."

"Do you know what I'm asking of you?"

"I know enough."

The uelfin's grin was unnerving. He wanted to slap it off that powdered whoremonger's lips. "What do you know?"

"You've pissed off a god. You need to get out of this city. You need to go where that god can't touch you. There is only one place like that, and it is on the other side of the world. Short of finding an acolyte of Gods Uldal or Mu, your only hope of getting there alive would be to form a compact with the wind spirits, which they would not give you."

Tears for the Moon God

The uelfin nodded.

"Perhaps it's too late, friends, but introductions are in order." Garam cut in. "Saijin, this is Wu Bane. Wu Bane, Saijin. Now you're properly acquainted, perhaps you can remove the knives from each other's throats."

"What knives."

"It's a, um, figure of speech. If I had known you would get along this poorly—"

"Enough, Garam." Saijin snapped. "Our guest deserves to know why we are gathered here. He must know what he is getting into. I will not have him making a snap decision he will come to regret at the critical hour."

"Then say your piece." Wu said. "But know I've made up my mind."

Saijin grew distant for a moment. His eyes became unfocused. He did not seem to be listening, even to be entirely with them. He snapped back to the present, gave his full attention to him.

"You'll have to pardon me. Given the circumstances, I have been, perhaps, easily distracted." he said. "With regard to my need of you, I have indeed angered a god. But to go along with the path he sets forward would be to doom countless innocents."

"I've never known an uelfin to care." Wu grumbled.

Saijin ignored him. "The specific god I have angered is Lanfin, God of Music. You see, there is but one taboo upon the use of his gifts, which applies to all uelfin. We must never sing in counter-tune to him. We are not to interfere with his designs. Rather, it is our place to aid him in realizing them. But what he wants is something I cannot abide. To give him what he desires would be to deliver devastation to mortal kind.

"There are others involved in this latest play of hands. Some lesser. Some elder. At the heart of their game sit the Wanderers, a man you are well acquainted with, and a spirit who is best left alone. They are plotting something, those who Lanfin walks in step with. Something I do not like. In order to ensure he does not get what he wants, I need the safety of Ur, so that I can sing again."

"You intend to violate Echo's Peace?"

"How do you define violation? I sing so that others may influence events in our world. I am not strong enough by myself to break any of them free. But there are older ways. Lost ways. Should I give them the opportunity, they may find what they need, and then perhaps we can stop God Lanfin's ploy from succeeding.

"What I need from you is simple transit. A way open to Nixir, where a convergence of certain powers is brewing."

"You'll have every uelfin outside of Cratom after you. Even some of them within the city will want you dead."

"Rest assured, they've already attempted to take his head half a dozen times. It has been just as many days." Garam said.

Wu regarded him. "You've put them down?"

Garam nodded. "They're getting smarter. Every day we waste here gives them another chance at success."

"Then we shouldn't waste any time."

"You don't want your stepmother dead?"

Wu's grin was full of malice. "I haven't changed my mind about that, but we'll have to speed up the timeline."

"No!" Saijin said. "No distractions. I must be out of this city at the earliest

Hunter, Pathfinder, Seer

opportunity."

"Quiet." Wu said. "Let the grown ups talk."

"He has a point." Garam said. "With every passing day, our situation becomes more precarious. The assassins they have sent so far have not been of my caliber, but it is only a matter of time before that changes."

"Which is why we speed up the timeline. Take her out sooner. We have what we need to formulate a plan. We can leave after she is dealt with."

Even two days would be too long—"

"Shut up, Saijin." Wu snapped. "You've got a Raukha assassin working for you. He should have no problem keeping you alive until we're done. Even if he is helping me rip that woman off her pedestal."

Garam turned pensive as he settled his regard on his client. "There is a potential benefit to you, as well. If Mistress Bane is preoccupied with trying to kill Wu, she will have fewer resources to throw at you. The uelfin who are after you will have fewer options at their disposal for dealing with you, and what is available to them will likely be worse."

"You say that as if he intends to operate in the open." Saijin said.

Garam smirked. "For someone who can see the future, you can be quite naïve."

"I'm leaving." Wu said. "Find me when you return to the Black Lamb. We have plans to flesh out."

He turned on Saijin, walked toward the doorway into the hall. Three steps from it, the hall was swallowed and replaced by a different corridor, a place of careworn carpets and dust glittering in lamplight, painting dirty walls in shadow. He stepped through, and let the door fall away behind him, leaving Garam to find his own way back.

He's been running from time for six days already. He'll be fine. And if he isn't, I'll have her head before long. I just need to keep the bastard alive until then.

He would keep his word. He was not beyond that measure of honesty. But if time ran out for the uelfin, guilt would lay at his own feet. He would feel nothing if Saijin died. And if Garam betrayed him, well...he would feel nothing for leaving him to die, either.

Baduhrak's Diplomacy

Beyond the break of Ung Sakh's jungle was liberation. Gone were the old ties. The old alliances and loyalties. The jungle was enemy land, of Saodein, but it was not hers alone. Saodein was just one nation within the spirit's embrace. There was Tulahk, as well, and if she was not misguided in her belief, that other kingdom enjoyed as much favor from her as her enemies did.

It was that playing of both sides among the spirits that rankled Lisandra. It was their penchant for neutrality that drove her to instruct Lisk to turn his prayers to Death Elder, Shah Jagat, when the ocean failed them.

No, Ung Sakh was not a friend to Lisandra Almaine, but she had been a warm enough host. The spirits were not loyal to mortals. There was no controversy in that. The fool believed in giving tribute, he might gain the favor of the forest, or the plains, or the sea, but he ignored a simple truth in his courting rituals. Those who would call themselves his enemy were just as apt to deliver offerings. They delivered them with as much frequency, as much fervor. So man pitted himself against man, and the spirit glutted. There was no winning this contest. The spirits abided mortals, but they did not love them. The spirits tolerated mortal intrusions, some of them did, tolerated the destructive ways of mortals, the fires set to their grasses, their trees felled, rocky slopes blasted to pieces and dark earth tunneled through. Tolerance was won through bribery. Sanguhr was the same as Saodein in this regard. Saodein was the same as Sarkahn's Fingers, his plains. As Rasheik's rope and all of its ranges and mountain peaks.

But Sanguhr was not beholden to Ung Sakh, not entirely. Her influence waned here. Whatever her relationship to Lisandra had been, it was not here that the jungle claimed dominance, and she did not have to think for the loyalties of the spirits who rose up in her absence, whose flesh she walked across, the length of whose bones she traveled.

She felt release. This was not home, but it was not enemy territory either. The conflicts between Saodein and the Fingers were not this people's to bear, and in their ambivalence was tolerance earned, so much easier to commodify, to win against mortal morality, the insights of the short lived. Perhaps it was easier for mortals to forgive, she could not be sure. But in this land was a different symbiosis.

Baduhrak's Diplomacy

Gonsai loomed in the far distance, his geometrically faceted wall climbing into the heavens, its heights shrouded in mists. A waterfall spilled forth from near its height, white water falling silent into an unseen pool. Trees dotted the open plains, but grew so distant from one another even the densest of their thickets could not be deemed a wood.

She had walked along this spare rib through Sanguhr's countryside for many hours, having seen nothing she would call civilized. A battered farmhouse. A herd of cows with shaggy mops obscuring their eyes, all of them, cow and bull, bearing horns. A number of children playing hide and seek among tall grasses, stamping down cattails within a shallow pond, making pathways among the reeds.

She could not help but smile at them. She had done much the same as a child, among the inland lakes and pools. Those bent reeds would not hold the weight of an adolescent, let alone that of a grown person, but they would hold for those children, keep them well above the cloying much. So those little ones tamped down reeds, rode over their bases with rocking, bare feet, let mud and water flow between their toes as they sprinted down existing pathways playing games of their own designs.

These were unburdened children. It had been too many years since the children of Sarkahn had been free of the terrors and the traumas of war. Since she had seen bright eyes, innocent smiles, on a child above ten. Her heart went out to these children. She hoped they would always know peace.

Zephos came with force enough to make walking strenuous, threatening to bowl her over if she did not choose her footing carefully, and on the winds he carried across the plains, the mists cleared. The sun's beating rays boiled away vapors, pulled back the morning fog to reveal the flat roofs and slab walls of dwellings, the front line of a village soldiering out of obscurity. Those homes were made of stones fitted together, a cyclopean puzzle, the uneven rocks fitted together and caked with clay mud. Ragged portals looked out over the planes, the stones about them cut and fitted with vitreous, glass. There was no wood among these houses to speak of. The doors were reed mats thatched together and bound into shape, sturdy enough to keep out the high winds, but they would do little against invaders.

Torch poles were staggered along gravel avenues between those houses. In the night, the heads of household must go out and light them. They might set a watch against the roads then. Looking for outsiders—raiders and thieves.

She closed in on this village, latched eyes onto a wider complex looming from behind those initial lines. There would be lodging there. She hoped there would be. Or was it a market of some kind, an agora? *Is that greater complex a pole house? Do their elders meet there?*

Life moved in the lazy way of the unbothered. The slow meandering of people along open streets. The children she had seen in the countryside, the farmhouse, those were peoples and a place where duties must be performed unselfishly. Where food was made, where seeds were sewn and crops reaped with the turning of the seasons, but this was no village for subsistence. This was a place where trade flourished and the people lived comfortably. Wealth was not concentrated in one set of hands, but rather the whole village prospered because everyone had their place. There had been a time when her village had been the same. Before Saodein arrived with all of her customs, and her way of life had changed.

There had been that time before skirmishes and war when she had been innocent, when all of them had been. A time when traders came to the Fingers from

Tears for the Moon God

Saodein and deeper within Sarkahn's embrace and within the Ergol range seeking what they pulled from their fishing expeditions and the grains they raised, seeking rich mud for their own gardens.

These Sangar villagers were prosperous, just as her people had been then. Their nation was healthy and hale. They did not know war, conflict, the resultant shortages of food, clean water, rebuilding after every ruthless attack. They were at peace.

And she envied them.

A mild pang in her chest, a hollowness within her gut. She had looked on generation upon generation of Sarkahni children with pity, because they knew nothing else. As she remembered her own childhood as a time of peace, a time of quiet joy not unlike what these people held onto, she could only hope that one day a new generation of children might know what she had known. The embrace of peace. That it was possible. Too many of her people had only known war.

Do they still know how to exist without it?

She passed into the village and her going went unnoticed except for the prying eyes of a few old biddies, who must be the village gossips. They sat and conversed quietly over cups of tea from squat chairs arranged around a mossy stoop.

That'll be the welcoming committee. She allowed herself a grin. *Might as well pay tribute.*

She veered toward a cluster of elder women all seated outside a modest home, approached and introduced herself.

"I'm Lisandra." she curtsied. "I've come all the way from the Fingers. Do you know where an old crone might find a decent bed and a bite?"

A plump woman favored her with a motherly smile. They might have been of an age with each other. The woman's hair was all curl and no color—steel gray, the curls so tight she could not have fit her pinky through any one loop.

Oh, that grin was welcoming enough, but there was the hint of something lingering in it. Something patronizing, if she was not just fabricating a narrative about the woman.

She had never been over fond of old women with nothing better to do than sit on the stoop and tell tales, but then she might be one if the chips had fallen well enough in her favor. She could settle here, if she could convince herself it was the right decision. She could abandon her people, but then she would live with unbearable guilt, until the day death came for her. Would he welcome her, then, knowing she had taken the coward's path. Knowing what was lost because she had.

The woman grinned sweet as sugar. "We keep an inn just that way, dear." she pointed toward the larger complex. "Though I'll warn you, it can get rowdy some nights. The young'uns do like to get on, and the walls are thin."

Lisandra followed her gaze to the broader complex. Stone walls cemented with mud could hardly be considered thin. It was clear to her these women were not over fond of outsiders.

She returned the woman's smile. "I'm sure I'll manage, thank you."

Another woman, her cheeks pooling around her jaw and her dark brown hair arranged in a neat bowl cut, piped up at that. "It'll be north. And a bit east, if you'd like to avoid ruffians. Isn't that right, Delores."

"That rabble come down from Nixir, aye." the first woman agreed.

"They're not all bad." The second woman said. "Just hungry, I suppose. There

Baduhrak's Diplomacy

can't be much to eat the other side of the wall, now can there be?"

"And that justifies—"

"Oh come. You'll scare her off the freeway entirely if you get to talking like that, missus. They're not all so bad. They've never attacked us now have they?"

"I suppose." Delores said, but she was glaring at the other woman. Her gaze softened as she turned it on Lisandra. "How long do you plan on staying, dear?"

"Rude." a third woman, who reminded Lisandra of some dogs she had seen, murmured. A pair of knitting needles dug into what might have been a hat or the corner of a quilt. She kept her gaze on her work, refusing to meet Lisandra's eye.

Lisandra put on a smile that made her cheeks ache. Whether the woman liked her or didn't, she would only become an issue for her if she believed she was being rude on purpose. So, she elected to kill the old crone with kindness. "Thank you for so generously pointing me to a place to rest my head, madam. I hope your evening sees you well."

She turned her back on the women, took three steps forward before Delores spoke up again. "Where did you say you're from now? The Fingers, yes. They're at war, aren't they? With Saodein. Why, pardon me for being so forward, but you must have come from that way recently."

"I did."

"How fair the southlands?"

"You can't ask that of a stranger." the woman with her knitting said. "She's been through an ordeal most likely."

"I have indeed, Delores. Was it Delores?" Delores' smile was honey sweet, but her gaze was hawk-like. "Yes, well, you and your friends have been quite pleasant, if I may say so—"

"You may."

"—And while this conversation has been enlightening, I really should be going. These shoes have not been kind to me, you understand. No benefit of a carriage either." She turned to leave.

Behind her, she heard the woman with her knitting say: "See now, you've offended her. Too nosy by half aren't you just."

Though she did not say so, Lisandra agreed. She struck out for the inn. A night's rest and a solid meal would see her better rested than she had been in quite some time. But the sooner she could leave this tiny village and its lazy way of life behind, the better. She did not want to believe she could be like this Delores, but knew if she remained here long, she may well become just that.

Lisandra doubted she had ever seen a proper inn. Her life, until the moment of her leaving, had been lived in isolation, restricted to the scattering of villages across a peninsula in the Fingers. She had never been aboard a watercraft larger than a fishing boat, and then had never ventured to the southern more peninsulas, the barrier islands splashed across the open sea. This was not a proper inn, either, but it had its charms.

The inn was more a tavern than a place for sheltering foreign company. She doubted very much they got much traffic from outlanders this far from any thoroughfare. Yet here was a lively common room filled with the sounds of laughter and stomping feet—men and women pinwheeling around each other in energetic sweeps, dancing to wild, country jigs played on fiddles, beating out a rhythm for the

Tears for the Moon God

music to chase after with their feet. Drinks passed over a long and narrow bar, which was one of scant few pieces of furniture made of wood in the place. The chairs and tables scattered around the edges of the room were all of metal—pig iron worked into shape, the components welded together as best she could tell. If there was not a Baduhrak trained smith in this village there had been once and not long ago. There were...*signs.*

An ornate clock hung from the lintel over the bar. Taps—she had only ever heard of them—sprayed beer and foam into tall mugs and pitchers. These were innocuous technologies. Gifts, perhaps, from God Hou Rok for a people he sought to court.

Strange, though, isn't it? She panned over the room. Those instruments were finely tooled and well in tune, and they were the only other scrap of technology she could conceive of as coming from that god's far away kingdom. The taps, the clock— she supposed the bar was an import, too—were juxtaposed against gas lamps, candles on the tables, the thatched mat doors so typical of this village's constructs. God Hou Rok had given, but he had only given so much.

What the god provided were toys, baubles, contraptions with narrow use and no cross over potential. Without comprehension for the complexities of these mechanisms, there could be no replicating them. Could a smith who did not know how to make a valve ever hope to put the mechanics behind those taps to use elsewhere? Could he be expected to make a hose with which to put out fires, or a more efficient means by which to irrigate fields? Could he dismantle a clock and reassemble it? Could he retool the technology that allowed those gears to keep time for machinery?

These gifts were meant to entice country folk to curiosity. Likely they came with promises of more to come, better contraptions, toys with other purposes and engineers to train these primitives in their use.

For the love of...Lisandra Almaine you let yourself relax. Saodein is not here. They are not coming for you. Why did she feel so stiff. Here was a moment in which to dance, to let herself cut loose, grant herself some kind of release. And she could not.

She could not.

Oh, let it go.

A wave of bitter emotion swept over her.

She had known so much kindness, so many hands held out for a stranger in her time of need, since leaving her home. The mercy of a saodeini family to let her into their home. The gift of a sturdy pair of shoes to take on the road with her, the darning of her socks, mending of her tattered dress. A spirit's mercy in allowing her a modest wash in the waters of its creek. Even the gift of fruit from that crabby, old fairy tree.

And now there was this to add onto the heap. The hospitality of a tavern with a spare room in which to house her. A mug if she would take it, and the possibility of a dance. A dance, for the first time in so long she could not remember the last time she had the chance at one. It had been months since she left home. Even longer since she had known enough security to feel at least somewhat happy.

But she could not accept grace. Could not acknowledge hospitality. Could not allow herself this moment of reprieve. Let her guard down and she might be convinced to stay. To be the refugee they saw in her, become a useless old hag like

Baduhrak's Diplomacy

those women she had encountered when first she arrived here. Like Delores. A professional gossip and nothing more.

What would happen to her then?

She approached the bar, flagged down its keeper. A short exchange saw some of her stolen coin passed over to him. It was not much.

A spare few pins for a room for the night. Rooms were upstairs, and she could take her pick of them. None of them locked, of course, and the barkeep, who was also the owner, would not have it any other way. She was lucky she had a door at all.

She found the room to be cozy enough. The furnishings all had the look of imports. A well kept bed, free of lumps. The cabinets had been varnished recently and still smelled of pine when she opened them. She was struck with the impression this room served the owner when the opportunity struck. When he was in the dog house, likely as not. Even the wing backed chair in the corner was well kept and well padded. It was the kind of place to inspire comfort, in a way that had been so lacking in her life for so long. Even home in the Fingers, such simple comforts were hard to come by. War torn countryside was not friendly to traders, and artisans had a habit of dying in raids.

Why can't I let go? She would have liked that mug. The conversation the locals offered. Maybe a dance with a handsome, old widower or an unattached youth. *Why can't I just be still.*

Something heavy being dragged across gravel awakened her. Dull scraping, the clatter of stones; several men were shouting at each other. At first she thought some kind of altercation had broken out in the village square, and she hurried to the window looking out on it. Through a slit in the curtains, she saw a massive crate coming off an equally massive wagon. The wagon's wheels were metal enmeshed in some dark material that looked much softer, and while the wagon bed was wood, the guard rails were similarly tooled with metal. Two horses were hitched to the construct, stout palominos, and they tossed their heads restlessly and snorted at anyone who came too close.

A team of four men, all locals, unloaded the crate according to a fifth's orders. The fifth man was not Sangar. He was not saodeini either. This close to Gonsai Wall, she could only assume he was Nixian. He was dressed in a leather jerkin, elbow high, fingerless gloves and boots that went up to his thighs, all made of the same material. Under these adornments, he wore in a loose-fitting, stone gray jumpsuit that looked to be made of linen, and a porcelain mask hung from his hip, opposite two long knives embedded in ornately tooled sheathes.

She wondered at that mask. It seemed significant. Designs like wheels with odd protrusions were painted in vibrant glazes along the left-hand side. There were those among the varied races who dwelt on Ul Sadh with such customs, and if this was like others she had encountered, she must assume it was something to do with coming of age within his tribe; or perhaps a betrothal rite. There were those spirits who sent their acolytes away with unique totems, too, and she would not rule out the possibility he belonged to one of those.

The Nixian marched ahead of them, guiding their steps as onlookers peered out from within open doorways or from behind glass fronted windows. The men carrying the container squatted in unison, slowly, their teeth gnashed together in

Tears for the Moon God

tight grimaces, the tendons in their necks and shoulders taught and bulging. They deposited their burden on the ground, earning a gentler smile from the Nixian, a flash of white that showed most of his teeth, and brought out wrinkles around his eyes.

He maneuvered around the container and to the wagon, and took from it a crooked, iron bar which he set against the crate's side, inside the gap between two walls. He wrenched it to the side in quick flashes, worked around the rim until he had pulled every seam loose. He cast the bar aside, and wrenched at the top of the wall to free it. It collapsed with a dull thump.

The other men gathered around the open side, and much chatter broke out among them. Locals had edged together in the meantime, sticking close to their homes and watching as the men did their work. They had their satellite conversations now, all eyes intent on the box.

The Nixian brushed past the men. He reached into the crate, and yanked at something. Again, and again, drawing it inch by inch from its shelter.

"What in all the world is that now?" she wondered.

Wheels creaked. Spider-like legs emerged first. They were comprised of various interlocking bars, all iron as best she could tell, or the more rust resistant carbon steel Baduhrak was known for. Exposed gears were affixed at the joints, and insulated cables were interwoven into them. The body came next, a wide expanse topped off with something that looked like a funnel and a tank beneath and somewhat behind it. This rested on a sleek body interposed between two wheels of the same kind as were on the wagon.

With the entire body of it free, the Nixian pulled at something, a kind of drawstring which looked to have taken some effort to wrench out, and let it snap back into place. The vehicle—*what else could it be?*—roared to life. He fiddled with something near the front end, and it's arms began to move.

"What the hell?" she breathed.

"It's a cadrewaller." the Nixian explained loud enough that the entire village could hear. "There are different models with different uses. This one is for harvesting grains. Hou Rok's gift to you all, if you'll trade with him."

Murmuring among the villagers. A wizened old man broke from one cluster of them. At almost the same time, Delores waddled forward to meet him and the Nixian.

"What does he want in exchange?" the old man said.

"Now, you leave the negotiating to experienced folk." Delores cut in. "What does he want in exchange, dear?"

"A small portion of your yield of wheat and barley." the Nixian said.

"Define small?" the old man asked.

"Yes, please do." Delores shed a withering glare on him. Lisandra suspected this man was the mayor, or some kind of magistrate over the village. Whatever he was, he did not welcome the nosy old crone's aid.

"He asks for an eighth of your annual yield, with potential to expand on that base in exchange for more equipment. No more than a fifth if he desires an increase, I assure you. However, the equipment he can provide..." grimacing, he spread his hands. "It is possible your yields will triple within the next two years."

"Now that sounds like a—"

"Deal." Delores held out her hand to the Nixian.

Baduhrak's Diplomacy

The old man stepped in front of her.

"I have some questions, before we agree to anything."

"Oh, come. Don't be a fool, Gregor. The offer is good and we'll have lost nothing for it."

"No, no, you're thinking too much in the now and not enough for the future." he said.

"Precisely." Lisandra whispered. "Any deal that looks too good to be true on its face, is."

The Nixian gestured for him to pose his questions.

"We'll need to know what kind of equipment you intend to bring forth, and how we'll take care of it if it breaks. Will you be training our people to fix this contraption, for example?" he gestured curtly at the cadrewaller. "If not, how often do you expect a Baduhrak Engineer to come by our village? Are there an abundance of people who know what to do with this thing in the area? In Sanguhr or Nixir?"

There was that inviting smile again. The Nixian pulled the old man aside, and they spoke in low tones as he guided him toward the tavern.

Lisandra decided now was the time to do some eavesdropping. Hou Rok's incursions across Sarkahn and inside Rasheik's Rope were well known to the Fingers. So, too, it appeared rumor of those dealings had reached this far inland for the people to be skeptical.

On silent feet, she crept past her door and into the hall, stopped at the height of the stairs with her back to the wall. They entered a spare moment later.

"I get the sense this is just the beginning, Jinga." the mayor said. "What benefit has your civilization had against Hou Rok's gifts? Is it anything like what's been going on in Tulil or Fyrna? His demands of them...well, the picture is bleak. I hear they cannot even spare enough ore to trade with the Jahhad Empire anymore. They used to be their biggest partner. And the profits they gain...with no other contracts, Hou Rok sets the prices for all of their—"

"Please, allow me to explain." Jinga gestured him toward a chair, taking up one for himself. "What is happening to the Sarkahni in those mining towns could never happen to your people. The people of those lands are crippled by their patron spirit's refusal to allow them to organize. He will not permit the development of sound infrastructure, so they are reliant on Tao Baduhr's rail system, a system which Sarkahn hates. They cannot organize into a proper nation, because any whisper of it would trigger Sarkahn to rage. He would lay them to waste before he ever saw an exercise in nation building succeed there, and because they cannot come together as a people, they cannot raise armies either.

"Sanguhr has no such problem. You are already a part of a broader kingdom with its own governing body, and your nation is well entrenched. Taking these gifts can only help you, and if you do not like the terms the god offers, you have your magistrates and your king to fall back on. You may file a formal grievance, and they will come to your aid. It is their obligation."

"How do your people fair?"

"We are afforded certain protections by spirits Hou Rok is not foolish enough to interfere with." Jinga explained.

Realizing she had been holding her breath since first he mentioned Sarkahn, Lisandra released it. She sank against the wall, let their conversation wash over her.

Tears for the Moon God

"The deal does sound reasonable." Gregor met his eye. "And your people...they fair well enough, do they?"

Jinga's expression turned dour. "As well as we ever have. Your people are not all kind to us, and there are few resources north of Gonsai Wall. Ul Sharak helps, but she can only do so much."

"And Sha Ruhhad will not release you."

Jinga chuckled. "No need to worry about him. What's a sandstorm except a reason to stay below ground. No, I do not worry about the spirit of the desert. I worry about these southlanders in your neighboring villages, and their reluctance to see our dignity as worth acknowledging."

"Fair point." Gregor said under his breath.

Lisandra tiptoed back to her room. A loose board creaked under her shoe and she cussed under her breath.

"Who's up there?" Jinga demanded.

She hesitated.

She stood up straight, spun on her heels and marched down the stairs.

"Pleasure to meet you, sir. My name is Lisandra Almaine—"

"And you're Sarkahni."

"From the Fingers, yes."

He rubbed his cheek. This close, she was able to pick out more of his features, which all together made up the visage of a handsome, middle-aged man. He was diminutive, not particularly broad across the shoulders. His eyes were tapered and rimmed with thick, dark lashes. His cheekbones rode high over a blunt jaw, and his complexion was the color of dark honey, providing sharp contrast to storm-gray eyes.

"It's not my place to tell you how to live." He said. "But I wonder why you chose to eavesdrop on our conversation."

"I wondered why an engineer was in this village. I did not suspect God Hou Rok's reach extended so far, but just last night...the bar...the clock and those taps. I wondered why your master gave these people such pointless gifts when he could grant so much more. It would only be coincidence your coming with something of use not ten hours later."

"Where the gods are involved, there are no coincidences." Gregor muttered.

They each flashed glances at him before settling on each other. Gregor had given voice to an uncomfortable truth. The gods were playing a game with Lisandra's life, and she suspected she would not like the end they had in mind for her. Here was a Nixian when she needed to get to Nixir City, one armed and with a god's teaching under his belt. One arrived right in the nick of time to see her through Sanguhr, or perhaps through the nation of Nixir, who might even be heading to the same destination as her.

No coincidences indeed. The Goddess of Fate was playing her hand. A bold move with death walking in Lisandra's shadow. Jinga had no such protection.

"I suspect they've put you here for a reason." she said. "But I wonder if it is to help me on my quest or remove me from their board."

"I have no ill will toward your people."

"Nor I toward yours."

"Where are you going?"

"Nixir City. I am to meet with some others there. I don't know who?"

Baduhrak's Diplomacy

"You're not with the Raukhas, are you?"

She shook her head.

"And after Nixir?"

"Echo's Rope. I intend to court a spirit there. Become her acolyte."

Jinga nodded.

Gregor was watching this exchange with interest, the conversation surrounding the cadrewaller and Hou Rok's promise of more treasures forgotten for the moment.

"You need a guide." Jinga said.

"I do."

"Then you'll have one. But I need to finish business here before we can go."

"I'll give you payment."

He looked her up and down. "Keep your coin. You look like you need it."

She bit back a retort. So often born from irrational places, her anger was not at Jinga but at the truth he told. She held her hand out for him, and he shook it.

"You'll be my guide as far as Nixir City." she said.

"I'll arrange for someone to take you the rest of the way to the Rope, if you please."

"I would appreciate that. Thank you."

He let go of her hand.

"I'll be ready to depart in one hour."

"Yes, well." Gregor cleared his throat. "Where were we?"

Jinga turned his attention back on him. Lisandra returned to her rooms.

She met him by the wagons at the agreed upon time. The tavern's owner had provisioned her with food, water skins, a tinder box and a medical kit for the road, and the old biddies she'd met upon her arrival to the village had scraped together fresh clothes to replace her ragged attire, and a pair of sturdy shoes that were a bit too wide in the toe, but fit well enough for her purposes.

If the neckline of the blouse was cut too low for her liking, it was at least clean and of good quality, and she suspected the pants belonged to one of their husbands. They were too wide in the legs, well worn and she needed a belt to hold them up, but there was a practicality inherent in the women's choices. Had she another option, she would not have left her home in the Fingers in the attire she had chosen. A dress was not fit for the road, and neither were those slippers. But Saodein had left nothing in their wake but a blown out ruin where her home had been. One more little insult to take with her on the road.

Jinga came in from the outskirts of town some time later. Gregor seemed satisfied with whatever exchange had taken place between them. Enough, at least, to send the Nixian off with a warm salutation.

Jinga helped her into the wagon bed, took up a seat at the driver's chair. "It's an eight day ride to Nixir City from here, and not all of the Sangar are friendly. If not for the wagon, I would strike out north, but the scarabs won't have a lift big enough to haul it up this side of the Gap. Not on this side of Gonsai's Wall, anyway."

"What kind of spirit is he?" she asked.

He tapped the reigns. The palominos pressed against their harnesses, and the carriage lurched forward, over hard packed gravel.

"That's an odd question."

Tears for the Moon God

She leaned against a travel pack situated near enough the driver's chair that they could make eye contact, watched clouds of dust steal away the village and its people. "Sarkahn is…particular. There are no highways across his plains. No formal roads in the Fingers. There are guideposts, of course, but no roads between them. What is there is enough to satisfy God Uldal and his acolytes, I suppose, but nothing of stone, or concrete. Rutted tracks shift with the seasons. When one path becomes too muddy, we follow another. The Fingers see heavy rain in the springtime. North more, they have no such problems. His territory is vast."

"He's fickle, then. Sha Ruhhad is the same."

The village fell away behind them. Stone structures became shadows in the distance as the palominos trotted onward into the day.

"Your people respect him?"

Jinga nodded. "We do."

"Give him offerings? Send him your young ones for training?"

His lips formed a thin line.

"I've struck a nerve."

"No. It's nothing like that." he assured her. "Sha Ruhhad is a recluse. He rarely takes acolytes. Most have been sun men. Our people see one born every two or three generations. Some leave and never come back. Some stay. We try to convince them away from his path when they do."

"If you don't mind—"

"We're a people with a task." he said. "Leave it where it lay, if you will. I'd rather not talk about it."

"And Gonsai?" she said, changing the subject. She was no stranger to the burden of a spirit's jealousy. Wherein they would claim to guard a people, they more often used them. Perhaps, the people were not even aware of how they were to be used. Set against each other.

Jinga shrugged. "He yields…for us. We tunnel through his cliffs, and he makes no complaint. I've often thought he might get some benefit from our mining operations. That we're simply clearing his veins or something. And there is the gap. I suppose if he was not merciful he would have closed it long ago, but he doesn't. In our legends, he rose out of the earth, beating his chest in defiance of two forest spirits who hated each other. One died, the other made her peace with him, and he was made king."

"Gonsai is the dominant spirit in this reach, then." Lisandra nodded. "He is your Sarkahn."

"He is one of those who came later. His grasp on power is tenuous. You'll see what I mean, I think, if we're unlucky."

"His lands are contested?" she raised a thin eyebrow.

Jinga snorted. "Memory can be its own poison."

This is a hard man, if I have seen one. She was reminded of her father, though Jinga was some twenty years her junior. This was a man fit for leadership. He was not unkind, but she sensed deeper structures working within him, saw bubbling to the surface hints of a hidden talent for steering conversations, guiding sentiments to the right conclusions. This was a man who could start a war, had he his way. Or end one.

"How far have you been into the world?"

"My home is part of this world."

Baduhrak's Diplomacy

"Home is beyond the world." she said. He met her eye, curiosity playing across his features. "Home is a place that travels with you, wherever you go. It is an anchor. Wherever you wander, it will always be there, waiting."

"And if it changes while you are away?"

"Then you can only adapt. New children are a blessing. War, on the other hand...." She turned her gaze away from him. The road smelled of horseflesh and dust and wheat. This was a world away from home. She could see it as nothing else. There was nothing familiar in these lands, nothing she could cling to, to bring her back to her center. But she was at peace.

For a moment.

For now.

"Your lands are in turmoil." he said. "I can see it in you."

"My ragged state was an indication, then."

"No. It's there in your posture. In your eyes. In the way you speak. You've seen bloodshed."

"Well you should know why." she said indignantly.

He teased the reigns, guiding the horses more eastward.

"I've been in the world." he said. "I took a ship once, off this continent. To another. I thought of it as an adventure, I think. In hindsight, it is always difficult to judge these things. For all my youth, I ached to be away. But when I was away, I found myself yearning always for home. In the end, I returned. Went to Tao Baduhr, like so many of my people, and learned some of his arts.

"It's important to get away, sometimes. I don't regret having gone. But I think we all feel a need to return to a place where we are known."

"You're not so bad." her gaze roved over the horizon. The iron rail was picking up heat, and she adjusted her arm against it, rolling onto an unmolested stretch of sleeve. The material this shirt was made of was thinner than her old dress, soaked in the heat more readily. "Were I meant to remain in these lands long, I think I might call you a friend."

"You may as well." he said. "We've a long road ahead of us before we get to Nixir City, and longer besides if you intend to cross the desert. You won't get far without a guide."

"Yet that guide will not be you."

He chuckled. "No, I suppose not. But if fate has brought us together, then perhaps I am needed on the path."

Reminiscences

Finding Sao Njack was no difficulty. He had not moved far from the pool containing the memories of the life he had lived since arriving, seemed intent on guarding it from intrusion. Or perhaps it was grief that held him close to it.

Xi understood that drive better than most. Even among the Wanderers, he had known loss far exceeding their own. At least, he thought he had. Shulraki Alran had lost little that was personal to him—a trade empire and the vast fortune he had amassed before the guild turned on him. There was nothing intimate in that, no one involved in his death he would miss. Ank was a mystery, but then he had never seen him pondering the life of another at the edge of any pool. He had never seemed to concern himself much with the loss of anything outside himself. Ever one for flagellation he might be, but the source of his eternal melancholy came from within. He had said as much when the sword maker asked. Had been closed off about the events precipitating his arrival here, but then that was not uncommon either.

Hanuman had lost a brother, yes, and perhaps his grief was greater. His entire people had been wiped out, but that had all happened before he was immured, and the culprits behind it were all entities beyond mortal comprehension. Politics had been involved in his downfall. The act itself was not personal. His taking was well earned, at least in the eyes of the gods.

But Xi knew grief in the loss of a lover. In the loss of his family. They had been taken by mortal hands, had been robbed of life long before he himself had been robbed of his right to rejoin them. Somewhere in the vast seas, his wife and their daughter were living out their afterlife, as was the man who saw him reclaimed. In Shao Luin's embrace was his family, and ruling over them a man he had given a sword, who had used that sword to spread his tainted influence across the world.

If I ever see him again, I will ensure he ceases. The thought came on like a rain of ashes, the echoes of utter destruction and its promise of absolution.

But Sao did not seem to want revenge. He did not seem to want much of anything save to live in those memories, to be taken of the succor of reliving those intimate moments with the people he had lost, who still lived in the world outside of these halls.

He understood that, too. In the prospect of living was the knowledge that those people had moved on. In knowing time had not pushed so far beyond the era of his life was the foreknowledge that the people he had loved no longer knew him, and could not return his love.

He found him where he had expected, sitting with his back against the wall across from that pool, looking despondently into its murky waters.

"What do you want?" he mumbled.

"Just to talk." Xi said, trying on a smile.

"I'm not in much of a mood for company."

"No one ever is in this place, but company is good for you. In sharing your pain, you lessen it. I can shoulder some of this burden."

"I don't want that."

The smile turned into a grimace. "You're depressed, but that will go away in time."

"With everything I once thought I knew."

"What you knew is passed." Xi unbound his sword belt and set the scabbard against the wall next to the once emperor's own. He seated himself, facing that stagnant pool. "All that you knew is gone now, but that does not mean all is hopeless. You walked into the world when the uelfin sang, and what did you see there?"

"A man who did not remember me."

"You saw hope."

A secretive grin spread across Sao's lips. There was no joy in it. "How ironic."

"Ironic?"

"His name is Dupec." He explained. "In the tongue of the Gil Garo, it means hope."

"There is significance in a name."

"So there is."

His grin fell away. "Love is complicated, Xi Didura. But you know that. You are a Cloud Man, too. Your parents must have tried, right? To kill you off before your curse could express itself."

"My time came far before yours. My people did not view my affliction as God Katcya's wrath. They believed it was a gift, of sorts. A complicated one, but one worth nurturing."

"They didn't seek to destroy you?"

Xi hesitated.

There had been a time when they had come to believe their efforts were not enough. Every Cloud Man since Hanuman had known such a time, when the essence of their condition ensnared an innocent, dragged them into illness or forced an unlikely accident on them.

But we were made of stronger stuff back then, weren't we? Whatever their thoughts about my curse, they had mettle these modern people do not. What does it matter if they had a moment of weakness? They pushed through it.

"When I was ten, my mother took me out into the woods. She took me to the river Shah, up close to its headwaters where the stream broke into rapids. She told me she would teach me how to swim, but the current was fast and there were many rocks in the stream. I could not see how learning to swim in that environment would be to my benefit.

"I suppose she had come to the idea that it was not worth it anymore. That *I* was not worth it. But love won out, as it often does. I stepped into the stream, and she called me back. She made up some excuse, I'm afraid I don't remember what it was. Not exactly. Something about the spring thaw and the current being to swift. We never spoke of it after that. I never told my father, and if she did, I never found out.

"It was the only time either of them attempted anything of the sort. It was also the crossroads I needed. I learned to control my power after that. It was not easy, but I did. Because I loved them, and they loved me. In love, I found a reason to push forward. To become better than I was. Safer."

Sao turned his regard on him. A wall came down, then. There would be that need for resistance, other walls to pull away when time and trust demanded it, but it was a start.

"Dupec's people don't tolerate cloud men among them. They believe, rightly, that the curse will bleed into everything they do. It's too dangerous to leave them alone. Most often, the parents kill them as soon as they are born. A midwife leaves a knife at the new mother's bedside, and they are given the room. The mother and the father understand the risks of harboring them. They could be exiled. But they don't always choose the knife.

"Dupec's parents chose the other way. They left him beside a horse track. They gave him his name, and they left him there to be found by a god. And a god took him in. He returned to them eventually. He *has* returned to them. He was among his people when the uelfin sang."

"You spoke to him?"

Sao's fingers found his sword. Xi followed his movements to it. His gaze roved over the scabbard, to the hilt which was wrapped in pink leather.

"I know that sword." He said. "It's name is Peace. An odd choice to hand to a conqueror."

"I was anything but that when Rein gave it to me. You might describe me as a sacrifice."

"Ah."

"Were the Raukhas around in your time?"

Darkness washed over Xi, infested his heart. Anger blossomed in his soul, and Sao took note.

"They weren't friends to you, then."

"They were a thought in my time. Nothing like they are now."

"They took something from you."

"They are the reason I am here."

Sao nodded. His fingers trailed away from the sword. He returned to his vigil over the pool. "They wanted one of his blades. They conscripted me and a few others into their party in pursuit of the cause. My father was an engineer. My cousin was an acolyte of Zangal. I myself was an acolyte of Salein, and useless for what they had intended, but they could find some use in my kin. There was a Katuwiti Spirit Caller with us, then, too, who they were using as a guide, to mollify the spirits on the way to the summit." The grin returned, and there was some joy in it. "Useless waste of his gifts."

"You were friends?"

"We became that, yes." He said. "It's all meaningless now."

"I made a sword." Xi said. "One to rival anything Rein crafted. It was my right

Reminiscences

as his acolyte—"

"I'm beginning to see why you were reclaimed."

Xi shook his head. "Neither the sword nor my apprenticeship under Rein was the reason. Those facts contributed, but they are not entirely why.

"In my day, the Raukha Cartel was in its infancy. Rauth Ku Lau, their founder—"

"I'm familiar with the name."

"Yes, well. I made a sword for him. He had a specific intent for it, and I obliged. It was in creating that sword I ushered in a cataclysm that eventually took my wife and daughter from me. The gods believed that had I never existed, Rauth Ku Lau would not have risen to power as he did."

"They were wrong."

"He did so anyway? I thought as much."

"If it pleases you to know, there is no record of him ever using a sword in the history kept by the Raukhas."

"I never did believe he needed it. The ocean spirit, Shao Luin, took a liking to him. Seemed to revel in the thought of her own death."

"How strange."

"What did they do to you?"

"They led me to the summit under false pretenses. Their leader challenged me to single combat and lost."

"A foolish mistake."

"More an accident. She did not know I was a Sun Man. In those days, I was prone to hiding it. Painting my skin and wearing masks and the like. People don't see our kind as people so much as things to be used." He shrugged. "Of course, they'll learn their mistake soon enough."

"Does this pertain to why you're here?"

"It does."

"And does it have anything to do with your lover?"

Sao nodded. "What would happen if you entered into that pool."

"I would learn more about you than you would ever willingly tell. I would lose something of myself in the process, however. There's only so much space within a mortal mind to house those memories. If I were to walk into those waters, and bear witness to your life, I'd lose some recollection for who I was. I might even take on some of who you are."

Sao considered him for a moment.

"If I asked you to, would you?"

"No, I think not. There are others who might." He grimaced. "One other. But you wouldn't want to invite his attention."

"The Elder." Sao sighed. "No, you're right. He seems...disturbed. Erratic, maybe."

"He is both of those things, but he is not evil."

"Evil is subject to interpretation." Sao said. "There are many things in my past I see as evil acts. Many regrets. And in each of those acts, there was justification at the time. Everything I did was with the intent of bettering someone's life, but in each of my decisions was a crime I committed against someone."

"That you regret those actions tells me you are not evil."

"Does it?"

"It does."

Tears for the Moon God

"Who is to be the judge of those things?" he asked. "The gods hate us. They are hardly impartial. The views of the spirits are mixed, but they are not impartial either. And mortals? They are just as prone to violence and deceit as we are."

"So there can be no judge. Is that what you're saying?"

"I'm saying there is no such thing as an impartial witness. What I am not saying, which is nonetheless true, is that in judging my own acts, I would view myself as a terrible force. A person who should never have been handed power."

"I see."

"Know this, though." He said. "A great upheaval is coming, whether I'm involved in it directly or not. All of the old players are involved in their own ways. Some of them unwillingly. But it will not be me who throws the world into chaos. I've just set up the chips to fall where they should land, if my wolf chooses."

"One day, perhaps you'll tell me." Xi said, knowing that day was not today, that Sao Njack did not trust him enough just yet to reveal all of his truths.

Xi climbed to his feet. He collected his sword and departed, leaving the pool and all of the memories it contained with its owner.

He ambled off, not sure where he was heading, but wanting for something stimulating to do...however ineffectual it might be.

Snare

"Peace, Tulukh. Be easy." Arrada cooed.

The boy was not having an easy time of it. Fits of rationality broke through the blood-cursed rage. At times, he almost resembled the youth Arrada had known. At times, all he could do was sob, plead for them to release him, or end it...whatever presented the fastest way past this turmoil.

Tursa was fairing better. His fever had broken a day's ride out of Gil Garo. A week later, he was still not well enough to ride, and the curse had not left his blood. Whatever he said, Arrada knew his condition was worsening. He had been finding isolated patches scattered about their camps where the soil had become a fine, lifeless powder, and the grasses had all died. Patches where the snows had been pushed aside to allow his father a place to rest his head while the work was done.

Were it not for Shi'an the Grass, his mentor, the man would have fallen over dead by now, would have become something unrecognizable to his children.

He tipped his nephew's chin back. The boy's teeth clamped down around a mouthful of thick leather. The glove had proven an effective enough defense against infection, for which he was thankful.

Shaede watched him from his bedside. Her husband held her hands in his, watched Arrada do his work with the same fearful expression his wife wore.

Karse was not a man easily shaken, yet the life, the vivacity, had been stolen from him. He looked as if he had not been sleeping. He could not be blamed for staying too long at his son's bedside, praying to whatever god might help him.

If Tursa was at full strength, he might be able to push back Tulukh's infection. But he would not have done. Would not have concentrated his efforts on a single child, even to spare his grandson this fate. To spare his Tulukh of this torment when others were suffering would be seen as deeply unjust by him. His family's needs had never come before the needs of his sect. It was a point of contention with his children. Arrada had learned to accept his place under his father's leadership, but Shaede must resent him so much for it. Particularly now, knowing that if her father recovered, he would not prioritize helping her son shake this off.

He pressed a bowl to Tulukh's lips. Karse leaned forward, his broad chin resting against Shaede's shoulder, his girth wrapped around her.

Arrada forced the boy's teeth apart. He tipped the contents of the bowl into his

Tears for the Moon God

mouth, and covered it, pinching his nose and holding his head in place, an attempt at forcing him to swallow. A scream welled in the boy's throat. He thrashed inanely against his cot.

"Where you are finding this strength in your condition..." he mumbled.

The scream died. His adam's apple bobbed up and down. The fight leaked out of him, leaving him panting and weeping as Arrada withdrew his hand.

"Did it work? What did you give him?" Karse asked.

"Something I'm not proud of." Arrada replied.

Tulukh's breathing eased. His eyelids fluttered languidly, threatening sleep. He had not been this at ease since the attack, would build a tolerance to this tincture eventually, and there was no telling whether it would fuel the curse besides.

"It's not a permanent solution, mind, but it seems the ticket is blood. It'll have to be fresh, lest it poison him." Arrada explained.

"Blood." The defeat was plain in Karse's voice, but then Arrada had not thought he would take well to this tincture.

"Blood, and opium." He said. "It seems he cannot sustain himself without the former, but we cannot risk giving him what he wants without a sedative of some kind."

"He will become addicted." Shaede whispered. "He will suffer when he cannot have any more?"

"Of what?" Arrada said. He pinched the bridge of his nose, refused to look his sister in the face. She was not the only one close to breaking for this boy. If she wanted him to live, there would be a price. There always was.

"Where did the blood come from?" Karse asked. "Not a human."

Though Arrada felt the insult in his uncertainty, he made no comment. He must remember Karse was grieving, not thinking rationally. He still believed there was a chance his son would not make it through this, and he may well be correct. The blood and opium could only last so long, in particular as opium poppies were not native to Tao Shein steppe. There were those who were bound to Shi'an, who were even now working to produce more opium, but they only had so much energy to spare, and he could not account for more of the plant being available to him with demand for it so high. Not any time soon.

"The blood came from a buffalo one of our hunters killed this morning." He picked up a clay jug and crossed to where Karse and Shaede were seated. "Place a thimble or so of vinegar in this each morning. Take it to a butcher, but do not go to the same butcher too frequently. They may start to suspect something is amiss with your family.

"Ask him to fill this urn with blood, and when you return here, add a pinch of this to it." He produced a sack from his belt pouch. "Only a pinch, mind. It is potent. Let it heat by your stove for a time. You do not want it to boil, only to become warm enough to steam off some of the vinegar.."

"How much do we give him?" Karse asked. "How often?"

"Every few hours. Enough to fill that bowl." He pointed to the vessel still sitting at Tulukh's bedside. "Ensure you do not miss a dose. It will be harder to bring him back up to the proper threshold if you let him sober up. He'll be dangerous then."

Shaede reached for the bag and the clay jug. She took them from her brother, set them in her lap.

"How long?" she asked.

Snare

"Before you run out of opium?" he asked.

She nodded.

"If you are conservative, you might get two weeks out of that supply. We must hope we can find a better means of controlling him before then."

"How can we?" Karse growled, balling his fists. "We have no resources. There are no traders this far north. There are not even caravans to raid."

"Calm down, husband." Shaede said. She turned to her brother. "Thank you for your healing. It is enough."

"I will keep looking for a solution, sister." He said. "Perhaps there is an exorcist among us I do not know of. An acolyte of Gur Tulain, or Ul Sharak maybe."

"Maybe there are some in another sect. We could ask the chiefs." Shaede said. She did not sound like she had much hope for it. The Gil Garo were not over concerned with healing curses. Their ills tended to remain in the realm of the physical. It did not do much good to have a healer who could not heal ailments of the body. He did not believe anyone would have been fool enough to waste their time, either. A deficit within their culture which they had dismissed too easily.

"If there is nothing else." He said.

Shaede nodded.

"I'll leave you to your son." He said to them.

He moved past them, through the tent flap at the entrance, and out into the winter snows.

The chiefs had erected a yurt to serve as their pavilion near the center of the Gil Garo war camp. Chief Arrak had taken helm in most matters that fell outside of the jurisdiction of one chief. Grief may take him, but he had driven it off for the time being by plunging into the work. The chiefs had kept to themselves what happened to Dupec Safar, and Arrada understood their logic. What might happen if the truth was revealed before the people learned to trust in Chief Ungol's lost son? With all of their other burdens, it would only inflame tensions further for them to know.

Dupec was an outsider. To many of their people, a Cloud Man newly returned to his father was already suspicious, especially given the context surrounding his arrival. That he would then be taken by their guardian spirit may worsen tensions between sects, between the people within them. Ung Kanh Dui was regarded as a myth by most, but there were still those who clung to the old ways. They would fall on their swords for him, if they knew; and drive a wedge between them and their brothers. They could not afford a fracture within their ranks, not against this enemy.

There were the odds of his survival to consider, as well. Dupec had not followed the forms. His loss in the Ung Tsang tournament meant he had entered that cave without the protections of the treaty between the spirit and the tribe, and maybe that treaty would not withstand this infraction. If he pressed the spirit too far, he may die, and then whatever rumors had sprung forth surrounding his status—whether he was alive, whether he would return—would be for naught.

There was much to lose from spreading the truth of what had happened in that cave. He did not know all of the details himself; only what Kuuda had been willing to tell him. Yet even as he believed the chiefs had the best interests of their people in mind, he did not agree with their decision.

Dupec Safar was a katcyakin. There was not a doubt in his mind that man would return, and when he did, if the chiefs elected to abide the ancient laws, he would be their master, the highest authority among the Gil Garo.

How do they intend to explain this to our people?

He wondered if Arrak intended to bow before him at all. His quieter style of leadership would imply he did, but his actions left too much room for ambiguity. Then again, his elevation was rooted in a technicality, a twisting of the law by that same outsider. Ungol should have been elevated in his stead. His son's loss had been deliberate, leaving room open for strife to take root, conflict to be manufactured between the Dumas and the Hakka.

He ambled down horse tracks amid knee-high snow drifts and bowed grasses. A fox stalked across the dunes, paused here and there, its ears twitching. It dug its muzzle into the snow, then leapt into the air, twisting into a dive and plunged into the bank to its hips. Its tail and hind legs wriggled as it struggled to free itself, and when it had, a field mouse was clamped between its jaws.

Arrada moved on.

Shaede's yurt was not far removed from the heart of the camp, and it did not take him long to find the chief's pavilion. No outward sign gave it away for what it was. In construct, it looked like any old yurt, but its proximity to the seven way crossroads from which the sect's camps expanded nullified any need for a greater delineation.

"Do not presume to have authority over me!"

The shout came from the other side of the tent, out of sight from where he was standing, but he would recognize that voice anywhere.

Father's awake? His heart sank. *Oh, this is not good. Not good at all.*

He hesitated to cross into the otherwise empty patch around the yurt. His father sounded angry enough to fight a stag in rut, and he was not keen to involve himself in his affairs. Not just yet.

"Calm down, Tursa." Arrak said. "You've only just awoken. You need rest."

"I've had plenty of rest! Now let me in! We have important matters to discuss."

"We will in time. When you are fully recovered."

Arrada steeled himself. He marched forth, around the yurt to find his father facing off against Arrak, with Gulang at his shoulder.

Kuuda emerged from the yurt as he was closing in.

Not now, Kuuda. You're only going to make things—

"Oh, this is just rich." Tursa seethed. "I'm out for a few days and you seize the opportunity to usurp me." The glare he set on Arrak could have crushed stones. "At least you picked someone competent."

"The Kirche needed a representative, Tursa. It was a temporary solution."

"Which has outlived its use." He snapped. "I am prepared to resume my duties."

His knees were shaking, telling the truth he would not confess. He was stronger now than he had been at any time since the attack, yes; but as Arrada had suspected, the poison was still working its way through his blood. This additional exertion was pushing him back toward that precipice. His stubbornness was standing in his way. He ought to be pulling on Shi'an's energy, using it to bolster himself, but he would not as long as the other chiefs were watching. He did not want to appear weak.

"Can you ride?" Gulang asked.

"Can I ride." Tursa chuckled. "Of course!"

Snare

"Bring around a horse, Kuuda. I'd like to see him make good on his word."

"As you wish." Kuuda moved past him, away toward the nearest yurt to negotiate for the use of a horse. It was not long before he had returned, the man to whom the horse belonged drawing it by the reigns in his wake.

"Father, would you just let it go? You cannot seriously think falling from the saddle will prove anything." Arrada intoned.

"I am not going to fall off anything." He said, and set his foot in the stirrup.

He did not even make it onto the horse before his legs gave out, shunting him onto cold, hard ground. He climbed to his feet, brushed himself off, and went for it again.

Kuuda stopped him.

"That's enough." He said. "You're too weak. Go back to your tent and rest. You'll be better tomorrow."

Tursa glowered at him. "Fine."

Kuuda guided him away, back the way Arrada had come from.

"You came here for a reason." Arrak said to him when they were out of sight.

"Yes. I wanted a word with Chief Ungol."

"He's inside."

"Alone?"

"If you wish it, we will give you a moment." Arrak said, earning a capricious glance from Gulang which he ignored. "Sauman!" he called sharply over his shoulder. "Come here."

Sauman emerged looking indignant. It appeared he still had not been forgiven for keeping Dupec's visitor a secret, another piece of information Kuuda had been forthright in passing to his siblings. He suspected his brother had come to a different conclusion about the apparition than he had, a discussion he did not believe needed to be had.

He passed through the tent flap, and into the yurt itself.

Several carpets and pillows had been strewn across the floor around a wood stove which kept the yurt well heated, almost to the point of being uncomfortable. Ungol was seated near a squat manger which had been stuffed with quilts near the stove. A patch of wiry fur and a hint of strangely human skin peaked out from a hole in those blankets. The skin framed one, hollow, infantile eye.

His attention snapped away from the creature. It made him feel nauseous.

"Your father is as fiery as ever." Ungol said.

"He will certainly try his luck until he runs out of it." Arrada said. "He's been like that as long as I've known him."

"All your life, then. Most of mine, as well." Ungol said. "It was a shock to find he had chosen Shi'an the Grass as his master. A spirit with the potential to bring prosperity to your sect, but not by the usual conventions."

"I suppose it shows he cares."

"One of his more endearing qualities." Ungol agreed. "You wish to have a word with me?"

"I do."

"So I assumed. What is it?"

"I want to ask you something. You are the only one I know to have had experience with curses. Did you ever try to break the curse on your son?"

Ungol's expression darkened. "No. Dupec's condition was known to us. He was

Tears for the Moon God

not the first Cloud Man to be born to the Gil Garo, nor even to my sect. They are not entirely common, mind, but common enough that the midwife, upon seeing him, laid a knife at Shaelein's bedside before she left."

"You chose to spare him?"

"I was not at all certain he would survive what we did. We set him on the roadside. I left him with a permanent memory of us, hoping he would come back to us when he had learned to control his power. I confess, I gave up hope of him ever returning after perhaps the fifteenth year."

"It took that long?"

"I did not give up all at once. At first, I believed whoever found him would teach him control and give him back. I was tempted to believe the stories about Ho'o spiriting away katcyakin children with nowhere to call home, but for all the drum circles, he never spoke of my son. I could only hope he was found, then. There were times I believed he had died on that roadside, that some animal had stolen his corpse away." A mirthless chuckle. "He did return, didn't he. Stronger than I could have fathomed. Strong in mind and in spirit."

He met Arrada's gaze. "What is this about?"

"My sister." Arrada said. "And I suppose my father, as well. Will you promise to keep this to yourself?"

Ungol hesitated, then nodded. "I will keep this between us for as long as it is feasible. If what you tell me puts our people at risk, however...well, I cannot put your family's interests before those of our people."

Arrada nodded stiffly. "My nephew was infected with the curse those Tului carry. I have found a means of keeping him contained for the time being, but it is not a long term solution.

"I feel as I am fighting a losing battle. Everything I have tried has been ineffective in removing the curse, but I feel I must keep trying. For Shaede."

"I see." Ungol said. "If his condition changes, you will tell me?"

"I suppose it is my place." He answered. "What happens if I fail?"

"The midwife left us a knife, but she did not stay to see that we used it. She gave us a choice. But if there is no cure...a chief's duty is to defend the lives and the health of his people. Your father well understands that. I think you do, too."

"I am no chief."

"No, but you are his son. He has imparted his morals onto you. If Tulukh poses a danger to your sect or your tribe, you will have to kill him or expel him. I'm giving you a knife, Arrada. Whether you use it is up to you. Until it isn't."

The look Ungol set on him was grave, full of the weight of choice and circumstance. His familiar's infantile face swelled, a wet wail expelled from some hidden orifice.

"Speaking of choice." He reached into the manger, stroked the mol fae's flank, cooing to it. "It's okay, little one. You are safe."

"I do not envy you your life, Chief Ungol. You have endured too many tragedies."

"Oh, I wouldn't say that. My best years are ahead of me, I think." He smiled warmly. "What is a few hard years."

"Thank you, chief. This has been...enlightening."

He bowed where he sat, and left Ungol to dote over that monstrous creature. He wondered, not for the first time, how such a kind, gentle man had come to keep such a grotesque beast. What had made him choose to climb down into Gandes Fae's cave, a place notorious for its horrors, and ask the spirit for a place as his acolyte. His training could not have been pleasant.

Arrak entered the yurt with Gulang as Arrada was leaving. They arranged themselves across the pillows—Arrak seated stiffly, Gulang sprawled languidly across a carpet.

"What did *he* want?" Gulang asked.

Ungol met his gaze. For a moment, he considered keeping Arrada's business to himself. He had given him a choice, but by the same token he must make a choice himself. He decided the health of the tribe was more important than one family's tragedy. Were Tursa hale enough to sit with them in judgment, he would have come to the same conclusion. He had given his life to his sect, had begun along the path before he ever contemplated vying for a position as chief. That it was his grandson would not matter to him.

I'll have to tell him before it is done. He would do it as a courtesy. Let Tursa know what was decided here, what would come of his kin. He was not convinced Shaede and Karse were the only ones harboring a sick child. With Tursa incapacitated, there had been no one to enforce a purge among the Kirche in the aftermath of the Tului attack, and not all of them would be as effective at keeping their cursed children, their spouses and parents contained.

"We have a problem." He said. "The Kirche have not dealt with their cursed kin. Arrada presents certain confirmation of that. Tursa's own daughter is among those who have restrained their loved ones and who are harboring them now."

"Which daughter?" Gulang said. Color was rising in his cheeks. It took so little to anger him these days. He had once been a measured individual, but something in him had changed with the attack at Gil Garo. In grief over the death of his son, he had become a man Ungol did not recognize. Irascible, his entire being folded around the idea of some divine retribution to be carried out by his own hand.

Here was more evidence of this festering darkness in his soul, something which might cause him to commit heinous acts when at last they brought their counterattack against the Tului, if he could not overcome it.

Ungol well understood his anger. He had been quick to curse the gods, God Katcya especially, for cursing his own son, for forcing a choice on him that could only end in tragedy for his little, insignificant family. He had done the right thing—he thought he had—but his decision had not made him any less human, had not shielded him from hurt, or the knowing that his own hand had shaped that decision, had denied Shaelein a right to motherhood. Gandes Fae had told him what would come, and he had ignored him.

Gulang's anger came from being unable to prevent fate from taking his son. He needed to move past that anger, to accept that Karsa did not die because he was weak, or because his father failed to prepare him for the life of a warrior, but because he was in the wrong place at the wrong time, poised to be struck down when his back was turned. Luck was fickle. Fate was apathetic. He might have believed differently once, but that time was passed.

It did not change what must be done about the Kirche. They would have to tread carefully there, but something must be done before the irrational actions taken on in grief among them spilled over into the other sects. Before the consequences of their refusal to make the right choice came to bear for them all.

"Which daughter is irrelevant." Ungol said. "The family has clearly folded around her child. Kuuda is likely aware of what is going on in her home and has said nothing."

"We will have to question him." Gulang said.

"He will only lie to us if we do." Arrak said. "We know what we need to know. Our task now is to act."

"What would you have us do?" Ungol asked. "Intervening in the Hakka affairs risks inviting a blood feud between sects at a time when we can't afford one. Those families have grown accustomed to the idea their loved ones will continue to survive. They may even believe they can heal them."

"There are no exorcists among us." Gulang growled. "None strong enough to force out the infection, anyway."

"You've tried?"

"It was the first thing I did, in the wake of the battle. I called for my people to come forward if they had any ability in healing. Most were simple doctors, acolytes of river spirits and the like. Sarri took similar action among his people. He came to the same conclusion. Even those who had some ability to heal ailments of the spirit could not heal this curse. One of my own recoiled from the victim in my presence. He believed if he had continued his probing, the infection would have been drawn into him."

"We need to eliminate them." Gulang intoned.

"We need to *isolate* them. Kuuda may well agree to purge his sect of the infected if he believes they will not be harmed." Ungol responded.

"We keep as much of this as possible between us." Arrak said.

"The other chiefs deserve to know—"

"But they won't. Not right now." Arrak cut in before Ungol could protest further.

Gulang looked on him appreciatively. It seemed they were of a mind in this.

"How do you intend to keep this secret when we will have to move large numbers of sick people out of their homes?" Ungol demanded. "Anyone who sees this will know the Kirche have been hiding infected among them. It will cause resentment in our own sects, as they will believe the purges we committed were an unnecessary cruelty."

"Or that the Kirche were too selfish to do away with their own." Gulang added. "If I am in my people's shoes, my belief becomes that my cousins among the Kirche were too self-centered in their grief to do what needed to be done, and that they put us all at risk by refusing to. If I am among those who buried their loved ones among the Hakka, I am also thinking Kuuda was too weak as a leader to do what was right, and that he put me, as a member of his sect, at risk by turning a blind eye to what was happening in front of him. I might think Tursa would never have put the needs of the tribe above himself, a thing his son refused to do. And I would question what kind of leader Kuuda must be to let the rot fester in his own household."

"Why do you believe it wise to keep this secret?" Ungol asked Arrak.

Arrak squeezed the bridge of his nose. He had never been this tired before taking up the mantle of high chief.

"What are we going to do if we cannot cure this?" Arrak asked. "We need those people alive, because we cannot find a means of countering this poison if they are dead. It was a mistake to kill our own."

"You did not view it that way when you were eliminating them from your own ranks." Ungol said.

"No, no I wasn't. But we were all still letting go of our loved ones then. We were not thinking clearly."

"We did what was necessary." Gulang replied.

"We did what was expedient." Arrak snapped. There was rage in his eyes when he looked at them. "It is a curse. Curses can be broken. Even those as strong as this one. We will take casualties in every engagement we have with them. You both saw what happened when our kin fell to their poison. How they...*returned.*" He shuddered. "How they turned on us."

"Like puppets dancing on a string." Gulang whispered. "The puppeteer our enemy."

"Then what would you suggest we do?" Ungol asked. "Isolate them, yes, but who will take them in?"

"You will." Arrak said. "You are immune to the poison. Something in your bond to Gandes Fae prevents you from becoming infected. When I saw you after the battle, you were bathed in blood. I can only assume most of it was theirs."

"I have a tolerance, yes, but that does not mean—"

"Your son arrived just days before the attack, Ungol." Arrak pressed on. "I do not believe Dupec brought the attack down on us, but he knew of it before it transpired."

"He took steps to see that we were prepared for it." Ungol growled. "It was Sauman's failing—"

"That's neither here nor there and you know it. He is where he is now because he believed he could save my son and Chakta. He also showed himself capable of keeping their power in check, with that nullification of his. *When* he returns, he will be invaluable in keeping them contained."

"*If* he returns." Gulang said.

Ungol kept his expression smooth, though it was not easy. His insides were boiling. He had believed himself beyond this anger, yet here it was to rear its head again. To remind him that healing was not all forward progress. That he was still capable of having the age old argument with himself.

You did this. You did. You sold yourself to Gandes Fae at the high price of ten men's lives and your own son's future. You are responsible for all the pain we have endured. You and only you.

"We will declare a curfew." Arrak said. "We will tell them we are nearing the Tului camp and must keep our precise position secret. That they may not retain lights beyond the doors of their yurts until we bring our attack against them.

"We will use this pretense to conduct searches of the Kirche's homes, but we will present those searches as visitations. Tursa's family will take helm on this matter. They are familiar faces. They will be better received than any of us."

"We'll have to keep an eye on them somehow." Gulang said. "They have already shown themselves capable of foolishness and deceit."

"We will go with them, then." Arrak said. The Dumas and the Kachin will be charged with transporting them to the Dumas camp, where we will have prepared a quarantine zone."

"And if they ask what need we have for a quarantine?" Gulang asked.

Tears for the Moon God

"My people may see to it that the purge is handled themselves if they believe it is in their best interest." Ungol said.

"Not if you tell them the truth." Arrak said. "A version of it."

"Any version that does not include the Tului curse and the Kirche's decision to hide them will be as good as a lie." Gulang said.

Ungol knew Gulang's heart, was of a mind with him in this. His own people were going to be put at risk for the Kirche's indiscretion, and while he did not believe it wise to kill those cherished loved ones immediately, he did not believe it wise to leave them where they were either. Especially so close to his own people, who had done nothing to deserve what felt so much like a punishment. A punishment for failing to kill his own son, when the midwife laid that cruel knife on the bedside table, the yurt he shared with Shaelein still stinking of fresh blood and afterbirth.

"If even one of them breaks loose, Arrak. If I lose even one of my people to that sickness, I will see to it that what you refuse to do is done, whatever your place among us." His voice held a cold edge.

"I will not leave you without help, Ungol." Arrak said, appealing to Ungol's sense of reason. "I would not do that to a friend. Among the Kirche are many acolytes of Shi'an the Grass. Two generations made pilgrimage to him in large numbers, following Tursa's example. You saw Tursa. He is healthy enough to walk mere days after having been infected—"

"A matter we will have to deal with eventually." Gulang said.

"If we cannot find a cure." Arrak said. "We will put out orders to have our best healers sent to them, to try everything they can to eliminate this sickness. They will find something."'

"They might." Gulang said. "There is a limit on my patience. That is all the more I will say. I agree with you that we need handle this delicately, but I do not agree that it is wise to keep these people alive. There are better ways to find a cure."

"There are no other ways I can see."

Ungol exchanged a tense look with Gulang. There was a conversation to be had among themselves later, when Arrak was not near. He would not have believed he would be back-dealing with his greatest rival among the chiefs before this moment, but he could not abide Arrak's choices, either. Knew that were Gulang still highest among them, he would not now be making the decision Arrak had. That had Dupec not forfeited his right to Ung Tsang, he would not be, either.

"It is undemocratic, making this decision without the involvement of the other chiefs." He said.

"We will follow the usual forms, then. If it makes you happy. But I do not see that another sect is better equipped to take them."

"Still, it is not our way to make unilateral decisions in matters involving all of our people."

"I agree." Gulang said.

Arrak's expression was unreadable. "I have other business to attend to."

He stepped forth, and left them where they stood.

Eat. It helps.

A lurid whisper lingered in Sauman's ears. He turned the desiccated fruit over in his palm. For all that he consulted what resources he had, he could not identify

Snare

what it was. It was segmented, not unlike the insides of those fleshy, citrus fruits they favored in Jahhad, but behind each segment was something paper-like, as if it was not a fruit at all but some kind of bud, a flower which had not bloomed. The skin was vitreous, almost waxy, and the coloring was a dark, uninviting shade of red.

Eat. It helps. The Tului woman's words rippled through him.

There were no seeds inside to plant. The fruit was already dead. He had seen to it that it remained buried in ice, in a chest he kept just outside his yurt for the game and ferments intended to sustain him through the winter.

The fruit lived in a jewelry box—a gift for a secret lover, delicate and sacred, yet controversial in its appeal—kept separate from anything that might touch his lips. He was unconvinced of the safety in touching it directly. Even as he held it, he kept it contained in a light kerchief, and avoided touching the frayed edge where the woman had bitten into it.

This small, delicate thing might be nothing, but he suspected nothing else taken off the bodies of those cursed Tului would prove as consequential for the Gil Garo as this mundane object.

This half-eaten piece of food. He snickered at the irony of it. *Still, it could save lives.*

"Sauman?"

He folded the fruit into its wrappings, and placed it in an ornately carved jewelry box, closed and latched the lid.

"Please, come in." He said.

Coltang ducked through the tent flap. He dawdled in the doorway, evidently trying not to be rude.

"Make yourself comfortable." Sauman gestured toward the carpets in front of his wood stove. The fire needed stoking, and a chill had taken his home when the tent flap fell open.

He fussed over a pile of firewood in a shadowed corner, selected a log of medium thickness.

"I don't mean to take too much of your time." He said. "I have a message for you."

"Oh?" Sauman heaved open the grate and cast the log inside. He slammed it shut.

Coltang looked troubled. He had not been himself since the attack, but then none of them had.

He could hardly be blamed for it. His daughter was several tens of miles behind them, alone but for the company of two chiefs' sons and awaiting the return of a man who might never come back from Duijus Kanh's cave.

They had all been told the same stories as children. Half-remembered legends of Ung Kanh Dui, the first of his kind, which were little more than a pretense to explain the way their world worked. Why they sheltered in their temporary city in the harshest months of winter, while dark spirits picked off the elderly and the sick—the disappearances noted and yet judged fair compensation for protection from who only knew what.

Coltang's nest was empty. If he was not sleeping, Sauman understood well enough why. But this discomfort felt newer, undiluted by the passage of time.

"Arrak dropped in on me not long ago. He is calling for a purge on our sects."

Tears for the Moon God

"Does he believe you've been hiding your sick." Sauman asked, keeping his features even. He had seen the piles of Tipik dead himself. He might have judged the other chiefs for their disposal methods, but he did not doubt they had done what was needed when the time had arrived.

"He did not say why it was to be done." Coltang explained. "Only that I should ask you to do the same."

"My sect is clean." Sauman said. "I saw to it that my most trustworthy people looked in on each and every yurt."

"Be that as it may, he asks that we do this. I did not get the impression he believes we are the problem."

"Another sect? Ungol's?"

"Fah!" Coltang batted his comment away. "Ungol would never fall so low. If his own son is any indication, he is the only one among us who would have no reservations in culling his flock."

"There is something dangerous in that."

"Still reeling from the Calling, then."

Sauman grimaced. "No, no. Nothing like that."

"Ungol is trustworthy. You're too young to have known him in his prime. If he has changed over the years, it has been in gaining wisdom, not losing it.

"I do have my suspicions. Nothing I would say with any certainty, but there is one irrational youth among us."

"Not—"

"No. No one who is willing to burn their dead would be hiding something as destructive as that in plain sight." Coltang's gaze was sharp on him, a quick flash and then gone. "Tursa was infected. He's been fighting off the worst of it, but there is no sense denying what is plain. His sect has not been told, but I suspect they know, too."

"Why Kuuda leads in his stead." Sauman nodded. "I suspected as much. One of mine watched him fall from his horse. His own men dragged him to safety, but it was a close thing."

"I'm surprised they didn't kill him then." Coltang said.

The air had gone out of the room. An awkward quiet settled between them, unbroken except for the crackle of fire against wood, the sounds of life going on outside.

"I'll see to it that another search is executed."

"Round them up, but don't kill them. Where to house them is still undecided. While our men conduct the purge, we are to meet to discuss our next move."

Coltang lifted the tent flap. Sauman watched him pass into the snows.

Is that the game he wishes to play.

He crossed to his squat writing table, where the box lay waiting for him. He snatched it up, and followed Coltang from the tent.

Arrak's intentions, it seemed, were aligned with his own. They had done the right thing, purging their tribes of those cursed with the Tului blood poison, but it could not be denied they had hobbled themselves in the same stroke. If there was a means to prevent their numbers dwindling in the coming war, they would need to find it, and quickly. One cursed tribesman held the potential to create a pandemic among them if left alone long enough. And here he was sitting on a crucial piece of the puzzle.

Snare

He so happened to know someone who liked puzzles. A disgruntled man ten or so years his senior who had recently parted company with his son. But not Arrak. Not yet. He would speak to Sarri first. Perhaps he had knowledge of what this fruit was, and if he knew, he may know where to find more.

Sarri's yurt was less inviting than it had been. As Bora sat at a low table near the stove, she was met with proof of a reality she was not ready to accept. Something had changed between them, and it was not difficult to identify its cause. It was not a flaw in her personality that drove him to it, not anything she had done, but her chief did not trust her. Who was her mentor had become a source of that distrust, enough for him to cast away all compassion for his son's woman.

Yet, he had summoned her here. She had not come of her own volition. A chief's summons was not an easy thing to ignore, and she would have been a fool to do so, whatever her relationship with the man had been. Stay away, and she would only drive up his suspicion. He had been more accommodating than the situation demanded thus far, stopping short of accusing her of misdeeds in their every interaction, denying her the succor of open hostility, the unearned approbation of the cunning tactician in service of a conniving god.

He arranged a kettle and a pair of mugs on the gilded table—a relic liberated from a Jahhad caravan, if the floral tooling at the edges was any indication. The flavor of empire was decided by how it defined its artistry, what suite of designs most befit its personal sense of glory. An empire's themes were first cast in iron and gold, woven into tapestries and carpets, carved into the legs and arms of its thrones and then repeated, and extrapolated on, across dining tables and chairs, couches, chaises, the molding at the edges of their ceilings and along their floors. The artist was the first propogandist, who set the spoke to the wheel for the god of the realm, its highest authority, to push downhill, to gain momentum as it traveled across time until it crashed against a rigid stone, and shattered.

What shape will Ung Kanh Dui bring? She thought idly as her lover's father poured white tea into those mugs. The lemongrass aroma perfumed the air, barely noticed as she reached for hers. *How will our society change?*

She imagined a future in which the Gil Garo staked out a plot along the edge of the Shan Lao river and built a true city, permanent and splendorous, to settle in as their capital. A world in which the lands not already claimed by Ao Lein, or Ruc, or Jahhad were governed by their chiefs, now magistrates in a sprawling kingdom under the explicit rule of a Cloud Man, who had been sentenced to exile hours after he was born.

A harsh world. Every sacrifice a necessity for our continued survival. What will we be without hardship? We will no longer be Gil Garo, not recognizable as who we have been for so long. He will not stop at carving out a kingdom for us, either, will he? No, his god is of ways and paths, of connections. If he chooses to build a nation, it will inevitably expand, because the God of Ways demands it. New roads sanctioned, new fingers reaching into older kingdoms, scoring away their traditions, clawing into their chambers to influence their politics, to shape them into something else entirely. We lose ourselves with every annexation. Every empire must.

Oh, what will we become? What will we become?

"Something troubling you?" Sarri asked.

He set a kugi board between them, and arranged nine pins for each of them at

Tears for the Moon God

its sides.

"Dupec." She said, and sipped her tea, elaborating not further.

"I'd have thought you were missing my son." His gaze was measured, giving away little.

They set about arranging their pins on the board in silence.

Some games required leaping without thinking, and others required long contemplation before any moves were made. Then there were those which were played in quick flashes, where strategies were built and countered so rapidly an observer might think each move was made randomly. Time decided, then. Time made a breathless back and forth of those games, but only a fool would approach them without strategy.

Tajima and Tirulain, Strategy and Games, goddess and god and flip sides of the same coin. Why was her mind on them? Why could she not shake the feeling they were, even now, climbing into bed together, sharing what passed for pillow talk between callous tyrants.

"Dupec is no concern of ours. Not yet." Sarri said.

"You are wrong." She said. "Dupec is our first concern. Right now."

"Tuluis Fel is our concern, Bora. Have you forgotten—"

"I cannot forget, but it doesn't matter. Dupec sits in the center of a tangled web. The intricacies surrounding his rise, I think, have shaken the pantheon before."

"The loyalties of the gods are always in flux."

"You're being intentionally obtuse. I expected better of you." She gestured to the board, to the pins set in its holes, all arranged neatly to provide most benefit to its players, while counteracting the array of the opponent. "You may have thought this game would be a nice distraction, but it's a prescient reminder of what our people have been dragged into."

He hid his scowl behind the edge of his cup, sipped. She saw his irritation there. It was hard to miss. He was tense, the lines in his face taut and his posture stiff.

"Why did you ask me to come here?"

"I wanted to talk about these Tului. You are much sharper than most. You might make a good chief one day, when I choose to retire."

"You don't trust me."

"I don't trust your god." He set his cup aside, retreated from the table to a trunk in the corner. He lifted its lid, rummaged through it, and returned with a parcel wrapped in sack cloth, which he set next to the kettle.

She reached for it, and he brushed her fingers aside. "We'll get to that in a moment."

"What is it?"

"A gift from Chief Sauman. On loan for the moment. He will want it back."

"Then it is not a gift."

"No, I suppose you're right. Nonetheless, it may be of relevance to us."

"In this conversation?"

"In general."

"What do you want to know?"

"Tirulain concerns himself with strategy as it pertains to games. Because he must inform himself of his allies and his enemies, it stands to reason he is well versed in history, anthropology...how mortals move and think would be relevant to him. In constructing games he believes we cannot win.

Snare

"I wonder, what is the nature of his relationship with the Rat Goddess."

"Goddess Ji Hara? Tense." She said.

"How?"

"In the same way most gods share tense relationships with her. She is a collector of information. Her spies are everywhere. Mice and rats. Most people throughout the world are rightly suspicious of both. Her record of all that transpires in the world is more complete than any god's, so they seek her out when they wish to have their questions answered, but she guards her histories jealously. She will not let them leave her library, and she is a gruesome beast, perfectly capable of delivering vengeance on any of them who choose to betray her.

"Tirulain needs her often, but he does not *like* her. They have been at odds before. At times, he has let her spies linger in his God House, to give her the impression of cooperation. When I was there, he had filled his citadel with cats, let loose hawks in the skies throughout his city. I'm told Goddess Liandal does the same."

"Did you—"

"No." She said. "I have never been to her library. What does this have to do with the Tului?"

"You said the gods were interested in Dupec?" he said, dodging her question. He made a move, opening the second round in their game.

She took note of the evasion. She would come back to it later, when she went over the details of this peculiar conversation.

She shook her head. "I wouldn't characterize it as interest. He was visited by a stranger who evaporated almost without a trace. You'd almost think it was a ghost, but no mortal soul is strong enough to break free from Shao Luin or Shah Jagat on their own. There is another possibility, but I'm reluctant to believe it."

"Wanderer." Sarri said, voicing her own suspicion.

She picked up her mug, drained it. "Do you have something more biting than this?"

A wolfish grin. He ventured to his trunk, liberated a bladder from its depths. He poured two fingers of spirits into her cup, which she knocked back as soon as he'd poured it.

He set the bladder aside.

"Let me tell you what I think." He said. "I think this Wanderer knew Dupec in a previous life, and that they did something together which offended the gods, who put pressure on God Lanfin to recall them."

"Close." She said. She was certain of this part. What lay in the wake of it was speculation, but a speculation which her gut told her was the truth. At least, a part of it.

"God Lanfin recalled the stranger, but he left Dupec alone. I don't think that's because Dupec was less guilty of the crime they committed. I think its because a cabal among the gods saw a use for him, and are *still* trying to use him. The Tului are an indirect means of controlling our movements, and by the same token, *his.*"

Sarri poured a draught for himself and swallowed it. He set his cup down, poured another for each of them.

"Why not seize his narrative directly? Goddess Liandal is hardly shy about doing so."

"Because she can't. Which would imply the Elder Gods are involved in some way. I would guess God Katcya. They hate each other. And he would view Dupec as his son, wouldn't he? In the twisted way the gods decide these things."

"Luck as a shield against Fate."

"And her allies. God Tirulain, for one. It seems to me they're working toward the same objective. If Goddess Ji Hara is entangled with them, then God Lanfin is, too. There would be a tactical advantage in involving God Hou Rok, as well. If only because he keeps his God House on Ul Sadh."

"How did you arrive at that conclusion?"

"The gods of music and language always work together. They have not been opposed to each other since God Lanfin shunned Oe in favor of the goddess."

"The rest?"

"Just a feeling. I haven't been able to shake it—" she knocked back the shot. "—since the night of the attack. What I can say is if they are all working together, our best advantage is in their disdain for each other. They've probably worked out a strategy among themselves, but I would be very surprised if each of them isn't also trying to undermine the others. And God Lanfin won't be able to recall Dupec this time. It'll be too soon after the last time."

"The Tului, then." Sarri reached for the parcel wrapped in sackcloth. He unfolded the layers wrapped around it, revealing a fleshy, dark-red fruit, or something very like one.

He passed it to her. "Careful not to touch it directly. It came from one of them."

"What is it?" she asked.

"I was hoping you knew."

She used a bit of the cloth to roll the fruit over, saw the frayed edge where it had been bitten into.

"What is it for?" she asked.

"It might be a cure." He said. "For the blood poison."

"Are there more?" she asked, then thought better of it. "No, of course not. If there were, you wouldn't be asking me to identify it."

"I might not have to, either." She said. "If we can capture one of them."

Sarri's expression changed. An unnerving mix of sadness and determination took him, and he reached for the parcel.

"One of them could identify it." She went on. "I'm sure you came to that conclusion yourself. But taking them alive would put us all at risk.

"I have a way around that."

He hesitated, his hand hovering over the fruit.

"My power is the same as Tirulain's, and he can't take it away from me. Ask the chiefs to give you freedom to send a small raiding party against them when we get close. Assign me to it. Ideally, you would be the leader of the party, but I don't think Chief Arrak will go for that. He'll cave to Gulang, who will suggest himself."

"He wants revenge. I see your logic."

She re-wrapped the parcel and handed it back to him. "We'll bring back a prisoner. I promise."

He took the parcel. "I hope you're right."

Tao Shein

Piled up corpses greeted Tao Shein as he entered what ought to be the Gil Garo tribe's fabled Shifting City. The city had entered the general canons of Ao Lein, Loc, and that self-important kingdom which called itself the Jahhad Empire. Stories of a city which thrived only in winter, when the driving snows buried his steppe and the prairie became treacherous for horses, impassible for the carts full of stolen possessions they carried. He had listened from his place within the earth as mothers told their children stories of these people, painted them as a terrible curse inflicted upon those entrenched kingdoms they took from. He had heard their justifications for these tellings. Had heard them demonize this people time and again, insisting always that their own people had done nothing to earn their wrath, and so they hadn't. Not to have earned the attention of the Gil Garo personally.

It was all a game to him, though he would not go so far in playing it as the Lesser Gods did. Those kingdoms dug wells, carved out roads across his wild plains, raised houses, palaces and mansions, whole cities almost overnight, it seemed, and with each new groundbreaking they drove a wound into his flesh. Like mosquito bites, they stabbed into the earth with their shovels, thousands at a time in disparate reaches, and he had not even the benefit of swatting them down. He had tried, in his spring years. But what hope he had of compelling these peoples to leave their efforts well alone had proven pointless excursions with increasingly frustrating results. These mortals were stubborn. When met with complications to their ploys for greater innovation they answered them with increased hostility, until what was left for the spirit was to yield.

He had never been good at yielding.

So the Gil Garo raided in their lands, and in raiding they delivered a thimble full of vengeance with his name tacked to it. To their end, they gained wealth, which was meaningless except where it granted them bragging rights. Whose mound of gold was tallest, who provided the heaviest tithe for Duijus Kanh? They needn't know he had a part in their ritual, that his hand guided the very activities upon which their culture was founded. Oh, how the spirits thirsted for vengeance against those who shunned them, who cast them aside, who in insisting on their own superiority thought to ravage the lands they occupied. How ignorant were those

Tears for the Moon God

mortals to the reasons they must suffer, yet they earned that suffering with their every feat of innovation, their every selfish act.

He saw those piles of corpses and a rage built inside him. A rare thing for an old spirit, to become so incensed at the sight of mortal carnage. Wars were fought across his back. Mortal blood seeped down deep into his flesh. He had tasted their torments. Had known a poison in the blood of those Tului for its bitter flavor against his tongue. There had been days when he demanded such sacrifice for his tutelage, but those days were long passed.

There were those piles of corpses. Thousands of Gil Garo dead left there in mass graves, for there was no time to bury them. It had been this way the last time. The dead mounded high and left in bitter cold to freeze. He had taken them into himself then, too, had given them that peace, to know a last embrace as their souls wandered the lands, to settle first in Gur Tulain and then follow Ul Sharak's band to Shao Luin, the Dead Ocean, where they may finally have peace.

The mouth of Duijus Kanh's cave was close at hand, but he could not endeavor their annual meeting with these dead looking back at him. The Tului were worse. Robbed of their innocence, some driven to madness for the evils they must commit in service of their lord. But what lord could command them to do this? Tuluis Fel had never been so cruel. He was an isolationist, jealously hording power to him, disseminating it to his people only because it gained him a following, broadened his cult. Few spirits were so perverse in their pursuit of power, yet Tao Shein tolerated him, for what was the other option? The spirit did no harm to the tundra he governed. He kept mortal innovation to a minimum, or compelled his people to make their dwellings of wood. Still, it had not been right to compel mortals to become his acolytes then, and neither was it now. The morality of man had no bearing on him, for it was a morality skewed in their favor, but there were those morals the spirits abided. Tuluis Fel ought to have embraced them. Ought to have embraced them then. When it counted.

He let loose a trickle of his power. The earth shook. Fissures opened in the earth, in his flesh. He thought then of Salein, of that misguided fool he had taken on as acolyte. Sacrifice...it was the only language the spirits knew. They made sacrifices for the mortals they sought to protect, and hoped those mortals would return the favor. But mortal greed tempted them away from the old compacts. It was not enough that the spirits provided. Mortal man demanded more, always more. He was never satisfied.

So, too, the Gil Garo thirsted for more. For better. But they retained something those other kingdoms, so entrenched in their territories, had lost. They knew respect for the spirits. And so he gave unto them the respect they were due. Fissures opened in his flesh, and he took those corpses under. Gil Garo and Tului alike. Alone among the people who occupied his steppe, they remembered the old ways, and remained faithful.

Bodies fell into the earth. The burial mounds were consumed. For the first time in centuries, Duijus Kanh and his concubines would have to hunt in truth. They may go hungry, or they may gorge themselves on what they killed. Surely, Meichekh, with her gifts, would keep them fed.

The last bodies fell beneath the earth, and he let those fissures fall shut, feeling whole again. Knowing Duijus Kanh would be offended by his actions, and that he would say nothing.

Tao Shein

He turned back to the cave mouth, and ventured toward it. It was time they handled this season's business, and he reclaimed the wealth those kingdoms had won in their pursuits of ever greater heights, the wealth they had taken at his expense.

The sun beat down from its noon height, out of a clear sky which yielded none to him. The most bitter days of winter were the cloudless ones, when what heat remained baked into the land was returned, when man discovered he was but renting the warmth and comfort of lighter months, the blazing heat of summer. Gorgus seized what was his, and left in his wake a bone deep chill for Shaki to endure. It did not matter how many quilts he bundled around himself, how dense the mittens or how long he let his deerskin boots lay in front of the fire.

He sat now on the edge of the long catwalk ahead of the chief's pavilion, resisting the chill on the air, Ho'o's insistent push. He had no ill will toward the spirit of The North Wind, but he could not believe the spirit was not contemptuous of him. Thera was ever his antagonist. What fitful rage he felt for her was like a bonfire, and her wrath was felt against him doubly so. Yet here, Thera's influence was diluted. The summer winds come from the south were in short supply. Bitter, howling winds descended from the north were more common, almost a daily occurrence for the last weeks. It was as if the spirit did not want her to see something, something of importance. Yet what had he to gain for keeping her eyes away from this land? What good did it do if her acolyte remained here?

His gaze flicked from one heap of corpses to the next. He would swear to the gods and the spirits both he had seen movement among those mounds. Was it one of the Swans? Could it be that Dupec had come to the surface, to rut through those mounds just as he had feared he would, dragging away corpses to feed his new master?

He was not convinced of his own safety, with the tribe now gone. Was not convinced Chakta or Tamlin would be spared this winter's harsh realities. Duijus Kanh had protected their people for as long as anyone could remember. For so long the story of his courting had become something of a folktale told at bedsides, what was remembered of the old pact passed from father to son and mother to daughter with each new flowering of youth, with each passage into adulthood. But the tribe was gone. Their dead lay in heaps. The Tului dead lay in yet others, some taller than the Gil Garo burial mounds, but only some.

How long will they settle for old corpses. What if Dupec's taking has changed the rules.

Creaking boards, rolling footsteps, announced Tamlin's arrival. He joined him on the edge of the step, several quilts wrapped tight around his chiseled form. He looked out on the plains, far beyond the mounds Shaki was so fixated on. Far out and to the west.

"Why could it not be Ruc? Or Ao Lein? They had better reasons to attack us. We raid in their lands, don't we?"

"They fear us, Tamlin. They would never attack us like that. They struggle against one of our sects. What would they do against all of us together?"

Tamlin shifted on his perch, lips downturned into a grimace. "It's distasteful. A blind attack. Rush in and flee. How far and how fast, no one can know, but they've gone well ahead of us. I guarantee it."

Tears for the Moon God

"Our fathers are capable men." Shaki said.

There it was again. A pale shape, ducking low, flitting from one mound to the next. The figure moved with such haste, kept so low to the ground, he could almost believe it was a wolf, but wolves did not hunt in daylight. Nor were they over fond of human flesh. He had seen victims of wolf attacks during the wandering season, their throats torn, entrails spilled out of the anus.

Wolves were master strategists. They preyed on the weak and the lame, targeted the vulnerable among herds of bison, cut them off from their kin with such ease it made a Gil Garo raid look amateurish. When they had worn out that tired animal—that poor creature so close to death, so new to life as to make no difference—they killed, and even that act was done with such cold, calculated efficiency it was hard to process what had happened until it was done. One went for the throat. Jaws clamped down, tearing through meat, crushing cartilage, lashing through artery and vein and crushing their victim's windpipe. Others still held the beast in place, harried its flanks, and as the lead element crushed their prey's throat, yet one more came from behind, latched teeth to that poor, sad, decrepit animal's anus, and dragged their intestines out from within them, hastening their death.

Brutal, effective, the wolf did not waste energy on its kills. It must hunt, for it must eat. In the pursuit of survival were hard lessons learned, was energy conserved, wasteful ploys removed.

"They are up against strangers. They'll lose the advantage of familiar terrain as soon as they cross their border. And then what?"

"They have Bora." Shaki said absently.

"What good can she do?"

Shaki only smiled. He focused harder on the mound he had last seen movement behind. Yes, that creature was human. Or as good as. If a spirit, it shared much in common with humans. But it was too pale to be one of theirs, and it was painfully short. A real stump of a thing, wide set and diminutive.

"What are you looking at?" Tamlin demanded, having finally seen fit to follow his gaze.

"Someone rutting around the burial mounds, I think."

"Where?"

Shaki jabbed a finger in the direction of those the Hakka had left behind. "White as a dead fish, shorter than Chakta by a head, and moving fast."

"Not her!" Tamlin vaulted to his feet, boots crunching in stale snow as he hopped off the edge of the catwalk.

"Sorry, what now?"

"Not her!" Tamlin repeated. "She's the one who took Dupec. Or...one of them. There were three. The Swans—"

"Would you sit down?"

Tamlin turned sharp eyes on him. The anger eddied, flowed out of him, and he resumed his seat. "I saw her when it happened. They couldn't hurt her. It was like she was made of stone or something. This absolute toad of a woman, and she just...destroyed them."

"Which one is she?"

"Why are you so calm about this?"

"Well...we've been wintering here all our lives." Shaki shrugged. "You expect to

Tao Shein

see them eventually, don't you? I just wondered if Dupec was with her?"

"You think he's—"

"Dragging corpses to the cave. Yes? It's a possibility, anyway."

"Drudge work?"

Shaki nodded. "Where is Chakta, anyway?"

"Hunting for jackrabbits. She wants stew tonight."

Shaki grimaced. "Gross."

Tamlin guffawed. "You're too picky."

"Okay just bear with me here. Chakta wants a stew made of the toughest meat known to man, that wasn't a question. Do you know if she's ever cooked it?"

Tamlin regarded him with a slack expression. Shaki could almost see the gears turning in his head. *Who does the cooking in the Krul household? Do you really think Coltang has the balls to make Chakta do it? He's a big man, but Tanta has him well enough in hand, and Chakta certainly isn't afraid of him. So, who does the cooking? Not Chakta. Definitely not her.*

Just then, a rumble took the earth. Vibrations rippled through the ground, soaked into the posts holding up the catwalk. They drove across planks, up Shaki's spine. He clamped his teeth together to keep from biting his tongue, and the vibrations climbed into his skull.

In the middle distance, mounds of corpses began to sink, bodies jostled by the minor earthquake tumbling out of order as the bases sank below ground. The piles jittered up and down, spread wider as more bodies tumbled across open earth and were consumed.

"What is this!" Tamlin lurched forward.

Shaki grabbed him around the forearm and pulled him back. "Stop!"

The last of the corpses fell into the earth. The rumbling ceased, but Shaki's heart kept racing, mimicking the steady vibrations of the land long after they passed.

"What was that?" Tamlin whispered.

"Tao Shein." Shaki said.

Mortal resilience was born out of a peculiar ability to weather change, to adapt to circumstance in a way that would drive a spirit to despair, a god--inch by inch-- to madness. Dupec had grown accustomed to sleeping on hard ground under God Uldal's care, but there had been the light of the stars for company then, the shifting seasons bringing with them their own, unique attributes--the smell of autumn on the air, winter's clean chill, mud and flowers in spring and summer's turgid, humid charge...the stink of his own body, rainwater, grass, life.

Duijus Kanh was a place in stasis. The temperature in any corridor, in any chamber was equal to that of every other, cold and dry, but to no degree unpleasantly so. The odors of the outside world, its seasonal shifts, all uniqueness come with those subtle changes were stripped away, leaving this place always smelling of dust and mold, and in its depths, lifelessness.

He could grow used to this. With months or years spent in close corridors, he would grow accustomed to this confinement, but now he felt discomforted by it. The sky and its celestial bodies were blocked by thousands of tons of earth, a ceiling he had never wanted, which he would rather not have. Those rare excursions taken in the night with the Swans, with Kachekh or Duichekh most often, were welcome

Tears for the Moon God

relief to him. A needed purge, a renewal of his spirit. He could feel safe again, whole, under the light of moon and stars, and knew he would be ill advised to mention either in the presence of his new master, this spirit whose hatred for the moon was all consuming, who would descend into the earth and remain there, so that he would never have to lay eyes on it.

But those rare moments of reprieve were complicated by their purpose. Meichekh did not attend him on these excursions to the surface, because she was out hunting. Hunting for game with the wolves. He did not eat what these spirits ate, did not consume the dead the Gil Garo had so carelessly left to spoil with the impending spring thaw, but he was not excused from supplying Duijus Kanh with those corpses, helping the Swans prepare them.

The first time had been hardest. He could not but make the needed cuts while turning the stiff faces away from him, so that those bodies could not judge him through lifeless, glassy eyes. No one lived under Duijus Kanh's protection without paying their dues, without carrying their weight.

It had taken far less time to grow accustomed to these acts of carnage, this systematic butchery he must inflict against his own people, their bodies, what had once held the essence of their identity. A woman's eyes, dark pools set in shallow pits where age had robbed her of vitality, stared up at him as he worked a crude knife through thick tendons in her shoulder, working with precision. A second body hung by its ankles behind him, a bucket beneath it ready to catch what blood remained to it. Its entrails had been taken from the hollow cavity beneath his sternum and arranged across a reed mat on the earthen floor. Kachekh performed the work of washing them down with a variety of dark wine the origin of which remained a mystery to him, and hosing out gut to be cooked down later.

He had assumed Duijus Kanh ate like a wolf. That all he consumed he took raw. His duties told him otherwise. There was a civility in the carnage, a sense of familiarity in every preparation, in the work of skinning and butchering, in the practice of cleaning entrails, in the methodical approach the Swans took to preparing everything he ate, everything they themselves consumed.

Man was like livestock to these spirits. They nurtured them in winter, kept them safe in their pen, and picked off those too weak or too ill to make it through the winter. Their actions were no different than that of those pastoralists of Loc and Ao Lein and Jahhad and any number of other kingdoms the world over. Yet in their chosen food source was all the difference.

I see why God Ao Nii finds him disgusting. He thought to himself as he passed the severed arm to Kachekh. *Then again, is this so much different than raising cattle? Can a cow think for itself? Does a goat not feel dread when its throat is cut? In a way, this is mercy. A quick death is preferable to slowly succumbing to disease, isn't it?*

Meichekh arrived then, a fawn slung over her slender shoulder. She cast it onto the ground next to the cadaver Dupec had been working on.

"Tao Shein is here to collect his tithe." She wore a scowl, the scaling around her eyes creased, drawing out monstrous features that must have been hiding just below the surface. He had never seen her angry before, and her anger was shared by her sisters.

"It's a little early to be doing business, isn't it?" Kachekh said, not looking up from her washing.

Tao Shein

"Had I my way, he wouldn't be here at all." Meichekh said.

Duichekh sniffed. "Had you your way, our grizzled, old wolf would be lord of the plains in his stead. Ambition is dangerous, Meichekh. Duijus Kanh is strong, but he is no match for Tao Shein. With or without us behind him."

"I just don't see why we should do all of the hard work while he reaps the rewards!" Meichekh stamped her foot. "All so he can have his petty revenge on those inconsequential mortals!"

Kachekh eyed Dupec then. Something in the way she looked on him was unsettling. She snorted, and turned back to her work. "You're not ready for that tale just yet, little cub."

"Is that the one where you explain the Gil Garo are livestock to you?" he asked.

Kachekh cackled, but the other two had gone silent.

"It's not quite that simple." Meichekh said defensively.

"Don't go pinning past hurts onto him, now." Duichekh said. "He's not the first to have asked that question. He will not be the last, either."

"If he succeeds where he failed before—"

"Quiet, Kachekh." Duichekh warned. "We agreed—"

"Agreed to what? To hide all that he was from him?"

They glared at each other. He felt himself shrinking in their presence, minimizing himself as the tension between them stole the air from the room, leaving him in an uncertain limbo.

"To leave it to Duijus." Duichekh said. "To decide when the time was right. He will handle it himself."

Close air pressed cold fingers into Tao Shein's skin, making the point without need for words that he was not welcome here. Duijus Kanh was no one he should fear, but these times were uncertain. The old alliance between the spirit and the first great chief of the Gil Garo was at an end, and a new treaty rose in its place. In a forgotten past, Dupec Safar had come into the title Ung Kanh Dui by the conventions of the old compact, as laid out within its bylaws. With the great river's flow diverted into a new track, some things must be changed, and still others remained the same.

Katcyakin were strange beasts, at the same time subject to time's unending flow and divorced from it. With every reclamation, there remained echoes. Their faces, their names, were known to the spirits and the gods, never to be forgotten by either. Their deeds were burned into their memories even as God Lanfin sought to erase them. Death was no bar to the katcyakin, for their deeds lived on long after them, stones thrown into the river, to disrupt its current.

Hundreds of names were etched into the walls, appearing in clusters of a dozen and more where past victors of the Gil Garo's tournaments had faltered, the well of their courage dried up and their feet unwilling to take them farther. The power of folklore on the impressionable mind was an incredible tool. More effective than bribery or blackmail in its ability to generate fear, of all mortal inventions, it was this tool that had proven most effective in shaping a people. In breaking them.

Hundreds of names etched into those walls, staggered at intervals so that the eldest names were always centered, always taking up prime real estate and well preserved in this place where nothing ever really changed. Those had been the truly brave ones. Each generation produced yet fiercer hearts and sharper wits. Each

Tears for the Moon God

generation pushed further and further into Duijus Kanh's cave, and yet it would be many generations yet before those names reached into his heart.

He paused alongside the wall and ran calloused fingers across the last of those etchings, which stood well apart from all that had come before it. There was the evidence of a claim to Ung Kanh Dui, which had been seized once and was again. There, written in a past that never was, defining a future that could never be again, was the name of the last to hold that title.

It seemed somehow preposterous that he had let the man pass him by, an entire lifespan drifted off like so much dust on the wind, having never attempted to meet him. *What could he have done with my power, then? With my might behind him?*

But those were dangerous paths to travel, dangerous thoughts. They were the kind that had started wars in the past, between spirits and gods, the kind both sides remembered even as they tried to forget. His fingers brushed the hilt of a sword at his hip—a heavy, single-bladed weapon, curved on the nose.

Bitter memories, those. How much better off are we with that monster still rotting in chains?

But there was the crux of the problem. When the Elder Gods spilled into the Waxing World, they brought with them whispers of cataclysm. They came to drag their lessers, kicking and screaming if it was necessary, back into order, to stamp them under their boots. They came with their thumb screws, their water troughs and performed what tortures they deemed necessary, what heinous acts they deemed valuable in reasserting the too crucial balance between gods, their elders, and spirits.

And when God Katcya's brood was involved, they were reclaimed. Every one of them who had come close to setting the Waxing World aflame had been taken into Lanfin's Labyrinth, to live out the rest of their days--and there would be many of those—in captivity.

But Dupec Safar was free. His very presence in this cave was a violation of long standing rules and principles which had kept the primal order in balance. He was free, and his lover was captive. Yet the Dragon of the East had sought to set things right, had come close to killing Duijus Kanh's favorite pup, had he not? Why, then, was Dupec here? Why was Sao Njack held captive?

He came to the heart of Duijus Kanh's cave, the locus from which his power flowed. He passed the threshold, an unremarkable widening of the tunnel. The Gil Garo had done well in their raiding this year. The mountain of fineries Duijus Kanh lounged on was far taller than it had been the year prior, which pleased him. The Swans would be furious for the loss of such a grand horde, but the spirit of the cave cared nothing for gold and jewels, for fine silks and the makings of what men believed was a good life. They would be sucking their teeth even now, cursing his name, making bitter statements about his character and their hatred for the part they must play in this cycle.

If Duijus Kanh cared, he did not show it. He never did.

The ancient exchange commenced, and he entertained it.

"What will you do with your cut this year?" the cave spirit asked, his rumbling voice lacking inflection.

"The same thing I do with it every year, old friend."

Hard, amber eyes flicked to the sword at his hip. "That thing never did suit you."

Tao Shein

"In winning peace, sometimes you must accept gifts you do not want."

"And in keeping balance, sometimes you must forego peace in favor of something less...palatable."

Tao Shein raised an eyebrow. Duijus Kanh was never one to maintain pointless conversation. Among the spirits who remembered the Wandering Period, he was perhaps the most remote. If they were, none of them, particularly fond of mortal company, few would deny a sense of kinship among their own kind, yet Duijus had never been particularly warm. Had never been one to extend his welcome to those others he shared his lands with.

And here he was, bouncing ideas off Tao Shein, inviting a dialogue which might even be called meaningful, for the first time in so many centuries he had forgotten when last he had been so amenable. It may well have been upon the rise of the first Ung Kanh Dui.

"What are you proposing?"

"Ung Kanh Dui desires a new compact to replace the old one. He sees himself as at an advantage."

"And so he is."

"What he wants, I cannot give him. But I believe you can."

"What might that be?"

"That ill begotten child, the emperor over the Nixians paid him a visit several days before he arrived in my cave. He left with him a truth I wish I had not heard. You deserve to know, Tao Shein, the scope of the problem we once entertained has broadened. Maybe beyond our ability to comprehend. There will be...echoes."

"There are always echoes. In all things concerning katcyakin."

"And that is precisely the problem he lays before us." Duijus Kanh righted himself then. Gold and silver fineries spilled over the mound like so many tinkling bells. He met Tao Shein's eye. "The katcyakin are a true race. The Elder Gods, Life, Death and Fertility, have sanctioned them. For now."

A hiss escaped Tao Shein's throat. "What is it he wants...from me?"

"To gather them. Those born across your steppe. He believes you will find them among the Tului. Where better to hide them than in a kingdom so veiled in secret even their own people do not know who rules them?"

Tao Shein grimaced. Bad enough the katcyakin had their bloodlines, but to have established them among the Tului posed complications in itself. There were things going on there he did not like to contemplate, events which made little sense.

Those lands should be barren, yet they flourished. The people should be starving, yet they thrived. Something was amiss in Tuluis Fel, and he suspected the Lesser Gods were involved in it somehow. Soon, he would have to interfere. If those bastard gods were meddling in his affairs, taking advantage of what ought to be a power vacuum two centuries passed could not have healed, then his intervention was paramount. He could not allow his steppe to go the way of Sarkahn, could not allow himself to succumb to the fate of the Plains Lord's predecessor. It was bad enough having one god put down roots in these lands without another trying to break off a kingdom of his own.

"Something is on your mind." Duijus Kanh said.

Tao Shein's grin was cold. *This whole thing is ridiculous. It's as if these gods want to revisit the old conflicts. Have they fallen so low they have forgotten?*

"I suspect you know what it is."

Tears for the Moon God

Duijus Kanh nodded thoughtfully.

"How many battles have we fought, do you think?" he asked. "And in how many of them has one of our own fallen?"

"There was Pantham Kris. Detained, but not slain. And Dosh Alaen, since replaced by Sha Ruhhad." Duijus Kanh said, stroking his beard. "There were rumors of Sal Fier's death in the late days of Harkahn's freedom, as well. He has since been replaced by Sal Seid, yes?"

"And what happened in the wake of those tragedies?"

"The waters of Sal Fier's ocean were poisoned for generations, until Sal Seid rose to power in his stead. As I recall, there were several spirits involved in the succession war that followed. It was only happenstance she emerged as the a new empress."

"Yes, and in the wake of Dosh Alaen's murder, what once was a vast forest became a wasteland. Desolation followed. Mortal kind could not but flee those lands in search of brighter pastures. The only people to have remained in proximity were the Nixians, and then out of necessity."

"And a harsher spirit rose up in her place."

"Two." Tao Shein corrected him. "Gur Tulain in the north, seizing on what little energy remained to her to set himself against Shah Jagat. A purposeful defiance in the face of the god, which he would not have been able to entertain without allies. And Sha Ruhhad in the south, a spirit who thrived on desolation, having no great love of humanity. Nor any desire to play politics with the spirits around him.

"Pantham Kris alone was able to avoid that fate, and then only because he had an obvious heir. Only because he remained alive, the reserves of his energy available for a like spirit to make use of."

"What is your point, Tao Shein?"

"In the case of Dosh Alaen, time's stream was set upon a different axis, and its flow went on. One was recalled, in those days, but the spirit was not revived. She remained well and dead despite the lives of all of those mortals in her realms having been reset. Do you remember how this world screamed?"

"I recall Lanfin paid his first ever visit to the Rat Goddess in the aftermath. He learned hard lesson that day."

"As did we all."

"You think Tuluis Fel is dead?"

"I do."

"His lands are still thriving."

"They were only ever barely alive."

"But they are not dead."

"Which means someone is keeping them alive."

"I see."

"I wonder if you can settle something for me."

"Yes?"

"Send Dupec east. Make sure he does not go to Tuluis Fel. Not yet. He will be needed there eventually, and I will make good on your request. He will have his katcyakin all in one place, and in the custody of his kin. I think it is for the best they keep them. I will need you to keep Ao Nii distracted for a time. His patterns have become more erratic lately."

"Mhmm. And there is a reason for sending Dupec east, when a departure of that magnitude risks...instability."

"Indeed. The hope is he confronts Salein."

"Ah, now it makes sense."

"Then you understand the importance of this?"

"Yes, I think I do."

"All that is left, then, is the matter of my cut."

"Take it, then. Take it all." Duijus Kanh gestured expansively to the mound of treasures. "But leave Dupec alone for the time being. He is not ready."

"You have a month, friend."

"I will do what I can."

The Freeway

Their journey took them onto the freeway, where, for the first time, Lisandra was able to see what true infrastructure looked like. Trade in the Fingers was mostly the seafaring kind, and what business they did inland was contained within Sarkahn Plain and the foothills of the Ergol Range. What roads were carved across the mountains were winding, rocky things, made with practicality in mind but not designed to contend with heavy traffic. This was a jarring departure.

Dirt roads joined a wide track of stone, like tributaries feeding a great river. The road was broad enough to accommodate six wide carriages abreast of each other. A platform occupied the center two lanes, and a cage of iron hemmed it in. Iron rails ran away from the platform in either direction, extending all the way to the distant horizons east and west of them, and thick cables hung from wiry poles between them.

A sharp whistle punched the air somewhere in the distance. It was followed by a sound that reminded her of the rare twisters which sometimes came with summer storms back home, making her heart pound as vibrations kicked up in the earth.

"What godless—"

Jinga snorted. "Engineers from Tao Baduhr built this. No, not me. This was before my time."

"The spirit of these plains must be furious."

"There is no spirit of the plains. I don't know that there ever was. This was all forest once. The reason this stretch is no longer covered is because Gonsai will not allow it."

"So this is his feet?"

Jinga nodded. "Far enough from the locus of his power that he can do little to stop the Sangar. There were attempts...a few weak efforts to swallow the tracks, but God Hou Rok prevailed eventually. Shock absorbers to deal with the occasional earthquakes when he gets grumpy, reinforced tracks...the highway itself is able to move independently to a certain degree if it's necessary. They even implemented sensors for...I'm losing you."

"I'm sorry. It's all a bit overwhelming. Sensors. Shock absorbers...it all sounds like a fiction." She rubbed her temples, her gaze fixed on the floorboards as the

The Freeway

rumbling grew louder, the whistling blasts closer, making her feel isolated and afraid.

"Come. Look. You're perfectly safe."

She supposed he must be right. The horses did not seem particularly affronted by the noise as they hauled the wagon eastward along the track.

"Sanguhr enjoys amenable relations with the west. Their technology far outstrips that of most nations across Ul Sadh, but it's a double edged sword." he was yelling now to be heard over the rumbling. She forced herself to look in the direction of the noise. If the horses had so much mettle, she ought to have too. "Ung Sakh doesn't much like the God of Smiths or his engineers. You didn't see much of our work in the jungle, did you? I thought not. Sha Ruhhad is the same way!"

Barreling down the track from the west was a behemoth structure of metal longer than several houses lined up one after another. The monstrosity was segmented like some kind of insect, the cars sleek and ribbed along their flanks and roofs. It gouted steam from a wide pipe at its height, iron bands raked around iron wheels that gobbled up tracks and shat them out again behind it.

Another blast of steam. That screaming whistle, loud enough to deafen. Broad fins flashed out around the sheer face of the foremost car, battled against a wind suddenly intent on resisting it. The sound it made was like roaring flame. The train slowed, the bars thrashing against its wheels, chugging, bringing it to land flush with the empty platform.

"We're not getting on." she breathed.

"No." he said. "Our journey is not taking us so far. This will go around Zangal's southern slope and come out again at oceanside. It's sister travels the other way, from ocean side into the foothills around Gaspar, but no higher. Rasheik has been tolerant, so far, but he will not have Hou Rok running tracks through his range. And Hou Rok knows his limits. He will not take on a Rope Lord, either."

"A tenuous peace." she said. "But that thing terrifies me."

"It is but a drop in the bucket." he was smiling. The train pulled away from the tracks, huffed to life and crawled onward, picking up steam again as it vaulted down the track, and left them to contemplate its leaving.

"A drop in the...*that* is a drop in the bucket?"

He shrugged. "It's outdated. The trains in Baduhrak are much faster, and more efficient. They run on energy they take in from the sun. Keeps things nice and clean."

She could tell he was enjoying this. Regaling her with tall tales about extremities of mechanical innovation which she could barely conceptualize. "They have flying machines, too. The first of them were probably being churned out when you were just a girl. They were certainly before my time. They used to require pilots, but with more recent innovations, they can essentially fly themselves. With someone to monitor them, that is. No technology is perfect."

"This is the power of the God of Smiths?" she said, regaining her faculties now the train was well and away from them. "Flying machines and...and trains."

He chuckled at that. "Oh no. No, any mortal with enough training can make those. He is what his namesake suggests. In the old days, he was an armorer for the gods, but if he still makes shields and breastplates, I haven't seen them. No, he is perhaps the weakest of his kind in raw power. It's his intellect. That's what sets him apart. That's why he was able to create all that he has."

Tears for the Moon God

"And shower fools with gifts and false promises." she muttered.

His expression darkened, but he met her with grace. For her part, she could not help but respect his restraint.

"What does this highway do?" his tone was disquietingly soft, introspective. "It disrupts the hold of a spirit on mortals, and gives them access to heights they could not otherwise achieve. Take that train, and it will see you across the entire nation of Sanguhr in less than a day. It will take us eight days to cross a fraction of it by horse. Were he not convinced we would use his devices to destroy each other, he might lend us aircraft that could take us to Gora or Sana or even Fang in that time. With enough fuel. His expression darkened momentarily. "There is never enough fuel."

An uncomfortable admission, that. But what can they expect when the spirits hate their god.

He cleared his throat, looked to her. "I'm sorry. I am sometimes a bit passionate about my god and his ways. I spent a great deal of my life in his city on its hill."

"I am no stranger to differing views. Or...difficult conversations. You Nixians are a peculiar people."

"We favor balance." he said. "We must."

She contemplated leaving. The firefly glow of lights in the distance to the east and north told her there were villages out there, villages near enough that she might lose him if she was careful.

Jinga was good company. She hadn't had anyone she could rely on since leaving her village in the Fingers. She watched him, sleeping by the fire, and contemplated what a different life might have brought them. Had they met under different circumstances. Again, she was taken back to who she might be without the war. Would she be entertaining leaving if not for that? Or was it Gandes Fae's answers troubling her?

No sense dwelling on it, now is there. But still, there was that shadow. An intervening distance between them she would not close. Liandal's hand was in their meeting, and the Goddess of Fate was not merciful. Among all the gods in their pantheon, she was perhaps the most cruel, the most vengeful. *What does she want with me? The Fingers were never that important.*

Which meant *she* must be. Enough to draw the attention of a Wanderer. Enough to draw the attention of the Gods, even to confound a spirit or two on the path. And now the guide she needed fell into her lap and she could only consider what this might mean for her future. What game was Goddess Liandal playing? Why had she written this man into her life.

Jinga stirred. His eyes snapped open. They touched on the fire he had started, which she had let slow until it was a scattering of tongues flickering over white embers. The night was not cool. These lands, as far north as they were, never seemed to be. There had hardly been a need for it, except to keep coyotes away.

He fixed his gaze on her. She flinched away from it.

"You were leaving?" he said.

"No." She would not meet his eye.

"Liandal's promise is poison." he said. "But it does not suit to flinch away from her before you can discern her cause. Her games...they're complicated?"

"I...I suppose they are."

The Freeway

"Never been caught in one before, have you?"

"You have?"

His expression was grim. He nodded.

"What uh..."

"If I tell you, will you stay?"

She contemplated him. What did he want from her? Did he not see the danger in them remaining together? He must understand her feelings, that however comfortable they were, there must always be that itch to flee. To deny this goddess what she wanted. Whatever that was.

"I-I don't know, Jinga. I'm with you, I think, as far as Nixir, but what happens after that...."

His gaze fell to the embers—embers to cast fire shadows across his face, roving patterns shaping his features, drawing out soft lines, pooling in the hollows of his cheeks, the low tide areas around his sharp nose.

"It's enough that you will not flee into the night." he said.

"I'm sorry I can't—"

"No. It's okay." he used his elbow to lift himself up, sat with his back against a wagon wheel.

There were those lights in the distance. Villages promising a departure from the games of the gods. But for how long? Goddess Liandal's gaze was trained on her, or Jinga would not have arrived when he did. And what protection did she have against her? How far did Shah Jagat's protection extend? The Elder Gods were stronger than their lesser counterparts, were they not? They had escaped the balancing of the Scales, had existed long before the Scales were made.

Jinga drew her attention back to him. His gaze was fixed on the coals, his arms wrapped around his belly, thumb rubbing the shaft of his forearm, over linens bunched near the elbow. The shadows played against his clothes, tugging at ripples and seams, shifting his silhouette. They painted the flanks of the palominos in red hues, deepening splashes of brown almost to black, like dried blood.

"Her attention is never welcome." his gaze flicked to her, an accusation in it. "No better than Gods Hou Rok, Mu, or Tirulain...or Goddess Tajima, so I've heard. It's never comfortable, feeling their stare on your neck. The lingering fixation of a god who you know, somewhere inside, does not wish you well. You are a pawn in their game. It is never anything more substantial than that. Even their own acolytes are but stones on a grand board, and you can never see how far their games reach. Only the pieces which surround your part. Worse, you know they have contingencies in place for if you die. You'll serve one or another of them because that is the nature of your life. You serve the interests of the player or their partner, and you have no choice in the matter.

"I was on Yu Danh Hao when I felt her eyes on me. I wasn't alone. There were others. We had all stumbled our way into Qin Loc one way or another. I won't get into why I was there. It all seems so foolish, now.

"The Raukha's found us. If you ever encounter them, do not give them what they want. Do not make deals with them. Do not even hear them. They name their own prices, and often the price they name is not what it sounds like. I was to take an official to the top of a mountain, where she was to receive a blessing from a spirit. All told, thirty-three of us climbed the mountain. Six of us made it back."

"What happened?" Lisandra asked.

Tears for the Moon God

She did not want to dredge up bitter memories, but she could not help herself. She was familiar with the Raukhas, but who wasn't? Everyone seemed to have a tale of a distant cousin, a friend of a friend, an acquaintance who had run across them and come out worse for it. Maybe they stumbled into one of their gambling parlors or whore houses—they were known to trade in all sorts of nefarious commodities, even to traffic people for their use. Had amassed a debt to them, and them all smiles as the legers grew. Maybe they didn't pay their dues, or fell on hard times and tried to negotiate, and ended up in a slave camp or a debtor's prison, or were beaten within an inch of their lives on the street. The stories were always second hand, always isolated to some distant land, some city far away from home, but she could have thrown a stone into a crowded room and hit someone with a story like it. Someone who swore to the truth of their tale.

And here was Jinga, her own acquaintance with a story to tell. A story she would take with her, chronicled and stored away as a warning...to herself....to others...to stay well away from those people.

"Hm." His lips spread into a cold grin. "The mountain is called Rein. The spirit does not take on acolytes, nor does he give blessings. He has never taken on an acolyte. Not once. The woman we were to escort to his height was called Helein. Helein Four Eyes. One of Gaul No Eyes officers. You don't want to mess with him. Not anyone he deems important." he met her eye briefly before returning to his observation of the fire.

"The mountain is not an easy climb. There are the usual dangers...avalanches, ravines, narrow escarpments...and there are other dangers. Lesser spirits don't occupy Rein's slopes beyond the snow line. But there are the gods who watch his heights...their acolytes...and Hod. There is nothing on those slopes which is friendly to mortals. Not even other mortals. We encountered a troop of one hundred soldiers on our way up who thought us easy pickings. I suppose they were not entirely wrong. I was just a medic then. I had some experience with healing arts. More than any of the rest of them. There are, I think, acceptable means of coming...apart. There were casualties on both sides. Blood in the snow. Wild carnage. I hope never to see it again."

"Fifteen of us arrived at the summit. Helein sought a sword. His skill in sword craft is unparalleled. A sword of Rein mountain will never need to be sharpened. It is imbued with properties according to its design. No two are exactly alike. And they have a fragrance. Each a unique odor. Few merchants know this. Even fewer that the swords are soul bound. To own one is to have conquered the mountain. To possess one is to have come into it by another means, but it will not yield its gifts to any who did not earn it. And the final price is death. A duel. Two mortals set against each other, most often who knew each other before the climb. Whether one of them knew what the ritual entailed and the other did not does not matter.

"I witnessed Helein cut down her opponent, a navigator with no combat experience who was deemed disposable enough to warrant execution. I was made navigator in his stead, and Helein walked away from the ordeal with her sword, called Indolence, a reward for taking life."

Lisandra hissed through her teeth.

"A sword in exchange for twenty-seven lives." he smirked. "Well worth it, don't you think. To this day, I don't know what purpose it served. Simply that God Hou Rok believed the endeavor had the flavor of God Tirulain's plots."

The Freeway

"The God of Games stands in opposition to Goddess Liandal, right?"

Jinga shrugged. "Sometimes. The most dangerous games they've played, as far as I know, have been the ones in which they saw fit to join hands. There is a way to win their game. I would not claim to know what it is. But there is, nonetheless, a way. And the Elder Gods resist it. Or why would they bring about cataclysm as they do? Why interfere if the consequences of this end are palatable to them?"

"You saw twenty-seven people die, and you still want me to stay with you?" she whispered, unwilling to believe it.

"I do. At least until we know what she's after."

"You said you never figured—"

"I never figured out what Tirulain's interest in Helein Four Eyes was. That does not mean I am clueless as to what part I was intended to play. I kept getting déjà vu, this feeling as if I had seen these happenings unfold before. The uelfin sing with God Lanfin to herald the beginning of a new era, but there is always strife in their song. They do not like their ancestral father, nor do they trust him. We can't hear it, but we can see the effects of these shapings in the land around us, in that feeling within us that says we have lived this life, sometimes weakly and at other times much more strongly, before."

She considered her own feelings. She had experienced that feeling before, if she did not want to admit it. There were deviations, certainly, but she felt the pull of...something on her soul, driving her east and north even before Gandes Fae revealed what he had to her. And there was the Wanderer. Shulraki. How much of this life had she repeated? How many of her choices had been autonomous? How many in service of whatever the God of Music demanded?

"I am certain of it. This meeting was not by accident. Nor was Helein's journey. We are called to our tasks. Lanfin can only push Time's River so far without creating devastating consequences for our world. I am sure I played some part in a forgotten past which demands I suffer in this life. I wonder, given our circumstances, if you are not the same.

She lingered in his presence, her eyes on the fire, and said nothing.

The Reaping

Like so many other drugs, the pool containing Sao's memories became like any other puddle. The stab of pain he must endure each time he peered into that window into his past lessened, and with it the draw to dive head first into those waters redoubled. He suspected it was not hatred for the substance that drove the addict to indulge, but a deep and misplaced infatuation, a love of numbness and all that it took away. In that pool was catharsis, a washing away over and again of the loneliness, the melancholy, so familiar in this inconsequential life. Sugar on the tongue, it could only remain so sweet for long. At some point in his time of imprisonment, since his shackling to these halls, this pool and all of its truths, he had developed a resistance, a tolerance, and yet still the cravings did not go away.

He found himself touching the contours of his life more and more frequently, spending less and less time in wandering this labyrinth, seeking out Shulraki and the comforts he offered. He had not seen Xi Didura in so long he was beginning to forget the sound of his voice.

The pool called to him, and his fingers played over it, surface tension dimpling the murky waters under his fingers as he waited for that peculiar, liquid light to pare back obfuscating layers and reveal some banal truth, some grand conquest, a moment in the building of empire, something from his life before power, before rule.

A glimmer lifted out of the depths of those waters, touched the far corner, drawing his eye. He watched it spread, licked soft, pink lips as the greater thrill of anticipation washed through him, rippled through his chest and out through his fingers, down his legs to curl his toes. Soon enough the light would push back fish and weeds, leaving in their place a perfect reflection of a moment in his life, taken from the point of view of god. He tried to clear his head, to think of a time before Dupec. To think of a time when things had been...uncomplicated. If there had ever been such a time.

A spiral current snapped across those depths, leaving the surface unmolested by waves or ripples. Muddy water, brown silts, languid weeds fell away. A window opened in their stead, pushing back algae, shifting pebbles in the shallows.

He plunged his fist through the surface before the memory had time to resolve,

The Reaping

and crawled. Knuckles digging into sand, his back arched hungrily over knees dragged through muck. Reeds tickled his flanks. Water pooled beneath his chin, flooded stone-gray reliefs, trapped the icy, wet chill against his skin.

He plunged in, the surface forgotten. The waters rushed in from every side, stealing his breath, dragging him into some unknown depth the light refused to touch, where his inner darkness could be explored. Salein's gift was not dissimilar, yet nothing within the spirit's power would allow him to reflect on his own memories, to relive them. Not since his first days in his would be master's care had he seen into his own past with such clarity, and yet he could not view this as a hopeful thing, or any kind of blessing. Within these waters lay a curse against his soul, his heart made to bleed again, to draw him into an endless cycle as he became obsessed with recriminating memories of bad times and good, and all of those memories were twisted into poisons. In revisiting those memories, he might find a form of healing, but he could not change what lay within them, and having no power to alter the course of his life, to change his fate, he was instead met with a stark reality. This was not healing but addiction, and he was powerless to overcome it.

How many times had he invaded another mortal mind, drawn forth truths from resistant people, compelled them to answer for crimes they believed secret. How much of the monster he became was born out of jealousy, that they could see their kin one more time, dead lovers, children, brothers and sisters; or revisit a place of tragedy and heal, truly heal! Perhaps it had been the first time some of his subjects had believed it possible to come away from war, or poverty, or some half remembered act of violence with closure, in peace.

Yet the more he sought the same peace—the more he entered this pool, the more he revisited the past—the more dependent he became on those momentary departures. As the waters pulled him down, another piece of him was taken, an old wound was picked open again, and there was no catharsis for him. No peace. No healing. Memory was his vice. A balm became a poison, and he refused to acknowledge that one thing, one voyage, one journey as witnessed from two different lenses could be both.

The waters were forgotten. He was going to drown. A pulse in his throat, his vision a black wall interrupted by bursts of light, explosions of white like so many fire crackers blasting apart a-rhythmically, without respect to distance, the spread random and ill conceived. Fang Ilra played her hand, and taunted him with the promise of a death that would never come.

The dunes of Sha Ruhhad were broken by spears of desiccated wood, old stumps and fragmented tree trunks frozen in time to remind his guardians that this land had not always belonged to him. That there had been a time life abounded and man thrived. Sha Ruhhad was a harsh master, a recluse indifferent to the perils of mortals, and the spirits who embraced him were the same.

But life finds a way, and the Nixians carved out a life beyond Gonsai Wall and within it. Gonsai stood strong against Ho'o's wild howling, the driving sands he cast against him, and within his embrace was shelter. For the Nixians, his shield was one mercy. Ul Sharak's bounty, another.

Sao kept close to his mother. He was not old enough to don the sheer, black shroud she and the other Nixians of age wore. Black, flowing cloth drawing in heat

Tears for the Moon God

from an open sky where Cyprus clouds promised rains that would not come. Too high and too thin, the clouds spoke to just how little influence the Goddess of Storms had in this reach, where everything remained dry until the monsoon season arrived, and then the rains were but fleeting mists, dampening the sands and retreating. Scarabs crawled out of the dunes in the morning, collected dew along their shells, siphoned it into waiting mouths and then retreated before the day's heat grew strong, into the sands and away. The fox slumbered in its burrow during the daylight hours, awaiting frigid night to hunt by moonlight.

Life found a way.

His mother waded into the band of Ul Sharak's great river. Around her ankles passed the spirits of the dead, eyes closed as if sleeping peacefully within the embrace of those green tinted waters. A wicker basket hung from her arm, and she collected produce harvesters up river had cast into the band. A porcelain mask was drawn over her face. He had been allowed one this year, having earned his right to adolescence, but the mask he wore was unadorned. Hers was embellished with lapis tiles, bands of gold foil hemming them in, giving the impression of scales under her eyes and chin, an homage to the river, her mentor.

He cast aside his moccasins and scrambled into the band after her, staying to the shallows. The current was not strong here, but boys his size had been swept up by it, cast far downriver before Ul Sharak saw fit to show them mercy. If she did.

Maize and squash and cords of millet flowed with the ever drifting souls. Wrinkled fingers brushed his ankle, and he leapt aside, coming close to stepping on another figure's chest.

His mother hissed.

"Show your respect." She said. "The dead belong to the river. We are guests to them. Or do you want this oasis to dry up, and us starve next dry season?"

"I'm sorry, mother." He whined. "I was just...startled."

She returned to her gathering. The basket was fast filling. She would need to exchange it for the other waiting on the verdant shore soon, settled there among the rushes.

"Ul Sharak is a spirit of renewal." She explained. "All that we have is given by her hand, but it does not come free. We honor the dead each year at the Sewing and the Reaping, because to pay respect to her dead, to all of those of the many races and ethnicities throughout our lands and others who pass along her band, is to ensure our continued survival. Be easy, my willful child, for the energy they give supplies nourishment to this oasis. They give their energy to ensure we have this."

She tossed a gourd and caught it, added it to her basket.

"I'm sorry." He repeated. "I'll be better."

"I'm sure you will." His mother said. "Now get me that basket."

She passed her burden onto him, and he carried it, struggling under its weight in the uncertain mud, back to shore. He grabbed the empty basket, and brought it to her. They filled it with potatoes, and sugar beets which his father would refine into sugar and molasses. Further down river from where they gathered, still others reached into the waters, collected rice and threads of kelp from deeper water. When he was old enough, he would join them, together with his mother, in the harvesting of grains. When he had grown taller and stronger, he would.

In truth, though being so close to the dead made him uncomfortable, it was a lesser discomfort than an ordinary day. At the ceremonies of the Sewing and the

The Reaping

Reaping, he was well covered, the mask hiding his face. Behind that mask, he could be like anyone else. The odd, golden cast to his skin went unnoticed. He did not have elders praying over him, or children mocking him or presenting ill conceived excuses for why he could not play with them, why their games of shadow tag, or kickball were barred to him.

At first, he had not understood.

He had fallen off a third tier balcony in the capital once when he was six. The fall should have killed him. A grown man would have been killed by that fall, but he had come out fine. Had not even suffered a broken bone. There had been a few scratches across his knees and elbows, a gash in his forehead, but even those marks had healed fast, without complications.

He had not known what a Sun Man was then, and could not have conceived of how it would impact his life. The kids locked him out of their games because the teams on which he played would win. The elders prayed over him because they believed his birth heralded an era of prosperity for his people. He was not a person to any of them. He was an idol, an object, and he had learned to hate it.

These days by the river, when he could don his mask, cover his skin, when the cast of his hands was marred by river water and he could be unknown to everyone if he simply did not speak, were the only days when he felt like one of them. But the day was fleeting, and as he carried the second basket to shore, his mother trailing behind him, he knew the time was coming when it must end.

Upriver and down, other families had completed their harvests and were returning to shore. The *thwack, thwack* of machetes chopping at thick stalks, the susurration of shovels driven into dirt, was drawing to a close. His mother took his hand in hers and faced the river. The sun was well past its zenith, and even now twilight's fiery hues were crawling across the western sky. There had been no Nixians on the east side of the river since the day's work began. There had been no crops planted there, either. The east side of the river was a wild tangle of brush and weeds, reeds and cattails taller than most men and so densely packed together that it was impossible to see beyond the first few lines.

Abasad's dark slopes and rounded peaks formed a rolling spine across the horizon, and before them were foothills, and then high, sweeping dunes, and those remnants of the ancient forest around their roots.

"Look to the dunes, Sao." His mother whispered. "Just there. You see them?"

Spread across a line of dunes, along their heights, were figures clad in white linen robes, robes which fluttered in a soft breeze he could not feel. He wondered if the dunes blocked that wind or if those people were in some other place, and were only visible to them by some trick of the waning light. Dozens of them looked down on their people, their families, their kin, looked across the river at the people they had left behind at the Sewing, when they declared their desire to study under the spirit of the river. Dozens looked on loved ones who had not seen them in months. Not since the beginning of the monsoon season, which had ended some weeks ago.

His mother's fingers pressed lightly against his neck, drawing him around to a hill near the center of the line. As twilight took the sky, a storm of vibrant colors displacing the near unbroken blue; as the sun crawled across Rasheik's Rope in the west, a woman climbed the slope of the dune, assumed her place atop that hill. She stood proudly, her back straight, her chin tipped upward as she looked down on the Nixians, now finished with their harvests.

Tears for the Moon God

Her skin was the color of obsidian, her head bald. Wide disks hung from her earlobes, and a choker of gold encircled her neck. She was clad in the same sheer, white linen as her charges, her robes hugging her figure and leaving her arms exposed. Bands of gold inlaid with lapis lazuli fragments hung from her wrists, clattered together as she lifted a slender arm to point across the band, at one family, another, another still. With each gesture, an acolyte broke from the line, descended the dune, crossed the river. They walked across the surface, unimpeded by flowing waters and cloying mud, and joined their families on the other side. One, and then another, and the next joined families who burst into tears and clinging hands, tight hugs and declarations of love and relief.

Of the dozens gathered there atop the dunes, a third returned to their families, returned to uncertain peoples suddenly granted catharsis after the long, fraught wait.

His mother's hand was on him, squeezing his shoulder. She raised her hand to the spirit. Several others along the western shore made the same gesture. Ul Sharak returned it. The spirit turned her back to them and descended the dunes to the east. The remaining dozens who had not returned repeated the gesture, and followed her away. Their families would go to Gur Tulain, to see them one last time, to speak to their dead before they passed along the river's band on their way to sea. They would have their release then, when they had made peace with their losses.

For now, they grieved. Mothers clambered onto the bank, dropped to their knees and wept. Children huddled around them, some too young to understand they would never see their brothers or sisters, their cousins, alive again. Those were the initiates who had failed in the last months, those who Ul Sharak had deemed unworthy of her. With one hand, she gave the Nixian people life, a bounty and a mercy against the hard months. With the other, she took, and with her taking, lives were lost. Families were broken.

And still, life found a way.

"If there is a way in, there is a way out." Xi mumbled to himself.

He scratched at a gap between stones with his thumbnail, loosening clastic silts in a bid to make the gap wider. If he could just release one of those stones, even a small one, he could confirm the basis of his latest theory. The labyrinth was endless. Even in its oldest passages, there was no escape. Even there, too many lives were drawn into pools, too many to count, and the halls surrounding them were too elaborate, a web which became ever more crazed the farther from its eye a Wanderer got. And this web had many eyes, one for each man who was immured here, and all of them overlapping at their fringes.

"The river has to be somewhere." He kept chiseling, glanced now and again at his sword in its scabbard where it rested against the wall of an adjacent passage. "Not down the halls, but maybe...maybe these aren't the only ones."

"An astute observation."

Xi jumped, raked his thumb against rough stone as he fell backward. He hissed.

Ank stooped over him with his hands laced behind his back. The paint on his face was running in places, and he was out of breath, panting, nose flaring with every inhale, as if he had been running.

"Don't scare me like that!" Xi growled. He examined his thumb. The nail was cracked, his whole thumb and wrist throbbing and in pain.

The Reaping

Ank turned to observe the wall, the spot where he had been digging. "What do you expect you'll find...if you open a wide enough gap?"

"What else? A way in." He righted himself.

Ank met his gaze. "You shouldn't do that."

"Why not?"

"We're in a God House."

"And?"

"This God House, like any other, is governed by rules. Now we must, of course, take into consideration the erratic nature of those who built this labyrinth..." he grimaced. "...perhaps *built* isn't the proper word. Regardless, we are in God Lanfin's house, and the walls, the floors, the chaise lounge in the piano room are all suffused with his power. He is an observant lad, that one, or why allow him to watch over time's flow. He is only a musician, after all."

"Who says anyone allows it?"

Ank clucked his tongue against his teeth, shook his head.

"I suppose I should let you get back to it." His arm swung out from behind him. He held out a stick, a green thing the thickness of a finger, which bore signs of having been twisted off a shrub, and then stripped of twigs and leaves.

Xi's gaze rested on it as he took it from the graemein.

"I've never seen a bush in this place." He said. "Or a tree...alive or dead."

"Yes, well, they are quite rare. But I've been blessed with uncommon luck, you see." Ank tapped his cheekbone, where a run in the white paint exposed a streak of skin like polished gold. "A keen eye helps, too."

Xi nodded. "I suppose that makes sense...in its way."

"Keep on digging if you must, but I should ask..." his gaze shifted to the sword where it rested against the wall, became unfocused. He convulsed, eyes fluttering, worked his jaw and tensed his fingers.

"Ask what?" Xi said.

Ank's steady, discerning gaze fell on him, then, taking his measure.

"Nice to see you, Master Didura, but I'm afraid I must be on my way."

He ambled away in the direction opposite where Xi's sword lay.

"Ask me what, Ank?" Xi called after him.

He turned a corner, and walked away.

"Strange people." He muttered, returning to his work. He dug the stick into the gap between stones and started grinding. "Incomprehensibly odd."

A Song for Violence

Ho'o whispered across the Sangar grasslands. Boisterous laughter became a soft chortle as he passed across those lands. Oh, how he wished that poor duo could see what slithered on its belly amid those grasses, using him, as it were, for cover. He ought to deny them that defense at least. Ought to make their lives a little harder, make them earn whatever it was they sought.

He made no move against them. He knew quite well who those unlikely traveling companions were, and wondered why the gods sought to bring them together. Hou Rok's engineers were one and the same in their mindsets. Build a mill with great big fins to catch the wind and hold it. Siphon its power off to use elsewhere, for something those mortals thought practical. Grinding stones together, it might be. Or housing raw power in some idle state, in an acid bath or some such, in metal housing. Draw it in and keep it, wasn't that always their way? And if he broke their fins of wood, or tarp, or what have you, they'd come back with metal stolen from the hills, refined ores spread and hammered into shape to form new fins, sturdier fins, fins he could not break.

If the mountains protested when they reached down with their drills and hammers, blow them to pieces! Oh, how it was their way. And if the oceans would not yield to them, was it not their way to armor their ships, place upon them layer on layer of iron, sheeting to protect the hulls from breaches. Forego the sails and use propellers. It was, indeed, their way.

Yet this one...he's not the same is he? He thought. He really ought to do something about those marauders coming to kill poor Jinga in his sleep, but why bother saving who should have been dead already? Lanfin might have nudged the river he so jealously guarded out of her track, but he could not budge her too far. Somewhere in his labyrinth was a pool that belonged to Jinga, to the Jinga who had lived in that time stream, the one the gods saw fit to recall.

He wondered if his son had found it yet. If the Halls of Time had stolen his mind as they were so wont to do, if the listless days in the stagnant abyss had already driven him to tempt death, to flirt with him, with knives or improvised ropes, or a loose brick torn from one of those drab, gray walls.

He chuckled to himself. *Now that one had mettle. And brains, too. Brains to*

A Song for Violence

know how to manipulate the idiots he surrounded himself with. How to topple this empire, make that king bend his knee.

What delicious irony, finding these two together. Lisandra always was good with her shield. Agnes will be missing her, the miserable toad.

Oh, let's see.

He thrust out his arm. A sword materialized and he caught it. The length of the blade was blackened iron shot through with crude veins of some vitreous material which reminded him of quartz. The pommel was walnut wrapped in black leather, and the sword exuded an odor. Baby's breath, infuriatingly enough. The odor was horrendous, but then it ought to be. Its maker had been loath to craft this weapon, had no great love for the man who commissioned it. The maker had named the damned thing Spite, for all the effort it cost him.

A blessed sword or a cursed one, it was nonetheless well balanced, light weight and single edged.

A gift from the Wanderers to you. He cast it before him, threw it hard.

He doubled over cackling.

Metal struck stone. Not the gong deep sound of something hollow hitting hard ground, but the clank and scuttle of something awkward striking home.

Lisandra vaulted upright. Her eyes latched onto the source of the sound. A sword lay spare inches from where her head had been.

Jinga knelt with his blades half drawn, his gaze on the sword between them. The horses slept, caring nothing for the disturbance, and the wagon was still. He eased his blades back into their sheathes, letting out the breath he had been holding.

Her gaze flicked to him.

"He's laughing." He said.

"Who?"

"Ho'o." He answered. "The bastard likes his jokes, but this? This is too far."

"Next, you'll scream at him." She said, getting to her feet. She dusted off her skirts. "Which will be about as effective as..."

She paused. There had been a sound, just then. Scattered stones. Reeds snapping.

"Don't put those knives away." She whispered. Her gaze flashed to the sword, panned across the grasses. Yes, the breeze seized those tall strands, caused them to whisper in the dark. The North Wind had seen...*something.*

And the sword?

She reached down, snatched it up by the handle. A quick swing, rolling her wrist, carrying the blade in a broad circle. The blade was as long as her arm, from shoulder to fingertip, but it was center weighted, well-balanced. She was reminded of a sword she had used in her youth, in the days when she had still been leading raids against saodeini occupiers, before age caught up with her, stole away her vigor.

Jinga watched her, a queer expression on his face. Did this old crone intend to fight? Could she?

She suspected he would try to cover her if she gave him that freedom. If she let him close, he would only get in her way. She needed free range to maneuver, needed him to understand, before this thing got well underway, what it was to dance with her.

She carried the sword in a decisive arc over her head. Fragrance burst forth, suffused the air with its cloying aroma—baby's breath in full bloom, that sickly sweet perfume. She carved down with the blade, leveled out as he backed a few steps away, giving her more space within which to work.

"You're not fooling anyone!" she shouted. "Come fight us like men, you cowardly shit heads!"

More of those sandpaper sounds. Their adversaries were fanning out, taking up positions.

How many? Half a dozen, at least.

A keening song drifted on the breeze. It tore lose from the throat of a hidden assailant, a fierce castrato cry.

Jinga turned his back to her, put yet more space between them.

"They're coming." He said.

The keening cry was joined by others, arranged in a half circle with the meniscus across from the freeway.

Monsters out of nightmare sprang from the grasses, wielding long knives in both hands. Too wide, red eyes looked out from pale faces, from under thick hanks of violently blue and green hair. Their features were extruded in a way that reminded her fleetingly of fish. Wide mouths, angular features pooling over blunted jaws.

Boiled leather armor covered narrow frames. They surged forth with serpentine grace, flowing through rapid, unfamiliar forms as they edged in close with flickering knives, testing her defenses, hunting for weaknesses.

She gave them no time.

A series of quick strikes. Black blade suffusing the air with its pungent scent. She swept through them, blade wheeling through concise forms, her feet carrying her through the gracile dance of death, homage to Shah Jagat, who walked in her shadow.

She spun around, a searching knife coming dangerously close to her ribs. Thirty years younger and the blade would have breezed harmlessly past, hitting nothing but air. It caught cloth now, tore a wide gash through just shy of striking flesh.

She snapped out with the sword's pommel, a vicious blow to the monster's teeth. Another boiled out of the grasses in her blind spot. Metal raked across skin, the blade slicing across her ribs, leaving shallow cuts in its wake. She stepped out of range of the knife, knee snapping up into the first creature's jaw at the same time, reversed her blade and back thrust at a high angle, taking the second in the throat.

From a distant place, she observed Jinga descending into the rushes, heard the gargled cry that precluded the song those creatures sang scattering, losing its sense for time, its cadence.

Her sword slashed across the belly of a third. Entrails tumbled from the wound, pattered against the ground as he stumbled away, clutching uselessly at the wound.

Another surged forth, desperation in his eyes as he swung wildly with both blades. She side stepped him. Two quick slashes across the pits of his knees, severing tendons.

He collapsed three feet in front of her. She closed the distance, raked her blade across his throat, and watched through ice blue eyes as he died. There was no

A Song for Violence

remorse in her heart, no grief, no need to wonder who these creatures might have left to worry over them when they did not come home. There was not even rage.

In that dispassionate place within her, she logged away two scraps of information from this encounter in the night. These were not Sangar, and The North Wind was with her. Another ally, should she ask for one. Temperamental he might be, but he had given her a sword. He had given her aid. She would not forget it.

Jinga returned to their camp. The iron musk of blood filled the air, displacing the sweeter fragrance exuded from the blade, pushing back the fresh, natural odors of earth and clean air and wheat. She tore off a scrap of wool underlining from one of the felled creatures, and used it to wipe the blade clean.

The cotton came away unsullied. She considered the black-bladed weapon, then, wondering what kind of sword drank in the blood it took. *What strange thing is this.*

"Goddess Liandal's?" she asked.

"He shook his head, expressionless, revealing nothing. "More likely God Lanfin's. Though what he wants with us, I don't know. They're uelfin. A long way from home, too. If I was a betting man, I'd say they hired a pathfinder to take them this far."

"To contest our arrival." She said. "Someone doesn't want us approaching your home."

He cleaned his knives and sheathed them, checked over the nearest corpses. He rutted through pockets, coming up empty of anything useful.

"They'll have a camp somewhere nearby." He said.

"Leave them to it."

He watched her, a queer expression on his face. "Why?"

"Why send so few? There are more of them out there. When these ones don't come back, they'll send others to investigate. That's why you leave them."

"They're uelfin." He said. "That song they were singing. Have you ever...no, well, I suppose you wouldn't have. It's how they glimpse the future. They have a small advantage in that, but the moment one deviates from the vision, it all falls apart. Most often they don't need more than one glimpse, but it takes time for them to regain access to those visions. Time we should use to put distance between us and any others that might be coming."

She looked down at the corpse at her feet. The blood pooling over ground looked no different than what she had seen leaking from so many humans. Its face, rigor frozen in a savage snarl, was little different than she had seen on those saodeini she had slain, either. To see the future, and use it to commit violence against two unassuming travelers, whatever walked in their shadows, was selfish, brazen and dumb. What could they build with such power? Yet they sought instead to destroy, to murder, to take life against some future they barely comprehended.

She wondered at what would lead such a people to travel so far, in force if she did not miss her guess, for the lives of two inconsequential strangers.

Preparations

Thin tendrils of smoke drifted from a bowl of smoldering herbs atop the wood stove in Tursa's yurt. The chief sat with two of his sons in the quiet gloom. He sat board straight while his sons lounged near the entrance.

Their presence provided no comfort to Ungol, and it surprised him that Arrak did not command them to leave their father's keeping. Certainly, Kuuda would have resisted. As acting chief of his sect, he would not have gone easily, and perhaps it was this truth that stayed Arrak's hand. Still, it did not help that the business to be conducted here was of such a delicate nature. Arrada, certainly, did not need to be here.

It might have been guilt that compelled Ungol to avoid looking at the youngest of Tursa's children. It might have been shame that kept him from looking the man in the eyes. Or, perhaps it was some measure of pity. There may come a time when their talk pushed Arrada to do something his siblings might find unreasonable. He had not been forthcoming with the attitudes of those others toward Shaede's indiscretion.

Off in the Tipik camp, Coltang would already be handling preparations ahead of the purge. In his own camp, Shaelein was already gathering the elders among them to see to it that those who conducted their purge were not seen as enforcers. He did not value putting his people through more hardship. Many of them were still grieving the losses of children, husbands, wives, mothers and fathers. Many a yurt had been filled with sympathetic kin of late, checking in on those who had lost someone, helping them along in their day to day struggles with the absences of those they loved.

In the wake of collective loss was not only grief, but a galvanizing of old bonds, a unifying of elements throughout the sect, within and outside of families. Everyone did their part. Everyone found their means of supporting the afflicted. In the days after raids in which the Dumas suffered large losses, it was to the survivors to come together, in remembrance and in aid, to provide help with the minutia of life among the Gil Garo, to tend horses, cook for those who would waste away in their sorrows.

Shaelein had done well to encourage the mothers among them, the widows, those who had lost what kin they had in years past, to provide space for the newly aggrieved to navigate their losses. Had settled them to work in groups to help along the mothers who had lost their children, the wives who had lost their husbands. This was the Dumas way. And he had taken measures to help the men in kind, setting them to work, giving them use. They needed those distractions. They needed encouragement. To feel like they were not useless, like they had not failed in their principled charges, of keeping their families safe and protected. To help them find other things to latch onto, and give new meaning to their pursuits of protecting what kin had survived.

He had needed them in the days following his own great loss, in coping with the knowledge that the future he hoped to provide for his son might all have been for nothing. They had come, then. Many had put their reservations surrounding the choices he had made as a young man, in courting and training under Gandes Fae, aside in order to see him, and Shaelein, set on the path to reclaiming some semblance of wholeness.

In returning that kindness, again and again, he found his own use. His own purpose. Denied his one shot at parenthood, left with a gaping whole where his son should be to fill with something else, he had come to understand a critical thing, which he believed Tursa understood better than most. He could not remain fixated on the loss of his child, because they needed him. In kind, he needed them. It was this that defined a family, and the Dumas was his. All of the Dumas must be his kin, for this was the place of a chief.

He wondered how much Kuuda understood of this concept. If he could rise in the absence of his father to shoulder this burden, bring honor to his station. He had seen those qualities in the man from a young age, but now, faced with the prospect of alienating himself from his sister, what would he do?

He could not decide.

"Come to shackle me to the stove this time?" Tursa snapped.

"No, chief." Arrak said tonelessly. "I have a task for you. I need you to gather the others among your people who took up apprenticeship under Shi'an."

"Why?"

"We have elected to perform a sweep of the sects for stragglers. I believe some of our people have taken to harboring blood cursed loved ones." He fixed Kuuda with a hard gaze. "You will have to conduct the sweep for the Hakka. Root out every afflicted person among your people and have them brought to the Tipik camp. Coltang is preparing a quarantine zone for them." His gaze swung back to Tursa, softening. "I'm sure you understand, friend, why this is necessary."

Tursa's gaze traveled to his elder son. Arrada wilted as Kuuda's attention shifted from Arrak to his brother, then to Ungol.

"What did you do?" Kuuda demanded.

"My question for you." Tursa growled.

"I did nothing unreasonable." Kuuda said defensively, his gaze still fixed on his brother. His jaw was set, and he had adjusted his position among the cushions. He was now sitting upright, and towering over Arrada. The fire glow from the camp stove set Arrada ominously in his shadow.

"Arrada?"

"He told me about your nephew, Kuuda." Ungol said. "It was my duty to ensure he was contained."

"Your responsibility as a chief is not to your family." Tursa said harshly. His

Tears for the Moon God

gaze set against Kuuda was like a thunderhead. "Everything you do must be with the greatest benefit of *all* of your sect in mind! How many of them did you let slip through? What might have happened if even *one of them slipped their binds!"*

"I did not think—"

"Precisely." Tursa said acidly.

"Tursa, if you will please calm down. The damage is done." Arrak interrupted, but Tursa ignored him.

"You saw, that night, what happened to our people. They rose up against us. Every one of them who was touched with that tainted blood became an agent for our enemies. A soldier in their army! How many casualties did we suffer *during* the attack? How many were killed *after!*

"And you thought it wise to allow their families, untrained in anything of this magnitude, to harbor them in perfect range, should they escape, to infect *all of us.*"

"Had I enacted the purge, you would not now be alive." Kuuda said coldly.

Tursa spat on the ground. "The Swans, my son, kill us for far less. You follow their example every day as a chief. Cull the flock. Remove the rot. If our sect is to survive to see the next harvest, we *must be strong!* I thought I raised you better!"

Kuuda opened his mouth for a rebuttal, and closed it again.

"Now go. Right now! Do the right thing."

Kuuda looked from his father, to Ungol, to Arrak.

"Don't have them killed. And leave Tulukh alone for now." Arrak said, earning a raised eyebrow from Tursa. "If it gets out among the other sects that your children chose to harbor an infected child in secret, it will create tensions we cannot afford just now. Tulukh will remain under Arrada's care until we have found a means of dealing with this affliction."

Kuuda came close to running from the tent. His face had gone a peculiar shade of red, and as he passed Ungol he made a point of shouldering him aside. A move that was not strictly necessary as Ungol was not standing in direct line with the entrance.

"Your weakness surprises me, Arrak." Tursa said.

"We risk losing far more of our people to this poison with our every encounter with the Tului." Arrak said. "We need to find a means of curing our infected, but we can run no tests without a stock of victims. We risk losing our war without them."

Tursa grimaced. "I don't like it."

"But you understand it." Ungol said.

"Yes." He said reluctantly. I'll gather the acolytes." He turned to his son. "You're going to find Kuuda. It will be your task to explain to these families why they cannot house infected in their yurts."

"Yes, father." Arrada climbed to his feet, and ducked out of the yurt without further comment.

"Is this wise?" he asked.

"I don't know." Ungol said. "But is it necessary?"

Neither of the other men answered.

A cold knot of anger had settled into Kuuda's gut. As he left his father's yurt, he was met with curious looks from those who had made camp nearest to the chief. Most of those would be his lieutenants, among them the brightest and most cunning minds among the Kirche, their wives and children.

Preparations

He paid them little mind as he marched brusquely past, and dodged the few questions those he had long seen as friends asked. He would have to tell them what was going on soon enough. He would need their help in the purge that was to come. *If they are not also harboring sick children.*

A feral growl escaped him.

"Easy, brother." Arrada said.

"This is your doing." Kuuda snapped. "You thought it wise to tell Ungol."

"I needed advice."

"And he told the other chiefs about Tulukh."

"It wouldn't have been necessary if Shaede had just—"

"Just what? She is his *mother,* Arrada!" Kuuda snapped.

"If he was to escape, what would you do? Father is right. You should have done what was needed before we ever left Gil Garo."

"If I had, and a cure for this affliction was found, our people would never have forgiven me. They might have sought to pull our family down. Father would no longer be chief."

"He isn't now." Arrada whispered. "You are."

"Only until he is healed."

"You tell yourself that if you must, but we do not know if he will ever be healed of this curse. You have seen him. He sustains himself well enough, but he is worsening by the day. Soon, Shi'an's power will not be enough to contain this poison, and then there will be nothing I can do for him except to keep him comfortable."

"As you have done for Tulukh."

Arrada nodded.

Kuuda turned down a broad channel among the yurts, led him away from the lieutenants camps and the feeble promise of an immediate solution.

"Where are we going?"

"To tell Shaede what is happening."

Arrada froze. "No, brother."

Kuuda rounded on him, his fury painted across his face. "No?"

Arrada shook his head. "No. If you go directly there, it will arouse suspicion among our people. They will wonder why she was the first person you visited, *before* you gathered the lieutenants for this purge."

"They will wonder just as much if we do not visit her at all."

"Then we will go while they are conducting the purge, and see to Boen and Alaar, too."

"Are you chief now?" Kuuda said cuttingly.

"You know this is the right choice."

Kuuda deflated. *What have you gotten us into, Shaede.*

He thought again about what he would do if her indiscretion was made public. If his nephew won free of his binds, or infected another person. He would have to kill him, then. He knew she would not be the one to do it. Her bond with him was too strong. A mother could not be expected to kill her own son.

But how many mothers had done exactly that, in mitigating the damage another curse might cause? How many had left their newborn children on the side of a horse track, or at the edge of the village? *The Swans would have taken most of those. It is their right.*

Tears for the Moon God

And the ones who survived and became men? How many of them were out there, having no connection to their home. Gil Garo tribesmen raised by spirits and gods, scattered across the world, having no idea of their parentage or the culture they had come from. Cloud men, one and all. Ungol was not the only one who had lost a son to that curse. He was the only one whose child had returned to them, but there had been that strange period when he was in his teen years, not yet a man, but close. A flowering of life like had never been seen among the Gil Garo before. There had been dozens of them born within a handful of years. The midwives had prayed to the benevolent Goddess of Fertility, then; had burned incense and given offerings of gold and silver and jewelry to the fickle God of Luck. They had been convinced God Katcya was angry with them, that he had seen fit to curse them with so many children who had been born to die in those days.

The knives had come out, again and again. The midwives lay them at bedside, or tossed them onto the still bleeding laps of the mothers, and turned their eyes away, left the families to do what they must. Many of them had.

And now, some twenty years later, they were again afflicted by a curse without a clear cure. An affliction they *must* confront. And he had shown nothing but weakness in the face of it.

Father is right. The thought tasted like ash in his mouth.

"Fine." He said. "*I* will gather the lieutenants. You go to the elders. We will need friendly faces among those we burden with this task, or we will be left dragging the sick ones out of the arms of their kin."

"When you tell the lieutenants what must be done, tell them to be gentle." Arrada said.

Kuuda set a conflicted gaze on his brother. "I will." He said after a moment. "I...I will."

Coltang's sect was not taking their new charge well. The purge was conducted with precision. Elders among his people were accompanied by warriors, two for every one of them. There had been need of them. Skirmishes broke out where parents refused to relinquish their kin. Some had taken to hiding their children in trunks or tucked away under blankets. Some had confessed to having tucked them away among their effects on wagons when the initial purge was happening.

The numbers had been low, but screaming matches between those families and their neighbors, many of them blood kin themselves, were becoming more prevalent as those loved ones were hauled away.

Tanta stood beside him as more and more of victims of the Tului curse were brought into the quarantine zone, a series of yurts and huts that had been donated by the other sects, what teepees could be spared by his own people. Mounds of grass had been dug out of the snows and were being dried over low burning fires and laced with oil. Some of his people lay the mounds around the quarantine zone, and those who had set up camp too close were pulling down their teepees and packing their belongings onto carts, to relocate to the fringes of the camp where they would be at less risk of being attacked if any of these victims escaped.

He had sent runners to Addula and Karakh, but neither had appeared just yet. He was not sure what he would tell them when they did.

The purge had yielded few victims among his people, perhaps two dozen all told, but two dozen was too many. Their number told him there had been

Preparations

sympathizers among those who had conducted the original purge, people among them who could be convinced to leave those families well alone. He would have them rooted out before the end of this day and brought to him. He did not much like the idea of punishing his own people, but there must be an example made of them. Those others with clean hands—and especially those who had seen their kin dead after the battle had concluded—would demand as much.

Exile is off the table, but perhaps a happy solution can be found here. Who else can be said to hold their sympathies? They might even be glad to be tasked with keeping this place secure.

"What's on your mind, husband?" Tanta was looking up at him expectantly. She hid it well, but he suspected she was as deeply saddened by all of this as he was. There had been losses among all of the sects. Those could not go unnoticed. If a quarantine was to be the eventually solution, did all of those others have to die?

"They were spared by someone." He said.

"And they will need to be dealt with."

"The problem is I understand what motivated this. It is not easy to look into the eyes of your friends and tell them they must kill their own children. Children you knew. It is not easy looking into the eyes of your friends as you feed them poison, or take a knife to their—"

"That's enough." She gripped his bicep gently. "It is past."

"But is it? The evidence of their indiscretion is before you." He gestured toward the tents, the thickening lines of Gil Garo from other sects carrying their own charges. There were none from the Chikata or the Dumas. It seemed their purges had been absolute. *Ungol, you have given your people a gift, haven't you. In your own grief, there could never have been a question for their sacrifices. They saw you abandon your son.* "They will have to be held to account, or there will be riots."

"How will you deal with them."

"I have an idea."

She raised an eyebrow.

He sighed heavily. "I think they will secure this site. They will be seen to be in the line of fire should there be a breach, and in setting it right, they may earn back some of the respect they lose for being held to account so publicly."

"But will they intervene if it becomes necessary? The did not before."

"They will not be the only ones here. Look. There is Tursa."

Tursa was emerging from the north, and behind him, a double file of others were marching toward the quarantine site. There were well over one hundred of them, and all of them wore grim expressions to match that of their chief. They fanned out as they entered the zone, and fell on the yurts and huts as those victims continued to be hauled, some thrashing and screaming through gags, into them.

Tursa approached Coltang and Tanta, as they fell into place. He was pale and somewhat gaunt in a way that was unusual for him. It had been many years since he had known youth, but he had become a wraith at some point in the last days. His condition was getting worse.

"I've done my part." He said. "Now it is up to you to do yours."

"The purge is nearing completion." Coltang said. "I am saddened to see so many of my own among the victims."

"How many were there?"

"Twenty-six so far."

"A low enough number to be justified as a few outliers."

"Yet enough to warrant concern."

"I did not know so many of your people had taken up your mantle." Tanta said kindly.

Tursa looked over his shoulder at the few left to mill about outside. Even those were approaching charges.

"This is only half of them." Tursa said. "The other half are needed elsewhere for the time being."

"For the counterattack."

"They didn't say anything about that." Tursa grumbled. His gaze returned to Coltang.

"Sarri's plan." Coltang said. "It has a chance, if it is executed well."

"We won't be catching up to their army for some time. I've seen the signs of their travel ahead of us. All of the signs of their passing are days old, swept over with errant dunes. They do not ride, but they make good progress toward their destination. Wherever that is."

"We intend to attack before they do."

"And what will my role in this attack be?"

Coltang gestured for a runner. One came sprinting across the quarantine zone toward them.

"Yes, chief Coltang?" he panted.

"You have something for Chief Tursa?"

"Right." He sprinted out of the area and into the camp. He returned almost as soon as he had gone, carrying a grain sack on his shoulder.

"What is this?"

"Seeds confiscated or donated from those who were known to have them. Opium poppy and valerian."

"Sedatives?"

Coltang nodded. "I cannot deny my surprise that Arrak did not fill you in on this piece, but perhaps he did not want to overwhelm you."

"He did anyway." Tursa said. "With anger. My sons—"

"Were doing what they believed was right." Coltang said.

"Were too weak to do what was needed." Tursa corrected him.

"Whatever your view, you are meant to have these, for your farmers to grow. A portion of the opium will be repurposed for the raid. You will find Gulang amenable to taking charge of it."

"And the rest will be used in keeping the victims sedated."

Coltang nodded.

"Do I get an explanation of this plan?"

"It is not my place to tell you." Coltang said.

"I'll pay a visit to Arrak." Tursa said. He turned on his heels and marched back the way he had come.

"Forceful as ever, isn't he?" Tanta quipped.

"He's getting worse." Coltang said. "I wonder how long it will be before he cannot fight this curse any longer."

"We will find a cure before then." She said reassuringly. "This raid. Is that not its intent?"

"It is, but with Gulang leading it...."

Preparations

"He is a competent war leader."

"He has also lost a son."

"You think he is weakened by the loss?"

"No, not that. I think he will do something reckless out of anger. Grief makes people unpredictable. It can make them cold and calculating, but I do not think it has done either with him. He will want revenge for what happened to Karsa. What he does when he arrives at their camp I can only guess, but I do not think he will come back with anything of use to us."

"Then why did you support him?" she snapped, a hot flash of anger darkening her features.

"Would you have done any different?" he asked.

"I..." her anger abated. "I don't know."

Shaelein was waiting for him when Ungol returned to their yurt. He took up a seat on the pillows next to her, and she spread a quilt over him despite the harsh heat suffusing the space. She had taken Dupec's baby clothes out of their trunk, and they lay spread across her lap, one of the tiny, deer hide boots pinched between her fingers.

He snuggled up to her, nuzzled against her breast, and she stroked his hair absentmindedly.

"Did they find anyone?" he asked.

"No." She said. "Not yet."

"The sweep is still ongoing, then." He sighed.

"Not for much longer. I left the old crones to their business. They seemed to think I had enough on my plate as it was. But they are finishing."

"We were thorough, then." He said.

"I passed our poppy seeds to Sarri." She said.

"Not Tursa?"

"Sarri said he would take them to the Kirche camp along with his offerings. He wanted to oversee instructions for how they were allocate himself."

"He doesn't trust Kuuda."

"Do you?"

"I believe he will do what he believes is right."

"Which is not the same as *what is right*."

She set the boot aside.

"This plan of his...."

"It is sound."

"But to have Gulang leading the charge."

"He led our people through hard times when he was chief of chiefs. He has never been one to let his feelings rule him."

"But he has never lost a child. Everything changes when—"

"He will do what he must. I have faith in him."

"I thought we were past lying to each other."

She edged away from him, and he looked into her face. Anxiety was etched into soft lines along her cheeks, and there was worry in her dark eyes.

"We are."

"Then why do you hide your concern?"

"I am not." Ungol said. "I worry for the state of our tribe, Shaelein. But I believe

Tears for the Moon God

Gulang will do as he must. He will have his revenge, yes, but he will remember that his family are not the only people depending on him. He has never put them first."

"It must be hard for them."

"Who?"

"The other chiefs. Tursa, and Sarri, and Coltang. And Arrak."

"And Gulang."

"They all have children they wish to protect. Coltang, Arrak and Sarri have all left their children behind. With our son."

"Waiting for him, yes. But they are well protected without us. Duijus Kanh will shield them from harm, together with his Swans. And Ho'o is a friend to our people. He will look out for them."

"What if Katcya comes to them?"

"He has an interest in keeping them secure." Ungol said, laying again his head on her bosom."

"He does not keep up with his kin." She said. "Never has."

"Hasn't he? The gods move in mysterious ways. Often they remain out of sight, leaving us to wonder after their intent, look for signs around us of their touch. He is no different."

"You believe he is watching over our son?"

"I believe he is watching over those kids." Ungol responded.

He did not know what possessed him to believe it, but he felt it was the only right course. It was a rare thing, the rise of Ung Kanh Dui among the Gil Garo people. So rare that the title had taken on the edge of conspiracy, had become folkloric in its nature. He himself had begun to believe no such people had ever existed. There were the stories they told each other, which must have some origin in fact, but in his youth, he had come to believe those men and women who had held the title were themselves simply competent generals who had ushered in uncommon eras of prosperity for their people. Duijus Kanh existed, as did his Swans, as protectors of their people, but by the same token, they fed and became fat on the sick and the dying among them.

He could not see what they had to gain from choosing an acolyte from among the Gil Garo people. He could not believe they were so impressed by mortal bravery that the simple act of descending into that cave, carving a name deep in its gullet, could be enough to entice them to grant such a boon. To imbue their hallowed powers into a mortal regent.

What did they stand to gain from it? In providing for the Gil Garo, they gained what amounted to livestock for their eventual consumption. They did not have to hunt across the plains for game, whether it be among distant, human settlements or in the fields and scarce thickets closer to home. But in taking on an acolyte from among their people, he could see no benefit. No equality in the exchange. The Gil Garo gained a power for themselves which would see them victorious in any conflict they engaged in, if they did not squander it, but what was in it for them?

And God Katcya? He was a creature plagued by endless curiosity. In the most ancient stories among their people, those that involved him, he came to the defense of humanity, yes, but sheltered them as his own secret, watching them grow, living among them, witnessing mortal innovations as a human diaspora spread across the backs of mountains, to inhabit forests, to cross the seas, to perform miracles in their artifice which allowed them to harness the power of water, of fire, of iron, in seeming defiance of the grand, holy order.

He had faith the god's curiosity would settle on Duijus Kanh cave, on the plains just outside and along the band of the Shan Lao river. If only to see what came of his son.

There were stirrings among the Gil Garo, as if they had been called to this task, to take on the Tului. But to what end? And he wondered, after Gandes Fae's intervention as conducted through him, what the purpose of those four young ones must be. Who's design they fit into. What they would do when the time came for them to play their part in the Greatest Game.

"What is on your mind?" Shaelein asked.

"Who else is playing their game?" he said. "If God Katcya sits on one side of the conflict, and I believe he does, then who competes with him?"

Her pawing at his hair ceased. "You do not think Fate is playing her hand?"

He shook his head. "She is always in these conflicts, but I do not think she is leading this time."

"Why not?"

He shrugged. "A hunch. A strange feeling, perhaps."

"Oh?"

He did not respond. Since the arrival of their son at Gil Garo, he had been plagued by the nagging feeling that this was not the first time events had played out this way. That even now, they were acting out the same play in the theater of war, and there was a sense underneath it all of subtle deviations, new hands shaping old narratives in order to suit their own ends.

Fate or good fortune had landed their son in their hands once more, and then ripped him away from them as swiftly as he had come. If he believed nothing else was certain about the events that had befallen them since then, he held this truth sacred. The gods had a purpose for the Gil Garo, and when they set their gaze on a people, chaos ensued. It always did.

But there was always a design. Even if mortals could not always see the contours of it, even if the design's themes outlived them, they played a part in its shaping. They became pieces to be moved against each other in the endless, Greatest Game.

What was clear to him...the Tului were on one side of this conflict, and the Gil Garo on the other. They had been pushed into each others arms, or there could never have been a conflict between them. The Tului were isolationists and the Gil Garo had no reason to enter their lands. They never had. But the Gil Garo were a raiding tribe, a tribe of nomads and horse warriors. No army across Tao Shein steppe could contain them when they rose to violence, not all of the sects at once. He had believed that before the attack. He still believed it.

He only wished he believed it was their own choices guiding them along this path. That the hands of those terrible gods were not behind them and their enemies, pushing them toward battle, pushing them toward war.

The Call of a Drum

Winter winds thundered against the sides of the chief's pavilion, but Chakta was at ease. Ho'o ran wild across Tao Shein steppe, calling his wild hunt to sew seeds of chaos into the lands. All the while, wolf song played across the night cloaked plains, call and answer, and a half moon loomed overhead; but the chief's pavilion provided sound shelter. Within its walls, she was secure.

Shaki made shadow puppets against a wall painted in firelight, and Tamlin rummaged through a trunk his father had left with him. She suspected it was in keeping of most of the trappings of his life...what was not strewn from hanging lines in the back of the single chamber, or laid across vacant benches, beckoning him to sleep.

He was uncommonly fixated on that trunk; was growing increasingly frustrated as his search for some forgotten object took him closer to the bottom of the chest. Its contents lay in messy piles near its base, yet her questions were met with grunts and half-formed sentences when she bothered to ask him what he was after.

"It's like they're egging him on." Shaki said. He contorted his fingers, held them up to the light. In silhouette, human fingers became a hare, head and body. "You think Dupec's out there with them?"

Chakta shrugged. She poked at the coals with a stick, sending flurries of sparks rushing into still, close air. "The Swans run with them."

"You would think we would have seen him."

"You think he's doing drudge work?"

"Could be. Thera made me catch air in buckets for days before she let me do anything serious."

"Catch...air?" He had to be joking. Then again, the spirits were wont to take things at their own pace. To do them in their own way. Catching air in buckets was of no more use than combing through silt on a river bank, and Galadir had pushed her to do that degrading work more than once. As a punishment, though. To teach her humility. "What was the point in that?"

Shaki shrugged. "I think she just found it amusing."

Chakta laughed.

"Found it!" Tamlin hefted a hand drum out of the trunk. The barrel was

The Call of a Drum

relatively flat, somewhat concave and tapered toward the base. The face was deer hide, tanned and stretched taut. His cheeks bunched around a satisfied smile. His eyes positively glittered.

"What do you plan on using that for?"

"What do you think?"

"Oh no, no. Don't you dare, Tamlin!" Shaki scrambled to his feet. He was charging at Tamlin before he was fully up. "Not tonight!"

"Oh come on! We used to do it as kids, didn't we?"

"It's not the same thing. He hates Thera! He'll knock this whole pavilion down if he finds out I'm here."

"Then don't come."

Shaki tried to snatch the drum out of his hand.

He held it close to his chest and stuck his tongue out.

"What do you even want with him?"

"Who says I'm not trying to sing with someone else?"

Shaki made another grab for it. Tamlin twisted out of his way.

Tamlin pelted past him, made straight for the entrance and the catwalk outside. Chakta contemplated him thoughtfully. *He's asking for trouble. He has to know that.*

But they had been without true entertainment too long. An entire tribe evaporated in the span of a day and a night, and they had as swiftly become each other's only company. She could barely stand Tamlin most of the time, but he had a point. Calling to the spirits, calling them to sing, was a winter tradition every sect followed. A night like this was perfect for it, though she did not value leaving the comfort of the pavilion.

"Fuck it." she said.

"No. Not you, too!"

"Who says he's even listening, Shaki." she said. "Besides, he's not the only one who likes our voices."

"One spirit isn't enough?"

She shrugged. "Maybe. But are you going to deny the other spirits if they decide to show up. And anyway, don't the four winds handle their conflicts in the south? I've never heard of them clashing this far north."

She marched after Tamlin. Shaki watched her go, a most incredulous look on his face. She wondered if he'd freeze right there, forget all about being a living, breathing human and become an ice sculpture for them to gawk at for the rest of the winter. He was certainly moving in that direction.

When she arrived outside, she found Tamlin seated on the edge of the catwalk, just outside of range of the pavilion's roof, the life-sized horse sculptures supporting the eaves. Horses rearing on their hind legs, their eyes wild, frenzied, reflecting this night's mood.

She sat across from him, crossed her legs. He set the drum between them, and it was begun.

He rubbed a calloused palm against the drum surface. The sandy sound was lost to the howling winds, but those very winds would hear it. They seemed to hear everything, appreciated subtlety as much as any bombastic rhythm. At least, The North Wind did.

The tapping started slow, the beats shallow, barely rising above the wind, the rushing grasses, the crackle and slither of snow. He beat the drum with more intensity. She could hear the unbroken pattern now, and closed her eyes. The sound she made, the accompaniment, came from deep in her throat, a vibrating current rattling through her windpipe, low and steady and undulating. Tamlin's voice joined hers, choosing a path unique to him, which wove in and out with hers, creating harmonies and then branching away, melding and scattering.

The wind howled across the plains, and the wolves raised their voices higher. They sang, and the wolves sang. Their songs merged together into an eerie, brutal cadence. She heard laughter on the wind, felt the watching eyes of those wild, terror struck horses at her back, and knew without having to look that Shaki was watching. Safely tucked away inside of the entrance, but watching nonetheless. There had been so little entertainment since the sects marched, and with Bora gone, he had not been himself.

They sang, and she was reminded of years past, singing on windy nights with her father. She passed those memories into the song, allowing emotion to shape it, notions of the past to give it form.

The wind closed in, whipped her hair loose and tousled it. Her voice broke with laughter.

It spiraled around Tamlin, pounded against the drum, adding to the rhythm he beat out as they sang. Beasts lowed, cougars screamed, all contained in Ho'o's hunting party. She felt the brush of fur against her cheek, a wet nose pressed against her crown, and wondered what creature had taken interest.

A soft tinkle. A bell chime. She squeezed her eyes tight, smiling knowingly at the new sound.

Laughter on the wind again, this time so close to her ear she felt heat against it. Tamlin laced his fingers into hers. The drum remained between them, and new hands beat out a rhythm against it. Still they sang, throaty and deep.

And Ho'o raised his voice in answer.

"Shadow lands
Windswept hall
Your friend is being creepy, why won't he answer my call."

Laughter cut through Chakta's singing. She resisted the urge to lay eyes on Shaki. To see that he had heard it. She did not want to look and scare Ho'o off. An enigmatic spirit he may be, but he was also flighty.

The drum beats picked up intensity. The cadence became lively and loose, barely holding to a coherent rhythm. Ho'o was having fun with them.

"Sitting abreast of the ugliest tree
Thera's boy is no kin to me
But Ho! He watches, he think's he's clever
Bless him, kids, he's expecting bad weather!

"Old Ho'o won't hurt ya

The Call of a Drum

He's not the kind
Unless, of course, he's of the mind
To get up to mischief!
It's not hard to find

"You young whips can help me if-ya-don't-mind."

He guffawed. His tone lightened and his cadence shifted, but the words he sang drove a chill into Chakta that had nothing to do with the bracing cold of the steppe in winter.

Was this a mistake? She wondered.

She kept on singing.

"Someone's a watchin' from the shadows
Peepin' across the open meadow
Someone's a watchin' from your shoulder
Wishin' you were all a little bolder

"First a little tickle from a lucky soul!"

Cold air tickled the back of her neck.

"A prickle, a trickle, a—oh, why do I bother!"

"Come on out, you old charlatan!" The North Wind snapped. "Quit being so antisocial, I say!"

New pressure, and warmth, against her knee. She opened her eyes, cast her gaze in that direction. Left. South. Away from Ho'o. She heard him laughing, still playing his rhythm on the drum.

There, filling her vision, was a man with the same flowing traceries as Dupec scattered across his skin. The pattern was different, but the effect was the same. He looked as if he swam in disturbed water, crystal clear yet marred by ripples coming from many directions at once. But his skin was golden. His hair a cold shade of blonde, loose curls spilling over his crown and down the back of his neck. He leaned in so close his nose was nearly touching hers, and her guts went to water.

Silver eyes shot through with chips of red, and green, and blue. Gemstone shades.

"Boo!"

She tumbled backward.

He flopped onto his back, laughing hysterically. Behind her, she heard Ho'o laughing, too.

Ho'o's laughter halted abruptly, as did the drum beats.

"Tell us a story, old man." he said.

"I haven't been in the business of telling mortal tales in some time, nephew." he said.

"Oh come now. They lived this one, did they not?"

"Ah. But that one is forbidden."

Tears for the Moon God

"Forbidden by who?"

"You know who."

"Who are you?" Tamlin cut in. She heard the fear in his voice, and suspected he was coming close to the same conclusion she had drawn.

"That's neither here nor their, young man. Particularly now, in such times as these, when we have so narrowly avoided one cataclysm, to run headlong toward another."

"Katcya!"

"Hey now! Don't ruin my fun, you nasty little windbag." Katcya snapped.

"But Katcya! I want to hear a story."

"And I told you that one is forbidden."

"Then what about—"

"Don't say it."

"You don't even know what I'm going to say."

"Recall, sir, that I am far older than you. And wiser for it."

Ho'o snorted.

What am I witnessing?

She backed away toward the entrance. Froze when Katcya's hand found her leg. His grip on her was vice-like.

"It's rude to run away from a god."

"I-I'm sorry."

"Are all of you humans so intimidated by me? You used to be so much more resilient." He grimaced. "I suppose it can't be helped. But this rude imbecile is not the reason I'm here." his gaze fell past her, on Ho'o if she did not miss her guess, though she refused to look at him.

"Actually, I thought you might deliver a message for me. It seems my kin have been a bit restless lately. The new ones will need a leader, but all of that has already been assessed and handled. One Dupec Safar is aware of what he needs to do, if not why. Of course, the why is not so important just now. There will be time for that later. If you'll be a dear, miss Chakta Krul, would you tell the kid to find me in my God House? I'll have answers for him when he arrives, but it is paramount that he bring a certain group of people with him.

"No, not you. Then who? She asks, because of course you do. To which I say all the old guard. Several people who tried to kill him once a long time ago, or maybe a long time from now." he screwed up his face in mock contemplation. "One needs protection from a god. Another is fawning over a god, but that isn't all that surprising, is it? There's a friend of his among them, I think. Or maybe a lover. I never was able to get a clear look into God Uldal's sanctuary. It shifts around too much. And there is the family of his former lover. No one he knows now, mind you. People he knew then.

"And don't worry about your father. Or yours." he glanced at Tamlin. "The first skirmish with your newfound enemy will be bloody, and many will die. But, how far away from the border would you say they are?"

His gaze fell again on Ho'o, one eyebrow hoisted up and his lips pursed comically.

"A few weeks." Ho'o said noncommittally.

"How long exactly."

"Seventeen days."

The Call of a Drum

"Precisely."

"You asshole. You knew that already!"

"Of course I did."

"Then why did you ask!"

"Reasons." he turned back to Chakta. "Something very special is happening in seventeen days, you see. Something very noticeable. So look to the sky on that day and be comforted. But remember. The enemy of your enemy is your friend. Until the moment arrives when your enemy has been dealt with. Then you should probably put a knife in your newfound friend's back."

What the hell?

He patted her leg and smiled. "Now go away. The wild hunt must continue on, and I have business to attend to elsewhere. That means you, too." he addressed Tamlin without looking at him.

Chakta met Tamlins eyes. She caught the impression of heavy furs and raw hide, a frock of wild, black hair in her periphery. Furs, hide and hair evaporated. The gust that chased after the departing spirit threatened to knock her flat. She scrambled to her feet, and marched toward the pavilion, careful not to run though her heart told her to.

When she had crossed the threshold, she finally allowed herself to relax. She had been a hair trigger away from a heart attack for too long. She found a seat by the fire. Tamlin set his drum next to the entrance and found a bench as well.

Shaki had the good grace not to say anything about their indiscretion. Ho'o nearly always showed up to the sound of Gil Garo drums, but in her memory there had never been a time that the drum circle had caught the attention of an Elder God. She felt like a puppet on a string. And suddenly, everything that had befallen them since Dupec's arrival seemed like it was no coincidence. Suddenly, she felt the cold eyes of the gods on her, and knew the worst of them must be watching. That the Gil Garo were being manipulated, and Katcya, God of Luck, was but one among many with hands in this game.

"What do you think he meant?" Tamlin said into the silence.

"I think he was pretty clear about what he meant." Chakta said. "We're supposed to go with Dupec. Dupec is supposed to go meet with a bunch of people who tried to kill him once. Probably some enemies of God Uldal."

"I don't think he's involved." Tamlin said. The fire reflected in his eyes brought out murky shades of red. By the omens, he was destined to be a great warrior. Fire in the eyes, the red cast within brown, was said to be the greatest sign, but she could not see him that way. Could not reconcile the arrogant prick she had known all her life with this dour creature reaching for a means to make it all make sense.

This winter was like none she had ever experienced. A man of the tribe and not was chosen Ung Kanh Dui, a title none had assumed in so long it had begun to taste like legend. An army spilled forth from Tuluis Fel had come down on them in the night, and now their people marched to war, to give answer to the slaughter they had committed. And she was here, one among three children of sect chiefs who would, soon enough, bow down before a man they barely knew.

Ung Kanh Dui would lead them. Ung Kanh Dui would shape them. But he should take them to the war front. He should lead their people in battle. And yet, perhaps strangest of all, an Elder God interfered. Drew them into a conflict with a different

Tears for the Moon God

shape, in another land, the rules of which they did not know, the enemy as much a stranger as the one who slept in the depths of Duijus Kanh's cave, maybe feasting on their dead, and learning dark arts from the lord of wolves and his concubines.

Lo, this winter had none of the trappings of the mundane kind. With the Gil Garo gone, and the corpses they left behind drawn back into the earth, the Swans went hungry. They must range across the steppe, seeking sustenance from other sources, as they had not been compelled to do in living memory. The old way was broken—perhaps just for this winter, perhaps for far longer. Their way of life had become unrecognizable, and she wondered if they would ever go back.

Never build a home where the earth drinks blood. She thought to herself. The chief's pavilion had been spared in the conflict. No fire was set against it. No battle had been waged within its walls. Yet it was surrounded on all sides by tainted land. Tao Shein consumed, and the grasses grew strong. The Gil Garo fed him, promising a bountiful harvest for whomever walked these lands in summer. By then, she meant to be gone. Leaving behind all memory of what had happened here. She hoped never to return.

"Any thoughts, Shaki?" Tamlin said.

"What did he say exactly?" Shaki asked.

Tamlin relayed everything Katcya had said to them, one more time. Shaki had asked too many times, had retained too little of what he heard. But there was power in repeating those words, in inoculating them to the ills which walked the mind in the face of an uncertain future. Madness came for those who seethed in silence, but the mind was a resilient beast. The words out in the open, the depth of their meaning explored, they three might hold onto their wits until the great thaw arrived.

Shaki took his moment of silence. He rubbed his narrow chin with the pad of his thumb, toying with his bottom lip. "What I keep coming to is this idea that we've lived this life before. Within that also, our future appears to be interchangeable with another past. To me, it sounds like our timeline deviates from another closely related one. We're falling into the same ruts, but we're finding ourselves there by different paths."

"What would Dupec have to do with that?"

"Isn't it obvious? He's the reason...or part of the reason, anyway, that we're in this branch of the River. He must have done something to offend the gods. Enough to force the River onto a different path, and make a tributary into the main flow."

Chakta lay her back against her bench, stared at the exposed rafters, the peaked ceiling behind them.

"You've got to wonder." Shaki said.

"Wonder what?" she asked.

"What Dupec did to earn the wrath of the Elder Gods, for one thing." Shaki said. "Why God Katcya wants him to do it again, for another."

"Who said anything about that?"

"Well, he did, didn't he?"

"I've never known you to make this much sense, Shaki." Chakta said.

"Neither have I." Tamlin agreed.

Shaki shrugged. "It's right there, isn't it? That comment about the old guard. If not him, someone has arranged for the people who had hands in making the last cataclysm possible together in Nixir. We must have been involved in some way, too.

The Call of a Drum

And somehow the whole problem was put to bed before the direct intervention of the Elder Gods became necessary.

"I think they leaned on God Lanfin. They must have pressured him to eliminate someone who was involved in shaping that cataclysm. And of course that person wouldn't be with the people in Nixir. He'd be voided from recorded history like everyone else God Lanfin recalls."

"Fuck." Chakta slammed her fist against the bench. "It's the guy!"

"What guy?" Tamlin was watching her now.

Shaki chuckled. "Of course."

"What am I missing?" Tamlin demanded. "Are either of you going to explain it to me?"

"The boot prints. All that water." Chakta said. "Dupec said he had a visitor that night before the tournament. Someone he didn't know, but not an enemy. Someone who knew enough to warn him about the Tului before they attacked us. Who could have known they were coming?"

"Any number of people who have nothing to do with God Lanfin." Tamlin said. "A conspirator, for instance. Or someone who wanted to ally with us."

"If they were trying to become our allies, they would have said so, wouldn't they? Besides, going to the son of a chief when he could just go to a chief himself doesn't make sense." Chakta said.

"The same could be said of a conspirator, if he was trying to defect." Shaki added. "Who was Dupec to anyone at that point. Just a Cloud Man. Long lost son of Chief Ungol, sure. But a complete stranger to all of us."

"An easy scapegoat." Tamlin said.

Shaki was shaking his head. Chakta found herself torn. There was a certain measure of sense in Tamlin's stance, but the gods were not prone to leaving mortal kind alone. In countless great dramas, they were involved in the tragedies which befell mankind to the neck. Their hands shaped catastrophes. The Lesser Gods, at least, played a game with human lives the scope of which no man could know, the goals of which were as unclear.

She sensed this conflict was shaping up to be like those. That whatever their role in this grand design, the lines had long been set, the teams chosen, the first play and counter play well and over. This game was in its advanced stages, and soon they would all see it for what it was. Whatever it was.

"Have you heard of the Wanderers?" Shaki said.

"No." Tamlin said, echoing Chakta's sentiments.

"What are they?" she asked.

"Not what." Shaki said. "Who?"

Counterfeit

The highway rode past a settlement of greater size, a shining jewel, as it were, laying out what was possible for those who accepted Hou Rok's bribery. Vagrants populated its cobbled streets, shaking tin cans and clad in rags. Working girls stood out here and there along the corridors with direct conveyance to the highway, boiling away into shadows as soon as they were well within the town. The thatch doors of villages past were gone and replaced by slick rectangles of a material she had never seen before, which Jinga explained was fiberglass. The signs which marked out street crossings were metal plates on slender poles, or hung from wires strewn between multilevel buildings who were only reminiscent of the architecture of the villages that had passed for their stone and mortar siding.

A clock tower stood within a fountain at the town's heart, and behind it loomed a structure larger and fatter than the dwellings and businesses they had yet come across. The building was fronted with crude columns, all hewn of timbers taken from the forest in the south. She wondered if the locals felled those trees themselves, or bought them off saodeini, or perhaps Tulakka, lumber traders. The town square was bright and spacious, and the locals had taken to planting fruit trees of some kind along the sidewalks, using something organic to break up the industrial landscape, and call back to the natural world from which the people sprang.

She was not greatly pleased with the way these people chose to live. The scattering of torches in the first village she had visited, in the villages she had seen after, were replaced with electric lamps—bulbous, glass orbs on corrugated poles, the mechanisms that allowed them to work kept well out of sight beneath sidewalks and intersections. There were pipes underground, too, so Jinga explained. Pipes carrying water and gas and housing thick cables through which electricity could be siloed into homes and storefronts. The buildings had their own heating elements, quite apart from the wood stoves she had grown up with.

Is this the price of compliance, or the benefit of peace? Few great mysteries had easy answers, and if history had taught her anything it was that the answers to such questions as they posed often pulled from many sources. Here were a people with few problems. They were not at war, and had not been for decades, maybe even centuries. Yet what was the point in peace if it meant capitulating to the demands of a god in shaping this way of life. The price lay in the vagrants, I the prostitutes, in how this population was striated. These were not a people who believed in cooperation. They were a people infatuated with avarice. Why else ought they have people without shelter living among them. Why else ought those with means sweep past them without a second glance, almost as if hoping in the act of ignoring their presence, those poor, unfortunate souls would disappear.

Jinga drew up short as they rounded the fountain, his gaze fixed on something she had not noticed. His expression darkened, eyes glittering with anger.

She followed his gaze to a cage near the steps of the town hall, one of several iron barred blocks before it. A swinging rope caught her eye momentarily, a noose hung from a wooden post, the stage beneath it rigged with a series of gears to collapse at the pull of a lever. There was a figure inside the cage, but she could not make out much beyond that. A figure clad in some kind of armor, who sat in the shadows cast by those bars, watching passersby march and ride along adjoining roads.

"What is it?" she asked.

"*He* is Nixian." Jinga spat. "Not all the Sangar are kind to us."

"Is it safe? Us being here."

He snorted. "Safe in that they have nothing I can't dismantle."

She nodded, not trusting herself to ask what was on her mind. *They throw this man in a cage, a spectacle for the locals to gawk at, to spit on, to do whatever it is the hateful are wont to do to the helpless. But what did he do? Why toss him into that cage at all?*

The sword The North Wind had gifted her lay in the wagon bed. She would need to find a proper sheath for it eventually, but she could hardly expect to do that here. Not with their sentiments toward foreigners, toward Nixians at the least, being what they so clearly were. If she could move freely through this town, perhaps she could find an armorer willing to part with a scabbard. She would take leather if it was all he had, but she would much prefer something wooden, or metal if it was insulated. She would countenance the less fluid draw if it meant the blade needed less sharpening.

"Can you do anything for him?"

Jinga tapped the reins. The palominos trotted onward. He guided them down a narrower lane to the east, down adjacent avenues which narrowed progressively until they would just admit the horse team and their wagon, and stopped at last at the side of a river. An inn rose up near the foot of a bridge, and a track on the interior side led toward a stable. He left the wagon, entered the inn and returned a few moments later with a balding man in his middle years, his gut tremendous and hanging over his belt.

"Any idea who he is?" Jinga was saying to him.

"Haven't been close enough." The innkeeper said. "I'd planned on sending a few up the way to grab him 'round nightfall, but with you here." He shrugged. "Maybe it's better you handle it."

"Alone?"

The innkeeper tipped his chin. "Aye, I can't countenance risking the lives of my men over something like this. Not if I can avoid it."

"I understand." Jinga said. "How much to take care of this?" he wagged his wrist in the direction of the wagon.

"Depends."

Jinga fished from his pocket a coin pouch. He opened it and pulled out a few coins, which he lay in the innkeeper's hand.

"The usual place, then. No funny business." He shambled toward the horses.

Jinga approached Lisandra, made as if to help her from the carriage. She hesitated, her eyes on the sword, and picked it up before allowing him the opportunity.

"We'll stay here for the time being. Delbert's a friend. But we'll have to be on before sunrise tomorrow. I intend to leave as soon as I've handled my business here. I hope you understand."

"It's about that Nixian, isn't it?"

He nodded. "Delbert'll help us get out of the city once I've taken care of that business. I'd move to retrieve him after we'd had some rest, but he's due to be executed tomorrow."

Lisandra raised an eyebrow at that.

Jinga sighed. "My people...we're not always able to come by the resources we need to survive. The outposts tend to fare worse than Nixir City, but they have their way. Mostly, they steal crops, but if things turn desperate, they might take it further. That's why these villages aren't all so kind to us. We trade with those who are friendly enough. The others don't give us much choice. It's steal or starve. We wouldn't if we didn't have to, but sometimes..." he looked her in the eye, seeking something from her she was not sure she could give. She knew desperation, knew the lengths one must sometimes go to in order to survive when faced with hostility from those around him, who had the resources to help but hoarded them. It was not in the nature of people to show kindness to strangers. She had done the same in Syrk's village, had she not? Stolen from those isolated people, themselves unlikely to help her if she asked?

He opened the door to the inn, let her pass through before him. "Thank you for understanding."

The door fell shut behind him.

She turned up her nose. "Delbert could do with tidying up around here."

Exposed eaves were wreathed in cobwebs, and piles of dust had been swept into the corners, yet still there were crumbs from some variety of bread or pastry scattered across the floor. A rat the size of her foot nibbled at refuse in the shadow of one table, and another barreled across the floor toward the kitchen as soon as the door clapped shut. She would have been very surprised if the place wasn't held together with cockroaches, if a war involving so many centipedes and spiders wasn't being waged behind soft wood wainscotings and grimy plaster.

At least we won't be sleeping here. I'd rather the wagon bed than this dump.

"Would you be offended if I left you for a time?" she asked, the thought of a scabbard on her mind again. "Will I be accosted by the locals if I do?"

"They have nothing against southlanders." He said. "No, I would not be offended. Do what you must."

"Thank you." She favored him with a warm smile. "I'll not be long."

"Take all the time you need. But be back before nightfall. I may need you."

Counterfeit

"I'm only going after something to keep this sword from biting my thigh."

"Ah, then you'll want Alaster Crouch. Best armorer this side of Gonsai Wall."

"Where might I find him?"

"Not far from here. Head west along this avenue until you hit Tulip Street. He's about three blocks north of the intersection."

She bowed at the shoulders. "I'll be back before you know I'm gone."

She marched out of the building, and as soon as she was past the entrance, sucked in a deep breath. The city smells might not be as fresh as anything on the road, but they were certainly favorable to Delbert's inn. She marched away up the street, sliding the exposed blade into her belt as she did, and tracked west in pursuit of this armorer.

First Delbert's Hovel, and now this.

She was beginning to wonder whether Jinga was blind. An armorer's house should not be in this sorry state. A reputable armorer, presumably, cut a tidy enough profit to afford the necessary repairs to ensure his roof did not leak when the rains came, that there were no gaps in the siding...that the siding was new enough not to show signs of bloat and rot.

This shop was the only thing on the block which resembled a business, and even then it looked as if it had been abandoned months ago. There was a display window but it was so caked with dust that it was difficult to see anything through it, and a lack of shadows on the other side told her there was nothing on display behind it besides. She supposed the small flock of vagrants pretending not to case the battered old houses across the street was explanation enough. There could be nothing of value in that place, but there was precious value in the structure itself for a people without ready access to shelter. A drafty cupboard was better than the street. There might even be a bed in there somewhere, a mattress at least. It would be filled with mold and smelling of cellar, but a place to sleep was a place to sleep.

How *did* one come by the necessities in a place governed by laws? It was not unreasonable to assume these people, so far removed from the highway and without cans to shake or barrels to beat on, might take up stealing to get by. That they might even have an odd shop or two in rotation for converting pilfered goods into hard coin.

A dusty avenue full of vagabonds. That's where he sends me. Her lips drew down into a thin scowl. She marched the few steps to the entrance, and knocked on a warped door, hoping no one would answer.

Footsteps the other side made a mismatched beat. The door swung sharply inward. The man who glared up at her was a bony, old thing—all sinewy and bent, with prominent knuckles on incongruously thick hands which dangled from long, ape-like limbs. Lank, white hair hung around a prominent bald patch, thin strands drifting over his shoulders, and when he spoke she was hit with a sour perfume, each syllable a slap in the face.

He looked her up and down, spat a gob of phlegm at her feet.

"Is that any way to greet a customer?"

"S'what they all say, isn't it? You sure you're not a tax man?" he shrugged one shoulder. "Tax *lady*, I s'pose."

"A friend of yours sent me." Her fingers found the hilt of her sword. His gaze flicked to it. Bushy eyebrows lifted and clamped down over narrowed eyes. "He

Tears for the Moon God

seemed to think there was an armorer here. Worth his salt, too.”

“I’ll be damned.” He said, ignoring her jab. “You been climbing mountains?” his gaze flicked to her again, suspicion traced across his features, perhaps a little bit of fear as well.

“Are you the armorer?”

“Depends who’s askin’.” He said. “Who sent you? If it’s a friend, I‘d know it before I invite you in.”

“A Nixian called Jinga.” She said.

He smacked his own forehead. “The engineer! In town is he? Could have paid me a visit himself, couldn’t he?” he grumbled. “Come, come. I’ll not have a friend of his waiting on my stoop. Sorry for my rudeness.”

He urged her past him, into the dilapidated, shotgun style shop. The interior had seen wear, but it was nonetheless well kept. The floorboards needed a polish, but they were swept free of dust, and the lamps dangling from the ceiling were a bit rusty but mostly shined around the rims. An offensively round cat was sprawled across a downy cushion atop a low cabinet near an empty armor stand. A leather jerkin lay on a work table opposite, alongside several, unfamiliar tools.

“What’s it gonna be, then?” he rested his knuckles on the table, his eyes again finding the sword.

“I need a scabbard.”

“For that thing?” he gestured at her hip. Well, then, let’s see it. Set it here.”
He slapped the table top.

She pulled the sword free of her belt and set it where he asked.

“You know what this is?” he asked.

“A gift.” She said.

He scoffed at that. “If a gift, the person who owned it must be dead. This here is Rein Mountain Steel. You’d think it one of the finest swords in circulation, and you wouldn’t be far off, but for a Rein Mountain Sword to function correctly, it requires a blood binding. That sword shouldn’t function for anyone but the person it was given to.”

“I’m sorry?”

“S’neither here nor there, really. You’d have had to leave this continent to get one of those the proper way. Most who make the summit never make it back down, so I hear. Problem is this isn’t an original. It’s a counterfeit. This here wasn’t forged by the spirit of the mountain, and that’s...” his gaze flicked up to meet hers, stuttered back to the sword. “...that’s one of the world’s great mysteries, isn’t it.”

“It’s history hardly matters to me—“

“Hardly matters!” he snapped. “*Hardly matters, she says!* You’re looking at a paradox, lass. No one knows who made these things or how, but they’re almost perfect reflections of the spirit’s work. I’d wager most sword smiths have never encountered one. There are always rumors, of course, but who’s chasing after them? No, what you got here is a rare treasure. Worth coveting, that is. Not a Rein Mountain Sword, but Rein Mountain Steel anyway.

“You’d wonder how I can tell, if you were smart. It’s in the fragrance. It’s too potent. With the real things, you can’t smell what’s in the blade unless you hold it under your nose. But this smells sickly sweet from feet away. No wonder you’d want a case for it.” He grimaced. “Last I saw the real thing was about thirty years ago. Can’t say I’ve ever seen a counterfeit this good before.”

Counterfeit

"Can you just sell me a scabbard so I can be on my way."

He chuckled at that. "I can and I will, but not without you knowing what this sword *means*. You might not care, but you're gonna humor me. Because I do.

"See, Rein never took on an acolyte. Everyone with any serious interest in the craft knows that. Never took on an acolyte because he never trusted no mortal man with his metallurgical knowledge. His swords never rust. Never need to be cleaned. They drink in blood and incorporate the iron and carbon into their cores, letting everything else evaporate into the air. They don't need to be sharpened, either. But what's real special about Rein's swords is each one has a particular flavor, a little trick imbued into the metal that can only be used by their true owner. That is, whoever was given the sword by the spirit."

"But this is a counterfeit." She said flatly.

"It is that, yes indeed. Which means someone had knowledge of Rein's own craft. Enough to be able to make a near perfect likeness of his swords. Whether they figured out the tricks from him or because of him doesn't matter. The point is someone was running around with knowledge they shouldn't have and abilities they could only have gotten by studying his way, but there's no record anywhere of that someone's existence. Not even in the Rat Goddess's library, if you'd believe it. At least, s'what the rumors have to say about it.

"So what you've got is a sword that shouldn't exist, which was made by someone who doesn't exist. Now there are plenty of rumors about how these swords came to be, but nothing conclusive. Me personally, I believe the creator was seized somehow. Dragged away by the gods, maybe."

Her blood ran cold. There it was again, certain assurance that the Wanderers, wherever they were, were tempting fate. There again, a tie to Shulraki Alran, guiding her along a path whose end she could not see, which spelled danger for her. Was this more of Goddess Liandal's meddling? Or was it something else? Ho'o had delivered this sword, a boon when she needed it, and yet now she knew what it was, what it mean—as Alaster Crouch had so aptly put it—she did not want to keep it.

"Funny thing." He examined that blade, rubbed his chin during a moment's pensive quiet. "About these swords. They're not blood bound like the real things. Seems the maker intended them to be passed from person to person. To what end, I won't claim to know, but I do know you'd be able to use whatever power is hidden in this thing if you knew which model it was."

She made an observation of that mottled blade, wondered at what it might be hiding. She was beginning to feel nauseous.

"Now about that scabbard. I've got one that might work, if you'll give me a moment." He said. "Just need to take a jot downstairs."

"As you wish," she breathed.

He shambled off for a door in the back of the room, vanished through it. The stairs groaned under his weight on the descent. It was not long before he returned with a wooden case, which was black and embellished with white flower patterns. The whole thing had been recently lacquered, the seams made to disappear for the way the pieces interlocked. Bands of gold encircled it at regular intervals, reinforcing it against splitting and giving it a more elegant profile. It was as fine a specimen as she had seen, a welcome surprise after an unwelcoming encounter.

"How much do I owe you?" she asked, reaching for her pouch.

Tears for the Moon God

He waved her off. "Nothin'. Jinga's an old friend. Besides, you've given me a real treat today. I'll probably never see a sword like that again. Gave up chasing down the identity of the maker a long time ago, too. Maybe there's a way to find out what happened to him, but if there is, I'm not fated to figure it out."

He chuckled good-naturedly.

She thanked him, barely holding back from wincing at the mention of fate, and slid the sword into the scabbard. It was a good enough fit. A little loose, but not terribly so. *There it is again. Fate, following me even as a god she fears lends me his protection.*

She bid him a good day and left the shop, intent on getting back to Delbert's before this day could get any stranger.

Ank

It's a wonder the gods should be so careless. Ank thought to himself as he stooped over the prone corpse of an uelfin.

If only it was that. To leave mortals alone with their thoughts was to invite madness into them. At least, that was the intent when the gods sought to construct their labyrinth. For so long, he had believed Lanfin's hand alone had carved out these walls from the rock, had drawn fel constructs out of the earth along the banks of Time's river, but it was a foolish belief. Spurred on by mortal ignorance, few learned to appreciate the nuance in its design. The detail that went into its planning. One mind, one fledgling god yet to come into the fullness of his power, could not have hoped to construct something so complex.

With each taking, the labyrinth expanded. The waters of Time's river drifted ever further from its chosen path, leaving new pools to fester, to be filled with forgotten memories, the essence of entire lives left behind in favor of whatever design the God of Music sought for the future of the Waxing World.

There were mysteries in these halls, mysteries he had dedicated his long life to solving.

Why deny the katcyakin their right to die, only to confront them with the prospect of death in his own spawn? He was no god of death, no reaper of souls. Certainly, it made a kind of sense to deny Shao Luin such potent souls, but Shah Jagat? Should he sanction the existence of this place, there must be death in its halls, and perhaps that was why these corpses littered the broken ground, but then why ought the Wanderers, all of them katcyakin, be spared this fate? Why leave them to wander, with their autonomy and their faculties in tact, at all?

He stooped over the corpse, pressed his fingers under the poor creature's chin, along the line of the artery there. He had performed this exercise countless times. The wonder at feeling a pulse there had long faded. It was no surprise this mutilated body still held a beating heart, that the body was still warm after all of its years, decades, maybe centuries lying still in these halls, its cheek pressed to bare earth.

The question of why those creatures remained alive had vexed him at first. There could be no explanation for it except in the denial of death his right to embrace them. But the god should have been at ease with their destruction, their passing into the hands of his uncle, or whatever Shah Jagat was to him.

There was rivalry among the gods, elder and lesser, that was true, but Shah Jagat was a neutral force among them. His exclusive domain in taking life, in controlling what he could not produce, in possessing it. Yet here was evidence that his authority was anything but absolute, that a Lesser God could simply refuse him, and that was no right the Waxing World gods should have.

Unless there had been others involved in the construction of this labyrinth. Hanuman had been forthcoming with answers. Who aided in the construction of this place? Why ought they participate at all?

Through his unveiling of those ancient secrets, he had given Ank a gift, though he could not know it. Not to know the full depth of it.

Mahan Mahain, Fang Ilra...

Why would God Lanfin seek to work with such volatile creatures? Did he have a choice?

He turned the uelfin's face toward him, looked into strangely virile eyes. Still, and yet full of life, and the eternal pain of dying. This was to be a punishment. Were the uelfin who had sung in counter tune to the god captured, he would be just as this one was. One more body clinging to life in defiance of death, one more to suffer this endless cruelty, and for the lone crime of mending what his father sought to break.

Mahan Mahain made a kind of sense. *What would impending madness in those trapped here do except bring him joy?* But a dose of chaos would not be enough for Fang Ilra. She was always and forever a breaker of things. Kings and gods had been made to bow before her will in his time of life. The Goddess of Fate loathed her, and there, too, was a mystery. Why would Discord turn on Luck? Why, when their natures complimented each other so intimately?

This labyrinth had rules. It had its own conventions, its own sense of normalcy and stability, and all of those things were necessary, for it could not exist otherwise.

And here, the greatest mystery of all. These mortal creatures had denied their father, had performed an act beyond forgiveness in betraying him, but he was a god. His power was greater than theirs, was it not? How, then, could they deny him anything? How were the uelfin, so delicate in their mortality, able to challenge him at all?

The only answer, the only answer that made sense, was that these gods were not as all powerful as they at first appeared. They could be challenged by mortals. He suspected the key to unraveling this paradox lay in Sao Njack's memories; but he was not fool enough to raid his pool, not brazen or stupid enough to follow in Hanuman the Elder's footsteps. To pursue answers in the lives they touched. He was he fool enough to permit the Elder to know him in the same way, either.

He could do nothing about Fang Ilra or Mahan Mahain, but it was not with them the power suffusing this place resided. Or, if it was, they had only touched this place. They were not its keepers.

It was a mistake for them to leave the katcyakin their lives. To let them wander among pools of raw memory, to leave them so close to the river, even as they sought to keep them out of it.

He took the uelfin's head in both hands. Blood still greased its shoulder where

Ank

the god had struck. Deep craters in the flesh of his chest and flank marked the points where the great snake's teeth had punctured. His neck was broken, as were the bones in the opposite arm, and his ribs and hips were crushed. He should have died a long time ago, but death did not walk these halls. Confirmation lay in Shulraki Alran for everything that was evident in this creature. Death could not have the Wanderers, for their deeds must be erased. So, too, death could not have the uelfin, because their deeds must never have been.

Yet time did not shift from its bed with their taking. No pool had opened in the wake of this corpse. It's soul did not flee, but he could not access its memories either. There was no answer for what it had done, what it had seen, what it had sought so adamantly to change.

But there was a way. In everything a way. Where there were rules, there were always means of exploiting those rules. Death did not walk these halls. Though life persisted, it's tie to time was severed, a wall formed to keep those who dwelt within the labyrinth living, yet unable to affect its passage from headwaters *on*, leaving fate to her own devices, and mortal man—if he were so unlucky—to her whims.

"I cannot fix you, you understand." He said. "I cannot mend your body, nor can I take you to death."

The pulse under his thumb quickened. Blood welled within the puncture wounds, pulsed forth and eased back into the depths of those wells.

"Help me, my friend." He said. "And I will help you in kind. Help me at the time of my choosing, and I will help you in this moment."

It had been a mistake to allow the Wanderers to retain a hold on their minds. A greater mistake to allow them command over their bodies. Or perhaps it was like the nature of their deeds, that some things could not be taken back. Some things must occur in the world in their absence, just as they had in their presence, because their father was elder, and those forces were far more potent than the Lesser Gods they spawned, because they came from closer to the source.

Blood founted from the wounds as the uelfin's heartbeat quickened, and spilled over his mangled flank to patter against the ground.

He closed his eyes, hunted through the flesh in spirit, opening a path between two souls which bound them together.

And he pushed.

He must know he was being watched. That Hanuman the Elder witnessed his deeds. He must know, and yet this was not an invitation. Not an invitation for participation, perhaps; but then, what was it?

Ank the Sanark was nothing if not secretive. His very history had been erased in some conflagration that went against everything he knew of these halls, which implied even as it obfuscated those critical memories, not just of the man but the people who knew him, that he knew something the Elder did not. That Ank the Sanark had stumbled onto some truths of this place and its great mysteries even he, who was first and oldest, had no knowledge of.

He could approach, and interrupt this peculiar vigil, or he could hang back and let it happen. It rankled him that he could not compel his feet to move, could not justify interrupting whatever it was the Graemein sought to do.

With a corpse. A rag doll barely clinging to its life.

Tears for the Moon God

It had all seemed so simple in the earliest days. In what memories of him remained, he had known some truths about the nature of these halls with such clarity, and yet now those same details were hazy, the intent behind them hidden behind layers and layers of other people's memories, the essence of too many lives.

There had been death for his brother, but not for him. The life of Heiman the Younger taken by Gorgus, what remained to remember him by enough to fill a crystal chalice and nothing more. Ao Nii had never forgiven him.

Ank lay the corpse's head against the patch of exposed earth where the tiles had been broken who knew how long ago. He climbed to his feet, using the nearest wall to steady himself, and found Hanuman standing there, watching him through silver eyes shot through with gemstone shades, a pensive expression etched into the lines of his cherubic face.

He bit back his questions, and waited as the Sanark regained himself.

Ank smiled, and his guts twisted into knots. There was something off about the other man. Something that had never sat right with him, even absent the mysteries surrounding his past. The Graemeins possessed two souls. One inhabited the body, the other a plane beyond the reach of the corporeal. Yet death in its many forms was not part of their arrangement, not part of the nature of their being. Graemlin had spawned these creatures. He was the father, but who was their mother?

The uelfin's legacy was known to all who cared to hunt after it. All life was born from rivers. It had been the way since the earliest days. His own people had crawled from the banks of a great river generations before his birth, had done so in the dark of the night, climbed onto the slopes of ancient mountains, crawled away into the forests to live in secret. Life seized in this way had given rise to a new race which was neither god nor spirit, and in this act had angered the greatest of those gods.

Humanity had been the first, yes, but there were those others—uelfin and graemeins—who had come later. God Lanfin's trysts with Oe for the uelfin. Their parentage was known, yes, but the nature of their gifts had not expressed itself until long after the fall of Hanuman's people. It was in the memories of those humans who had lived near Oe's band he had first seen those creatures crawl from the mud. But Graemlin was different. There were mysteries in the birth of Ank's people he would like to have known.

Who was their mother? Who was she? If the Great River spawned this life, who had provided the essence of their being? Not Graemlin alone, it couldn't be. The River was not enough, was it?

It was with us.

But that had been different. Within the river was a seed, then, its source knowing nothing of its presence, so it was said in the stories his people told. But how much of their history was truth? How much had been lost in endless retellings before Katcya fell in love, before he had given life to his sons?

Tell me of you, Sanark. Trust in me. I am not your enemy.

Ank stumbled toward him, that smile still painted across his face, inviting nothing save his frustration.

"You've always been a nosy thing, Elder." He snickered.

"Who rides you, Ank?" he demanded.

"Ah, a peculiar question." A wild glint entered Ank's gaze, something far more manic than he had ever seen in the man. "Completely irrelevant at any rate. The

Ank

soul is weak. It cannot hold this form. It must rest.”

“Then you are the Sky Soul.”

“We are birds of a feather, you and I.” he said. “Too curious for our own good.”

Hanuman’s gaze drifted past him to the corpse. Blood still poured over its flank, which should not have been possible, locked in stasis as that body had been. As all of them ever were.

“I did what was right.” Ank said. “He is free.”

“Free?”

“Yes, that.”

“How?”

A maligned grin spread across the Sanark’s face. “Wouldn’t you like to know.”

“What game are you playing?”

“All that exists must be bound by rules.” Ank crooned. “Life and death, two sides of one coin. Why do we never die, Elder? Why did we ever assume these creatures were themselves dead?”

“I never assumed—“

“But you did. In the earliest days. When they first showed up here. Why ought you ever to assume otherwise? They did not move. Their eyes were glassy and open. They were stiff with rigor. Some had even voided themselves. What must you have thought, except what I did.

“But why should they be allowed the embrace of death if we were not. Are they not dangerous to their god? More dangerous than us, to be sure.”

“Say it plain, Ank. Tell me what you know.”

“So you can stow it away with all of those pieces of other people?”

“We can help each other.”

“Did it ever occur to you that I do not want to leave? That I believe my taking was a gift to the world? I am not like you, Hanuman.” He tapped his temple. “Think, for once, of the damage you would do were you to be flung out of this tomb. Think of the consequences for all the lives you would touch.

“Why did the gods see fit to let you live? It was not mercy guiding their hands. They understood, just as I do, that everything we did in the day of our lives was such an affront to mortal kind we were deemed too dangerous even to die. Our very essences, our histories, must be erased, or the world would suffer.”

“You are a fool.” Hanuman intoned. “The gods do not *like* us. We are pawns in their game. Do you know what lies at its end?”

“I have an idea. But move aside.” He made a swatting gesture. “I need rest. I would advise you not to linger too long here.”

Hanuman stepped aside, let him pass.

He turned corner and slunk off, down an adjacent passage.

“What did you do?” Hanuman asked, watching him stumble over broken ground on his way to whatever place he might find respite.

Ank loosed a guttural chuckle, a sound to make the Elder feel sane.

“You’ve wanted to know that for a very long time, haven’t you.”

He did not answer.

“Do you know how soulbinding works? What it is? There’s a mystery in that, isn’t there? With all of the might in their hands, why would the gods not rip away our power? There would be no need of this place if they simply *plucked*—“ he snatched at the air. “—their essence from our souls. The spirits have ever done just

Tears for the Moon God

that when our will has turned against them."

He slinked off, relying on that wall to hold him upright.

What did you do, Ank? What in the name of all the gods and spirits did you do.

Game Maker

The night of the raid arrived as if a thief had stolen all of the days between. Sarri marched across the Kachin camp, the moon half full and steadily waxing above him.

Clouds scudded across its path, catching silver light across their crests. He suspected the winds were watching—holding their breath back as each waited for another to slice across the plains, to be the one to herald the beginning of battle, for the winter's harsh chill was abated.

Ho'o would do them no kindnesses now. It was Thera they needed.

He closed on Gulang's yurt, unremarkable except for its positioning, and signaled for the diminutive figure trailing him like a shadow to wait. He flashed five fingers over his shoulder. He did not expect this conversation to take long. He was only here to warm Gulang to an idea. After that, he would leave this place, go to Tursa's camp or Sauman's. He had business with both of them; though, until this night was ended, he supposed none of it was pressing.

He pulled aside the tent flap at the entrance and passed into the relative warm of Gulang's yurt. His sons and daughter were all gathered there. Their mother busied herself with painting their faces and bodies with lines and images of ritual significance. They were going into battle, and this time they would be prepared. She worked on Saafha's chest now. Gaulakh wore the paint in the family style across his neck and shoulders. The Kachin had never been much for direct depictions of their token animals and spirits, not like the Cuu. Instead, across his neck and shoulders was written script forming the rough shape of spread wings in black. Smears of ashy white had been dragged across his cheeks and the contours of his abdomen. He wore a gilded choker like his father. An inset band had been cast with lilies and rushes in the Jahhad style, a much more feminine and posh array than the simpler and thicker band his father wore. Leather bracers crossed thick wrists and hugged his ankles, and he had donned a woolly bear's skin, the whole thing having been tanned all at once and bifurcated along the midsection so that it resembled a cape draped over his shoulders.

His younger brother, Saafha's embellishments were similarly garish. He forewent any furs, but sported shoulder pads embellished with porcupine quills,

Tears for the Moon God

and feathers danced in his hair, laced into the head of a sinuous braid that ran down his back.

He remembered seeing Saafha fight in the Ung Tsang tournament seven years back now—it must have been. He had been uncommonly cruel, the blows he dealt brutal and efficient. A very different style than the cocky, almost flowery way his elder brother fought. A style which had not rubbed off on the twins, as he had seen, which both would have done well to pay attention to.

There was nothing to be had in battle but bloodshed and hurt. Every man who had seen it knew this truth. There was the manic, frenzied drive to survive moment by moment, a drive not governed by anger but bone-chilling fear, as each moment came with a renewed certainty that Shao Luin's embrace would take the warrior, leave behind a mutilated corpse for his family to grieve.

It would be worse against these Tului, when Gulang's raiding party closed in on them. These were not an enemy who left dead in their wake. What would befall each of them if they did not watch themselves—did not do away with the gaudy, grandstanding postures and ridiculous challenges those three had grown so fond of—would be infection, a claim on their souls perhaps. They would be denied the absolution or relief of feeling Shao Luin's tug on their souls, of being awakened in Gur Tulain, of a dreamless sleep afloat in Ul Sharak's band.

Saafha met his gaze, and he tipped his chin in acknowledgment. Those eyes were cold as ice, hard as granite.

Watch out for your siblings. He thought to himself. *They are not ready.*

Gulang followed his second son's gaze to him, and his expression turned stony. Fire lingered behind that grim expression, a bad sign for what was to come. It was no secret to him why Gulang wanted to lead this charge, and he was not yet convinced the Kachin chief would let go of his grudge long enough to see to what must be done. But he was not here to pass judgment. He was not here to chastise Gulang for his selfishness or his ego, though neither was in short supply this night.

"Come to see us off?" Gulang asked.

Saerin looked up from her painting.

"I need your ear for a moment, chief." Sarri said.

"Absent my family?"

Sarri nodded.

Gulang marched past his sons. Sarri retreated into the moonlit snows outside, drawing him out after him.

They marched a little distance away from the yurt, so that his sons and daughter would not hear this exchange, though they would all see the impact of it soon enough.

"Where is she?" Gulang asked.

Sarri gestured over his shoulder. His follower emerged from the shadow of a nearby yurt, crossed the snows quickly, without making a sound. She lowered the hood of her deer skin coat as she closed in on them, revealing planar cheekbones, hooded eyes, hair bound in an unfussy knot at the back of her head.

Bora looked up at the Kachin chief, and saluted.

"I don't see why we need to do this in secret." She said. "They're going to know."

"They will know about *you*, Bora, but they cannot know about the true nature of our plan." Sarri said. "It will only frighten them."

Game Maker

"You underestimate my children." Gulang said.

Sarri avoided his eye. It was not his children that worried him. Not really. He may not approve of Gaulakh's grandstanding or the codependence Sircha and Kachukh often showed toward each other. He might not approve of Saafha's brutality, either, in the way it revealed itself when he was in the thick of it. That boy showed no compassion. A man like that was perfectly cut to be an effective warrior, but he should never be a leader.

Gulang himself was his worry, and that concern would not be abated until the raiding party he commanded returned with their charge.

"Everything is ready?" he asked.

"The opium has been packaged and distributed." Gulang responded.

"Good." Bora said. "Down to business, then."

"Yes, about that." Gulang said. "What good does any of this do if we cannot get near enough our quarry to apprehend them?"

"Worst case, we send a shock to their system when they realize we have fangs. Right now, I think they believe us to be crippled by this infection. They may even believe we're playing into their hands, and in a sense, they would be right." Bora said. "But we have some tricks up our sleeve they don't, and tonight, we're going to show them a couple of them."

"You still believe your god is acting against us?" he asked.

Sarri had been wondering the same thing. The games of the gods were, if the Gil Garo tradition was correct, complex things the full breadth of which was rarely accessible to the mortals ensnared in them. The Gil Garo were being goaded into a battle they did not want. That was true. But why? He thought he had some idea, but there was too much left to conjecture for his tastes. He much preferred to gather intelligence on his enemies, through reconnaissance and other methods, before attacking them.

By contrast, Bora's approach seemed to favor hit and run tactics, an arena he had little infatuation with.

"Best case?"

"We apprehend someone important to them, and they respond. Either by attacking us or running hard for their reinforcements."

"Neither outcome bodes well for us." Sarri muttered.

Gulang nodded grimly. "You're sure—"

"Sorry for interrupting, but no. I'm not *sure* of anything. But I know how Tirulain operates, and I don't think he's working alone."

"Clearly, he isn't. The Tului all seem beholden to one spirit. I think it best to assume they follow a plains lord, and if so, *he* is working with God Tirulain."

Bora nodded. "I thought the same, though I think *working with* him is too generous. God Tirulain has no interest in working *with* anyone. He may conspire with the other gods for a time, but the spirits...unless this spirit is strong enough to stand against him, he is using it."

"Which does not meaningfully alter our predicament." Gulang rubbed his cheek absently. "You have a target in mind?"

Bora nodded curtly. "I do. To start with."

"I was under the impression you had thought all of this through already." Gulang growled, a sudden wave of irritation sweeping over him.

"I have." She assured him. "I've considered the nature of our enemy's raw power. Their greatest strength is also their greatest weakness. There is no diversity in their talents. They all seem to be acolytes of the same spirit, and they possess a hierarchical command structure framed around a small number of individuals, almost like a hive mind. If we can tap into that, then I can follow the channels up to the leadership. Once I've done that, we'll have our true target. His location and his identity both."

"At which time we create a distraction." Gulang said.

"Long enough for me to neutralize the target, yes."

"You cannot think I'll let you do it alone." He intoned.

"I wouldn't dream of it. Which is why your son will go with me." She looked pointedly in Sarri's direction. "You recommended Saafha."

"You did?" Gulang's eyebrow rose precipitously. "I was under the impression you did not like him."

"I do not think he is cut out to be chief." Sarri said. "However, of your children, he is the most calculating. Gaulakh, though not a bad choice, will be needed elsewhere."

"Making noise." Gulang said knowingly.

Sarri nodded.

"And Sircha and Kachukh lack the experience to handle this sort of thing delicately." His gaze fell on Bora. "A trait I would argue you share with them."

"I can't argue with that." Bora said. "But I'm also the only one who can neutralize the target. The rest of you have skills better suited to direct combat, but those abilities aren't well suited to crushing an opponent in the way we need."

"I understand that well. Nonetheless—"

"Peace, Gulang." Sarri clapped him on the shoulder. "No amount of plotting and scheming will eliminate all traces of risk from this. You know that better than most. Saafha has a good head on his shoulders. He will have no trouble keeping her safe while she does what is needed. Trust in them."

"I..." Gulang met his eye, saw the assurance in his gaze and was mollified. He turned his back on him. "Saerin will be finishing with the twins by now. We should be going."

Sarri watched Gulang's broad back as he set off for his yurt.

Bora turned her gaze on him. She was smiling. "That went better than I expected."

"Did it?"

Her smile broadened, taking the corners of her eyes in its twist. "I thought he would ask me to stay back. Or demand that he accompany me personally."

"He would have been in the right."

"He would also have doomed the rest of our troop. Most of the pressure will be on them until I'm done."

"How long can you keep this commander under control?"

"Long enough to incapacitate him by other means." She said. "That is...as long as he doesn't figure out the rules before the game is over."

"What happens if he does?"

Her smile fell away. "Then we'll be in trouble."

"God Katcya protect you." He prayed.

She giggled. "Oh, I'm sure he has better things to do." Her gaze shifted over his shoulder, south down the war path toward Gil Garo.

Game Maker

He dipped his head and shoulders in a slight bow. She mirrored him.

"Come back safe." He said.

"I intend to." She replied. "I have a date with your son when this is all over."

He snorted.

She spun on her heels, and marched across the snow dunes. He watched her go, and wondered again what she saw in his boy. Shaki was so very unlike her, but then...his wife had been a light in dark places. Perhaps Bora was drawn to that flighty, idiot boy for much the same reason. For the cynic, there must be a reason to press on, something to make it all mean something. Something to fight for, to protect. Something they might cherish. It was often something fragile, and complicated in that it piqued the cynic's curiosity, and refused to be understood. In that it did not settle tidily into a little box.

Shaki was not a man in the traditional sense. Not in the way Sarri saw such things. But he was brave, when he wanted to be, and sincere.

We may have this thing in common. He mused as he ambled away through the drifts. *We may take different roads to it, but the conclusion is the same. That boy, pain in my neck though he may be, needs protecting. To keep him good. To keep his light shining.*

One day, perhaps, I'll pass the torch to her. One day, maybe, she will be my daughter.

A rare smile curled his lips, and around him what few stragglers were still about outside their yurts shied away. He had never been particularly charming, had he?

Aeranha always did say I looked murderous when I smiled. He cackled, and those few scampered away into their yurts. His late wife might have had a chuckle at that, too, were she here with him now. Oh, how he wondered how Shaki took in so much of who she was, having never known her. Or maybe...maybe he had seen what became of his father, an embittered old loner, devoid of a sense of humor about much of anything, and had simply filled in all of the spaces in himself with the needlepoints needed to chip away his father's armor.

Wouldn't that be something.

He whispered a quick prayer for the safety of his son, and another for the raiding party for good measure, whispered them for the silently watching winds to carry away, away to God Katcya, in hope he would find them in good humor. In hope that that so mercurial god would keep his loved ones safe.

Bora followed Gulang into his yurt to find his children had all been done up in war paint. It seemed an oversight that they would observe the traditions in a contest of this nature. She had foregone her own adornments, had chosen nondescript clothing for the occasion.

Foolish grandstanding. She thought to herself, but did not comment.

Even without their warpaint, the feathers laced into their braids, the pilfered trinkets adorning their arms and legs, wrapped around their necks, they would be running a high risk of exposure once in the enemy camp, a risk she would have thought Gulang smart enough to mitigate. They did not even take to wearing these adornments on raids across the countryside. The grease paints had long lost favor for hit and run strikes, as the preparations for those assaults took too long, left too much room for their targets to move off before they could assemble their cavalry for the initial sweep.

They mean to make this about revenge, don't they?

She stood near the entrance and waited in silence for Gulang to make his assessments. To deliver his instructions to his children. And she hoped he had done better with his selection of the other participants in this raid. That he had not decided to select exclusively from within his own sect. Those people would be too easy for him to command. They trusted him. None of the Kachin would ignore his commands, or push back against him, and that was the problem.

Sarri did not trust him, and she did not either. It was not that he lacked competence. He was, perhaps, the most successful of the chiefs in his campaigns across the steppe, but she feared his heart was guiding him. That revenge would take precedent over the mission, and he would lose sight of what he was being called to do as a bloody rage took over.

It was a mistake to allow him command over this force. A mistake they would all pay for if he could not keep himself contained. Even Sauman, untested as he was, would have been a better choice for this errand. She would have preferred Sarri, but anyone with the dispassionately hyper logical disposition required to burn all of his sect's dead in the aftermath of battle would be better than a man grieving the recent loss of his son. She met gazes with Saafha, found she was looking into a mirror. Behind the carefully composed, neutral expression was a cold fire smoldering in his eyes, tension in his posture. He had positioned himself such that he faced away from his father, so that he was the only one not looking directly at him.

In that exchange, she thought she sensed dread. Wondered if he would seek to position himself close to Chief Gulang, to pull him back from the edge if he became too frenzied, too incensed in the heat of it all. But she could not afford to let him linger at his father's shoulder. Sarri believed he alone among Gulang's children would be up to the task of accompanying her, that he alone possessed the skillset required to compliment her power.

"Bora will be accompanying us on this raid." Gulang said, and left it at that.

The twins exchanged queer looks, and Gaulakh stepped forward with a protest on his lips. Saafha barred him moving any further, but he could not stop him speaking.

"She's barely grown." He said. "It's bad enough we're involving Kachukh and Sircha, but at least they're family. We know what they're capable of. Her?" A knife-like thrust of his arm in her direction. "She's a liability."

"Quiet Gaulakh." Gulang said. "She's coming."

"What *is* the meaning of this?" Sircha asked. "She's an acolyte of the God of Games. You said yourself the chiefs chose to take her with us to prevent him finding out anything about—"

"Dupec Safar, yes." Gulang said. "It was Sarri's decision to take her with us. It is his decision to leave her in our company now. And he is right. The edge she provides may be pivotal to our success here."

"But *why?*"

"Because she is, at her core, a strategist. She was the mastermind behind this plan, a fact you will all keep to yourselves. I do not value the idea that the others involved in this raid will see it as a doomed mission from the start because she was involved in shaping it."

Game Maker

Sircha quieted, but her gaze remained steadily fixed on Bora, wondering. Kachukh, too, watched her, but there was far less doubt in his gaze, in the set of his jaw. He was thinking it over, piecing together the features of her abilities, rumored or actual it didn't matter, trying to see the bigger picture. He had always been more tempered than his sister, more discerning.

Saafha shunted Gaulakh back. When his elder brother was well in hand, he turned his full attention on her. "What game are you playing?"

His mother clucked her tongue, shooting him a glare at the same time.

"A deceptively simple one, as it happens." Bora replied, striking a confident tone. She looked up into Gulang's face. She had to crane her neck to pull it off at this distance. "If you don't mind, I'd like to get started."

He gave her the floor, earning the confusion of all the gathered others.

"I need to touch each of you, and anyone else who will be involved in this game."

"It is a raid." Gaulakh muttered. "Not some simple child's game."

"It will be both, insofar as it is anything at all." She said, meeting his gaze, dagger point for dagger point.

She started with Gulang. A dark flash passed under her fingers and traveled up his arm, across his chest to settle over his heart. He flinched as the disruptive presence seeped into his skin, taking on the form of a toy shield.

She performed the same seemingly insignificant ritual with Sircha, Saafha, and Gaulakh. The strange ether settled in the shape of a horse against each of their flanks. Then she closed on Kachukh.

"You'll be the most important player in my game." She said. "It is imperative you do not make direct contact with any of our enemies. Not skin to skin, anyway."

"Why?"

"Because you'll be our flag bearer." She said. "If you are captured, it will plunge the mission into jeopardy." She panned over his other siblings. "Unless you can bring down the assailant before he passes the line."

She pressed her fingers against Kachukh's wrist. The blot of darkness traveled across his arm and settled against his chest, taking on the form of a barrel-sided tower with a lone window. She almost chuckled at that. It was strange to think of Kachukh as a damsel in distress, but in many ways he would be exactly that until this errand was completed.

She passed the floor back to Gulang, who was watching her impassively throughout all of this.

"Saafha, you'll be with Bora. Your task is to find our target and take him captive. Bora will neutralize him."

"Understood." He said.

"The rest of you will be with me, creating a distraction. We'll be drawing heat away from Bora and Saafha together with the others." He said.

"One thing you should all understand. My power is indiscriminate. We'll all be bound by the same rules as our enemies, which means you have to have a concrete understanding of the rules in order to play safe. Our enemies won't have the same advantage, but that doesn't mean they'll be less dangerous to us."

"And you've chosen Storm the Keep as your game." Saafha said.

She nodded.

"What are the rules?" he asked.

Tears for the Moon God

She explained them in detail, and as she did, a malicious grin spread across his lips. A deepening dread took the rest of them, not least their mother, who seemed on the point of speaking out against the whole idea until a look from Gulang silenced her.

"I'll explain everything to the rest of our company before we depart." He said.

"I wouldn't have it any other way. The optics of me taking command would be terrible." Bora grinned at him. "Just make sure you're not touched by them."

"It'll be hard to prevent that happening." He said. "With their use of shadows."

"That's why I said not to let them *touch* you. Their shadows will be meaningless in this fight, as long as they are bound by my rules. They won't be at first."

"They might not be at all." Gaulakh said.

"There is no such thing as a fight without risk." Saafha said. "It would be best if we operated under the assumption they won't be."

Bora nodded.

"You'll bring them back safe." Saerin whispered. "I've already lost one child. I will never forgive you if I lose another."

Bora approached her, took her hands gently in hers. "Don't worry. We'll be back before you know it."

"It's time to go." Gulang said behind them.

Bora released Saerin's hands.

Saerin and Gulang exchanged a tender embrace. She gave each of her children a hug before letting them all go on, and stood by the tent flap, watching them cross the drifts until they were beyond her sight.

The number of those chosen to outfit their company was fewer than Bora had expected. When they arrived at the edge of the Kachin encampment, it was to be greeted by ten horses, all outfitted with saddles, travel packs and, by every appearance, the weapons each of their owners favored. One horse was absent any weapons sheathed or otherwise. She assumed the roan was intended for a spare mount.

It would be hers to ride, now; and she thanked the gods and the spirits for it. She did not relish the idea of riding behind one of Gulang's children. Even less, sharing the saddle with the chief himself.

She panned over the four mounted warriors in their seats. They all wore ceremonial war paints, though these had foregone the gold and silver fineries. A whip slender Kirche man sat tall in the saddle. Deep smile lines were carved into the ridges framing his lips. His features were wide and blunt, looming over a skinny neck which heightened the pie plate roundness of his head. A barrel chested Kachin man—his arms so hairy, me might have been mistaken for a bear—was drawing his horse around as she closed in with the chief and his kin. Behind them and holding the reigns of three horses in his right hand was a broad shouldered beast of a man a head shorter in the saddle than either of the other two. His eyes were an uncommonly light shade of green, and his dress and the patterns painted across his arms and cheeks marked him as a member of the Chikata sect.

She recognized the last of them. A woman from her own sect, Berni was possessed of a smug kind of beauty even in the waning half of her life. Flowing, silken hair ran loose down her back, and high cheekbones rode the rims of round, hooded eyes. The men who knew her gave her a wide berth. They knew better than

Game Maker

most who she was, what she was capable of. There was something off about the woman, some darkness in her. Though she was not surprised to see her here, she wished Sarri had chosen someone else.

"What are you doing here?" Berni asked, a cold regard settling on Bora.

"The same thing you are." Bora said without inflection.

She spat on the ground, a gob of mucus piercing through the snow, and drove her horse around to face Gulang. "I did not agree to sending kids to die." She said hotly.

"Your concerns are misplaced." Gulang said.

"Really? I see three of them in your company. Every one of them untested."

The round faced man behind her chuckled. "They'll have to face their test sooner or later."

"On a raid." She said. "Not like this."

"This is a raid." The Kachin man with the bear-like arms said gruffly.

"You know what I mean, Guruhl." She growled.

"She will not be your responsibility." Gulang cut in. "The chiefs took it upon ourselves to assemble a company whose strengths complimented each other. Bora possesses a skill we will need. That is why she will be coming.

"If you have a problem with our choice, you can take it up with Chief Sarri when we return."

"You can't be serious. He would never allow a kid to run headlong into this kind of danger. Simple contact with the blood of those monsters could bring any one of us down, and you expect us to babysit a bunch of toddling children when the odds are already soundly stacked against us."

"I would tend to agree." Said the Kirche man.

"Your judgments are noted." Gulang said, his tone expressing to everyone that the matter was closed.

Gaulakh's gaze settled on Guruhl, followed his broad chest to his saddle. "Where is your friend?"

"Sitting this one out." He said. "The cold of the open steppe will be too much for him. Monkeys of that kind are not accustomed to this climate."

Gaulakh nodded. "He'll be okay with you rattling the Chain when he can't see what you're doing?"

"That is none of your business." Guruhl said.

"Akhi, take point." Gulang said.

The Chikata man nodded curtly. He trotted his horse forward. Gulang mounted a black stallion with a splotch of white running the length of its nose, and guided it up to take position behind him.

His children and Bora mounted their horses, and Berni slid up to her flank. She looked her up and down.

"No weapon?"

Bora reached down and pulled a buck knife from a sheath hidden beneath the hem of her deerskin coat. She flipped it around and held it out for Berni to see.

"That's it?"

"I don't need anything else." Bora said.

"Spoken like a fool."

"Berni." Gulang said in warning.

She edged her horse away.

Tears for the Moon God

Bora replaced her knife in its sheath.

"Where are they, Akhi?"

Akhi lifted his head, inhaled sharply through his nose. His chin twitched north and then slightly east. "There. About fifteen miles."

"Closer than I would have guessed."

"They've been maintaining about that distance on us for some time. They seem not at all concerned with opening the gap."

"As if they want us to test them." Gulang mumbled.

He's a hunter. Bora thought. She let her gaze drift from him to the others. She knew who some of them belonged to, but she was not foolish enough to believe knowing who they trained under could give her a complete understanding of their capabilities. There were always nuances in the way acolytes of the same spirit or god used their abilities, and time opened many doors where it concerned their capabilities. Feeling the pulse in the land was only the start for most spirit callers, and for a soul binder, the process of conditioning the soul could take years, even decades, to truly master.

Berni had gone out to sea to court a minor spirit, a fairy queen in truth, and had come back with a host of formidable powers most would not have thought possible given the nature of her mentor. Kachukh had gone into the mountains in pursuit of his mentor, had stayed close to home and chosen a spirit who was fairly indiscriminate about who he took on as acolyte. He had not been particularly ambitious, and neither had Sircha, who had openly chosen Dadang. Their choices had been critical in shaping a strategy for dealing with the Tului, especially when considered against how others who shared their mentors had fared during the attack.

The Kirche man was a mystery, but it was not a stretch to assume he had followed in Chief Tursa's footsteps. Shi'an the Grass was very popular among the Kirche, and he was known to be fairly indiscriminate about who he took on as acolytes, as well. Guruhl was a mystery. She did not know what he might be capable of, but she had seen him in Gulang's company often over many winters, and had come to understand he was a trusted confidant to the chief, a man who commanded the respect of most within his sect.

She had witnessed the tournaments in which Gaulakh and Saafha participated. There would be no surprises from Gaulakh, who had chosen Sildein, liking the flash and spectacle inherent in the Range Lord's aesthetic, and having idolized Chief Coltang when he was younger. She did not know who Saafha was beholden to, but knew he had chosen a dark spirit who claimed dominion far from Tao Shein steppe. He had been gone on pilgrimage for several years before returning. No few throughout the sects had believed him dead. Not all the spirits the Gil Garo called upon were friendly to them.

And the powers of the chiefs were a secret to no one. Stories of their leaders were crowd favorites among the people of every sect. Ungol, hated and loved by his people in equal measure for his decision to court Gandes Fae. Arrak, having spent so much time wading into Shan Lao's band to impress his would be wife that the spirit forced him into service. Tursa, who chose to forgo the warrior's path in favor of Shi'an the Grass and the promise of full bellies and good health for his people. Coltang, who chose Sildein when the challenge of courting Rasheik the Rope proved too much. Sarri, who was the first of his people to go to sea, giving Berni and so

Game Maker

many others the wish to see that vast, borderless expanse for themselves, and came back riding a horse born of water and sea foam, wearing Byr's pulse on his soul. Sauman, whose infatuation with the world's great mysteries had led him across Rasheik's Rope, and fell into the care of Ul Surta, mother of the streams. And Gulang, ambitious to a fault, who in failing to court Tao Shein himself trekked farther, beyond the waters of the Fyrni sea, and found a place under Sarkahn instead.

If he could keep a level head. If he could remain in control long enough to see this mission through. He would prove an asset like none of the others gathered here. But if he lost control. If his composure broke. If his lust for vengeance proved too strong to ignore, he would prove the undoing of them all.

Akhi kicked his horse into a canter, setting the company into motion behind him. Berni shed a last, withering look on her before passing her up to ride behind Gulang, and Bora fell into step in the middle of the pack, near Sircha and Kachukh, while the others formed a guard around them.

Pulse of the Land

Echoes of a life once lived and dashed to pieces, potential futures unexplored or seized in the wake of a dramatic closure, lingered with Dupec in the stillness. He had not wanted to be Duijus Kanh's acolyte. Maybe he thought he had, that it was this underlying condition he had been seeking in rejoining his family, but were those his wants, his beliefs? Or were they someone else's, a stranger and a man who wanted for him a life he had not asked for. A tribe who gave everything to the wolf in his cave, in exchange for a flawed sense of protection that left the sick and the weak exposed?

He had wanted his family back, but as he lay on a bed of dried grasses, soft light emanating from a lantern on the floor and glinting off some of the gold and silver treasures which made up Duijus Kanh's horde, he found this family, this *idea* of kinship, left much to be imagined. That he had gained back his parents to have them ripped away, that his people had gone off on the march to war and might not return...what was this except divine intervention, a subtle torment for him to endure as the gods sought to structure a game around the nature of his life, the path he followed.

In quiet hours, witnessed by darkness, there was no peace for him. In quiet hours, witnessed by fate and all of her terrible devices, were nightmares wrung from a soiled cloth, the waters pulled from the river's edge, reminding him of all of those unknowable things he had lost.

He could not help but to fixate on the details of that other life, what it must have been like. *Why* had that other Dupec gone mad? What must it have taken to drive him over the edge, when the logistics of running an empire, what must have been constant battles fought against countless peoples, had not done the job?

It's a blessing I don't remember.

It did not feel that way.

What time he had with his father and mother had been fleeting, and his people...how could a man know himself without knowing his roots? He had not been with them long enough, not to have gained any trust from them, and certainly not to know them. If God Lanfin had ripped away his history and his future, Goddess Liandal his autonomy, then in their absence it was God Uldal who drove

Pulse of the Land

the arc of his life onward.

He would not like this fate. Had been very clear that this place, this spirit, was not to have any part in his life. What would he say when his acolyte returned to him with a wolf pelt on his shoulders and a host of spirit given gifts he had not sanctioned? It would not matter to him that the gifts had been given without him asking for them, that the conventions for attaining them had gone ignored.

Shuffling steps drove him out of his head, back to the present and his sleeping chamber. He glanced toward the tunnel beyond, a narrow, unlit passage which adjoined onto the cave's main thoroughfare. Diminutive and stooped, her proportions toad-like and hideous, Kachekh shambled into the room. She hissed and shielded her eyes at the greater light of his chambers.

"Gah! It stings!" she flapped her wrist in the direction of his lantern.

He hastened forward to shield it. "I'm sorry, Lady Kachekh."

"Just my name will do, young pup." She said. "Now come. You're with me tonight."

"Is it night already?"

"Something you'll become aware of as time goes. Night and day are separated by more than just light and a few odd orbs." She said. "Now put that out. We've only so much time to get done what needs to be. Tak won't help you much with what you'll be doing."

He pulled back the lid, earning more protestations from the Swan, and blew out the wick.

"Least there's enough airflow from above to keep you breathin'."

She shambled off the way she had come. In the greater darkness, he was forced to bend over and pick out his path on his hands.

"Don't take all night now!"

He found the edge of the tunnel and pulled himself up, used the rough rock as a guide as he set out to follow her.

"Come along." Her voice echoed down to him. "Come, come. But don't hurt yourself. I'm no healer."

He followed the sound of her voice as she led him down dark passages. His vision adjusted in stages, never quite rising to true clarity, as he trekked after her, occasionally bumping against an unexpected outcrop, or stumbling over a dip in the floor.

They emerged from the cave mouth to starlight and moonlight, the breezes hushed and soft and the air bitter cold against him where his skin was exposed. Ho'o kept his distance, but winter lay heavy on the land, and in the far north as they were, its bite was like knives dragged across his skin.

His breath misted the air, and his deerskin boots crunched through snow crust as he marched after her, shivering against that bitter chill. The cave was not warm, but deep in its confines it was not particularly cold, either. He would welcome the comfort of those tepid, stable halls and hollows when he was at last allowed to return.

"Good night for it, don't you think?" She stood facing the moon with her fists planted against blocky hips. "Let's see."

He followed her gaze to the moon. It was nearing full, but there was still some time left before it gained its corona, before the night of blood returned. He hoped, after all the Gil Garo had been through, Ao Nii would not let down his gate here.

Tears for the Moon God

Not in Tao Shein, among the vulnerable.

In the far distance, a wolf howled. Its call was answered by several others.

"Wolves don't hunt alone, you know." She said. "When the old ones know they're soon to die, that they can't keep up with the young'uns anymore, they drift to the back of the pack. Give themselves up for the cougars and the bears, and whatever else might try for the young'uns, don't they. It's altruism, really. Death is no gift, but if it purchases survival for the strong ones, well then maybe the pups will grow up healthy.

"The cougar or the bear, it doesn't matter. They'll take a pup as soon as an elder."

He thought of his people, their treaty with these spirits.

"The Gil Garo are the same. It's what you're thinking isn't it?" she turned hard eyes on him, but her tone remained glib. "Only problem is they've forgotten the essence of our deal. There is the pack, and then there is their alpha. The Gil Garo sects have theirs, I suppose, but the tribe as a whole hasn't had one in, oh, who knows how long." She waved the thought away.

"They used to send us the brave ones, but they forgot the old deal there, too. Strength is not what the old wolf cares about. Not physical strength anyway. I always did think that little contest was a silly thing.

"It's the strength of your heart that matters." She flashed a crooked smile at him, then. "Are you keepin' up, kid?"

He pulled away from his observation of the moon, to the wider world, to the tall grasses of the steppe that seemed to go on forever, to the mountains in the distance, and the river. Its waters ran black in the night, reflecting moonlight in glittering bands and whirlpools.

His fingers and toes had gone numb, and his breath came in shallow gusts. Any deeper and the chill would bore into his lungs, choking him.

"Isn't that just about right." Her grin turned mischievous. She hobbled over to him, snatched up his hand and examined it.

"Flex your fingers for me?"

He tried. They bent slower than they ought to, refused to move far without stressing his tendons and joints.

"That's what we're trying to get past."

"The cold?"

"Vulnerabilities like that, yes." She said. "Every spirit, no matter how lowly, has a gift to impart. Some do work alone, but as wolves don't, we will not either. Now, you know how this all works, do you?"

"Know how what works?"

"Spirit calling. What else?"

"To some extent."

"Right, then. All the power we control is regulated by our lover. As his concubines, the expression of his power, through us, is influenced by our own natures. But it all comes from this cave. It's properties. It's depth. A cave's power comes from absence. It's as much an expression of the power in the earth as in the air. So the winds don't like to run too deep into our humble home, and the only earth spirit who is brazen enough is Tao Shein."

"Who regulates Duijus Kanh's power."

"I always did think you were brighter than a brick." She guided his hand toward

Pulse of the Land

the earth, through the snow, until his palm lay flat against hardened dirt.

"Now consider for me why we spirits exist at all. What happens when we die. Oh yes, it has happened more than once. More than once on this continent, as it happens.

"But close your eyes now, and reach down into the earth. Feel the air around you."

Dupec obeyed, closed his eyes, practiced a meditation God Uldal had taught him in the earliest days of his training. "What am I looking for."

"No judgment, now. Let it come to you."

"Are you sure I'll be able to find it? My arm is quite numb."

"Did I not just say?"

He stood there, doubled over in the freezing cold with his arm buried almost to the shoulder in the snow as the breath fluttered in and out of him. How much time went by lost meaning as the blood within him drew back from his limbs, leaving them stiff, and swollen, and blue.

There came a pulse. Another. A rhythmic beating not unlike his own heart. He opened his eyes, met her steady gaze.

"The land is alive." If you stayed there long enough, you'd feel more pulses than just one. Different rhythms belonging to different spirits. What you see in me is the most refined expression of my spirit, but it is not all of me. Not even most."

"This is your pulse?"

"Hardly." She spat. "No, that's the old wolf. Linger a bit longer and you'll feel it. It won't be hard to find if you pay attention."

He reached down further, let himself drift. As she said, the pulse was joined by others. A steady thrumming, a fluttering thing quick as a rabbit's, and one more, which beat slower than the rest, but was stronger than all but the first.

She nodded. "There you are."

"You can feel my heartbeat?"

"Your soul." She said. "An entirely different rhythm. Not like the first few who came to us, either. They didn't have a soulbinding." She reached for his arm and wrenched it free of the snow. "That's where our power comes from. It's where yours'll come from, too. You remember those rhythms when you call on us. That's how you do it."

"Just feel for you?"

"In any land. Wherever you are. No matter how distant. Remember this if you remember nothing else. Everything is connected. Layers and layers and more layers all connected and in harmony, as long as we live."

"And if you die?" he asked.

"The land dies with us. Your people starve. The soil loses its life. The rivers dry up. The trees grow brittle as dry bones. Nothing grows, and people like you and your kin...well, they leave unless they're fool enough to risk their own death.

"That is, until the echoes of our deaths cease, and the way is paved for another spirit to take our place."

"How...sad." He said.

"Oh, now don't go bringing down the mood. You're doing so good."

She took him by the hand once more, and led him away toward the mouth of the cave. Just within it, she halted and spun him round to face the deeper darkness further within with surprising force.

Tears for the Moon God

"Now feel for my pulse again."

He bent down to place his hand against the rock, but she snatched up his arm before he could. "Not like that!" She released her hold on him, and he stood. "With your spirit. With your soul."

He closed his eyes, fell into a meditative state, let go of himself, his judgments, his attachments. Layer after layer of the man, Dupec Safar, yielded to a greater stillness. Were he to reach out in this state, a pathway would open, to take him wherever he might wish to go, but he stayed his hand, allowed himself to drift. To feel the cold against his skin and let it be as it was. To feel the uneven ground under his feet, the press of still air against his skin.

He let go, and in letting go abandoned that sense of self with all of its complex desires, worries, attachments. There again, the strong pulse of Duijus Kanh awakened, but it remained outside of him, felt as an echo of him. There, too, just beneath it, was the steady pulse of Kachekh, who she was as expressed by the land. A spirit baked into the stone of those walls, low and stable, and secure.

"Reach for me." She whispered.

He reached out toward that pulse, and his soul blended with it. The pulse beat within him, her rhythm shielding his heart, worn in his soul, the raw expression of her being entwined with him.

As her pulse settled into him, the cold was driven back. Blood flowed back into his limbs, came with warmth and not pain. Breath filled his lungs more fully, the labor of breathing no longer burdened with harsh, stinging cold. He opened his eyes, and found he could see well into the darkness, could see deep into the gullet of Duijus Kanh's cave as if it was lit by an unencumbered sun.

"There you go." She said, puffing out her chest with pride. "That's it. That's it!"

"It feels...pleasant."

"Yes, well, that's why I have you first. Why I did the first time, too."

He turned his gaze on her, and melancholy and confusion washed over him.

She took notice. "Now. It was never as bad as it might seem. There are gifts in loss, too. In your loss, anyway."

"Why is it that you can remember me, but I have no memory of you? Or anything from the time you're speaking of."

"Because you're human." She said.

"I don't see—"

"Leave it there for now." She insisted. "It's not worth getting into those details just yet. There will be a time, I'm sure of it. The old wolf is a better person to ask, anyway. He's better at explaining these things."

His shoulders sagged, and Kachekh's pulse fell away as the fight leaked out of him. As his moment's triumph was marred with all of the complicated feelings he had for that past self and what it meant. "It just seems so unfair."

She reached up and patted his cheek. "Be glad you don't. You suffered more than any man I'd ever known."

"And I'm doomed to suffer more."

"Now that's a matter of perspective, young pup. You've got some of the most unlikely, most predictable friends waiting just outside this cave for you to return. And when you do, they'll whisk you away on a grand adventure like you never could have had in that other life."

"But *why*?"

"Because the person you are now does not need to become the person you were then. You're free, Dupec. Free from all of the scars you bared back then.

"Think of it like this. You lost a lover, but it's like you never knew him. And the two of you...well, the world is probably better off without him in it. You're better off. You have your father and your mother, both alive. You have an opportunity to be one with your people again. There is enough good in your present that a future you missed is not worth dwelling on.

"So don't."

"But—"

"Nope. No more of that. Now come with me. You'll be longing for some rest and a little warmth after everything."

She guided him into the cave. Like an obedient dog, he followed.

Water Bearer

On it's face, the square appeared unoccupied, but Lisandra knew better than to hold anything at face value. If an ambush was to be sprung, the enemy would not telegraph its presence. Or if they did, it would be in bating their enemy into a trap. She had learned that no one who fought battles, who was on the ground level in protracted wars, believed in the causes they executed. The common soldier of Saodein did not believe he was doing the right thing, that in the pursuit of annexing the Fingers there was some moral virtue to be had. Sure, there were the propogandists ever extending their tentacles into the pool of minds that governed a nation, but the soldier knew better. They knew they were less than dogs, that their purpose in the grand scheme was in giving life to an idea they might not even believe in.

They were tools to be used, means to an end. They held no illusions about their purpose. Most often, it was not even a matter of the soldier viewing the freedom of that external force as bad for their homeland, for the world. The resilience of those soldiers was an incredible thing. Most often, it was the abject resolve of a man who believed, in killing others, he would bring some security, some prosperity to his family. If he was killed in action, they would never suffer poverty. If he was captured, they would be trapped in uncertainty.

So it was that every saodeini soldier she had bested asked that he be executed, his body left where his fellow soldiers could find it. And she had, time and again, obliged. Perhaps it was the warrior's code. A reciprocal relationship between reason and mercy. What she did to others must be equivocal to what they could do to her. And if she had no family, she had people who depended on her. There had been those times in her past. There may even be those in the present who viewed her as worthy of such care. Of such concern.

She stood with Jinga on a street clad in shadows, hugging a building and observing the square. If there were guards—*of course there must be*—there must need be conflict. Knives and swords drawn, the fight waged and concluded, and the losers taken care of. She knew if she proved victorious in this skirmish, she would leave those dying men in plain sight, and pray that they were found before death came to them. This was not a land for Shah Jagat. So close to the band of Ul

Water Bearer

Sharak's river, these people would give their souls instead to the spirits. What a loss it would be. To forfeit their souls to spirits who cared nothing for them, to collectors of the dead with no conception of the hubris with which they exerted their powers.

Squatting low, Jinga eased onto his toes, swinging a hair past the edge of the building they hid behind to get a better view of the square, its clock post, the court house or city hall or whatever the monumental structure was to these people, and the cage and the gallows just in front of it—both waiting to satisfy their purposes with the coming of the sun.

Cold light cast scattered shadows across cobbled streets and brick sidewalks. The hands of the clock chugged forth with each passing second, the minute hand moving fluidly as the second hand clipped past. In the greater silence of the night, she could hear the gears inside clacking and screeching as teeth bit into each other, as they slid away.

Jinga drew back. He rose, using the wall of the stone dwelling for support, and met her gaze.

Surety. Resolve. Whatever trap lay out there, he would spring it. Whatever devices these people used for surveillance, he did not care. She saw it in his eyes. In the stone set of his jaw. In his upright posture.

She reached for her sword, but he stopped her—wrist coming down on the back of her hand, forcing the sword back into its sheath.

"Keep watch." He said.

She nodded.

He rushed around the side of the building, glided into the square. He cut a straight line across, making directly for the cage. She expected resistance as he approached it, retaliation, but none came.

She squatted low, slipped onto her flank and edged forward so that she had a clear vantage of the clock tower, and the square, the cage and its contents.

Jinga closed in on the prisoner, the man who would be executed come the morrow if he did not succeed. As he approached, he dug into the pocket of his loose-fitting coverall and pulled free a pair of what looked like awls, and a length of wire.

He stooped next to the cage, and she saw the prisoner was smiling. They exchanged quiet words as his hands closed on the cage door, as his fingers roved across its upper edge. He dug behind the bar with one of his tools, then ran the wire and fidgeted a bit.

Soundlessly, the cage door sprang open, and the Nixian prisoner climbed out.

Jinga swung it shut, worked the upper edge of the door a bit more. The prisoner hustled back up the way he had come, and he chased after him.

Lisandra slid back around the corner. She took the hilt of her sword in a loose grip as she righted herself, prepared for a fight if one became necessary, but no one came. No alarms sounded. No watch emerged from joining streets to apprehend the prisoner newly freed, or his conspirators.

The prisoner pitched to the side, almost bowling her over as he fell back into the cover of the shadows. Jinga took a last look over his shoulder before turning corner to join them.

"Hi." The prisoner panted. He thrust out his hand. "I'm Kiresh."

She firmed her grip on the sword.

His gaze shifted from her face to her hand and back. A sad look stole over him.

Tears for the Moon God

"She's a friend, isn't she?" he asked Jinga.

"You can trust her." Jinga looked pointedly at her hand.

She uncurled her fingers, dry washed the back of her hand against her skirts.

"What are you doing here, anyway? You should be back home with your father. He must be worried sick."

"He was with me when I was captured. Mining expedition. I went out to collect some water and..." he shrugged. "...well."

"Gonsai's doing?" Jinga asked.

He nodded vigorously, a bemused smile drawing light into bright, innocent eyes. "He's been grumpy lately. Won't even let the guides through the gap on a consistent basis."

Jinga's expression darkened. "We're getting out of here." He started walking down the street, in the direction of the inn. "He's in one of his moods again."

"Something like that." Kiresh agreed.

"I thought you said your people had an amenable relationship with the spirit." Lisandra intoned.

"We do." Kiresh said. "But the spirits don't share our ideas of morality and such, do they? He lets us dredge up ore inside him, but we dug up too much this time." He explained. "Sometimes shit happens. Sometimes he gets pissy. We're still friends at the end of the day. We've just got to apologize really hard for making his tummy hurt."

He chuckled.

She glared at him, and he was silent. "The spirits are nothing to trifle with—"

"It's alright, Lisandra." Jinga cut in. "Not all of the spirits are as guarded as Sarkahn. Gonsai provides for us in his own way, on his own time. As do all of the spirits of the desert."

"They could stand to do a little more." Kiresh groused. "Especially that fat slug, Salein. He's been withholding water. That's why the old man sent us out on a collection run."

"Then our blessings are in abundance." Jinga said grimly. "The Scarabs?"

"Doing their best. We're going to have to start raiding again soon, if things keep on this way."

"For clean water?" Lisandra asked, more curious now than angry.

"Food, too. Our reserves are holding fine for now, but Ul Sharak only gives us so much. We have mouths to feed. These fools have been reluctant to trade with us since—"

"Since nothing. This cycle never ends. We sew our seeds in the soil in spring and reap our crop in late summer. The stores last longer than we have a right to, but there is never enough to sustain us." Jinga explained. "Lucky for us, I got a few villages to accept machinery from Baduhrak to help with their harvests. They'll trade with us."

"If his taxes aren't too high this season." Kiresh grumbled.

Jinga said nothing.

They marched the rest of the way to the inn in silence.

A breeze was coming in from the east—floating around corners and prancing down lanes. Mice, watching from cracks in the foundations of houses, from gutter wells embedded into sidewalks and streets, from within the eaves of roofs in need of new tiling, shied away as she passed, averted their gazes from the Sarkahni woman and her Nixian traveling companions.

Some leapt down from their vantages, skittered away into the earth and its intricate mazes, webs of cracks and cave tunnels, to make the long march home and report what they had seen.

When they arrived at Delbert's hovel, they found him waiting on the stoop. He looked like a drowned rat, bloated and sweating and anxious as he was, and Lisandra found his thoroughly harassed disposition somewhat satisfying. If he could be bothered to hustle about like this all the time, perhaps his inn would not be in the state of disrepair it was. She might even enjoy the idea of staying there, then.

He snatched two travel packs off the step and waddled up the short walkway to them. The packs slipped out from under sweaty palms and hit the ground with a dull *thunk*.

"These are yours. Plenty of food in them. You'll need to ration the water, but you know that." His gaze spread between Jinga and Kiresh. "Everything you need for the trip is just there."

He spun round in a jagged circle, casting his gaze briefly on the last of the packs still situated on the stoop.

"I'll get it." Jinga said, and moved past him.

"You don't have to—" Delbert took a step in his direction.

"No, no. It's no imposition." Jinga waved him off over his shoulder. He approached the step, snatched up the pack and shouldered it.

"You're sure you don't want to take the horses?"

"I'm sure. They'll only be extra mouths to feed once we cross through the gap."

"If we do." Kiresh said.

Jinga shot him a warning look.

"Gonsai's giving you trouble again?" Delbert asked.

"Mind your business, old friend." Jinga said. He smiled warmly at the squat, anxious man. "Thank you for your help. We'll be out of your hair now, okay?"

"O-okay." Delbert produced a dirty handkerchief from his vest pocket. He dabbed at his forehead. "If there's anything else I can do."

"You've done enough." Jinga said. "All we need from you now is to forget we were ever here."

"I can do that, friend." Delbert whipped the kerchief behind his back and bowed. "Always a pleasure."

Kiresh and Lisandra shouldered their own packs. Lisandra bowed under the crushing weight of hers, but she refused to let it drag her down. Twenty years younger, she would have had no problem lifting it, but time had taken its toll against her bones as it was wont to do. No, she would not ask for help with this, but she could not deny she wanted it. She gated after the Nixians, up the street and toward the river, and across the narrow, wire-framed bridge that crossed it.

"The gap isn't far from here." Kiresh assured her, noting the way she stooped under her load. He wisely did not offer her a hand with it. He contemplated her a moment longer, and she wondered if he would peel the rucksack off her back. "You're going to need better cover than that."

"I factored that into our arrangement." Jinga said over his shoulder. "Delbert will have made sure we had robes tucked in with everything else he provided us."

Tears for the Moon God

"Robes for what?" Lisandra asked. *It'll be hot as all get out when we reach the desert.*

"To keep the sun off. Exposure can be as deadly as any lance tiger."

"Noted." She growled. "Let's get on with it then."

And they marched, out of the town, into the plains, then northeast away from the Freeway. Gonsai's Wall, that marvelous, canyon bluff rose in the distance. In the night, it was clad in shades of blue and gray, looming tall against the endless sky, the last bulwark against the dead lands of Sha Ruhhad.

She wondered what those lands were like. She had never seen a desert before, had only her imagination to rely on in painting a picture of what such a place could be like. Inhospitable to all but the toughest of creatures, it must need be a wonder to her any human civilization could thrive there.

She would wonder only a little longer. Soon, they would be through this gap in Gonsai's Wall and she would be swallowed by the endless dunes. Then she would see the Nixian way, their way of survival.

Adara Yun

Ordein the White, Right Hand of God Ao Nii, marched down the wide, main thoroughfare where parade processions once passed. Those times were ended long ago, before he or his grandparents, or their grandparents had been thought of.

Generations gone, and a vibrant history buried. All that remains is bloodshed, a corrupted gift for us all.

Behind him, the Crystal Palace shone with moonlight, so many needles thrust into black fabric, piercing holes through which stars might shine. Before him, in the distance but clear in its details, the forward gate at the edge of the city. Crystal bars were closed now, and a smoky substance swirled within the forest of columns framing it to either side, drifted along on unnatural currents within a long block carved all over with friezes across its height.

A secret history lived in those friezes, in frescoes ground into the walls of hidden chambers within the depths of the most ancient of the God House's dwellings. In root cellars were depictions of reverent worshipers bowed in prayer at altar bowls filled with clean water. In barracks halls, where new recruits once slumbered, telling processions of acolytes all clad in white with flowers laced in their hair, dancing in this very street, and handing out pastries to gaggles of smiling children. In the god's own private chambers, so it was rumored, there were depictions of him, too. A Moon God who smiled, who knew so much more than grief and anger and regret. A Moon God who did not suffer, but thrived. Depictions of him making curious observations of rock formations and still pools, of him playing in the ocean's depths while flocks of birds flitted by and tall ships drifted along on the currents. Depictions also of the spirits with him, spirits who now loathed him, and gods of all stripes sharing his table. Unafraid, drinking from crystal goblets, laughing and hugging each other and him tight like old friends or brothers and sisters.

What would I do to see those days returned?

But there was no going back to those days. In the earliest of them, humanity—his people—had been a secret kept by a very few within the pantheon from the host of their kin. A secret people unsanctioned which the spirits shielded from harm, for as long as they had been able. But no secret remained that way forever.

Tears for the Moon God

No, there was no going back to those times. Too much bloodshed, too much hurt, had been suffered. Too many grudges endured—between the gods, the gods and the spirits, the spirits among themselves. Too much darkness, too much dread, too much fury. What short lived peace may have existed in those times had been dashed to pieces, and though the greatest of those responsible were long gone, sealed or dead, it was to their kin to uphold old grudges, ensure the memory of hatred remained even as the specific details, the *why* behind it, was forgotten.

He arrived before the gate. His gaze fell on the friezes high along the bulkhead, traced a line across. Sirens singing songs in saccharine voices were frozen in time there, bare chested and half-submerged in deep waters. Gulls winged overhead as ships drew anchor in a distant bay. Mountains gnawed at the horizon, under the light of a vague orb that could be the sun or the moon.

His lips turned down at the corners. *Or neither.*

"Fascinating, isn't it?"

He had not noticed the newcomer's arrival, but he supposed that ought not be a surprise. It was the way of pathfinders to hide their steps, when they did not want to be noted by others. More even, it was their nature to arrive unexpectedly, at precisely the place they were needed.

He eyed the pathfinder. A man of the Magura, or perhaps the Sha'ron; he was dark-skinned, his complexion very nearly mirroring the night. He carried a catch pole—one end sporting a wide, leather loop and the other weighted with an iron ball which rested against the glossy flagstones. Streaks of red ochre crossed his chest, and dot scars rode the ridges over his eyes, where his brows had been shaved away. Still more dot scars crossed his chin, a double file descending from his lips.

He sported an earth-tone, linen tunic and breaches, neither of which were common of those two tribes, which he may well have adopted at some time during his decades long tenure in God Uldal's keeping.

He made a studied observation of the frieze, snorted, and turned his attention to Ordein.

"I'm told you want to go somewhere."

Ordein nodded. "Somewhere ill suited to your newer initiates."

"Few places are out of their reach."

"The winds permit no sanctioned road from taking shape where they must travel, Timin." Ordein said. "And what the Empresses abide must naturally be impermanent. Their movements and their domains are not fixed in the way of mountains and forests."

"You wish to go to sea?" Timin's eyebrow shot up precipitously. "Hire a ship."

"Is that any way to…" Ordein cut himself off before he could say something he might regret. He would have preferred Jaunz Faedrin or Suli, if they could have been spared. Timin ever rubbed him the wrong way. "What you do now will help both of us greatly. Your order and mine."

"It's gotten that bad?" Timin's expression turned pensive. He returned to his observation of the frieze. "Do you think times were ever as simple as they appear in those scenes?"

"I confess it is hard to conceive of my god as having ever been happy." Ordein sighed. "He is…erratic. He favors isolation with alarming frequency. He has begun talking to himself when he believes he is alone. The content of those…*conversations*…does not bode well for us."

Adara Yun

"A coming eclipse?"

Ordein said nothing.

"Ah. Then God Uldal will need to be informed."

"As will the others. God Mu, and God Shakh. They will need to call their forces to them, prepare for what may be inevitable."

"Have you any idea where the stair will come down?"

"When he decides, you will be informed."

"I'll ask my god to allow for a pathfinder to remain stationed here." Timin promised him. "Now, where is it you wish to go?"

"To the last person who might talk some sense into him."

Timin chuckled, and the sound made Ordein's blood run cold. "I see, I see." He patted Ordein fraternally on the shoulder. "You must believe I wish for death."

"If she agrees, it will not be you I call on for aid."

"You'll need my god, and who is to say he'll cooperate with you. A lowly acolyte of a rival god."

"The right hand of his oldest friend."

"He has a few of those."

"You have your task." Ordein said indignantly. "Perform it."

Timin hissed through his teeth. "Aren't you feisty today. Okay, then."

He squared himself in front of the gate, a distant look stealing over him as he performed whatever internal operation was necessary to extrude a new path from the ether. The bars of the gate fell away like sand, leaving a clear opening beyond. Within the gate, a new path emerged. Rolling waves boiled away toward endless night in every direction he could see. In the far distance, ship sails slashed across the stars low along the ridge where water met sky. The path opened, and the road it let onto was one to mirror the stars. Valiant, blue stars wended away under the waves, forming a broad, serpentine road, the edges falling into chaos where the krill which gave it shape drifted too far from the main mass of their kind, radiated outward and made the fringes hazy.

Walking the path were ghost entities, humanoid and faceless, and emanating a light to match that of the countless millions of krill. Dozens of them shambled forward, an eerie procession marching toward an unknown destination, and each of them carried a lantern in its upthrust hand.

Timin took him around the hips, guided him forward, and through.

Ibrim marched with the other initiates toward the palace. The procession followed the main thoroughfare through the city, and no few citizens saw fit to take the time to deliver blessings and words of encouragement to them as they followed the acolyte charged with their delivery this day.

Seun walked in his wake, a half step behind him, but his attention was not for where they were going. It seemed he had been through enough of these dosings that the fear of being driven further into madness no longer bothered him. Instead, he kept a watch on the gate behind them, a monolith of suffering Ibrim was not yet ready to confront again.

"What is Master Ordein doing there?" he said, munching absently on a hibiscus calyx.

Ibrim stole a look at the gate on reflex. There was a man clad in white robes, a strange cap with lace netting dangling from it hiding his face. The man's dress was

Tears for the Moon God

far more elaborate than what even the senior most acolytes he had seen wore, lending added weight to his station.

"Who is he?" he turned back to the palace, leaving the man and his acquaintance to their business.

"He's God Ao Nii's right hand. He's responsible for keeping the children out of harm's way during full moon nights."

"Is he now?"

"It's not that I expect you to care." Seun said, picking up on the indifference in Ibrim's tone.

"I take it he doesn't usually come this far into the city."

"Not without an escort. He's usually riding a palanquin, hidden behind a bunch of curtains. His counterpart is like that, too."

A wave of melancholy passed through Ibrim. His shoulders slumped around a longing sigh. "I miss my palanquin."

"I never saw the point in those." Seun said. "What's wrong with your feet. Or a horse. It just seems awkward traveling that way. With a bunch of burly men grunting and shuffling their feet around you."

"Grunting?" Ibrim snorted. "If they were so loud, they would be flogged. It is the highest privilege to carry the weight of your rulers. You must treat it as such."

Seun guffawed. "Are you always this out of touch?"

"Whatever do you mean?"

"Look! They've opened a gate!"

Seun took him by the cheeks, spun him around to see what he was seeing. In the process, he nearly shoved another initiate to the ground.

"Watch it!" the initiate snapped, glaring up at them.

Ibrim barely heard her. The gate's bars were gone, and in their place was a moving, vibrant image of a wide open sea. A glittering path cut across the waves, and a troupe of glowing men marched along it, all holding lanterns high from straight arms.

"Who are *they?*" he hissed.

"No idea. But you need to start walking. You're holding up the procession." Seun said.

Ibrim looked down at his feet. A small gulf had opened up between them as he stared, frozen, at the portal into the open sea. He cussed, turned round and hustled up the line to where the others were still marching.

"This is your fault, you know." He snarled.

"You're the one who was getting all emotional about forcing people to carry you." Seun said, hustling to keep up with him.

"No one was forcing them!"

"So they had nothing better to do than lift your moving bed?"

"It's not like that." He panted, having finally closed the distance.

"Look." Seun gasped. "No one likes royalty, Ibrim. Sure, they like the idea of it. Nobody wants to make the big decisions. But royalty...royalty sucks. The sooner you realize that, the better off you'll be.

"That life is behind you, after all."

"For now."

Seun chuckled. "Ibrim...you live here now. It'll be years before they let you go back home, and even then, you'll be a danger to everyone around you as soon as the

Adara Yun

moon is full."

"What are you saying, Seun?" he said venomously.

"You're a moonkin now." Seun replied. "That's all. A moonkin first, and then *maybe* a prince. Although the way you put it, you weren't going to be king anyway."

Ibrim glared at him. "This conversation is over."

"Okay." Seun twisted around to get a look at the gate again.

That he was completely unfazed by Ibrim's quiet seething made it all the worse. He was right, but he didn't have to be so callous about it. Whether he could go back to his homeland or not, whether his subjects would even recognize his authority when he did, he was still a prince gods damn it. This *peasant* had no right to talk to him like this. No right at all.

The trade winds brushed Ordein's cheeks, stroked his robes and yet left his veil alone. Byr was no fool. He knew well not to interfere with the moonkin, and in particular the two trusted enough among them to sit at God Ao Nii's side. For his part, Ordein took solace in that if Byr was here, the four winds were not, and unlike them, Byr would keep the business of a moonkin come to visit upon a sea spirit to himself.

Ruhanni's ocean was rarely placid in any of its reaches, full of life and energy as it was, but the sky remained clear, the storms far distant. He found firm footing on the path the Lantern Bearers followed, his shoes barely sinking under the surface of the waves. Firm enough footing for a mortal man to walk by, if he could withstand the rolling currents underneath, if he could keep himself from tripping as he marched forward.

So much about the sea was unstable, so much in flux. This path would exist as long as the Lantern Bearers had a reason to march, and when their trek was finished, when they came within sight of some coastal port where safe harbor was possible, they would fall again beneath the waves, their flock of krill scattered against the currents.

"How long do we have?" he asked Timin.

Timin shrugged. "How far are we from shore? Do you see storm clouds on the horizon?"

"No."

"Long enough then."

"You're certain?"

"Not at all."

"Then we should hurry." He trudged on, the living road sucking at his moccasins and making the footing treacherous. Sooner or later, his legs would give out. Fatigue would grip his muscles, and pull him under. He was no acolyte of a water spirit, he could not walk easily on fluid. Few of them could either.

Timin was having an easier time of it. He stepped sure footed, paused at the right times to avoid being carried back by a rolling wave. The lantern bearers provided ample light to see by, which made the going easier, but it was nothing if not frustrating to see that the pathfinder so deftly navigated these waters. To know that he could extend nothing more than bad advice to him in helping him navigate these currents.

"Where is she?" He demanded.

"Watch your tone, now, old man." Timin said.

Tears for the Moon God

"Well?"

"Close. Close enough, anyway." His gaze was on the distant head of the column, where the lead element of the procession served as navigator and guide for them all.

"Strange how quiet they are." Ordein mumbled, taking in one Lantern Bearer after another in quick succession.

"No mouths with which to speak." Timin said absently.

In the middle distance, a gout of white froth burst from the deeps. Mists crashed around a dark, glossy fin which was large enough to be a ship's main mast. The fin cut a graceful arc through cool air, trailing threads of glittering water.

Deep lethargy threatened to pull Ordein down, into deep slumber. He wrenched on the soulbinding power within him, and a granular aura spread across his flesh, waves of healing energy driving back the influence of that creature as its fin slid back under the waves.

He looked to Timin, noted the lag in his steps, the way his eyes fluttered. He spread his influence to embrace him, threads of gray energy twining around him, forming an envelope to drive back the spirit's influence.

"Thank you." Timin gasped. "I thought for sure I was going to fall asleep."

"If you'd have done so here, you would have drowned." Ordein growled. "I can't risk you succumbing to such a fate. But if the Manta is here, the more problematic beasts will not be."

"Safer for that." Timin mumbled.

"Sorry?"

"We're safer for that." He repeated louder.

"Are you okay?"

"I think so."

"Then let's get moving. We have little enough time as it is." He laced his arm under Timin's shoulder, taking up the burden of his weight.

"It'll wear off soon." Timin promised.

"Yes, I suppose it will." Ordein agreed. "Just accept my help for now."

"Gladly."

"Easy now." They trudged onward. *At least it was only that. At least it wasn't something worse.*

Strange to think of a Fang in the depths. To know a mountain spirit of such power was so capable of free movement. There was no telling how far that beast was from its locus of power, and yet its influence remained this potent. Enough to pose a true challenge to two seasoned acolytes of the gods.

He did not like being in these waters. Did not like traveling across any of the three oceans. It was not natural for mortals to travel by sea. Theirs were the mountains and the streams. These vast, depthless waters held too many mysteries, possessed too many ways to bring about a mortal man's destruction.

The sooner we are out of this place the better. He would not be here at all, not having come of his own volition, if he had any choice in the matter. But *she* was here. The only spirit left who Ao Nii trusted absolutely, the only one who might be able to talk him out of the contest he sought. *She* was here, and with her the last hope of stopping what seemed so inevitable. Another clash between the Moon God and the Sun. A deep, festering madness for all of those who had known him. Even the children who had escaped him would not be spared. Even those who had never sworn his vows.

The procession halted before the great gate in the cliff side, beneath the palace in all of its glory. Darkness swallowed the crystal cave, a strange sight in a city in which everything drank in moonlight, in which everything seemed to shine.

It lurched forward in fits and spurts, and Ibrim craned his neck to see what was happening at the head of the column. He had been wondering what this was about since they were called from their barracks, since the acolytes came for them. They had been receiving their doses of seething, scarlet madness in the privacy of their chambers since the day of their initiation. Whatever the reason for their summons, it could not be as simple as that.

Lord Faez A'doelle had become such a regular presence in his life he had almost come to think of the former slave as a friend. There was comfort to be had in familiar faces, and there had been so few of those in his life since he arrived.

The dosing had become easier with every day passing, just as he had promised, but with each new day, his anticipation grew. The last few dosings had been abnormal, as these things went. Nearly every time he had been infected with the aura of madness it had driven him into a deep yet blessedly brief state of depression. Almost of suicidality at times. It was no easy task to hold onto a god's grief, no easy task to contain it. Frantic thoughts had ripped through him, sharp pain, the strong desire to end it; and he was left each time drained, unable even to lift his head as he lay there, reeling, and Priest A'doelle drew his coverlet over his body, tucked it under his chin. As he performed his healing of the bloody scratches where Ibrim had raked ragged nails across his forearms, or dug deep into his thighs, the cuts in his lower lip where he had bitten down on reflex.

But those last few healings...it had not been grief he felt within the embrace of that madness. Not grief, but a frenzied panic, a bone deep fear which refused to surrender for hours after the initial injection. Lord A'doelle had taken to staying by his bedside for all of those hours, running a gentle hand across sweat-slick hair, dabbing at his forehead and cheeks with a clean kerchief.

He had been so grateful.

What is this all about, then? Another test.

The file chugged forward a few steps. The initiate at its head, the tak moran woman he had noted on initiation day, passed into the cave mouth alone. Another initiate sought to follow her, but the acolyte barred his way.

"What's happening?" Seun asked. He bobbed on his toes, trying to overcome his shorter stature to see what Ibrim saw. He looked ridiculous.

"They're letting us through one at a time." He said. "It seems that way anyway."

"I wonder why."

Ibrim shrugged. "An audience, maybe? Or an interrogation."

"They've never bothered to question me and I've been here for months." Seun pointed out.

"I wonder about that frequently." Another acolyte was admitted. The line chugged forward once more. "If you've been here as long as you have, why are you still with *us?*"

"I had to get better first."

"But you're not better."

"Better than I was. It would have been unsafe to let a starving Tului Blood Lord into the general population. Maybe I can't infect other people, but you know how I get at night. I used to be just as bad during the day."

"You tried to eat people?"

Suen scowled at him. "No."

"As good as."

"Not at all. Draining blood isn't the same as chomping on..." he sagged. "I see your point.

"In any case, they wouldn't let me participate in these tests until I was at least well enough to keep myself contained around people. Although, I still get cravings. I guess that's to be expected, isn't it."

"In what way?"

"I can smell their blood. Like a mosquito. Yours. Everyone else's."

"I commend you for your restraint."

The line chugged forward once more.

"It's not like I'd just attack any old person, you know. Even at my worst, I had standards."

"You liked attacking princes?"

Seun made a retching sound. Ibrim rounded on him, ready to scold him for his rudeness.

"I'm sorry." He said, wiping mucus from his lips.

Ibrim glanced toward the ground, noted the tiles, and more importantly his shoes, were dry.

"Sorry, it's just...royals. I had never met one before you. Mostly I fed from peasants. People from the southern kingdoms sometimes stumble across my country's border. We use them as breeding stock."

"Despicable."

"No worse than you people making use of slaves."

He opened his mouth. Shut it again.

"Really, what's the difference between your palanquin bearers and our hapless breeders. At the very least, we have the decency to recognize the horror of our own need. You raise cows for slaughter. We raise people. We still have enough compassion not to put them to work without pay. Some of them are even given the gift of infection if they sire enough offspring. The equivalent of becoming a minor noble in your kingdom."

Nausea ripped through Ibrim's guts. He swooned.

Seun reached out to catch him, and he took an involuntary step back.

Hurt reported in the man like a firecracker, blooming bright and then fading behind a mask of indifference.

Ibrim felt that hurt reflected in him as guilt, knew he had just driven a wedge between them. And this poor man his only real friend.

"I'm sorry." He said. "I didn't mean—"

"It's okay."

"You're sure?"

Seun nodded.

The line chugged forward once more.

"I'm sure your land is beautiful." Ibrim said half-heartedly.

"Yes and no. It would be, but our king...he's a monster. He really is."

"You did say no one likes royalty."

Adara Yun

He chuckled at that, his expression brightening slightly. "I did, didn't I? I suppose now you know why."

"Not really, but I am trying to understand."

Seun smiled up at him, eyes a-light and glimmering like obsidian. "Thank you."

"Yes, well." Ibrim averted his gaze from him. It was awkward, people being vulnerable, threatening to get their feelings on him. He didn't like it one bit.

But he supposed if any lowly peasant absolutely *must* inflict their emotions on him, it would be far worse if it was someone else. He was frequently annoying, and he had taken a meal against his blood once, but he was coming to like the poor fool. To care about him surely not, but there was a middle ground to be had, wasn't there? A king did not feel particularly close to his subjects, but he did feel some responsibility toward them. He supposed a prince could feel something of the kind. Supposed, perhaps, he felt some responsibility for Lufir Al Seun.

He is a nuisance, though. There is no sense denying that. A nuisance and a pest, but likable enough I suppose. Better than these other ones.

The Lantern Bearers froze. Their feet came together in unison, their postures rigid, lanterns swinging in their hand as the waves rolled under them. For a moment, Ordein thought the road would dissolve under his feet, and with it any hope of returning to the God House of the Moon, any hope of surviving. If the seas did not simply swallow him, there were those spirits who inhabited them to do the job. Twelve Fangs riding the depths, submerged so that even their peaks were hundreds of feet below the surface. Predators of many stripes dwelling in the light touched reaches close to the surface and deeper, in those places where light would not touch, where the spirits courted God Mu and called him friend.

For a moment, he believed he would be dragged under the current, but Timin's hand on his shoulder—a light, reassuring squeeze—steadied him.

"They're not done yet." The pathfinder said.

"Good."

At the head of the jagged double file, the seas quaked. Dense waters whorled away and scattered; white crests rode their edges. They hugged the contours of the winding, iridescent road, disturbing the masses of krill, stirring them up and casting them aside, causing the road to narrow until its borders lay under the feet of their sentries.

The Lantern Bearers lowered themselves onto their knees as a deep well formed at the source of the disturbance. They arched their backs, touched their foreheads to the road, lay their lanterns before them and prostrated themselves for the greater spirit in their midst.

He knew the time had come. That the spirit he sought had taken notice.

From the well rose a woman with skin and hair like porcelain. Sea water covered her slender form, the currents whipped into a frenzy and contained like lace fringe along the bodice, quieter waters cascading over her belly, across her hips, down her legs—sheer and yet entrapping clownfish, and angelfish, eels and red kelp, trapping them like textile patterns, drifting and casting illusory shadows against her. Her features were refined, yet cracks as in dry mud crawled over her cheeks and forehead, and her eyes were the unrelieved black of obsidian.

Princess Adara Yun, lone daughter of Empress Ruhanni, stepped sinuously onto the path; and as she did, Ordein slipped his arm free of Timin. He lowered himself onto his knees, touched his forehead to the waters and was prostrate.

Sensibly, Timin followed his example.

Adara Yun glided across the glowing road, white and glowing like the moon shining down from so high above them. Krill were drawn into her flowing gown, lending their light to her, blue stars drifting among the kelp and those fish too small and weak to escape her. She was like the night sky in all of its splendor, like the ocean's very depths in her ferocious beauty.

She stood before them, reached down, cupped Ordein's chin in shockingly warm fingers, and lifted him so that he could do nothing else but see her in her every, ethereal detail and be struck with awe.

"Stand now, both of you." Her voice was melodious, soft and deep, reminding him of the low ringing of temple bells in his homeland.

He obeyed, climbed to his feet. He barely noticed the chill, wet fabric clinging to his shins and torso, where his robes had made intimate contact with the waters, the scattering of krill snarled into the fabric, glimmering to match those contained in her raiment.

"That's it. Good." A faint smile touched her lips. His spine went to water. "Now, what would a moonkin be doing in my mother's domain?" Her gaze traveled over Timin, giving him a moment to breathe, for the muscles in his chest to loosen and his lungs to work more freely. "You must be Uldal's."

Timin nodded vigorously.

She returned to her study of Ordein. "Is it the usual dance, then?"

He nodded. "Yes, your highness."

"How far gone is he?" she asked.

"There is time yet to reclaim him, but it is a close thing. Soon, he will be beyond even your influence."

Her grin broadened, becoming a dark and ugly thing. Her eyes seemed to blaze, yet they remained their eerie, liquid black. "The Right Hand seeks peace, yes? It is your place to calm him."

"It is what I am called to." He agreed.

"But you have failed."

"That remains to be seen."

"Yes, I suppose it does." She let that terrible grin fall. "Nonetheless, you must know he will not come to me of his own will. He will be too embarrassed. Too full of fear. Even in his youth he was never the direct kind. He *hated* violence, in fact."

"Then it should be that he is spared from committing violence against—"

"Do not assume you know him simply because he has allowed you to dip your fingers in that *cursed* cup." Her gaze grew distant. She turned away from him, to ponder the movements of the moon through the endless abyss of the night's sky. "He is pining over it again, isn't he? Dragging it close and pushing it away like a lush in recovery."

"He has been doing so for weeks."

"Then you waited too long." She snapped. "Too much time wasted watching for signs and waiting for certainty to support your suspicions when both were ever present before you.

"He will attack Gorgus soon. You feel it. Do not deny what is plain. In daylight when the Sun God is at his strongest, he will throw himself at him, and drag him out of the sky. Pray they take their contest elsewhere. That you do not witness it. It will be worse than the last time.”

“W-why?” Timin asked.

Ordein shed a warning glare on him. *Rescind your question. Please. For your sake and mine.*

But the question floated between them, and Timin did nothing to call it back.

Moonlight touched her face, a light caress. She smiled, and the smile was that of a woman remembering a dear old friend long deceased, recalling those pleasant memories so complicated by the lingering aftertaste of his taking into that next life, and away from her.

“Because *they* are involved, pathfinder.” She said. “And unlike you, he remembers. He’ll seek to defend them as he has always done, but who can say if he will recognize them in his madness? Who is to say he will know friend from foe when the day comes.”

Timin stole a glimpse at Ordein, his confusion worn on his sleeve.

What do you tell God Uldal when we have left this place? That is what you want to know. What do you tell your god? That it becomes increasingly certain God Ao Nii will turn on God Gorgus in the coming days, certainly. But what of these others, who the spirit will not name. Will you ask me what I know of them? Will you hunt after what is plain.

“I cannot help you in this, moonkin.” She whispered. “You are too late.”

She glided away, up the column. In her wake, the Lantern Bearers rose in pairs and trios.

Timin cleared his throat. “We should get out of here.”

“I think so, yes.” Ordein said absently. *And just like that, our last hope has gone. What can we do, then? He will not be contained. I fear we will not be, either.*

Timin opened a gateway before them. Within it, the shifting path was cast aside, and the city and the palace on its bluff in the God House of the Moon replaced it, in all of its cursed splendor, its glorious putrescence.

Ibrim’s turn had arrived. He stood before a veil of unrelieved darkness. Even standing at the cave’s mouth, he could not see anything beyond it. Matte blackness looked back at him, an unbroken abyss.

The acolyte stood at his right, one arm thrust out to bar him entry. Seun had long quieted, the excitement of Ordein’s unexpected presence behind them now, and the imminence of his own passage into that chamber keeping him calm and compliant.

The acolyte craned his neck toward the void as if listening for something he could not hear. He retracted his arm.

“Go now.” He said.

Ibrim hedged. He was not ready to confront whatever peculiarity awaited him in the chamber. After the last time, he had few illusions left about the nature of that place. Trust was a thing in short supply for these acolytes, for the hall itself.

“Go!”

He jumped. Stepped forward.

The veil pressed in cold around him, and darkness swarmed in from all sides, leaving him blind to everything around him.

He stepped forth, one foot in front of the other, navigating by touch. Cold terror leaked down the back of his neck, into his chest and outward. He kept on, knowing

Tears for the Moon God

well if he paused in his pursuit of whatever lay within this chamber's embrace, he would never start again.

A faint, pulsing glow broke the darkness somewhere far ahead of him, there and gone like a heartbeat. He stepped, and stepped, and stepped again, forced himself to make for the source of that light.

Another pulse, brighter than the first.

Cold hands wrapped around his ankles, clambered over his shins and thighs. They slid under his initiate's robes, pressed firm against bare skin, too many to count and all of them like ice. He screamed, kicked uselessly to get rid of them, and they remained. More hands joined the first, wrapped around his flesh, pawed at his torso, pinched his flanks. With each new hand came added weight, as if he dragged slack bodies in his wake, dragged them ever onward toward that strange altar pulsing and strobing in the distance.

The chamber was empty of sound except for the wet slap and rubbery squeal of those hands latching on and then being dragged against his skin. The air was eerily still, leaving just the feeling of those loose-flowing robes and the hands traveling over him underneath.

He lifted his leg to step forward, and those hands yanked it back down, keeping him frozen in place. The altar pulsed, granular, cloud-gray light interpolated with white orbs and spangled patterns coruscating from the source, washing over him like a powerful wind as he stood there in his place.

Animal panic welled up within him, but he could not summon the nerve to cry out. He was silent before that altar, still and blind, and helpless.

The light ebbed, drew in on itself. It oozed across the floor, granular energy pulsing and rippling unnaturally as it ran through stubborn darkness and toward him, waves rolling ashore at high tide, spilling over sand where the land met the sea.

There within the embrace of that aura was a man clad in white silk, the sleeves flowing and splayed across the floor around him. Glossy, black hair fell over his shoulders and swam around him across the floor. His eyes were as black as the abyss woven between them, and his skin was the white of glazed porcelain. His features were refined, almost feminine, and it was hard to discern what kind of build he must have under so much loose-fitting silk, but he suspected this man was thin as a wraith; starved, though he could not fathom how he had become that way.

Black eyes found Ibrim, settled on him, and he could not look away.

"I know you." He said. "You came here once before, seeking my aid."

Comprehension donned on Ibrim, and he gave in to the roving, discomfiting hands, allowed them to drag him onto his knees, so that he could bow before his new lord and master, the Moon God, Ao Nii.

"Your Holiness." He said. "My sincerest apologies for any rudeness you might have suffered."

"Quiet. I need to think." Ao Nii snapped. "It occurs to me you could not have suffered the same fate which drew you here before. Your tormentor is not alive. In the traditional sense.

"Why do you want my power, prince?"

"It is pride." Ibrim said to the floor. "My first brother will be made king. My second will be master at arms. My sisters will be left to manage the day to day affairs of the interior. Maintaining the treasury and the like. What, then, is left for me?"

Ao Nii made a strange sound in his throat, like a cat giving warning to an invader in its territory to flee. A guttural sound, it sent a tremor across Ibrim's neck, down the length of his back and into his hips, where the dregs of it stayed, a perianal tingle.

"Are you worthy of me? As you are now." He demanded.

"I hope so." Ibrim whispered.

"You were once, but you were disloyal. You betrayed my trust in those days, when you came to understand I could not give you what you wanted. I *would not.*" God Ao Nii intoned. "I wished to guide you away from your path, and you refused me. Without *him* your motivation is weaker, but then...perhaps, with him absent, you will not seek to abandon me again."

"I will not abandon you, my god." Ibrim said forcefully. But he was confused. He had been in this room before, certainly. Perhaps that was what the Moon God meant, but he did not think so. Something in his tone suggested a deeper history than what lived between them, echoes of catastrophes of the personal kind. Events he had lived through, had witnessed in the flesh, yet if there were such bitter memories to be had, they were not within him. Nothing in his past would suggest he had any tie to this creature, save what he had earned in climbing his staircase.

"We will see." Ao Nii said.

Ibrim chanced a subtle regard for his god. From his vantage he could see nothing higher than his chest. The god held a crystal goblet in his off hand, twisted it between his forefinger and his thumb. The goblet was filled with a substance that reminded him of pond water, murky with algae and silt.

He doesn't mean for me to drink that, does he?

"I suspect you will come into my gifts quite rapidly this time. Your soul will remember, even if you do not." The glass stilled in his hand. He set it aside, and it was swallowed by darkness. "If you survive my test. I hope you will."

The darkness crashed in from every side, denying him sight of his god once more, and he was ejected forcefully on a high wind. He slammed into a distant wall, head and neck cracking against rough stone.

He fell into a dreamless sleep.

Ao Nii climbed to his feet. He plucked the crystal chalice containing the last of his lover's memories from its place on the floor. Through his eyes, the chamber appeared as it always had. A vaulted stage occupied the back of the chamber, and a monolith carved over in ancient runes stood sentry atop it. The domed ceiling culminated in portrayals of his closest allies, frescoes depicting elusive Shakh, Mu and Uldal, and the only man he had ever loved.

Heiman, what would you do if you were in my place. If I had died and you survived me?

He sighed, and crossed the chamber to where the acolyte's body lay in a crumpled heap, his head lolling limply over sagging shoulders, bony wrists resting limp against gray floor tiles.

This one will be a problem.

He lifted the acolyte's chin gingerly, let it drop. He ran his fingers across the back of the poor fool's head.

Granular energy leaked from his fingertips into the wounds. They rippled. Blood drew back into his skull, leaving his hair dry and clean. The wounds inched closed. Within a handful of breaths, it was as if those wounds had never been.

He hauled his acolyte onto his shoulder with his free hand, and carried him out of the chamber.

Along the wall were the corpses of too many failures. More than a dozen so far, and his work was not done. Those were the liars, the cowards, the ones who had refused to approach his altar. He had no use for such feeble creatures.

One day, these acolytes may have to drive him back, work with the others to push him into his God House, away from the land where he might do harm to the mortals he so cherished. He might kill a few of them when that day came, even if they were strong enough to resist him for a time.

The world around him waxed with power, but he had always been a weak god. In times like these, when gods like Gorgus—*Murderer! Whore!*—and Uldal grew in power with every passing year, he waned. These were no times for darkness and gloom. He knew the contest he wished to have with the God of the Sun would be an exercise in futility, yet he was swift reaching the end of his rope.

Gorgus followed him, chased him endlessly across the sky. He kept his vigil over this house and all of its people as if he had not created the conditions for this madness to spread with his own hands. As if he had not been singularly responsible for Ao Nii's grief.

As if he did not kill my Heiman himself.

And now the bastard had gone and sided with Lanfin and his sympathizers. Had elected to side with those evil, inhumane creatures Liandal and Tirulain. He did not need to see the evidence before him to know his brother's mind. Nor did he need the cooperation of Ji Hara and her horde of rodents to know those other three had joined hands. Their stink was all over these happenings, from the recall of Sao Njack to the arrival of this very prince at his doorstep.

And he knew what they wanted. What all of them wanted so badly they would violate the rules they themselves had set in place all those many thousands of years ago.

They tossed a liability in my lap, didn't they? He squeezed the acolyte's flank. *But there may be a way I can use him. If he proves to be made of stronger stuff than the broken mess Lanfin stole away.*

He chuckled, thinking back to the events that had led Ibrim Alghoul here. *Savagery. Pure and simple. How strange to think I would find myself liking someone as hungry for blood as the late emperor. What a terrifying, fascinating, endearing individual he was.*

It was no mystery to him why the Dragon of the East was recalled, either. His wolf had been a terror in his own right, had done unspeakable things before Sao's recall, but his sins had been localized. Isolated.

If Dupec Safar was the kind who might set a continent ablaze to see his ends through, Sao Njack was the kind to set their world on fire. And the poor fool had nearly done just that.

He adjusted his grip on the cup. His fingers vibrated with adrenaline as it slipped a hair too far, threatening to spill its precious contents.

If there was ever a man who could take up Heiman's legacy...he may have found him at last.

His lips broke open around a manic grin, every tooth exposed, his cheeks

Adara Yun

tingling around suppressed laughter. It had been too long since he had felt so alive. There were stirrings throughout the world now of a kind he had not seen in so long he had forgotten what true uncertainty felt like. The most mercurial of the Elder Gods were in the Waxing World, playing games whose ends no one knew, whose shape would not become evident for some time yet; and he suspected he was a pawn in them. That he was being used, just as the Lesser Gods used their acolytes in the games they played with each other.

If the Elder Gods saw fit to involve him in these, his most unstable times, then their ends must be cataclysmic indeed. But he would not make their games easy for them. He would not allow them control over him.

This one will be key, I think. If Gorgus can be made to step aside, then Lanfin will be mine. If Lanfin is left vulnerable, then perhaps I can finally have peace. But one step at a time. Find a purpose for this boy. Set him in the right place. He will be needed soon enough, but first he must be tested. Beyond what can be accomplished here, in the safety of my house.

Ibrim stirred. He found himself in an unfamiliar chamber, which was nothing like the side chamber Facz A'doclle had taken him into after his first visit to the cavernous hall within which he had met his god what must have been some hours ago.

He was not the only one waking. Yawns escaped from several mouths. Joints popped and crackled. Robes whispered across even flagstones. He righted himself and stretched, tipped his head back and forth, and looked around him. The chamber's walls were as opaque as those in the audience hall, but the material they were made from was a clean white. It might have been marble, but it was too slick to be anything of the sort. It was strangely glassy, polished, free of any visible dust. The floors were tiled with glass, which looked down into depthless space, a world of stars and darkness.

His heart thundered in his chest for a few, brief moments, until his brain could catch hold of some semblance of rationality, and he was able to convince himself that the floor was very much stable. That the view was an illusion, and he was not seated atop a thin pane of glass, which was all that separated him from plummeting into the endless vacuum of space.

When he had calmed himself, he panned over the other figures gathered there. There were perhaps fifty of them. There had been so many more awaiting their turn to enter the chamber. He wondered what had happened to them. If they were simply in another room and waiting for the same events to unfold as would here. He suspected they were not. That they had failed the test laid before them by their god. That they might very well be dead.

Seun was huddled in a tight ball next to him. He looked at peace and in deep sleep, which was a departure from those fitful nights when he could only cry out in pain, when he must convince himself he would not starve for his lack of access to fresh blood. Ibrim had heeded his warnings not to come to him in the night, but he had been sorely tempted more than once. Those screams would go on for hours. It was a wonder his friend—*how in the name of our god did that happen*—slept at all.

Here he was, fast asleep and vulnerable. A man a spare few years younger than Ibrim himself, if appearances did not lie, who was perfectly, entirely, and for the first time since he had met him, at peace. He reached toward him. Reached for

Tears for the Moon God

flowing hair, to draw it out of his face, push it back behind his ear, and froze as a vaguely familiar voice cut through the relative quiet.

"Leave him be. He needs his rest. He does not get much of it as it is, does he."

Ibrim's gaze shifted to the man who spoke. He found himself pulled in by red-rimmed black eyes, suffused with a madness which swam just beneath the surface, which was suppressed for now, but would be for who knew how much longer. He shied away from God Ao Nii's gaze; and, retracting his hand, noted a slight quirk in his god's lips, an easing of his posture which did not appear the result of his obedience.

"You were drawn to him before, as well. Do you know that? If Fate must write in her diary of extraordinary feats by extraordinary creatures, it is mine to enjoy the smaller stories, those chance caught intimate moments between such ordinary people."

Ibrim suppressed the urge to scowl. He kept his features even, and maintained his silence. It was not easy. *Ordinary? I'm a prince of Tulakh!*

But he understood his god's point. He did not over much like the idea that he might be in any way close to Seun, that he might truly care about him, but he *had* decided he cared for him. In his own way. On his own time. It was not at all beyond the pail of expectation that God Ao Nii might pick up on his feelings toward the Tului commoner.

"Even the great and powerful have their moments. The ones that never make it into their histories, the tales written about them. I recall a time, it seems so long ago now, when I felt such kinship with another man. I knew, for the first time, I think, true and pure love as we sat at riverside, casting lines into the water, stringing earthworms onto hooks. It was no grand thing. We made no proclamations of our intent. We didn't have to. I knew him, and he knew me; and in that moment, as we sat there in the quiet of a mountain valley, patiently waiting for fish to tug on our lines, I knew I had stumbled blindly onto the very thing his father had spoken of so often, which I had never understood. It is a thing for which there are no words, I think. Your people have many for it, but none truly describe it."

In his periphery, Ibrim saw him make a staying gesture, as if to say he understood he was being far too vulnerable himself, that he may be making Ibrim uncomfortable. And he was. Whatever Ibrim felt for Seun, he was not inclined to call it love. Certainly not of the romantic kind. Not anything like what his god was describing.

A light chuckle from Ao Nii compelled his attention back to him. He was so much larger than life. He took up so much space in Ibrim's view, and yet to look at him...he was no larger than a common man. Tall for one, sure, but not so much as to be noteworthy. In every way, he looked human, and if his dress and the way he maintained himself spoke to a time long passed, then it was only expected that he should put on display the vestiges of a culture he felt comfortable with. Which spoke to him. Whether it be alive and hail or dead and buried in so many layers of silt.

Seun stirred, spread himself out. He yawned and stretched arms and legs in a way that reminded Ibrim of the cats that prowled Tulaen's palace, the mousers.

Ao Nii's gaze roved over the gathered mortals, those who had passed his test. He nodded, as Seun righted himself, and rubbed the sand out of his eyes.

"Good. You've all awoken, then." The god said.

Adara Yun

Seun looked about himself. His gaze settled on Ibrim, and he grinned. "You're here! Which means you must have passed."

He surged forward and embraced Ibrim. And Ibrim pushed him away more forcefully than he intended. He chuckled lightheartedly at that, and the former prince did not miss the mirth in their god as he set his focus on them once again.

"You have all passed the final test you will endure in my God House." God Ao Nii said. "Those of you who survive your descents into madness will have your places among my acolytes. But I have not gathered you here to congratulate you, to stoke your egos, nor to give you a false sense of security.

"I must apologize to all of you. If it were not for my grief, and all that has come with it, you would not know the burdens you have suffered. If not for me, you would never have encountered the terrors you did on the climb. I am sorry for that. And more, I am sorry I cannot simply say now you have arrived here it is over. Now you have been through your trials, it is done. When the next full moon arrives, you will all encounter a madness like you have never felt in your lives. I am responsible for that, too. Years from now, when you have learned to command that madness, it will become your duty to force me away from the world below, and I am sorry for that, too.

"My grief has never known an end. It had its beginning, which you know well by now, in the death of someone I cared deeply for."

Ibrim noted the way he looked down at the crystal chalice in his hands. The same one he had in his possession in the chamber beyond. The one filled with pond water.

"I suppose it does not help any of you to know how deeply I loved that man. Nor to know he was mortal, like all of you." His voice took on a warble with those last words. He cleared his throat, avoiding all of their staring eyes.

Ibrim felt a pain in his chest whose source he could not quite identify. He felt for this god, suspected some part of his own emotional turmoil was related to a kind of symmetry in their fates. Here was a god who felt guilt, and guilt for the people he hurt, even as he was above them, or should be. Here was a prince who had led a cozy life in an opulent castle while down on the streets, many of his people suffered, and struggled one day simply to make it to the next. He had buried those feelings of guilt so deep he thought they must have died away. It was his penchant for empathy, his ability to comprehend *why* the lower castes of Tulakka society did suffer, that brought Ibrim to believe his brother, Hassan, would make a better king than the first in line for succession. And though he would like to believe himself above it all, incapable of feeling for the peasantry anything but contempt; there had been times, behind the sheer veil of his palanquin, when he had seen those desperate, dirty faces, and thought to himself: *there must be a better way.*

"I cannot promise any of you a happy life, but know this. I have allowed my doors to be cast open, my staircase to touch the earth, to inspire hope. I have allowed it also to encourage others to take up this distinction. That they are the first line of defense against me. When I am driven over the edge. That *you* will stop me from killing and maiming the very people I so love, because that is my choice. If I must be driven so often into madness, if so much else must be unforgivable, at least I have brought and given strength to a people who might keep me in check. Until I can regain my faculties again."

Tears brimmed in Ibrim's eyes. There was not fear in his heart but true sorrow.

Tears for the Moon God

Here was a god who understood with perfect clarity that he was a detriment to the mortal races. Who understood he could not but harm them in the worst imaginable ways. But here, too, was a leader—so like his brother—who sought to mitigate that damage in whatever way he could, to protect the multitude at the expense of the few. Who might even spare those few such turmoil, if he had any choice in the matter at all.

Ibrim watched God Ao Nii's lieutenants exchange words before the entrance to the palace as he was escorted away. Faez A'doelle had been charged with his escort, and a dozen others followed behind the acolyte in a loose cluster.

Seun walked at Ibrim's shoulder. He was not his usual jovial, frenetic self. Rather, he looked as though he had been through an ordeal. He was gaunt, his cheeks lacking some of the fat he was so accustomed to, and in those hollows, the waxy cast of his pallid skin, he was made to look older by perhaps twenty years. As if he had aged that much in the span of a handful of hours.

He wondered if this was the effect of battling his curse, but he did not ask. It seemed wrong to. As if in asking, in concerning himself with this man's health, he would be pulling aside a curtain, revealing an intimate secret Seun would just as soon no one knew.

There's no questioning that. I would be exposing him as some kind of freak. Someone who might even be contagious. The rest of these people would shun him, then. If they haven't already.

He shook his head. Seun's fingers wrapped around his forearm, held on too loosely. He looked down at him, noticed the labored breathing, the way his lips had grown rough and cracked. His steps had become drawn out, his feet barely leaving the ground.

Faez A'doelle set a brisk pace which Seun was having difficulty keeping up with. Ibrim slowed, and Seun's fingers slipped away, leaving ample space for a chill to inhabit his flesh. To leave him feeling as if something shapeless and incomprehensible had been torn away from him.

"Seun?" he said.

Seun missed a step. He pitched forward, and Ibrim rushed in to catch him.

"What's wrong?"

Seun shook his head. He whispered something, but the words came out too low for Ibrim to hear.

"I'm sorry. I can't understand..."

Seun pawed his robes. He lost his balance, and the bulk of his weight bared down on Ibrim's arms, leaving him the burden of keeping the Tului boy upright.

Wrinkles creased his forehead, deepened substantially with every heartbeat. His cheeks began to sag. Folds cut into his neck around his voice box, and the tendons which were barely noticeable there before became obvious; traced bold, sloping lines from the edges of his mandible to the join in his collarbones.

He was losing...volume? Depth? The effect was strange. In life pouring from this man to feed his curse, he had begun to deflate, lose vibrancy. He was like a wilting flower, withering in hot sun and humid air.

Faez drew up short fifty paces ahead of them. The other acolytes had kept pace with him, and he signaled for them to remain where they were as he doubled back to examine his flagging charges.

Adara Yun

He took up the burden of Seun's weight, at the same time pushing Ibrim out of the way. He eased him onto the flagstones, in the middle of the road. On the fringes, denizens of the God House paused to make observations of the anomaly. Most dismissed the affair and went about their way, but a few lingered. Watched from the wings as so many in his own court were wont to whenever there was fodder for gossip to be had. Some things were universal. Reassuring and rude were two sides of the same coin. He was not sure what to make of their interest. Especially now, when they must know as well as any of these new initiates or their handlers what was coming.

This more unusual drama may well have come as a relief to them.

"What's wrong with him?" Ibrim said, watching as a granular aura crawled over Faez, gray as clouds in moonlight.

"He's sick." Faez said low enough that he alone would hear. "He has been fighting this curse a long time." He reached into an inner pocket in his robes, produced a tiny, ridged fruit of a kind Ibrim had seen once before, on the night he had barged into Seun's rooms.

He pressed the fruit to Seun's desiccated lips. Seun's eyes rolled into his head. His lips worked, but they would not open wide enough to admit the fruit. His teeth were locked together behind them.

Faez retracted the calyx. He popped it in his own mouth and chewed.

"Hibiscus?" Ibrim said, the name of that fruit coming back to him too late.

"The plant...is outlawed in his home country." Faez said as he worked the calyx between his teeth. "Because it contains a high volume of iron. They don't make use of raw iron in their kitchenware, either, because they risk some of it leeching into their food if it rusts."

He reached into his mouth and removed the chewed up mass. "These are far more palatable than rust or blood, but they don't work as well as either. Blood fuels the curse. Raw iron...hibiscus...they weaken it. The infusion is too direct. And there are other compounds in hibiscus that help to wean these creatures of the blood poison, as well. Things that compel the healthy cells to regenerate."

He pressed the wad into Seun's cheek, and retracted his fingers as Seun's teeth unclenched. He managed to win free before they came down again.

"Strange, isn't it?" Faez looked up at him.

He nodded.

Faez reached into his robes and liberated a handful of the fruits. He passed them to him. "Take them."

Ibrim held out his hands, and Faez planted the wad into them.

"You two are close?"

"I wouldn't say—"

"You give him one of these if he starts showing signs of withdrawal. Until the curse has been broken, he will be reliant on them. It will be some time yet before it is."

"But these can break it."

"Not on their own. Not if the victim continues to imbibe blood."

Ibrim grimaced. *How far did I set him back that night?*

He pocketed the calyxes.

Seun's color was beginning to return. The wrinkles in his forehead and cheeks were beginning to recede. He was regaining some of his fullness. As his adam's

Tears for the Moon God

apple bobbed up and down, worked to draw the chewed up calyx, its juices, into him. His eyes fluttered open.

"Wh...what happened?" he asked.

"Have you been following your diet?" Faez asked.

"Y-yes." His voice cracked.

"To the letter? No blood of any kind? No meat?"

"No." Seun said.

"Then perhaps this is just the natural effect of being afflicted by so much of our god's power all at once." Faez said thoughtfully. "We'll keep you away from the palace for now." He looked at the parapets and towers, its domes and wide arches. "There isn't much reason for you to go that way, anyway. You've gained his approval already."

He gestured to Ibrim. "Help me."

Together, they helped Seun to his feet. "Come. You have my permission to take rest for the rest of the day. Both of you do."

"T-thank you, Priest A'doelle."

Faez regarded him over his shoulder. He snorted, and then marched away.

Storm the Keep

A bonfire glow rose up in the distance. Silhouetted in its embrace, figures marched along tight lanes between camp tents. Thick clods of white smoke drifted into the sky. The Tului were not interested in hiding their presence. What need should they have for stealth? They must know where the Gil Garo were. They must feel they had nothing to fear from them.

Their raid in the night had gone off well for them. They had taken few casualties, could even now wield their power against the tribe with savage efficacy. They might even delight in the prospect of a strike in force from their enemy, a chance to display their might on home turf, where the Gil Garo would be disadvantaged.

But they would not expect a raid of this nature. A small party infiltrating in stealth, a hit and run with a specific target in mind, with whom their command structure might be destabilized.

At least, Bora hoped it would.

The odds *were* stacked against them. The Tului camp was far larger than she had assumed. Such a small force had been composed for the initial attack. She had assumed they prioritized mobility on the way to some predetermined destination where they would regroup with the larger force, but it seemed her assumptions, the assertions of the chiefs, had been grossly overconfident.

The camp was a sprawling, well organized complex. Trenches had been dug into the drifts and ice and snow cleared away to form a web of channels which would allow for an ease of mobility for their forces if they needed it. This was not a ragtag band of untrained soldiers. This was a war camp in truth, comparable to any she had seen from Ruc or the Jahhad Empire. Pickets were staked outside of tents and horses were bound to them, dashing any notion she had of them being a force exclusively composed of infantry. If these tall, bulky stallions were an indication, at least some of the Tului were skilled riders, further disadvantaging the ten Gil Garo closing in on their camp's borders.

Gulang signaled the company to slow their pace, and she dragged on her horse's reigns, bringing it from a swift canter to a trot as the others did the same. He turned his horse westward, following a bone chilling breeze, and drew to a halt a short way off.

The others gathered around him, assembling their horses into a rigid line.

He observed the wide line of tents, the ditch before them which was filled with dry weeds, a defense that bore an eerie similarity to the trenches the Tipik had erected around their quarantine zone.

"They'll have sentries out, watching for invaders." He said.

"Then we should leave our horses." Berni said.

"We'll be at a greater disadvantage without them." Akhi protested.

"We may have to take that risk." He responded. "Can you pick them out, Akhi?"

Sircha drew her horse forward. "No need. There are posts there." She pointed to the northwest edge of the war camp. "There." She pointed closer to the center, and then at regular interval from there to the east end of the camp. "There, there, and there."

Akhi's gaze fell on her. He seemed impressed. "They'll have other defenses."

"They'll notice if we eliminate their eyes." Gaulakh said.

"It will take time." Gulang said. "Which favors us. Can either of you identify any messengers."

"By their movements," Akhi said. "There are four, all moving away from the sentries."

"When they are out of sight, let me know."

Akhi and Sircha both nodded.

"They're gone." Akhi said after a moment.

"Do you believe they know we're here?"

"If their master is a dark spirit, there is a chance they can see us even at this distance. But their actions do not give me that impression. If they have seen us, I do not believe they know what they are looking at."

"Then the rest of you will feign a retreat, come around to the northwest side of the camp. I will incapacitate the sentries on that side." He said. "Guruhl, you will take helm until I have rejoined you."

"There is a pen near that outpost." Sircha said. "The kind used for livestock. Their are humans inside."

"Captives?" Gulang asked.

"I don't know." She said.

"They smell different than the Tului." Akhi added. "Healthier."

Impressive. Bora thought. *To be able to detect anything from this distance. Is this what decades with a god does to you?*

"Investigate it. But do not get closer than is necessary. If they are ours, we will liberate them."

"And if they are not?" Guruhl asked.

"Leave them." Gulang said.

"Understood." He said.

"Go." Gulang commanded. "It's time I shut their eyes."

Guruhl brought his horse around. "You heard the man!" He kicked it into a canter, and led the troop away.

Bora chanced a look over her shoulder at the chief as they left. He straightened in his saddle, and a frenzied aura rolled out of him, like thrashing currents, coruscating waves of amber.

He let loose a loud, sonorous cry, and a surge of emotion built in her. A feeling as if she could accomplish any feat she set herself to, as if nothing in the world could touch her. Wrath and confidence built in her soul, and had it not been for Guruhl's position at the helm, for his insistence on maintaining his steady, neutral pace, she would have kicked her horse into a gallop then, and charged headlong into the camp.

The sensation ebbed, settling into her like a warm wind, and she was enlivened.

"He has their attention." Akhi called back from his position ahead of her.

"Then why are they seated?" Sircha asked.

"Because they have ceased to believe we are dangerous." Guruhl said. " Your father has taken their fear into himself, and eased their minds. It is the power of his voice."

He brought them around and northward, striking straight for the camp's western flank. He kicked his horse into a gallop then, and they charged straight for the trench.

They closed moments later, horses leaping over the wide trench and rumbling across the other side. A wild aura flashed into being around Guruhl, churning, a vibrant shade of orange like sunset. He reigned his horse in almost at the feet of the sentry there, and lashed out. Sunset orange energy pounded the child-like Tului, knocked him flat on his back. The Tului was catatonic, his eyes open and searching, his body refusing to move.

Berni swung from her horse while it was still galloping. She rolled across hard ground, a scimitar in her outstretched hand, and took the sentry's head from his shoulders. Guruhl turned his horse around and returned at a trot. The others amassed around the fast aging corpse.

Bora watched as the man's youth leaked out of him, as wrinkles creased his forehead, his cheeks pooled around his chin and his neck sunk inward. A short distance off, Berni punched her sword into a snowbank. Guruhl took the reigns of her horse as he passed it, and brought it back to her.

He looked down at the decrepit body. His gaze shifted to the head.

"That was short-sighted." He growled. "You could have been exposed."

"He's dead." She said sharply.

"He was in hand." Guruhl growled.

Gulang's voice had died away, and he was closing in from behind. In moments, his horse was jumping the trench, and he was wrenching on the reigns to drive it to a stop.

He came back around and looked over the sentry's body, then up at Berni, who was returning the scimitar to a sheath attached to her saddle.

He found Bora, then, a grim cast to his features.

A Tului man emerged from a nearby tent, a youth of perhaps twenty. His gaze fell on them, and he turned to run away.

Berni's hand whipped out. Melt water ran across her palm, whipped out like a blade, its edge frothing madness, and took the enemy in his flank. At the same time, Saafha dropped from his horse.

The Tului keeled sideways, blood welling from the wound. Saafha pelted after him, shifted course to catch him on the side that was not bleeding, and snatched the man up by his hair. Sickly, green energy oozed across the back of his hand. A darker miasma leaked from the Tului's head, joined the mass of green ooze and settled into his skin, blackening the back of his hand. The darkness faded, and he

Tears for the Moon God

tossed the Tului soldier away.

"Can you tell me where your leader is?" he asked.

The Tului rolled onto his back, winced and clapped his hand to his side. "Which one?"

"Both, I think." Saafha said.

Bora looked into the man's face. His eyes were unfocused, but for the distance she could not see more than that.

"The Crow is at the command post. The Scarlet Baron is in his tent, feeding."

"Feeding?"

"The Crow demands we ration our stock until we reach home, but Baron Keirn does not abide his orders. He demands fresh blood. It is why the pen is one short."

Several of the Gil Garo exchanged looks of disgust. Berni spat on the ground.

Gulang's expression was stone.

The soldier jabbed a finger eastward. The edge of a low, wooden fence was just visible where two lanes crossed. "It is not my fault. I told him he shouldn't. Do not tell the Crow."

He looked on the point of weeping, as if he suspected Saafha was a superior officer and would report his indiscretion to this Crow. As if he believed his punishment for enabling this Scarlet Baron to do as he pleased would be severe.

"I tried to stop him—"

"That is of no consequence just now." Saafha cooed. "Where is Baron Keirn's tent? I'd like to have a word with him."

"Please do not mention me to him. He will be angry." The soldier gasped.

"He will not know who I have spoken to, I promise." Saafha said. "Now, please tell me where I can find the Baron."

The soldier twisted his neck. His free arm rose, and he pointed up a north-faring passage. "That way. Close to the heart of the camp. You will see the banner staff. He will be east of it in his tent. It is red. You will have a hard time missing it.

"Can you tell him to stop taking the livestock? He will not listen to us."

Saafha left his side and returned to where the rest of them were waiting. He looked up at his father, seated tall in the saddle. "We'll go now, if you have no objections."

"Go." Gulang said.

Bora swung down from her horse. She guided it to the chief.

"We'll go on foot. We'll be less likely to draw attention that way." She looked pointedly at Saafha. Clad in war paint as he was, it would be hard enough to avoid notice without offering the enemy a better vantage point to see him.

"As you wish." Gulang said.

"Remember your role, chief." She intoned.

A curt nod told her she was understood. She joined Saafha, and they marched away together.

Bora's chosen hunters had all gone into the war camp. Gulang had chosen a position close to its edge. If they needed to make a hasty retreat, it would not take long to win clear. He did not want to take any chances.

Kachukh stood behind him, in the center of the circle he had carved into the earth, according to Bora's specifications. It rankled him that she should have such influence over the events to unfold here. Even more that he should have to be here,

Storm the Keep

blind to what was happening in the field, tending to a pack of horses when he should be doing something more useful.

He wanted blood. Wanted the Tului to suffer, but at his hands. Not at hers. Not at his sons' or his daughter's. He wanted to seize one of them, and then another, and another, and watch the life leave their eyes as he pulled his scimitar out of their chest. He wanted revenge, to avenge the death of Karsa. But he must remain here, feeding nothing to those flames.

She had made good choices. He may suck his teeth at them, but she had seen the strengths of everyone in their party, everyone she was aware of anyway, and had formulated a strategy with Sarri's guidance—he was certain it was not the other way around—which had the potential to work. But he did not understand the nature of her power. Not fully. It was not a common choice among the Gil Garo to seek apprenticeship to a god, and the one she had chosen.

Conniving son of a bitch.

Sarri may trust her, but he was not as sure of her. She was an acolyte to one of the worst and cruelest gods in the pantheon. God Tirulain had seen something in her character that he *liked*, which should give them all reason for concern. Should have from the moment she declared her choice, from the very moment she set out on pilgrimage. He was not even sure where God Tirulain's house was. How much of the world she had seen in her pursuit of him.

Going far from home could change someone's loyalties, lead them to believe something of their own people they would never have concluded had they stayed closer to home.

But he was being unfair. As he stood at the edge of the circle, with Kachukh behind him stroking his horse's snout and showing all of the gentle care that had led him to believe the boy was not cut out for battle, he faced a reckoning. He was jumping at shadows, placing blame for what had happened to his family on everyone but the person who had failed him.

Had I done better.... But he could not follow that path. He could not allow himself to venture into the warrens of despair, the bleak places that hid in plain sight and beckoned a man to succumb to his own weakness. Those paths led nowhere he could afford to go.

Somewhere far afield, the first detonations thundered. More followed in quick succession from several strategic targets throughout the camp. Guruhl had done his job. Even now he would be making his way back to their rendezvous point, at a slow pace. He had little to fear from these Tului.

Clouds of white smoke billowed outward from the sources of those blasts, fat columns rising high in the air. The west-faring breeze swept them onward, diffusing the smoke, increasing its efficacy by dispersing it over a wider range.

Opium. He snorted.

"What is it, father?" Kachukh asked, coming up to him. "Has it begun?"

"Stay inside the circle, Kachukh."

"I don't see what good it does—"

"Bora must think highly of you. She has made you into the most important piece in her game."

Kachukh drew up short at the edge of the circle, a foot or two behind his father. "I don't believe she likes me much."

"It's not about being friendly, son. One of the things you must learn in this life, if you are to rise to your station among the Kachin. It does no good for your sect to place friendships higher than utility when you seek to form your strategies. On a summer raid, there will always be risks, but you will jeopardize your entire raid every time if you seek to replace those whose abilities are of use with those whose company you enjoy.

"Sometimes, the former will become the latter. Seldom, the latter becomes the former. Most often, those latter kind become dead."

He felt his youngest son's eyes on his back, knew he was contemplating his words. What they meant.

"She held me back." He said.

Gulang watched the clouds of opium smoke drift. Watched as bursts of scarlet light began to radiate from near those places. He had chosen the pens. Akhi's scent tracking abilities had revealed more than one, as staging grounds for the first wave of attacks.

The Tului, it turned out, were even more craven than he could ever have suspected. The pens resembled the enclosures ranchers in the countryside used for keeping sheep and chickens, but they all contained humans. Humans who were not sick or cursed with blood poison, who were nearly all fitted with cylindrical devices on their necks, which when twisted allowed blood to flow from their arteries, a discovery that had enraged him more than the sickness the Tului had afflicted so many of their own with. It was hard to think anything could have made him feel a rage deeper than that blood poison—than watching his people turn their blades on their own, become puppets dancing on the strings of these Blood Lords.

He watched as the clouds drifted, watched as those scarlet blooms rose and ebbed away almost as soon as they had, when they crossed into the smoke-laden junctions, sought to put out fires which would as likely kill them as put them to sleep. He hoped most of them did not get back up, that they died in those clouds, and by the same token felt they deserved far worse. Going to sleep and never awakening was too good for them.

"She made the right choice. Your mentor does not trade in wanton violence. He is a shield bearer."

"And Sircha is the sword." Kachukh said dejectedly. "Will I even have a use in this raid?"

Gulang turned to face him. Behind him, he saw Chuuta ambling along the ditch, stopping here and there to touch the earth. He would tire soon if he did not find something with more than a weak pulse to draw energy from. Winter was not kind to people like him, whose abilities were ill suited to combat. But Chuuta had not been chosen for his fighting ability. He was a clever shit, the best kind, and was skilled in setting traps. Even now he was at work, the gears turning, making preparations for their escape so that they were not followed.

He looked down on his son. "You have an impressive mind, Kachukh. I ask that you use it."

Kachukh's gaze shifted to the line in the dirt. "They can't harm me, can they? Even if they do come at me with blades of ice, they could never break my skin."

"They can't move you, either. As long as you stay in that circle, they can't touch you."

"Is that why she wants me here?"

"I believe so."

Storm the Keep

"Then I am to be our ace in the hole."

"And you should be honored by that. It is a show of immense respect that she believes you are capable of this."

"But what is my purpose?"

"Perhaps the most important purpose there is. To buy time. If they capture you, it will put us all in danger. I suppose she believes your abilities will make it difficult for them to gain ground. We are playing a dangerous game. She sees in you a use which none of us are as well positioned as you to take on. Mitigating risk, son. Something you will have to do if you become chief one day."

The Tului were coming now, swarming on that reviling pen where they kept their livestock. Gaulakh had wondered at what the soldier Saafha had taken control of meant. He had not had to wonder long. The sight of those people, filthy and dressed in ragged wools, every bit of exposed flesh caked in grease and dirt, came close to costing him his composure. It had taken Guruhl's full strength to hold him back, keep him from running off into the nearest tent and murdering the Tului soldiers bunked up inside it.

A sweeping cloud of opium smoke was spreading through that section of the camp. He held a wet cloth over his mouth and nose, but even from this distance, he could still faintly smell the cloying aroma of opium on the air. He held a long knife in each hand. One lacked a blade, was a simple, unadorned hilt of iron wrapped in hide. The other was wickedly curved, almost a sickle. A vicious weapon.

With the work done, the detonations going off and Guruhl somewhere east of him and finishing with the last of the parcels, it was time to return to the rendezvous point, and he did so reluctantly. He wanted violence, the taste of it. He wanted to know these Tului bastards had gotten theirs, but there would be plenty of time for that before they were done. Saafha would see the job done even if Bora didn't. He had faith in his brother.

Red glow rose at the edge of his vision. A wave of assailants marched onto the path, shadows shifting and flowing under their feet. He pulled on the pulse of Sildein, tensed his right hand. White fire thrust from the bladeless hilt, took shape to match the bladed long knife in his left hand. The tents, the ground, were cast in harsh hues, the nearest shadows driven away and those behind the tents stretched long and dark to paint the tents in the next row over.

She wants a distraction, she's going to get it.

He hefted the dagger in his left hand, and threw it. It soared across the blank space between the Tului and him, punched through the point man's chest, through another soldier, and carved a deep gouge into the shoulder of the man behind him. He made a snatching motion, and the blade changed course, returning to his hand. The hilt slapped against his palm obediently.

Three bodies fell. Dozens surged past them. Shadows flickered under their feet as they pelted forward, and evaporated as soon as they got close. Ice crawled around them. Blades whizzed through the air. He raised his left hand. Ice shattered. Blades dropped and broke against hard ground. The nearest of the Tului bowed under the pressure of heightened gravity, a generalized assault, and he rushed forward, blade of white fire lashing out, cauterizing where it cut, denying them any chance of infecting him with their blood.

He whipped his iron long knife into their ranks. Several hit the ground, some voluntarily.

Blood flew from open wounds. Life left their eyes.

He retreated to a safe distance, called his blade back into his hand. He turned, and ran for the rendezvous point, thought for vengeance set aside for now. A rigid focus had stolen over him. He had kicked over the hornet's nest. Now it was time to goad them onto more advantageous ground. Time to get back to his father and his brother, where the Kachin could have their pound of flesh in truth.

"Hold on." Bora said. They had reached the Tului banner staff.

Saafha's peculiar abilities had done most of the work of seeing them this far. Though she would have liked it if Gulang and his children had prioritized blending in with their attire; his abilities and apparent lack of empathy had rendered the loud paint and jewelry a moot point. He had no care for how much damage he inflicted on the enemy, and she supposed this was the right mentality to have when traversing enemy territory. She had seen nearly a dozen Tului soldiers brought down in fits of immense pain and fatigue at his hand now. Some had been so ravaged they had simply laid down their arms, curled into tight balls, closed their eyes and died.

His particular flavor of spirit calling was unpalatable, but then most were. In their ability to destroy, the Kachin were unmatched. Their sorcery heinously efficient. And she had little room to speak ill of Saafha's methods. Double edged sword though her own soulbinding may be, it possessed a similar potential to maim and control. She did not have to wonder any longer why Sarri had been so confident in this man. Why he believed he would be best suited to accompany her on the push into the Tului encampment's heart.

But the banner staff—a crow with its wings spread bold in black across a snow-white sheet of linen—provided an opportunity she would be a fool not to take. It's positioning, on the other hand, left plenty to be imagined. She did not like the idea of being exposed longer than was strictly necessary, and there was nothing around the banner for tens of feet. It occupied a blank space in the camp which was hemmed in by a circular conveyance, the center of the web. The nearest tents all looked toward it, and she suspected the soldiers inside them were high officers, elite soldiers who had been tested in many battles within their motherland. Or perhaps these were among those who maintained the border, prevented any intruder from coming back out again.

Isolationism was a difficult state for a nation to maintain. There were always those who coveted what they could not have, who loathed mysteries. She could not believe the kings and high officials throughout the various other nations who called Tao Shein home could have been content to stay away from that border indefinitely. Could not believe Ruc, in particular, would have seen fit to leave those lands alone, being the north-most of the southern kingdoms as it was.

"Don't be a fool, Bora." Saafha said. "Whatever advantage you believe you will achieve here will be met with tenfold the risk to you and us. It is not the right place to make a stand."

"Who said anything about that." She said absently. "If anyone interferes, handle them."

"Do not—"

But she was already moving, already closing in on the flag. When she was

Storm the Keep

within two strides of it, she removed her dagger from its sheath and set to work. Hunched close to the ground, hoping her lack of adornments and diminutive stature would help her stay well concealed, she dug the point of the dagger into the earth and dragged it back, and repeated the motion as she backpedaled around the banner.

Her heart pounded and she cast glances at the nearest tents every few seconds to make sure no one had begun to take notice. The dagger made a dull grating sound in the dirt as she scraped it back, backpedaled a few steps, dug it in and dragged it back again. Saafha maintained his position in the shadow of a nearby tent, watched the circle as avidly as she did, and occasionally fixed her with a tired expression, as if she was a child and he the sitter watching her get into mischief for the thousandth time.

She closed the circle, and touched it with a trembling finger. Ink-like energy poured from her fingertip into the shallow trench, and followed its contours from the point of contact around and back again. She felt an echo in her soul, and knew Gulang had staked out a circle himself, expending the reservoir of energy she had left within him for precisely that purpose.

She backed away, rushed back to where Saafha was hiding, rolling her steps to prevent herself making much noise.

"Satisfied?" he asked.

"Yes."

"And what was the point in that?"

"For this to work, everything must be equal. But it wouldn't do us any good to carve out the Keep around the Baron's tent. It would be too easy for them to regroup there."

"And the banner is a better option because?

"It's far enough removed from Gulang to give the others room to maneuver. The line will have materialized halfway between this post and the other one. The game commences now."

"It didn't when you touched us?"

He touched the inky pictograph on his chest.

"The rules needed to be defined and the positions executed before it took effect." She said. "Now let's go. We're wasting time."

He sucked on his cheek, but followed her as she darted from the shadow of one tent to the next, following the outside edge of the broad way to its eastern edge. From her vantage, she could make out a dark shape in the middle distance. The tents surrounding it were all white, and this one was well enough removed from the rest to identify it as the dwelling of someone important. She might have suspected it was the lodging of this baron from its positioning alone, but the darker color provided confirmation.

Saafha barred her from going any further, pressed his finger to his lips and squatted down.

She eased onto her laurels beside him, and watched.

An altercation had broken out in that direction. Raised voices.

The baron's tent flap flew open and slapped the tarp wall. A fine featured man with a pointed chin who looked no older than her stormed out. He spun on his heels as another emerged somewhat more primly behind him. The second man's face was narrow and vulpine, and wavy, blonde hair spilled over his shoulders. He was

Tears for the Moon God

dressed in bright red silks, a matching bib of rougher material saturated with darker blood tied around his neck.

The man with the bib looked even younger, perhaps in his teens, but he was aging rapidly, his plump cheeks hollowing, the lines around his mouth deepening. He was losing mass, as well. His arms and neck thinned under restrictive sleeves and a tight collar. The effect reminded her of a water skin being emptied.

"How dare you!" the baron, he could be nothing else, bellowed. His voice was incongruously deep, belonging to a much bigger man.

"You deserve much worse."

"The absolute outrage. To treat a nobleman—"

"You are under my command." The other man, who was clad all in black from his neck to his ankles seethed. The cut of his dress was utilitarian. A leather jerkin clung tight to his chest, and the shirt underneath was thickly woven wool. His slacks were the kind military men in Ruc wore, and his boots were bronze shod, encasing his ankles and shins. "Which means you will abide by my orders like everyone else."

"But I am not like everyone else!" the baron snapped. "And you would do well to remember it. Or should I report of your insolence to our king?"

"Do what you wish, but should starvation rack my soldiers, it will be you who answers for it."

The baron stomped forward, seized the other man around the collar and dragged him close with surprising strength. The other man was nearly dragged off his feet.

"Listen to me well, Crow Durin!" he hissed, bearing fangs still glistening red from his recent meal. "If Tuluis Fel discovers you have been smuggling iron into his lands, he will have you executed. There is no question of it. Possession of iron means death. It is the law."

"Then perhaps it is best if you suffer an accident before we reach the border. My soldiers will not starve out before we arrive then. Do not test me, Salus al Keirn. If you choose to glut yourself again, you selfish whore, you will not make it to Tuluis Fel to make any report. And you will find no one in this camp willing to rise to your defense for it."

Crow Durin shoved him back. Baron Keirn's fingers were wrenched loose, snapping like green twigs behind the force with which he pushed. He stormed away, leaving the baron holding his mangled hand, the fingers already straightening out and sliding back into place with grotesque popping noises that reminded her of corn kernels in a hot skillet.

Saafha pulled Bora around the tent, into deeper cover, as the Crow stamped past.

"You'll pay for this!" the baron crowed.

He spun round and marched back into his tent, flinging the entrance flap aside aggressively and vanishing inside.

"What do you make of it?" Saafha asked.

"You're asking me?" she said. "The ruler of their nation does not trust this Crow. Otherwise, why place a watch on him. It seems he is right not to, if the Crow is willing to violate their laws to see his ends met."

"What of the iron?"

She met his steady gaze, and shrugged. "Maybe a weakness?"

Storm the Keep

"Or a cure." He eased around her, crept down the lane. He was not bothering to hide himself now, and as she followed in his wake, she was certain he had the right idea. What soldier would come within sight of that tent now. They must all have heard the exchange. They would be reluctant to leave their tents now, which served her just as well. It would make the work of capturing the baron easier.

Even better. He won't be missed. They might even believe the Crow made good on his threat.

They closed in on the tent, took up positions to either side of it. She strained to hear what was going on inside. Aside from the intermittent wet gasp, some suckling sounds that made her deeply uncomfortable, there was nothing to indicate the baron had company. A victim, perhaps, but no dinner guests.

She signaled for Saafha to remain outside, slipped the tent flap quietly aside. He watched as she crept past the wide threshold, and took up a post just outside, holding the flap open enough that he could watch through a slim crack.

Guruhl had finished with the last of the parcels. The first explosions were already going off, the first in a long chain of detonations which would see most of the southern half of the war camp inundated with opium smoke.

"How long do we have?" he asked Akhi, who was leaning on a fence post. Behind him, men, women and children huddled in close clusters. He did not value the loss of these people, but knew there could be no other way. To free all of them would overburden the Gil Garo, but these people had no immunity to opium, had no tolerance. Many of them would die, but with the toxification of their blood with harsh sedatives, their deaths would serve a greater purpose.

He told himself it would. It did nothing to ease the guilt.

Many of those people did not belong to the Tului. Most bore resemblance to the Ruc'an. Some few looked as though they might have hailed from Ao Lein once. They had lived through enough suffering. Most people would have been driven into madness having witnessed half of what these people likely had. They knew they were going to die. He could see it in their eyes, in the way some of them looked upon him with hope, and whispered admonitions to their children—cooed to them or told them stories. Worse than that, they welcomed it.

A cold rage built deep inside him, but he would not let it consume him. He could not afford to. He saw that lingering anger reflected in Akhi when he met his gaze. Heard it in his voice as he answered.

"They've taken notice. Maybe a few moments."

"Time to go, then."

Akhi pushed off the post. He did not look back at those people as he followed Guruhl away. Another series of detonations marked the second cluster of opium bombs going off. The nearest of them shook the ground under their feet.

Scarlet glow emanated from several points all at once. The nearest of them was perhaps a hundred paces off.

They broke into a jog, and fled for the rendezvous point.

Three...two...one!

The last round of explosions went off. Smoke struck the sky behind them, and he reached for the soaked rag tucked into his sleeve. He pressed it to his face as the first tendrils of smoke rolled into his path, barely dared to breathe until they were well clear of it.

Tears for the Moon God

Berni did not flee when the detonations went off. Her aura shielded her, a bulwark against the intrusion of those opioid compounds. She waited until the first wave of Tului emerged to survey the damage, hiding in plain sight within the thickest clouds of smoke.

The Tului gave the smoke cloud a wide birth. Even so, some succumbed to the effects and collapsed under the weight of what must have been an overwhelming high.

She watched, satisfied, as the smart ones fled to a safe distance, as the idiots among them plunged into the cloud and almost immediately collapsed. One of them made it almost to her feet before he fell, seizing up and gasping for breath, making his situation that much worse.

She watched him struggle to breathe, reveled in his pain as he rolled around—wild, desperate eyes gazing up at her, realizing she was there.

"Well now, let me help you with that." She reached down, pressed a long, slender finger to his sternum. "Now, now. Hold my gaze."

The power of her mentor bubbled within her, rippled through her arm, out of her and into him. He breathed in deep like a fish on dry land.

All that air and none of it to breathe. She mused. *But that's no problem for us. No, it is* not.

Chained to him, she felt the alveoli in his lungs expanding and contracting, the outpouring of oxygen into the blood and the return of carbon dioxide. She felt the flow of metabolites traveling along quite unbothered in his bloodstream, and the release of restrictive hormones. She attacked these channels with surgical precision, not denying him breath but making it easier. Doping him by increasing his capacity to metabolize those chemicals, the opium in the air, making it easier for his body to access it, to take it in, to hold it. Making it harder for his cells to expel those pesky toxins.

She watched as his features went slack, felt echoes of the chemicals inundating his brain. Hormones squirted from parts of him like geysers, hammered him with so much pleasure it must almost be painful.

His heartbeat slowed. His lungs rose and fell, rose...and fell, rose...and...fell.

She watched the light leave his eyes, smiling all the while. This death was too good for him, that was true, but it satisfied to feel it happening, to feel the life leaking out of him, a neural leach mimicking the actions of his cerebellum, his brain stem, behaving like both and yet with the self awareness those higher order parts of the brain assigned to rational thought. The body did not know what was happening to it in dying. The mind conveyed the message, and fought tooth and nail to prevent it happening, went into panic mode and sought to compel it back into some semblance of life even as the houses that allowed it to function died, became less and less able to self regulate, and then gave up.

She had not known how much she would enjoy the sensation until the first time she had experienced it, to know what passed through another person when they met their end, and have none of the risk of succumbing to it herself.

She withdrew her finger as the last dregs of life went out of him. The candle was snuffed. The fire doused. Smoldering embers remained for some minutes after the death took hold. The body twitched. Nerves without guidance from the brain fired randomly. The bowels evacuated, and rigor took over. Eventually, the muscles relaxed, and the bacteria in the corpse's gut flourished, beginning the process of decay, but she would not stick around for all of that. She would not feel it anyway.

Mother Gusula's knowledge of the body was analytical, pristine and complete. Her teaching had been...*educational*...for the art of killing. Had been well fashioned for a certain, minor form of healing as well, but that was Father Ferg's domain. No, Mother Gusula culled, and as Berni saw little value in bolstering the capacities of others, beyond what might make the fight easier for her, she had chosen the more wicked one. The one more abiding of her...*proclivities.*

She stood up, and walked out of the cloud, circumventing dying soldiers as she did, stopping to drag her sword across a throat or two for her own peace of mind.

What Gulang didn't know wouldn't hurt him, but now it was time to return to him.

She passed the perimeter of the cloud of smoke, and found herself surrounded by those Tului who had been intelligent enough to flee from it.

They lashed out almost as soon as they saw her, but they were already too late. Their motions were sluggish. Several of them dropped their weapons, clutched their throats.

"And here we arrive at the other end of the knife." She said for the nearest of them to hear. "Don't get too close to me, and I might let you breathe."

She patted the nearest of them on the shoulder, looked into confused eyes. The soldier dropped to her knees, her skin withering, advanced age descending over her like a hammer trained on an anvil.

They collapsed. Every one of them close enough to be affected by her did. And she walked away unharmed.

"Those pesky fairies, right? That's what you get for attacking Gil Garo."

A naked woman was laid out atop a long table of white pine. A dowel-like device dangled from the side of her neck, where a thick vain was pulsing weakly, struggling to supply her brain with oxygen. Wide, round eyes fluttered open and closed as the baron's hands roved over her body, grasping and squeezing, one thumb rubbing circles around a blood greased nipple. Her chest and thighs were covered in blood, and the baron stood at one end of the table, his mouth and nose buried in her crotch, which had been shaved smooth.

His eyes were closed, a manic snarl wrinkling his brow as he lapped at her genitals with increasing vigor.

She whimpered softly, her pupils dilated, gaze shifting from an ornate writing desk in one corner to a pewter pitcher on a low stand near the entrance, and then settling, pleading, on Bora.

The woman's breath caught, and the baron's eyes flicked open, snapped onto the intruder in his domain. He latched onto her breast, used it for purchase as he dragged himself up. His shadow, where it lay against the floor, split into three and began to dance, the silhouettes all performing different actions. One climbed onto his lap, reached for his hip where she suspected a hidden weapon lay. Another made a clock hand shift toward her own shadow, painted across the tarp behind her. She dodged out of its reach, while the last sought to close in on the other side.

Baron Keirn's scarlet eyes were fixed on her. Dense, pink threads of drool dangled from his chin, a trance-like hunger pushing out all else but the prone figure before him.

Tears for the Moon God

"When it rains, it does pour, doesn't it." He mumbled drunkenly. "You made a mistake coming here, woman, but fear not. I will take care of you."

Bora recoiled. Her mind was racing. She was having difficulty forming thoughts. Her gaze darted from him to the woman, back and forth, back and forth. The nearest of his shadows lurched toward her. She leapt back, crashed into the table.

The pitcher wobbled, crashed to the ground with a dull bell's toll.

"Come here, dear. It will not hurt."

The woman's horrified expression told her a different tale. Whatever he intended for her would be no painless thing.

She ran around to the side of the table where the woman's head lay, putting as much distance between them as she could manage in the cramped confines of this tent. A bed on that side interrupted her progress. Metal dug into her shin, and pain exploded in the limb.

Need to get close. Need to touch him. The thoughts came as a maddening tangle, driven into echoing chaos by adrenaline.

He shoved the woman's legs closed, and climbed over her. Manicured fingernails dug into the table, and he lunged at her with explosive force.

She lurched to the side, narrowly dodging him.

Blood welled from a fresh gash on her arm, but she was certain he hadn't cut her. She found a shadow slinking away from her as he struck the bed, as he righted himself, shook off the confusion at the head injury.

She clapped her hand to her arm, retreated out of range of those shadows, but they were coming for her again.

Saafha stormed into the room. He put himself between her and the shadows. Violent, green ooze ran over his shoulders, down his arms; thick ropes tumbling onto the floor.

"Wait for your opening." He said inflectionlessly.

He stepped forward, and lunged.

The baron took the impact. His head darted forward, teeth bared, hunting for exposed flesh.

Saafha's fist slammed into his jaw, snapping his mouth shut. Fresh blood weltered over his lips as he gasped.

"Now, Bora!" Saafha hollered.

Without thinking, she rushed into the space between them.

A thick sob issued from the baron's throat.

Saafha's whole arm had gone mute black, and he was climbing off a now writhing Baron Keirn, leaving him to grapple with his pain.

Bora reached out, dark energy shrouding her hand and wrist, and clapped her hand against the baron's neck. She held it there, fighting to keep it in place against his incessant thrashing, as black wrath poured from her into him, fled into his robes and across his cheek.

"Caught you." She gasped. "Caught you."

The baron's blood-smeared fingers climbed up her arm, seeking the wound. A wave of nausea spread through her, and she choked it down. The baron's shadows ceased dancing, reunited as a single entity. The luminous, scarlet shade of his irises faded to a dark brown.

Saafha reached for him, then. He pressed his own fingers in the same place Bora's hand had just left, and vibrant ooze leaked into the baron's flesh. A black substance emanated from him. It passed into Saafha's hand, and faded.

"Be a good boy, Baron Keirn, and come with us back to our friends."

The baron's gaze grew unfocused. A milky cast settled over the dark irises, as if frost had settled against the lenses.

He climbed onto his hands and knees, climbed off the bed, and stood with them.

Bora produced her buck knife from its sheath. She pushed the frightened woman's head back, pressed it to her neck. She closed her eyes as she raked the knife across the woman's throat, and stepped back as soon as the cut was made. She wiped the knife clean against the baron's bed spread, and returned it to it place as the woman gave a last gargled cry, and died.

Saafha held her gaze. "This is your first kill."

"Yes." She said softly.

"You did the right thing." He pressed his hand into the small of the baron's back. "Change your clothes."

The baron began to strip. He moved on a trunk and rummaged through it. Bora looked him over, noted the way the veins in his limbs pulsed, how she could make out the color of his blood though his skin.

He donned a fresh robe in the same color, one suited to daily life, which was hemmed with lace at the collar and the cuffs. He produced a soft, clean towel from the trunk and wiped his face clean.

"I'm ready." He said.

"Then come." Saafha said.

"You have a terrifying power." Bora whispered.

Saafha grunted. He guided the baron to the tent entrance. "You're certain he cannot call on the pulse of his master?"

"Positive."

"Our kin are waiting."

A storm of other people's thoughts surged within Lufir al Durin's mind, a dull roar crowding around the edges of a pocket of silence. He listened to strings of commands given by his Blood Lords to the peon soldiers in their companies, the return of information gathered by them. Smoke bombs had gone off near the pens at the camp's southern edge. The soldiers who got too close were incapacitated. They believed the clouds were suffused with some kind of poison. The enemy had been sighted in several locations, none of which seemed important excepting the pens.

One here, two there...their total number could not be this low, and yet the same faces kept appearing—lightning strike flashes, snatches of imagery, tents and scarlet auras, explosions, pockets of fast spreading airlessness. The soldiers were dying. Some could not draw breath. Others were mangled ruins bleeding from several places at once.

He clamped his right gauntlet shut.

White fire burned in the shape of a blade, and their shadows could not come closer than thirty feet to the man who held it. Men fell to puncture wounds and deep gashes, but they could not identify the source. A Blood Lord was taken by a ghost, and to glance in its direction was to see it vanishing into the shadows, as if it had never been.

He latched his left gauntlet into place.

Tears for the Moon God

They've infiltrated our war camp in stealth. Their intent must be sabotage. Destroy our food supply. Starve us out before we reach the border.

He drew a hauberk of fine chain over his shoulders. The links tinkled together like tiny bells as it fell over his waist.

A young woman lashed out with whips of compressed water, which parted muscle from bone effortlessly.

He slid his foot into a bronze-shod boot, and laced it.

A pair of shadows quivered nervously against the tarp wall near the entrance.

"Come in." He said.

A runner parted the flap. His appearance would suggest he was forty or so years old, but he was much younger. A new initiate, one of those who had risen to some status from the pens, having fostered many children in his short life. Durin did not know his name, and did not care to hunt after it. The initiate was of little consequence to him. Had not even developed the telepathic link more seasoned acolytes of Tuluis Fel used effortlessly.

The initiate saluted.

"What is it?" he asked.

"The Baron is missing." He said.

"I see."

What could they gain from him? What do they believe they could gain?

He closed his eyes, opened his mind to the tumultuous storm of active, foreign thoughts. He targeted the Blood Lords, those who had made contact with the enemy, and relayed orders, switching from one to the next, a blurred string of orders disseminating rapidly from him through direct channels into them. He had turned many of these himself, a privilege and an honor for those who displayed strong loyalty.

"Form a perimeter around the one who overrides our breathing."

"Command your soldiers to cover their faces with dampened rags and snuff those fires immediately. I do not care how many we lose to see it done."

Our spirit calling is being disrupted. We cannot draw on Tuluis Fel's power. A Blood Lord snapped. A surge of fury accompanied his message. Behind it and somewhat more muted, fear registered in the minds of nearly all of his soldiers.

"Fall back. Await further orders. Alert me if anything changes."

That one had been turned by Baron Keirn.

"What is the status of your company?" he asked another of Keirn's men.

We have been cut off. We cannot use our spirit calling.

He opened himself up to all of those Blood Lords Baron Keirn had turned. All of those who had been turned by them.

"Fall back. Do not engage the enemy."

To those he had turned.

"Split your forces. Send teams to handle the pens. Bring the hammer down from the east. Form a wall on the southwest side. Cut off their exits. If it is possible to secure Baron Keirn, do so, but do not allow him to leave our camp alive."

He slipped on his other boot and laced it up, taking his time about it. There would be a commander among these forces, someone disseminating orders from a location he believed was safe. He intended to handle him personally.

When he opened his eyes again, he saw the runner still standing there, one flat hand pressed against his forehead, the other arm stiff behind his back.

Storm the Keep

"Bring me my horse." He said.

The runner darted out of the tent. Durin ventured out behind him. He sucked in an icy breath, and exhaled hot vapor.

"I kill a chief tonight." He thought, and let the thought drift along to his forces. The pocket of silence returned, and the thoughts of all of those others became frenzied, wrathful and hopeful by the same measure.

This will be a night of blood. He thought to himself. *They will learn again how outmatched they are. They will know the wrath of Tuluis Fel.*

A large force moved silently westward, their defenses drawn down and shadows rippling around them. If Bora had made contact with the baron, her plan had failed. The Tului were still able to use their powers. Those frenzied shadows were all Guruhl needed to confirm his suspicions.

It had been too long since she departed with Saafha, and though she was in good hands, the two were grossly outnumbered. The enemy had taken notice, were even now amassing ahead of a counter attack the scope of which was disproportionate to the stealth raid they encountered. Ten Gil Garo may have justified the deployment of a few hundred troops. The people of the southern kingdoms thought so. But the military command here had deployed near enough their entire force. They were taking no chances...may even believe these ten were bait to draw them into an engagement with a larger force.

He spun round, threw his blade into the horde of soldiers marching for the west edge of camp. Some way off, the lead elements were already shifting course, moving south around the camp's edge. He needed to disrupt their movements, force them to split their company and lay chase. He could lose them among the tents, hide in plain sight if he needed to.

The blade punched through a row of soldiers, taking several in the chest, piercing through ribs, finding hearts and lungs and vulnerable, soft tissues. He clenched his fist, and the blade returned, driving point first through another row of marching soldiers. A pushing gesture brought it back around, but by then the lines had broken. Waves of troops were breaking from the lines, orders being barked by frustrated commanders.

Gaulakh raised the fiery dagger in his right hand, drew down his left. The nearest soldiers hit the ground. Bones split through skin along their joints, ribs crunched, teeth gnashed together in rictus snarls.

He called his blade back to him, guided it through a snowbank on the way back to strike home in his palm, cleaning some of the tainted blood from it.

Ice flowered beyond the range of his influence. Jagged Shards bloomed under his feet. He leapt back, out of range of them as they thrust skyward in tight columns.

The enemy reached for him, and were forced to their knees.

Too many bodies. He backed off, releasing his hold on the area where those Tului had fallen, allowing gravity in that region to ebb as he sought to remove himself from the conflict.

He considered using his ace in the hole to cover his retreat, blind them to his movements, but it was too soon. He needed them following him. If they gave up too soon, they would simply return to the main body, and then his efforts would have been for nothing.

Tears for the Moon God

As he ran, he caught sight of Berni breaking away from a smaller force all compromised by her abilities. They writhed on the ground, pawed at their necks. A maniacal grin was smeared across her lips. She was enjoying this.

She tipped her chin in his direction, and walked away, choosing a different path down which to travel, one which would take her more directly to their rendezvous point.

He spun round and launched his knife into the mass of followers. It left his hand with a thunderous bang, soared across the gap, took another file of forces down.

He twisted his wrist, calling it back, washing it in packed snows, taking it in hand.

Shadows licked at his heels. Ice sprouted where his feet had just been. A plume of vitreous daggers shot out of the ground ahead of him, and he rolled out of its path.

He pelted off again.

He was getting tired. He did not know how long he could keep up this pace. He may be a fast runner, but he was not built for tests of endurance, was not made for sprinting over vast distances.

He spun round to face his attackers, let go the white fire riding the empty hilt of his blade and sheathed them both without looking. He clapped his hands together and drew them apart.

A spectrum of colors soared into the space between the Tului and him. Vibrant reds and greens and blues, an aurora akin to anything that lived in the sky at night in the northmost reaches of Tao Shein. It unfurled like vast wings, flew outward for a span of several dozen paces to either side.

He turned and ran with renewed vigor, not watching to see if the Tului chanced passing it. They would be met with no resistance if they did. Those auroras carried no ability to harm. But they would give them reason to consider their movements, would breed a caution in them if they were anything like the people of those southern kingdoms the Kachin so often raided from.

Streams of red light converged on a growing river east of Gulang's position. He watched the hammer form, hunted across the horizon for the anvil, but a mirror glow was not evident anywhere to the west. The orders these Tului had been given must have involved traveling in stealth, but he had no illusions about the nature of this assault. It would come hard from the west, seeking to close off their routes of retreat. A competent general did not show his whole hand to his enemy. The hammer was too obvious, too flamboyant. The smaller force would be there, the larger seeking to blind him to their movements.

As the streams moved down from the north and amassed in the east, Berni emerged from among the tents. A satisfied smile lightly touched her lips; a manic, murderous glint in her eyes. She had killed this night, had taken her time about it if he knew her as well as he believed. She was no afterthought in the planning that went into this raid. Sarri had chosen her deliberately, had seeded several others into the discussion, all of whom were less qualified for this kind of mission than she was. He had wanted her here, and Gulang suspected his reasoning lay in just how much she enjoyed it. The killing, reveling in watching the life drain out of her victims.

If she had been born to a different tribe, she would have been a murderer. Cold blooded, intelligent and cunning, she would not have settled for the humdrum of city life. She would have found a way to sate her addiction, and it would be far less palatable than anything she did in the summer months under Sarri's command.

She closed on him, positioned herself at his side, and watched the mounting glow push across the southern side of the camp, watched them come.

"Did you run into any problems?" he asked, though he already knew her answer.

"Nothing I couldn't handle." She said. "They are not so different from the Ruc'an. They see a woman and they think she must be an easy target."

"They pressed their advantage."

"Too far as it turns out."

"Did you cross paths with any of the others?"

"I saw Gaulakh running away from a mob." She met his eye. "He will be fine. He may not be as skilled in the use of Sildein's power as Chief Coltang, but he is not stupid. He knows when it is pointless to stay and fight."

Gulang nodded.

Behind them, Kachukh made polite conversation with Chuuta, who had finished with his preparations. The anvil would not have an easy time reaching them when it came, but he would not be at ease until all of his soldiers had returned. The longer they remained inside the camp, the greater his anxiety grew. He did not like being so distant from his remaining children, did not like dealing with such uncertainty.

He worried about Saafha. He was capable in ways his siblings were not, almost as bad, in some ways, as Berni. He did not revel in causing pain, but neither did he feel any remorse for the pain he inflicted on others. He did not place value on the nature of a kill, did not see honor as a valuable commodity in combat. In many ways he was less vulnerable than any of the others, but he was deep behind enemy lines now, and would have his work cut out for him getting out now. That hammer was amassing in front of him, carving a thick line between Saafha and Bora, and the rest of them.

Come back to me. He thought to himself. *Do not be brave, my son. Do not choose now to make a foolish mistake.*

Akhi paused to test the air, hunting for presences near enough to cause a problem. Guruhl halted a few paces ahead of him.

"Is something wrong?" he asked.

They had found a pocket of stillness in the chaos spreading through the camp. He did not relish the idea of being found again. The few skirmishes they had encountered thus far had been one sided. Small bands of soldiers, too few in number to pose much of a problem for them working together.

But the tides were turning now. They were still well within the camp and removed from Gulang and the greater safety of familiar ground. In the east, a bonfire glow was amassing. Narrower streams were filtering into the greater mass just north of them. The smoke from the first wave of detonations was beginning to ebb. Some of those fires had been snuffed out already.

The Tului were organizing ahead of a brutal counter attack, and there were just ten of them. Five of them spread across the camp and making things messy for the Tului, two with their target in hand if things had gone well for them. He did not

Tears for the Moon God

value the idea of dallying here longer than was necessary, did not want the needless complication of trying to break through that line, two men against thousands.

"I've had a thought." He said.

"Now is not the time to deviate from the script." Guruhl growled.

"I won't be long." He said.

"What is this thought?"

"I want to find the other force. The one they don't want us to see."

"What do you hope to gain, Akhi. You will be disgustingly outnumbered. Vulnerable."

Akhi shrugged. "I just want to bump uglies with someone important for a change. Is that so wrong."

"Can I convince you to abandon this thought?"

"I think no."

"Then be quick about it. And do not take any unnecessary risks."

"Oh, I doubt they will notice me."

He stepped back into a nearby shadow. Darkness crawled across his shins, climbed over his body, a mass of writhing serpents. The change took seconds, and Guruhl lost sight of him.

"Be careful, asshole." Guruhl turned away and hurried southwest, out of the camp.

Bora watched as the lines converged a hundred or so paces from where she hid with Saafha and Baron Keirn. Quiet whimpers issued from the baron, but she could not focus on him. The pain in her arm had lost some of its intensity, but with every movement of it renewed agony shot across her shoulder and into her chest and neck. The strip of cloth she had fastened over the knife wound there was still bleeding, and the cloth was soaked through and beginning to freeze in the winter air.

She needed to get to Sircha. She could have healing then. Saafha's abilities had proven grossly ill suited to providing medicine. His training as an acolyte and a raider both had left him deficient in the ministrations of first aid, and she knew nothing of the science. She had become a liability even as she provided a boon. Even as Tului soldiers amassed south of them, others were marching en masse away from the conflict, north toward the banner post where they might have their spirit calling restored, if they had figured out her game. Droves of them had been impacted by her stealing away the Baron's power. Their shadows obediently mirrored their movements as they passed, proving her theory had been correct.

There was a hierarchical order to the Tului ranks, which left no room for fluidity. Channels of power ran down from the top, making of each rank a subordinate caste to the rank above them, which meant superior and subordinate shared a bond akin to the Chains some spirits assigned to their acolytes. Like Ungol's mol fae familiar, or the langur monkey Guruhl almost always kept with him, which he had left behind for this raid.

The lines of retreating soldiers dwindled more swiftly than she had assumed they would. It seemed most of the Tului outfit were descended from a different lineage, likely with the Crow at the top. Saafha signaled a move, waited for the last of them to pass. He darted across the path, the baron trailing him obediently.

She gripped her wounded arm and barreled after him.

Storm the Keep

"There! The Baron!" A soldier screamed.

Oh no. Oh no, oh no, oh no. She bolted for cover as a smaller troop splintered from the main force and laid chase. Saafha spun as she passed him. The first lines of soldiers made contact.

He lashed out with whips of sickly, green energy. They latched onto a half dozen Tului soldiers. He spun, wrenching on thick ropes of green light, and six bodies slumped. Six spectral entities ran away from them in the opposite direction, lashed out with clawing fingers and snapping jaws at the soldiers behind them.

"Run dammit!" he snarled.

She realized she had stopped at the edge of the pathway, turned and ran after him.

"What...the hell...was that!" she gasped as she pelted along in his shadow.

"Never mind that now. We need to get away from here!"

The baron ran between them, keeping pace with Saafha as Bora lumbered after them. Saafha paused to engage the enemy closing in at their backs. Oozing, green ropes flashed past her, struck home against bodies, ripped souls from flesh, and those souls turned on their allies, brought them down by scores.

He ran after her, after the baron. Shadows snapped at her from behind as a fresh wave of soldiers lay chase, shadows made longer for the better light along this channel. They clawed at her heels, opening fresh cuts in her thighs.

She screamed, and pelted on harder, putting as much distance as she could between her and her attackers. Blood leaked into her pants, peppered the snow through fresh tears in the fabric.

She ran until her lungs burned, until her legs jelled and threatened to jam up under her, and ran still harder.

Fresh shouts from the soldiers brought new bodies into the conflict. Tului emerged from adjoining avenues, pressed in from the fore.

There was nowhere left to run. They were surrounded. She spun, hunted desperately for an exit. Her knife was in her hand, having found its way there as if by some instinct. If she was going to go down, she intended to fight until she could not any more.

"What now?" she wheezed.

Saafha's cold regard took in the Tului closing in from every side. She saw the calculations running through his head and wondered if they had arrived at the same conclusion. If even now he was reaching toward acceptance for the inevitable. There was no strategically expedient move she could make. Until her game concluded, she could not fashion rules for another. She could not draw on her soulbinding to increase her odds of success by snaring these monsters in a series of rules which would give her the advantage. She could not kill these soldiers if she could not touch them.

But I can touch them.

Saafha clapped his hands together. Threads of mucosal ooze retreated, coalesced against his skin, crawled across his torso, his arms, his legs.

Every game has its risks. If they can't infect me, so be it. I can exploit my advantage.

She hunted through the ranks, her gaze darting from soldier to soldier, taking in the details of their uniforms, looking for nuances in their designs.

In the second row, hanging back slightly from the rest of the soldiers, was a man who looked about twenty, who wore chain armor over his reliefs. There were others clad in similar dress, but none as well equipped as him.

Her gaze fell to the snows, to the shadows those soldiers cast, the frenzied array all reaching with blades in hand toward them. Four danced around the feet of the hanger back.

She cocked her chin in that direction. "There."

Saafha followed her gaze.

"I need an opening."

"You're wounded."

"It won't matter."

"If you die?"

"Then the game is over."

"We cannot afford the risk."

"We have no other choice."

The Tului attacked.

Shadows pressed into the space around them as the mob surged forward.

Saafha lashed out with cords of sickly energy. They latched onto the nearest attackers. He wrenched the whips back, and two bodies tumbled. Two wraiths lashed out at the nearest soldiers on that side.

Bora surged forward. She burst through the gap Saafha had opened, bolted straight for the commander.

His shadows boiled toward hers.

She dove. Momentum drove her straight into his arms, his sword knocked to the side and out of range as she made full contact with him.

The shadows surrounding Saafha contracted, snapped back into single entities. Soldiers stumbled, threw up their arms, fell back, skidded toward him and the baron at his back.

The Blood Lord collapsed under her weight. She punched her dagger into his chest, and rolled off him.

He seized up. Age descended on him like a hammer beating a copper sheet. In moments, he had gone from a youth to an old man, a desiccated husk of who he pretended to be.

Saafha moved on her. He hefted her into his arms.

The soldiers nearest them collapsed, age falling on them as heavily and as swiftly as it had on their master. They writhed, kicking up powder snows, showering the path with fresh flurries.

Saafha hauled her away, pelted through the snows with the Baron following them like a lap dog on the heels of its owner.

She laced her good arm around his neck, held on for dear life as he ferried her away.

"That was...a stupid...*stupid*...." He gasped.

"It worked, didn't it?"

Not...the point!"

She looked back at the mess in their wake. Several bodies still twitched. Most had gone still.

Every good plan holds a fatal flaw. She thought deliriously. *How short-sighted. How damned short-sighted.*

Storm the Keep

Whips of water flowed from Sircha's arms. Meltwater trickled over ground, pilfered from the vast stores locked up in the snows. With another decade of experience working with this power, she might be on par with Shaelein Safar, but she was outnumbered, and did not have the benefit of her brothers to draw the enemy away from her.

Another ten years and she might have been equal to the challenge, but as it was she could barely keep those soldiers out of range. Shadows moved unnaturally across the snows, hunting for weak points in her defenses. She stepped out of range every time they got close, lashed out with her whips, only managing to carve away flesh by happenstance.

Her breathing was becoming labored. This force was not large. She should be able to handle them. But those powers complemented hers too well. The edge of a water whip became sleet and collapsed, was replaced by a fresh flow of blood-tinted water. The Tului closed from three sides. They were edging forward to close off her retreat.

She lashed out to either side, catching two soldiers among dozens along the chest, but the cuts were shallow. The Tului did not go down like they were supposed to.

She backpedaled further, a mistake as it turned out. A shadow crawled into range, latched onto hers. She couldn't move. Couldn't break the contact.

Shit.

Her arms dropped to her sides. The Tului pressed their advantage. They closed in on her, hemmed her in. Ice became water became ice as she fought to maintain control of the flows.

Shit.

She lashed out, riding on battle training that had taken on the edge of instinct. Frothing madness boiled from her in a torrent, knocking the Tului closest to her back, sending them rolling away on rip currents.

The contact was broken.

She turned and ran away, feeling like a coward and running as fast as she could anyway. The ranks split around the roiling whitecaps and pursued.

If I can just make it back. If I can make it to father.

She pelted away with those dozens at her heels, closing the gap opened by her attack too quickly. She would be exposed, trapped again and useless if she did not find her way back to the rendezvous point quickly, or at least to another raider. Gaulakh must be somewhere close. If she could find him....

Just get back. Stay alive. Get back.

Shadows snapped at her ankles. Ridges of ice flowed around her, cutting off hope of shifting course.

She ran south. Ran and ran. A sword whooped in her direction, narrowly missing her shoulder. Ice became water along her left flank and she plunged through it, rode the current to its conclusion and kept running. Kept running like a coward. Kept running like a useless, ineffective *coward.*

I should not have come. I should have stayed home. Mother was right. We were not ready.

Akhi saw the aurora unfurl. A weaker showing than what Coltang was capable of, but he was impressed nonetheless. Gaulakh had taken quickly to Sildein's power.

Tears for the Moon God

He might well surpass the Tipik chief one day.

He smiled as he marched unseen within the ranks of Tului making speed for the western edge of their camp, turning southward to hem in the most obvious retreat path the Gil Garo might take. He passed by soldiers with stony faces, all of them sharing some resemblance to the Gil Garo, and most giving the impression of a child army. There were men barely old enough to hold a sword among them. Men in their middle years were a rare sight.

He chewed on that, thought it over. The Tului may be a short-lived people, but he did not think this likely. He had seen the way the youth leaked out of them too many times now to believe this strange virility was natural.

The youth they clung to must be some kind of illusion, a reversal of age from their drinking of mortal blood perhaps. He had heard stranger things in his time in Shakh's God House, if it could be called that. A forest shrouded always in oppressive darkness, as if night never broke, never yielded to God Gorgus's touch.

He slipped between two soldiers, narrowly avoiding touching either, and took in their scents as he traveled. Sickness like curdled cream, faint spices, pepper, sour melon. He cataloged their odors, the faint and subtle nuances in their blood, flowing from the flora of bacteria against their skin, deep in their guts. He could follow those scents to the ends of the world if he wanted to, pick them out across continents. It would be no trouble following the Tului even once they passed their border. If they managed to get that far.

As they disbanded and returned to their home cities, he would know precisely where they were, be able to lead the Gil Garo straight to them. It was this which had driven him here. This task that seemed so important he could not simply let go of the opportunity. This troop would find its way back to the rendezvous point eventually. He had not lied to Guruhl when he said he would be quick. The force was closing in swiftly now, and there was another matter he thought it best to attend to.

As those shadows flickered over ground, he was met with an even greater advantage. So many shadows provided all the camouflage he needed to remain unseen. The shadows, such a potent weapon for the Tului, became fuel for his immaculate defense.

He traveled up the line, deftly navigating between gaps just large enough to see him through, taking in scents which rankled, and all the while closing in on the lead element.

He remembered his time in the God House of Hunters, the others who had come to train alongside him from disparate places throughout the world. There had been that Magura gentleman, the one who was always smiling. A man who had chosen a path he might have considered himself had he no obligation to return to his people.

A pleasant man, was he not? I'd like to see him again one day.

He breezed past another pair, brushed one of their hands, leaving a fragment of his aura mingled with his scent buried in the soldiers soul, and suppressed a laugh as he turned a glare on the man next to him.

"Don't touch me." The one snapped.

"I didn't." The other said.

He left them to their bickering.

A nice chat would be good. Catch up on old times. I wonder what he's doing these days.

Storm the Keep

He wondered then about these Tului. He knew well the odor of sickness, had helped the medicine men among the Chikata identify infections in the past. Often, those advanced afflictions had simple cures. Some herbs administered over a duration of a few weeks often saw their victims returned to health. He wondered if it was the same for these people, if this thing that plagued them was less a curse and more a disease. If the cure for this sickness was as simple as administering the right herbs over a span of so many days or weeks.

And if it was, then maybe they could cure their own of the affliction. Maybe they would not have to cope with the infection much longer.

A peculiar smell emanated from the pocket of one of those soldiers. Something floral and tangy, if it was not precisely fresh. He slipped his fingers carefully into that pocket and came away with a delicate ball, which he slipped into his own pocket as he left the soldier in his wake, a fresh, quiet quarrel passing between him and the man next to him on that side.

He decided he would investigate it later. The other soldiers had nothing of its like on them, and that creamy, sickly odor was not as strong with him. A weak correlation, but one worth noting. It may have been that he was newer to this disease than the others, but he did not think so. He shared with them the virile youth and flickering shadows underfoot, both signs the infection was well into its late stages. Like so many parasites, it had settled happily in the soldier's body, making a home for itself and striking a balance with its poor host for its own benefit.

No, this was not a man new to these powers. But his body was fighting against the parasite harbored within him. Was pushing back against it if that fainter odor was any indication.

He passed between two more soldiers, the odor emanating off them much stronger, hiding behind a layer of pungent onion and pepper, telltale signs of men who had not seen a wash in some time. He wrinkled his nose at that sharper odor, and filed it away with all the rest.

Guruhl seized a soldier's face with a hand the size of an oven mitt. Raw energy pounded into the man's skull. He leapt back, ran to a safe distance. The man's body exploded, the explosion taking limbs from the nearest soldiers, knocking those behind them back for several feet.

He pressed forward, hunting for the Blood Lord among them. Quick flashes took in the soldiers even now closing in on him at his flanks. He danced with their shadows, stepping in the gaps between them, narrowly avoiding strikes for his own shadow, twisting so that it spun away from them as they closed in on it with clawing fingers, outstretched blades.

A sword whizzed through the air, mirroring one of those shadows as it struck for his neck. He ducked under it, barreled forward, and caught the Blood Lord around the midriff.

The shadows snapped back and together. The Tului soldiers nearest him recoiled.

Power leaked into the Blood Lord's stomach. He tossed him aside and kept running.

A vicious explosion rumbled through the earth. Showers of snow and earth blasted away from a newly formed crater.

Tears for the Moon God

Soldiers all around him dropped to the ground, clutching their necks, age descending on them like a thief.

He barreled into the next wave, clapping hands to bodies, imbuing exposed stones with raw power as he bolted through the hordes. Shadows snapped back into place. A fledgling respect was beginning to bubble forth in him for Bora. He had not believed she would be of any use to him or to the other raiders in this errand. He had been wrong.

The cunning little shit.

With every new contact, skin to skin, palm to body, another shadow snapped back and left a pocket of safety at his flank, in front of him. Explosions rocked the earth, compromised footings, blasted grit skyward to block out light sources that would have given the Tului some advantage.

He pressed onward, always southward, ever southward, ever closer to the rendezvous point as scarlet auras winked out, as ice stopped flowing from the soldiers.

The belly of the snake was in chaos. The hammer was collapsing in the center. New bodies filled in the gaps and were dispatched with brutal efficiency.

He caught another Blood Lord across the neck with a brutal swing of his arm. Explosive power leaked into him as four shadows snapped back into a single shape painted across bloody snow and rutted ice.

And he was running past. Blood and gore blasted out of shape, peppered the ground. Another wave of Tului soldiers vibrated across the ground and died.

He pushed through the last elements on the southern side of the mass as more broke off to lay chase, goaded them onto a losing path. He was close now. Akhi—*that bastard*—might have his own plans and he hoped they were worth the risk, but he could not think too long of him just now. He would bludgeon him half to death when he saw him again if whatever he was on about didn't prove worthy of his insubordination. He'd see the punishment done even if he had to go through Gulang to get to him.

But now, he was beginning to enjoy this. The taste of payback was sweet. The Tului were learning hard lessons, and he relished the act of delivering them.

Do not think of us as weak, you bastards.

He lumbered down a narrow avenue between pristine tent rows, ran his hands along posts, across the flank of an unattended horse, across stones and the exposed edges of weeds.

In his wake, explosions rang out, showering his pursuers in dirt, piercing them with pebbles speeding along like arrowheads.

He could see Gulang in the distance now, could see Berni and Chuuta. Swords flashed out. The first lines of the hammer had made contact, were seeking to drive them away and were suffering for it.

Bodies dropped to the ground in scores, some clutching at their throats and others at their bellies. Gulang's voice rang out, and a fresh wave of confidence pounded into him. The Tului laying chase, the lead elements of the hammer, were made frothing mad with it, and he lashed out with the other side of Sarkahn's power, sewing agony into them, bleeding it into the air around them as Berni robbed them of breath.

He panned across the scene, found Gaulakh rushing past the last line of tents separating him from his father, saw that he was not followed.

Storm the Keep

Where is Sircha? Not dead. Please not that.

She should have returned before either of them. They had left her closer to the rendezvous point with instructions to return as soon as her parcels were in place. Had left her with the warning not to linger too long, not to invite more chaos than she could handle. But the girl was a hot head, not at all like her twin.

Had she listened? He hoped she had. If she had not, she would be in a compromising position, alone in enemy territory and surrounded. These Tului were too much for a woman untested in combat as she was. He would have preferred if the twins had stayed back with their mother, had told Gulang as much, but he had left the decision up to them. Had left a choice of this magnitude, with the potential to kill them both, up to *children.*

Don't let this become another regret for your father, Sircha. He cannot handle another of his children dying. He is barely hanging on as it is.

He spun round to face his attackers, drew his scimitar from its sheath and dug it point first into the earth. He ran with the blade skidding through dirt and ice, pulses of power riding its edge into the soil.

He retracted the blade and ran the rest of the way to rejoin the others. Behind him, explosions rippled along the entire length of the line. Tului bodies exploded into shrapnel. Bones splintered. Chunks of meat flew in every direction. The belly of the snake was shattered, broken and reeling. Echoes of the blasts thundered through the air, robbing the scene of other sounds, of clanging metal, of tinkling ice, of snarled curses and bellowed orders. Horses threw their riders from the saddles. Forelimbs shattered. A pile of ruined corpses formed a steep embankment behind the line, and already more Tului were clambering over it, more horses were pouring around the sides.

Cussing, he backed to the edge of the circle.

Where are the others?" he yelled over the battle sounds.

"They haven't returned!" Gulang shouted back.

"How long do we wait for them?"

Gulang lashed out with his power, felling dozens of Tului soldiers, causing some few to fall from their saddles as intense pain flowered in them. "Until we cannot."

Guruhl rushed into the circle. He found his horse and leapt into the saddle. He kicked it into a gallop and exploded out of the safety of the circle, into the chaotic array of oncoming attackers as a cavalry unit broke from the infantry lines' flank and mounted a route along the southern edge.

His sword came away from its sheath. Power rushed down its length, white hot and dangerous. He carved lines through soldiers, along the flanks of horses as shadows danced under their feet, seeking to disrupt its footing. Explosions rocked the ranks behind him in quick successions. Savage detonations broke up the charge. Berni was on horseback now, too, making a sweep along the other edge. A vibrant aura emanated for several feet around her, and those caught in it clutched their throats, eyes rolling, horses collapsing under them as their blood acidified in their bodies, as they were denied precious oxygen.

She closed in, her aura enveloping him, providing a protective layer against the nearest elements of the Tului army.

"Where is Akhi?" she called.

"Finding the anvil!" His sword bit into the shoulder of a Tului horse. They galloped past, an explosion ravaging the charging element as the horse keeled forward, its head dipping.

White fire blasted forth behind them, erupting from Gaulakh's right hand and engulfing a fast closing complement of infantry who was attempting to regroup from the first wave of explosions.

The kid's got mettle. He lashed out at a horse warrior who was clutching his throat, struggling to draw breath.

Berni guided her horse away from his, down an open channel in the ranks, heading straight for the infantry contingent. The body slid from the horse and detonated before it hit the ground. The blast shattered the limbs of three other horses and sent their riders flying.

We can't keep this up forever. He thought as a new flash of white fire blasted from Gaulakh's open hand. *That anvil will be closing in soon. We need to retreat before it does.*

Bora watched the lines marching past. They seemed far more eager than they had to rut out the invaders among them. A full company of soldiers were marching toward the engagement racking the southwestern edge of the war camp in double time. Blood Lords were shouting orders, a measure that seemed redundant when a telepathic link was available.

Unless these are the ones that have been cut off. No. Those have already retreated.

Explosions echoed in the distance. Showers of earth rose and drifted along on the breeze.

Astair is watching. Will she intervene?

She wondered what other spirits were watching the engagement. If Tao Shein was angered by the brutalization of his body, or if he reveled in the suffusion of fresh blood into his lands. If Gondol the Witch had come out of hiding to watch the conflict unfold. The murky band of her creek was near enough on the eastern side.

She shook herself. There was no time to allow her thoughts to wander to those other spirits. To Sersu the Cricket, or Lardar, or Semh. All spirits whose sources of power were housed in the east central reaches of Tao Shein steppe, all of whom were of little consequence as lesser spirits in his embrace.

The Tului forces marched by. Explosions rocked the south. They needed to get past, win clear of them with the Baron well in hand.

Saafha leaned close to her. His breath came out in harsh gasps. The Baron, at his shoulder, watched those lines and made quiet conversation, as if the three of them had been friends for many years.

"What did you do to him?" she asked.

"It's—"

"Not important, yes I know. It is strange, though. He's like a dog."

"Just another kind of game." He said. "Do you have any ideas for getting past them?"

"Well, I can barely stand." She said. The pain in her arm had ebbed, a bad sign. She had lost too much blood already. Her strength was waning. The bandage had become a rigid band of ice glued to the wound, which had the benefit of stopping the blood flowing out of it, but was even now threatening her with hypothermia. "They are south of the line. In our domain. Skin to skin contact would render their powers useless, but it will not help us with their weapons. If they know how to use them."

"If we make contact with a Blood Lord."

"How would we? We would have to break through their ranks on foot. There are too many of them for your power to be much use."

He observed the lines cutting a path across the camp, keeping them well away from Gulang and their hope of leaving with their lives.

"Psst!" a hiss a few tents removed from them drew her attention. She saw Sircha there, hiding in its shadow, head and shoulders poking out around it.

Saafha gestured for her to come around the back, to join them.

She disappeared behind the tent. Quiet footsteps grinding against snow. She appeared around the back of the tent they hid behind.

Her gaze fell on the Baron, who was still talking to himself as if none of this was of any consequence.

"You know, the blood takes on such bitter notes when they're afraid, but the bitterness can become something like the astringency you southerners associate with dry wine if it can be matched with something more pleasurable. I like it best that way. A nice, dry red, I think. I often drug them before I take a meal.

"Of course, not too heavily. The drugs will come through with the blood. Enjoyable though they are, it would do me no favors to be seen deeply intoxicated in front of my peers. No, a little...."

Her gaze flicked to Bora, to the sodden, frozen bandage around her arm. "You're wounded."

"Can you do something about it?" Bora asked.

Sircha moved in close to her. She unbound the bandage and pried it back. "Hold still."

She ripped the bandage away.

A fresh flash of pain surged through Bora. She hissed through clenched teeth. Fresh blood weltered over the cut.

Sircha placed her hands above and below the wound. A sensation like warm water flowed over it. Trickles leaked deep into the cut, tickling her flesh as the muscle knit itself back together. The skin knit shut, leaving only dried blood to remember the wound by.

"Thank you."

"Now how do we get past them?"

Bora looked out at the troop rumbling by. She considered what new potentials might lay in the addition of Sircha's skills. Her power was a better match to these Tului than Saafha's. She could deal with the ice if they sought to attack in that way. Saafha could handle the shadows easily enough.

"I think you take point." She said. How far can you drive a current?"

"I don't know. Pretty far." Sircha said.

"Far enough to reach the other side?"

"I doubt it. This power is still new to me. I've only been with it for a year."

"If your running? Can you keep it going?"

"Yes."

"Then maintain a current around us. When we reach them, Saafha will handle the rest."

"I see." Saafha watched the lines pass. "If they see the Baron—"

"They'll pursue."

"Some of them are on horseback."

"Does your power work on horses?"

"No."

"Then target their riders as much as possible. If you get a shot at the Blood Lord, take it."

Saafha nodded.

"Time to go." She said.

Sircha hesitated.

"Now!" Bora cried.

She jumped.

Bora was already running before any of the rest of them set out. Sircha made up the difference. She whipped out her arms, yanked in the direction of the nearest snowbanks. Snow melted. Water flowed forward in a double line of raging white caps. Saafha and the Baron followed in their wake, Saafha already extruding oozing whips from his arms.

The waters knocked aside the nearest soldiers. Whips flashed through the air, struck several of the nearest figures, ripped their bodies away from their souls. Ghouls slid off bucking horses, surged into the rank and file.

"The Baron!" a soldier hollered.

The waters ebbed, and redoubled ferociously. Saafha's whips latched onto new bodies, drove their souls from them. The nearest lines recoiled. Soldiers split off in pursuit. Horse warriors broke off from the southern edge. His whips found those who got too close and pulled them down.

They cut through the line and won clear on the other side. As soon as they had, Sircha released the torrents, flung them to either side to bowl over horses and soldiers, and they bolted.

Akhi was near the front of the column now. He could pick out the lead elements of the troop from here, the Blood Lord leading the company plainly visible three ranks ahead of him. Even now, he was calling out orders. They were closing on their target, could taste violence in the air. Squads of infantry formed up in squares, carving out a blunt head for the assault. Cavalry units were organizing into a wedge to the south, readying to hem in the retreat.

It all seemed so useless to him. So disproportionate and yet so heinously rigid. They were fighting ten enemies. Ten Gil Garo raiders were hardly enough to warrant such a massive show of force. They were slowing themselves down with these preparations, giving time to their enemies to regroup and retreat. And that was to say nothing for whatever nastiness Chuuta had prepared for them.

They would have done better to organize themselves in smaller units and perform a sweep down from the north, pushing the Gil Garo out. But then, he supposed this was all to his people's benefit. Not least for what it told him about their tactics.

This was an army well trained who had not seen real combat in who knew how long. They used methods which seemed taken directly from the scholarly writings of Goddess Tajima's strategists. They were not as adept at handling the hit and run tactics the Gil Garo favored as the Ruc'an, or the Jahhar, the Loqui or their cousins in Ao Lein. Not accustomed to dealing with guerrillas and saboteurs, who were plentiful among the Gil Garo sects.

Storm the Keep

Have they even considered we may have anticipated them? That they are running directly into a trap?

They certainly hadn't anticipated anyone like him infiltrating their ranks. They might believe all of the Gil Garo were beholden to local spirits like they were. A flaw in their thinking which left them vulnerable, for the Gil Garo worshiped gods like anyone else. It just happened the gods they worshiped were different than those the more organized kingdoms in the south favored.

A lambent, amber eye, the pupil a fat slit riding the overlarge iris. A body sheathed in impenetrable darkness, its form hard to distinguish, giving the impression of a large beast with a slick hide. He remembered first laying eyes on God Shakh, and channeled that fear sense into him. He blinked his eyes, and the world was painted in different shades. Weak auras emanated from the Tului within his line of sight. He saw them cast in warm splashes of color, clouds of dusty rose radiating from them to mingle with each other. The heat of their bodies was mirrored by deeper shades of blue and violet where their shadows crisscrossed the snows, and those mounds and ice sheets took on a black tint, the colors inverted.

There was heat in those shadows, too, if it was much weaker. A suffusion of energy drawn down from the soul, which meant the Tului expended energy to maintain them. Energy they would need to recoup, which placed a burden on them even if a small one.

How much energy do they need to expend to keep those shadows alive?

He followed a channel between two squares each five rows deep and five long. Followed it straight to the head of the column, where the Blood Lord on horseback trotted back and forth, inspecting his squads from the saddle. He could pull him down, but what use would that be. He would only alert the others to his presence then, and the hunt would be on.

He fell into rank with one of those compliments and waited for the Blood Lord to return, masked his aural signature so as not to startle the beast under him. Animals used to being prey were more attenuated to sensing a Hunter's presence, but their second sight was not absolute, and avoiding detection was of great consequence to God Shakh. One might say hiding in plain sight was the true essence of him, that everything else was simply in service of avoiding prying eyes.

The Blood Lord returned. He tipped his nose up and inhaled deep. Horse flesh, earth, the brittle odors of snow and mud, brighter boot leather. The scents came to him mingled together. Behind them were deeper aromas. Sickness, the iron tang of blood, the heady musk of man flesh, mingled bacteria and sweat, faint ammonia barely perceptible through layers of cloth and tissue.

He compared that scent to the catalog of others he had filed away, noted similarities in the odors, the kind he associated with familial ties. There were those who possessed it and those who did not. He blinked again. The world was cast in shades of gray. Sizzling whites disrupted the gray scale, electromagnetic disturbances, aural intrusions. There were similarities between this Blood Lord and many in Akhi's immediate range. He noted those, too. Dark voids rippled along the contours of their bodies, rolled along them in absence of the brighter shades of activated auras. The shapes differed in nuanced ways, spike frequencies differentiated individuals from each other, but some bore a resemblance to those dark spots flitting around the Blood Lord's body.

He wondered how many behind him were linked directly or otherwise to this

Tears for the Moon God

commander, how the ripples would spread when his chosen task was done.

The Gil Garo were in sight now, but they were distracted, dealing with the hammer, putting up the good fight.

The Blood Lord came within two paces of him.

He drew a knife from his belt and surged forward. He leapt for the horse, rolled under it, hamstringing its forelegs as he passed. The horse pitched forward, throwing its rider amid cries of alarm from the soldiers. Akhi rounded on him, dragged his head up and slashed his throat.

Blood sprayed the snows. Age shattered the visage of a young man. Behind him, bodies dropped to the ground. Dozens, and then hundreds.

His suspicion proved accurate. The chain of command was absolute. Many of those soldiers died. Blood Lords of lower rank slid from horses suddenly wild with fright who broke into wild charges away from the soldiers. Full squads dropped onto the ground, writhing and clutching at their necks.

He pelted away, dropping his defenses as he traveled. They would cost him too much now that he was on the move, and the shadows provided no defense he needed with the anvil in chaos. The chain of command had dissolved, leaving Blood Lords attempting to bring order back to the horde of others all falling over each other to put distance between themselves and the perceived threat Akhi offered.

He thought again of the Magura man he had met in the God House of Hunters, a man of an age with him, who had gone over to the Raukhas to become a Lamb. Assassinations were a better use of a Hunter's capabilities, but against an enemy like this, such a short-sighted endeavor as this caste system propped up provided the only weakness he need exploit.

The heart can be healed given enough time. He recalled that man saying. *But the mind...once conquered it can never heal. Men remember what hurts them. Lock it up somewhere deep down and inaccessible, until the moment it comes time to remember. Cripple the mind. The flesh is of no consequence. It is the mind that is weak. Cripple it, and the man never recovers.*

He smiled as he ran. If the Tului remembered nothing else about this raid, they would remember what ten men had cost them. Their food supply, yes, and a full company of their soldiers.

Gulang's gaze snapped to the east. Beyond the gouts of white fire, among the flickering, long shadows cast by it. A diminutive man with a barrel chest was running toward them.

Akhi.

Behind him, the anvil had revealed itself. It was in chaos. Bodies writhed in the throes of death by scores, by hundreds. He wondered what had come to pass over there. What Akhi had done that could have caused such a conflagration among the Tului. Many of them were barreling away to the north. More were amassing around horse warriors, and even those were having difficulties keeping their horses contained.

Guruhl was sweeping down from the east, making swift progress to reunite with them. Berni occupied a pocket of writhing bodies dwarfed by the summary fall of the men of that other force.

To the north, Saafha and Bora had emerged. Two others ran along in their wake. A blonde, prissy looking man in scarlet robes, and a woman taller than Bora

Storm the Keep

but only just.

Sircha. Thank the gods for setting her path before her.

He breathed a little easier, and blasted a fresh wave of power away from him, suffusing the area a dozen long strides ahead of him with all of the negative feelings he had taken from the Tului leading the charge for the circle.

Bora's arm and flank were covered in dried blood. Saafha's lumbering steps spoke volumes of the shape he was in. But they had succeeded. They had taken this baron.

A force of hundreds were in pursuit, ten paces removed from them and barely out of range. Their shadows danced ahead of them.

"Gaulakh!" he bellowed.

Gaulakh turned to him, followed where he pointed. He broke away from the his engagement further east, sending a wave of white fire behind him to catch any Tului who came too close. He flung his knife at the lines of pursuers, guided its movements with his left hand. It punched through the rank and file, dropping several.

Guruhl changed direction, cut a line across those ranks, laid into them with his sword.

Gaulakh retreated, changed course and followed at their flank toward the circle where Kachukh was awaiting them.

A horse broke through the ranks of followers. It's rider jerked the reigns, bringing it around and in front of the Gil Garo forces. He was clad in heavy armor, leather and chain, plate gauntlets and boots which rode his calves almost to his knees. He set a scarlet eyed gaze on Gulang, and charged.

Crow. The word bubbled into the fore of Gulang's mind, and his middle son's face loomed at the fore, framed by black, all consuming rage.

Bellowing, he snatched at the sword belted to his hip, wrenched it free as he charged forth to meet that horse mounted warrior.

The Crow dropped from his saddle, a heavy claymore already coming free of its sheath. He swung the blade, ice coalescing along the edge, pulled from the air itself. A barrage of glassy Shards followed the arc of the swing.

Gulang leapt to the side and kept coming. He brought his blade up, stealing raw terror from the soldiers in the Tului camp and pressing it into the steel.

Metal clanged against metal, the impact driving tremors high into his arm.

He forced the Crow's arm wide, brought his sword around.

The Crow kicked snow loose from a low mound. Needles of ice pierced Gulang's flank. Bora, Saafha, Sircha and the Baron rushed past, making for the circle.

He did not have time to wonder what would happen when they reached it. Blades whirred through the air. Ringing impacts echoed after them. Metal bit into metal. Savage blows were parried and thrown aside.

Shadows danced under Gulang's feet. Fresh cuts bloomed across his body, shallow gashes. The Crow was playing with him, seeking to weaken him with his shadows, slow his movements ahead of a final blow.

His blade opened a cut in the chain hauberk along his flank, bit into the Crow's flesh. Blood weltered from the shallow wound and the Crow hissed, his sword changing hands as that arm dropped uselessly to his side.

His shadows shot forward, doing the work his arm could not, making contact with Gulang's shadow and wrenching open deeper cuts as ice flows shot up around

Tears for the Moon God

the Crow, forcing him back and away.

Blood leaked from several places along his torso, arms and legs.

The fight was close to its conclusion, and he was losing. Black rage and adrenaline kept him fighting, kept the sword coming up to meet renewed blows, to shatter ice as he leapt between shadows, seeking better ground behind him.

Berni charged into the gap between them. Her hand came down and took hold of the collar around Gulang's neck. She dragged him for several feet, brought him back into the circle and dropped him there.

He wheezed through a brutalized throat.

The Crow was running for his horse, preparing to mount it.

Kachukh helped him to his feet.

"The horse! Get on the horse!" he yelled.

He climbed to his feet. Chuuta and Gaulakh had taken hold of him, were tossing him over his horse's back. Guruhl took its reigns in hand, maneuvered it around.

The others were amassed in the circle, the baron included.

The Tului were retreating back a safe distance.

He watched from his prone position in the saddle, gripping the pommel horn for purchase as his horse leapt the trench, carrying him away. Watched as the Tului formed up for a charge. As Chuuta tossed a burning rag into the trench. As fire blossomed in the ditch, and the sickly sweet aroma of opium filled the air. Formed a wall between the Tului and them.

Bora was in the saddle with him. Her hand was on his back. Darkness filled his vision, and oblivion replaced it, driving him down into unconsciousness. Into a dreamless sleep.

Crow Durin watched the Gil Garo retreat. He had not felt so vulnerable since his turning—since awareness of Tuluis Fel blossomed in his mind, and began a constant watch through his proxies, an observation of his behavior which would follow him for all of his life.

His mind was empty. The storm of thoughts from outside places was no longer crowding his mind, giving him these moments to be with himself, alone for the first time in four decades.

He wondered at the power of this people as he watched them retreat into darkness.

He needed to rethink his strategy where it concerned these Gil Garo. He had suffered an embarrassing defeat this night. The death toll was staggering. The pens on the south side of the camp had been compromised, and what survivors were still housed within them would need to be bled of whatever poison those raiders had used.

They should not have come this far. Should never have succeeded in their endeavors. They had come away very nearly unscathed, a bitter fact he would harbor in his memory as he considered what strategic endeavors would need to be undertaken to prevent another defeat of this magnitude.

His commander was still out of range, still blind to what had occurred here. He would have to make haste to reconvene with him, ask for fresh forces to be sent. Absent a more expedient means of communication, he would need to send a runner. Let General Saraed know his company would be striking camp once an account of the damages had been taken. That they would be making double time back to the

Storm the Keep

border where their main force awaited them.

He would have his pound of flesh for this. He would pursue those chiefs and their people when the time was right and he had the advantage of home terrain. This insult would not go unanswered. But now, he must strike a retreat. Engage with these beasts of men no further. Not until he had reunited his force with General Saraed's.

He would have to let him know of Baron Keirn's capture. It would not suit to lie to him. The general would see through the lie effortlessly. He might be court marshalled over it if his commanding officer saw fit to alert the Order of Scarlet Wings to his failure. To the loss of one of their own.

He hoped he would be spared that fate. That he would live to see his day of blood, when next he encountered these savages.

But now. Now I must wait. Now I must gather intelligence, take it to General Sarae, as quickly as possible. He will need to reassess his own strategy.

That conniving god...that conniving bastard god.

"Stubborn *ass!*" Berni seethed.

She watched Gulang's body flop around on the back of Bora's horse as they galloped away from the war camp. The enemy was not chasing after them, a matter that gave Bora relief. They were in no position to contend with them on the retreat, and Gulang badly needed healing.

Some of his wounds were deep, in need of more care than a fledgling acolyte of Dadang could provide. The bonfire glow of the camp had lost its red cast as the Tului let down their guards and regrouped.

She wondered how much damage they had done to them. Akhi's move against the anvil had fallen well outside her calculations. She would not have believed, *could not* believe, one man had taken down so many soldiers by himself, but he had exposed a greater weakness in their ranks. The hierarchical order to their troops concentrated power at the top in a way she would never have believed was so direct. She had expected disruptions in their ranks with the felling of their leaders, but she had never believed it would progress so far. The Tului had in their hands a double edged sword.

Getting close to their commanders would be difficult. They knew tactics, and while those tactics were clean and straight forward, their response time was too swift, the way they conducted themselves when met with opposition, even if small, was nothing like what she had expected from an isolationist kingdom.

This force had seen combat before they ever arrived at the Gil Garo's doorstep. That Crow was a formidable one, as well. To have handled Gulang on even ground, to have bested him in single combat...he would be a dangerous foe indeed, and she suspected he was not near the height of command in the Tului army. That there were yet more ranks above him, several degrees of separation between him and this people's commander in chief.

Guruhl, at the head of the column, signaled for a halt. He slowed his horse and dismounted, then rounded to where Bora sat in the saddle, still clinging to Gulang to stabilize him.

"Sircha!" he growled.

Gulang's only daughter dismounted her horse. Astair gave breath to the world, driving westward as snow began to drift out of a clouded sky. The glow still

Tears for the Moon God

emanated from the horizon, but it was dimmer, and smaller. They had traveled some miles, and the horses breathed heavily, their hides slick, feet stamping aimlessly. They needed rest.

Guruhl and Chuuta pulled Gulang from the saddle and lay him against the snows. Gaulakh, Kachukh and Saafha watched as Sircha knelt beside their father, laid hands on him and closed her eyes, searching.

"Can you heal him?" Guruhl asked.

"He should have known better." Berni muttered. "He let his ego get the better of him, the incompetent—"

"Quiet, Berni." Guruhl snapped.

"Most of his wounds are minor, but the deeper ones...I can close them but we'll have to hand him to a more practiced healer when we get back." She looked into her father's face.

In sleep, he was at peace in a way she had never seen from him. The kind thrust upon a man at his most vulnerable moments, when he was not in command of himself.

She went to work. The minor cuts and shallow punctures in his flesh knit back together, leaving just dried blood to remember them by. The deeper wounds remained mangled ruins, but slow trickles of blood stopped flowing from them, and the flesh along those cuts lightened to a dull pink under clots of a darker crust.

The men helped him onto a fresh horse, and Guruhl drew out the reigns and tied them to his saddle horn. Chuuta remounted, and they set off again at a slow trot. The chief's children wore stony expressions as they struck out for the Gil Garo camp, and Bora wondered what they were thinking. Whether they feared for the loss of their father still, or felt some relief at his healing.

A Song for the Forgotten

Soft singing roused Ibrim from his sleep. He had been dreaming of his family. His sisters had been arguing over something...something menial. Hassan was trying to intercede, nudge them along a path both were reluctant to venture down, at the end of which was common ground. Hassan had always been like that. Putting his nose into other people's business when it was clear he was unwelcome.

He was so unlike the rest of his siblings. Ibrim could not deny he had a penchant for vanity and excess, that he might even be a bit shallow. But for all the gold and jewels, the status and power, foisted upon Hassan I Alghoul, he alone could leave it all behind and feel nothing whatsoever untoward.

Samara and Nimira, Abellard III...he felt no such longing for their company, but Hassan he missed deeply. So hollow was life without his brother by his side, to temper him.

That song was riding a deepening crescendo, clamoring for hidden reserves in the singer's lungs. The singer's voice was deep and sonorous, and reminded him of water—something depthless, the true breadth out of reach of human ears, suffusing these halls and chambers with a foreign power.

He bunched up his pillow to block his ears, a futile effort to drown out the sound. *The nerve of this bastard! Where is his sense of decency.*

The song was joined by the cascading beat of hurried footsteps rushing down the hall outside. Footsteps carrying several bodies toward his chambers. If they were trying to sneak about in these barracks, it did not do to sing that guttural dirge as the one among them did. It did not do at all.

The pattering ceased, and his door warbled open, revealing in silhouette several figures occupying the doorway. He could just make out the balled cheeks and taught tendons in the neck of the singer among them, and then another was stepping through, into the moonlight.

He had never seen a creature quite like it. It resembled a human, but dodged the proper vestiges by narrow degrees. Pallid skin reminded of a dead fish. Its eyes were an aggressive scarlet, too wide and too large for its face. Cheekbones were ridged with scaly spurs that ran from the edges of a smashed-looking nose along the sides of its face, and below a wild frock of sea green hair, it had no discernible ears.

The creature reminded him of a snake.

He recoiled against the wall at his back, the pillow dropping away as he scrambled for anything that might serve as a weapon. The best he could do was a belt laying at the foot of his bed, where he had discarded it atop the coverlet. The buckle was wide and heavy, and he held it by the notched end, ready to crack skulls if these monsters got too close.

They loomed in the moonlight, the singer positioned just outside the door, some with their heads tilted and gazes unfocused, listening to some peculiarity within the song the shape of which he did not want to know.

The nearest of them pulled a long knife from his belt, stepped forth. Silken robes of a kind not made for fighting swished and swirled around his shins as he stepped in close to the bedside.

Ibrim lashed out with his belt, and the creature caught it with his free hand, caught it without having even to look at where it would land. His assailant's eyes were unfocused like the rest of them. He was barely aware of his surroundings.

The creature wrenched the belt out of his hand. It burned across his palm as leather bit into flesh, and he screamed.

"Quiet." One of the others hissed.

"Do not make this more difficult than it need be." The assailant intoned.

Whimpering, he curled his knees up to his chest and set his forehead against them. If he could do nothing else, he could blot out their existence, keep his gaze trained on the rumpled bedsheets beneath him, the edges of his bare, honey-toned legs. He was not one to care whether he died with his dignity.

His father's face crowded next to Hassan's, his sisters and his elder brother, and twisted into a shapeless mass as each vied for his attention, as he tried to fix the second prince's soft features, so like their mother, into place, so that he could die thinking of someone he loved.

The singing cut off in a garbled, monosyllabic plea.

A sound like stacked wood rolling off the back of a wagon. A body hit the ground.

In the wake of the death, a second singer raised her voice to replace his, and was cut off almost as quickly.

Several blades rasped out of their sheaths.

Ibrim's chin snapped up. His gaze fell on the entrance to his chambers.

Framed in a miasma like a bloody mist, eyes shining a luminous red to match the attackers, was Seun. Ice crept across the threshold, climbed the door frame, and twin shadows danced out from under his feet, each wielding a long knife like the one the monster in front of Ibrim had been about to use to end his life. Knives flew through the air, mirroring those the silhouettes carried. Throats were slit in quick succession as the temperature in the room dropped.

Ibrim's breath misted before him, obscuring the face of the final assailant in time for a knife to sail out and thrash against his throat. Mangled cartilage and gore wobbled around an exhaled breath as the body dropped to its knees and keeled forward.

As Seun walked over the scattered corpses, new voices rose in the hall. Shouted orders. Marching feet.

Ibrim's heartbeat thundered against his eardrums.

A Song for the Forgotten

The first moonkin acolyte crossed the threshold. His gaze flickered over the corpses and Ibrim, then landed on Seun. The bloody aura around him had faded, and his eyes had returned to their usual, muddy brown. He was panting, clutching his side.

"You took long enough." He gasped.

"What is the meaning of this?" the acolyte demanded.

"What does it look like. A god wants Ibrim dead, and it isn't the one we serve."

"But these...these are uelfin! We have no bad blood with them."

"You do now." Suen said. "I need sleep. I'm going to bed."

"Wait."

But Seun had already gone.

The acolyte's gaze hung on Ibrim. "You know who these creatures serve?"

"I don't even know what they are."

"They're demigod children. Much like the katcyakin. But their father is God Lanfin, the God of Music."

"Keeper of Time." Another acolyte intoned, and he recognized his voice.

Faez A'doelle loomed in the doorway. "Report what you've seen to God Ao Nii. Do it now." He said to the acolyte.

The acolyte bowed and left. Faez twisted around, shouted behind him. "Clean this mess up!" He turned again to Ibrim. "Come with me. We'll get you situated somewhere more secure until we have a better grasp on our situation."

"What does God Lanfin want with me?" Ibrim asked, rising.

"Who knows? The gods are prone to attacking each other when they sense a weakness, or a potential benefit to them. What this is, I do not know. Only that it means we will require a calculated response."

He took him from the room, and led him through the barracks in pursuit of safer reaches.

Thera had come to Gil Garo, carrying with her warm breezes from the tropics far south of Ul Sadh's coasts. Her touch on Shaki's cheeks invited relief from the bitter cold of a northern winter, from Ho'o's wild, howling winds, for The North Wind was far away from here, and would be for some time.

With Thera came the promise of coming spring, a taste of sweet grass and floodwater. Her influence would wane with time, and by nightfall of the next day, she would have gone completely. He thought about calling out to her while the opportunity still held, but decided against it. He could feel it in the bond he shared with her, in the tether that bound his soul to hers, that she was preoccupied, worried over something far beyond his ability to understand, and the source of that worry was somewhere north.

North...where Bora is. With my father. He sighed, and climbed onto his feet at the edge of the long platform outside of the chief's pavilion. Chakta had gone off to check her snares for small game, out amid the snows and tall grasses. She'd been lucky of late, catching the occasional jackrabbit or prairie dog. Small game was always in abundance if the hunter knew where to look, and Chakta had a gift for tracking paw prints across the mounded snows, rooting out active burrows.

Tamlin had packed the snows into the crude shape of a man, and was using it now for target practice. He knocked an arrow to the gut string of his short bow, took aim and loosed. The arrow thunked home in the figure's chest, where its heart

Tears for the Moon God

ought to be, and a shower of white powder and ice chips was blasted away.

He trudged through the snows to his target, pulled his arrow free and then fussed over packing the crater it left behind with more snow, to cover the damage it had done.

A quiet day, and a peaceful one, it seemed their worries were abated for now. Be it that Thera kept watch over her acolyte, kept what gods might wish them ill at bay, or that God Katcya still lingered too close for any of those nefarious actors comforts to make their plays, or even that Duijus Kanh and his concubines were enough, life had taken on the ease of humdrum mundanity. The quiet banality of routine.

If it was not what he wanted, it was at least comfortable. For the time being it was. If Chakta and Tamlin could just leave that drum alone, they'd all be fine. They hadn't touched it since that first night, in which Ho'o and God Katcya—both mercurial, often violent entities—had joined them. If they were shaken enough by those events to leave their playing well alone, then he could count his blessings they wouldn't be inviting a repeat anytime soon. And he would do just that.

"It's a stupid tradition, anyway." He grumbled, too low for a returning Tamlin to hear.

A keening cry broke through the quiet, a sonorous, coruscating rhythm. Someone far in the distance was singing.

A doe lifted onto its feet and took flight in a shower of snow, a yearling fawn driving through the banks behind it.

As the snows settled, Tamlin's focus snapped in the direction of the distant, northern horizon. Chakta was scrambling through drifts, a pair of jackrabbits strung up by their hind legs and slung over her shoulder. She pelted hard over treacherous, uneven ground, hunting for the nearest tracks where the Kachin camp had formerly been arranged.

In her wake, several figures rose up amid the snows, climbed fluidly to their feet. Two hung back as the others lay chase, pursuing Chakta on surer feet, the deep snows providing no barrier to their progress.

She hit the nearest track and pelted down the lane. Tamlin was already calling on his spirit's pulse as she found her footing and galloped toward them. Around the edge of the pavilion, horses whickered and snorted, heedless of the impending danger these foreigners posed.

As they closed, what he had initially taken to be Ruc'an raiders materialized as something else entirely. They wore cloaks that drifted around their ankles, all of silk and frocked with dense furs. Their skin was far too pale for them to be of the Ruc'an, their features oddly stretched and flattened, giving them an almost snake-like appearance.

They drew long knives from under those as they marched diligently across the drifts, dropped onto the track behind her as Tamlin knocked an arrow.

He let fly. One of those monsters caught the arrow mid-flight and tossed it aside. At the same time, the singer holding back quieted, and the song was picked up by his peer.

The monsters broke into a run, moving sinuously over surer ground, closing in on Chakta.

Thrilling static vibrated along Shaki's limbs. He felt for the pulse in the breezes, Thera's pulse, and pulled it into himself. Her energies suffused him, drawing out

A Song for the Forgotten

barbed tendrils of electricity to crawl across his skin, to drift down his arms.

He suppressed a surge of panic, ignored the ball forming in his throat. These were not friends, but they were not Tului, either. He had seen those corpses, had seen those people on the night of the attack in the hundreds. He knew the look of them, and they were nothing like these, sharing only red eyes in common. Red eyes and pale skin, and even then the Tului were not this pallid. These creatures looked dead.

He stepped forward. Too fast to be followed with the naked eye, he had breezed past Chakta, putting himself between her and the closing troupe of monsters. Lightning thrashed across their ranks. The song ended and was picked up by another singer. The lightning recoiled to roll across his exposed forearms. Steaming craters marred the path, but the creatures were unharmed.

How?

Tamlin knocked another arrow. He drew the bowstring back to his cheek. The arrow head glowed with vicious light, and he loosed.

The arrow struck home in the dirt at the feet of a pair of those heinous creatures. Earth exploded under them. Mangled carnage, meat and gore sprayed across open air, spattered the snows.

The singing went on as the two hangers on sped forth, trailing their fellow hunters as another pair fell back from the charging line, and a new singer took up where the last left off.

Shaki lashed out with another wave of lightning. He backpedaled, putting several dozen feet between the assailants and him as the lightning thrashed across their ranks, missing all of them yet again.

How are they dodging me? They shouldn't even be able to see those attacks.

He fell back another step, placing himself just ahead of Chakta. He reached out as she closed on him, wrapped her in his embrace, supported her head and neck like a newborn and stepped back once more. In a jarring instant, they were atop the pavilion's deck. Tamlin rushed in to join them.

"How are they doing that?" Tamlin gasped.

"I...I don't know. But we need to get away from them."

"We can't." Chakta glanced pointedly in the direction of Duijus Kanh's cave. "They're not here for us."

"So what? We die here? If we can't hit them—"

"You hit them just fine. How?"

"I don't know. Maybe they were too distracted by you to see what I was doing." Shaki nodded. "I'll cover you."

Chakta was shaking her head. "Let me try something."

She pulled away from Shaki, who realized with a wave of embarrassment that he was still hugging her tight to his chest. Realized, too, that he was doing it for his own benefit. These creatures terrified him.

"Give me some space. This could get weird."

He retreated several steps. To her other side, Tamlin did the same.

She spread her arms, closed her eyes. Waves of coruscating power flowed into her like flowing waters. At the foot of the platform, the snows were scattered as if by raging winds, yet Thera's breezes held.

"Get ready, you two. I've never done this before and I'm not sure how long it'll last."

Tears for the Moon God

"What are you doing?" Tamlin asked.

"Interfering with their senses." She said.

The snows billowed forth, drove across the intervening distance like a wall. The wall glittered with stolen sunlight, shimmered and spangled as it collapsed over the closing attackers.

"What the hell." Tamlin whispered.

The wall of glimmering snows crashed soundlessly over them, but they toppled one and all as if struck with a physical force. Utter silence fell over the plains, driving out even the subtle sound of the breezes sifting across the snows.

Now. He could see the word painted across Chakta's lips as if she screamed it.

He drew on his link to Thera. Lightning struck across the line as Tamlin loosed another arrow. Earth exploded forth, stealing away the last of those unnatural snows, leaving behind a trail of corpses.

"There." He panted. Having so much of Thera's power running through him left him exhausted, feeling as if great holes had been burned into his spirit. He collapsed onto his knees, leaned back and lay across the ice rimed planks.

"What the hell, Chakta." Tamlin said. "Where did that come from?"

"It was just an illusion." She said.

"But—"

"But nothing. If they'd been expecting it, I doubt they would have been thrown off balance that easily. And who says there aren't more of them."

"If they come back, we have the Swans." Shaki pointed out.

"You know they don't come out in daylight. God Gorgus won't tolerate it."

"They must have known that." Tamlin said. "Or why bother attacking when they know we are alert."

"Why bother attacking us at all?" Shaki said. "Why do we suddenly have so many enemies we've never met? First the Tului attack us unprovoked, and now whatever these are."

"I think I know what they are." Chakta said. "At least, I know who they serve."

"Yeah?" he asked.

"They dodged your attacks like they knew what was coming. I think they could see the future somehow. Which means they must be servants of the God of Music, right? They've got to be God Lanfin's."

"Have you two been seeing mice lately?"

"Why?"

Tamlin cussed. "The Rat Goddess. She must know we're here."

"Bingo!" Shaki said, punching the planks for emphasis. "The snake and the rat run together. If he knows we're here, she does too. And if she does, how many other gods are watching us right now? Waiting for their turn."

"This is because of Dupec." Tamlin grumbled. "What else could it be."

"That isn't news." Chakta said. "No sense acting surprised now."

"You're not?"

"Why should I be? The guy is half god himself."

"Let's get inside." Chakta panned over the snows. She adjusted the pair of jackrabbits dangling from her shoulder. "I don't want to give that bitch more material for her archive than we already have."

"Who's to say she doesn't have mice in the pavilion?" Shaki asked.

"We'll flood them out, then." Chakta said confidently.

A Song for the Forgotten

Just when I thought things were finally getting back to normal. He accepted Tamlin's offered hands and climbed to his feet. They marched into the pavilion, leaving those monstrous corpses for the Swans. Without their usual stock of sick and elderly tribesmen, and with the Tului corpses long buried, they must be starving.

Hopefully they have some idea what to do about these people. He thought, taking a last look at the scattered, dismembered and disfigured corpses before passing into the greater warmth and comfort of the pavilion. *Hopefully they know how to stop them.*

Ibrim sat at the little table in the corner of the barracks' rooms he had been taken to. With the guards outside the open door, he did not feel safer. Those creatures had breached a God House, after all. The whole city was suffused with Ao Nii's energy. His influence touched everything within it. They had managed to pare away every defense it possessed, infiltrate deeply enough to land themselves at *his* doorstep, and if not for Seun...if not for him....

He shuddered. *I'd be dead.*

The furnishings in this room were the same as in his or Seun's. A small, white oak table and matching chairs of simple design. A camp bed with a rather thin mattress. A wardrobe near its feet. The vitreous wall looked out on a different scene than his room.

The vantage was farther removed from the gates and the palace, and to look out of it was to look out on the city proper, its residential districts sprawling almost to the very edge of the island this city occupied. Beyond, the city and the island yielded to impenetrable darkness, stars, and a distant, strong glow which reminded him of hearth fire, the vibrant array of oranges and yellows splashed across the wall opposite it. That glow had been faint when first he arrived. It had been growing stronger of late.

An acolyte marched into the room. He was roused from his observation of that distant glow, where he was sure the God House of the Sun, seat of God Gorgus, lay. Somewhere in the gulf between sun and moon, the God of the Sky, God Shirad, must maintain his own domain. He wondered what a place like that must be like.

He twisted around, found Faez A'doelle crossing the threshold, and in his wake, a man he did not recognize, who was dressed in elaborate, flowing robes, who carried a halberd in his right hand, whose face was veiled behind a rigid fall of scarlet lace.

"Ibrim, this is Jule the Red. He is Right Hand of God Ao Nii. He wishes to ask you some questions." Faez said.

"Your participation will not be needed." Jule said to him.

He bowed, and then took his leave.

Jule gestured to one of the guards at the door, who hurried to him. He passed the ornate halberd to him, and beckoned him return to his post.

Jule took the unoccupied seat opposite Ibrim. He leaned back against it, striking a too casual pose as his hard eyed regard fell on the Tulakka prince.

"You don't look like much." He growled. "Powdered nobles rarely are."

"Is that any way to—"

"Quiet." Jule snapped.

He closed his mouth, but settled against his chair in the same fashion Jule had done.

"You don't know much about respect, do you? No, I do not give you leave to answer." He raised a hand in warning. "You are speaking to the Right Hand of our god. You will sit up straight, and speak when you are told to speak."

Ibrim did not rise at his demand. He did not speak, either. He had dealt with these types. He understood far more about them than he did the common rabble. He would gain nothing from this man if he complied with his demands, and he had too many questions to entertain a one sided conversation. Those creatures were not human, and they seemed to know how he would react before he did. Almost as if they possessed precognition.

He had never heard of any creature with such abilities. Had never known a God Lanfin who cared a wit about mortals. What god so afflicted would concern himself with taking on acolytes?

"Those uelfin chose your rooms to attack for a reason." Jule said. "Do you know why?"

Ibrim did not answer.

"*Now* would be the time to speak."

He grinned. "I have a suspicion."

Jule laced his fingers together, set his wrists against the table. "Elaborate."

In the interim between the attack and this man's arrival, he had been given time to think. Isolation had a way of allowing a man to make sense of things he may otherwise have missed.

"It's something Ao Nii said to me."

"*God* Ao Nii." Jule corrected.

"Yes, I'm sorry." He said. "Our god implied this was not the first time I had come before him. He said the last time I had been looking for revenge. That I betrayed his trust, or something like that, when it became clear he couldn't give me what I wanted."

"God Ao Nii does not sanction mortal revenge." Jule said. "He understands the affliction well. He would rather us not follow his example, as, I am sure, he explained to you."

"In so many words."

"Nonetheless, an uelfin attack is a rare thing. Usually, God Lanfin handles his grudges personally, and succinctly. He values clean outcomes. He does not like messy solutions to complex problems.

"What I fail to understand...is what problem he finds with *you*."

"Is that—"

"Yes. Speak." He gestured curtly for him to say his piece.

"I don't know."

"You don't? Most often, a god does not attack unprovoked. Unless the contours of the attack can be construed as a move in their Greatest Game. God Lanfin saw an advantage in removing you from the board. Why?"

"As I said. I don't know. But perhaps the person who arrived at *God* Ao Nii's doorstep in this forgotten past did."

"Perhaps."

"He did say—"

"You have made that abundantly clear. As has he."

"You've spoken to him?"

A Song for the Forgotten

"Of course." He spat. "Our conversation did not bear much fruit. That is why I am here. Speaking to *you*. The imbecilic prince who has, inexplicably, earned the wrath of a rival god. One, I might add, who does not view our god as a friend."

"I can't speak to that." Ibrim said. "Except to say I know less than you do."

"If God Ao Nii remembers you, it is likely because you lived once before."

"I can think of no more plausible explanation."

"Quiet. I'm thinking."

Ibrim fell silent, watched Jule the Red's face for tells that might give him some insight into what was behind all of this.

"May I supply a thought?" Ibrim said.

Jule gestured for him to speak. His expression, however, did not speak to any amenable disposition on his part.

"Was I the only one attacked?" he asked. "No, I don't mean here. I mean in general. Was I the only one attacked by these *uelfin?* Is that what you called them."

"That is what they are."

"What are they?"

Jule glared at him. "If you must know. They are the descendants of God Lanfin with the Crystal River, Oe. A Great River."

"I thought he was betrothed to the Rat Goddess."

"Oe was his first lover."

"Understood."

"You wonder whether you were the only one attacked. I wonder why you believe you were not."

"Because if the person I was, when I first visited our god, was invested in revenge, there must have been a target of that revenge."

Jule's expression was unreadable. He stood abruptly, and rounded the table.

"Is that all?" Ibrim asked.

"It is."

"Then you have what you need."

"I do."

"What about me?"

"What about you?"

"Will I be safe?"

A cold laugh issued from Jule. He said nothing more, but left, collecting his halberd from the guard at the door on his way past.

A Coming Eclipse

The road was marred with craters and ruts this close to Gonsai wall. It provided unstable footing for Lisandra as she labored under the weight of her pack, at times falling behind Jinga and Kiresh as she picked her way across the uneven ground. Twenty years younger, she would have had no problem keeping pace with them, but time was not kind to mortals, and it had left her weakened. What stamina and strength she possessed in her middle years waned with the coming of senescence.

Her foot dug into a pothole she had missed in her survey of the terrain. The ankle twisted painfully, and she gnashed her teeth together. A soft groan gusted through curled lips. She lifted her leg, pressed her foot gingerly against a level patch between ruts where cartwheels had passed countless times, depressing slick mud, molding it into shape before it dried and hardened, accepting the depressions as a semipermanent feature.

Wild country sprawled toward the horizons east and west of them. Open plains riddled with deer tracks, creeks and streams. Spirits abounded within the streams, lesser kin of deep lakes and aquifers. They would provide healing if she could reach them, if she could entice them with some offering against what she carried in her pack. But the road did not come close to the waterfalls spouting out of Gonsai's face, the pools and streams they fed.

The sun bulled through its evening stations on its way across the horizon to light up the other side of the world, and the moon loomed in the sky with it. Its presence so early in the evening, when there were still shades of blue in the sky, sent a shiver down her spine. She had seen an event such as this only once, nearly thirty years ago. Her village had been blessed in the days that followed for its isolation, but even there, one saodeini woman who had come to live among them as a youth, when Lisandra herself was barely a woman, had been taken by the affliction at noontime, when the moon blotted out the sun and darkness reined.

They had found her in her home in the aftermath. There had been holes in her roof, blasted through the walls. Holes large enough to stick her head through if she had been so inclined, and through one of them she had seen her. The woman, middle aged by then, was bound under so many layered straps it was hard to comprehend how she had secured them all in place. Straps bound her forehead,

A Coming Eclipse

arms, chest, legs, and ankles to her kitchen table. Several knives were embedded into the wall next to her front door, and one was still wobbling back and forth as if it had just been planted.

She was dead before any of them had time to notice her. A crushed windpipe, from struggling against a bind at her neck, where a chest strap had slipped too high, but it was the look in her eyes that stayed with Lisandra all these years later, the blissful smile plastered across her rigor frozen lips. She had been happy to die, at peace for having had an end to it all.

"A bad sign." She mumbled.

"Hmm?" Kiresh said.

"The moon being up so early." She said.

"Oh. That."

Jinga turned to check on her. At least, she suspected that was his intent. She shifted her pack on her shoulders, stepped forward. Her knee buckled under the weight, her foot slamming into a pothole. Sharp pain lanced up her ankle, and she winced.

Gods! Did it have to happen when he was looking. She thought as the pain dulled. She took another step forward, and collapsed.

"Kiresh." Jinga said.

"I'm on it." He rushed over to her, unlimbering his pack and casting it aside in the dirt. Her ankle was in his leather-sheathed hands before she could protest. Bright green eyes became pitch black as he surveyed the wound.

"Don't worry, ma'am. I'm an acolyte of Zangal." He said.

"That means nothing to me." She growled.

"I'm a healer. Of a kind."

"He's a midwife." Jinga ambled over to join them. He squatted next to Kiresh, rubbed his chin as he watched his nephew do his work. "A very skilled one."

"What's a midwife going to—"

Warmth bloomed in her ankle, sailed up the shaft of her leg and down into her foot. It was chased away by a tickling sensation that left a pocket of pleasant coolness behind. The pain in her ankle was gone, and renewed strength had replaced it, a sensation which permeated every muscle in her body.

Suddenly, she was awake. Alert in a way she had not been in years. She felt twenty years her junior, and perfectly capable of shouldering that silly pack for hours yet to come, quite as if she'd never known its burden.

He set her ankle down again, his eyes returning to their natural color, and stood.

Lisandra climbed to her feet, tested the straps of a pack that seemed now half the weight it had been.

"Don't overdo it." He warned. "You had a sprain. It's healed now. I took some energy from the earth and passed it into you, as well. Something I would have done if you had let me back at Delbert's."

"I feel like I could march the whole night away." She almost shouted.

"Yes, and that's the problem. The energy will strengthen you for a time, but there is a cost. I've given you energy now, but it isn't yours. It isn't coming from a place native to you. You'll wish I left you alone when it wears off. I promise you the after effects won't be pleasant."

"Well let's go then." She gestured up the road.

Tears for the Moon God

Jinga grimaced. He stood up, spun on his heels, and set off down the road. "We'll go until nightfall."

"How long will this last?" she asked, following him as Kiresh scooped up his pack.

"Long enough." He said. "Long enough to get to the checkpoint at Gonsai's Wall, anyway."

"It's safe there." Jinga added. Our people keep an outpost for travelers. A place to rest our heads and refill our water skins before we enter Sha Ruhhad's lands."

"We won't have a week with that moon." She shot a look at the gray ball in the sky, sheathed in thin, atmospheric mists as it was.

"I meant to ask, before you fell over...*why* is that a bad omen."

"You're not old enough to have witnessed the last eclipse." Jinga said. "But you've seen your share of full moons."

"I suppose I have." He said uncertainly.

"Eclipses are like those, but worse." Jinga said.

"Worse?" he asked, his attention focused on Lisandra.

"During a full moon, acolytes of God Ao Nii spill into the land at one location, razing the countryside until they are stopped. But some of them still cling to something like sanity on those nights. The strongest and the most experienced protect the weakest. It is their way.

"But during an eclipse, his rage is so strong it compels even those acolytes into madness. Anyone who has lived in his God House for a time will be affected by it." She thought of that woman. *Vira.* She had been sixteen when she came to live among them, too young to be even an initiate. She never spoke of her childhood. It seemed there was a great deal of sadness attached to those memories. She had left her whole way of life behind, but then...so many who came over from Saodein in those days had done the same. She had learned early to leave those questions unasked, to leave them with their privacy. "Worse than that, it won't just be one city, or one nation, that's impacted by him. If an eclipse should come, everything on this side of the world will fall into madness. Everyone who has lived in his God House, all over this hemisphere."

Kiresh had paled several shades at her explanation, and now walked on in silence.

"If it makes you feel any better," she said. "Nothing is certain. The god is angry. The moon in the sky in daylight tells the tale of that. But he has walked away from a fight before. He can be calmed."

"Pray to God Katcya he is." Jinga said. "If I can live the rest of my life never witnessing an eclipse again, I'll count myself one of the lucky ones."

Answers

The baron lay in the center of the yurt with the chiefs arranged around him. All save Tursa and Gulang were present. Days had gone by since the raid, and though Gulang's wounds had been attended to, he was not strong enough to leave his home just yet. Guruhl stood in for him as a representative of the Kachin, and Kuuda, despite his indiscretions, took up for Tursa, who was off making observation of the most recent opium harvest.

With them was Akhi, who had accompanied Sauman for this meeting, having claimed he had matters of importance to discuss with the rest of them, a claim Sauman had been eager to verify.

A previous debriefing had left a bad taste in Ungol's mouth. The raid had gone according to plan, but he did not like that Bora had been shoehorned into the preparations without the consent of the other sects. Sarri had kept that detail to himself, and while it seemed the raid might have failed without her, that she had played a pivotal role, it rankled him that so many in the party had been so young. He understood the motivation for placing Kachukh and Sircha in the party. He had not agreed with that either, but knew Gulang would continue to press for their inclusion despite the obvious shortfalls in allowing them to join it. But Bora had been an unnecessary complication in an otherwise sound scheme.

That they had discovered a weakness in the Tului ranks hardly mattered. They did not have the means of refining iron into an ingestible form, and the Tului would be much more reluctant to place prominent commanders in vulnerable positions now they knew they were exposed.

Gulang's wounding posed another complication. The healers who oversaw his treatment said he had not been infected, but with him incapacitated, another sect was left without their leader. Guruhl had taken up as acting chief in his stead. He hoped it was only a few days, that Gulang would have a swift recovery. He respected Guruhl as a warrior, but the man lacked the temperament to be chief. He was not the compassionate sort.

The baron's shadows flickered across the confines of the tent, striking for the gathered chiefs, and the baron tested the strength of the ropes binding him in place. He did not seek to use his command of ice to attack them. Ungol doubted he had the strength to wield it anyway with Guruhl's binding on him.

"You think you've had a great victory, don't you?" the baron raved. "That you've taken something from my people worthy of their concern. But I am unimportant."

His confessions came out with a desperate edge to them, and Ungol suspected nearly every word he spoke was a lie. He would be denied the luxury of telling mistruths soon enough, but they had other matters to address first.

"You've come to present something for our consideration, Akhi?" Arrak said.

Akhi produced something from his pocket, a dark red, segmented mass that looked somewhere between fruit and flower. Seeing it, the baron hissed.

Arrak's gaze snapped to him. "Is this something of importance to you?"

The baron did not answer, but his gaze was fixed on the fruit in Akhi's hand.

"I think his reaction verifies my suspicions. I took this from the pocket of a Tului soldier while I was pursuing the head of the anvil." Akhi said. "Sauman came across a similar fruit when he was setting fire to our dead."

Ungol looked around at the other chiefs. Surprising him, Sarri did not seem particularly bothered by this news.

"You've had one of these this long and you did not think to tell us?" Coltang demanded.

"I was not sure what it was, or whether it would prove consequential to our efforts." He said. "I passed it into Chief Sarri's keeping, believing he would be able to puzzle out what it was, but he did not know either."

Coltang glared at Sarri. You've all elected to set up a quarantine among my people, and here I find two of you were aware of a treatment and withheld your knowledge. I believed you a friend, Sarri."

"And I am. But what harm may have come from passing this onto you if it worsened the state the Kirche infected were in. If it heightened their power? We had no way of replicating it, either. Even with Shi'an's influence so heavy in Tursa's sect."

"Still, you should have told me."

"What I do know," Sauman continued. "Is that the Tului woman who passed it into my possession used her last breaths to inform me that it was helpful to her in some way. I am led to believe, and Akhi shares my sentiment, that this may be some form of treatment for the curse these people bear."

"Lies!" the baron growled.

"Your vehemence tells another tale." Arrak said.

"Arrada has a better grasp on horticulture than either of you." Kuuda said. "You might have thought to bring it to my sect for study."

"The fruit in my keeping was just a fragment. It would have been much harder to identify it given it was already half eaten." Sauman explained.

"Still."

"Your sect was also compromised during that time." Ungol said.

"A matter that has been resolved." Kuuda countered.

"Nonetheless, it would not have been in our best interest to pass something so consequential to you." Sarri said, agreeing with Ungol.

"Now you want to be the voice of the dissent. You harbored Arrada's secret, did you not?" Kuuda's tone took on a dangerous edge.

"Peace, Kuuda. There is no need for hostility." Arrak said. "What is past is past. We must now focus on what is present before us." He turned his attention onto the

Answers

baron. "What is this thing?"

"That is none of your concern." The baron's shadows thrust outward, straight for Arrak's feet. They recoiled, splayed apart as if they had struck some kind of barrier.

Guruhl grit his teeth.

"It's not easy containing me, is it?" the baron taunted. "Not as easy as some lowly piss-on!"

"If that is all, Akhi, I ask that you leave us." Arrak said.

Akhi bowed. He passed the fruit to Sauman, and took his leave.

Arrak began to pace, keeping to the edge of the yurt, out of range of those darting shadows. "This fruit has some effect on your people. We have been made aware that iron, when taken orally, nullifies your powers for a brief interval. We do have the means of ensuring your tongue remains in contact with raw iron. If it becomes necessary, we will expose you to it."

"You would kill me." The baron snapped.

"What a loss for us." Sarri said sardonically.

The baron's gaze snapped to him. "If you did not capture me for the information I possess, why target me at all?"

"He has his point." Ungol said to the room at large. He fixed the baron with a stony regard, cold and stalwart. "What you fail to understand is that we do not need your cooperation to obtain the answers we seek. In fact, it was never our intention to capitulate to your demands in pursuit of the information you claim you have."

"No? But surely you know I am chained to my spirit. He will know precisely what is befalling me in your company, and will seek to fight you off with all he has."

"A bluff if I have ever encountered one." Ungol said, though he was not at all certain he had the right of it. He was familiar with the jealous regard of a dark spirit, what it meant for the acolyte who courted it. Gandes Fae was one such as that, but therein was the crux of the problem. For the baron, anyway. If the spirit he was bound to was as active in his affairs as he claimed, it would come down to a clash between two dark spirits with investment in their pupils. Who would win in such a conflict remained to be seen, but he knew well his own apprenticeship under the spirit had come with a conditional immunity to the poison suffusing the baron Keirn's blood.

Gandes Fae's touch lived in his soul. It would be harder to shake than a simple blood curse. Harder still, for he was not alone.

A warbling sob issued from a shadowed corner of the yurt, from a manger he had positioned there ahead of this meeting. The cry drew the baron's attention, and a confused expression stole over him.

"What is that?" he whispered.

"My Chain." Ungol responded. He turned to Arrak. "If you will give me leave to begin."

"Not just yet, friend." Arrak said. "There is one more matter I would like to see to before we move on."

He turned his attention on Kuuda. "Given the nature of this parcel, it does not look like it bears a seed. Can your people grow more of these?"

"I will ask my father. He will have a better idea. But I would not rule out these things containing seeds. Most fruits do, and though these are more delicate than

Tears for the Moon God

most, I must assume they are mature enough. Now whether those seeds are viable is another matter."

"Then I ask that you go to your father. Return to me with what you have gathered."

"As you say."

Sauman approached Kuuda and passed the calyx into his possession. Kuuda took his leave, a scowl painted across his face. He could not be blamed for desiring to see what came of the interrogation that would follow, but if the fruit amounted to a cure, they must prioritize growing as much as possible as quickly as they could. It would be better to know sooner, rather than later, if this avenue was viable.

Arrak nodded in Ungol's direction. "You may begin."

"I will need you to restrict his shadows, Guruhl. As much as possible. I cannot perform this feat without making direct contact with him."

Guruhl stepped forward. He drew on the power of Range Lord Ergol, his mentor, and pressed two fingers to the earth. He held his other hand out in the direction of the baron, and clenched his fist. Power surged through the earth, rumbling underfoot, and the shadows froze in their poses, leaving enough room for Ungol to cross the intervening distance.

"I cannot hold him long." Guruhl said. "He is a slippery one."

"You will not have to." Ungol twisted his fingers, and the quilts in the manger parted. An infantile wail interrupted the quiet, and spider like legs clacked against its iron banded side. Eight, compound eyes peeked over the edge, and a mass of wiry hair slithered out behind it, dropping onto spindly forelegs as the hindlegs stabbed into the cracks between wooden planks for purchase. A fleshy, hollow eyed face like an infant child swam within the creature's fur, preceding a naked, round-bellied torso and nubby shoulders and arms that descended into the harder carapace at the elbows.

Air was pulled in through a double file of spiracles along the mol fae's flanks, and distorted the face into a horrific, bloated ruin, the eyes and mouth forced unnaturally wide as another wail escaped it.

The baron recoiled from the creature, but it remained on the fringes, watching as Ungol placed his hands along the sides of the baron's head and locked eyes with him. A black cast swam over his irises, spread to encompass the whites of his eyes, driving away light and leaving in its place voids like burned pitch with an oily shine that caught the light and snuffed it.

Power surged through the mol fae, earning an elated gasp from it, and suffused Ungol's body. Cold bloomed in his guts, and spread like sheets of ice across his limbs.

He guided the baron's mind to the proper memories with his questions, drawing him into a hypnotic trance. The baron's spirit master did not resist, as he had believed it would, but set aside its defenses, allowed him full access to the baron's mind and all of the answers it contained.

"What is the use of these fruits." He asked.

Memory's waters surged forward, to the fore of the baron's mind, and he thrust himself into them, plunged deep into that inhuman creature's psyche, to live in the moment he had first encountered this fruit, and gain comprehension for what it was, what it *meant*.

He spoke as the memory played out in his soul, and the others listened.

Answers

"A truly terrifying power, he has." Guruhl whispered as he drew away from the shadows, leaving Ungol to do his work without the added protection of his magic.

"What is he doing?" Sauman asked.

"Delving into the baron's memories. Dredging up everything he needs." Sarri explained.

"I once saw him use this ability to lock a Ruc'an admiral in a loop of his worst memories. The admiral was so distraught he impaled himself on his own sword, simply to see the end of it." Sarri said. "And people call me cruel."

Quiet, all of you." Arrak said. "Listen to him speak."

"The fruit is not a fruit at all. It is the protective casing of a flower. Hibiscus, which is high in iron, and possesses other properties which are anathema to the Tului. It was first processed into a tonic, which was given to those afflicted by the spirit in the days before it rose to power. Before it fashioned of itself a king over mortal men. This knowledge is privileged, known only to the order this baron belongs to."

"Then it is a cure." Sauman said, stepping forward.

"Yes, though a slow acting one. Its effectiveness is unquestioned, but it may take as much as a year to completely purge the curse from the blood. Its efficacy depends largely on how long a mortal has been an acolyte of the spirit. For our people, it should not take long." Ungol explained. "Who is this spirit king, baron?"

The memories swirled, became an amorphous thing, and settled again on an unfolding scene. A grizzly spirit, grotesque in its dimensions but resembling a great bird, not a crow but something similar, emerged before him. The spirit glutted on the blood of mortals, piercing its beak into their soft bellies and draining them dry.

It's great, glistening eye peered out from the side of a corrugated head, blue streaks interrupting the consummate black, as its regard settled on Baron Keirn.

"The spirit, the king and the kingdom are one entity. Tuluis Fel is its name. It has ruled the lands in the north for thousands of years, having been born as the spirit of an underground river the first Tului tapped when they sought to settle there.

"How strange."

"What is strange, Ungol?" Arrak intoned.

"A branching of streams. The Tului and the Gil Garo, two sides of the same coin. We were once one people. The Gil Garo are, I believe, those who chose to keep to the old way. The Tului became agrarian, enjoyed a brief period as seal hunters and whalers along the arctic coast. Tuluis Fel's influence descended over them like a shadow in those days, but it was not without a cure. Not hibiscus. A spirit of healing who lived in the ocean, who has since been driven off. It is with this spirit the flower casings first flourished, and in this way...if I am not mistaken...the flowers were imbued with a murky reflection of that power, a power expressed again through iron, which was taken from iron, as the spirit is one of a mountain under those waters."

"Then we know who our enemy is, but why have they chosen to attack us?"

"The baron's memories yield no answers. The order came down from the king, with no explanation given. They will seek to break us, scatter the remaining members of our sects, hunt us into extermination or bring us into their fold. This man does not know why."

Arrak nodded. "That is enough, Ungol. You may remove your influence from the man now."

The mol fae wailed in protest.

"I cannot." Ungol said. "There is something in this man my master desires. A question he wishes me to ask."

"Then be quick about it. I would rather not lose another chief to these people."

Ungol nodded. He posed the question the mol fae demanded of him. "Why does the moon god grieve?"

"A strange question." Sarri said.

The baron's answer came from his own lips, with no need for Ungol to step into his memories to find it. "The gods hold the answer. The Wanderers...God Lanfin...they are the source."

"What does this myth have to do with us?" Ungol asked, and the question was for himself.

"They are not a myth. The Halls of Time...they exist alongside the river. The spirit knows. He knows! The Moon God grieves for a dead man, and rails against God Lanfin. The eclipse. It is coming. God Ao Nii will come...and we must all fear for what arrives with him. He will come...and our people will die...if we cannot stop him."

Sober eyes met Ungol's gaze as he pulled out of the Scarlet Baron's mind in steps, careful to leave his faculties intact. "He will come to make peace...and our way of life will die. We will kill the wolf! We must kill the wolf!"

Ungol stepped away from the baron. Exhaustion washed over him, and he seated himself alongside his familiar. They had their answers. Gandes Fae had his. But what did this mean?

Arrak approached the baron, then. They had what they needed. It should not have come as a shock that he would take such swift action, but riding on the heels of this revelation, he was nonetheless caught unprepared when the chief took hold of the baron, and snapped his neck.

A visceral crunch. The baron fell to the ground, his shadows snapping back into one form as age stole over him in the unnatural way it did with all of the Tului embraced by death.

Ungol looked around at the others. "We are being manipulated, aren't we?"

"Just as I suspected." Sarri said. "But by who? Surely, God Ao Nii is not coherent enough to orchestrate such elaborate plans for us."

"But he is a part of this." Ungol said, his gaze fixed on the dead baron.

"If an eclipse is imminent, it will be God Gorgus who bares his fangs against God Ao Nii, whether he wants him or not." Guruhl said. "It has always been his way."

"But why God Lanfin?" Sauman asked. "Why now?"

"The Wanderers." Ungol said. "You don't think—"

"I have suspected as much for quite some time, Ungol." Sarri said. "The visitor to your son in the night. He left water behind. It seems they were able to escape God Lanfin's labyrinth for a time. Long enough to influence events in their favor, though I struggle to comprehend what they might want."

"That seems simple enough." Sauman said. "It would be freedom, I think."

The quarantine zone was a demoralizing sight. The healers were taking it in shifts, getting barely enough sleep to recover their energy before diving back into

Answers

the drudgery. So little of it resembled the kind of care Coltang was accustomed to.

The enemy had the high ground in this fight. The other chiefs may not want to admit it, riding high on Gulang's recent victory as they were, but even that had not been the success he desired. Another chief incapacitated, even if temporarily, was not a loss they should take lightly. They had taken someone important from the enemy, sure, but they had lost someone of equal importance to his own mad desire for revenge. Gulang had been a liability from the start. Any other chief would have been a better option for the job, and whether he agreed to it or not, whether Arrak's relatively weak position would have allowed him to skew the conversation in a different direction, hardly mattered. He was lucky not to be dead.

They would be lucky if they weathered this winter.

Without the protection of the Swans, the entire tribe was more vulnerable than they had been in ten generations. Likely even longer. There was no certainty that Dupec would pass whatever tests of character and strength Duijus Kanh foisted onto him, and even if he did, he would not return to them for some time. His fate necessitated a departure into the mountains, across the spine of Rasheik Rope, and maybe he would draw on God Uldal's power to see him to his destination, maybe that would make the whole errand faster for everyone involved, but it would do nothing for them when it came time to cross into the lands of Tuluis Fel.

The sick were here, and their affliction had become more pronounced with every passing day. The demand for blood was growing. Its effects on the accursed were lessening, and opium came with its own complications. Dependency, withdrawal. When it came time to ween their kin, how many of them would die from the shock to their systems? He did not trust the ministrations of blood, either. It seemed to fuel them, even as the opium drew their eyes closed, left them floating in blissful aplomb. Eventually, the victims would gain such a tolerance to the drug it would hardly impact them anymore without administering near lethal doses, and that, too, would come with risks.

For the victims of Tuluis Fel's aggression, a high toll was mounting. A bubble had formed around their care, with so many factors dependent on the continued ability of simple men and women to perform small miracles. If Tursa's farmers overtaxed the land, it would never rebound. The spirits would be angered, might turn on them for their efforts to preserve the lifeblood of their tribe in their way. They might simply collapse from exhaustion one day. They could not sustain themselves and see to this rapid harvest at the same time. They must choose between themselves and their people. Eventually they would have to make the selfish choice, preserve their own lives at the price of a shortage of opium and valerian root.

And the healers? There was only so long a person could keep going at this pace. Working through the day and night, emptying bed pans, restraining victims who had broken their binds until new ropes could be procured, knots retied, bodies bound to cots and sticks shoved between their teeth, fastened behind their heads with butcher's twine. Some of them had been infected in the past days, had been bitten while they tried to fasten gags in place, or exposed to tainted blood when a shadow flashed out from under a patient who sobered faster than expected to slice them open. More than a dozen healers had been killed by their patients in the days since Gulang set out for his raid, and the week was not over yet.

Every death was a loss they could not afford. The promise of an increased

Tears for the Moon God

burden on the whole operation. And with just two curse breakers among them, two who had no power to subvert the effects of a blood curse, two who between them could contain it for a time, the perimeter was more vulnerable than he would have liked as well.

When Ungol arrived at the quarantine zone, it came as a surprise. Most avoided this place as much as possible. Even the other chiefs had given it a wide berth until it came time to ask after something from him, or, in the case of Tursa, to oversee the transfer of medicine and herbs to him for dissemination among the healers.

Ungol marched up to him, but his gaze was on the tents, flitting from one to the next as screams punched the air from one, as his healers ran to that tent to restrain another victim who had broken through his binds. He waited for the call to help restrain him. He hoped they would call on him. At least then he did not have to worry about whether another had become infected, or had simply been strangled to death by a power mad tribesman.

"What brings you here?" he asked.

"I want to discuss something with you. About the baron's testimony."

"If you must call it that." Coltang said.

"Yes, well, forced or otherwise it is still his truths we heard. It is strange, though, isn't it?"

"What is?"

"When I delved into him, I met no resistance. A spirit that powerful should have attempted to push me out. Especially if he was guiding his acolytes against us. Yet he did not resist. I could almost convince myself he *wanted* me to see what I saw."

"That is troubling." Coltang lifted his gaze toward the sky, where thin clouds scurled across a vibrant, winter blue ceiling.

"Perhaps. Perhaps not."

"There is something you are not telling me."

"I am concerned for our children." Ungol followed his gaze, unwilling to meet his eye. To see his worries reflected there. "I gather the target of those Tului was Duijus Kanh, but it does not make sense that he would be, does it? Else why taunt us into following them away."

"They may have sought to push us out so that a secondary force could attack."

"Which would be a fool's errand. Duijus Kanh is an ancient spirit, and a powerful one. And if they sought to kill him off, they would find themselves going toe to toe with Tao Shein."

"I see your point."

"The baron did not mention him by name, either. In fact, he seemed to think this impending eclipse had little to do with the old argument, which is troubling me even more."

"Who is his anger directed at, then."

"It hardly matters."

Coltang waited for him to elaborate.

He sucked in a breath and let it out through his nose, slowly, calming his nerves. The whole affair had him thinking he was missing something, some critical detail. It was not Gandes Fae's way to interrupt him when he sought to draw on his power. He had never done so before, and yet there had been truths he had been after in the Baron. The mol fae had conveyed dissatisfaction at the man's answers, signifying there was more to these events than he was aware of, that the shape of this conflict was of a greater scope than just Tului against Gil Garo, one tribe waging war against the other.

"The Tului believe he will seek to strike at God Lanfin. The problem I see is a lack of connective tissue. God Ao Nii's traditional enemy is God Gorgus. He has never sought direct conflict with the God of Music that I know."

"I can't say I've heard a story like that either." Coltang said.

"This hibiscus. It may be the cure we've been hoping for." Ungol said, trying to steer the conversation in a lighter direction.

"How sure is it?" Coltang asked.

"From what the Kirche say, it is what is sounds like. At least a balm against the blood curse's poison. Probably more than that. But it will take time to express its effects. Whether we can mass produce it in the same way as this opium is a different matter. Kuuda is asking after that information as we speak."

A commotion was rising in one of the nearest tents, a struggle ensuing.

Coltang jerked his head in that direction, and Ungol followed his gaze. "Perhaps we will have some hope then. If it can be mass produced."

"We don't have much of that these days."

"No, I suppose we do not. But it is a start."

Coltang moved on the tent, intent on sparing another healer from a terrible fate.

Yura

Shaelein was among the elder women when Ungol found them. They sat in the confines of a yurt belonging to Yura, the eldest among them, who had reached her eighth decade that year.

Yura had developed cataracts ten years past, arthritis in her hips which made it difficult to ride a horse. Her husband had been taken by the Swans almost twenty years past, but they had spared her, year after year, and perhaps that was God Katcya smiling down on her. Or maybe the Empress wasn't ready to claim her just yet.

He suspected she would not have survived this winter if they had remained in Gil Garo, and was glad they hadn't. Yura was a chronicler of the histories of the Gil Garo tribes. In her were the stories of their people, which she had passed down to three generations now. And she was Shaelein's grandmother. A woman she had grown to respect over all of these years, who had outlived his wife's mother and father. Her mother had gone with the Swans, her head held high, so Yura claimed, when a sickness fell over her which made breathing difficult. Something Shaelein or another healer would have been able to mend had she been younger, with the reserves to handle the shock of the purged.

Her father had gone the way of so many others, had fallen in a raid in summer seven years gone now. He had gone the way he wanted to. Not quietly, but leading the charge against a Jahhad trader's caravan in the south lands.

They had been as much a family to him as his own, had been around longer, had made better decisions, but then Ungol had been the son of a chief himself, and a chief wore a target on his chest always. To lead was to carry the weight of a people on his shoulders. To lead was to accept responsibility for all of his people. Gaulha had been captured in Ao Lein, and his head had been mounted on a pike outside the capitol. Ungol had gone to Gur Tulain to see him one last time before he departed for the Empress and her land for the dead on the ocean's floor. As he had done with his mother, and Shaelein's parents, when they had fallen.

Shaelein's smile was a light in the claustrophobic gloom of her grandmother's yurt, which drove the cold embracing him back more than any fire could. She climbed to her feet.

Yura

"I'll only be a moment." She said to the other women.

Ungol gestured for her to stay where she was. "There is no need. I have news for all of you."

"Not orders, I hope." Yura said.

"No, not that. Though, I think, you will want to organize around these new developments."

"Good." She said shortly.

He crossed to where his wife was still standing, kissed her cheek and wrapped his arm around the small of her back. A light squeeze, and he placed some distance between them. This was not a moment for romantic entanglement, and it would be a show of disrespect to hold onto her in the presence of her elder.

"I've come from questioning the captive together with the other chiefs. Tursa has been informed of our findings. Guruhl is on his way to inform Gulang, as well."

"What have you found?" Shaelein asked.

"There is a cure." He said. "We believe Tursa's horticulturists will be able to produce it at a similar volume to the opium they have been growing lately."

Yura hissed through her teeth. "Not a false trail, surely. How certain are you of this cure?"

"I am certain it will work, though it will take some time." Ungol said. "It was there in the memories of our captive. And in his response to seeing it."

"It is a tincture?"

"A plant, which can be administered as a tea." He said.

Yura contemplated him through unseeing eyes.

Shaelein laced her fingers cautiously into his as a wave of whispers washed through the seated others.

"So strange, these tidings." Yura said.

"You have a story, grandmother?" Shaelein asked.

"I would like to hear one if you have it, Elder Yura." Ungol said before she could answer.

"Another matter for our consideration?" She asked.

"I would invite the elders to place their minds to this task alongside the chiefs, if you would." He said.

"What is the subject?" she asked.

Shaelein was looking to him with renewed concern. Her grip on him tightened.

"A story of the relationship between Gods Ao Nii and Lanfin."

"Ahhh." She panned over the others, and her expression grew grim. "Few stories survive among us of the earliest days of our tribe, and this is older than them. Your son might know of this entanglement, if he was told anything of use by his god. The moon once had an amenable relationship with the master of all songs, but in the earliest days, before the lands of the world were fixed in place, before the Iron Spirit descended into the earth and the Spirit of Salt dozed off, and the lone lord of fire chose peace, their relationship soured."

"Then they have known hatred for each other for as long as we have been." He said.

"Longer." She replied.

"You have this story?" he asked.

"Yes, and it is a peculiar one. But does it present an academic interest to the chiefs, or are we ensnared within it?"

Tears for the Moon God

"I suspect the latter."

Another wash of whispers descended over the elders, harassed sounds, speculations about their part in the grand games of the gods.

"I see." Yura cleared her throat, drawing silence out of her peers, and beckoned Ungol and Shaelein to sit.

"This will take some time to tell."

"What is going on, Ungol?" Shaelein whispered.

"I suspect we will have a better idea of that soon." Ungol said. "What is known to me is that our relationship to the Tului is closer than we anticipated. There is a story there I would tell, but let your grandmother speak. We are in need of her insight."

"To tell this tale, we must go back to the first days, when a war between gods and spirits was raging, the subject our right to continue. To be. To draw breath and live until we died.

"We are not like them. Not like spirits, and not like gods, both of whom trace their lineage back to the same source. Our emergence was unsanctioned. Our blood was drawn from the river, our bodies stirred up from the silts within its band. A river without a name, or the name has been lost to us for countless generations. No mortal people within the world remember its name, nor do any people who spilled forth from it remember the name of her enemy, who was lover to her.

"In the relationship between God Lanfin and the river Oe is a reflection of the relationship between the great river and the father of the gods, or so the story I have heard is told. God Lanfin won the love of the Crystal River in the young times, when both were juvenile and prone to whirlwind romances, and from their tristes spilled forth the uelfin, who are neither god nor spirit, but rolled forth from the rapids near her headwaters."

"Then God Lanfin must have some love of mortals." Shaelein intoned. "Surely he could not see his children and hate them."

"It was not love for mortals that inspired God Lanfin to yield his seed to Oe, and it was the act of using it to draw life from her waters that saw them split. God Lanfin did not want a race of people capable of singing as he did in the world, but that is another story, which is not needed in the telling of this one." Yura responded.

"In those earliest days, the world did not look as it does now. Small islands populated it, and the spirits who governed them were weak. The gods ignored them, and believed they were well in hand, but the spirits grow in power as they amass new lands. The most recent example, I think, is Sha Ruhhad, who rose to supplant a dead spirit in the lands across the rope. In rising to replace her, he gained in power to rival the Rope Lords either side of his domain, but he was not strong enough to kill the forest altogether, and Gur Tulain rose in the north to meet his challenge. Their contest has since ebbed, leaving the wastes in the south and the forest in the north, and Ul Sharak to act as mediator between them.

"In the same way, the islands marched across the seas, waged war on each other and grew to encompass vast territories, until but six remained to command the rest, and were chained for the sin of coveting such power by the gods, and the spirits of the Tetract, who together bound them in shrines. This knowledge comes from the traditions of the Nixians, who fashion themselves as stewards of Sha Ruhhad, and serve as guides through his lands."

Yura

"The Great Kings, yes." Ungol said, at last taking his seat among the women. Shaelein followed his example, if somewhat more reluctantly. "But what do they have to do with the moon."

"They were friends to the Elder Gods in the days before their chaining. Elders who thought to use them against their children, but one among them harbored a secret. The first river spilled forth man unsanctioned. In those days, the mountain lords we know were not as they are. The power of the eldest of them has waned, and the younger have grown. It is the way of our world that such things must always be in flux. Their ranges have split, and in many places, new lords have taken over where the older grew too weak to defend their claims. The mountains are ever at war, the mountain climbs in might and supplants the spirits of others, until a Range Lord's claim is uncontested by any other, and then that Range Lord might become a rope in his time, commanding vast territories until age shakes his bones, and he is pulled down by a more powerful entity.

The eldest lords are those who have struck down their enemies, or made amenable pacts with them. The eldest of them are Ban and Echo, who were once Range Lords within the same Rope."

"I see." Ungol said.

"But how could they be? Shaelein asked. "Ban is halfway across the world."

"The seas rose to meet the challenge of the Great Kings, and the Empress Shao Luin shattered the spine of their master. She carved out her land for dead mortals in his domain. But in the earliest days, man sprang forth to occupy that rope. God Katcya found them in the forests, and chose a lover for himself from among them. A woman who sated his endless curiosities for a time, with whom he fostered two children. The first of the Luckborn. A Cloud Man, and then a Sun Man, who God Ao Nii fell in love with.

"For a time, man walked away from the forests in the night, marched across the spine of the great rope, descended from Echo's Range and into Gora's lands. They settled in new holdings, and when the empress seized her claim, crafted boats to cross her waters in night's embrace, followed ice shields to new lands to fashion new settlements in those forests. The Great Kings followed their migrations into conflicts, and shielded them from the eyes of the gods still loyal to their father, until dawn rose over the horizon to meet them, and they were discovered by God Gorgus, who took with him this news to his grandfather, initiating a war for the survival of mortal kind with God Katcya as leader in this conflict.

"Little survives from the era of this war, but what is known to me, what survives in the tradition of storytellers, is this. God Gorgus killed the Sun Man who God Ao Nii loved, and earned his hatred forever thereafter. God Lanfin, in seeking to break the moon and deny God Katcya his greatest general among the gods, gave him a gift in the aftermath, and at the same time conspired together with the Elder Gods to erect what we know now as the Halls of Time at the edge of the river which gave us life. He broke his mind with this gift, but in the way of such madness, God Ao Nii did not know it for what it was. The gift was in fact a curse. The monthly migrations of the moon, the contests which see him struck from the sky when he seeks to smite God Gorgus, are a result of his fury for what was taken for him, and his grief for what was lost, but God Gorgus was never his enemy. It was God Lanfin, working in the shadows, who stole away the brother, the Cloud Man, and locked him away where he could not be found. It was God Lanfin who invited the madness

Tears for the Moon God

into him, in service of a master who has since fallen away from the world. And it is God Lanfin who has seized each of the katcyakin strong enough to stand against the holy order of the gods since then."

"The Wanderers." Shaelein breathed.

"One of whom managed to escape for a time." Ungol said into an unsettling pocket of silence as the elders considered Yura's words. "Who warned our son of the coming attack from Tuluis Fel. An entity the chiefs have come to understand is not the name of a kingdom or a people, but the spirit who inhabits those lands."

Yura's mouth clicked shut. Her gaze snapped to him. "What have you discovered, grandson."

"We are being used." He said. "By who, I do not know." And he told the women what he had learned in his questioning of the baron.

He came away from Yura's yurt shaken. There was no question the gods had snared the Gil Garo in their web. That even now they were marching them into a clash which should never have been. The feeling, so pervasive, that all of this had happened before, was stronger now than it had been since the raid on Gil Garo. That they were revisiting steps they had already taken in some forgotten past or future.

When a new Wanderer is reclaimed, what happens to the rest of us? His life made forfeit, what happens to the people he has left behind?

He worried over the idea, following avenues into streams of consciousness which became more confusing the farther he traveled down them.

Tuluis Fel, a spirit with absolute control over the people who inhabited his lands. Tuluis Fel, who was working with at least one god in orchestrating this war between distant cousins.

That the God of Music was involved, and the Wanderers.... *How did he escape? Surely such a feet should be impossible.*

But the man who had visited his son could be nothing else. All of the evidence pointed in that direction, and perhaps he was a free agent in all of this, or why warn them of the coming attack. What else had he passed on to Dupec? *Enough to draw him into Duijus Kanh's cave, to be taken in by our protectors.*

But why? Why was it so important to these Tului to see Duijus Kanh dead? And if it was so important to them, why did they flee after the initial attack. Why did they not take a greater force with them? Why not wield their full strength against the unsuspecting Gil Garo?

They could have crushed us with a greater force. We did not know they were coming. They had the element of surprise, and yet they sought to draw us into their borders rather than crush us when we were distracted, and confident in our ability to defend ourselves against any force brazen enough to attack when we were at full strength.

A summer campaign would have made more sense. This makes none.

He marched deeper into the Gil Garo camp, intent on his yurt and rest. There would be little of it to be had with so much on his mind, but a lesser peace had settled into him. Arrada had taken a look at the calyx, had found viable seeds within it. Even now, he was taking those seeds to Tursa, together with the remains of the calyx, intent on testing the tincture on his father, who would take on the role of first to be administered this treatment in order to ensure the other victims were

Yura

not poisoned by it.

There was potential in those seeds. Potential for a return to normalcy for the Gil Garo, maybe even a means of preventing them becoming infected to begin with, if they could be distributed to the men and women who would see battle in the coming weeks.

But still, he found himself bothered by the deeper implications of what he had learned from the baron. Something was coming with the eclipse which he suspected had not been seen in thousands of years. Something which may even predate the Gil Garo's emergence as their own people, and he could not help wondering whether the Goddess Liandal's hand was in this, too. If she was even now writing a fate for him, for the other chiefs, which would see them subsumed into the Tului ranks, turned to their cause, to become a fighting force in the name of her designs.

She had always been among the worst of the gods for the way she played their games. A wicked mistress whose diaries captured the lives of mortal people of consequence, and brought about the destruction of whole tribes and kingdoms through the maneuvering of a few, well placed levers. This had the flavor of her style. And if her hand was manipulating one side, it would be God Tirulain on the other, seeking to oppose her in whatever way he could.

Breaking Camp

Sauman looked up from the papers scattered on the low writing table before him. Akhi looked in on him, the tent flap entrance of his yurt held up on one, thin arm.

"You're letting out the heat." Sauman said, returning to his study of a leger detailing the Chikata's supply of foodstuffs and medicine.

They were running low on gauze for binding wounds, which meant he was going to have to direct the healers to safeguard what they had on hand ahead of renewed conflict with the Tului. This period of noninterference could not last, and there was still the prospect of new infections spreading among those he had provided to the Tipik. Food was less of a problem. The supply of hardtack and dried fruits would hold for now, and game was abundant throughout the steppe. If the need should arise, he could negotiate with Kuuda for help with growing foodstuffs to supplement their stock anyway, and there were a few acolytes of Shi'an the Grass among his people besides.

They had never gone hungry in the winter months, and he did not intend to set a new precedent for starvation among his people now. Even if the march did challenge them in other ways.

Akhi stepped inside, and let the flap fall closed behind him. Cold settled close to the ground and was quickly driven off by the heat emanating from the camp stove near its center.

"The Tului are moving." Akhi said. "They broke camp two hours ago, and the trailing elements are beginning to clear away northward, making speed."

"They've decided to run away, then." Sauman said.

"It is likely a greater force awaits them."

"Which we are better equipped to handle now we have a means of treating the infected."

"Will we pursue?"

"Go to Arrak and tell him what you have told me. He will want to break camp quickly and lay chase. It will be better for us if they do not convene with their secondary force before they can be dealt with."

"Why the change now?" Akhi asked.

Breaking Camp

"Because they are licking their wounds now." Sauman responded. "They are vulnerable, and they will have the advantage of familiar lands if we allow them to reach the Tului border. It is better to send back a few stragglers to their waiting forces, to let them know we are not as weak as they believed.

"If they hold back their best and most seasoned war leaders, they will be far less vulnerable, and the Crow has already proved himself to be a match for a chief. We cannot allow him to fall under the protection of someone even greater."

Akhi nodded. "If you will give me leave, then."

"You are dismissed."

Akhi left him to his legers. The work of a chief was never done, it seemed, and in laying chase behind this wounded compliment of Tului soldiers, it seemed his work would double again. It would be some time before he could rest, and he needed it. Needed to clear his head, too.

This all seemed so familiar to him, as if somewhere within his body, echoes of these events had been stored in memory. As if he was going through the motions of something he had done before, and all of these moments were being forced upon him by someone else's hand.

He wondered if the Goddess of Fate had her hands in this, if her intervention was why he felt this way. If it was written, a destiny for him to follow, for the Gil Garo to fall into, then to what end did she seek to use them? What did she have to gain from this conflict?

He wished he knew.

Arrak watched as his people packed their belongings, hauled trunks and furniture, bundled quilts and rugs onto wagons. He watched as they dismantled yurts, rolled tarps out in cleared spaces in the snows. As teams of men hauled heavy camp stoves and braziers over to be packed up and readied for the long ride, and horses were tethered to crossbeams and hitches with lead ropes, bits fitted into their mouths and saddles slung onto their backs.

Gulang stood with him. He was still a little pale, and favored his right leg a little too heavily for Arrak's taste, but he was awake, strong enough to walk again, and that meant he could take over leadership of his people from Guruhl, a blessing of a kind in its own right.

Recovery had been swift with him, leaving the rest of the chiefs to breathe a little easier. Guruhl would prove an asset when it came time to wage battle on these Tului, which he suspected would come soon. A road march was no place for healing, that was true, but that they had a means of healing the victims among them would be enough. In the night, energy could be stolen from the plants on their path, which he suspected would come to be known as the Dead Path when summer arrived and the lands they traveled were left barren. He would spare no thought for the damage they did to the grasses and the soil, the acolytes of Shi'an among them, for the price was worth paying if it kept his people healthy, if it gave to them the means by which to overcome this affliction.

He only hoped this cure purged them of their curses swiftly, so that the numbers of their soldiers could be bolstered, and the sick among them could return to health without too much complication.

This road had already proven a burden to him and his kind. More of a burden than he would have believed possible. If it would have benefited them, he would

Tears for the Moon God

have demanded they turn back, go to Gil Garo to settle in for the hard months, but to do so would leave them where the Tului knew how to find them, would invite another attack, this time in force. And the lands, though familiar to them, would prove no advantage. They would be pressed against Shan Lao River then, left without the option of escape.

No, this needs to be done now. When they are still reeling from the recent assault on their forces, and afraid of what a greater force of our people could do to them. It will be worse for us if we wait, and they will not ignore us if we turn back. They will pursue us all the way home if we do. They have made that clear.

Gulang leaned toward him, shifting his weight onto his good leg as he did. "What are you thinking, old friend."

"I think we are being led into a snare." He said. "Being pushed toward a pointless conflict. And I think it would be foolish to ignore it. If we could."

"We agree, then." Gulang drew back, to watch the preparations under way. "It would not be wise to ignore them. They might run amok through the countryside, spill out into other kingdoms then. By next winter, they might have overrun our neighbors in the east, leaving behind a bigger mess than we could hope to contain."

Arrak observed the man. No scars remained to remember his healing, nothing to call to any injury, but he could see the wounding in his steady gaze, the way he seemed to look past the people as they pulled down their yurts and packed their things in their wagons. He could see, in his features, the marks of a failure, and found he could not understand why the man should feel the way he did. He had brought his entire troop home alive, and there had been so few of them to begin with. And the toll in blood had been steep for the Tului besides. Their food stock was sabotaged, and though the opium would leave the survivors' systems in a matter of days, the withdrawal effects would have killed some of them. There had been those who died from inhaling so much of it in the initial attack, as well, and the line felled by Akhi's meddling.

The raid had been a success. A greater success than he could have hoped for. And yet here, his sometimes stubborn and often irritable friend looked out on the world through the eyes of one who had lost a great deal.

Perhaps it has finally hit him that Karsa is not coming back. That no amount of blood drawn from Tului veins will ever see him returned.

"We're being led into this, aren't we?" Gulang said. "I can see it in the other chiefs. The uncertainty. Should we go with Fate or run away from her."

"You feel her hand in our movements, too?"

Gulang nodded. "I have been thinking it over, and yes, I believe she is involved, but the movements of our enemy do not follow the usual patterns. There is no one among them I would deem so important that her interest would settle on them long. And the same is true of us. The one among us who might hold her attention, if it were so, would be Ungol's son, yet he sits out this conflict. His fate is written such that he must be drawn away from us. Gandes Fae said as much, did he not?"

Arrak nodded, and watched as in the distance, the Cuu broke camp and drove their horses northward, to beat their hooves into the snows, and fashion a road for the rest of them to follow. Sarri was somewhere up there guiding them onward, showing his resolve to his people, that whether the future of his sect was certain or not, he would lead them into it.

He should be up there leading the march, and yet he felt none of that resolve

Breaking Camp

himself. Thought the Hakka might see him for the fraud he was. He did not deserve his place as chief of chiefs. He had not earned it.

"What I cannot wrap my head around, is why?" Gulang said. "Why us, and why now?"

Arrak sighed. "I have been grappling with that myself. There is nothing for the Tului to gain from attacking us. We do not even claim lands for ourselves with any sense of permanence. Just the lands outside Duijus Kanh cave, and then only for a few months. If they had waited until summer, they could have attacked him while he slept. They would be at a greater advantage if they had, with us out of the way. They might even have succeeded at killing him."

"Duijus Kanh was never their target." Gulang said. "Dupec Safar—"

"Do not start with the accusations—"

"Listen to me." Gulang snapped. "Dupec Safar is the only one who makes sense. They did not attack until days after his arrival. Their agent arrived almost at the same time as him."

"We do not know that." Arrak protested. "Besides, they did not stay to see him dead, did they? They are in conflict with us. Not him."

"Your view is too narrow, Arrak." Gulang growled. "Dupec is under watch from your son and two other chiefs' children, and two of them were present after the Wanderer visited. That a Wanderer visited him in the first place would be more than enough to draw Goddess Liandal's eye, but she would want him alone. He would be easier to manipulate that way.

"Even then, there is the matter of timing. The Tului forces arrive on our doorstep just after him. His visitor gives warning to him that they are coming. Not to us, but to him. And we have all gained a sense as if we have lived through these events before, that we are even now repeating the same actions we once did.

"Wanderers are locked away outside of time, and this one knew Ungol's son. Knew him personally, and well enough to stay his hand when he sought to attack him, or do you think a newly returned pathfinder and a Cloud Man does not have enemies he might seek to kill before they could bring harm to him?"

"What is your point, Gulang?" But he thought he knew. Gulang had been suspicious of Dupec since the night of the attack, since finding out from their children, his own among them, that the Cloud Man had been warned of the coming assault. That he had *known* it would happen.

But it had not been Dupec who refused to pass that knowledge along. And if Sauman was being twisted into knots by a god's own hand, what could they have done to prevent the attack happening? What guard could they have used against her?

And still he found himself wondering. Wondering what it all meant. Why these events had befallen them, and what need the gods could have for them.

"You told me, in the aftermath of Ungol's questioning of the captive, that the baron believed an eclipse was imminent. And I have since spoken to Ungol, who consulted his only remaining in-law, who in turn told him a tale connecting the gods of the moon and music, as enemies."

"He mentioned as much to me, also." Arrak admitted, though he did not want to be speaking on this matter. It was as if the words resisted him, the subject, so prescient to their current predicament, became a cloying mass in his throat, and his mind flitted away from it.

Tears for the Moon God

You will not have me, Liandal!

The sensation passed, and yet within it was confirmation for all he had long suspected. They had become pieces in her game, and though her influence may be subtle, it was strong. Binding them to a path.

"There are still missing pieces in this design." He whispered.

"No, there are patches in your comprehension of her strategy which she is pressing into you because they are inconvenient. Arrak, there is nothing about this that is difficult to understand."

"Then what conclusion have you arrived at?"

"Dupec lived once before. We are being set upon a path we traveled with him in that past life, and he is being held at arm's length in order to ensure we do not succeed." Gulang said. "He is not our enemy, he is our greatest asset, and we are being pushed to leave him to his fate, so that fate can ensure our destruction."

"Then we must turn from this path." A deep chill ran through Arrak Sarr as if he had been doused in Shan Lao's waters.

"No. That would be the wrong answer." Gulang said. "The Tului would see our retreat as a sign of weakness, and they would seek to regroup and exploit it."

"But we cannot follow them into a trap, either."

"No, you're right about that." Arrak saw he was shaking. "We need to uncover who the other players are. Set a trap of our own."

"It is clear enough, isn't it?" Arrak said. "We were gifted a Cloud Man, which would have drawn God Katcya's eye if he was not involved already. And God Ao Nii will be involved in some capacity if an eclipse is coming. Which means his moonkin will be involved in this somehow, too."

"Then it is on that day we should stage our assault." Gulang said. "Hold our forces back until the moon crosses paths with the sun."

Arrak touched his cheek with trembling fingers. "I will think on it."

"Do so quickly. We must assume the Tului have factored the eclipse into their preparations. If nothing else, we must seek to slow them down. Deny them the advantage of making a stand at the place of their choosing."

"We will discuss this when we have bedded down for the night. The road will be a good place for thinking."

"I will look for you when my people have been settled." Gulang squeezed his shoulder reassuringly, and stepped away to return to his own people, and see to the last of their preparations before they set out for the road.

Sky Souled

"Thinking again?" Ank's emergence was as jarring as it ever was. The man had a way of gliding about as if his feet never quite made contact with the tiles.

Shulraki had known few people capable of moving so quietly, and nearly all of them were assassins or thieves, the kind of people whose livelihoods depended on moving unseen.

He looked up at the Sanark, who was standing at his shoulder and looking out over the vast lake of fouled memories uniting the various crossing halls into a single organism.

He grinned, the corners of his narrow eyes wrinkling. Shulraki had grown accustomed to feigning joviality in his life as a merchant. Just now, he wanted to be alone, but it would be rude to dismiss the sanark, and there may well be use in talking to him. Even more than the Elder, Ank was an enigma. A man for whom honesty was a vice, who would rather not answer a question at all than lie.

Men like that tended to die young...in Saodein, anyway. In his time. Yet, Ank was ever a step ahead of everyone else around him. Even here, where collectively, the scant few residents of these halls had committed some of the most heinous and cunning acts in the Waxing World's history.

Here was a pool filled with scum and vitriol, with tragedy and loss, with laughter to make the eyes water and the belly hurt. A pool full of memories with no borders....

Collateral damage in our little game.

"Just that, yes." He said. "Will you be staying?"

"Oh, I suppose." Ank eased onto his haunches.

He turned back to the pool. If he let the silence stretch between them, perhaps the sanark would go away. Then he could go back to what he had been doing. Testing his will, playing games with probability.

Would he walk into the lake or wouldn't he? *The question of the hour!* Would he plunge head first into the closest thing to true escape from boring, consistent banality in this listless, sprawling hell?

"You seem upset." Ank said.

"I'm afraid it's a chronic affliction."

Tears for the Moon God

"As, it seems, are these quiet moments at lakeside. What do you think it is, anyway?"

"You're oddly glib."

"Ah, well, I am a man of two minds. What can I say?"

"Chose to wear the white paint today?"

Ank chuckled. "So?"

"I think it is what it looks like. A whole bunch of memories without enough left of their identities to keep themselves contained like the rest. Given its location, I can only assume it came about because two of us were recalled in quick succession."

"An interesting idea. Well...I should be going."

"Oh, but you have so much time on your hands, don't you?" Shulraki said. "Stay. Please."

"I'm afraid I have things to do elsewhere. Important meetings and the like."

"I'm sure they can wait."

"Well, they could, but I've already settled the matter at hand, haven't I?" Ank shot to his feet. He sauntered away.

"What would that be?"

A dry crunch brought him around to where Ank was standing. He was leaning against the corner where the nearest hall let out. He held a piece of fruit in his hand. *An apple? Now where in the names of all the gods did he find that?*

"First." He said around a mouthful, gesturing toward the lake with the apple. "I thought you were going to do it this time. I no longer think that's likely."

"No?"

"Well, you've made a friend, haven't you? The new one. Maybe talking to him would ease your mind. It seems to be the writing on the wall, anyway. Now."

"Then you've gained the ability to read minds. In addition to locating things you shouldn't have."

Ank looked down at the apple in his hand. "Oh this? There's a tree off that way." He gestured curtly over his shoulder, back into the section of the maze where Shulraki's actions and their echoes were housed. Deeper still, he would find himself in Ank's own territory, and then Xi Didura's, if he elected to travel that far. There was no need, of course. Xi was not in the habit of staying close to home. It seemed he was not fond of dwelling on old memories. Even the good became touched with bitterness as time went on, as a man lost hope. In accepting his life held no meaning, that even those he had loved had moved on, the best times became the worst, the brightest memories became the bitterest.

"You know, you're thinking about all the wrong things, Mister Alran." He said. "What would have happened if Sao *and* his lover were immured here at the same time. How many lives do you think were impacted by them, as opposed to just one or the other."

"Far more than are kept here, I suppose."

Ank sniffed. "All of them."

He chucked the apple at the lake. It sailed far into the gullet of a corridor on Sao's side of the break, landed with a hardy splash somewhere well out of Shulraki's sight.

Shulraki watched it fly, lingered on the place where it had landed. When he turned his focus back to Ank, he found he had gone. *As quiet as a mouse, isn't he?*

Sky Souled

The apple drifted out of the corridor amid coruscating ripples of memory, lives lived and lost crashing into each other as the ripples drew away from their source.

Then there is life in this place, after all. But...if there is life, death should be here, too. Shouldn't it?

A Quiet Place

A narrow strip of land cut a sinuous path between the edges of two ice shielded lakes. In winter, the spirits, Tanchik and Chuklha slept beneath the fine sands in their depths, and a bounty of fish drifted languidly along nearer the surface. The ice shields were incomplete, dotted with open windows where sun touched waters broke across ice so thin to walk along its surface would be to risk death.

The Cuu had descended on the ice where it was thick enough to support them, dug into it with chisels and awls, carved out chunks and dropped baited lines into the waters, and hauled away a bounty of bass and walleye, returned to firepits filled with embers and layered grasses, to smoke their catches and preserve them.

But Bora held back. She kept close to Sarri, as the Chikata and Tipik broke camp and drove their horses across the land bridge, the acolytes of lake and river spirits among them clearing the way of deep snows and treacherous ice sheets that might break the ankles of their horses.

The going was slow, leaving ample time for the haul to be taken in, leaving time for the Cuu and Dumas to finish the work of smoking those fish ahead of the long march north. The land went through a change in these reaches. Where once glacial ice had risen to form the slopes of a long enduring mountain, myriad lakes like these, brooks and dells, spars of sedimentary rock, of shale and sandstone were all that was left to remember it. The Cuu would be taking the rear this day, a transition affording Arrak's Hakka some protection in the belly of the snake as the double file of marching warriors and camp followers neared the border with Tuluis Fel. Gulang and Kuuda had taken to arranging their forces in a defensive array, ready to spill out and form serrated edges for the spear should they witness an attack here. Such choke points were vulnerable, and though the Tului fled, they would want for blood before long. Their reinforcements were somewhere over the horizon, beyond these twin lakes and the pass they guarded.

In another two days they would be on Tuluis Fel, and already the lands had taken on a cast of unfamiliarity, the shine of absent knowledge to remind the Gil Garo they were not home anymore. These were no lands for raiding. They were not lands for living, either, and what settlements rose up in this reach were well defended. Farms marked out by tall fences, trenches forested with long timbers cut

A Quiet Place

into points along their meaty heads. Goats and sheep brayed and bleated behind those walls near enough for them to hear, while the residents within the rare outposts cowered within their homes, waiting for the Gil Garo to pass.

These were not a people accustomed to war, not truly. But they knew conflict, or why would they seek to build up such heavy defenses, position guard towers behind their walls which looked less like houses and more like the tree stands the people of Ao Lein sometimes employed for hunting, mere seats atop ladder poles, narrow platforms providing footholds for the sentries to look out on the world.

They had passed two such outposts before they arrived at these lakes. A third rose up along the outside edge of Tanchik Lake, and the lakeside border was more strictly watched than any other front. The people knew their enemy. Knew the Tului way of using ice to their advantage, and shadow, for there were torches at regular interval along that border, sending up smoke even in daylight.

Sarri's gaze was fixed on that settlement. There might be a dozen families living within those walls, all contributing to the tending of livestock and the raising of crops, and then just enough to feed their people. They would be dedicated to the spirits of this reach, would find the idea of travel well beyond those walls an uninviting prospect. Civilizations like these were so often fearful of the outside world, and it showed in that all of the watch towers within sight were manned, and all of those eyes were trained on the columns marching across the strip, the activities of the Cuu and Dumas as they did their fishing well away from the village.

"What do you make of them?" He said.

"Those pens are stocked somehow." She responded.

"Yet I see nothing to tell of recent conflict here."

"Considering how close they are to the border, it may well be that they have some relationship with the Tului. Some kind of treaty in place."

"I see no evidence of that, either."

"The fortifications tell you a different story?"

"They speak of a people *expecting* conflict, who will not shy away from it when it comes."

"Yet the Tului are a greater force than them. We've seen how organized they are."

"And we know now they need breeding stock in order to maintain their food supply." His words came out as a growl. He had not seen what she had, yet the idea of it was enough to drive him into a quiet, simmering rage.

"Consider, then, the need for genetic diversity. They cannot hope to maintain a healthy population among their...*charges*...without replenishing their supply now and again."

"What are you saying, Bora?"

She contemplated the fortifications. The array of them. The lake would provide ample space for a people who commanded flows of ice to cross, should they seek to attack, but ice could be broken, did not stand up well to impact, could be melted or converted to water by an acolyte of even a lesser spirit with enough practice. And she did not believe this was a people without such acolytes.

It would be better to go overland. There would be gates on the landward sides, somewhere. Even an isolationist people would have need of the roads for hunting, to gather supplies, or seek trade for medicines and other goods they could not easily come by. Food may not be a problem now, but there were always other concerns to be met. Wood for fires would need to be taken from the countryside. Water drawn from the lake itself. They would need healers, and these lakes were bound to minor spirits, none of them with enough power to cure the sickness the Tului brought with them. They were not spirits of exorcism either.

"Consider what it might mean for a village like that to comply with the Tului. They may hold quorums, elect to send their own people to the Tului to bolster their breeding stock in exchange for...for peace. For survival."

"Who would do something so despicable. To send their own children..."

"In their shoes, would you see fit to do differently. Their compound could be overrun with a large enough force, and the Tului have that. They took a whole army across the steppe to meet us. It would be nothing for them to storm the village and take every last one of those people for themselves, but there would be no advantage in doing so. And there is the matter of their own numbers. Surely, they have as much need to diversify their population as the Tului.

"I would think the exchange would run in both directions. They send their people to the Tului to foster children, which the Tului keep. Perhaps the Tului release some of their kin to them after a measure of time spent in service."

"From different villages. Well enough removed from them that they may sustain themselves. People who would have been conditioned for this task." Sarri's expression darkened. "Then they are even more despicable for it."

"Yes, but then they may have entered into a state of symbiosis with the Tului. The terms being mutually beneficial, the sustained trade in human stock ensuring they are not attacked...unless they cannot provide. But those lessons would have been learned by now." She rubbed her mitten shielded hands together, trying to bring warmth back into them. She was not accustomed to this measure of exposure, not used to being so long away from the heat of her yurt.

"Do you think they would see us as an enemy, if they knew what we were here for?" she asked.

"I think they see plainly what we're here for." He said. "And see us as an enemy anyway."

"Because their way of life may be threatened by our coming. But what if we bring them something more to their benefit than what they have now?"

"A gift?" he eyed her suspiciously.

"Yes. A token to win their favor."

"What do you suggest."

"Send an envoy across the ice. A nonthreatening company, just a few of our people. It may help if you go in person."

"To what end?"

"To deliver a boon they likely do not have. Hibiscus, Chief. Enough seeds that they can grow their own crop. They may need to do it in secret, or risk drawing the wrath of the Tului down on them, but to have it...if they don't already. They can only benefit from having it on hand if they refuse to comply."

"Which benefits us in that it removes another potential food source. We starve them out by drawing their allies away from them, making new allies among the border tribes."

"Exactly."

"And if they attack us?"

"We retreat. The Cuu will already be joining the march by then. It will be easy enough to avoid losses.”

“I see your point.”

He backed away from her, marched down the stretch to the nearest group of fishermen. A brief exchange and one broke away, ran south, toward the camp where the remaining forces were packing their belongings ahead of the march north.

All of war is a game. She thought. *Isn’t that right, God Tirulain? And the victor in any war is the one whose schemes are the most underhanded.*

If we waste this opportunity, what will it mean for us? We will be in enemy territory soon. This war does not end at the border. That is where it begins.

Sarri was joined at the lake’s edge by Kuuda, who came with several others all carrying heavy sacks at their sides. The efforts of his horticulturists had proven successful, as they transitioned away from growing opium, wielded the life of the land in growing hibiscus from seed in the night, and watched the blooms flourish and recede with each morning.

“I hope this is worth it, Sarri.” He said.

“I don’t believe it will be.” Sarri said.

“Then why bother?”

“Something you must learn if you are to rise in the place of your father. Sometimes the risk is worth the reward, even if the outcome is unknowable. There are villages in Ao Lein and Ruc who fear an attack from us with such intensity they are willing to part with a portion of their crops to see us pass without incident. They give us this tithe as an offer of peace, knowing it will not earn them favor with their capitols. Those grains and food crops are meant to fulfill their tax debts against the thrones, but they do not have the luxury of housing large forces who might pose a challenge to us. They are the forgotten places in their kingdoms. With no garrisons, they are vulnerable, which would make them easy targets for us if they did not seek to appease us.

“I believe these people are the same. They see an army and quiver in fear of what might befall them. They know the Tului well, but they do not know us. They are undecided, friend. They do not know if we will attack them, and so bolster their defenses against the possibility. But they are loyal to the Tului, I believe, because they fear them. Given this...” he gestured to the parcels in the hands of Kuuda’s men. “They will have a greater defense against the threat looming across the border. And they may see in us a distraction for the Tului, a complication to them that may see them through to a better way of life.”

“You believe they have *friendly* relations with the Tului?” Kuuda said skeptically.

“Friendly is not the word I would use.”

“Shall we?”

“I think so.”

They struck out across the ice, spread out so that their weight would not threaten collapse at any one place. They stayed along the perimeter as they traveled, where the ice was strong enough to support them and the risk of collapse would not send them into deeper water than they could stand in.

As they neared the village, Sarri produced a length of white cloth, held it high over his head.

Tears for the Moon God

A sentry descended from his perch and out of sight. Silence descended as they stationed themselves in sight of the wall, but at a safe distance from arrow fire should those people become hostile.

The crunch of snow under boots; a small force approached from the north side. All of them were armed and wearing boiled leathers. They stepped onto the ice, came within a few paces of the Gil Garo party and halted.

A middle aged man among them, bulky and with a wild beard crossing a blunt jaw, stepped forward.

"Move on with your forces." He boomed. "We have no desire for conflict, but we will defend ourselves if we are pushed to it."

"We have no fight with your people." Sarri said. "We have simply come to negotiate."

"To what end?" the man demanded.

"A gift, to secure your friendship." Sarri gestured to the men arrayed behind him. "I am Chief Sarri of the Cuu Gil Garo. This is Acting Chief Kuuda of the Kirche Gil Garo. We march for Tuluis Fel to answer an attack on our people, to war."

"Then go to your war. It is futile."

"You see our forces." Kuuda said. "They cannot stand against us."

"We know the Gil Garo." The man growled. "Raider nomads. Your exploits have done harm to many in the east and south. You are not like them. They will see to it that your entire civilization is destroyed and subsumed into their own. Your way of life will come to an end as their curse spreads through your ranks.

"We have learned our lessons. There is no means by which you can stand against their poison. They will turn those of you who are of breeding age into livestock, and take the rest of you for food. Those strong enough they will corrupt, and you will become soldiers for them. You are fools to attack them."

"This gift." Sarri said. "It is a cure for their poison."

Quiet chatter washed through the ranks of the villager's party.

"There is no cure." Their leader growled.

Kuuda gestured for one of his men to come forward. He took the sack out of his hands and unbound the leather cord around its neck. He opened it, and spilled a handful of calyxes onto his palm.

"Steep these in water near boiling to make a tonic, or eat them raw and whole. They will reverse the effects of the poison. If done before the infection sets in, they will prevent the disease before it can take hold. If done late, it will take time for the full effects to bear out, but they will still reverse this poison.

"We have brought seeds as well, so that your people can cultivate your own stock. But I would recommend you hide your fields from prying eyes. Keep them secret until we have concluded our business. We will be done within the year."

The leader looked over the calyxes. A hungry expression stole over him at the sight of them.

"This is blood bane?" he said. "I have only heard of it. It is outlawed in their lands. They say it came from the sea long ago, when the spirits battled with each other. A gift from the dugong."

"We know nothing of this." Sarri said. "But it has worked on our own people. Some are already returning to themselves, and they were infected weeks ago. They are returning to sanity, losing their craving for blood."

"Their shadows have stabilized." Kuuda added. "All because of this."

A Quiet Place

"Then it is." The leader's gaze flicked from one of them to the other, hunting for a lie in their expressions. "What do you want from us?"

"We want your allegiance." Sarri said.

"To exchange one cruel master for another. The price is too high."

"We do not raid in your lands, cousins." Sarri said. "There is nothing of value for us in doing so. We did not even know you were here until we struck north.

"We will leave you to your lives. All we ask is that you do nothing to support the Tului in the war effort. Whatever tax they leverage against you must go unpaid. But they will be too busy with us to come for you before the spring thaw arrives. If we are successful, they will have been crushed before autumn returns, and you will never have to deal with them again."

"Just that? No tax against us? No raiding on our village."

"Just that."

The leader nodded. His gaze fell on the calyxes. He turned to the others, hunted through the ranks of middle aged men for any dissent. Finding none, he turned back to the Gil Garo chiefs, marched forward and stuck out his hand.

He spat in his palm.

Sarri imitated him, and they shook.

"We have a deal." The leader said.

Kuuda stepped aside as his men passed their parcels into the hands of approaching villagers.

"We owe you a great debt." The leader said.

"You owe us nothing." Sarri said. "Your friendship is enough."

"You truly believe you can break them?" he intoned.

"It will not be easy." Sarri admitted. "But we have never met an enemy greater than us."

"You may have with this one." He said.

"We will see, friend." Sarri said. "We will see."

A Name

Meichekh emerged from the cave with Dupec in her wake. She had not believed her grizzly wolf's promise that the boy would pick up the various powers, a sense for the pulses of the lands and elements associated with her humble home so quickly. Duijus Kanh may well have been too optimistic in his assessment. After all, who was to say how much a soul remembered of the conditioning it endured in a life it never lived? A life stolen from it? But Dupec had taken no time in identifying their pulses in the land. Kachekh's stable heartbeat, as much the mossy, old stone as the woman herself. Duichek's fluid grace and odd candor. Her own breezy, cold perfection, so keen on winnowing away strong barriers, intimating herself to her lover.

Blood painted the snows somewhere off to her left, a short distance away. Blood and mortal flesh scattered across a too vast distance. Violence had happened here, in daylight, when she and her sisters slumbered, all of them curled up near their lover.

Are those children among them? She wondered. The gods did not make a habit of attacking in daylight, for risk that Tao Shein himself would bring his sword against them. Hate him, she may, but she must confess the Plains Lord was no slouch when it came to fighting. There was a reason the gods gave him a wide berth, a reason they did not simply strike at the heart of Gil Garo in midwinter when the sun was still high in the sky.

This broke sharply from the precedent they had set. She could smell the taint of a thoroughly conditioned soul behind that flesh, the denial of Shah Jagat's touch on those bodies. Mangled they may be, but they were still alive. Each one of them trapped in a strange loop within time, and awaiting the moment they were seized by their master, or some servants of him, to be taken away and home, where they must live in this broken state forever.

Lanfin!

She traipsed across the snows in the direction of the carnage, intent on ensuring those children were not among the bodies. If they were not, she would have to adjust her opinion of them. It had been many hundreds of years since the Gil Garo knew their way in truth, and half as long as that since their capabilities

A Name

had begun to decline. Her opinion of them had long declined along with it.

"What's wrong?" Dupec asked.

She flinched, then turned around and smiled serenely at him, the scaling around her dark, liquid eyes bunching and fraying slightly as the individual tiles formed spurs along her cheeks and forehead. "Nothing you need worry about."

He followed in her wake as she found the proper path, and marched toward the dark, broken shapes banded across it.

An arrow stuck out from a crater in the earth, and she smelled Rasheik's essence on it, felt the echo of the Rope Lord's pulse weakly, as if the acolyte who drew on him was not yet mature enough to have strong command over his power. Within the snows, a second pulse which was older and foreign echoed, and it was there, too, in the crystallized blood smeared across the ground between limbs. In craters scattered haphazardly about them, there was a third presence, a third pulse, and she recognized it immediately as the flighty, somewhat chaotic rhythm of The South Wind, Thera.

"Oh, this is good." She said. "Strong forces abound here, right under my nose, and I hadn't the slightest clue."

Dupec came to her side, observed the scattering of entrails, the shattered bodies, the flayed limbs. "These are uelfin. Are they Oe's or God Lanfin's?"

"Oe has no part in this." She said.

"Then God Lanfin has made his move." Dupec whispered. "This must be retaliation for the Dragon's intercession."

"Call him by his name, dear. You shared a bed for years."

"I don't know him, mistress." Dupec protested gently. "He's a stranger to me."

She reached up and smacked him. "Soon, you'll be among his people, and then you will know who he was. Save your ruminating for then."

"What do we do about these?" he asked.

"Leave them." She growled. "Their god will come for them before long."

"Then would it not be to our benefit to take them away before he can have them?"

"And do what with them?"

He raised an eyebrow at her.

"Fine, fine. You go on, then. Gather up my sisters and tell them I'm in need of them. But stay close to Duijus Kanh this night. There might be more of them close by."

"What will you do once the bodies are taken care of?"

"What do you think?" A subtle but menacing smile told a tale of mischief. "We'll hunt."

It did not take long for Dupec to find the other two Swans. His vision had improved substantially in the short time since he had begun his training with them, and walking into the gullet of Duijus Kanh's cave was like walking any other path in broad daylight. He did not have to strain to see the ridges and pits in the walls. He did not have to rely on flows of dank air to tell him where he was in relation to the surface, or where a chamber branched off from the main tunnel.

Stranger still, he did not need to attach himself to the pulses of Duijus Kanh's concubines to retain such clarity. At some time in the past weeks, he had shed the need, and what had been a struggle to maintain became an innate sense, as if in binding himself to the Swans, he invited permanent changes, mutagenic shifts in his own composition, and became something more than he had been. The summation of so many moving parts he barely understood, a conduit for a depthless, ancient power.

He marched past countless names etched into the uneven walls, in crude variations, the handwriting of hundreds of Gil Garo ancestors. The record of their travels into this cave formed a loose chronology. Weathered names barely distinguishable from the stone behind them were framed by scattered, vivid carvings made generations after their original scribes had died and gone to Shao Luin. With each step forward, he was met with fewer of the illegible carvings and more of those newer ones. In the presence of names was the history of the Gil Garo, and in that history, the makings of a stronger society. Each passing generation yielded to braver men and women. Ung Tsang and Ung Tsong became emboldened to push further and further into the cave in pursuit of a fabled title they would likely never bear.

He understood the significance of it, and yet felt it as an alien press in his soul. So many had passed along this path. Countless generations had observed the Gil Garo traditions, lived among them their entire lives, had never known success in courting these spirits. He was alien to his people, and they to him. Gil Garo by blood, but not culturally one of them. Where Chakta and Tamlin had been with their people for decades, he had been with them for days.

He was unworthy to lead them, and yet if tradition held, he had already been decided as their chief. Not chief of one sect but all of them. A Dumas exile come back after so long away to assume a title that had not been worn by any among them in so long they had begun to think the very concept of it was a myth.

On the surface, Meichekh stood vigil over uelfin corpses, the remains of warriors sent by a god who wanted him dead, who had attacked what few people his tribe had left behind.

Why did they leave them here? He had lingered on that for too long without answers. Had been too afraid to ask his spirit keepers. What answers they did provide him when things took a turn for the philosophical were often painful, inviting difficult subjects he would rather had never been addressed. Too many of their answers pointed back to his night time visitor—that man who said he loved him, that stranger with the scar on his chest, who insisted the puckered mass was his fault, that *he* had been the one to stab him.

He had begun to resent being alone. Being alone meant being alone with his thoughts. Thoughts which had a tendency to wander into troublesome territory, and stick there in a land all questions and no answers, no answers he could stand to hear.

He arrived in the chamber at the base of the cave, where its lord slept on hard ground behind two, pallid, deformed women. Both of them doted over him as he slumbered. The horde of treasures that had been there when first he arrived in this cave was absent. Gone off to whatever secret hold Duijus Kanh kept, if it was still in this hole in the earth at all.

He cleared his throat, drawing their attention away from Duijus Kanh and to him. "Meichekh sent me with a message."

"What is it now." Kachekh groused.

Duichekh sighed. "What trouble has she stirred up for us this time?"

A Name

"No trouble." He said. "None that she created, anyway."

"Well, spill it boy!" Kachekh demanded. "We don't have all night."

"Don't we?" Duichekh asked.

"There was an attack on the Gil Garo camp." He said.

"Who would be such a fool as to attack the Gil Garo in broad daylight. Tao Shein ought to be throwing a fit!" Kachekh said.

Duijus Kanh leaned forward, taloned fingers tracing thin tracks across his bare jaw. "Quiet, Kachekh. Let him speak."

"A squad of uelfin...maybe a dozen, attacked and were dealt with by my people, master. They were sent by God Lanfin. At least, that's what Meichekh believes. She's asked me to send Kachekh and Duichekh to her, to help her dispose of the bodies."

"She came to this idea herself?" he growled.

"She seemed content to leave them there for the god or his acolytes to find. We talked. She decided it was better to get rid of them."

"It seems I continue to underestimate you." Duijus Kanh climbed to his feet, and shambled past his concubines. "Go to Meichekh. If Lanfin has made his move, we should be prepared to counter him. This will not be the last of his indiscretions."

The Swans nodded. They took foot and fled the chamber, to join their sister on the surface.

"Walk with me, cub." He said.

Dupec fell in with him as he crossed the chamber, and they emerged in the tunnel outside. They ambled up the slope in silence for a time, before he halted, and turned cruel, yellow eyes on a patch of the wall which was mostly devoid of names. A scattered few, all of them relatively old but not so far gone they could no longer be read, formed a jagged line building from the densely populated upper reaches toward a single name standing alone, etched into the rock in linear script. *His* script.

"I prefer my solitude. My concubines, I permit to remain close because they please me. I enjoy their company. It is not a common thing for me. But the Gil Garo have produced those I have come to respect from time to time. Brave enough souls to venture far down into my cave. *These* are the bravest among them." His gesture encapsulated all of the names in that narrow line. "Pioneers, of a sort. Each one was terrified to carve his name into my flesh.

"They are the bravest of your people. The ones who wore my power in their souls, because I desired to know them. In your last life, I found you more commendable than any of them. Until you lost your way."

Dupec's gaze was fixed on his name, written there on the wall, the last of them all. It was not that Duijus Kanh had not been candid about this matter. It was not that he did not know the name existed where it was. But there were uncomfortable truths embedded in those letters. *He* had not carved them there. *He* had never carved anything in these walls. The Dupec who had done so was a stranger to him, someone he had never known, who he doubted he would recognize had he known him.

They were back to those uncomfortable truths again. Back to discussing the things he would rather remained buried.

He ran trembling fingers over the letters of his own name. *Dupec. Hope.* He looked into his master's eyes, and said: "I am not him."

Tears for the Moon God

"Who are you, if not Dupec Safar?" Duijus Kanh challenged him.

"Have there never been two men of the same name, whether within the same tribe or not?" Dupec responded.

Duijus Kanh stooped, so that he was at eye level with Dupec. So that they were on the same level. It was an odd gesture, but he did not comment. He understood what it meant that this spirit, so powerful he had earned the respect of Tao Shein himself, brought himself down to meet his acolyte. That he thought highly enough of him to show, in his way, humility.

The spirits were seldom so moved.

"You are every bit the man who carved his name in my wall, Ung Kanh Dui." Duijus Kanh growled. "The monster came later. His cause was justified. The gods do not care about mortals, and the spirits you railed against were no friends to me. A tyrant, and a liar. They had long needed to be dealt with. But the monster was flawed in that he was broken. He could not build anything. He needed to lean on someone more whole, or everything he touched would devolve into chaos. For him, the Dragon of the East sufficed for a time, and then he, too, saw the madness within, and realized he could not be the cure for it. He was, after all, the man who created it. Its source.

"What could you have accomplished absent that intervention? I ask myself this, and I cannot fathom…"

He rose again to his full height, thrust fingers in the direction of that name. "That man should have been recalled. He should even now be wallowing in his misery within the Halls of Time. But he was spared, and he came back to me, and now he seeks to reject what I helped him become. I refuse it."

Dupec looked up into his face. Uncertainty plagued him. He was not the man who carved his name into that wall, he was *not!* But he was akin to him. To this moment, their experiences had been nearly identical, or so he suspected. Otherwise, why lead him by the nose to this place. Why deposit him in the very place where he might resume the mantle he had donned in that past life, and become the thorn in the side of the gods he had been then.

"Why won't any of you let this go?" he asked, and the question was genuine. Ung Kanh Dui or not, it did not seem to matter to them what happened when he left this cave, but he believed this to be a calculated apathy. Something simmered beneath the surface, and they had all been keeping it close to the chest for too long.

"Because we are those who sided with God Katcya. The old alliances are fractured. Some of us were not born before the old conflict was resolved, but we know his heart. We understand it. We are those who agree."

"Then maybe…maybe it's me. Maybe, I can't let it go." He looked to his name carved into the wall. "I think we should talk about what I want out of our compact. For the Gil Garo."

"Then you must accept your place as leader over them. As my representative in all matters concerning them. What do you want from me?"

"Peace, Master. I want peace."

Jinga

The Elder wandered along the corridors of the Halls of Time. Now and again, he paused to regard a murky, shallow pond, to disturb it with his fingertips, watch as fragmented memories played out. Most did not contain anything worth noting. Most did not give rise to the imagery he needed. This reach was a scattered array like any other, but of clearer design. There was some semblance of intentionality in the way these pools were arrayed. If Xirakura had been at the fringe of Sao Njack's life, then whoever these people were, they had lived in proximity to him, or perhaps under his rule, for quite some time. There were Nixians among them. A crossing corridor revealed sweeping views of dark forest, battle lines breaking around the boles of trees, the figures swarming over root-threaded ground bearing torches held at arm's length, which shed light on hooded heads and leather jerkins, gloves and boots that rode high over forearms, shins and thighs. Earth tones, to blend in with the stones of Gonsai's Wall. Their camouflage granted them advantage here, in this reach of what could only be Ung Sakh's jungle. But she was not cooperating with them.

Tree roots snapped up to meet boots. Limbs quivered and drew down to catch the raiders across the chest, to crush in throats, beat down skulls. Heavy fruits dropped onto them, and fairies clouded the air, snapping tiny fangs around exposed flesh, being wrenched away, murdered by their victims.

Ripples crossed the pools and they returned to stillness, and still he wandered. These people were not important to him. Not important enough to shed light on the content of Sao Njack's character, the state of his life. He found nothing interesting in the wanton slaughter battles wrought. Those machinations of kings, those *human* conflicts, paled when set against the events he had lived through, in the countless lives he had dipped into—windows opened, doorways flung wide to reveal screaming creatures, burning forests, the entire horizon engulfed in flame.

Tak's cold eyed regard settled on him in his mind's eye. He shivered, and willed the image of that creature away. He had been different then. Violent. *Dangerous.* Not a pacifist, but a monster within whom lay a singular power to destroy. Not even Shol Barak, lord over all of the winds, who with a single act could steal the breath from all those who lived, bare down on mortal kind and leave behind a world for spirits and gods.

Yet he abstained. He reminded himself. *He sided with us.*

He dipped his fingers into another pool, disturbed its placid current. Carp drifted languidly within its reaches in one moment, and in the next, scattered scenes revealed themselves, scenes drawn from a life lived out in caves and mining tunnels, and he saw within them a golden-skinned boy not ten years in age, squared off in the gullet of an expansive cave. The walls were lined with home fronts, so many luminous blocks thrust out of the walls, their windows facing down rope drawn elevators, platforms burdened with cargo, and people stood along those verandas, watching.

How much can be revealed about a man from this view. How much does knowing the child benefit me.

But the image he looked into did not remain still, did not stay focused on the boy. It jittered and shuttered, flitted down narrow corridors clogged with other people, other Nixians, and he realized there was an element of desperation in the way this figure traveled. That he might, in fact, be panicked by the very sight of that boy standing in the heart of the cave, on the floor where open troughs lay to either side of him, long as the cave entrance was, nearly as wide as its floor. And this cave...it was the largest he had ever seen. Its far end was swallowed by darkness.

He retracted his fingers from the pool, and stepped into it, waded into its depths. The waters dragged him down. He could not breathe. For several, agonizing moments, his brain betrayed him and he began to believe he would drown. His lungs constricted, tugged at his throat, dared it to draw in breathe in this aquatic world, and he was dragged deeper. Deeper, until the waters broke around him, and he inhabited the Nixian man's skin, peered through his eyes, and his autonomy was stolen away, leaving a bare thread of his consciousness in tact, enough to know this man was not him, that he was not a natural element of this vision.

The phages attacked, swarmed in from every side, tore away chunks of his identity until all that remained of him was that single, raw thread—one tie, a rope he might pull when time came to resurface, when he had seen enough.

His joints ached. He had done hard travel just the day before, had only returned this morning to his home, and then to sleep off the worst of the road's ware on his aging body. He was not the young whip he had been, but he must endure the strain a little longer. He must get down to the cave's broad floor, and do so quickly.

A distant rumbling brought him up short. He stole glances in several directions, looking for openings along the crowded balcony he might use to get closer.

Need to find a lift. Where is a fucking lift!

He shouldered aside two onlookers, a couple who both hissed indignantly at him as he shoved them aside. Gloved hands gripped a rough hewn rail, his exposed fingertips grated against the grit. He panned over the sheer side of the cave, down below, looking for rope elevators, platforms rising toward him. They should all be rising with that rumbling coming closer, vibrating the walls of their homes as it was.

I DON'T HAVE TIME FOR THIS! MY FUCKING SON! GODS DAMN HIM!

His gaze latched onto a series of ropes twenty paces off. The platform was still two stories removed from his rise, but it would have to do.

Jinga

Heart thundering, he pelted down the granite pathway, bowling people over as he went. Their curses chased after him, the last attempted to grab a hold of him and he swatted the clawing hand away, his thoughts for nothing except getting down there, getting to his boy!

He vaulted across a half flight of stairs and over a railing, snatched hold of a rope and slid down its length. His feet thudded heavily against the platform, and he rammed the driver away from the control console before slamming the lever down. Rope spilled out of the slots in the lift's rails. It plunged past three rises before he slammed his foot against the brake pedal, bringing the platform to a tooth rattling halt.

Amid protestations and many cuss words from the driver, he shook off the force of impact and vaulted over the rail, then sprinted across the pit on unstable feet. The rattling in the earth was picking up intensity, vibrating along his shins and into his torso. From this distance, he could hear the great exhale as built pressure released behind the coming beast, the spirit of Salein Lake, deep underground. Waves thrashed against stone, a dull roar emanating from the tunnel as he closed on the trenches.

His singular focus remained on his son as he leaped over the nearest trench, rolled and came down hard on his shoulder fifty paces from the boy. He ran down the length of the track. His son's attention was fixed on the tunnel, as if he knew no danger from the beast fast careening up its gullet, chewing up space as its many limbs sped overground.

He closed on his son amid screams and useless cries of warning from the well populated walls either side of him, screams that were swiftly drowned by the roar of agitated water and the thunder of too many feet rising from the deeps.

He latched onto the back of his son's coverall. The hood dropped down, revealing a shock of red-brown hair and the golden back of his neck. There wasn't *time* to get him out of there, and in his desperation, it was all he could do to hug the poor, idiot boy to his chest, shield him with his body.

Waves crashed across the back of the cave. An animal wail cut through the raging sounds of spilled water rushing for the trenches. He looked up in time to see the spirit break through the pass.

A gargantuan worm. Skin the color of crude oil, thick with glistening slime. Human arms and legs pumping under its mass, countless limbs picking over uneven ground, whipping up frothing mud as the waters came forth from the deeps, carried along by the lake spirit himself. Salein's gargantuan face, round and white as the moon, hollow eyes turned up in agony toward the ceiling, its teeth gnashed together in a rigid grimace. He stared, transfixed, as the length of its body curled toward the ceiling and crashed again earthward, and it ran, skittered on so many feet toward him and his son, around them, and away. Mists and harsh currents exploded around them, leaving a hollow pocket of mostly dry earth for them to inhabit as the world around them was drowned in white rapids, the rises choked with onlookers stolen away in favor of frothing, mad chaos.

And the waters settled.

And the trenches swallowed the bulk of them, and funneled them away into reservoirs throughout the city and the mines, to refill what had been nearly depleted over the dry season.

The spirits provided. In their own way, on their own time, they provided. And

Tears for the Moon God

the gods looked down on him in that moment and smiled, for it was no act of mercy that saved him.

Katcyakin. Golden Skin. Sun Man.

My son.

He let go of Sao Njack, who was named in honor of his father, who bore that name to honor the last elder to have served in the name of the Njack family. He held on loosely, and Sao twisted in his grip. And he hugged him tight, and they wept. Sao for his fear, and Jinga for knowing his son had saved him. That the gods had smiled down on them in the moment of his birth, had given to his family and his people a true and pure gift, and he was here and now alive, they both were, because that ephemeral, mysterious creature, God Katcya, God of Luck, had deemed them worthy.

He was seated in a broad, multi-use chamber. The walls were the same, rough hewn stone that dominated the rises throughout the city proper, and the home it belonged to was removed from the walks fronting the cavernous pit of the cave. A cave whose spirit Hanuman had begun to suspect was dead, or why did a lake dominate? Why were there no other elements present in the harrowing of this core, the whittling away of the walls this deep in Gonsai's domain?

Hanuman wore Jinga's skin, a flesh coat harboring his soul, leaving him enough left of his rationality to know he was not Jinga in truth, that he might flee from these scenes whenever he chose.

If he chose to leave at all.

Living within the flesh of another mortal made him feel like a parasite, feeding off the blood supply of another until he was sated, for a time, but there was always need for more. Always that desire to walk blindly into another pool, to experience that same succor even as it chipped away pieces of him, left him less than he was, more unstable and volatile and unpredictable, even as it drove the other Wanderers away from him.

Jinga sat at one end of a sturdy, oak table. The table was crowded with books and old maps, histories and guides to the lands in other nations, even those that thrived or faltered in reaches well removed from Ul Sadh, which lay across vast oceans, on the other side of the world.

A bank of windows framed one side of the table, looked out on a narrow hall illuminated with electric lamps connected each to the others by loose, insulated wires. Those had been among the first things Jinga had learned to make when in his early years as an apprentice under a Baduhrak engineer. It was those lights that had given the man an interest in the craft, and which had ultimately led him to take his vows as acolyte of God Hou Rok of Smiths.

There was a price for learning, which his son—standing over the other end of the table, looking over the gathered tomes and trying to select out the one of most interest in the moment—refused to accept. Any number of local spirits would provide a boon to him. There were those in the Ropes framing Sha Ruhhad's desert that would deliver immense prosperity to the Nixian people if he chose to take on the challenge of courting them. Spirits of rivers who excelled in healing arts, of forests and mountains and vast plains who might help them to grow food crops, or preserve them longer. There were those like Ul Sharak and Gur Tulain who excelled in healing curses and purging ailments of the spirit.

Jinga

And there was Salein. A name which vibrated against the tip of his tongue, barely suppressed. He did not know how much longer he could go without suggesting Sao Njack descend into the cave this city occupied, down deep into its gullet, to confront the spirit there, ask for a place as his acolyte. But his son did not want him. Did not want to confront any spirit who might accept him without a struggle.

Sao reached for a book well removed from him, the very one Jinga knew he would. He dragged the thin, leather bound log to himself, a log that had been written by a Nixian spirit guide, one of those selected by the elders to escort foreigners across the desert, who himself had taken great strides to locate and converse with all of the spirits who inhabited it, and there were not many. His accounts drew so many in when time came for them to choose who they would apprentice under. The stories it told were complex, flavored with intimate descriptions of the land features which in life were so dull, awash in shades of gray and ochre, so much more alive on paper than they ever were by sight. He had hoped his son would see sense, leave that text well alone. There was only one spirit enshrined in those pages he had ever cared about, and it was the one most likely to kill him if he laid chase.

Sha Ruhhad himself. He thought grimly. *Even a Sun Man would have trouble with him.*

And that was precisely the point, wasn't it? All his life, Sao had only wanted to feel human. It was why, so many years ago, he had placed himself in the path of Salein. Even then, as young as he was, he had known something was different about him. There was that time he fell from a fourth floor balcony and landed in a heap on the cave's floor, entirely unharmed, not a bone fractured. There was the time Jinga had found him missing in the dead of night, and his favorite toy gone with him.

He had been heartbroken then. Relieved when his son returned looking confused and a bit dejected. Even more when a then ten year old Sao had wrapped his arms around his father's hips and hugged him. There were tears, then, dampening the front of Jinga's coverall. Ho'o had answered his call, only to reject his plea to spirit him away. It seemed The North Wind had his lines in the sand. He would not take this child from his loving family, but whatever else they had discussed remained secrets for Sao alone to carry. They had never spoken of it again.

His challenges had begun small, and had become more and more reckless as he passed through his teen years, until his every manic act became a challenge to death herself, and this was no exception.

"Put it down." Jinga said. He could not help it. He had raised this boy from the cradle, had done so even as it lingered in the back of his mind that he may not be the boy's true father. No one knew how God Katcya spread his influence, but popular myth in Nixir held he impersonated men in courting their women, and lay with them as a lover.

In Sanguhr and Saodein, across Rasheik's Rope and throughout Sarkahn Plain, there were other accounts of how he went about it which were far more innocent, and yet the thought had lingered, and festered, until the night Sao courted The North Wind. If he was not certain of Sao Njack's parentage before then, he knew beyond doubt after that incident, the boy had chosen him. That nothing short of his death could break the bond they shared.

He would not see him die for being a fool. It was a father's place to protect his child from harm, to shield him from the ills he might suffer for his own inexperience. But his boy was a man now, and would be leaving him for a time. How long depended largely on which spirit he chose to hunt after, how long an apprenticeship under that spirit lasted. He wanted to be supportive, but at the same time he wanted his son to recognize he did not need these increasingly dangerous challenges to feel human.

If he would only let himself see it.

Sao ignored him, and thumbed through the pages, pointedly making a show of contemplating the other spirits described in vivid detail as he closed in on the pages he wanted, the particulars surrounding the most antisocial spirit to inhabit the lands north of Gonsai Wall.

Is this how he came to know his power? The thought echoed in Hanuman's voice, seeming to come from a great distance.

He arrived at the pages in the heart of the book, buried where to find them the avid reader would need to cross through the terrain of several more reasonable spirits. There had been others in Jinga's lifetime who sought the mentorship of Sha Ruhhad. Most of them never returned to Nixir City. Their families grieved their losses. Sha Ruhhad, so unlike Ul Sharak, did not grant the mercy to these families of showing their taken souls to their kin before they were stolen away to Gur Tulain.

A few of those mothers and fathers, and siblings, had ventured up to Gur Tulain, and most of them came back with nothing more to go on than that their children had passed. Almost certainly, they had. *Almost. And that hope, that little thread of it, keeps every one of them looking north, or at their doors, waiting for those kids to walk through them.*

Sao sat at the other end of the table, set the open book on the table in front of him.

"I keep thinking it over." He said. "And I keep coming back to the same conclusion. I could go after any spirit in the desert. I could go after Gonsai himself if I wanted to, and he would probably accept me with open arms, grumpy as he is, but what would any of it mean?"

"You would bring prosperity to us all. Security. Gonsai is not a bad choice. Though I would rather you—"

"Salein is not worth considering."

"Why not, son?"

"Because."

"Because he is too easy? He hasn't taken on an acolyte in near enough fifty years, and the last one died five years before you were born."

"What does that have to do with me?"

"A Sun Man would have no trouble securing his mentorship."

"Not you too." Sao said quietly, and there was a dangerous undercurrent in his tone. They were coming up on the very source of his greatest insecurity. The reason for all of his stunts over the years, and a conversation Jinga did not want to engender. Which he had avoided as best he could every time it came up, because the answers he provided to his son's earnest questions were never enough. And how could they be? He had no concept of what it was like to be a Sun Man, one of the Nixian people and at the same time apart from them. Always apart, held in high

Jinga

esteem and shunned by the same token. Who could know what it felt like except a Sun Man, to be loved for what he was, and left there, with only his family to acknowledge who he was beyond it. Even some of *them* struggled.

"I'm sorry. I didn't mean to imply—"

"That I should put my people before myself? It would be the honorable thing to do, father, but it would kill me. Is this all I am to them? Not a person but an idol, to be protected until I can deliver some golden age to them?

"I don't want that! I never have. And really—"

"I'm on your side." Jinga cut in. "But that isn't why I want you to consider another path. There are spirits who remember the old times, before our civilization was founded. Salein is one of those. If you will not go to him in pursuit of his tutelage, maybe he can help you in other ways."

"What can he do?"

"His domain is memory, and he has lived since those ancient times. He is older than some gods, you know. It's strange to think about, but he is." Jinga folded his hands in his lap and met his son's eye. "At least consider going to him. If anything, he can help you decide which spirit is best for you. He might even tell you how to win their favor."

"And if that's Sha Ruhhad?"

"You're a man now, son. You can make your own decisions. But I'm still your father, and as long as that remains true I'm going to do what I can to protect you. If you want to chase after shadows on a lifeless plane, I can't stop you. But I can at least make sure you're equipped to pursue him. Even if I don't like it. What else can I do?"

Sao nodded, seemingly mollified.

A rare fury had settled over Jinga Njack. An advanced, clammy-cold rot festered in his guts. A confused storm spiraled across his head, half formed thoughts dancing in and out of focus as he marched, stiff-limbed and square-shouldered down a hall in Tulaen's Palace.

Let it not be true. He wouldn't have...how could he!

What devil has possessed my son? Who is this beast he has become!

The roots latching this flowering of anger to fertile soil had been there from the start, he supposed. Since he ceded his claim to his son, his role shifting from parent to counselor, from counselor to aide, from aide to something less effectual than a common drudgery maid. He had been losing Sao for a long time now, had been sleepwalking toward this conclusion since he placed his support behind the idiot boy's decision to take the Nixians away from their home. What good had it done them, sending scarabs and miners, engineers and harvesters into Sanguhr? What peace had it brought?

Tulakh should have been a bridge too far, but there had been reasons and justifications for invading that kingdom, too. A kingdom who felt the threat of war on two fronts became a dangerous thing, indeed, but Sanguhr had never been the Nixians to hold. They were never meant to be stewards over the south lands, and had he known his son intended this war to be one of occupation rather than a simple battle for independence, he would never have agreed to it.

Nixir had been fine before the first skirmishes broke out. There had been as many Sangar villages who would trade with their people as not, as many who thought fondly of them as viewed them through a less savory lens.

No, I should have spoken up when he courted the elders. He growled deep in his throat, a feral sound. The creases in his forehead and at the corners of his eyes felt deeper. The old aches in his joints, the arthritic stiffness in his knuckles and his wrists felt sharper, more insistent. He was too old for this. Too old to be chasing down beasts masquerading as men. He had never expected his son to be one of them.

What choice did I have. He smacked his cheeks, ran his fingers through straight, steel-gray hair. The black had long since receded, leaving behind narrow streaks near his temples and sprinkled about his bangs. "I didn't have a choice."

It felt like a cop out, thinking of his son's gift like this. A gift that had turned out to be a curse, one more wedge hammered into the space between father and son by the gods in the latest extrapolation on their great game. He was all used up, tired of laying blame on Goddess Liandal for all that had befallen them, tired of blaming Fate for all that Sao Njack had become.

She might have had a hand in shaping him, it was her way; but she was not responsible for who he was. Who he allowed himself to be.

He found the door, an unassuming, oak rectangle recessed into the slate-tiled wall, where the emperor of this sham society had taken to meeting with his generals.

He snorted. *Generals. As if every one of them wasn't a common thief five years ago.*

He twisted the knob and slammed the door inward. It blasted against the wall, startling several of the young men gathered within. Some of those were Sangar. Most were Nixians. All of them were scum.

The door swung back, warbling as it traveled, as he shoved aside one of those men, a man who reached for the long knife at his hip—Sao was well aware of his power, had taken to allowing every one of these people to keep their weapons on them when in his presence. What could *they* hope to do against a Sun Man? There was nothing to fear for him from mere humans.

The sword slid half out of its sheath, then slammed back home as the general met Jinga's gaze. No words were needed, not even a sound. The man saw the storm in Jinga, and chose the wisest path.

Jinga turned the storm in his son's direction.

"What the *hell* has gotten into you!" he demanded.

"I'm not sure what you mean." Sao said placidly.

Jinga noted the drum and sword leaning against the wall behind him, neither of them within arms reach.

"What you did to those girls." He said through gritted teeth. "Did I not teach you better! Where have your morals gone! They can never recover from what you did!"

"Ah." Sao said, in that infuriatingly flat tone. "Who told you?"

"So you can mutilate them too?"

"A simple question, father." He leaned back against his chair, a cocky grin parting his lips. He looked so like his mother, and yet he could never have imagined her behaving like this. She would never have allowed him to show such disrespect to her, either. To speak to her as if she was a naive child. "Sometimes in politics, we must do unpalatable things in order to make our point. The Tulakka royals

Jinga

were...regrettably...hesitant to accept our rule. They needed reminding why they ought to capitulate peacefully. As it happens, one of them saw wisdom."

He gestured to the seat next to him, where a reed-thin man with a wide face and hooked nose sat. The man was younger than Sao by a handful of years, and seemed uncomfortable having his attention on him, as if he had done something heinous and unforgivable in being here. And perhaps he had.

"This is Hassan Alghoul. He has proven quite reasonable, I must say. I do believe he cares deeply about his subjects. I could not say the same for the rest of his family."

"So you bonded his sisters together, blood and bone."

Hassan stiffened.

"Quiet, father. He did not see what happened in that chamber. I gave him that kindness, as will you."

"Don't talk to me like that." Jinga snapped. "I've come to tell you I'm leaving." He turned hard eyes on Hassan. "If you have any respect for your sisters, you'll run as far from my son as you can." Snapped back to Sao. "I'm going home. Don't look for me. Don't come home. You're no longer welcome. If you insist on being this *thing,* this *beast,* you can do it without me. I'm done."

Sao looked as if he'd been struck, and it took him long enough to recover that several of his advisors, these thieves and cretins turned generals in his ranks, these backstabbers and connivers and manipulators, noticed. Most looked away. Most had that much sense.

"You're done when I tell you—"

Jinga spun on his heels and marched out of the chamber.

"YOU ARE NOT DISMISSED!" Sao shouted after him.

"I'M QUITTING YOU, MY SON! I'M QUITTING YOU FOREVER!" Jinga roared. "EVERY ACTION HAS ITS CONSEQUENCES. TAKE THIS TASTE OF YOURS AND HOLD ONTO IT! IT'S ALL YOU'LL EVER HAVE OF ME AGAIN!"

His face had gone scarlet with the force of his own shouting. He felt drained, exhausted, as if he had never known rest. And that sickness roiling through him redoubled. Had he known this was the way things would turn out when Sao was a child, he would have been harder on him, would have spoken up more, would have shown him the right path as best he damned well could.

He ventured through the arc of his life, every bittersweet memory with his only son, hunted for the moment when everything had gone wrong. When he had failed.

As he marched away, the thought came to him again and again, unbidden and relentless, stubbornly refusing to die.

What did I do wrong? What did I do wrong? What did I do wrong?

Life had gone and passed Jinga Njack by. He had gone and gotten old, hadn't he? He supposed he might have made different choices had he known his life would pan out the way it did. He might have given into Dinei's wishes to have another child. They'd have a son or a daughter, then, who had no illusions about becoming someone powerful, someone...monstrous. She would have had someone around when she fell ill, and maybe their second son or daughter would have been able to give her the care she needed, or barring that, to find someone who could. At least she would have had one of her children near her when she died, if Shao Luin must claim her.

Tears for the Moon God

And if we had grown old together? If she was sitting here with me now... His gaze drifted to the empty chair the other side of their hearth. It had been hers. No one sat there now. His own brother could not take it, and though he might look at Jinga and see a man who had never learned to let go, who could not move on...well, he didn't understand love, now did he? Not that kind, anyway.

Maybe they'd have grandchildren, and if they did, they would be in their late teens by now. Sao had been coming into the prime of his life when last he saw him. There had never been any hope of him having kids, of course. Even had he not been a katcyakin and sterile, he was built the wrong way for it. Was invested in the pursuit of men, and they did pine after him when he was younger. *Before he found....*

Sighing, he rubbed his temples. Flames guttered and bloomed in that soot-stained hearth, lapped at a kettle he'd hung there. Some things were best done the old fashioned way, and though he could just as easily build something more convenient with which to make his tea, he had long ago decided it was not worth the effort or the upkeep. Besides, nothing he made could have made his tea taste better, and boiling the water over the hearth reminded him of a home he had long since left, a home filled with warmer memories than this one.

His life could have been so different. He might have had a house full of laughing children, and that would have been...well, it would have been just fine. He would have been happy with that life and its lack of complications. This house might feel a little more like his parents' home, then. It felt so cold and lonely, now.

The kettle whistled and a gout of steam blew straight from its spout, and he shambled to the kitchen, where he picked out the cupboard he needed and selected two mugs from it. He set the first on the counter, stood there with the other cup clutched in his fist, a queer sensation stealing over him.

Now why did I do that? He was not expecting company. His brother, Syrj, was not due back from the mines in the western reaches of Gonsai Wall for a few days yet, and Kiresh had not called on him either.

He shrugged, and set the other mug down. "On the off chance."

He pulled a porcelain serving tray out of another cupboard, set the two cups onto it, and took it back into the sitting room, where he set it down on the quaint, little end table between his chair and Dinei's. He took up a fire poker from a wrought iron bin next to the hearth and hooked the kettle on it. It would be some time before he was comfortable touching it, and boiling water made for bitter tea anyway. He set the kettle on the tray, then returned the fire poker to its place.

As he settled back into his seat, a knock came at the door. He looked to the second cup, then at the ceiling above it. *Is that you meddling again, Goddess Liandal?*

He righted himself, and shuffled off to the front door. For several seconds he stood there looking at it, willing whoever was on the other side to move along and leave him to his quiet. The knock came again, a pathetic wrap of the knuckles so light he wouldn't have heard it at all had he stayed in the sitting room as nature intended. He was in no mood for visitors today. Those days when he felt like talking to much of anyone were becoming scarcer with each passing year, and he was beginning to accept the idea that he very well might prefer to die alone. Kiresh and Syrj would never let it happen, of course. They'd come to understand his predilection to solitude as some kind of disease, but what was there in the company of others except poorly suppressed pity and reminders of everything he tried so desperately to forget.

The knock came one last time, even weaker than the last. He grumbled out a curse for Goddess Liandal on the on chance, and pulled the door open.

The seconds following dragged out in mutual silence. He thought to slam the door, but couldn't bring himself to do it. By the same token, a great sadness washed over him, and though his eyes remained dry, he could just as well have cried right then and there. Collapsed onto the floor, sobbing irreconcilably like the pathetic creature he was.

He stared. At his guest. All of the pieces were there. The features were familiar, and yet his mind reeled, refusing to assign a name to the man standing across the threshold from him, the man who looked so much like his mother, who nonetheless had his father's cheekbones—Jinga's cheekbones.

"Sao?" he croaked.

"This was a mistake." His son said, and for his part he agreed. Hadn't he told him to stay away? Hadn't he complied with this one wish for near enough twenty years now?

Sao made a quarter turn away from him. One foot in front of the other, he began to walk away.

"Wait."

He froze in mid step. The toe of his boot descended ever so slowly to the ground, and he remained where he was, as if ensnared by a sorcery that would not allow him to leave.

"Just...why are you...here?"

Sao looked away. Jinga could not see his face from his vantage, could not see anything at all but the back of his head, where red-brown hair formed a whorl somewhat left of center and a snatch of golden skin peaked out from under his collar.

He was not dressed like an emperor ought to be. He wore the hooded singlet his people favored, and leather armor over it. The leather was cracked in places and it looked worn.

"I came to apologize." He whispered.

Whatever Jinga had been about to say had failed him. He stood there, gaze flitting from the back of Sao's head to the nearest of the lights in the corridor to the stoop to his own bare feet.

"All I can say is I'm sorry. Nothing else feels...right. It would all just be excuses anyway."

He took a step forward.

Jinga snatched at the air short of his son's collar.

"He's going to do something terrible." A watery edge had entered his voice. "And I can't stop him.

"I tried. So hard. But he won't listen to me anymore. He's barely himself and..." he drew a long breath, held it. Released. "I'm sorry. I'm just so sorry."

"C-come inside. Please."

Sao faced down the hall, and though he would not look at Jinga, it was apparent he was trying to see him. In his periphery. Oblique details taken in without the pressure in meeting his eye, one man to another. His father might see the truth of him, then. But though he tried, he couldn't hide that truth from him. He

Tears for the Moon God

was...*delicate.* Whatever had come to pass since their parting had left him much more fragile than Jinga remembered him being. He was not at all sure what to think.

"*Please* come in. Have a cup of tea with me. We can talk."

Sao stiffened. And nodded rapidly. His gaze traveled to the floor of the corridor, and he ambled past his father, boots scraping against stone as he dragged his feet.

Jinga closed the door behind him, and followed him up the short hall into the sitting room, where he led him to Dinei's chair, and the chair was occupied for the first time since she had died.

They sat in silence for a long time, both staring at the flames. Sao was the one who broke it. And when he had, it was for his father to wish that silence could have gone on indefinitely.

"He's going to wage war on Hou Rok." He said. "He's got the Ul brothers involved."

Jinga hissed. He knew Crolus and Bradus Ul quite well from his time in Tao Baduhr. They were clever bastards, but they were also some of the dirtiest, most conniving people he'd had the displeasure of meeting.

Sao began to recount his tale, and in fits and starts, it came together. Before long, he was sobbing. Shaking with the effort of keeping the worst of it back.

And as he recounted all that he had done and that had been done in his name, Jinga listened. If redemption could be had, it was not something any mortal man could give. He knew, then, that he had made the right decision in leaving when he did, and knew too he would see his son to safety if it killed him. He had not forgiven him, not for what he had done in Tulaen. For every affront to the humanity of his subjects—to rulers and leaders the continent over—there would have to be forgiveness, too. But he was not ready. He would protect his son because he saw in him a new flowering of moral fiber, but forgiveness would have to come later, when all of this was no longer fresh.

One truth remained to guide his actions now. Sao Njack had given up everything. His titles. His power. Even his lover. He had given up all of it, and a man willing to do that must have gone as low as he could go. From deeps clad in darkness, a man was given the opportunity to see the light but once, and he had. In giving up the life he had built, he reached for it. And maybe, just maybe, if he kept straining to do better, be better than he was, he might just touch it. Might hold it. Might be good again. Might even be whole.

Water boiled over the edge of the pool, and Hanuman was flung from it. He rolled across the corridor and slammed into the cyclopean wall, its every stone a jagged puzzle piece grinding into soft flesh, making rags of his deer hide tunic and cotton trousers. His teeth slashed shallow lines into the meat of his cheek as they clamped together, filling his mouth with the iron tang of drawn blood.

He peeled himself off the wall, one stiff arm thrusting out, palm rasping against the cutting edge of a broken sheet of flint.

Blind groping. Water ran across his eyes, streamed from his hair. His head was full of air. A few moments from now he would have a searing migraine. For now, it was as if someone had saved him from drowning. His lungs seized. Water mingled with thick threads of saliva was flung past his lips with every hacking cough as he keeled onto his arms. They shook as he tried to crawl away from Jinga's memories,

Jinga

desperate for dry ground, somewhere, anywhere he could gather himself in relative safety.

The auras were coming. Clouds at the edges of his vision had already begun to form, and though he tried to blink them away they came on stronger, stronger still. Lights popped and whizzed across his vision, stole away stone, and pond scum and brown water, sky and narrow sunbeams and clouds. And he was left cold, adrift in darkness, haunted by the echoes of Jinga's last thoughts.

Where did I go wrong? What can I do now?

His heart raced. The fog crowded his thoughts every time he tried to push it away. A battle was in progress, and it came on with a rare ferocity. Within that cloud were unseen razors, the cuts unfelt as they stole away chunks of him, bit into his soul and dragged out memory after memory. He could not be certain which chunks belonged to him, what was *him,* anymore. This biting away, chewing, digesting of Hanuman the Elder had long stopped hurting.

Who else did they take? What else of consequence?

He barely remembered Heiman. He remembered his face, but not his voice. He'd lost that in the first two centuries or so of isolation. He remembered the man but not the boy. Had fleeting images of a youth barely into his teens smiling as he locked arms with another man, who shared his cherubic face, his skin tone, who shared with Hanuman the crazed array of spangle lines creeping across every inch of his skin, the gemstone chips suspended in his silver irises, the marks of an Elder God.

"I am Hanuman." He gasped. "Son of Katcya. And Heiman is my brother."

He remembered the array of huts all made of driftwood drawn down from the headwaters of the great river as it cut its path across the mountains, remembered digging irrigation ditches to draw those waters into channels, into fields where grew wild rice, and corn, and squash; yams and beets; sorghum and pole beans. He remembered making molasses, hunting for bee hives in summer, in the heavily forested mountains where he would one day meet his closest friend and mentor. And he found he could not remember the face of that friend, either. Could not even remember his name.

Terror lashed through him. He whimpered. Matted locks dripped water into his sodden lap. Rivulets ran across his cheeks, obscuring tears.

"I...I am Hanuman the Elder. Son of Katcya. My brother is Heiman the Younger. My mentor is...is...is...." He sank against the wall behind him. One leg slid out. His heel touched the edge of a pool. He retracted it as if he'd been burned.

"I am Hanuman the Elder. Son of Katcya. My brother is Heiman the Younger. I was trapped in the Halls of Time because...because...as a punishment...for, um...."

"FUCK!" he slapped himself. "FUUCK!"

"I told you, you shouldn't be messing around in other people's memories." Ank's voice came from almost at his shoulder.

When did he show up. "Leave me alone."

"How bad was it this time? What did you learn, no, no. I don't care about that. What did it take from you, old man?"

"I am Hanuman the Elder." He whispered.

Ank leaned over him. He could just make out the other man's shadow crossing his head and chest, but could see nothing else. After so long spent outside of reality, immersed so deep in another's life, it would be some time yet before his vision

Tears for the Moon God

returned. He did not like the Sanark being so close to him. He felt raw...vulnerable, and weak. So much weaker than he ever had before. So much more delicate. Like a crab having just molted its shell.

"I am Hanuman." He whispered. "My brother is Heiman. My father is Katcya. My mentor is...is..."

"Is Echo." Ank supplied.

Like lightning, the image of an old man—a man who favored a green tunic and brown trousers, who went bare foot everywhere he traveled and whose stern, almost translucent eyes held a manic edge which rose not hotter than arctic ice— was fixed into his mind's eye.

He breathed out a relieved sigh. "Echo. Echo the Rope, now."

"Was he not always?"

Hanuman sobbed. It was unbecoming of him in the presence of the Sanark, this man he knew nothing about, despite his best efforts to know everything about him.

"I take that as a no. But then, that doesn't interest me, either." Ank said. "No, I think what you *can* tell me, now the time has come, is *why* you want to know so much about this particular Wanderer, Hanuman. You have never taken such an interest in any of us. Not this obsessively."

"I took an interest in you."

Ank chuckled. "Oh, but that's different and you know it. Your only interest in me lies in what you don't know because you can't know. You've been invested in the story of my life for who knows how long, and all because you can't *find* it.

"But here, right in front of you, is a piece of Sao's story. And you've found yourself invested in other fragments, haven't you? Pieces taken from all manner of other peoples who consorted or conspired with him at one time or another."

"It's Dupec." Hanuman said. "Why not him, too?"

There was a pause as Ank contemplated something. The flashes and streams were ebbing now. Sight was returning ever so slowly, and the migraine was coming on with it. That would last for a few hours, or a few days. He would need to rest until it went away entirely. This had been a close shave. Too close for his comfort.

Shulraki's advice bubbled up to the forefront of his mind as Ank settled in for what seemed an unavoidable conflict. *You could just ask him.*

He realized he was at his limit. He'd managed for who knew how many thousands of years just fine, had even begun to think no such limit existed. That he would be able to press on indefinitely, combing over countless memories, but the human mind could only take in so much before it broke. And even once it had, how much stress could it expect to endure before the shattered pieces of what remained could no longer be rearranged, glued back together. Before they returned to being sand at the river's edge?

"What have you been doing all these years, Ank?" he asked. "You are spare with your words. You barely bother to show your face to the rest of us. Are you not curious about why each of us was trapped here? Why the gods saw fit to recall Shulraki from *death*? Or why they built this miserable place to begin with?"

"Do you find a need to be curious about truths you already hold?" Ank said. "No, I'm not curious about why this place was built or why Shulraki was recalled, or what the simple forging of a sword could do to earn its maker a place among us. And I am not curious about why Dupec is still out there, either.

"It might have escaped you, but it is, I think, entirely possible that we *should* be here. That this is just what each of us deserves for upsetting the balance."

Hanuman scoffed. "What *balance?* There are millions of us crawling across six continents this side of the Heart. More on the other side. All toiling away for nothing because the gods cannot handle *what we are*, Ank. What we represent."

"And that is?"

"Change. Growth. Evolution."

Ank grew silent. Hanuman's vision had cleared enough to grant him a hazy impression of the man. He wore white paint over his skin, red traceries connecting his eyes to his chin, more blots crossing his palms and fingers. At some point, his Sky Soul had pressed forward, and he suspected it was this erratic, often unserious soul leading at the moment. The Earth Soul had never been this talkative.

He fixed his gaze on the man's face. "Some irony, isn't it?"

Ank contemplated him. "What irony?"

"That they would confine me in a place so close to home." He said.

He climbed unsteadily to his feet, shuffled past the Sanark. It was time he left this where it lay. He knew what he needed to do, now. It had been hubris to think he would not have to confront Sao eventually. That he might have to cooperate with him. And after Jinga, he was surprised to find he wanted to. That he might even see some of himself in the other man.

In another world, if he was whole and hale. In another world in which they were not confined to this place, for their minds to rot and madness to seep in at the fringes....

We might have been friends.

"Where are you off to in your condition?" Ank asked, watching him go.

"Mind your business, Sanark." He said.

Ank chuckled. "As you say." He marched off in the opposite direction.

Hanuman paused, twisted round to watch the other man go. *Not even a little curious. How odd.*

He shrugged, continued his pursuit. There was something he wanted to get off his chest. Something he had spoken of to no one in all of his years of confinement. It was time he let it out. Finally and truly time.

Why not Dupec? Some part of him knew, without need for verification, that Ank knew far more than he let on. That for all of his long silence and frequent stretches of isolation, he knew far more of the workings of this place than most of them. Might even know why Dupec was not among them.

Father uncloud my vision so I can see. He thought to himself. *Why these particular people? Why have you brought them to me? Why* now *do you believe all of the elements are in place for us to play our hand.*

He could not even remember what their strategy in this great game his cousins insisted on playing was, and yet here he was, doing as he was told once again, and hoping his volatile father knew what he was doing. That all would be well in the end.

It hadn't been in so long.

Tears for the Moon God

Part 4:

Turning Away

Under the Heart Tree

Mortals shed their bodies when they died. The mortal soul vacated its flesh, leaving behind a shell it no longer needed, for those who survived it to look upon, grieve over. A husk for them to caress, to look upon and remember better times when this person they loved had been with them. Last words spoken before last moments. Old memories of children running around, all knees and elbows, grass stained, or covered in dry dusts, filthy in myriad ways and speaking to their parents' frustrations. Irritation which felt like hollow blows to the gut in those moments after bearing final witness to this still, too pale figure, if they were given the luxury.

The spirits provided a balm against that grief. Some few, most of them isolationists, set forth their rules and conventions, and under their own terms provided last rites, closure, to the survivors—the family of the deceased, their lovers and their friends. It was their way, to provide a few last moments, spoken words or the simple sight of the soul adrift in the embrace of a shallow, wide, slow-moving river, drifting along for them to view. To know their loved ones would soon find a greater peace, in Shao Luin's embrace.

Sao Njack's mother was dead. Some irony there, for she had been an acolyte of Ul Sharak. How many bodies had she prayed over. How many had she given over to the river, and the forest at its headwaters. She had been dead nearly three months now. Had died in absence of her husband and her son, while they were abroad across the vast ocean, the same ocean which would be her final resting place when Empress Shao Luin took her.

He should have been there with her in her final moments, when sickness swept over her with the suddenness of a wave crashing ashore, white crested and hard edged and unyielding. His father should have been there with her. His cousin there for them as he was now, a shoulder to lean on, a rock of support when times were too hard and the grief too overwhelming.

He was here now, in the forest, in Gur Tulain. Nearly three months gone. In the gloom of the hermit's forest, he would see his mother once more. One last time, to

Tears for the Moon God

say goodbye. To make peace with what befell her, and apologize for having been absent when she needed him most.

He needed to be alone just now. His father was off somewhere closer to the river, where heavy bows burdened with dense, yellow fruits curled over narrow, moss-strewn embankments. Where the band of the Ul Sharak river was shallow enough to walk across, wide enough that the light of the sun just touched on it, and the souls of the deceased who had finished their reflections on the lives they had lived, had seen those they loved if luck had been with them, climbed into the band, crawled into the heart of it, and lay down one final time.

To drift.

To close their eyes against the brilliant light of that sun, and drift away on the current. Away from life and all of its hurts. Away into their promised after, to dream and dream, and be welcomed into the great reunion with those they themselves had survived. To meet their ancestors.

He needed to be alone. He suspected his father needed this time to gather his thoughts, as well.

What do I say to her? I'm sorry I wasn't here. I hate myself for having been away when you needed me. You were too young. I am too young!

He punched a nearby aspen, leather cushioning the side of his fist, preventing it from chafing against rough bark. Higher up, the wizened bole gave way to newer growth, and where dappled sun touched it near its height, where twisted branches thrust out to catch and cling to spade-like leaves, the bark resembled white paper. Under leaf litter and the sagging bodies of rotting fruits, an intricate web crisscrossed the forest floor, every root running from one tree to the next, and all of them interconnected.

Gur Tulain was not a forest in the same way that Ung Sakh was. He was not a friendly spirit, and did not share his territory with myriad creeks and streams, fairies and fairy trees. Gur Tulain was one tree, his roots telling the truth of him, while the boles and wending bows of those trees told the lie.

Souls of the departed drifted through the gloom around him. Warm light spilled from them, like so many kerosene lanterns emanating from within their bellies, the light spreading to touch every part of them, to touch upon the boles of those ever climbing shoots as they reached for fruits the size of two fists put together, to eat what no living mortal dared to.

He averted his gaze from them. He was not ready yet to pursue his mother, to see her among them.

The path he set upon approached deeper shadows, where the oldest trees grew in dense clusters, their overlapping canopies pressing darkness into the land, making a theatrical display of those warm auras spilling forth from the ever wandering souls, leaving behind sunlight and the softer color pallet of a forest in daylight—all those greens and browns and pastel yellows exchanged for ash gray, storm gray, and iron blue.

His feet carried him forward, and his mind wandered into a deeper quiet. Thought fled, leaving behind a soft-edged core of raw emotion, those feelings he had been denying himself on the road from Nixir north, through the desert and the dead lands, where dark spirits thrived and drank up sorrows as raw life passed them by, and into this forest. This place he had not suspected he would find so soon. That no one suspected they would find before they were ready.

Under the Heart Tree

Into darkness. Into silence. His feet carried him forward, and the core spread wider along its edges, filling him with scattered vibrations, Shards of glass to flow with his blood, to creep along the inward edge of his skin. A hard ball formed in his throat. His eyes watered.

I will not cry. I will not cry.

Roots dripping shaggy mosses vaulted up before him. He stumbled over the first few, before his vision adjusted to the greater darkness. Salein's press tickled his spine, a curtain of water flowing down his back, icy cold and beckoning. His mother, clad all in black linen, filled his mind's eye. Her face was hidden behind a porcelain mask embellished with lapis plates and veins of gold, to resemble reptilian scales. His mother, seated next to the sweating body of the victim of a vicious curse, alone in the room with him, the light of a single candle illuminating a hooked nose and hooded eyes, her gaze intent on her patient.

I'm sorry.

Tears threatened to spill forth from his eyes, to fall over soft, golden cheeks, draw down around his narrow chin and fall into the loam. The gloom broke ahead of him, the soft light of true lanterns spilling forth from the bows of a gnarled, ancient tree.

By that light, he saw a man. A man reaching overhead, reaching for the forbidden fruit.

"NO!" he bellowed. His grief forgotten in a momentary surge of panic, he charged.

The other man flinched, reached for a sword.

Sao sidestepped a sudden upthrust from the unsheathed scimitar. He drew his own blade, the Rein Mountain Sword which had cost him his last chance at seeing his mother alive.

Peace danced, an extension of his arm, as he batted away brutalistic blows from the other man. He registered in quick flashes the strange character of the other. Odd feathers, some black and some crossed in vibrant yellows and reds, danced over his head as he flowed through curt sword forms. Broadly muscled, he nonetheless moved with the fluid grace of a seasoned fighter. The precise shade of his skin was difficult to discern in this lighting, but his complexion was broken. Spidery lines in a lighter shade ran across every exposed inch of him, a crazed mass of patterns that reminded him of disturbed water, like ran in the clearwater creeks in Gan Forest.

A stop thrust took him just under the collar bone. Fire laced through the meat there, driving those first tears from his eyes even as the other man, the absolute fool, fell back, his own sword clattering against roots.

Shaking fingers traveled across his chest. Shaking fingers covered in spider veins, a patterning Sao had never seen before. Shaking fingers to mirror his own, as he touched the edges of the shallow wound he had suffered.

He met the stranger's gaze, an involuntary reflex, and saw his own shock reflected back at him. Watched the other man's gaze rake over him, taking in details in quick snatches, details he had missed.

Peace dropped from Sao's hand, clanged against the other man's sword.

"D-don't." Sao said as the stranger closed on him.

Bloody fingers found his chest, pressed against his sternum. They traveled over his flank, and the stranger snatched up his hand. Thick callouses rasped against his

Tears for the Moon God

exposed fingertips. The stranger lifted his hand so that he could see it better, noted something he had missed, his peculiar skin tone.

He spoke in a language unfamiliar, a simple utterance but one with no context to shape it.

Sao shook his head. "I don't speak that."

The stranger growled something else.

Sao pointed to the bows he had been reaching for. He shook his head, cut a line across his neck with his free hand. The pain was beginning to dull, but he would need proper healing.

We should have taken Kiresh with us.

The stranger nodded. He leaned over, picked up his sword, keeping his gaze fixed on Sao. With it in hand, he stepped back out of this expanse.

When he was well gone, Sao perched on a fat root near the base of the tree strewn with lanterns, picked up Peace, and slid it back into its sheath.

He watched the gap between trees where the stranger had faded into the shadows.

Shambling footsteps, the thunk of something heavy and blunt striking the ground, marked the approach of a newcomer. A squat figure emerged. His back was horribly bent, his spine twisted. Toad-like features were drawn out like pulled wax around a wide chin. A few strands of white hair crossed his bald scalp, and he clung to a knobby staff twice his height as if he could not keep himself upright without it.

He was looking off in the same direction Sao had been, weighing the value of speaking his mind.

He shrugged.

"Strange happenings, eh?"

Sao glanced over at him, then returned to his observation of the dark patch the stranger had retreated into. "Who are you?"

The old man spat in the dirt. "You're traipsing along in my forest and you want to know who *I* am? Don't be daft, boy."

"Ah. My apologies, spirit." He stood up and bowed, winced at the pain in his chest.

The hermit's gaze flicked over him. "You look surprisingly content for someone just stabbed."

"He did stab me, didn't he?" he chuckled, regretted it immediately.

"Looks shallow enough. You could do with some stitches, I'd guess. Didn't bring a healer, did you?"

"You'd know that well."

Gur Tulain nodded. "Yes, I suppose I would."

"What is he?" Sao asked. "No one has ever...."

"He's a Cloud Man, boy." Gur Tulain said. "Your natural undoing. You'd do well to stay away from him."

"On the contrary. I think I'd like to see him again one day."

"You've a death wish, then."

"A wish, certainly. I'll give you that."

Gur Tulain shrugged. He turned to go, dragged himself after his walking stick. "Suit yourself."

"You know his people. Can you tell me where to find him?"

Gur Tulain snorted. "He's Gil Garo. Best wait for winter, when they come together. But you'd do well to stay away. Trust in an old man's word. Nothing good can come from arguing with a man like that."

"Who says I want to argue?"

"What else can you do? Not knowing his language. Or his customs. You don't know nothing about him, in fact." Gur Tulain said. "I stand by what I said. You'd do best leaving him alone. Staying in your corner of the world and what not. Better for everyone involved that way."

Sao watched him shamble away into the shadows. He made a last observation of the tree with all of its lanterns. *The Heart Tree. Gur Tulain's own heart. It's as if Goddess Liandal has written it herself. And if she has...we'll meet again, won't we, stranger.*

Bait

Squat shrubs and narrow pine shafts dotted the slopes to either side of a shallow valley. Scouts from the Chikata roved the hillsides on foot, hunting for signs of the enemy. If they had taken the high ground, they would be at an advantage, and though the trees provided little cover, the hills themselves might hide a force on the leeward side, waiting to spring a trap on them.

Arrak was wary of those slopes. He much preferred the vastness of the open plains, where his line of sight spanned miles wherever he looked, provided plenty of warning of an incoming attack.

They were at a disadvantage in this terrain. Could only hope the area was as unfamiliar to the Tului as it was to his forces. Those scouts were vulnerable. Akhi alone had the advantage of true camouflage, was the only hunter among the Chikata, one of a spare few who had taken up the mantle of apprenticeship under God Shakh, and there were no acolytes of God Uldal among them. Not now Dupec was gone.

The spirits may favor them in this conflict. He hoped they did. But whose loyalty these fell under he could not know. They were too close to Tuluis Fel's border. Too much rode on suspicions that may prove inaccurate. If the spirits of this land were beholden to Tuluis Fel himself, then the land itself was compromised. They could not trust their footing here. Could only choose to believe what was plain before them.

Tao Shein abstained. In this conflict, he had not shown himself, had not contributed his might to either side. But Tao Shein was not the only spirit of these lands, and he did not command loyalty from all of them. Many abided his rule out of fear, and fear was an unreliable crutch for any entity. Fear drove those who sought power to reach into the depths of their souls and draw out rebellious features, to seek the downfall of their hated lord. There were those loyal to him, of course. Those who held no fear for him, like Duijus Kanh or, perhaps, Tuluis Fel himself. But those loyalties were marred by resentment, anger, loathing for the creature they supported. It was not love of the spirit but mutual benefit that drove them to engage in some symbiotic relationship with him, and those loyalties did not extend to mortals. Not often.

Bait

Duijus Kanh was an exception, not the rule. That he saw fit to defend the Gil Garo was written in the annals of a history, the contours of the story blurred by countless retellings and all the years that had come and passed since the pact was formed.

It would be the same for the Tului. The spirit who guarded them may even command the loyalty of those who dwelt in his lands, and that may be a thing born out of trust. The worst kind of complication.

They were going into this conflict blind to the nature of their position in the grand order of things.

And those hills.

An itch formed between his shoulder blades. He sifted through those trees for signs of life, signs of watchers. The Tului would not be foolish enough to keep all of their eyes forward on the path of retreat. Their scouts would even now be in those hills, reporting their findings back to the Crow through telepathic links if he was in range, receiving orders by the same channels.

Another advantage over the Gil Garo. Another complication to drive anxiety deep into his core.

The trees provided ample cover, an immaculate mix of shadows and pole shaft trunks, the snows denied access to the ground nearest those trees by dense needle coverage high in a loose canopy where some of those bows still clung to pinecones.

Akhi listened to squirrels chattering back and forth, watched rabbits break into bounding runs. Their winter fur was as white as the ground they covered; distinguished from the deeper snows farther removed by their motion. Listened to the soft, rapid sounds of their breathing, smelled the blood flooding their veins, pumped by a hummingbird heart as they dove for cover.

He did not concern himself with camouflage. There was nothing to fear from these woods. If he was spotted, well the Gil Garo column was hard to miss, and he was not far removed from it.

Odors filtered into his nose. The bright scent of pine sap exuded from those trees. The odor of old blood where a deer had fallen to a wolf attack, its entrails spilled out and reeking of rancid fat. Peat moss and raw earth, the dusty odor of old snow. Human activity underpinned those natural aromas. Shit covered under a layer of brown pine needles, the stench of unwashed bodies leaking from several places at once, sweat and oil carrying the musky tang of hormones, cortisol and others, the dead smell of old leather and the sweet, savory perfume of damp hair.

The perimeter of the forest was sparsely populated with pines; and hardy shrubs with woody, green stocks ran wild in the intervals between them. A spare few scent tags came back to him, the marks he had placed on the Tului he passed on his way out of their camp the night of the raid. Some few of those had been chosen as scouts, it seemed, which was unfortunate for them.

He tracked their movements by that unnatural smell, an odor burned into their spirit, a perfunctory explosion of his own secretions blasted into them, subsumed into their bodies where it would linger until he died.

He picked across the forest, laying pursuit, a greater mass some miles off yet where the Tului held their main force back. They were not moving, a sign he suspected meant they intended to take advantage of the familiar ground, use it to set up an ambush, some kind of snare they thought the Gil Garo blind to.

Tears for the Moon God

I suppose they will have to be for now. But his errand did not demand he turn back yet. There would be time for them to regroup, prepare for the assault, when he returned to them.

It would be foolish for them to do battle here. This was country for harassment, for sewing confusion and picking away at the enemy. It was not well suited to large scale battle, and they would know that, having passed this way on the march to the Shifting City, *his* city.

They may have intended to use these hills and thickets to their advantage on the march north, winnow away the Gil Garo forces before a broader assault on more favorable terrain. As it was, there was nothing in this valley that would provide them the greater advantage.

This was a quiet place. A place for observing. A mutual exchange transpired here. The Tului watched the Gil Garo. The Gil Garo watched the Tului. Reports filtered back and forth between camps and leading elements, and the war effort turned cold, was tempered by a mutual need for subtlety.

He looked into the bows of a nearby tree, sited a Tului scout hidden among the branches. He unlimbered his bow, drew an arrow from the quiver at his hip, knocked and let loose. The arrow struck the bole of the tree high in its branches, missing the Tului agent but inciting movement from him as he sought to get out of the way.

Answering fire returned, missing by a wide margin.

He knocked another arrow, waited patiently as the Tului took position, seeking to use the branches for cover as he took aim.

He fired.

The arrow thrust through the Tului's eye. His body dropped from the branches, a sack of meat tumbling through sturdy bows. It pinwheeled on the way down, struck the dirt.

He left the arrow embedded in the corpse, left the corpse to rot in the snows.

One more pair of eyes eliminated. If the Gil Garo must go in blind, then he would ensure the Tului did, too.

Coltang called a halt at the mouth of the valley pass. Ahead was dense forest, and the low reaches were shielded by a dense wall of fog, which should not have been for the dead of winter did not provide free moisture to whip up such clouds. He picked out the nearest boles within that shield.

Already envoys from the other sects were galloping along the fringes to meet him. Sauman emerged with them, noted the heavy fog, this most obvious sign of some nastiness set against them by the Tului. He sawed the reins. His horse reared and dropped onto its forelegs, driving to a swift halt at his side.

"Strange, isn't it?" Coltang said.

"Can you break through it?"

"The heat of my fire may displace the curtain, but there will be others contributing to it."

"And lying in wait for us to venture into it."

"Yes, I think so. They want us blind. Who knows what they've set up in there."

"Nothing good."

Coltang shook his head. "Of course not. Where is Akhi?"

"I sent him with the scouts. He should be returning soon."

Bait

"He will be close by."

"We need wind. Or water. Someone who can wield either. Or perhaps someone who can wield both."

"The Cuu are fond of the winds."

"That they are." He summoned a runner to his side. "Send for Chief Sarri. And pass word to Chief Arrak that we will halt here for a time." He panned over the hills to either side. "I want twice as many men in the hills as we have now. If they encounter Tului scouts, they are to kill them."

The runner bowed in his saddle, guided his horse around and set off down the column.

Crow Durin observed the snare he had set for the Gil Garo. A choke point where the valley let out on a broader plain, where the trees began to grow thicker together and denied solid footing for the roots of lesser plants to emerge. The soil here was nearly depleted of its nutrients, so much was the demand for sustenance from those trees. The ground was littered with dead needles, and little snow fell far below the canopy. Light dappled the forest floor where sun beams broke through, and shadows loomed heavily over ground.

The terrain with all of its shadows gave advantage to the Tului, but he would not spare more of his forces than was needed to hold this choke point against the Gil Garo columns. The main force was already disembarking, heading deeper into the wood, moving on the border with Tuluis Fel, and no one of importance had been left behind.

He remained to oversee the work of setting the stage for this conflict, but he, too, would retreat before the first clashes arrived.

Tului forces clambered into those trees, secured harnesses to their trunks and climbed using the tension in those ropes for support. Casks of melt water dangled from their hips. Bows were slung across their backs and quivers at their hips. On the ground, still more dug shallow holes, filled them in with rocks and broken glass, drew sticks over them and covered them with layers of brittle twigs and pine needles, blending in the edges so that they would not be identified easily.

The Gil Garo would regret ever having pursued them. They would see many casualties in the coming hours, and all to the Tului benefit.

He passed orders telepathically to his scouts, recalling them from their positions along the fringes of the Gil Garo column. They would be critical in springing the trap. In goading the Gil Garo into it.

"Fog?" Arrak asked the Tipik messenger.

"Yes, fog."

"I see. Yes, send additional men into the hills. Sarri is ill suited to this task. I will go myself."

"Should I alert him?"

"Run back to the Dumas position. Tell Ungol to prepare for an assault from the rear. If a trap is forthcoming, they will seek to push us into it. His position will be the most vulnerable."

The messenger galloped off. Arrak kicked his horse forward, intent on meeting Coltang and Sauman at the head of the column.

"Tell Gulang and Kuuda to maintain eyes on those hills!" he shouted behind him. "I do not want them separating us!"

Tului filtered in and out of the trees, their shadows dancing around their feet as they hurried forward. The scouts were active now, moving against the Gil Garo column though they were few and far removed from each other. He followed the movements of the ones he could trace, relied on smell to decipher the movements of the others.

Smoke filled the spaces between them, a noxious, bitter odor of burning pine oils which muddled his senses, made keeping track of those others difficult. He blinked, and the world was cast in shades of blue and green, animals dozing in their burrows and running about among the bows cast in warmer shades, and still warmer glows marking the figures of the nearest humans, the Tului among them.

He saw them moving on the Gil Garo column. The Tului's main force was moving away from the valley, but some stragglers remained. The rear elements were taking longer to join the march than they should, much longer than usual. They were on the march, yes, leaving scouts in their wake, but they had not yet fully retreated from the pass.

They let us get this close?

He broke into a run. He had tarried in these woods long enough. Sauman was positioned at the head of the column. He felt the tug of the scent tag he had left on his chief in his nose, pulling on him as he sprinted through the woods, toward the column, turned along the slope of the hill and ran for the head of the column, where the Tipik had taken point.

Arrak, too, was moving in that direction, and swiftly. He would be on them soon.

Three chiefs of seven in one place. They'll be vulnerable. Perhaps that's what these Tului bastards are after.

He wondered if the chiefs comprehended what would be lost if they were taken down here. Wondered, too, if they had not learned their lessons from previous encounters. The Tului were no fools. They understood the chain of command, how disrupting it would lead to chaos, knew the powers of all of those chiefs, too, if he did not miss guess. They may well be counting on the chiefs to do something brash, to place themselves in harms way. And if it was this that motivated them, then springing the trap would prove fatal for their assault. They would not come out of this unblooded.

Arrows sailed from the hills, bit into the flanks of horses at the edges of the Kachin file. Horses went down, tossed their riders from the saddles. Shouts rang out as others fought to get their own beasts under control.

Gulang twisted in his saddle, an arrow sailing past him as the Tului broke over the hills, set fire to burning rags and tossed clay jugs into the valley where they burst into flame underfoot.

The horses nearest those flames bolted, forcing a stampede as they sought to get away. Riders were cast into the dirt and trampled. Other warriors turned and charged into the woods.

His bellowed orders were lost in the commotion as the column buckled, and Tului soldiers pushed the horses forward, into the waiting jaws of their trap.

Bait

Horses blurred past Kuuda, many of them riderless, as the Kachin ranks buckled. Arrows flew from the hills, buried their heads into horseflesh. Burning jars sailed through the air and broke at the feet of the Kirche lines. Riders lost their mounts to the storm of tramping hooves thundering across the valley. Warriors sought to bring their mounts under control, were failing everywhere he turned.

He heard Gulang's call behind him. Heard the bellowed war cry and felt a storm of triumphant emotions surge through his soul, an echo of Sarkahn's power driving out fear. The horses nearest him calmed, but too many had been lost to the frenzy. Too many were even now running into the hills, running away from those flames.

He kicked his horse forward, drove toward the obvious trap awaiting him and the rest of them at the head of the column. There was no help for it. There was nowhere to run, nothing he could do to win free. His horse galloped past others, did not slow until it was nearly at the mouth of the valley, and a wall of fog rose up around him, blocking off sight.

Coltang watched Kuuda stream past him on a horse too fearful to be brought to reign. He knew then the nature of this trap, knew how the assault was to play out.

Arrak arrived and reigned in alongside him. He looked out at the fog.

An unsettling chill stole over the Tipik chief.

Arrak dragged on the power within him, the power of Shan Lao, the River Spirit. He cast his arms wide, and brought his hands down. With them, the fogs settled. Water rolled overground and collected in rivulets which swam around the trees.

Coltang watched as the air cleared before him, as horses screamed and riders cried out.

Arrows stabbed the earth. Ice Shards blasted away from the sites of impact. Long shadows licked at the flanks of horses, at the feet of the Gil Garo as they ran past, into the mists ahead, where Arrak's influence could not touch.

"This is madness." Coltang bellowed.

"Sauman!" Arrak called. "Now would be the time!"

Sauman dropped from his horse. He slammed his fists into the earth. Vibrations rippled away from him, seismic waves coruscating from the point of impact.

From the hills, a wrathful roar. Waters rushed past the trees, down around the valley and into it. The Tului scouts lost their footing, fell into the torrent and slid across fresh mud and wicked sheets of slush as the waters ran straight for Sauman's feet.

Blood wept over his arms, extruded from his pores, slid across his neck and face, rendering him a red ruin.

Cackling. Cruel laughter as the waters split and frothed, as Sauman's blood mingled with the motes gurgling around his fists and feet.

Arrak drew reign. He pushed into the space opened up amid the fogs before him, cast the waters ahead into a frenzy as Coltang moved his own horse forward in his wake. He wielded a wicked hammer in each hand, his gaze fixed on the trees, flung both into the air and at them.

Impact.

White fires flashed across the canopy. Wood splintered. The tops of trees crashed earthward and were swallowed in those torrents of water.

Entities emerged from the waters along the hills, swarmed the Tului scouts, snuffed out fires as they ran amid the horses behind them.

Horses galloped past, riders were dragged behind them, their arms caught in the reigns, unable to break free.

Sauman watched as short lived spirits lashed out at each other, fell onto human victims, clawed and bit, flayed skin, gouged away chunks of meat.

A horse stumbled ahead of him, its leg snapped and it slid across the ground. Shadows stormed across the waters, riding the currents, engulfed the fallen rider.

Blood spray fanned across air and spattered the nearest tree trunks. Coltang's hammers worked the canopy, adding to the chaos and confusion as Sauman's fledgling spirits fed on the Tului and the waters around them ran pink with their blood. And he was sated with the power wrought in their souls, the taint in their blood denied purchase within him, the spirit of the playa lake he belonged to, bound to his life force, demanding this killing, the passage of the energy of those dead into her.

Ul Surta could not survive without him. Would not survive long after his death if she did not find a new regent to replace him. So feeble, so prone to dissolution, the spirits of such lakes seldom took on acolytes. They rose with the spring thaw in the mountains, as alluvial fans birthed newborn spirits, spirits who cannibalized each other, who merged their energies, comingled in the mad struggle for survival at the fringes of the vast dessert beyond Rasheik's rope. The shallowest of those lakes were gone before summer was well underway, their waters drawn into living creatures or wicked away on hot currents as the sun baked the land, were killed by an indifferent god.

She reveled in this feeding frenzy. He felt her excitement in him, knew he would not need to feed her for years to come if this war played out as it must. The blood, the essence of the Tului soul, would suffice. His tithe would be accounted paid before the summer arrived, and he would not have to return to her.

He felt her lust for blood within him, a frenzied, manic glee to match the ravaging of those scouts on the hillsides. Knew a thrill he had seldom experienced, which sickened him and made him yearn for more. More blood. More chaos. More death.

And still the Gil Garo surged into the wood. Into the trap. Still the ranks were in chaos, out of control. Still the shouted orders of the chiefs behind him were met with indifference, if they were heard at all.

The blood kept flowing. And he reveled in it. And he was at peace in this world of chaos and death.

Ul Surta drank in energy, glutted herself on the raw essence of mortal life, and was full.

Tului soldiers descended from ropes dangling from tree branches ahead of those swinging hammers. Their flaring lights and vicious impacts. They dropped into the waters and ran, their legs pulled out from under them as the currents dragged them toward Arrak, as Arrak infused them with controlled bursts of energy and watched as they died.

He walled them off in the embrace of those waters, stole away their energy and gave it back to them. Flesh rotted away too quickly. Heat radiated through bodies as their ability to self regulate was denied them.

Shan Lao was not a kind master. His power was no warm embrace but a cold,

Bait

seething anger held in suspension as Arrak pulled it into himself, and loosed it on the Tului in this camp.

He watched as Tului soldiers flailed in the band, watched as the lucky few escaped onto dry land before he could take them. He twisted round and looked to the slopes, where strange creatures like fish with human limbs—their bodies too long or too fat or too short, mouths wide and gaping, bodies framed by thick, slab limbs, and eyes rolling in their sockets—carved away chunks of meat and swallowed them down. Watched as they turned on each other, a gluttonous frenzy.

He flinched at the sight of them.

Sauman's power was not one he coveted. It was a power bent on destruction. A lake spirit was to be a spirit of healing, but the one he had given himself to was incapable of anything other than destruction.

She fed. It was all she did. Fed on chaos and violence. And he was the hand that fed her. The true power in their relationship, for her life was forfeit without him, and she well knew it.

How many have we lost? He wondered. *How many more than them?*

They were retreating. Coltang watched as they ran away into the forest, ran as fast as they could. He did not pursue. They had done enough damage. He had taken enough life this day. They ran, and he let them go. Let them go back to their people to declare to them their victory. That this trap had been sprung successfully, and they were the survivors. They were those who were worthy. Those who had escaped.

He watched as horses close to death kicked and squirmed against ground. As blood and gore wept from them and was dragged past the lead elements of the column on waters manifest by Arrak and Sauman. This fight was over. There was need now for healing. Need to pick through the remains in search of survivors. Need to tend to their dead.

The Tului retreat was an act of cowardice, but then, this attack was that. A conniving, deceitful foray into the realms of possibility, as orchestrated by a man without mercy, for whom the idea of honor was alien.

He held up his hands. His hammers snapped against his palms, and he tucked them into holsters at the sides of his saddle.

Time now for a new grief. Time now to answer to the people for our blindness.

He turned his horse around, and returned to a column settling into itself, turned to a broken mess.

They had driven the Tului off, but they had lost this engagement. Their losses, he was certain of it, were greater than those of their enemy. There had been so few of them to begin with.

Humility in Knowing

The auras didn't stay away long. Halos wreathed Hanuman's vision, wicking away details in his periphery. The world beyond each single object in focus became an impressionist painting, and the lines wavered and spangled, as if the whole construct, the whole of the Halls of Time, was underwater.

He navigated the passes on wobbly legs, clamping onto rocks, thrusting his fingers into the gaps between them where pebbles and grit filled in narrow spaces for support.

Not far now.

His head felt as if it had been filled with bullet ants. As if molten metal had been poured across the base of his skull, and even now flares lapped at the meaty tissue underneath the bones. He should not have remained in Jinga's memories as long as he had. He had known better. Knew from experience how debilitating the pain must be when he lingered too long in any one pool.

This was the price for his greed.

He turned corner, stumbled over a tile vaulted half out of the earth, and collapsed in a heap. For too long he lay there clutching his head, his teeth gnashed together, cheek meat clenched between them.

He started to crawl. Use one leg as an anchor, the other to propel him forward. He clawed at raw soil, and each time his fingers danced over liquid, he pulled back, shifted course, circumvented the treacherous pool and all of its promises of knowledge and self-destruction.

He clambered onto his knees, reached out to take hold of the low stones of the nearest wall, and climbed to his feet.

I will have my dignity, at least, when I approach him. I will not come to him wriggling across the ground like a common worm.

His hand trailed through open air. He took three jogging steps forward, and crashed into the length of a wall opposite. Swirls of gray and brown formed gloss layers at the corners of his eyes, but the stones straight ahead, which his eyes were but inches from, were clear. Rough edges. Gritty faces. A gap in the stones let out onto a view of another hall running up to this one, and he wondered if there was a different maze beyond it. If that other maze had its own conventions and rules. If

Humility in Knowing

this labyrinth sat atop something older, maybe the crude roads and narrow paths all climbing toward his ancient home. The single-room hut he had kept on the mountainside, overlooking the village where he had been born. The hut where he had lived with—

Who? Did I have a lover? No children, certainly. They would never have allowed....

A chuckle escaped him.

No choice now. Right, Sao? Is that not why they left you here to rot... "With the rest of us?"

He shuffled down the length of the wall, rounded yet another corner. He knew where he was now. He had been here before, amid the chaotic scattering of pools with loose relations to the last immured among the Wanderers.

Just ahead sat the man. Though he looked barely into his twenties, the set of his eyes belonged to a man much older. His golden skin was smooth and unmarked. His build was that of a runner, lithe and compact, but the hard edges had begun to soften from indolence. He had sat beside this pool far too long. It was time for him to go.

Will he?

The wise man's gaze, drunk with melancholy and sobering because it was, turned onto Hanuman, and a light smile broke across his full, pink lips.

Hanuman stilled, his feet grinding pointedly into sand as he drew up short. They held each others gazes, saw each other's hearts in that moment, and the Sun Man's smile fell away. He broke eye contact, returned to his vigil over the pool, the arc of his life.

"What do you want?" he asked.

"What we all do." Hanuman said.

Sao looked Hanuman over. His clothes were sodden and ragged. His hair had lost all of its volume, and wavy threads of it clung to his cheeks and forehead. The crazed lines crossing his limbs, neck and face were interrupted by errant drips and narrow streams.

"You look like shit." He said.

Hanuman made a little sound in his throat.

"Come. Sit."

"You'd offer me a place beside you?"

"When you put it that way." He rolled his eyes. "You look like you're standing at death's door."

Hanuman dipped his head and shoulders in a slight bow. He shambled over to where Sao sat. If he had wanted to, he could have taken the Elder's head from his shoulders right there, and left him to whatever fate befell the would be dead in these halls. There were no healers among them, that he knew. Maybe Ank had such gifts. He supposed he might be able to reattach the man's head to his body himself if he tried, but then...were he to violate the man so thoroughly as to dismember him, there would be little point in piecing him back together. There would be nothing he could do about the blood loss, either, or any infection that may come from his actions.

Nimira and Samara had been fine. Yes, they had been. But the throne room had been recently sterilized then, and they had been given access to healers after the deed was done. Here, there were no guarantees.

Besides, it would do him no services to kill the man. He was already as good as dead, anyway. He was just barely holding himself together.

What was a life if your sense of self had been stolen away? What was left for him, then, except misery and regret.

Hanuman the Elder slid down the length of the wall at his back, onto his haunches, and then to be seated almost at Sao's shoulder.

"It's time we talked." He said.

"Given up on plundering the memories of my kin?" Sao sniped.

"Yes."

Cold settled into Sao's guts. He did not turn to meet the Elder's regard. There was no need. Or maybe the truths that lurked there frightened him. Maybe the idea this man had finally accepted defeat, the futility of his own pursuit, terrified him.

What was a man to do when he had lost hope? Or was it that in losing hope he gained clarity, even peace? Was it not this way with Shulraki? He had come into this place without hope of leaving, had been unconcerned with escape from the moment his feet touched ground in these halls. What regrets he held were in being drawn away from death, which he had earned more than once.

But Hanuman did not seem at peace. He seemed terribly bothered by it all. If he had lost hope, it had not been replaced by any inner peace. If he had lost hope, in its place had come a deep dread, or something very like it. A sense of vulnerability antithetical to all Sao Njack had believed he was. A conniving, manipulative tyrant did not feel such things as vulnerability, did he?

Of course, I was that for many people. I was far more insecure, then, than any of them realized. Everything was a show. Everything a display designed to incite fear, and through that ambient fear, loyalty. If they feared me, they would remain under my thumb. And as long as they were there, I had nothing to worry about.

And yet I worried constantly. About everything.

"I want to show you something." Hanuman said.

"Why the sudden change? You have made it clear enough you have no intention of sharing anything of interest with me."

"I meant not to, but things change. I am...forgetting. Forgetting the important things. It's no longer worth it to me to pursue you in the way I have been."

"What could be so important to you, after having spent so much time willingly divorcing yourself from your memories."

"Sacrificing who I am in order that I might know the rest of you more intimately than you know yourselves." The Elder chuckled. "Times change. People do, too. Your father thought you had it in you to become good again."

Rage built in Sao unbidden, and he stuffed it down. "So, you've found my father's memories." He said in a tight voice.

"It sometimes feels as if Fate's hand is present here, guiding me away from what I need. Or, perhaps it would be better to say what I want."

"She has no power here."

"Doesn't she?"

"In another god's house?"

"Is this place a part of the God House of Music? Or is it only bordering it?"

"What are you getting at, Elder?"

"Do you know what rankles me so? Gods this pain." He cupped his cheeks in his palms, rubbed his temples gingerly. "Not since I was immured have two katcyakin shared such a close bond as you did with Dupec. But Heiman was dead long before this labyrinth rose. Shah Jagat took his spirit into himself, as was his place.

"You and your lover? You pose a question with your very existence that I cannot answer. I suspect the gods could not find an answer to the problem presented in you two, either. Or you would not now be here and him free."

"I'd have thought your fixation on me would go much deeper. You've been on my trail for twenty years now, haven't you?"

Hanuman grimaced. "Time does not move in the Halls."

"Yet a window opened into the world outside tells us that it has been at least that long since I was born. Which means it has been at least that long since I was reclaimed."

"Out there." Hanuman whispered. He eased his head back against the wall, closed his eyes. "I thought...perhaps it was something to do with...well, that doesn't matter, does it."

"You thought it was because of something I did. Something the gods would have seen as much worse than what Dupec sought to do.

"It was. I seized the last opportunity I had, when I realized what Ur was, *where* it was, and I asked your father for a favor."

"You never told your father you were not blood kin to Katcya, did you?"

"What difference does it make."

"It made a difference to him."

Cold became ice, a dagger lodged into Sao's abdomen. He had never considered what it meant to his father not knowing the truth. He had believed, even young as he was, that Jinga did not want to know in truth. That he would view anything he said as a lie, to spare his feelings.

"I thought, perhaps, they had a use for him. I think that is still true. But there is another matter. Something I didn't consider until just hours ago.

"What happens when the river moves too far? It has happened before. A flood."

"A flood?"

Hanuman nodded.

"What does that entail?"

"There is a lake at the edge of your domain, where it adjoins to Shulraki's. Shulraki often goes there when he feels like giving up. I think he believes if he plunges into it, he'll die. Or, at least, he'll have his own identity shredded into pieces, and it will be something like dying."

"Will he?"

"I don't know. But the lake was the result of so many lives being recalled once, and then again. Taken back, to allow those people another chance at living. First, without him. Then, without you. You were immured too close together. The essence of those people's lives became too unstable, and their histories lost all meaning, merged together and became something without reason, which did not follow the contours of any rational design.

"Something similar happened after a spirit of the forest was killed in what is now the area north of Gonsai Wall. The ancient people from which your people descended...they lived in that forest. When the spirit died, the lands died, and so did the people who lived in them. Lanfin attempted to resurrect the spirit, but diverting time onto another path could not fix what was broken. The spirits, unlike us, cannot

Tears for the Moon God

live again once killed. If time is pushed onto a new path, they remain dead. So, your people were revived in a dead land, one racked with her death throes, and died again in the tens of thousands. The pressure placed on time's stream was so immense it threatened to destabilize all that existed in the world, and he was forced to find a new path for her to follow, in which Dosh Alaen remained dead, and your people were able to resettle elsewhere.

"In order to make this work, a god had to step in as a stop gap until the people could be evacuated. An Elder God. It was Eiman Vol, then. The God of Preservation."

"But now think on it. Dupec killed a spirit. Forced a god out of his home. Did who knows what else in his time. Your impact spanned four continents. That is Fang. That is Gora. That is Yu Danh Hao. That is Ul Sadh. How much more devastation would have been created if those lives had been snared in the reclamations of two katcyakin. How much larger would the lake have grown?

"But come with me, Sao Njack. I have something to show you. I want you to see it. I think it will make sense of much more than you would like to believe. Not least, why these halls were made for me."

Sao looked on him then, and saw the sincerity in his gaze as he set it against him. That he meant every word he said, that he was, perhaps, done with the obfuscation of truths, and would, indeed, meet him in the middle.

He nodded, and Hanuman climbed shakily to his feet. He took a last, long look at the pool.

"I cannot plumb the depths of your soul, Sao Njack. Not now. Not if I wanted to. And no one else within these walls would risk losing what I have, even to know the simplest of your truths."

"Then I will come with you." He said. "This once."

"Once is all I ask. Just now. Before it is too late."

"Too late in a place without time?" Sao mused.

"How much time is left to us, Sao Njack? If the gods believe this prison no longer suffices to hold us?"

Sao helped him to his feet, placed his weight under him. They marched away, and though he did not feel good about what he had agreed to, he suspected he had made the right choice. Leaving those memories behind, leaving them vulnerable, felt far less wrong than he had believed it would, but it did not feel right either. Nothing about this turn of events felt right. Nothing at all.

The lake was on Shulraki's mind again, but he had shoved the urge to go to it down. Instead, he ambled along the corridors in Sao Njack's domain, seeking by less traveled avenues the Sun Man and a conversation that might take his mind off it. He was not ready to take the man up on his offer of aid, not to remember what he had forgotten in dying before his scattered Shards, but then...perhaps he could be convinced to see reason. Perhaps, if he was pressed, he might accept the healing his friend offered.

But all of that was to be seen. Time had a way of bringing men around to acceptance for the things they wanted so badly to hide from. He had been immured, yes. The Gods had seen fit to pry him out of death's hands and place him here, but they had waited seven years to do so. That first year had seen him wandering about Gur Tulain's forest, to be visited by no one. It had seen him step willingly into Ul Sharak's headwaters, lay down within her embrace with her gentle hands cupping

Humility in Knowing

his head as she prayed over him, and sent him on his way. Her face, dark as obsidian, her features refined, almost doll-like and her head an elegant, evenly proportioned oval, looking down on him had been his last memory before awakening in darkness.

He remembered Zangal, at once man and beast, grizzled and hairy and diminutive and thin, and strangely effeminate—he had expected other than that from a Fang. Zangal had stripped him of his clothes and scored him clean with rough pumice stones, had set him ablaze, inviting agony as his soul was purged of all the ills it had endured in life. He recalled how Zangal had lamented that there was not more of substance to him, that he had come an incomplete being.

What a strange time that was.

He had been awake when Zangal cast him down again into Ul Sharak's currents, had been awake as he passed through the gap in the base of the mountain, and was born into death. He had seen the Guardian of the Gate in all of its ethereal glory where it coiled around the entrance to the Land of the Dead, and had set eyes on Shao Luin, the empress, in depths so far removed from the surface the sun's light refused to touch, and darkness flourished, and what light was to be had came from grizzly fish and corals, and the auras of the countless souls who roamed her lands among ever shifting oozes.

He missed that place. Yearned for the promise of relief, that he would be permitted once again to be graced with such simplicity, such peace, as she offered. Death was a gift. A gift God Lanfin had denied him. That he needed constant reminding that *this life* was worth living, that he *should* cherish having been given this second chance at living, was yet more evidence that living in this plane was not at all worthy of mortals. They belonged to the spirits, were meant to pass into that blissful plane, to be embraced with open arms by the empress and her king.

Thoughts of Xi came unbidden to him as he turned corner. He was close to his destination. Just at the end of this hall, around one more corner, Sao would be waiting for him and he could let go of these thoughts for another while.

Shao Luin's embrace would never give him peace, would it? There is too much hurt there for him. Too much of it inflicted by her king.

His lips turned down in a tart frown. *But perhaps he has the capacity to forgive. The ability to understand. Her embrace is for everyone. Enemy and friend. We must all be equal in death, or we would be compelled to live out an unending struggle for dominance, over each other, as we did in life.*

There can be no worse hell than that.

He chuckled. The irony was palpable. There was a worse hell than conflict, than aggression, than dominance and submission...and the politics of civility. It was all around him. It was everywhere he traveled, and it was inside him. It was, he reflected, an unconscionable kind of hell to place those whose greatest asset was their mind, their capacity to reason, in a place where no such efforts were necessary. Hell was banality in all things. Hell was the minutia of a day without end...without change.

He rounded the corner, and his heart stopped. There was the pool containing the arc of Sao Njack's life, but the man himself was not there.

Forlorn, wary and tired, he approached the edge of the pool. He sank onto his haunches, tested the waters with trembling fingertips.

Murky waters clarified. A fleeting glimpse of something intimate, of two men

Tears for the Moon God

embracing each other within the confines of an expansive yurt, stole across the depths. Sao clung to his lover, who shoved him away, peeled him off and dashed him against the wall. And between them were two corpses, a length of steaming, black metal, a broad-bladed claymore he recognized as the sword his friend had taken to setting against the wall just there, just beside this pool.

Two corpses. One, a man who bore substantial resemblance to his lover. The other, a mol fae, the infantile face and torso nestled into the black fur on its back gone slack, black blood pooling around it. Its legs were still twitching as rigor set in, and its many, glossy eyes had gone dull.

Sao looked upon his lover with eyes full of regret, the lines of his face etched all over with sorrow and fear in equal measure. And Dupec Safar, his grizzly wolf, wore his anger like a bonfire. Those eyes, so full of betrayal, so rife with shock, fell on the Nixian, and there was fear in them, too. Fear, and the beginnings of tears.

He ran out of the yurt, and Sao sank against the wall, and cried.

He retreated from the vision, realized with alarm that he was seeing the moment all they had built between them was lost. The love they shared was twisted into something sick, something foul, in this moment, and there could be no going back.

Sao had killed his lover's father.

He recoiled, stepped away from poolside. All at once a great wave of grief took him. He did not know where it came from, or if it was beholden to a single source. He did not want it, either.

He retreated from the pool and its contents, from the hall where Sao had spent the last twenty years, as these things were measured outside. He fled, then, back the way he had come.

There is no hope for us, is there. He thought as he sped away. *Is this not why he couldn't let go? Is it not why I refuse to remember my own sins?*

If there is no hope, then what is the point in all of this.

He slowed, having cleared the hall and its adjoining corridor. He eased up against a nearby wall and caught his breath. And thoughts for the lake returned.

I've done what I set out to. The woman has her shield. Sao has learned to let go of what haunts him. At least, for now. What happens to him beyond is none of my concern. My queen stayed dead, as well. There is no better news I can have than the knowledge that all of those I wanted so badly to see gone are dead.

There is nothing left for me here. No, no, he is his own man. A friend, yes, but one of convenience. The bonds we share are less than we may perceive, and all predicated on what we do not wish to confront.

Loneliness. Regret. Anger. All of those things we seek to bury in each other, where they are easier to bear because they are not our burdens, they are impersonal to us.

There is nothing left for me here but hopelessness and despair. And it is time.

It is time.

He shambled onward, down this hall and toward the breech between Sao's domain and his.

It is time. Time to surrender.

The Heir

Getting into the Bane estates was no easy task. The mansion was a sprawling expanse, the kind with wings, and rooms with extravagant names—most of them calling back to long forgotten heads of house, or important members of whichever family had occupied them before the House Bane moved in. Liudao Bane had put his own touches on the sectors of the estate he frequented.

What had belonged to his first wife had been purged by his second. If Garam knew her at all, she had seen it done as soon as she moved in. Or, perhaps, she had kept the most expensive of her possessions for herself—had dresses taken in, jewelry polished and appraised. What she didn't keep, she would have sold, or passed to significant underlings, but all of that was before his time.

Evening's dying light painted echoes of cross barred windows across the wide corridor he ambled down. It was inconvenient, masking his presence. He could not be sensed, but he was not invisible. The eyes of the guards he had met in the courtyard, in the lower halls, slid past him as shadows coalesced around him, his environment providing him the same kind of camouflage that had made it impossible throughout his time with Shakh to identify what shape the god took, what kind of beast he was, save to see his piercing, yellow eye looking back at him, or the ridge of his spine, the edge of a leg or a sweeping tail.

The shadows danced around his figure, moonbeams breaking against dark flesh, mingling with royal blue carpets and rugs with kaleidoscopic weaves, to splash across crisp wallpaper—its pattern matching the textiles, the textiles matching the drapes. Whatever her nature, the mistress of the house had taste.

A guard's hand shifted toward his hip, where a rapier was sheathed. He'd be one of the elites, the rapier for rushing tactics, to buy him enough time to draw on whatever nasty sorceries had earned him this position. Liudao Bane did not deal in 'ifs'. He did not hire those without skill, without documented histories of competence to defend his home, his family.

Garam froze where he stood, slowed his breathing.

The guard tracked down the hall a few steps, hand on pommel, eyes darting every which way.

His shoulders relaxed. He glided more than walked back to his post, and Garam moved on.

The room he was looking for was well removed from the happy couple's chambers. Samil was not keen on his mother. He had displayed a surprising amount of suspicion in their few interactions, even daring to ask pointed questions about Garam's activities when she was not in their presence.

He was more than just her anchor, her tether to the family wealth. When he assumed the title of Lord of House Bane, would he remain the politically expedient choice as ambassador to Cratom? He had no ties to the throne in Ung Roc...would be seen as a liability. He was too close to the uelfin was he not? But then, if not ambassador, his mother must have other plans for them.

Too bad. He's a sweet kid.

He ducked into a room to his left, the door framed by bean plants in full bloom despite the season, the stalks rising to a height with him.

This is new. He contemplated the delicate, bonnet-like blooms as he slid the door open, and slipped through. *Must have picked up a new hobby.*

He had never grown accustomed to the predator's second sight. Years beyond his apprenticeship under God Shakh, the sudden shift in colors, the rigid clarity was disorienting. His pupils felt stretched and loose, his irises sitting awkwardly at the edges of his eyes as he took in the room, its quiet opulence.

Samil's furnishings were almost educational in their nature, as if each piece he added to this collection, the trappings of a life, were chosen deliberately for the purpose of learning something, engaging with a new art, parsing out the secrets behind the sciences. He would climb high as an acolyte of Hou Rok or Tajima if he chose. Or there was that school in Oppi City that earned Sha Burak his place among the Eight Hands. She could do worse than to send him there.

He paused. *She'll never have the chance if we're successful.*

The walls were lined with honeycomb shelves, and most of the spaces were occupied with odd trinkets—puzzle boxes, animal skulls, stone or gold tablets. A host of books were interspersed among them, so many the room felt cramped and claustrophobic.

There in the back was a curtain-framed bed which bore no discernible heat signature, though a faint, organic odor emanated from the mattress, where Samil had spent so much of his life sleeping.

There was no truer reflection of a person than what lingered where he slept. In his bed was isolated years worth of information. Were he so concerned, he could use his preternatural sense of smell to determine what ailments his quarry had suffered and when, the state of his health, whether he had shared this bed with another person, how many and how long ago, and he could identify who those others were if he swept through the streets long enough.

But he was not here to go sleuthing. No amount of information regarding Samil's health or habits would make Wu's task any easier. He reached into his belt pouch, slipped on a leather glove and used it to remove a black-bladed knife. A lamb's eye was engraved into it near its base.

He rubbed it down with an oil soaked cloth, and the smell of lavender stole away Samil's own scent, and the less important odors of old bones, and dust and raw stone, for a moment.

He tossed the blade on the bed, where it would be noted by whatever maid came to turn the room over in the morning. All that was left was for Wu to come through

The Heir

on his end, and the first act in this deadly show would be concluded.

He retreated from Samil's quarters, fixing the true sent of the young man in his memory where it would never leave. With that scent, he could trace him to the ends of the world and back again, and the heirs of House Bane would never escape him, neither Wu nor his brother.

He had done his job, and in doing coveted his best means of reprisal should this operation run foul. If Wu betrayed him—if he betrayed Saijin—he would hunt them both down, and he would kill them. He would not grieve for them either.

In the night, Cratom was changed, but not all that came of its metamorphosis was blissful. Merriment abounded in the low streets near the rivers. Laughter and shouted conversation blurred together. A shapeless, dull crescendo broken by cackles and jeers rose to a fever pitch and then died down, as brothels and taverns and opium dens swallowed patrons down cavernous gullets, glutted themselves on hard coin and the stink of human debauchery.

Thieves filtered in and out of those crowds, unseen for the number of bodies smashed together. They resolved like so many ghosts, cut purse strings and evaporated again. Blasting cold from the south whipped mists into maddening cover at riverside. Lovers cuddled together on benches and docks at riverside, while cutthroats used those mists for cover, dashed heads in with bricks and stones, beat their quarries with iron-barred fists or slid harrowed knives across throats, leaving their victims to choke on their blood on those close, romantic walks.

Like so many others, Cratom was two cities wearing the same skin. At surface level, it was a place for debauchery and romance, where parties could be had, matches made, marriages officiated by uelfin paid grossly to see the arrangements done. It was a place for reading fortunes, scrying and palm reading and other pseudosciences to flourish and be embraced by those with the gift, who shaped small futures with their songs, and listened for grander designs in the songs of their god. And beneath that patina of innocence, of sweat-stained sheets in candle-lit chambers and the feigned cries of ecstasy their visitors paid handsomely for; beneath those wrinkled, Goth women teasing crystal balls with arthritic fingers and casting chicken bones into hearths; beneath the sickly-sweet perfume of opium, the glaze-eyed stares of those who imbibed, transfixed and stuck in place for hours; beneath it all were the bones and muscle fibers that kept it all working.

Prostitutes must be kept in order and maintained—kept free of embarrassing infections and infestations, trimmed, and plucked like prized geese, and smelling of heavy oils and perfumes; scoured clean and their bowels irrigated free and clean of what gifts their patrons left in them. So, too, the women needed to be served with trenchers of herbs to keep seed from taking root, and when they failed, with secret services to have those fledgling humans taken care of before their bodies could be distorted, before they became fodder for fetishists, their value reduced by the ravages of childbirth and them left to debase themselves further, further, exchanging what remained of their dignity at the hands of greasy, aggressive, and dangerous Johns for whom they were not objects of pleasure, but experiments, test subjects for their lecherous theories, to be used up and discarded. A fate all of those who practiced the trade would endure eventually, when age brought to their bodies ravages of its own.

There were structures in place to hold them together, then, to stave off the

Tears for the Moon God

weathering effects of time for a while, until even those creams and ointments, cut and stitch jobs no longer worked. Whole industries flourished around those surface level pleasures. Opium for the patrons of those dens—the highest grades were sold to those with coin to spend—who would evaporate back into those mists, who would go home once more when their time here was done, and remember fondly each sweet moment, every offensive act and reminisce about how it had been unlike anything they had imagined, or could imagine. A perfect vacation from the humdrum of their daily lives.

And for the locals?

The usual industriousness held in those parlors and on street corners and in broken down hovels on the high streets, well removed from the entertainment districts. Dealers hawked dirtier product, often cut with junk substances of other kinds to stretch the supply. Loan sharks propped up addicts on borrowed money, and then hired out thieves of more discipline than those cut purses to get it all back, or strong men to meet those borrowers at their homes, or on those street corners when their banks reclaimed those properties, and bludgeon them half to death as warning. Rivals sent out hired hands to dismantle their competitors operations, saboteurs and assassins to destroy what weaker men had built. And all the while the city turned its eyes away, and visitors shed their scales in rooms wreathed in white smoke or suffused with the alien scent of other bodies, sweat and shame and the heady perfumes used to cover them.

Rhul saw these lives unfold, so many petals unfurling across the tracks laid by bitter thorns, and knew the flower, the city, was sick. That at its center was a poison sweet as nectar, and he would find it eventually.

He remembered the wounds Garam had inflicted on him, and felt the wrongness in those memories. Was it that his core willed him to remember? Or had the impression of those wounds been stored in some part of Wu Bane's mind that belonged to Rhul alone, laying dormant until he was again split off from the Core.

He wondered, as he walked down avenues populated with vagrants, offensive piles of human shit and rubbish, if there had been others like him. If his evolution, his development into a *being* was happenstance or if there was precedent for it in the splitting off of Shards, the fragmentation of the mortal soul, in others. If God Uldal himself convened in closed quarters with his Shards, and gave them names and spoke to them as equals. How much independence must they have gained, how many quirks in their character, in the countless thousands of years the god had been alive? What did that do to the god's mind? What was it doing, even now, to Wu?

He focused on his feet, paused to take in his surroundings. He contemplated resisting the orders he had been given. They were innocuous enough for the moment. Wu hated his father's wife, and he thought he hated her, too. But that hatred was a product of what lingered in the core, where control was sourced from, along with everything that made Rhul who he was. He was not at all certain he shared his hatred of the woman with his core, or if that hatred had been forced upon him.

He knew her son should not be a part of this. His younger brother, as these things were judged, did not need to be brought into it. But Wu had been listening to Garam, and Garam had been listening to Wu, and the two of them together had decided they must involve the young man.

The Heir

He focused on keeping his feet still, keeping himself planted in this place. *Go back. Forget about this errand. Find a safe house another day. Delay, damn you. Delay!*

His feet betrayed him. Synaptic pulses compelled him forward, and a wash of shame and anger traipsed through his head. He was not sure if those feelings were his, or if they had been imposed on him, some curse in the nature of his god's magic to keep him in check, to keep him in control. Did he feel guilty because he liked Wu? Was he angry at himself for attempting to resist him?

He thought not.

As he pressed on, he found himself wondering if anything he felt, anything at all, was real. If it was, all of it, an extension of Wu Bane's will. If the guilt, the yearning for true autonomy, was his own or if Wu felt those feelings toward him, and so bred the need and the reprobation of it into him as his proxy.

Most of all, he wondered what defined personhood. If he could remember his own past as a separate entity from his core, could he be so defined? What was personhood if not an attachment to an identity? And if he could identify himself by a name, if he could have a history, if he was born and born again with the same attributes, the same face and the same soul, could he ever be human?

The cloying aroma of baby's breath predominated, shoving the scents of other blooms into the recesses of the flower shop as Wu lingered in its shadow. In the dying light of evening, paper lanterns shed rays of golden light through the display window, bars crossing recently waxed floor beams, lending a closeness and intimacy to the tiny shop.

Poppies, daffodils, monkshood, a hundred other blooms were arranged in intricate bouquets, populated deep trenchers where they grew unencumbered, a garden tended to diligently by a decrepit Goth who had been as gray and hobbled and old when he had been a child.

He struggled to remember his name. It was there, on the tip of his tongue. An acolyte of some lesser spirit of Guldanh forest, his one concern this hobby turned trade turned enterprise. Haffa was among his best customers, had been even then. His other clients included several well-to-do madames, uelfin soothsayers, and no few matchmakers of varied reputation.

Even now, at this late hour of the evening, the shop was populated with runners and apprentices come to collect bounties for their masters. Wu's presence here would be noted if he lingered much longer, bent over one trencher and then another, feigning investigations into the blooms, a futile hunt for flaws.

Somewhere else in the city, Rhul was stalking through dirtier streets. Among the bones of Cratom were vagrants and murderers and thieves. He could only hope that his Shard remained hale until the conclusion of his pursuit, that he had not made a mistake in sending him on this errand, so far removed from him and vulnerable; but Garam was the only one in the city who could track him that he knew. There could as well be another acolyte of God Shakh or one of those rare spirits who cast the roads God Uldal grew into dissolution, and were they here, they would reveal themselves soon enough. By night's end, if he did not miss his guess.

By night's end, his own presence here would be made known to the Mistress Bane, and then every assassin in the city would be hunting him, all of the best and brightest shining stars in her arsenal. Even now, Garam was laying down his piece

Tears for the Moon God

at the family estate—inside a room that would be vacant at this time, its occupant just arriving at the door of this shop—and her none the wiser.

Saijin's vision swam. His head was full of cotton and his limbs didn't want to move properly. His wrist felt unfamiliar under a hand loosely gripping a wine glass filled almost to the top with a wet, sweet red from who really cared where.

Was it a vintage? A good year? *Did I ever know?*

He chuckled to himself.

At some point in the last hours, he had regressed into a kind of infantile meandering, had taken to pacing on wobbly legs, his arms drifting seemingly of their own will through twisted arcs and languid, geometric patterns as if the very act of moving in this wide, wondrous world was new to him. As if he had not been visiting these chambers at the height of his very own whorehouse for the better part of two decades now.

He hip checked his chaise lounge. Wine sloshed over the edge of his cup to shower a vase full of lilies, staining their petals in spatters of pink as it sluiced off of them to be sucked up by too dry dirt in the vase that held them.

He looked down at the flowers. Rage bubbled in his guts, flashes of lightning scraping at the fog in his head, igniting ephemeral gases to heat a suddenly blank, white mind into a violent inferno. He snatched up the nearest lily beneath its calyx and wrenched it off its stem, crushed it in his fist and cast it over the back of the chaise. He reached for the next, tore it away and threw it, and the next, until all of them had been ripped from their stems.

Panting harshly, the wine glass still clutched gingerly in his free hand and half of its contents peppering the rug underfoot, he collapsed onto the seat, and wept.

It was in this prone position, chalice hugged to his pallid cheek as runnels of salty fluid jogged across his cheeks, that Garam found him.

The Hunter emerged in the doorway onto the veranda, taking the back way in as Saijin had, time and again, demanded of him.

It did not do to be seen in the keeping of a Lamb. People did talk, after all.

Garam panned over the room, found him lying there, both useless and emotionally compromised. Though he did not say anything untoward, anything at all, it did not take much imagining to arrive at what he was thinking. It was there, written all over his face. The passive judgment. The exhaustion.

Oh, his Hunter was well and fed up with him, and he supposed he had a right to be. Whatever pay Saijin had offered him was nothing when counted next to his life. If an assassin held anything as sacred, it was his ability to continue drawing breath. Death couldn't like their kind. Or if he did, his antithesis and friend, the god who gave life, must loath people like him. People who stole away futures and possibilities from others for coin or for some misguided sense of pride. If it was ego that guided them, then it was Ego they should answer to in the end, a most terrible force indeed.

But whatever judgment Garam held for him, however tired of this Seer's drunken antics he was, he nonetheless crossed the short expanse of tile and carpet between them, slipped slender, muscled arms under him, and hauled him off the lounge. He even took care enough to mind that what remained of his employer's wine did not spill as he carried him away like a small child. Like *his* child.

"This is...undignified." Saijin grumbled.

"If you can walk, then you can have your dignity, sir. But we must be leaving. It is close to time."

"Time." Saijin snorted. "Isn't that what's gotten us into this mess? Some irony that it should be fleeting now when there was so much of it to be had then."

"Shh." Garam adjusted his hold on him, snatched up the bottle he had been pouring from. "Take this."

The bottle rose to flush with his hip. He took it, and cradled it to his chest.

"There's a good boy."

"Where are we going?"

"First, to a safe house somewhere around the slums."

"No, that will never do. Why go there, when I can stay here. With all of my comforts."

"Here, there is a good chance someone will find you."

"But you've masked my scent, haven't you? Made me impossible to find by conventional means. Or unconventional means."

"I have no such power." Garam whispered. "I told you that."

"Then why have the other uelfin not come for me?"

"They have. But I have been close enough each time to deal with them. I will not be tonight."

"But...the *slums*?"

"Near them, yes. With any luck, not in them."

"I suppose that will have to do, won't it."

"It will, yes."

"Will you carry me all that way. I'm quite heavy." He chuckled hysterically. "All this wine and good food. I've gotten fat, haven't I?"

"No, sir. You are light as a feather."

"Liar!"

"Would you prefer to walk?"

"Is there a carriage waiting for us?"

"No."

"Then yes, I think that's wise."

He rolled into Garam's fingers. Garam firmed his grip, clutched him tighter to his chest.

"You're far too drunk for that, sir. If you must, take a ride on my back. I will have to set you aside if we encounter violence on the way, of course, but it is somewhat less conspicuous, I think, than this labor of...this labor."

Saijin snorted. "Fine, fine. I'll take what I can get. But lets be quick about this. And you be quick about whatever this errand is. You can't expect me to hunker down in some Goth *peasant's* home all night, now can you."

"I will not be long."

He set Saijin down, and squatted down for the uelfin to mount him. Saijin wrapped his arms around his hunter's neck, the half-empty wine bottle clutched in one hand, the chalice in the other.

Garam took him around the legs and lifted him off the ground. He marched toward the front entrance, and they ventured past it.

The guard watched them pass in silence, though Saijin knew quite well he could not be trusted. Few strong arms in the city could be with Adam Five Eyes' favored lieutenant curled around the arm of Lord Liudao Bane. It had been almost

Tears for the Moon God

impossible to peel an assassin off of her when he found himself with a need for such heightened security. Nearly impossible to find one willing to protect him, even if his protection meant forsaking her orders to manage other, less important affairs.

Garam had not been an easy find, no. There had been much courting involved. *Courting. Now there's a funny word. Like flirting with a potential lover. Oh, how I'd like to—*

"Sir, if I may ask—"

"Yes, you may."

"—could you please direct your thoughts to something less unsavory. Or, at the very least, adjust your position."

"What's the matter?"

"Your erection is pressing against my spine."

"Oh. Sorry."

He shimmied his hips, and snuggled himself in tighter around Garam's shoulders.

"That's not quite what I meant." Garam said under his breath, but Saijin did not notice. His thoughts had taken him away into whimsical fantasies, leaving Garam to his work. He pressed his wine glass to his lips, knocked back the rest of its contents, and cast it onto the floor, where it shattered.

"Don't be long, okay?" he mumbled.

A harsh sigh gusted past Garam's lips. "When this is over, we will have arrived in Nixir. Which means the sooner Wu Bane's business is done, the better for you and I. If for no other reason than that, I will make this as quick as I can.

"But please, sir, could you think of dead puppies or something? Anything at all? This is getting uncomfortable."

Rhul considered that he might be looking in the wrong place. Wu's logic was flawed. Any dwelling suitable for a safe house in this district would be populated with vagabonds and junkies. Any reasonably dry alcove would be teaming with them. Any shot-out building, empty of life, would be difficult to keep that way. They would be playing a losing game. Word would spread of a place where vagrants disappeared. Before long, that word would arrive at their enemy's doorstep, at Mistress Bane's doorstep, and who would she send after them then?

Or is this Wu's intent?

He wondered at that. Could Wu keep parts of his mind secret from him? They were cut from the same cloth, two pieces of the same whole, but the Core retained some privileges that were not extended to his Shard, at least not yet.

He had never tried to push against those walls. Not to delve into his Core's mind, pick apart the barriers which might exist between them. He had never thought to do such a thing, and yet now he found himself sorely tempted. His Core had not been bad to him. Had come to his aid swiftly whenever the moment demanded; but it was no act of altruism that motivated him. Kill Rhul, and he would lose a sliver of his soul, the power contained within it. A Shard must be aware of his station, but also the nature of his being. Otherwise he risked entreating the Core to an eternity of longing, a state of incompletion which would last, possibly, even beyond the day of his death.

Who could know what happened to a broken soul upon death? Who but Shah

The Heir

Jagat, or Shao Luin.

He explored the offerings across this barrow for the damned. Stable hovels, long abandoned as the money left this once industrious neighborhood, became dens for vagabonds and whores—those too broken and addled for the brothels near the river. They slept under ragged coats on matte, wooden floors which were as often warped from rain shed as in tact.

His passing was noted by those whose sleep was fitful, for whom withdrawal came like dozens of knives slicing and cauterizing raw flesh, like hammers shattering bone.

This is the wrong choice.

He searched for the bond between Wu's soul and his. Through that bond, communication between them was made possible, but it was limited. All energies which extended outward from the Core were meant for its benefit. Most were the kind intended for surveillance, but why were such redundant structures needed? A fragment of a soul could not hide from its most stable element for long. It could not run for long, either. Even as he walked these wending lanes, sifted through wreckage, meandered across halls and down staircases, he felt an absurd longing, a tug against him, a *need* for reunion.

He could not deny existence in this state was uncomfortable. Home was a secure place. Life, for him and, if his suspicion proved correct, for any Shard, was vulnerability, a terrifying prospect. Birth, then, was to know true fear, to be cast out into the world and endure, as cruel whims were foisted upon him, and suffering pressed in from every side.

And death? Each involuntary passage out of the world, to rejoin his core...each completion, every conclusion of his short life, was met with a wiping away of his essence, the sanitation of his unique attributes in favor of Wu Bane, the origin. The source. Yet he knew it was coming. Each time, he knew what awaited, recalled memory of the sensation, of annihilation.

And this is why I wonder. Am I the same person who was expelled last time? The time before? If I remember my death. Each time, and however vague the details. If I have this measure of autonomy, and can think for myself, come to my own conclusions even to know that what Wu intends is wrong, is bound to draw the wrong eyes to us...then am I not worthy of his life? Are we not the same?

But that was a dangerous thought. It invited...*possibilities*. There was the order of things. There were rules, and comfort in keeping with those rules. Expelled, he witnessed the world unfold around him, knew it was a flawed world, that he did not belong here, and felt that discomfort grow and grow as he navigated its bounds with borrowed knowledge to guide him, his identity or lack thereof a byproduct of his attachment, a symbiotic link to this other, who lived in this world always.

He thought of the Graemeins, who possessed two souls. He had seen both sides of Jaunz Faedrin's personality. Or Wu had. Nonetheless, he recalled the manic, maligned glee which overran God Uldal's second when Sky Souled. So different from the patient, grounded man they had grown so accustomed to. A mercurial force, bad tempered, with a penchant for mischief, fragments of that other soul were sometimes imbued into his Shards, and when it was just two of them, as it must be whenever the man left Sana's Horn, one full soul must occupy that body, the other remaining well in place. There could be no blending of personalities, and so they were always separate, always at war with each other, two personalities

Tears for the Moon God

vying for dominance, one which did not belong in this world and the other...what happened if the Earth Soul died? Was the Sky Soul left with a body to dwell within, a corporeal form through which it might extend its will?

He was on the edge of the slums now. Those abandoned dwellings were fast becoming less common. He contemplated turning back, noting the way light spilled from nearly every window in every squat, tile-roofed home, the lesser state of disrepair from a lighter neglect. A chipped tile here. Frayed paint hanging in ribbons from a shabby facade there.

He contemplated turning back. Wu would want that. Had been explicit enough about his desires.

But he was wrong. Those slums were the express property of Mistress Bane, they must be. Those addicts were as rejected goods to her, and he suspected many of them were hiding from her agents. What would they do if they discovered Samil Bane among them? If, in his innocence or ignorance or both, he divulged to any passerby his name? Would they shunt him into the street, fearful of the wrath closing in on them, which might ensnarl them so tightly they could not hope to come away from it alive? Would they hold him as ransom against their debts?

But that was little different than what Wu and Garam had planned for him. They might even seek to employ a few of those drifters to look after him, shell out a few coins for—

Don't be a fool. They'd take that payment and seek out the nearest opium den. They'd be followed then. Back to us.

He drew up short before a modest cottage. The windows in its face and under its eaves were dark, the curtains drawn.

This will do.

He hopped a picket fence and crossed the shallow, brown lawn. A pair of lilac bushes framed the stoop. He circled the yard to the back door, leaving the cozy, front entrance to itself, and once there, drew out a pigsticker from within his shirt, and used to work the latch. He shoved the door inward, revealing a slice of a kitchen carved in moonlight, and eased the door shut behind him.

Someone lived here. He suspected they were asleep somewhere deeper in the house, thinking nothing was amiss. They would have to be dealt with, before Wu or Garam returned.

They're not going to like this. But they were wrong. So very wrong. They were not going to be here for days on end. Wu had been clear enough about his intentions. *We're going to kick over the hornet's nest and carve a path out of the chaos. But if she finds us with her son, she won't hesitate to kill us where we stand. She can't find him before Wu finds her, and she will if we remain on her ground. Better to keep him here, in mind your business country, until this is over.*

He wondered, as he ventured deeper into the house, if Wu heard his thoughts. If what he was thinking was clear to his Core, if even now he was trying to unravel what it all meant. What new defiance had taken his Shard.

There were dangers in that too. Dangers for both of them, if either cared to think on the implications of Rhul's actions, this newfound defiance. That it was allowed even as it was not sanctioned. Were they now equals? *No. Not that.* But neither were they master and servant. Not now. Not ever again.

A tinkle of chimes over the door. The sudden arrival of cooler, river-scented air.

The Heir

Scuffling boots dragged across waxed floorboards, pausing here and there as the newcomer bent to make closer observation of a bushel of flowers, run a pianist's fingers through streaming ivy which dangled from pots hung from the ceiling on delicate hooks, and twined its curling stems around the crosshatch bars of lattices.

A greater warmth drove out the chill, drove Wu to look up from his own meaningless appraisal, to regard a young man who looked so like their father. Liudao Bane was in the tilt of Samil's eyes, in the delicate structure of his face, the curious quirk of his lips that, when taken together with dark circles under those light-brown eyes—the way his gaze settled on everything it touched a hair too long—bred into him a sense of somber longing, or perhaps disappointment.

To look at him was to see a boy who had everything, and who wanted for nothing, and yet yearned for something to long for. Something he could not have described, even to himself. There was grief there, a long, festering kind which lingered even as the sharp edges smoothed over, leaving just the hard core, the polished stone, a grief so close to the boy's identity it became his identity. To remove it, to let in a little light, would be to reshape who he was, into a person he did not recognize.

Yes, he had inherited so much of their father. So much of his uncertainty, perhaps some of his wisdom. But the man Liudao Bane was in absence of his elder son must be different than the man he had known. *How much has he changed in my absence?*

Jealousy ravaged him suddenly and unexpectedly. *He stole my life. My title. My inheritance. My* father!

The rage beat through him like a drum, the cadence slowing, blood settling back into regions of his body outside of his head, away from his temples. He was calm. He *must be calm!*

There, too, was revulsion.

He didn't mean it. He didn't choose it, not any of it. He's as much a victim of his mother's brutality as you are.

Samil's back straightened. He twisted on his heels, stepped across the aisle to regard the contents of a trencher just opposite where his long lost brother stood, and Wu's breath caught.

He bent to get a closer look at those tulips. *Yellow tulips, how fitting.* To take in their fragrance. Stood up again, resurfacing.

Chug...slam! Chug...slam! Wu's heart thudded against his ribs.

Time slowed, a cold, hard knot settled against his diaphragm, stealing his breath. He had thought himself prepared for this moment. He had been wrong.

Samil's gaze lifted from the trencher, found him. Like a fawn struck by sudden light, harsh and white and blinding, he froze. That somber regard snagged on details in Wu's face, so many similarities the resemblance could not be incidental. Could not but mean...something. A warped mirror reflected features back at him, things he had seen before in himself, in their father. More than just two Goths staring at each other over a trencher filled with fluted blooms in pastel shades. More than two distant cousins looking at each other.

He had Liudao's nose. A fat, round thing interrupting softer features, seeming even more out of place for that he had not yet gained the age lines which made it look at home on their father. He had his rounded chin, too, but he was thinner by several degrees of magnitude than their father, who in his years as ambassador to

Tears for the Moon God

Cratom had packed on substantial weight. Even before Wu's abandonment, his stepmother throwing him to the wolves and the wilderness, to die, if hope would have prevailed. If fate had not chosen a different path. Even before his abandonment, the lord of House Bane's belly had been a barrel, his cheeks plump and pinching around his mouth, his flesh dimpling across his brow in a way unbecoming.

A gasp escaped Samil. A gasp which woke Wu to the harsh truth. He was not here to make amends. He was not here to invite kinship with this boy, this boy who must think he was seeing a ghost, for his brother was dead.

No.

He was here to play abductor, to seize this boy and take him away, and do so with as little commotion as possible.

"Do I know you?" Samil said.

"You might have once." Wu answered.

He reached across the trencher, grasped Samil around the forearm, and dragged him around the side.

The shopkeeper did not turn to face them, did not note the odd scuffling somewhere in his shop. He was engrossed in pruning a small shrub, setting wires against slender branches. His attention was needed elsewhere, and what ever happened in a flower shop, anyway? Who would dare cause a ruckus in his store.

"What are you—"

"Quiet now. I'm not here to hurt you. But you need to come with me." Wu said for him alone to hear.

"What is the meaning of this?"

"I'll explain everything, just come."

He felt Rhul somewhere in the distance, a presence like a blister in his mind. He latched onto that piece of his soul, opened a road just there, where the door onto the street was located. In doing, he let go of himself, let go of those crucial threads of his identity even as he exerted his will. The doorway opened into a quaint bedroom, sparsely furnished, all cast in shades of gray where moonlight passed through lace curtains.

A bed, its dressings tussled and the comforter half on the floor. A chest of drawers near the entrance. A closet, its doors open wide and revealing clothing on wooden hangers, a trunk bound with iron bands lingering in their shadow.

He marched for the portal with Samil stumbling after him, his protestations rising in pitch. The shopkeeper looked up from his pruning, noted the Acolyte of Ways dragging his quarry through a window into a distant place, where two paths adjoined in defiance of what was right. Watched as the pathway closed behind them.

Was that the Bane lordling? He vaulted out of his seat, palms slapping the surface of his desk.

"This is bad this is very bad." He hissed.

He barreled around the pay desk, hip checking the flower pot on his way by. It crashed against the floor, terracotta Shards scurling in every direction as he thundered past, and out into the street.

"HEY!" he shouted at the nearest patrol. "HEY!" he waved his arms frantically overhead. The patrolman, seeing him, marched to close the distance.

The Heir

"WHAT IS IT?" he boomed.

"KIDNAPPING!"

The patrolman was rushing now, brushing past him, into the shop where the offense had happened. Finding nothing, he spun to face the shopkeeper, who had been trailing him like a shadow.

"Who was it? Where is he?"

"Don't know. Looked to me like he took the Bane brat. He left on an unnatural path. A *godly* path."

"One of God Uldal's." The officer growled. "The Bane boy, you said? No, this can't be. This can't happen."

"It has, sir."

"Nonetheless." He marched from the flower shop and away, and in his wake the shopkeeper slid onto his haunches, back against a trencher full of flowers.

"No, this can't happen. She'll retaliate sure as she is who she is." And he made a silent prayer to the Goddess of Fate. There would be blood in the streets before sunrise. Blood running like creeks across the low streets to feed the river.

For good measure, he prayed to her, too.

Garam set Saijin down on the stoop outside an unassuming dwelling just beyond the border of the slums. The back entrance bore no signs of having been forced, but he had not expected it to. It was a perk of being sworn to God Uldal worthy of his envy that they could simply appear where they wished without need of the usual conventions of picking locks and scrubbing teeth.

Wu's scent emanated strongly from somewhere on the second floor of this house, and was mingled with the even more potent scents of two others, which suffused the entire home but were most concentrated near where the pathfinder had staked out his base. The salted pork odor of sex, the intermingling of those two bystanders odors, gave the impression they had cohabitated and been involved with each other for many years, and had the unfortunate affliction of being too poor to afford the simple comforts of new mattresses. More, an older stink of blood and viscera told him the woman had given birth on that bed more than once.

Lingering odors of garlic, and yeast, and sugar, of burnt oil and iron, emanated from the other side of this door. He knew he would enter onto a kitchen even before the door was fully open. Saijin twisted around to view the quaint interior of the cottage where he would be staying, and wrinkled his nose at what he found there.

"You can't really expect me to—"

"Yes, I can."

"Fine." He sulked.

"Drink your wine, sir. You'll feel better about it."

"You're quite right." He unstoppered the bottle and took a long pull from it.

"Oh, this is interesting."

A fourth odor emanated from upstairs now, a familiar, spicy, floral odor that reminded him of late summer blooms. Samil Bane had arrived, his ambient scent interrupted with those fresher bursts which must have come from a brief contact with the flower shop where Wu had expected to find him.

Unexpected, too. There's no difference between the core and the Shard.

He had not been paying enough attention the first time he'd encountered the two, it seemed. Their scents must be identical, for he could not make out Wu's scent with his Shard present.

One more factor in the balancing act between we of the Huntsman's Triad. He mused. "Our pathfinder has arrived."

"His timing is impeccable." Saijin said.

Garam giggled. "More than you know, my dear."

They stumbled through into the bedroom. A keening cry was coming from somewhere down the hall. A dull *thunk* and then silence.

Rhul emerged from the greater darkness of that hall. His right glove was spattered with blood, still glistening and wet. He was otherwise unspoiled.

"This is not what I wanted, Rhul." He growled, releasing his grip on Samil.

Rhul made to move on their brother, flinched back when Wu moved into his path.

"We should bind him." Rhul said.

"Come back to me." Wu commanded.

He focused on himself, as two pieces of one whole, as those pieces reuniting to form one entity, the complete picture.

A wall rose up between the two pieces, resistance like he had never felt before in the connective tissue between them, as if something had scarred over.

His gaze snapped to Rhul, cold surprise mirrored in his Shard's expression.

"You can't." He whispered. "Can't resist me."

"Not for long, no." Rhul agreed, and there was caution in his tone. It seemed he had not intended to do...whatever he did. Did not believe such resistance possible before this moment.

"You defied me." Wu said.

Samil scrambled around the bed, intent on putting something, anything, between himself and these two, who by every appearance were twins. A confusing detail, for his parents had never mentioned two elder siblings before him. Had only ever mentioned the one.

Wu Bane. My brother, Wu.

"This shouldn't be possible."

"It's certainly something that shouldn't leave this room." Rhul said. He turned his regard on Samil then. "He looks like us. More like our father than I would have guessed."

"*My* father, you mean."

"You don't see it, do you? You view me as my own person. You give me a name, and my identity is attached to that name. You've even allowed me to retain some measure of my memories, from other separations. I am not *you* any longer, Wu. I am what you manifest through a weakness of your own resolve."

"That can't—

"It is standing in front of you. All the evidence you need. Every bit of it."

"Why did you choose this place, Rhul." He needed to change the subject, get away from the implications of this, that he had, in some sense, created a life independent of his own, which was bound to the same soul.

His mind was wandering too close to Shulraki Alran, to what his god had told him of the man. Seven years his Shards had survived beyond him. They had fallen into roles, had adopted guises outside of him, their own identities. How much of that was of his choosing? How much of what they did beyond the death of their core was free will?

No, he did not want to think about this. Could not afford to think about this. He needed to recall Rhul back into him.

"Not yet." Rhul said.

"You have a window into my mind, then."

"I have always had that window. But it is not a door. We are not equals. Or, at least, we weren't. I don't know what we are now."

"Will you cooperate with me?" The words came through a constricted throat.

Rhul nodded. "Of course.

"You ask why I chose this place? It's unassuming. It falls just outside her territory. She'll scrape clean every hovel in the slums until she satisfies herself that her son is not being kept somewhere so obvious. Then she'll broaden her scope to include the places occupied by her enemies, those she believes to be enemies within her own ranks, and then beyond. To those she barely suspects could be working against her. She'll come across us soon enough, when that barkeep at the Black Lamb spills the beans about our connection to Jaunz Faedrin—"

"You're working for a Hand!" Samil ejaculated. Eyes wide with fright, he edged back against the wall, but there was nowhere to go. He began to climb. "What do you want with me?"

Wu shed a tired look on him. "Stop. Please. You're going to hurt yourself."

He slid back onto the floor.

"We need to bind him." Rhul said.

"Like you did with the owners of this house?"

"Yes."

"That's unnecessary."

"He'll start screaming for help soon. These walls are poorly insulated. Someone will hear."

"I said there is no need."

"I heard you. I disagree."

"You said you'd cooperate with me."

"I did."

Wu spread his hands.

"Fine." Rhul said. "We'll do it your way."

"Come home, will you? Your task is done."

Strangely, Rhul smiled. Wu didn't quite know what to make of it, was left in confusion as Rhul said: "Life is...fraught with complications, isn't it? An uncomfortable state. Yes, I'll welcome the invitation, now we understand each other."

"I don't know that we do?"

"Just as well." Rhul shrugged. "It's a beginning. I doubt either of us will truly grasp what has happened between us for some time yet."

He stepped around his other half, positioned himself so that their backs were pressed against each other, their limbs parallel.

Just then, the door swung open. Garam stood there in the gloom with a piss drunk Saijin swaying back and forth behind him, a mostly empty wine bottle clutched in his fist.

Garam looked Wu and his Shard over. "Well, don't do *that*."

Wu stepped forward. Rhul ambled around him, positioned himself so that the two were both facing the doorway.

Garam stepped into the room and to the side, allowing Saijin entry after him. He shut the door behind him.

A muffled scream issued from somewhere down the hall, and Garam twisted round to look in that direction. "You left them alive?" He arched an eyebrow precipitously as he returned his gaze to Wu.

His Shard cleared his throat. "Sometimes showing mercy is beneficial."

"You agree with him?" Garam asked, ignoring the Shard's interruption, and, more generally, his presence.

Wu didn't answer, which was answer enough.

Garam nodded slowly. His gaze traveled to the other side of the bed, where Samil was pressed against the wall, looking thoroughly overstimulated as recognition for the hunter dawned on him.

"You." He whispered. "You're in on this?"

"I am." Garam confessed.

Shock fluttered away. Samil's eyes narrowed, his nose wrinkled and rising over curled lips. "What is the meaning of this!" he demanded, stamping his foot on the carpet. "Has my mother not been good to you."

"Your mother hasn't been good to anyone." Wu said.

"Oh, you would say that. Gone running off into the forest as you did. She was heartbroken, you know! She looked for you for days. Even sent hunting parties out to find you."

"Is that what she told you?" Wu said flatly. He turned then to regard his half brother.

Samil flinched back, with the unfortunate side effect that he knocked the back of his head against the wall.

"Your mother is a liar, Samil." He said. "I don't hold it against you. She's very good at what she does, but its over now. By the end of this night, she'll be dead, and we will all be gone. I intend for you to take her place. She has trained you for exactly that purpose, hasn't she?"

"That's immaterial."

He pinned Samil to the wall with his gaze. He would not blame his brother for what had befallen him, but he could not leave him blind to what his mother was either. "She told you her tale and you ate it up because she is your mother, and whatever your relationship with her, she is someone you are hard wired to trust. After all, if she does not have your best interests in mind, how can you justify her treatment of you, of everyone around you?

"You are aware of her role in this city, aren't you?" He did not need an answer. It was written all over his brother's face. "For her to sit at the center of her web, commanding the respect of a Hand's direct subordinate, to be respected and feared by every assassin, strong arm and thief in this city, she herself must be despicable. She must be cunning. She must be cold and calculating. And most important, she must be perfectly willing to do terrible things to get what *she* wants, regardless of who she hurts in the process.

"And this is a woman you choose to believe."

Samil lip quivered. His gaze slid from Wu's face to his knees.

Saijin brushed past Garam. He gripped Wu's shoulder. A brief moment followed in which Rhul looked as if he might cut that hand off, but he restrained himself.

The Heir

"Ease up on the kid." He said. "He's a very sweet boy."

"Which would make him ill suited to the task we have in mind for him." Rhul cut in.

"How shocking." Garam sniped. "Good sense coming from the king of leaving open loose ends."

Rhul glared at him.

"Your mother tried to kill me." Wu said. "I was six years old. She had already done away with my mother, and extorted a gifted matchmaker into pairing her with our father under threat of violence by then, and I was in the way. She had you, didn't she? But as long as I lived, you could not inherit our father's estate and the vast fortune that goes with it. His title as ambassador to the uelfin places him in command of power like no other Goth in this city, and she wants that for herself. She'll almost certainly have him killed off as soon as it becomes obvious the king favors you to replace him, and she'll feel nothing about it.

"As for me, she left me tied to a tree in deep forest, away from any obvious road or path that someone might travel down. She tied me to the damned thing herself." Color was rising in his cheeks, and his voice had taken on a hard, grating edge. Saijin's hand had come away from his shoulder, and the uelfin had taken several steps back.

"It's only sheer, dumb luck that a pathfinder found me and took me back to God Uldal. That lone act of kindness is what spared me from death, and *she is going to pay for it!* Tonight. With her life.

"When this is over, Samil, you may assume her place or you may not. I would hope you do, and guide this city into a brighter future than it has been allowed over these past twenty odd years. I won't try to make the choice for you. But whether or not you do take up her mantel, come morning, you won't have a mother. Her time has come." He whispered those last words, the rage draining out of him, leaving a cold, iron ball to settle in his stomach, his skin vibrating with draining energy.

"She left you for dead?" Samil whispered. "She...she killed your mother." He sank down the wall. "Why don't you hate me? She gave me everything she took from you."

He crossed the room, seated himself on the edge of the bed, where now the owners of this home should be sleeping soundly. Instead, one was unconscious and the other screaming down the hall, the sound of his voice only barely audible through his gag and the closed door.

He took his brother's cheeks in his hands, lifted his head so he had little choice but to look him in the face. To see the grief mingled with anger there, the press of true catharsis edging in from all sides as he confronted this boy who had done nothing wrong, told him the truth as he saw it, and sought to forgive him.

"You were just a kid, Samil." He said for this innocent boy and him alone to hear. "And I loved you."

He let go of Samil, who remained there, seated with his back against the wall, looking up into his long lost brother's face, a confused array of emotions vying for dominance.

"Stay here. Rhul will protect you." He rose and joined Garam. "Time to go."

"Wait!" Samil said. "Take me with you."

"No." Wu said.

He focused on the door before him. In the space of a breath it had collapsed

Tears for the Moon God

inward and opened onto a path he well remembered, a street just outside the gates of the Bane estates.

Garam looked through the portal over his shoulder. He snickered. "Funny. It feels like I just came from there."

"Go." Wu ordered.

Garam marched through, and he followed him like a shadow, into the hornet's nest.

Courting A Spirit

This was no place to make a stand.

Wide channels spanned the gaps between sawtooth lines of trees, and these grew hail and strong, denied the moon its touch on the land, robbed it of starlight. Clearings dotted the landscape where old trees had fallen, where new shoots rose out of the loam, and dense, downy mosses dominated those clearings. Yurts had gone up in those lanes, and makeshift torches provided ample light in the channels between, but in the distance, beyond a bleak void, their lights were echoed. The Tului had struck camp within sight of them. The gulf between the two camps was not large, but Ungol had no illusions about what would come were they to mount an attack in the night. The Tului had taken their time, had been here long enough to raise defenses, and they knew this terrain. Knew where pitfalls would hinder progress, where steep drop offs made uncertain footing.

This was their land. They had arrived, were made more confident for their knowledge of this terrain.

And reinforcements were in reach now.

An eerie silence hung over the Gil Garo camp. There would be battle on the morrow, when they closed the gap, refused the Tului the luxury of running away. There would be little sleep for any of them in the night. The trees blocked out the moon, but he was certain it was nearing full. It had been too long since the new moon. Nearly a month gone on the road.

They had played into the hands of their enemies. All advantage lay with the Tului. For the Gil Garo, the minds of their leaders would prove the only balm against the deaths that would arise with the coming dawn. With the arrangement of their forces.

He sat amid the pillows before the wood stove at the center of his yurt, and knew tomorrow's battle would prove the pivotal moment in which the Gil Garo staked their claim against the Tului. Knew that in the coming hours, they would either fold under the weight of their losses, or come out victorious, and strike deeper into the forbidding nation beyond this wall of trees.

He hoped they proved worthy. That this march had not all been for nothing. That his people lived on beyond this night, and the culture he had known all his life was not erased.

Shaelein had retired, but her sleep was restless. The familiarity of their camp bed had proved no comfort to her, and she slept lightly, woke often. She was concerned, and he shared her concern. More rode on their victory than simple triumph. If they died here, any hope of finding familial bonds with their new returned son would die with them. They would be broken then, wouldn't they?

Broken, and their son broken in ways he could barely comprehend. Survival must be his priority. Survival for a people, for a culture. Survival for two people who had given up on fostering children with the death, for it was that in its way, of their son. Survival for a son resurrected from the ashes of a burdened life, who he would like to see again. Alive and in the flesh.

He did not want their next meeting to be in Gur Tulain, with the certainty of a descent into Ul Sharak's band on the horizon, knowing there was no turning back. That Dupec had lost again what he had only recently reclaimed. That *he* would lose all hope of seeing his son grow into himself, would be denied witness to the beauty and the honor of a full life. This thing he had forsaken with his courting of Gandes Fae, which he had been destined from that moment to live in absence of.

Hope was finding Dupec Safar after all of this had concluded, and knowing he had years, and not days or hours, to know the man he had become.

The forest felt like home to Akhi after so long away from the God House of Hunters. Trees grew close together, allowing shadows to pool between them. Torches and lanterns perched on overturned crates outside the yurts of his kin illuminated channels for their trespass, and made of the darkness beyond an impenetrable shield, swallowing all of the space between this and the Tului camp. He saw clearly enough what lay between the two encampments, the ocean of space seemingly unmolested by Tului traps and fortifications. In the days ahead of the Gil Garo arrival at this, the place they had chosen for their battle, they had not concerned themselves with the usual conventions. Pine needles made a thick, prickly quilt to dress the lands there, and though channels had been cleared among them by marching feet in their thousands, there had been some effort, perhaps by the spirits who resided here, to draw that coverage back, to protect roots and seeds buried under them, keep warm against the winter's chill.

Yet a quiet stole over the wood. In night, the trees breathed deep, expelled oxygen into the air that mortals could breathe a little easier while they dreamed, but in winter, all was asleep. The bear crawled into its den, and stayed there until the spring thaw arrived. Wolves hunted after rabbits clad in coverings that matched the snows, a natural exchange of one camouflage for another as the lands went to sleep and dreamed of better times, and the birds all stole away south, into the tropics, leaving just those who would fare well in these brutal reaches—owls and other predators—who he heard calling to each other in the distance, warning competitors off for these were their lands, their territories. Their hunting grounds.

The messenger who had called upon his yurt had been of uncertain footing, had floundered for answers to his questions when the summons was given. Chief Ungol wanted to see him, but they would not meet at his yurt. No, the edge of the war camp called, and he answered the summons, and Chief Sauman knew nothing of this meeting. Not yet.

He would tell him what transpired here after this business was concluded, of

Courting a Spirit

course; but the chief was elsewhere, his head pressed close to Chief Arrak's, a summons having been given to discuss the strategy the Chikata would be called to with the coming of morning, and the first blooding between the Gil Garo and the Tului, for the spirits of these lands to imbibe.

He saw the chief beyond a last row of yurts, which were arranged in a jagged array, denying clear lines of sight to the enemy scouts if they should get too close, and pathways for them to follow into the camp should the Tului forces seek a surprise attack in the night. The perimeter, so arrayed, would make for nasty fighting, and served as a deterrent for the time being, allowing them to bide their time, prepare for an offensive that might favor them.

Nothing good ever came of battle in dense forest. The canopy did not yield well to sunlight, leaving the gloom and long shadows to pull at the eye. The boles themselves disrupted the line of sight for both the enemy and the attacking force, but their enemy had the advantage of familiar ground. They had been here before, knew the lay of the land, and knew how to use it to their advantage.

This kind of battle did not lend well to the Gil Garo way. Cavalry would be useless here. There was too much risk of injury to their horses to mount a broad scale flanking assault. They would have to forego them, bring the fighting to ground, an intimate exchange of blows with an enemy whose shadows provided the ultimate defense.

Archers may help, but the Tului would have them, too. The intervening space between these camps would be contested, and he could only hope Arrak saw fit not to place his hopes on a frontal assault there. Instead, to use it for what it could be. A distraction, from the bumbling idiots groping around in the dark the Tului might think they were. War was simply a raid whose scale and scope had grown unruly. It was a game of subterfuge, designed to weaken the spirit by attacking the mind. Man became his closest to beast in these clashes, could not deny that piece of him any longer. In the moment by moment play of weapon against weapon, warrior against warrior, the monster in man was awakened to its true potential. Battle was no place for rational interests, but someone must maintain his humanity, or the entire effort crumbled.

Ungol awaited him at their predetermined meeting place, and he bowed when he was before him. A show of respect for a chief who had already lost everything, who did not know how much he had lost.

"You asked for me?" he said.

"I would like you to accompany me on a walk." He said. "Guide our steps, if you can."

Akhi nodded. "Where do you wish to go."

"Out." Ungol gestured toward the forest, in a direction that would take them well away from the Tului camp, adding further confusion to the nature of this errand, denying him validation for his prior assumptions."

"You do not wish to see the enemy lines."

"I can see plainly enough what they wish to hide."

"Then what is your goal."

Ungol ventured off in the direction he had pointed. Akhi followed at his side.

"I've been thinking. The Tului have chosen this site for a reason. They have all of the advantages here. Should they desire, they have all of the conventions in place to whittle our numbers down through ambushes. Our lines of communication are

Tears for the Moon God

not as efficient as theirs. We possess no telepathic bonds to exploit, which leave us at a further disadvantage in that those lines are vulnerable to being cut. They have few weaknesses we can readily exploit. Shadow and ice are both in abundance. The trees will dilute Sildein's power, making the going harder for both Coltang and Gaulakh, should they seek to use their strength to force those shadows back. Our horses will not be of much use either."

"We've arrived at the same conclusion then."

"If we wage battle here, without making certain preparations, we will lose. I wish to make those preparations now. Which is why I've called on you. You can sense them, can't you? The sleeping giants among us."

Akhi said nothing.

"Lakes. Creeks and streams. Minor tributaries all may serve to hinder our progress. Even the steep side of a hill, a sudden shift in terrain, may work to disadvantage us. We know nothing of the terrain we are fighting on."

"We have scouts for that reason."

"Ah, but that is not my concern."

They walked on in silence for a time. To Akhi's eyes, the world was rendered in vivid detail, the gloom no bar to his sight.

"The spirit the Tului worship, who they are all bound to, is the spirit of an underground river, one which likely feeds the water spirits in this reach, or is fed by them. Tributaries running into him, water expelled into cave chambers and then up through wells and springs into the lakes and ponds here. Those will likely be loyal to him, and, by extension, to the Tului.

"But what of the lands? The ground we walk on is Tao Shein's. This forest is supplied with waters from deep underground. The roots of pine trees run deep. But they collect as much from snow melt and rainwater in the spring and summer months. And what nutrients it receives...they will come from the land before the water. Forests and plains share in common that they are places of renewal. Death is important for its ability to sustain life. From decay, new growth flourishes. But what does that say for the relationship between the people of these lands and their spirits?"

"What are you getting at, Chief Ungol?"

"The spirit of this forest sleeps only lightly. The trees here do not drop their leaves with the coming of winter, which means it does not hibernate in the way so many of the creatures who shelter in its embrace do. Rather...it is the lakes and streams who sleep.

"Now come, into a place where the light does not touch. And watch my back."

Ungol stepped forward, hastened away from the camp and its imposing glow. Away from the camp of the enemy. They marched into deep wood."

"You asked me to follow you...to ensure you could return. To make sure you did not lose your way on this path."

"I cannot mark the trees if this errand is to be successful. Doing so would anger the spirit. This is why we do not build lasting cities, Akhi. Why the Gil Garo have always been nomadic peoples. The last of our kind on the steppe. Tao Shein gives us his favor, because we do not carve wells into his flesh. Duijus Kanh provides his protection, because we give him our weakest, the old and the dying. Our relationship with the spirits is one of noninterference, and they view us highly for our dedication to controlling the populations of those empires and kingdoms who wound them so frequently.

"This is the secret the chiefs have kept for as long as we have been a people. We do not serve our own interests in being the barbaric people we are. No, this is the truth." He said when Akhi began to protest. "We are not a *kind* people, as these things are measured by men. They believe us a cruel people, murderers and thieves. But our place in the grand designs of Tao Shein are as his immune system. We keep him healthy, by eliminating the parasites infesting his hide. What would the spirit of a forest think of a people who refuse to do it harm, who enrich it with the blood of its enemy? The lakes and the streams may be loyal to Tuluis Fel, but they are replenished always by waters from the sky and the ground. The trees, though...the trees care nothing for the loyalties of these waters. Their concerns are different. They do not share the same drive to bolster the population of men in their lands. They seek, with every fiber of their being, to destroy them."

"So you suspect. But what if the Tului choose to build their cities of stone?"

"Wood is in abundance here, and the mountains are far off. The mountains are patient, certainly, more so than the forests, but the resources they provide are not renewable. The trees grow and die and are replaced by new growth, but one spirit remains the dominant force among them, one to whom all others in this reach are beholden. Out of respect, or fear, or love...maybe all of those things.

"Our task this night is to find it."

He halted. The lights of those camps were a memory now, the last dregs of firelight gone away and obscured behind the boles of countless trees.

"Kneel. Lay your forehead against the earth." Ungol instructed. He prostrated himself on frosted ground, in the midst of this dense growth of trees, in a patch amid sinuous, warty roots.

Akhi obeyed. He knelt, crawled forward and lay his forehead in the dirt.

"We come, spirit, to hear your voice. To see you." Ungol said. "We come as a show of respect on the eve of battle, with a promise against your good will. Come to us, spirit of the forest. Let us know you. Let us see you. Let us speak."

A deafening silence hung around them. Akhi heard his pulse beating in his ears. The smells of the forest suffused him, and he focused on them. Dirt and snow, hair caught in the bark of a tree where a deer had rubbed up against it, old blood where a rabbit had become food for a coyote. Death and life working together, the cooperation of many elements in sustaining the wood.

Light footsteps crunched over the snows. Footsteps to know the spirit's coming, that it had answered their call, watched them through eyes full of wonder. Who were these people who had come before it, who had ventured into such a vulnerable position, who sought it out so willingly, when none else of their kind would.

"My daughter bears the wounds of your passing." The woman whispered. "Do you seek now to make amends."

"We do." Ungol said.

Akhi grit his teeth. So vulnerable, even with his gifts, the spirit could as easily kill him as snap the neck of a stick doll. He did not like being so exposed before her, knowing nothing of her nature.

He saw her bare feet just before him, the bangles of carved wood laced around her ankles, the hem of a skirt composed of moss and twigs and animal hair. Her skin was fair, matching the snows, but mottled with darker patches like the dirt under it. He wondered if her form changed with the seasons, or with day and night, as some spirits did. He wondered if she would see fit to help them, or break them here and now, swallow their corpses under clawing roots and drag them into the land to feed her.

He wondered, too, if Ungol's gamble would aid them. If even with the spirit's cooperation, they would be met with such disadvantage the Tului would win over them.

They had all of the advantages. What the spirit might provide in the way of aid may not even matter in the end, if the offensive proved too great. If reinforcements arrived to bolster them.

These people were accustomed to working in the confines of deep wood, weren't they? The resources they pilfered they took with the knowledge that the spirit would retaliate. And they did not care.

What was she to them? What was she to the Gil Garo?

He watched her feet slide away as she twisted, placed herself squarely in front of Ungol. Watched as her hand reached under the chief's chin, and drew him out of his bow, to kneel before her, and bear witness to all that she was.

"What is your name, spirit?" Ungol asked.

"It is Dosh Urul." She crooned. "Daughter of the Shattered One."

A crude family portrait lay across the squat writing table at Arrak's knees. A child's aimless scribbling gave shape to three ropey piles, finger marks done in grease paint which made up in creativity for what it lacked in content. A jackrabbit stood at the side of a smiling boy who held his parents' hands, but the Sarr family had never owned a pet. The dreams of a young child were wild, eccentric things, so pure in that they came from a place of innocence.

In this quiet moment, the wood a still place filled with the crunch and whine of restless boots cutting paths through old, shallow snow, he lingered over the painting, a reminder of what he was fighting for, who was awaiting his return when it was over.

I will survive this.

He would go to Gur Tulain when the fighting was done, when Tuluis Fel had been de-fanged. See his wife one, last time and then leave with his son. They could forget all of this winter's conflicts then, move on and into a life that reflected something of its old character.

If Tamlin survived his own trial.

The sweet, innocent boy who had drawn this picture had gone and left in his wake a strong, discerning man—one who understood survival, knew when to fight and when to leave the fighting to more accomplished hands. He had Duijus Kanh to protect him, a line of defense his sect was dispossessed of, which meant Arrak must approach tomorrow's battle with caution.

His yurt's entrance flap parted, admitting Sarri, and then Sauman.

"Any changes?" Arrak asked them.

"No." Sauman said, taking a seat.

Sarri seated himself against a cushion near the wood stove. He produced a water skin. "Something for the nerves."

"Ungol's gone ahead." Arrak said.

"Then that much is settled." Sarri removed the stopper from the skin. He passed it to Arrak.

Courting a Spirit

"Now may not be the best time." Arrak protested.

"I see you've been pining over your son's handicrafts." Sarri's gaze traveled to the crude family portrait. "You're in good company, Arrak. I miss my son, too."

"I should leave." Sauman said.

Sarri clapped him on the back. "Don't be silly. You might learn something useful if you stay."

"Why always the patronizing—"

"We are hard on you, Sauman, because you are new to your role. Tomorrow, I think, you will rise to it."

"I have been chief of the Chikata sect five years now. I would not call that *new*."

Sarri snorted. "Despite all of those claims made against me, I have served in my post almost as long as you have been alive. I remember when you set off across Rasheik's Rope. I thought you wished for death."

"No need to be crass." Arrak said.

"No, I understand. Ul Surta was not my first choice. I had my eyes on Alar Vashan. I was surprised when Gulang's son came back wearing his power." Sauman snatched the bladder from him. He took a long pull of its contents. "Tastes like horse piss."

"Close." Sarri said.

"Ul Surta was a matter of consequence. I was dying. Yes, I was. I had run out of water. It did not occur to me that what animals inhabited that part of the desert did not drink from her lake. That was all it took. A taste of her waters, and our souls were bonded.

"Her power has served me well nonetheless."

"Saafha learned hard lessons from you." Arrak said. "I believe you were the reason he cited for pursuing the spirit. Ten years later and with a guiding post to keep him on the path."

"I did not take him for a fool."

"I am just surprised you two made it as far as you did. There are things in that desert that defy logic. Then there is the problem of roaming those lands without a guide. The spirits there...they do not take kindly to strangers." Arrak said.

"Seems the spirits in this reach don't either."

A silence descended between them. Sarri took back the water skin and drank.

"Careful. We have a battle to fight tomorrow." Sauman said.

"Leave me be." Sarri said over the mouthpiece. "My son is far away and I've been dealing with his girlfriend for weeks. I miss the idiot."

"It could be far worse." Arrak intoned.

Sarri shrugged. "She's not bad company, I guess. Smarter than him. If I may confess, I have no idea how those two ended up together."

"Let me never have children." Sauman mumbled.

"They're not all bad." Sarri said. "I would give my life for my son. Might have to one day."

"That is the risk we take, isn't it, friend." Arrak said. "But that day is long in coming, if it arrives at all."

Gulang sat with Guruhl outside of the other man's yurt. His children sheltered with their mother for the night, and she told them stories of the Kachin conquests before their time. Told them of battles fought against the Jahhar and Ruc'an,

Tears for the Moon God

bounties taken and blood spilled. Stories to capture their minds and set their spirits on fire, to embolden them in the coming battle. Times of uncertainty demanded these exchanges, to bring confidence to uncertain kin.

But he could not take part in those stories. The eave of battle had always put the itch in him, made live wires of his nerves. A clay jug filled with spirits rested between them, and both were bound in heavy quilts against the cold.

"The eclipse will be tomorrow." He said.

"Don't start with that, now." Guruhl growled. He snatched up the bottle and took a swig.

"It is my hunch. The Tului have led us here to make a stand. Their actions would imply they expect reinforcements. They have made no effort to observe our troops, our positions. They have not taken advantage of this moment to stage a raid."

"Night combat does not suit them."

"It did in Gil Garo."

"Where there was moonlight to fuel their shadows. When we were not aware of them."

"Still."

"A hunch? No lunar charts. No star gazing?"

"The moon has been in the sky with the sun, Guruhl. You have seen it in the breaks where the canopy lets up." He snatched the jug away from him, took a long swig himself. The bottle was approaching empty.

"The question is not whether it occurs, but whether it benefits us." Guruhl said. "I think it does."

"Then you are a fool."

"Maybe." Guruhl chuckled. "Maybe."

"They will destroy us, you know. If not by ruining our bodies, then by crushing our spirits."

"Do you have sand in your vagina?" Guruhl said. "Would you like me to gather some snow?"

"I am just saying we will not be who we were on the other side of this conflict. We are hardly who we were now."

Guruhl squeezed his shoulder. "You are grieving, friend. It is understandable. But do not let the grief consume you. All is not lost. We are who we are, and will be that until we are gone. If the spirits have any favor left for us.

"Speaking of. Why does Arrak insist we do no damage to the trees. Shattering them benefits us. We lose nothing by coating the Tului with splinters and Shards of wood."

"Because he believes Ungol will succeed in his errand." Gulang took another swig.

"And Ungol is doing what exactly?"

A wicked smile broke across his face. "Courting a spirit."

Guruhl nodded solemnly. "Who's idea was that?"

"Mine."

"Conniving shit."

"Ungol was happy to lend his support. We cannot rely on the gods in this, but the spirits of the land have always held a favorable opinion of us."

"And you wish to use them, knowing the Tului may have the same advantage.

Courting a Spirit

Knowing the spirits may see them as favorably as us. Especially here."

"Tuluis Fel is a river spirit. The river runs underground for most of its length. All of those springs...the lakes and ponds feed on his waters, are imbued with power through him. But the land is Tao Shein's, and Tao Shein is our friend."

"Tao Shein is of unknown loyalty." Guruhl said. "What if the spirit kills Ungol. We will have lost a powerful asset against the enemy, and the Dumas will be shaken."

"It is a risk."

"One worth taking?"

"I don't know."

Coltang waited at the edge of camp. The trees beyond were shrouded in silence, an ominous sign. In the distance was the glow of the Tului camp, and the intervening darkness concealed all that he suspected lay out there. The Chikata scouting parties had turned up no sign of Tului spies among the trees, and he had seen no sign of them either. No activity within their camp to denote they prepared for battle. They slept soundly, certain sign of their confidence in the position they had chosen, in their ability to use these woods, the hidden treacheries the landscape provided, to their advantage.

But he could not think of them just now. Ungol had gone into those woods, taking with him the last hope they had of turning the tides in this battle. If he was successful, they might have a chance. He had been the obvious choice for the task.

Coltang could not have gone to court the spirit of the forest. He would have been seen as an enemy, having cast his hammers against the trees at its fringes. Sauman and Arrak would have been viewed with a similar contempt. And the others...Tursa's affliction would have left him too weak to be seen as a strong ally to the spirit in this conflict, and Sarri's cold detachment would have invited no certainty in her. Gulang would not have negotiated at all, but would have sought to force her hand into a bargain. He was too much the conqueror for those delicate conversations.

Ungol was the right choice, but he worried for his friend. The spirits did not share human conceptions of loyalty, kinship or morality. They were unconcerned with the battles mortals fought amongst themselves, except in the power of those altercations to destroy. Fire was no friend to the tree. Corpses scattered across the earth may be seen as an insult to them.

There was too much uncertainty in this. Too much riding on a narrow chance at success in the face of a clash orchestrated by the gods.

A hollow wail washed over the canopy. Tree trunks creaked and swayed, showering the ground with brittle needles, shaking loose pine cones to thud against ground.

He stepped back. His gaze roved through the darkness, hunted for signs of the spirit, found nothing.

He settled himself as the wail died away. Its echoes felt in his soul, in vibrating nerves and knots in his throat and stomach.

Ungol had made contact, and the negotiation was begun. He waited for his friend's return, denied himself warmth and comfort at the side of his wife in favor of this disconcerting vigil. He needed to see the Dumas chief return, to know he was safe. Whatever the result of their encounter, he needed to know his friend was safe.

A Deepening Sickness

Shifting shadows crowded the edges of Ibrim's vision. In the eternal night gloom, figures danced crooked jigs in dark corners. Clambering arms pawed at slick, vitreous walls, raked at floor tiles, and vanished as soon as he tried to look at them. He was not sure if this sickness of the mind was the result of his daily infusions of God Ao Nii's fouled aura, or if those shadows were cloudy flashbacks, stunted by anger and fear and unable to develop into full apparitions in his mind's eye, but whose origins lay in the uelfin attack of a few night's prior.

He couldn't sleep. To fall asleep risked not waking up. He could not call it death, that final sleep, but he was sure the god or the spirits or both lurked in those shadows, watched from quiet places and waited for their opportunity to strike him down. Paranoia was his only protector. The acolytes patrolling the halls—a new feature to remind him of his vulnerability—were no comfort. Seun, in the next room over, was compromised. How long could he hold onto his strength. He had fallen, hadn't he? Fallen wracked by withdrawals from the cursed blood poison he had lived with since almost the day he was born. The Tului boy's strength waned, and he was certain some of the fault for his worsening condition lay with their god. His healing took on the edge of an infestation, an assault on the body, and who could say whether this exorcism was helping or harming Ibrim Alghoul's only friend more.

Those shadows seemed to laugh at him, to double over their slender bellies, clutch at their guts, their heads and shoulders shaking, and some animal part of him could not shake the idea that these shadows, these writhing figures, these desperate entities were real. That they were in this room with him, and every one had a mind and a soul.

It's all by design, this madness. First it's shadows. Then come the hammers to chip away the mortar holding you together. Soon, they'll be inside. Past the walls, in the palace halls, flaying me open with their teeth.

"What will be left, then."

Faez had not come to him in several days, now, he was sure of it. Time had taken on a strange edge when the shadows arrived. He lapsed into sleep at odd times, woke up not knowing how much of a day had passed. Faez had not come, but

A Deepening Sickness

the infusions had continued. Every day, before sleep seized him or after he awoke, cold sweat soaking through his night clothes, spasming with a sourceless terror whose beginnings lay with those last minutes of absence before his eyelids were dragged down, and he was defeated.

Who will protect me if Seun is not here? Who will keep the monsters away?

A hot, crimson flash flew out of him like a sparrow's wing. The shadows danced out of its path. The razor struck the little table across from his bed, cleaved it cleanly in two.

He recoiled against the wall, squeezed his eyes shut. If he denied himself the sight of what had happened, what had sprung from him, it couldn't have happened. If he could not see it, it wasn't real.

He lay there with his knees grinding into his sternum and his nails digging into his shins for what seemed like hours. In the wake of the unwilling expulsion, a hollow formed along the edge of his arm, a ridge of absence running from his shoulder along the outside path to the pit of his elbow. Cold oozed into the spiritual chasm. Slimy, digging fingers fluttered across the rift. He eased the afflicted arm away from his body, and a list of sharp objects flitted through his mind, implements he could use to cut it off before the infection could spread, before more of him could be compromised.

Where is he? This is his fault! His fault! HIS FAULT!

Where was Faez A'doelle? Was he not supposed to be protecting him from those...those freaks? If Seun must fall to sickness, a blight on his soul, should the bastard once slave turned soldier not be here guarding his door? Cutting off his arm or burning it before...before....

Before they are born?

He was not sure what would burst out of him when this strange infection took its course, but he was suddenly certain beyond doubt the rupture would be violent. Those first breaths would be seized while blood weltered over tiny bodies. The arm would shrivel up! Yes, yes, it would shrivel up like a green shoot left in the baking sun too long, and he would die then. He would die, and...and...and it would be over.

Bliss! Peace at last! How exquisite.

And dread. The preamble to any death must be a deep dread. A gut curdling comprehension that the undertaker was on his way, the barrow being constructed, or filled with gold and silver and gifts of silk and sweet cakes or whatever he'd take into the afterlife with him. Of course such myths, with all of their staying power, never held water. What use did Ul Sharak have for gold and silver? What bounty had she ever asked for? No, those were the makings of status, remembrances for the power and the might of a royal house, and he found he cherished them. He dreaded that his death would go unremarked, that his own family would not know he had gone beyond their reach. They would not come to visit him in Gur Tulain forest, or follow the band of Ul Sharak's river from its headwaters.

His death would be unremarked, except in its capacity to breed new life into those squirming, maddening *things!* Not even they would remember his passing.

But Seun? He'll remember, won't he? It will be his tears shed over my corpse that give me validation. That I was someone. *Someone of consequence. That I was someone, in someone else's eyes.*

A new flash of crimson stabbed out of him and struck the wall. Thunder sounded at the sight of collision. There were voices outside. In the hall. Running footsteps.

The sentries, those new ones who had been stationed there to watch over him, took notice. They were coming to him, to put him out of his misery maybe. Coming to him with a promise of absolution, of destruction.

And now they must care. Now they must care.

The sentries marched past, and he saw his madness reflected in them. Paranoia pressed itself into their features. A strange unwinding of their reservations twisted their features into manic grins, their teeth gnashed together, eyes wild and unfocused. Left others with vicious snarls to snatch harassed glances at the shadows, and still others to contend with a deepening sorrow as they dragged their legs after them, compelled to move down halls swift filling with fledgling acolytes as the Moon God's touch spurred them on toward the stairs and then into the streets.

He turned from his watch over the hall and marched to the vitreous wall, looked down into the city and saw the same frenzied abandon in the movements of its denizens. Clods of burning crimson light enshrouded clustered figures rendered dark by its cloying embrace, and they were being goaded toward the gate even as they launched themselves at each other.

Madness prevailed, and he yearned for it. Violence was imminent, soon to be upon him, and he reveled in the promise of blood, in the taste of it.

They will take notice of me soon, and I will see them all dead. See the ones who ignored me for so long brought low, and watch the life leave them.

His gaze flicked to the shadow people. He watched them fall over themselves laughing and nodding vigorously in agreement with him. People would have to die. But not Seun. Never him. He must survive this night, even if Ibrim himself did not.

His gaze shifted to the palace on its wide shelf. A bonfire glow soared from the tallest tower, and several lesser pyres rose up around other towers as a granular, gray aura spread over the lower domes. The granular aura rolled from the palace over the bluff and cascaded into the streets below, divorced masses of bleeding crimson from each other, as the people down there broke contact and ran with all the haste they could muster toward the gates.

He left his quarters then, left behind what few possessions he had been given, the safety and security of familiar trappings. A disheveled acolyte raised a belt knife in a shaking hand, his grip on it firm despite a greasy layer of sweat staining the leather under his fingers. He raised the knife to his own throat, held there for a moment as clarity washed over him, driving back the insane longing for crucial moments. He whispered a prayer, and slashed.

Blood painted the neck and shoulders of his pristine, white robe. He stood there as Ibrim watched him, and what the Tulakka prince saw in his eyes was relief. He fell to his knees and keeled over, smiling all the way down.

Ibrim stepped around him, careful to avoid getting the dying man's blood on his shoes.

They'll have to notice me. They'll have to care.

He glanced over his shoulder as he joined the frantic rush to reach those stairs and the exit, and saw no one in his wake.

Where is Seun? I'll find him. I will find him. I will protect him, and they will praise me for saving my friend.

He broke into a run, intent on catching up to his friend, his only friend, to

A Deepening Sickness

become a shield for him as he had been when Ibrim had needed one. To be his sword when his hand was empty and his back was exposed.

He ran, the walls blurring around him, as still others took blades to themselves, sought to end it before it began—this madness they all must wear in their souls. Ran in pursuit of a Tului commoner and exile, a Blood Lord who had turned his back on the way of his people, on the spirit who claimed them.

But the boy he had befriended, who he had grown fond of, was not with those others. The man he might one day come to love was behind him.

An internal battle between two flavors of madness raged within Seun as he stepped into the corridor. On one side, the irascible plague of grief and anger God Ao Nii's surrogates had pressed into him; on the other, the sick hunger granted him, a gift to a good servant, by Tuluis Fel. He had never been one to fear what might befall him. He had never been one concerned with pomp and spectacle, or the pursuit of power. He had been a liar, that was true, but to spare those others who had come to him in the night, the one other who had come a second time, and a third, the indignity of knowing him in truth.

Lufir al Seun had been born in the pens, had sired many children in his virile youth and had been bled for the succor of the Tului who kept him. There were nearly forty of his children being raised as he was, as livestock for consumption by the other Blood Lords, and he had been given this curse as a gift. Freedom, titles befitting his new station, the right to rise among the people and lay claim to something better than he would otherwise have had.

He had not known of the hibiscus, the cleansing power of iron, in those days. Most of those he sired were still children. They had a chance at a life if he could break them free, and he knew where they would be. Where some of them would be when he won free of this hold the dark spirit, Tuluis Fel, had on him.

All was according to a grand design, and when the moonkin madness arrived, a new curse to compel the old one into dissolution, it had not been fear or pride, grief or anger that came over him, but a reckless kind of bravery. A willingness to sacrifice himself to protect those others, to see them through this day, and all that unfolded when the moon crossed paths with the sun, when his god waged battle against his hated enemy.

He marched into the corridor, and saw Ibrim Alghoul rushing down the hall ahead of him, knew the pampered prince could not survive this conflict on his own, so used to letting others fight his battles for him. This was no place and no time for noble foolishness, nor regal spectacle.

He broke into a run, his shorter stature placing him at a disadvantage, stooped as he passed the dead acolyte at Ibrim's door and raked his fingers through the blood. He set it against his tongue, sucked it down and swallowed, and renewed life took root in him, bringing his curse flaring to life to rail against the affecting madness and its false promises, to drive it back into the corners of his mind and hold it at bay.

He ran after Ibrim, intent on saving the only friend he had ever known, so that he would not have to be alone again. Not ever again. So that he would not have to endure this burden by himself.

The God of Ways

The moon cut a line across the sky in plain sight, despite the time of day, and Lisandra watched it as she made haste to follow Jinga and Kiresh on the path. They were in Gonsai's shadow now, the wall looming to block the horizon, leaving just sight of the sun at its noon day peak and the moon swift closing on it in her sights.

Soon, the moon would eclipse the sun, and throw the world into darkness. In the nearest settlements, what peoples traced their lineages back to that mad god's domain would be taking measures against him, and against themselves. Strong bindings would be placed on their bodies, chains fixed to heavy weights, leather cords wrapped around their torsos and belted behind tables in dark cellars. Men would be burying themselves under makeshift cairns in deep woodland, or securing themselves in the high bows of great trees. Whatever it took to see them through this day, to stay their hands from doing violence against their chosen people, they would see it done. They *must* see it done.

She thought of that old woman in her village, the one who had been found when the eclipse had passed, dead and a ruin of herself in a house locked and bolted from the inside when she was still sane enough to take such measures. She thought of all the others like her who lived in this world, and wondered how many of them would not survive, how many would break their binds, return to places where mortals were plentiful, how many villages would be faced with their wrath as the madness suffused the lands, as God Ao Nii brought low his hated foe.

"We need to find cover." She said.

Kiresh followed her gaze to the sky.

"There will be safety in the wall." Jinga said.

"Will there?" Kiresh said absently.

"Gonsai will protect us." Jinga insisted. He picked up his pace, leading them at a trot toward the wall and what shelter it promised.

She found she did not believe him. What lay in Gonsai Wall might resemble safety for a time, but where mortals lived there was always a chance a forgotten moon child lived, too. If it was possible for one to blend into the fabric of her life in the Fingers, it could happen here as well.

She pursued, keeping speed with him and knowing at the same time she would come to regret it eventually. That the price of Kiresh's healing would come to bear for her when the energy leaked out, and the damage would be so much worse when it did.

She tested the sword in its scabbard at her hip, the counterfeit made for a man long dead by a man who never existed, and smelled the saccharine odor emanating from it as she slid it an inch out of that scabbard.

She did not trust in Gonsai the way Jinga did. Had not seen what protection he provided. And who could know where the great staircase would touch the land, what would arrive when it did.

No one was safe. Even those hulled up in their fastnesses in discrete places, the Nixians in their caves, the Sangar in their stone walled homes in towns and cities across this kingdom.

No one was safe when the Moon God was angered. No one was safe from his wrath.

"Shaki? Sha-Tamlin!" Chakta called. She watched as the moon invaded the day lit sky. The clouds which had been present that morning were driven away, leaving an open arena for the moon to make its challenge.

The moon was fat full and fast marching across that field. In an hour or so, it would be passing into the sun's path, blocking its light to cast the long shadow on the lands below. On *these* lands.

Shaki and Tamlin burst out of the pavilion. Both cast worried glances toward the snow dunes and the river. Ho'o whistled down from the north, his voice picking up volume as the winds ran from soft, chilling breezes to gales. She felt eyes on her, watching from deep shadows, suspected they belonged to the Swans, that they were keeping vigil over them, waiting for the moment they were needed.

Duijus Kanh slept in daylight. They ought to be sleeping, too, but as if drawn out by a magnet, they were there. Their presence felt beneath those high winds, before and behind the emanations of wild energy from the full moon, which had begun to pulse with red light, which had begun to stir up madness in its kin.

Shaki looked to the sky, saw what she saw, and flinched.

"Eclipse." He whispered. And Tamlin followed his gaze to the crimson shrouded moon, watched with them as it cut its war path toward the hated enemy, made its challenge for all of them to see.

"What do you make of it?" Shaki said.

"This is bad." Tamlin glanced back at the pavilion. "We need to find cover."

"Not there. We'll be exposed there." Chakta intoned. "The cave."

Tamlin's gaze cut an arc from the moon in the sky to the barely visible entrance to Duijus Kanh's cave far off in the distance.

If we leave now, we can make it. Go down and wake...but no. He won't accept us, will he? Not like that.

"The cave." He agreed.

In the distance, a melodious keening rose up. A familiar sound which curdled her blood. Voices raised in song. There were more of them than there had been before. Where before there had been dozens, now there were hundreds, a full bore assault coming straight for them.

"Not them!" Shaki said. "Not again!"

"Run." Tamlin said.

Tears for the Moon God

He did not wait for them to begin. He leapt from the long deck and bolted in the direction of the cave, and as he did, the first figures rose up among the snows, like phantom ghouls they emerged, and marched to close a net around them.

Chakta vaulted over the deck's edge and ran after Tamlin. Shaki followed in her wake. *The cave. We'll be safe there. We'll be safe if we reach the cave.*

Those creatures broke into a sprint, weapons out and running to intercept them.

Chakta dragged on the pulse of her spirit, pulled down his power into her. She wielded it as she had done that night when first these monsters attacked, and lashed out with illusory sounds, a pocket around them expanding to encompass as much territory as she could manage with her inexperience in the use of Galadir's arts.

The first lines of attackers tilted their heads as if straining to hear the song their brothers and sisters sang. Tamlin pulled a skinning knife from his belt, held backward in his right hand as he pelted toward that cave and the safety it offered; and Shaki lashed out with electric lances, taking two of those dozens down just ahead of them, another pair after them.

They ran, and the creatures closed the net, cut off their path of retreat, hemmed in the sides. They were drawing closed at the rear now, swarming them, intent on pulling them down and removing an obstacle from their path as a second group broke away from the first, and made speed for the cave itself, where Dupec and his protectors lay in wait for them.

Dupec. They're after him. They're going to kill him. Her thoughts came in a frenetic tangle as she fought to quell her nerves, to weaponize her anxiety and turn it into something useful. Something she could use in combat.

Shaki lashed out with electric barbs in every direction, left smoldering corpses to be replaced by fresh bodies, and it was all she could do to hold onto her illusory song, a counter melody she hoped, hoped to all the gods and the host of spirits, would cancel the song those monsters sang, rob them of precious insight long enough for them to counter, to form a rebuttal to the argument being lobbed against them, break out of this tangle of swarming, writhing bodies.

In the sky, the moon closed in on the sun, its aura flaring to life to match the sun's crown, promising blood and chaos, fire and death, bringing its vengeance to bear before them, as it was writ in the sky.

Xirakura watched through a patch of clean glass in his otherwise dirt caked window as the moon marched across the horizon. He had seen this event only in his mind's eye as elders told stories of the moon's long hatred for the sun to gaggles of wide eyed children at fireside. Had been one of those children watching as the spirit caller who preceded him wove together the framework and cast shadows in the flickering light with dolls made of twigs and woven cloth, to tell the story of a god driven mad by grief.

In all of his years of life, he had never suspected he would live to see it, would be caught in its embrace, in the path of totality even less so. The moon marched across the sky, and in the lands and the sea, spirits took note. The lesser among them cowered in fear, and he heard their whispers in the breezes. A north wind was blowing across Faed City, bringing with it warmth and fair weather. Zanzark was brooding somewhere beyond the city's borders.

The God of Ways

He felt an itch building across his belly, and knew the Chained One had come aware of the march of the moon on its warpath, and wondered if he also felt fear. Or if that itch was an echo of his laughter as the ones who in the earliest days sought to bind him now sought to drive each other out of the sky, to raze the lands and break them with their contest, and leave one and other bloodied and near death's door.

He wondered, too, how the other gods would meet their contest. The moon and the sun were vital to mortal kind, but he did not believe their purpose served the others of their order in the same way. Those immortal entities could survive without food crops to sustain them, without the tides to carry them across water, or heat to bring on the rains. He wondered if they would let this contest come to pass, or if even now they sought to contain those creatures among them who threatened to bring their balance of powers to its knees.

He felt the Empress's fury in waters churned suddenly and sharply to violence, and the anger of the lesser spirits she commanded as echoes of her own. And he knew the waters would not rest until this clash had concluded.

Somewhere out there, the God Houses of Sun and Moon would make contact with the lands, and violence would spill forth from them. He hoped it was not here. That he would escape this day without seeing any blood shed.

He knew he would not escape. That even now the place and time of this contest had been set, and he was well within the path of ruin. Soon, those creatures would spill forth into the land, and their hosts would come with them. And the Magura were unprepared. The traders in their craft on the water's edge were not prepared. None of them were prepared.

He ambled to the table at his bedside and picked up a rawhide cord. He laced it around his midriff and tucked himself into it, and then fastened his gourd in place. It may not be the done thing to be seen in his natural dress in these lands, but he would not have any interruptions to his craft. He would go to that medicine man who shunned him, and place himself in his service. Surely, a mounting catastrophe of this magnitude would make him see sense. Surely he would leave behind his prejudices, invite a helping hand into the fold.

Xirakura could be of use to these people. He *must* convince them of his use. *There is no one in this land who can stand against a god. They do not remember the old ways. They will be of no use in this conflict, and their people will not survive if they cannot meet the challenge against them.*

He ventured out of his rooms, and then out of the inn, into a street where he went unnoticed. The Magura were too busy preparing for the inevitable. Traders among them were too preoccupied with gathering their effects and getting out.

When the moon crossed paths with the sun, they knew there would be violence, and none of them who had the option at hand wanted to be around to see it. He did not blame them for their fear.

God Uldal sat atop his hill, the doorways onto countless paths spanning the world below and beyond flitting in and out of focus, revealing well traveled roads and newly set passages which required his sanctioning or denied his touch. He saw new paths converging, a crossroads inviting into it three powers who ought to remain separate, and knew the newest play of hands in the Greatest Game was underway. Knew, too, that the time to choose a side had presented itself, and he

Tears for the Moon God

could not deny its pull any longer.

A falling star punched the ground, another following parallel to its path. Both stabbed straight down out of a clear, blue sky, as two gods with grievances against each other so long in building and so well maintained that neither would run away from their contest, denied the Goddess of Storms her claim as writ in the clouds she sent to crowd its edges. In a disparate place, well removed from this one, a second crossroads was writ into the annals of time as still more forces loomed in a city off the coast of a vast bay, where once a hand rose up in the name of his father, and carved that name into the records of history with a sword that never was.

In his stead stood a Spirit Caller, a man of a tribe long forgotten by most others who inhabited the world, which kept to itself as stewards over an ancient shrine, and he was marked by the lover of the monster he had sworn to guard, marked by His hand, to carry out His will.

In another place, an old crone who had lost her shield made swift progress to reclaim it, but was hindered by attacks from singers loyal to a snake; but whom was driven forth by the hand of fate, or would be if God Uldal's oldest friend did not walk in her shadow. No, Fate's hand was on the father of a man who never was, driving him to move her onward, into the place where she *should* cease.

In another still, three children of chiefs looked into the sky from the winter home they had known all their lives, which resembled nothing in their memories, and watched as the moon and sun closed on each other, watched and hoped the spirit of a cave would protect them. He shared the uncertainty of those children, and knew a fear deep in his soul, a pervasive infestation as he had not felt in so many generations as to lose count of them. Those measures of time were for mortals. The arc of his life was far longer, and yet the memories he held of his time of life were few.

A resurgence of melancholy stabbed through the fear, and he was reminded of a village in the mountains, then towering peaks and jagged slopes, which were now just more than hills, their tops round and green, their slopes rolling and plunging into deep, lush valleys. He was reminded of a people who lived in forests, and only came to the river's edge at night, to drop offering into it, and gab and laugh and make merry as a god walked among them, intent on a certain house high up slope, at the forest's edge, where he would meet again with his lover.

A man who shined like the sun, and was killed by him.

Before him, on the hillside, sat his three most seasoned acolytes, each of them ready to lead his forces into the world. Beyond the hilltop and its many doors were amassed all of the others, hundreds of them ready to go into the world, where, for some of them, death awaited.

He cracked his jaw, parted his lips, and called out for all of them to hear. His voice rolled over them like thunder. All but two had gathered at his call, for he had denied those two word of his will.

"Darkness follows in a woman's footsteps. He passes his watch to the Father of Roads. The Moon weeps tears of blood for the lover he lost, and knows new anger at the reclamation of one who he sees as friend! The Hunt is called. In the Name of God Uldal, the Hunt is called. We go to defend the people, *spawn* of the Great River! And I go to meet my friend, to push him back, to spare him the embrace of death! A fate no god should know!"

He rose, and with him the other three. His lieutenants descended the hilltop in

The God of Ways

three directions, and opened the doors into three places. The rank and file of acolytes marched for the doors, all fixed on those crossroads, places where energy built and chaos threatened to rule. Stony faces looked back at him as the first ranks passed into the world, heralding the arrival of eclipse for the first time in thirty years, and the arrival of madness to those kin of God Ao Nii who had chosen a different path, a different life.

He hoped they had seen it coming. That even now they were bound to tables with old belts, or barricaded in root cellars. That they would *survive* this day, and know not death's cold embrace either.

Strike at the Heart

Somewhere across the world, daylight touched on mortal faces turned up in horror, and the moon marched to block the sun as two gods sought conflict with each other, but there was no moon in the sky over Cratom. In the city, a new unfolding of the Greatest Game was underway, and Wu an unsuspecting pawn in the broader conflict between the gods.

Fate scribbled frantically in her diary, snaring lives in her designs as her rival and newfound ally toiled in the north to place the pieces in his game where they might lay slaughter, and hobble the efforts, the complex designs of their enemies.

Ao Nii marched across a day lit sky halfway around the world, and here, memory of him was forgotten. His taint was abated, his attention so fixed on his ancient enemy that other gods could carry out their plans for this city with impunity, unbothered by the influence of others who might stand against them.

The eyes of the gods, their enemies, were turned away from Cratom, leaving exposed those pawns of most influence in the eyes of their betters, in the eyes of elder figures who sought to wield them against them.

There would be blood this night. Wu tasted it on his tongue, reveled in the thought of it as cold settled over him and the streets of the city, so teaming with life, were ensnared in the Greatest Game. He would have his revenge this night, and no one would stand in his way.

He marched on the fortress of his enemy with Garam in tow, the Hunter casting nervous glances at shadows as they marched up a hill street toward a sprawling mansion, its shadow looming heavy over the slope, painting the facades of nearby dwellings from behind a fence of wrought iron spears, the monster's own teeth.

The fence was patrolled by agents of Raukha, strong men armed with mauls, with hidden knives scattered across their bodies, barrel chests and bald heads and gazes cold with murderous intent.

The gates were flung open, and from them spilled new entities. Men threw open the doors of his childhood home and marched down the pristine, stone path as trees kept in bloom by unnatural forces showered the yard with white petals, a fall to mirror the stars scattered across the wide open sky.

Firelight played against hard faces as they swarmed past the guards and spilled

Strike at the Heart

into the city in search of the mistress's young son, his brother. He pressed himself into a shadow, the paths he traveled scattered into disarray under his feet, denying those among them who specialized in tracking sign or symbol of his presence. Behind him, Garam blended into the shadows and was lost to their sight.

They lingered in that shadow as figures darted past them, as Lambs spread out along side streets and traveled down alleys, most intent for the slums. No few marched on the red light districts, or made headway for the streets choked with revelers and carousers celebrating the night at taverns and in brothels and opium lounges and gambling dens that would soon find themselves at the heart of violent insurgencies.

There would be innocent blood spilled there, too.

The last of them well away and in pursuit of conspirators, of enemies they would use this excuse to destroy, he moved for the gates and those strong men.

And Garam moved past him, a blur crossing through scattered shadows, closing in on his targets with fluid grace, a black bladed dagger in his hand.

He reached up, unconcerned by the roving eyes of those strong men, slid his blade under one man's ribs, turned as he wrenched it free and carved a line across the other's throat. The gates still open, he marched onto the path between them as their bodies fell, and blood painted the road around them.

Wu followed. Snowy petals to mark their passing. Boot prints in blood to tell of their presence. He marched toward his long awaited fate, and down in the city a commotion rose.

Screams of terror and rage echoed up the hill to greet them with the promise that violence had been done, and with it, a keening song sung in many voices. A song that should not have been, for the uelfin were no part of this conflict. And the uelfin had come.

Haffa saw them coming. Uelfin not of his tribe descended on the streets, rose among the rank and file of revelers in the streets below. He heard their song, a song sung in so many voices it would be impossible to snuff them all out. God Lanfin brought war into the streets of Cratom, the city looming on the bank of Oe's band. At last, after all of these years of silence, he brought his song to bear against her, brought his uelfin to challenge the sanctuary for her kin.

He had never wanted them. The earliest of the uelfin who spilled from her banks he had sought to murder as soon as they passed into the world, as soon as air filled their lungs, but she had shielded them. Had railed against her lover, a feud spurred on by her desire to keep these children, to deny death's embrace from taking them so soon.

He had not wanted them, yet he used them. Had used them for so long it seemed he would never breach this tenuous peace between the god and the river. Here was evidence of a change come over him. The god brought his loyalists into the one place the world over they were restricted from entering, and broke with a tradition thousands of years old.

The uelfin were coming, and he could not ignore them.

He marched to the edge of his balcony, gripped the rail, opened his throat.

Sonorous song spilled forth from his lungs, drowning out the confused screams and panicked shouts of the humans in those streets, the Goths and others, visitors and residents of the one true stronghold along Oe's band. The one settlement she had ever sanctioned to thrive along her shores.

He sang, and other uelfin joined his song, others loyal to the Mother. Sang a song of lament, of grief for what was lost, what would be. Flashes of the future arose in his mind's eye, a moment by moment play as he and his kin sought to arrest control from those enemies, to force a silence, deny them their sight.

He sang, and in his song was a call to the river, to her descendants, to rise against these creatures. To see their blood paint the streets below. To see them dragged into the river and buried under her silts, their last breaths choked off.

Within the song sung in the enemy's voice was a shaping, the beginnings of an ugly thing, a future in which the gods prevailed and man was thrust into servitude beneath their heels, crushed and destroyed, their civilizations razed, spirits dashed against stones and murdered, opening wastes in the world as the people died in scores, in hundreds, in thousands.

He heard the Father's voice behind their song, heard in it his intent. That they would be spared as his chosen people, to rule over all of those others they sought to command, as kings and lords the world over.

A false promise.

They should have known, should even now be railing against him. As Cratom broke the taboo, and sung in counter tune to those uelfin and their father, he knew the uelfin of Cratom faced extermination if they could not push these creatures off. Knew that what was decided in this clash was the fate of his people, his way of life, and that the god's loyalists were all too keen to see it done. To see the destruction of their cousins, those who had pledged themselves to the river.

Samil vaulted upright on the bed as the song arose to greet Rhul and his captive in this house that belonged to none of them. "What is that?"

Rhul crossed to the windows, drew a curtain aside and looked out on the street. No one was in sight. It seemed Mistress Bane's agents were not on them yet, had not become desperate enough in their pursuit of her son, the heir of House Bane, to spread their net this wide. He heard the warring songs in streets not far removed from where they were hulled up, and let the curtain fall.

"Strange." He whispered. "Whatever it is, it is not intended for us."

"Oh, it is." Saijin drawled. He lifted his wine jug to his lips and took a long pull. "God Lanfin has made his decision. He is no longer content to watch from the wings as our people use his gifts for our own gain.

"He is coming to mend what was broken with my *sin*."

"What sin is that?" Samil sounded worried. He watched the uelfin apprehensively, waiting for the truth to be unveiled.

Rhul's gaze settled on the uelfin, and what was painted into his soft features was not concern but simpler frustration.

The bottle thunked against the carpet where Saijin leaned against the wall—scattered light crisscrossing his pallid skin, illuminating scarlet eyes. "There is one taboo on an uelfin's gift." He wagged his finger, following its progress with unfocused eyes. "We are *never* to sing in counter-tune to our Father, lest he smite us.

"There have been others. Oh, no, Rhul Bane, I am far from the first to violate this taboo. Every one of us who has was born *here*. Each of them stood alone, raised their voice in protest. It was all a futile effort, really. What have any of us accomplished in the *grand* scheme.

"He wants dominance. Always has." He belched loudly, and covered his mouth, his throat working to keep down worse. "Thus far, I think, he has been satisfied with seizing the bad actors, tossing them into his halls where they can do no more damage."

"Wouldn't that have a destabilizing effect on time?" Rhul said.

"Why would it? We're not God Katcya's brood. All of the elements of our emergence are here, in this world and well enough contained. He simply does not want death with her many appendages to have us.

"But he's coming now. His forces precede him, but he will come before it is over. I think."

"What possible—"

"That's just it. It's not some remote possibility that bothers him. I can hear it in his voice. He is shaken. He did not expect us to resist."

Then we need to leave. Now!"

"No, no." Saijin waved the idea away. "*You* need to defend us. Buy time for your Core to finish what he started. He will not leave until he has."

Rhul returned to his vigil of the street. Words refused him.

God Lanfin is coming. What chance do we stand against him.

"Oe will protect us." Saijin said, his words slurring. "What good are we to her if we're all dead?"

Samil met his gaze. "What good is she to us if *she* is dead?"

Saijin cackled. "What you humans fail to understand never ceases to surprise. We were never her guardians, kid. She is ours. Why do you think God Lanfin has left us alone this long? He loathes our kind, remember? No, he has left us well enough alone here for a reason. He is *afraid* of her."

"Not enough to stay away, it seems." Rhul mumbled.

"Well, the situation has changed, hasn't it?" Saijin snapped. "It's not just two katcyakin in the world these days. There are thousands."

Eclipse

A keening song filled the air, washed over Lisandra's back as she pelted after Jinga and Kiresh. They were close now, the gap just ahead of them. If they could just make it past, then perhaps they would find a force awaiting them, a garrison stationed at some way point near the entrance into the canyon who might relieve them in combat, bring themselves to bear against the uelfin laying chase.

The song broke, a chorus of cackles interrupting the harmonious, high singing. That sound made her blood run cold.

Figures emerged along the uneven shelf at the walls height. Broad, meaty shoulders dipped and twisted as they dragged themselves forward on long forearms, their wide, long heads turning this way and that, taking in sight of the Nixians, Lisandra, the insurgent force hammering after them, closing the distance with weapons bared and hangers back opening their throats to belt out verses replete of lyrics.

They crowded the cliff edge. Some came on with children at their sides, or cradled in slab arms. Some plopped down lazily on their rumps, ham-like legs splayed open, wide feet dangling over the edges.

She watched as more and more gorillas emerged atop that cliff to watch the drama unfold below, wondered at their presence. What it meant. Whole harems arrived together, the intervening spaces between them enough to keep the males happy, to prevent conflict in the face of this mortal clash. They watched, and the gap grew closer, closer still.

They were so damned close. A hundred or so more paces and they would be inside. Just that, and then Gonsai, if Jinga's suspicions proved correct, would come to their rescue, would save them before they were enmeshed in what could only end in slaughter, in their deaths.

The earth rumbled under her feet, threatened her footing as she hurried on. Those gorillas watched from atop the rise, hundreds of them gathered for this vigil over the south lands.

A gargantuan beast swung into view. A towering figure like them, its head round, its face white as ash and streaked with red across its forehead and wrinkled cheeks. It vaulted off one wall, spun round in mid leap and slammed into the other. Leapt back to the first and struck lower, lower still, and then slammed into the ground with a tooth rattling *CRASH!*

Eclipse

Jinga stopped short ahead of her. She nearly ran into his back for trying to draw herself down, slow and then halt with him. Kiresh was backing up, away from the wall, back toward the uelfin, their murderous pursuers.

Is something wrong? Is this not supposed to be our...our protector?

Gonsai towered over them, filling the gap to a third of its height. Thick, slab forearms were shielded behind gilt gauntlets inlaid with jade ridges in the shapes of great trees, scenes of forest and bluff, river and shadowed valley rendered in arresting detail. His fists were shielded in ropes of thick chain, the knuckles encased behind cook-pot housings. A white crest ran from the top of his head down his back, parting a sea of dense, black fur.

He reared onto legs so densely muscled they might be mistaken for stone themselves, bulging boulders cemented together with fleshy mortar where thick tendons contracted under his weight.

The spirit spread his arms.

Vines shot from the walls, twisted together to form thick, braided ropes and then chains that he caught in bulging, veiny fists.

He dragged on them, stepped back as he increased the tension, and doors carved out of shale and granite and raw ore crawled out of the walls, grated across the floor of the gap. They closed off their best hope of retreat, barring them and their enemies alike access to the wall, and safety.

She surged forward, and was barred by Jinga from moving any further.

"He'll kill us." He whispered. "If we break through that wall, he will kill us."

"You said—"

"It doesn't matter now. Gonsai will not help us." He said, and for the first time she heard an edge of fear creeping into his voice. Knew his hope of a clean exit had died with the spirit's intervention.

The gorillas amassed along the heights watched on as the uelfin closed in behind them, and she turned to meet them, dropped her pack from her shoulders and drew the counterfeit sword from its sheath. If she must die, if it was her fate to die here having accomplished nothing—having left her people to the Saodeini occupiers and their greed—then she would die on her feet. She would stand and face this terrible foe, and die swinging her sword for their throats.

It was the way of a warrior to die in combat, or spend her waning years jumping at shadows and laying awake in the night. She had been tested. Again and again she had been tested.

And she was ready.

Jinga unslung his pack, dropped it at his feet and pulled the drawstring loose. He rummaged through its contents.

"Is now really the time to go...." She did not dare take her eye off the approaching force, a full company of those uelfin, all charging with their arrogance on them, advantaged by that future song.

"I was going to sell these." He came away with an egg shaped object the size of his fist in each hand. A loop was fixed to the tip of each bauble, and the sides were beveled to promote a firmer grip.

He clamped his teeth around the tin loop in the height of one of them and wrenched a thin, cylindrical stopper free. He hefted the object and threw it with all the force he could manage.

A preemptive, collective flinching away among the rank and file of charging

Tears for the Moon God

uelfin near the sight of impact.

A violent explosion.

Earth erupted. Bodies came apart in explosions of gore. Still more were knocked flat, cut open where metal fragments from the explosive lashed across them, opening deep gouges and puncture wounds across their flanks, punching through the tender gaps between ribs to strike lungs and hearts.

Some twenty bodies fell to the initial blast. Another two dozen were knocked back by the blast. The uninjured among them scrambled away from the sight of impact as he pulled the pin on the second bomb, reeled back and threw it into their ranks.

The lead elements surged on, and Lisandra stepped into Jinga's path, intent on defending him as he pulled two more of those strange parcels free.

"Is this what Baduhrak engineering looks like." She said.

A manic grin spread across his face. "If you only knew."

He tossed another bomb. It detonated, opening a crater in the ground as more bodies flew away and apart, gore showering the nearest uelfin soldiers, and the sound of that detonation drowned out the singing for precious moments as the front ranks made contact.

Kiresh drew twin short swords from their sheaths at his hips, and they stepped forward, Lisandra dropping into the opening movements of a dance she knew well. A dance of death, flashing steel biting into bodies as new eruptions rang out, drowned out raised voices, denied the uelfin their access to that future.

They fell to her sword. One and then the next. Another.

Dozens came to fill the gaps. Carving knives and swords licked out to dig into her flesh, driving her onto the defensive as she sought purchase on shaking earth, fought to keep her movements loose and fluid, to steady herself against the rocking, warbling quakes as the gap fell shut behind them, and Gonsai sealed himself in.

Ibrim thrust out his elbows, knocked down those who were in his way as the stone doors out of the barracks loomed high and wide before him.

They were open. A stream of acolytes and initiates all wearing crimson light poured out of them in droves to join the chaos beyond. The rolling wave of gray crawled after the masses. He broke into a run as soon as he was past those doors, drove straight for the distant gates and the staircase into the world below.

Would anyone challenge his passing on the way down? Would there be those in the mortal coil who sought to join these ranks?

He hoped so. There would be a chance for recognition then. As a survivor of the long march down the staircase, embraced by the taint of madness, to survive the conflicts with those people with their cudgels, and hammers and maces and swords. He would fell them like trees, touch down on the earth and sew violence into whatever reach he arrived at while the staircase loomed behind him, pure white steps echoing the moon's light, painted with the blood of so many countless others, those brazen enough to make the challenge.

He would survive, and he would rise in the favor of his god because he survived. He would know the taste of that beautiful, sweet praise, that his god saw him and saw a man worthy. That he passed this test, came into a new world in which he again possessed power, status, influence. He would earn his right to be seen.

He vaulted over acolytes taken in the throes of grief, sobbing as they bashed their heads against the flagstones, or drove knives deep into their own flesh, or clawed at their eyes, ripped them from their sockets. And he ignored them.

Those were the weak. Those who lacked his strength of will, his certainty in himself. They deserved to be where they were, falling on their faces, grieving and denying themselves the succor of a power they had so vehemently sought out in the months or years before this great convergence came to bear.

He wove between these figures clad in his small clothes and nothing else, and he was not alone in the way he was dressed. Others spilled forth from houses and from side streets in the state of dress of those who had been struck dumb by fury. Those were his people, he realized. Those who embraced abandon, the truth of mankind—that it was violent, foul, and lewd, that it sought always to benefit itself, whatever the cost to others.

He witnessed a truth unfolding before him. A personal truth, deep held and unmolested by the norms and expectations of a society he had never embraced, a family who had only deigned to embrace him out of some familial sense of obligation. He could run from all of those who sought to place him in a box, constrain his desires, and in doing so he would be free.

Free to be this agent in the grand scheme, to become chaos, to sew it into the world around him and know his perfect right to have peace. That the suffering of others was no bar to his carnal need, that if he so demanded, he could take what he wanted, and no one could stop him.

Recognition be damned. He may ask for it and receive none. But if he demanded it. If he demanded respect, power would follow. Status would follow. All those things he cherished would be his. If he only demanded it.

He punched an acolyte ahead of him in the back of the head, knocked him flat against the flagstones on his way by, and surged onto the stairs. Down below was a world unsuspecting, a world wherein he could have all he ever desired, a chaos unfolding even as he rushed headlong toward it, unafraid, unconcerned. Down below, he would earn his place in the great order of mortals, and carve out the beginning of his rise to power in their blood.

It was his right. As a prince. As an acolyte of God Ao Nii. *It is my right!*

Mistress Bane

The entrance to the Bane estates was unguarded. The halls sprawled out before Wu Bane and Garam, enticing them to step easily. He sensed a trap in the silence, wondered if the mistress was aware of them, had known of his presence in the city.

Garam stepped into the hall, lifted his nose and inhaled.

"They're waiting for us." He said, his eyes fluttering open.

"Then we should meet them." Wu said.

They marched down the entrance hall. Fine china rested on ornate tables along this central corridor. White roses frosted the lips of vases. Portraits lined the walls, of past dignitaries who had held the station his father had occupied for so long. Figures from other families, all sharing in common with him the wide faces, mono-lidded eyes and planar cheeks of the Goth people.

They passed through shadowed reaches in pursuit of a greater light from the series of bay windows fronting the broad courtyard at the center of the complex, where he had so often taken tea amid the blooms with his mother, before her disappearance.

As they neared the crossing corridor, a knife flashed out from darkness. Wu met that blade with a dagger drawn, steel flashing in the low light, a ringing sound echoing away from the contact.

He ducked under a following blow, pulling his other blade free of its sheath and thrusting, stabbing into the meat of the assassin's neck.

Others broke out of the shadows, all bearing black bladed weapons, swarming on Wu and Garam as they descended into the fray.

In the distance, sticks beat together, a clattering, hypnotic rhythm to accompany the sounds of steel biting against steel.

Shadowed figures all clad in black from their necks to their toes. Soft whispers of boots against carpet. The easy groan of ancient floorboards protesting under the weight of those figures as they converged from two sides to meet the acolytes of Ways and Hunters.

Wu dropped into a crouch and bounded off his heels, his knife biting into the thigh of an assassin and drawing away, leaving blood to well over cloth as the assassin shifted his weight onto his good leg and pivoted out of the way of a trailing

Mistress Bane

swing from his other blade.

Garam faded from sight.

Steel rang out against steel somewhere farther removed from him as he met another Hunter. A blade rasped against dense cloth, found a home. Another body dropped.

Wu pitched out of the path of a dagger bearing down on him from above. An errant pull slammed him against the floorboards as something heavy struck him from behind. He reached up, made contact with exposed skin and bled his power into the assassin there, denying him his tether to the spirit he served.

The greater weight abated, and he rolled onto his back, carving a wide arc across the assassin's ribs.

A dagger punched a hole in the floorboards next to his cheek, missing by bare degrees.

He smashed the hilt of his knife into the assassin's elbow joint, shattering it.

"Urngh!" The assassin recoiled, and he drove his other blade into his stomach, disemboweling him.

He rolled over, hamstringing another and shoving him aside as he climbed to his feet.

Clack, clack, clack. The percussive music suffused the hall.

He barreled forward, throwing two assassins off their feet as he charged past them, seeking better light by which to see.

Shadows swarmed to close the gap. Harsh light flashed and smoke spilled into the hall. A piercing scream issued from an assassin's throat as Garam materialized in the gloom at the crossing.

Assassins swarmed him as Wu sought to join him there, forcing him to correct his course as several knives flashed out at once. A white flash as another smoke bomb exploded at Garam's feet.

The Hunter leapt out of its path as the explosion reverberated, unnatural force from the detonation throwing him back as the nearest wall shattered.

Wood chips danced across Wu's path.

An arrow punched through glass, whizzed past his head as he pitched sideways.

"Damn you, Jensen!" Garam bellowed.

Another flash bang imbued with festering power rolled into his path and he kicked it down the hall.

Wu pelted into the crossing and around the corner as the latest charge exploded, blasting away chunks of wall, shattering porcelain, sending flower petals and mangled flesh flying in every direction.

"Watch it!" came a booming voice as another assassin emerged in the crossing, a burly brute who bore a vague resemblance to Dupec.

He lashed out with a slab-headed hammer. The head slammed into the ground, and the floorboards reverberated.

"Run!" Garam shouted as the ceiling caved in, the wall into the garden coming down behind him.

Wu broke into a sprint, out into the courtyard. Several arrows thrashed across the expanse all at once, punching holes into soft ground, blasting holes into the scattered trees, smashing stone tiles.

He rolled into the shadow of a nearby tree, hunted across the roof for signs of the assailant.

Tears for the Moon God

There.

He shook a throwing knife out of his sleeve, cranked back and threw it.

The archer fell back against the roof. The dagger whizzed by.

He readied another as the archer rolled to the side and righted himself, aiming a crossbow at the place where he hid. The second dagger caught him in the throat.

Garam fought four assassins at once, lashing out with knives, a flurry of blows parried, shoved aside, as he flashed in and out of focus.

A dagger left Garam's hand and was replaced in the next instant by another. The first sailed across the yard, catching a would be attacker in the throat as an impending blade came for Wu's back.

Wu scrambled out of the way as another blade flashed for his eye, reached out as the man with the hammer emerged behind him.

He sought flesh, missed, spun away from the hammer and ran to a safe distance. The hammer's impact rattled through the ground. He missed a step and collided with the ground.

More assassins were pouring out of the adjoining halls, surging forth to take position behind trees. Another assassin lunged, dove into a water feature, a coy pond which had no place in his memories.

Blades of compressed water flashed away from the pool as he rose, cloaked now in those waters.

Black specks floated in Wu's eyes. His lungs constricted.

Weakly, he loosed a dagger, caught the assassin in the shoulder, distracting her long enough that he could win free.

"Run, I said! Their Shepherd!" Garam thrust his dagger in the direction of the pond.

More water blades whizzed away from it, and pelted through an opening made by Garam, seeking the doors, shelter, a means of getting away from the Shepherd and his peculiar, dangerous abilities.

Clack, clack, clack. The rhythm obscured the sounds of their footfalls. Garam fell into step with him, slashing at assassins to either side as he pursued.

"Where is she?" Wu said.

"Not far from here." Garam pushed past him. The assassins laid chase behind him, their progress hindered briefly by the narrow door into this wing of the mansion.

"The Shepherd?"

"My master." Garam growled. "The piece of shit."

Smoke.

A loud crash as a wall gave way. Charging feet. The weight of impact struck Wu hard in the ribs. He was vaulted off his feet, carried through another wall, into a guest room, thrown aside.

Assassins boiled out of the shadows.

He struck the bed. Knives thrust into it, and he pitched to the side, opening one path and rolling out of another into a connecting hall. As he climbed to his feet, throwing knives left Wu Bane's hands, struck home in one man's eye socket, under another's clavicle.

The bull crashed through the wall next to the open door into this room. He tensed his fingers, knuckles bloodied ruins wearing splinters.

Wu backed away, ran down the hall.

Mistress Bane

He opened another path, into the hall the assassin had taken him from, leapt through and clamped it shut behind him.

Garam was nowhere in sight. He backed up the hall, shadows shifting along the walls, threatening renewed violence.

He was alone now. Exposed, and alone.

The cadence of the song shifted. A call and response, echoing shouts from God Lanfin's uelfin. Something was coming, and Haffa's lament took on a tortured, desperate edge as he resisted with the others, resisted the song of destruction.

Along the riverfront below, cargo boats, grain barges and ferries choked with tourists and citizens cut their lines, fled into Oe's band and greater safety. The press of that rival song drove needles into his brain, washed his body with fire, and still he sang.

In the streets beyond his matchmaker's house, steel rang against steel, screams lashed out, adding their own chaotic melodies to the song the uelfin sang. The air was suffused with raw energy. Thunderous booms echoed as another force which had no investment in this battle navigated the lanes in search of something, someone, who was not here.

The Raukhas took advantage of the chaos in pursuit of their aims. Enemies were struck down in the visions of the future he saw. Flashes of the road behind him where innocents died in scores. Where the masses quaked and shivered, desperate mothers clung to children, shoved them through crowds toward boats already too far away for those little ones to swim to, which would not take them in even if they reached them.

Smaller gondolas, fishing boats and leisure craft became the subjects of other fights as innocents of all stripes sought to take them for themselves, driven into rabid clashes with deadly results as he watched on.

Glassy eyes looked back at him, imploring him to stay death's touch as he railed against the insurgent force, his focus elsewhere, his nerves rattled.

A god's voice took on sharp edges, drove into his mind and cut him off from the vision he sought, the shaping he structured. The song died in his throat, and he crumpled, fell over the balcony and into the street, and the masses trampled him.

Tension built in Saijin's mind, driving back the drink with sobering visions of death and destruction. He kept vigil over the events unfolding in the city as God Lanfin's harsh, echoing chants fused with those of his loyalists, emboldening them with the coming of the god himself into the world. Drawn down into Time's River, leaving himself vulnerable, exposed to the machinations of other gods and spirits.

And a new song rose up to meet him—a song in a woman's voice, low and melodious, a contralto matching his power and his range. The great snake was stirred awake, and she was angry.

The assassins in pursuit, Wu searched his mind for an obvious place, a place where his stepmother would feel safe, secure and well away from the conflict spanning her stolen estates. Blades whizzed past him. Daggers bit for his flanks, missing by spare degrees. Walls exploded and smoke filled the air, blocking off sight in one hall and then the next.

He drew on his power, planted himself in new halls to find them teaming with

Tears for the Moon God

shadows bearing black blades and heavier weapons. A staff sailed across his shins, knocking him onto his back as a following blow from its weighted end arced for his chest.

He rolled out of its path, down an adjacent corridor, opening a new path as he did, and arriving in a dining chamber.

Still more blades sailed out of the shadows. *How many men does she have!*

He crawled across the floor, breaking into a run before he had righted himself. A short sword sailed into his path.

The assassin crumpled, blood flying from a vicious neck wound.

"I found you!" Garam said.

And he was running with him, out of the room, into a connecting hall.

"She'll be in her safe room. She'll have your father in there, too." Garam said. "Are you ready for him?"

"I'll have to be." Wu said. But he had not anticipated his father being present. Some part of him had hoped the man would be away on some errand in the capitol, well removed from this house. It had been a misguided hope, informed by his feelings. But he had hoped nonetheless.

He did not value murdering the monster in front of the man who had chosen, for better or worse, to love her.

Garam took helm, led him down an adjoining corridor, a bank of windows to one side looking out on a smaller garden and the sprawling estate beyond. They passed Samil's room, where a conspicuously placed dagger had carved the hornet's nest from its branch spare hours ago.

Down another hall, and another, until they were deep within the bowels of the mansion. Assassins broke from shadows as they passed. More knives sailing. Arrows punching from adjoining rooms as they passed.

And then Garam slowed, and slammed his shoulder against a locked door. The door did not give.

Wu held him back when he mounted another attempt.

Assassins poured into the hall from both sides, a force amounting to a small army.

"Let me." Wu said.

He opened a path in the place of that door, shoved Garam through and climbed through after him.

On the other side of the door, the first assassins arrived. They beat against it, sought to bash it down and were rebuffed.

"MOVE!" came a gruff shout from outside.

"Hurry now." Garam said.

The chambers they had entered were lavish. A four poster bed dominated the chamber, lace curtains woven with intricate, floral patterns shrouding the sides. The room was windowless, a box containing so many fineries it began to resemble a museum for lost treasures.

Mistress Bane valued opulence. She had only embellished these chambers more with his long years of absence.

Garam found a bust in one corner and wrenched the head to one side.

A lock in the floor thumped open. The edges of a rug fluttered.

Garam wrenched it aside.

Behind them, the door to this chamber warbled open, revealing the silhouette of a wide chested man, with a lithe woman standing just within his shadow. She was dripping wet.

"In! Now!"

Garam wrenched the trapdoor open. Wu rushed down the steps it hid and Garam slammed the door shut behind him.

"Wait, no!" Wu shouted as the door fell into the floor.

Go to your victory, Wu!" Garam said on the other side.

"What is the meaning of this, Garam." The wide chested man demanded. "Have you betrayed us?"

"On the contrary, I have simply chosen a different master." Garam said.

"Move aside!" The woman demanded.

Broken pottery clattered to the ground.

"You'll pay for that!"

"I'm sure the mistress can handle herself."

Wu contemplated opening a path back into the room. The trap door would serve well enough as a medium. His thoughts were dashed by the hard voice of another.

"Come here, my son."

Ice ran in his veins at the call. It was a voice he recognized, though not the one he had expected. A voice which surfaced from his earliest memories, the voice of his mother.

He turned in slow motion, descended the steps one at a time, entirely uncertain of himself in this moment. He emerged, and saw there a woman clad in fine raiment of silk. A woman who shared with him his cheekbones and eyebrows, his diminutive stature, full lips. She was carved out of his memories, exactly as she had been in those days, as if not a moment had passed since she left him.

"Mother?" he said. "What is the meaning of this?"

Another woman sat idly behind her. She was clad all in white, a flowing night robe sheer and cleaving to her body. He would not have said she was beautiful. She bore signs of a working woman's struggles. Hard lines etched into her forehead, steel streaks breaking up raven hair. She wore a placid expression, an expression he well remembered. It was the same one that greeted him when she had bound him to the trunk of a tree deep in Guldanh Forest, when she had left him for dead.

Grief for the Moon God

Ordein the White observed. It was all he did. The lace veil, customarily pinned in place against his cap was undone, and obscured his aquiline face to the lips, pronouncing to all that were present in these dungeons that the time had come for this trial. The moon marched across the open sky, the crystal city marching against its usual path to meet the God House of the Sun, where soon blood would paint its streets, and these streets in kind would become a scorched ruin, homes once places of safety caked in layers of soot, their facades melted and twisted into strange shapes.

He had lived through an entanglement of this kind but once, and it had been his undoing. Even now he could feel the madness coming over him, and knew it was worse for the acolytes fussing over bindings, shoving chips of wood into the mouths of young children, in these dungeon halls. Sobbing, screaming, pleas for mercy echoed back from dungeon cells as acolytes moved from one to the next, shackling youths to the walls with heavy chains and thick, iron cuffs. As they imprisoned them for their own safety. Fearful eyes looked back in his direction, not daring to settle on his face, keeping enough of themselves in tact to mind the forms.

The work was done quickly. Each of them stood in the hall, joining lines cuing up along its edges, iron doors fell shut and bolts were locked in series against them. Each room home to a dozen children, each held by restrictive bindings away from the rest, out of reach of them. Some of those binds would snap. They had when the day came three decades past. In the aftermath of this day, they would descend on these chambers, remove the survivors to safety, drag out the corpses of the fallen and return them to their parents.

Grief would follow. Grief from the children for the mothers and fathers they had lost. Grief for the parents whose children had not survived.

The acolytes, all clad in white with silver embroidery along their cuffs and collars, haunted expression on every face, some gazes already growing distant as the madness seeped in at the edges, compelling them to fight harder, joined those cues along the halls, joined as they finished their work, awaited the march forward.

As the last of them finished, he turned his back on them, and marched forth from these dungeon halls, bringing them into the palace. The last of them barred

Grief for the Moon God

the door behind him, and they marched through the lower halls, the gloom of a perpetual night's sky broken and crimson and shot through with harsher shades of fire orange and white as the light of the sun pushed back the brutal hue of God Ao Nii's taint.

Somewhere in the distance, the gates were drawn open. Star shower punched into the earth and the staircase mounted the pillars in its wake as a deep shadow crossed the land. The eclipse was beginning, and he was suffused with a bone deep grief, a self effacing melancholy marred by thoughts of flagellation, of cuts to his flesh and the sour taste of bile in his throat as he struggled against pain he inflicted on himself, penitence for a life spent in sin. A life given over to a violence he had, for so long, shunned as a youth at Wyte Landing, the port stronghold of the tak moran.

He remembered holding a fire mane cub in his hands, tiny flames sputtering to life around its neck and down its back, dancing over thick gloves of woven iron sheathed in dense leather. There had been a time when he had yearned to be a warrior among his people, when the desperate desire to possess one of those creatures so blessed by Tak the Fire had been all consuming. But that was the wrong path. Peace was the only path the spirit accepted. The Rahad must be his regents in the world, delivering his message of pacifism.

If only I had joined them.

He led the march into the streets, the palace shrouded all in violent shades and granular, gray auras behind him, raw energy spilling over a high bluff at his back and into the streets, spurring the masses toward the doors. They did not want to be caught in that embrace, did not want to be under its influence, for in that embrace was a dread to match their rage, a grief so binding they would turn their mad hatred on themselves.

It was in a mortal's nature to seek life, to run away from death. To know death was a mortal thing, to know it was imminent, inescapable; but to witness it was to know the unknowable. To fall into its embrace was to embrace, in kind, finality. The *end*.

Madness swarmed in at the edges, prickled across him as a red light began to emanate from him, and he stood aside to let the others pass, left them to their march, turned away from them once again and marched into the city, toward the ever burning sun and all of its false promises. It would be to him to stop his god, to drive him back together with the others who had chosen peace, and many would die for it.

Many would die.

Ao Nii emerged, the crystal chalice left on the floor of the chamber behind him. With his passing, Jule removed the pins in his veil, let the thin curtain of red lace fall over his eyes and nose. It was time, at last, for the Moon God to move against his enemies, and he felt free.

An aura of madness emanated from him, snuffing out the purer light in the hall beyond his chamber, darkening shadows in the gloom to an oily, unnerving black. He lifted his chin, long hair and flowing robes dragging across paving stones in his wake, and regarded Jule from the corner of his eye.

"Go to your forces, priest."

Jule marched ahead, his halberd stamping to mark a ringing rhythm in the quiet

Tears for the Moon God

hall as the echoes of a greater chaos in the streets of the city below came to him. His own madness came on as a wave of wrathful anger. Paranoia leeched in at the edges, threatening him with a descent into the same chaos that gripped those acolytes in the streets, that suffused the halls of a dungeon below as children were bound in place, gagged with wood to bite on, to spare their writhing tongues, save their teeth from grinding against steel chains that would not yield to them.

He left his god's side, and his god watched him go. And his god walked the other way.

Ao Nii marched up a winding staircase, intent on the sanctity of the tallest tower in his god house. Granular mists rolled away from him, down the staircase, into the halls below, crawled after Jule the Red, his greatest general. He climbed those steps, and a thirst built within him. A thirst which could not be sated except with the taste of the sun's own blood.

He would bring all of his fury against that god this night, demand he step aside, let him have the one he wanted, truly wanted, after all this time. God Lanfin was in the world now, hiding in plain sight but subject to the rule of the Great River. For so long, he had held himself back from the world, remained in the safety of a God House outside time, where its passing would not affect him.

And God Gorgus knew where he was, what he was doing in the world below, what he sought to do in furthering the plan his faction among the Lesser Gods had set into motion with the capture of Sao Njack, who was the best hope mortal kind had of asserting their right to freedom, their right to be in absence of the boot heel grinding against them, the work of the gods who hated them in breaking their spirits, crushing them into the dust.

Somewhere out there, a Rope Lord watched from his place of safety forces amassed in his shadow. Somewhere out there, gods marshalled their forces, to lay pursuit against him and the monster he would destroy, to hold each other back for painful moments as the latest play of hands seized on the lives of a few critical figures, spun fates for them in service of a greater design.

And the uelfin sang.

And they sang for their survival.

And they sang for their destruction.

He heard their song and knew the gods had made their moves, that even now across the world there were those who they manipulated in grand designs which would have greater effect. And he knew this new unfolding had blurred the lines, stolen away old hatreds and rivalries in favor of alliances which were never meant to be.

The Arbiter would take note. And he would tip the scales. Soon, he would tip the scales. His hand would be forced, and these new tidings in the Waxing World would yield to an era of decline for all of those who dwelt here, for he would be left with no option but to see it done, to preserve the tenuous balance between this world, the other, and the Heart.

He climbed the stairs, his robes lapping at the steps, hair fluttering about his head, crossed the threshold into the highest chamber, loomed in the window and looked out, across the horizon, as the east faring edge of his god house crashed against brutal spars of rock, slashed through streaming clouds, and made first contact with the god house of his enemy, the God House of the Sun.

Grief for the Moon God

There on a bluff to match his was a stepped compound, the blocky, tile roofed buildings sheeted in gold and glimmering to catch the light of the sun behind it, the burning ball baking the tiles of a place of light and fire. Poppy red banners fluttered in the slipstream breezes, soldiers formed phalanxes in the court below the rise, along an expansive, central walk. And from a tiered monument to the Sun God's power, fire surged into the sky, a wave of vitreous, burning plasma, a geyser blast of raw power, and he saw before it the one he sought.

A figure with three heads, one human, one of the jackal, both framing the head of a falcon, and all crowned in circlets of gold forested with gilt tines. A strip of linen was wrapped around God Gorgus's hips, and he held out his hand in a mirror gesture of Ao Nii's own, inviting battle, a clash to rend the land itself into ruin.

And God Ao Nii leapt from that window. And he soared over the city below, over the sprawling, militant compound of the God House of the Sun, and landed on the roof of the Sun Palace.

He seized God Gorgus by the falcon's throat. Momentum carried them over the rear facing edge of his house, and two burning stars, one robed in golden light and the other crimson, fell to the earth. Stars careening earthward, the gods beating each other over the heads, gouging fingers seeking eyes, faces contorted into feral snarls. The ground rushed up to meet them, a city sprawling to either side, and in the sky above, the moon passed into the path of the sun, a black ball making a crescent of that golden, burning orb. They slammed into the heart of a city on the edge of Shao Luin's ocean, and plasma and flame and scythes of red madness flashed away from them.

And the homes of innocents toppled all around them as their descent, their long simmering feud, came to a head, and the Magura of Zanzark Plain, the Magura in Faed City, were caught between them and around them. As they were forced to bear witness to the razing of their civilization, and were powerless to stop it.

The uelfin drove forward along the flanks. The last bombs exploded among their ranks as they split around Lisandra and the Nixians, and Jinga drew his swords. The uelfin sought to surround them, and Lisandra stepped back and around Jinga, taking the right side as Kiresh moved to take position on the left, their backs to each other as Jinga drew his own blades.

They launched into a frenzied assault as the uelfin came, rank after rank. Her blade flickered and lunged, an extension of her arm, suffusing the air with the cloying, pungent aroma of baby's breath, noxious and sickly sweet. The blade whirred and stabbed, found flesh, dug in and retreated.

A wrong step. A blade grazed her ribs and she clamped her teeth down around a scream.

She back stepped, a mistake that gave the uelfin precious moments to mount their offensive, seeking her vitals with their blades as the song returned in force, earnest and insistent, granting advantage to the uelfin who heard it, giving them insight into the moves their quarry would make before they knew which way they would strike themselves.

Kiresh's talents could only help her along for so long, and she was beginning to feel that familiar, mounting pressure in her joints, the fog crawling in at the edges of her mind, exhaustion pouring into her, threatening to break her focus, slow her movements, give yet more advantage to her attackers.

Tears for the Moon God

Soon, her body would give out.

Jinga's blades flashed and bit, raked across ribs, cut open throats. Bodies fell around them and the uelfin climbed over them, compelled them back into the ascending force at their rear, where the ground was more level, where there were no mounded corpses to recall their brief, early successes against these creatures.

She lashed out with her sword. The intended target shifted out of its path before it had a chance of reaching him. Unfocused, scarlet eyes looked past her as his sword flickered toward her ribs, reeled back and came forth for a stop thrust to her thigh. The point rasped against bone, and she buckled.

The sword came down over her head, and Kiresh was there to accept the blow, one blade parrying and the other seeking a home in the uelfin's throat.

The uelfin reeled back out of its range, stepped to the side and lashed out. Another came in from the opposite side, baring down with his blade for Kiresh's back.

Lisandra swept her sword across his ankles, and he leapt over it.

She winced, a fresh wave of pain blurring her vision as her movements forced blood from the open wound in her thigh.

Jinga placed himself in her path, blades flashing, bodies falling in his wake.

"On your feet, now." He grunted. "You can't die on your knees."

She pushed off her knee, eased back onto her good leg and sprang forward, charging the nearest uelfin with her sword in front of her, driving the point into flesh with a guttural howl.

A death charge to match the dirge suffusing the air, those uelfin harmonies taking on a bitter edge, harsh and defiant. A small part of her mind recoiled from that sound, wondered where this sudden shift came from, why they sounded so...so angry. It was drowned under the haze of battle, the mists of wrath, the insistence on her own right to die honorably, if she must die. To feel Shah Jagat guiding her hand in this conflict, drawing down into her a blessing to steel her against death's final embrace, to goad her on for still more moments, bring his wrath to bear against these cretins.

A dark pulse echoed in her heart. Shadows flickered. Crazed and shifting, they snapped back and forth under the feet of the uelfin and the Nixians and her as the moon crossed into the path of the sun, marched into its path and snuffed it.

The eclipse had begun.

Katuwan watched twin stars fall from his vantage along a street market deep in the city. Lura set aside a round fruit and followed his gaze, and they watched the balls of fire and crimson light drop from a sky where the moon crossed the path of the sun, a moon black with rage.

The stars thrashed earthward.

Impact.

The earth shook violently under his feet. He reached out a stabilizing hand to Lura as she lost her footing. Gouts of flame, motes of raw energy, rolled over the buildings for several blocks, stopping short of the markets and them, of shoppers milling among the stands.

Silence.

A soft, fitful murmuring from several places at once. Hands reaching blindly to touch others. Pulling them aside, drawing them away as the first to sense danger

Grief for the Moon God

broke into jogs, away toward the docks or the gates.

Lura's grip found him. She turned him around, dragged him after her. And they ran. These shelters would not stand long against the raging torrent of fire and light in the distance.

"Xirakura." Katuwan said.

He pulled free, ran a few steps in the direction of the conflagration. Lura's grip clamped down on him again, seized and pulled.

"We can't leave him."

"Husband!"

He spun, wide eyes settled on her.

"Do not run to your death. Do not think he would be as much a fool as that."

"He will want to lend his hand to these people." He protested, shaking her hand free.

"Not there!" she insisted. "Down to the water. He will think to wield water against them, or to heal who he can."

"He cannot hold a spirit in his condition."

"There are many of power in the sea. He will trust in them."

He gave up the argument. A curt nod. He followed her, away from the market, south toward the docks and the sea.

Zanzark cowered away from the impact. His voice filled Xirakura's ears as he ran through the city, away from the sight of impact. Acolytes in white robes, cuffs in the shapes of static flames encircling their arms, swarmed into the area where buildings lay in ruins, roofs caved in, walls blasted outward. Already, they were dragging people out of the wreckage, dragging them to a safe distance, if any such thing could exist in this city, where two gods whose very nature was destruction railed against each other in a flurry of blows and blasts of raw flame and blistering heat.

Burning stones soared away from them, crashed into buildings as Magura and traders still caught in the city ran away screaming, as mothers cradled the mangled ruins of their children and their spouses dragged them back, intent on keeping what remained of their families from succumbing to the conflict.

Fires took the nearest homes and storefronts, flashing walls blasted across them, and the fires spread across the city, consuming whole blocks in seconds. Those who had lost their loved ones wailed their sorrows, and the song of their grief filled the air, warring with the panicked screams, stampeding feet that swallowed those not fast enough or sure of foot to keep pace with the throngs seeking the walls, seeking whatever exit they could find.

He ran with them, seeking a place of safety, seeking anywhere he might be able to gather himself, regroup, find the courage buried deep inside and wield it in the way of his people against these insurgent, wrathful gods.

Blistering heat thrashed at his bare back and legs as he ran. A horse on fire galloped, screaming past him, set fire to a wagon filled with grains as it crashed into it, impaled itself on a broken timber and died.

He pelted past it, down toward the docks and the greater safety of an ocean whipped into raging, white capped waves. He saw a stream of those white robed figures, fear painted across stony faces, their horror made palpable as they carried broken bodies away.

Tears for the Moon God

He needed a place of safety, just for those moments while he emptied himself of his soul, drew in a spirit, any spirit, with power enough to meet these gods in conflict.

The earth quaked under his feet, and he was not certain if it was the terrified throes of Zanzark or the echoes of the fight between those creatures out of story, those nightmare specters locked in conflict.

He needed a place of safety, if only to buy time, if only to make what challenge he could against the gods and their fury. Needed to add his weight to the people, lend his gift to their cause, push back against these impossible powers, even if it cost him his life. Even if he could do nothing save keep the worst of their violence from spilling yet further into the city, denying life to mortals, denying them their safety, shattering the vestiges of their lives into ruin.

He needed to help. If he must seize a spirit and drive it kicking and screaming into himself to see it done, he must take that risk, swallow down its fearsome might and wield it. Wield it for the protection of all of these people, until the gods saw fit to intercede.

King and Empress

In a shrine far removed from the conflict in Faed City, a spirit in chains was burned. Hissing steam, smoldering flesh against his flank. He groaned as white hot pain bored into him, cutting through skin, through the thin sheet of fat to press against muscle.

Gora looked to the chains binding him to the floor, he lifted his narrow face to the ceiling, beaded braids clattering together as he closed his eyes, and through his second sight was filled with visions of a twilit sky, the moon crossing into the sun's path, and knew the source of his pain.

The wound would heal. He was not so weakened by these chains that he would witness this burn become a scar, a pocket in his flesh to mar his transcendent beauty. The voices of spirits raised in anger, whimpering from hidden places where they held themselves away from a conflict they should be—their wrath a sword thrust forth, their courage a shield against their hearts and minds. He knew their fear, but he could only see it as cowardice.

He climbed shakily to his feet, the weight of his body an unfamiliar burden against legs unused to supporting him. He had been away from the world too long. The spirits had forgotten the way. Even those who had served him as his greatest generals in the times before their betrayal, his sealing as they turned their gazes away from him, were not as they had been. He heard their voices among the rabble, heard Sufa Salein's whispered curses as he marched across his forest. Heard Ouran the Giant's rage in the mountains as he came down to meet him. He heard in them outrage, yet they did not seek to march from their homes, did not move to join hands against these creatures.

They moved instead to defend the borders of their territories—amass what lesser spirits loomed in their shadows to defend their domains—should this conflagration spill forth into what territories they had carved out of his kingdom.

He called to his ill-gotten son, Ba Gora of the central plains, and was met with silence. To Zanzark and Shahalanak, the spirit of the aquifer beneath his plains, and they flinched away from him. He called to the mountains and the forests and the plains, to the winds sweeping across his domain, and was met with a similar quiet.

Trapped, sealed away in this place, they knew his power refused him. Knew he

Tears for the Moon God

was not strong enough to compel them into his service, a feat which had once come easily. But there were other ways to see his will carried out. There were those in the seas who had railed against him in the earliest days, those who remained from a time when his conquest was ended.

His eyes flashed open, and he drew in the power of the lands, drew in all that he could hold, a fraction of a fraction of the power he had commanded in his prime. The glyphs along his shackles emanated searing light, Tetract energies drawing them to life, bringing four ancient powers against him and seeking to crush him under their might.

He called to the empress, heard her laughter in his ears as if she stood beside him.

"Your hubris is ever as great as it was." Empress Shao Luin said. *"But you will have no aid from me. The seas remember, Gora Soft Touch. The spirits all remember."*

"Then you will stand by while the gods raze the countryside, knowing nothing of their plans for you?"

"They have no power to break me. They have learned."

"Remember, woman, the taste of life. The one you rode against the gods."

"He is my king."

"Take my prince. I will see to it he does not die in your embrace."

"You have no command of mortals." She spat. *"They are mine, now and always. They have always been mine."*

Will the oceans be safe against their power?"

"In this I choose no side."

"The gods seek what they have always sought. They have the means now, or will soon. Will you stand aside when they come for you. They *will* come."

"They will not!"

"There is still the one who wishes you dead, removed from the saddle, slain like all of those you embrace."

"He is of no consequence to me."

He sensed her fury. Waves of raw rage thrashing against him, waves cresting and slamming against his lands, shattering docks where mortals labored to see their vessels cast off, to know the safety in her embrace.

"Take him, Empress. Take him."

He raked long nails across his chest. Blood weltered from shallow cuts and evaporated, suffusing the air with the scent of iron.

He watched as thin tendrils of smoke danced in the air before him, watched as they took form, the echo of a human figure. He pressed his hand to the naked figure, reached behind the veil of gray flesh, past his belly, and imbued the idol with his power.

"He will not die for receiving your power, Empress. And you will know the thrill of life. Do not squander my gift, for it is fleeting."

"Fleeting always." She intoned, and the essence of her slid away from him. But the power within the idol redoubled. The power wrought in those chains redoubled, forced him onto his knees, and he fought against it.

His chosen priest, the shamanic entity, Xirakura, was too important to see dead for his involvement in the presence of warring gods. He gave him a shield, for precious moments, to see those gods cast aside, to see their conflict taken away from his lands, to wound someone else, to burn against the flesh of a different

King and Empress

tyrant.

His teeth snapped shut around a pain filled groan, and the spirits all quaked in fear, for his will was made known in the bond he shared with his regent. A Great King was active in the world again, chained and beyond the reach of his true power, but able to affect what transpired beyond this shrine in a way they had never suspected he could.

Empress Shao Luin contemplated her domain from the seat of her throne. Mortal souls suffused with green light illuminated the streets and alleys of a sprawling city. Coral forests sprawled across the ever expanding settlement in imitation of the true forests they had known in life, in the earliest days before human life was known to the gods, before the first wars broke out. Eels drifted between houses in myriad styles, all built of stones mortared in place with dense, calciferous silts and oozes.

She watched them from a throne made of bone white coral, her raiment composed of kelps and corals and luminous creatures trapped in a perpetually spiraling current about her thick, domineering form. She looked out through cold, amber eyes, the vicious eyes of predatory mackerel, and watched as families reunited with those loved ones who preceded them into her domain, as laughter washed over them, as children taken too soon rode by on the backs of ghost sharks, watched by their ancestors from chairs scrapped together from driftwood or made of rusted metal and taken whole into her depths from shipwrecks.

She glanced over and down, to a throne set against a lower step along the high shelf, a canyon wall overlooking the abyssal plain her city for the dead, her serene afterlife for mortal kind, rested against. To regard a man of mixed crow and Katuwiti descent. A man whose impassive regard was fixed on the settlement, on a particular place within it where a woman of Qin Loc told a story to her children, smiling though a veiled sadness hid within her.

Alone among these mortals, she had married a katcyakin, had fostered a family with him, and that katcyakin was taken. She had been refused him, but he had not been seized. No, the other had made problems for her, but there was still hope, however slim, of the first returning to her. The sword maker who had given Rauth Ku Lau the means to see a change sweep over the world, to become such a threat to the gods elder and lesser that the sword need be seized from his hands, and the maker punished with eternity in life, in a place outside time, where the severity of his crimes could not be wrought so successfully against them, and man would again be pressed under the thumb of the gods.

She had held onto Rauth Ku Lau, this man whose black hair flowed with the currents, who wore the beads and disks in his braid, a pale reflection of the Great King of his homeland. This man who had once housed her in his body, and given her the first taste of life she had ever known.

Gora's wishes were unknown to her, but the succor of life was not. And it had been long since she had witnessed it. His confidence in this prince among Spirit Callers to house her, even briefly, awakened in her the old argument. To expose herself so risked death for the ocean, would see countless millions of lives added to her waters, but the afterlife they sought denied them. Without her, there was no city in the deeps, there was no reunion with family and ancestors and kin. There was no hope left with the Dead Sea herself dead.

Tears for the Moon God

But those gods would not leave her to herself in this conflagration. She had seen the first waves of cloud men enter her domain. Infants all, who would never grow old, who would never be anything but what they were. Age did not claim the dead.

Her gaze drifted from Rauth Ku Lau to a sprawling complex, all of barrel-sided structures with open roofs where cradles claimed the dead and the mothers of stillborn children doted over those children of others, visiting upon them to nurture them, to hold them, when the grief for what was lost grew too strong.

There was a place inside that complex in which all of the infant children were covered from their crown to the tips of their toes in crazed lines, spangle traceries covering muted flesh. Most had come within the last two decades, and more were still pouring in. All over the world, cloud men were being born and then killed within moments of their births, were being ferried down Ul Sharak's river, passed under Zangal Mountain and into her domain, to be kept by her against the ills of a cursed life.

She was no fool. She had known this tide for what it was, an event of such significance the gods could not look away from it. Could not leave the rise of a race among the katcyakin alone. And they would not leave her alone. Gora Soft Touch was right about that. They would come for her before it was over, if only to see to it that those children, the men and women who emerged later when their own fates were decided, were denied her embrace. That this force did not fall into her keeping, for even dead the katcyakin held power. They would be the same as those uelfin, and she would be driven to defend her domain against all who came for her.

She growled low in her throat, and Rauth Ku Lau looked up at her, twisted around in his throne in order to see her clearly.

"What is it, my queen?" he asked.

"I am going for a time. See to it that your people are well protected. I fear I am needed in the lands above."

Hard eyes yielded to something softer, curiosity quirking his thin eyebrows, twisting his wide-set mouth into a consternated grimace.

"They have made their move, my love." She said. "The gods will stand in unity it seems, intent on lobbing a last great insult against we and our way."

"I will see to it they are protected." He said, turning away to take up his observation of the city of the dead.

She rose from her seat, climbed a swift current to the ocean's surface. It was time those gods knew their place. She only wished she was happy to make her position clear. What would come of this would be to fix their attention on the oceans, not just her but her contemporaries, Sal Seid and Ruhanni. They would know the wrath and the fury of the gods for her intervention, but she *must* intervene. She must.

A hunter prowled the streets of Faed City. Down an alley in the low city, the docks barely visible half a mile away, the walls to either side of the claustrophobic expanse were a collage of timbers yet unvarnished for the dry season held, and the back ways were of little importance to a people obsessed with commerce.

A crimson beacon arose in his sights. He blinked, and the world was washed in shades of gray, blue and magenta. And that crimson light remained, a figure secreted away in a back room in that house while two Magura citizens kept watch on a barred door from outside.

King and Empress

Another Magura man sat on the slab stoop outside the dwelling's back door, secure behind a wooden fence in the yard. A chicken coop was situated against it, and the chickens inside fluttered their wings restlessly, preened themselves and clucked back and forth, voicing their concerns as that glow leaked around the contours of the door.

He smelled the familiar perfume of cortisol and adrenaline emanating from the men in that home, the faint odor of musky, days old sweat baked into the weave of thin cloth and the wilder, grease aroma of hair and skin oils, of bees wax, though the substance was not in common use for cosmetics among this people, and old wood from great trees which were not common in the plains the spirit, Zanzark, controlled.

The hunter climbed the wall as deftly as any cat in his homeland, and dropped down in a yard devoid of grass, a patch of bare earth tilled up in narrow, mounded rows where the first planting had been done against the promise of coming rain. A wind chime dangled from the eaves of a squat shed, long bones and metal coins clattering together as south faring gusts drove across the city.

He would not find the Spirit Caller here, but his trail would betray him. From the front porch, as he left, it would take him to the man's own feet, where he would kill him in the name of his god.

But first, lend a hand to chaos, free the tamed moonkin, cut loose the binds.

He crept up to the door, a wickedly curved knife in hand, and descended on the bald, young man seated on that stoop.

Fires raged in a district far removed from here. Glass crawled over ground. Crimson and gold light slammed against each other, and even here the echoes of those clashes rolled through the earth.

He pressed his free hand against the guard's mouth and nose, and carved a line across his throat, tipped the head forward as the man clawed at his hand, reached with shaking fingers for a blade at his hip. Blood welled over his torso, leaving the hunter clean.

He leaned the dying man forward, leaned his torso against his knees. His blood fell in curtains to patter against the earth, to feed it with the essence of his life, and the hunter moved on, slid a window in the back open and climbed through.

It was a gross oversight that this people had never embraced more sophisticated locks for their doors and windows. Had never worked gears in their forges. Getting into this house quietly would have been made much more of a challenge had they done.

He stepped onto a hardwood counter top, ducked under a series of cast irons dangling from hooks from the ceiling, and climbed onto a floor obscured by a batik rug, the dyes arranged in spiral patterns around an intricate depiction of the lunar phases.

Yes, the woman in those rooms missed home, and she was not the only one who had settled here. In this city.

Dried herbs hung from the adjacent wall. Limes blackened and dried on strings in front of a window with western exposure. The other two men bore resemblance to the first. Both were in their twenties, thin and tall and well muscled, and lighter complected than most of this tribe.

They sat in silence, cast nervous glances at the door off the side of the table, situated next to a short hall which led into the sitting room, the front room. The

Tears for the Moon God

spirit caller's musk was stronger there.

He stood between them, listened to the fitful, muffled groans and thrashing coming from that other room, where their mother was bound, may have even insisted on her own binding, her own confinement, before the madness took hold.

One wore a coin pendant on a fine, gold chain around his neck, the other stud earrings in his lobes. Both wore the traditional dot scars along their brows, signifying their betrothals. They would be missed.

He reached out, cut the first one's throat, spun and slashed as the second vaulted out of his seat. Both dropped heavily against the table. He lifted the one by his braids—long braids which ran in neat pleats down his back, and yanked the chain free, a trophy to take after an easy win.

He pushed the slot bar back and let it fall, opened the door into that chamber.

Laying prone against her bed was a stout, light-skinned woman, her wiry hair streaked with white and worn natural. She withered against the leather straps, fingers twisting into warding signs, her teeth gnashed together, eyes squeezed shut and leaking tears.

He made quick work of cutting her binds, freeing her to raze the streets in the name of a god she had shunned, whose touch lingered in her soul, a curse she could not break, which she must bear until her death, and he suspected as she righted herself, swung her legs over the edge of the bed, that death would come soon.

He left her there, ambled down the hall, threw open the front door. A sorrow filled wail rushed in to gobble up all the air in the house. A wail filled with spurious horror, a spontaneous outpouring of grief. There was that pungent odor, the trail marred by other scents, scents of other people, of oxen and horses and dust. But it pervaded his senses, drove deep into him, and he marched into the streets unseen, and followed it. Followed it deeper into the city, toward a stranger unaware of his pursuers, as others closed the net from other places.

There were the spouses they must find, who they must seize. Hunters would even now be on their trail, following those vulnerable people to secure a fate for them worse than simple death. A fate according to the designs of tyrant gods, a goddess whose schemes had led his god to take a side in the unfolding conflict, and betray his closest allies.

Tuluis Fel

The moon stole across the sky, but for the trees it was blocked from Ungol's sight. Where the Dumas arrayed behind him—their horses left staked to posts in the camp at his back, to be tended by the noncombatants and their Kirche guard—could catch a glimpse of the sky. The trees grew far enough apart to admit them that view. Their heads were tilted up, their postures stiff in the face not of battle—a familiar force—but of the contours of an unknowable force. What would come with the arrival of the eclipse? Were their moonkin among the enemy? Among them?

Those entities hid in plain sight, the ones who had escaped the halls and towers, the roads within the God House of the Moon. And God Ao Nii was enraged, or would he not now be taking his city across the arc of the horizon, away from the sun, always and forever away.

The Tului were stirring. He heard the dull rumble of their approach, gripped the pommel of his scimitar. Battle was not for the brave. No, battle was for cold hearts and monstrous minds, the blow and counter blow a language written in actions, a conversation between two forces to whom words had failed. And there had been no words exchanged between the Tului and the Gil Garo. There could be no reasoning with a people bent on the destruction of the hated foe, no room for diplomacy without bloodshed. And he did not want it.

The first lines broke into light washed terrain, came running over ground as one legion, streamed around trees with shadows snapping around their feet in frenzied anticipation of the blood they would have, the converts they stood to gain, to replace the numbers they had lost, to *feed on.*

He raised a clenched fist. *Hold. Do not be goaded into their snare.* His gaze touched on the trees, passed over them, ignoring soldiers spilling forth between the gaps, the avalanche sounds of their boots thundering over uneven ground, deftly dodging roots, ducking under low branches, their weapons bared and teeth gnashed together in snarls of rage to drive back fear. Rage to drive away panic, to push out cowardice, a most human element.

He opened his hand.

Arrows hissed out of the trees overhead, took Tului soldiers in the neck, punched through their chests and out their backs. Ice flowered along the boles of

Tears for the Moon God

those trees, shot up their lengths. Gil Garo archers fell from their places among the bows, run through with jagged, glittering Shards; were swarmed by soldiers.

He watched men and women he had known for many years converted into blood thirsty monsters in seconds. The archers rose, their eyes glowing, and joined the charge on the Dumas position.

We arrive at this place, as phages intent on the destruction of a parasite, to be dragged kicking and screaming...into the void.

He dragged his broad, hooked sword from the sheath at his hip, angled it before him.

"ATTACK!" He bellowed.

The Dumas boiled forth to meet their enemy, ran into the trees. Clangs and biting clips echoed back to him as his people made contact, drove the attack deep into the woods, where they would be lost to his sight, lost to each other amid deep shadows, and forced them to fight alone against this enemy, alone and with stubborn resolve their only true shield.

He hoped they remembered the hibiscus calyxes tucked into their pockets, their boots, wherever they had secreted them away. Flowers to drive back poison, fruit to keep their blood pure.

He kicked his horse into a trot, and hoped Shaelein fared well. It was time he found her.

The Tipik beat a track through the woods well removed from the first clashes with the Chikata and the Dumas to the east. Sarri's Cuu forces remained behind, intent on a destructive charge of their own. Their chief had foregone his horse, for he did not need it. In a battle of this magnitude, every effort must be met with absolute resolve, with the steadfastness of mind to meet the charge head on, uncompromisingly. No weakness could be permitted.

Sarri had chosen his place well, lay in waiting for the right time, the moment his charge would sow most confusion. Waited for the Tipik and the Kachin to gain their positions.

Coltang's hammers were in his hands, fingers twitching restlessly around their shafts, the reigns looped around his dominant wrist, the better to guide his mount forward.

This strategy bore no resemblance to the Gil Garo pattern of raiding. It was enough to drive a man near panic. Unfamiliar tactics for an army unprepared for a woodland assault; could there be any worse fate for a people reliant on mounted charges, flank attacks, unsubtle uses of force?

Trust in Arrak. He thought to himself. *He is no fool.*

He signaled for his forces to turn to the east. The Tului camp was in sight at his right, distant enough that the passage of so many clad in deer hide might pass unnoticed. The Kachin remained on the path north, left them to take the eastern flank while they posed for their own assault from the west. Twin pincers designed to squeeze the main body of the Tului force out of their encampment, to deal with the secondary force they suspected would come from this direction.

If we can destroy this force before the second arrives... There may be hope then. But hope had never been worth much for the Gil Garo. Hope would not lead them to an easy victory. Fate had turned on them. She was not on their side.

Tuluis Fel

The sounds of fighting washed over the southern half of the battlefield. Sarri watched from his vantage on a low hill, the stream before him and the Cuu arranged in blocks behind. He sat atop a horse made all of sea foam and green-tinted water. The creature was bound to his soul, a gift of Byr for his trouble, and the others of his tribe left a pocket around him and his ephemeral stallion, their horses stamping restless hooves, tossing their heads, daring not to move closer.

Ice broke down within the stream's banks. Water gurgled over stones. Blood seeped into the land where the Dumas made first contact. As predicted, the Tului spared no time in launching a frontal assault on the camp, but this was a diversion. The forces they took against the Gil Garo were few, the main body hidden somewhere else, readying for their own play.

Sauman's forces flooded the forest, leaving the bend in the river at their backs. Squads of five and ten warriors flowed among the Tului. Arrows rained down from the branches, picking off the Tului at the fringes while the serrated turtles drove into the enemy's flank, forced their lines apart, were engulfed by the superior force. He watched as dozens of his men were cut down. Jagged ice cut lines through them, broke them apart as arrow fire continued to rain down. Return fire flashed through still air, dropping Arrak's snipers from their positions with too little effort.

He left them to it. Left them to march into the stream, where the currents ran strong and the ice refused to take firm hold. Into the band with his power on him. He drove it down into those waters, watched as the currents were whipped into an array of whirlpools and rapids, listened as cold laughter echoed across those currents.

The spirit of the creek fought against the insurgents, the invaders in its band, as its own life became a weapon in his hand, the essence of it yielding to the birth of new spirits, spirits too weak to live long on their own, who dragged its power into them to sustain them.

He charged, carrying the waters of the band behind him, fragile spirits emerging as demented infants, clawing at each other, gnashing dagger teeth around throats, drinking in the essence of their brothers and sisters, becoming child-like, surging into adolescence as they charged after him.

He ran into the fray bellowing. Ran with the waters, ran for the enemy, ran to save his kin.

The newborn spirits fell on the Tului, forced them under raging torrents. Blood flowered. Pink ran with white. The stain of blood poison mottled the corporeal forms of those twisted fiends as they ravaged bodies, flung them aside and away, rag dolls in the jaws of a feral dog.

The enemy broke rank and retreated. The Chikata pursued them. New forces surged forth to bolster the line, broke bodies with twisting shadows, produced walls of ice to meet Sauman's fel spawn, which climbed and then shattered, whizzed past and found homes in mortal bodies. Their makers converged on him, intent on the destruction of the covering element, the man whose assault threatened the security of their position.

The Chikata rallied around him. Squads converged and pushed deeper into the wood, bringing the fight to new enemies. Screams and rage-filled hollers mingled with the sounds of clashing steel, breaking ice, the *thunk, thunk* of shrapnel piercing wood.

Tears for the Moon God

"I don't understand why we aren't fighting, father." Kuuda said.

The Kirche had not entered the fray with the rest of the sects. Were being held in reserve at Arrak's command. There was nothing to be gained from leaving an entire sect out of the fighting, not least when their forces were the most resilient against this enemy.

Tursa's yurt had become a claustrophobic container, denying him hope of success in this battle. Of being a part of that success, should it be won.

Tursa patted him lightly on the shoulder, a comforting gesture from anyone else turned patronizing, as he had only ever seen his father show such kindness to children.

"The Tipik cannot defend the sick among us." Tursa said. "Until they are well healed, we must assume our duties as guards over them. Consider what might happen if they escape?"

"Still—"

"Still nothing. We have our task." Tursa snapped. "Personally, I agree with Arrak's decision. Shi'an the Grass provides some protection against infection, and through him, we are given the means of producing more of this hibiscus. Our task, then, is to find the best means of administering it to those who are newly infected."

"Which we have done."

"What is an army without medics?"

Kuuda fell silent as Tursa met his gaze and held it. An incongruous sadness stole through him at that look. He so often forgot how long his father had lived, how many friends he had survived, how many of them must have met violent ends. Time was no friend to a warrior. Time stole so much from a man, gave him memories to hold onto, not all of them comforting.

"Fighting is a means to an end, my son." Tursa said, and brushed past him. "We're wasting time. Where is your sister?"

"Which one?"

"Alaar. Shaede. Does it matter?"

"You could stand to be less irritable, old man."

Tursa snorted. He pushed open the tent flap with an emaciated arm. His strength had been returning for some time now, but he still wore the vestiges of an infirm, the skin and bone texturing common to those who were near the end of their fight. Whether the outcome was good or bad, the sickness stole away yet more of him, leaving behind a wraith, though it had been long years since his father had looked anything but.

"Look out there." He said.

Kuuda looked over his shoulder, through the flap. Lights rippled across the sky in the distance. An aurora in the west, spreading eastward as it was picked up by another's hand, a joining of two of Sildein's acolytes, Gaulakh and Coltang, to signal the coming charge into the enemy camp, to signal the second open in this grand, bloody dance.

"We are outmoded. Their general is a cunning man. He has proven as much. He will not be alone, either. The task the other sects have set upon is simple. The total destruction of the enemy before its reinforcements arrive. Our task is the complicated one. To hold back and watch, remain fixed in place when the wounded inevitably come pouring into our camp. Every one of them will have succumbed to

Tuluis Fel

the poison, will need to be restrained and treated with the antidote to that poison, and then healed of their wounds before they die.

"Your wish to be in the action is selfish. It is inspired by a desire to be part of the celebration after all the blood has been shed and the bodies buried, but the time after battle, even in victory, is a time for grief. There will be dead. You will know some of them. You will loathe who killed them, even as you cannot put a face to the ones who did. And you will grieve.

"War is not a time for laughter. It is not a time for celebration. It is a grueling march to the ends of foreign kingdoms, the steady capture of more and more land as town streets and forest floors run with blood and gore. Someone has to clean all of that up. Dress the wounds. Tend to the fevered until they are well past the point at which you believe their souls might flee.

"That is why we remain here, Kuuda. To await the end, when our work begins."

He let the tent flap fall, and returned to his former place before the wood stove. "Now come. Sit. Conserve your energy. It will be needed when the time comes."

Kuuda joined his father, seated himself. He would not look into the other man's face. Would not meet his eyes. His anger had not been abated by Tursa's speech. It had been emboldened. Emboldened, because he was of no use as long as he remained here. None of them were.

"There is another reason we have been left behind." Tursa said softly, the heat leaving his voice. "It is not just our people who are here. There are those who cannot fight among us. Those who were never intended for combat. Those of the other sects who have lost their ability to hold weapons and ride galloping horses, and children. So many children.

"Who will protect them? Who stands between the enemy and our legacy? The children are our future. The elders the keepers of our past. If the Tului reach this far, it will be our duty to cover the retreat, so that our kin have a chance at life in our absence. Or our entire race, our way of life, the Gil Garo way, will end here. So it is our task to be what the others cannot be. To do what they must not do. And hope we are not needed before it is over."

"I...I understand." Kuuda said. He settled in then, the fight leaving him at last, and accepted his place among the Gil Garo. Not as a chief of war, but as a defender. The last defender.

Wrath for the Sun God

Timin had never liked the Faed City, its dusty streets teaming with urban odors of shit and piss, dust whipped up by clawing breezes, and the fresher, salt brine of open sea. He was a man for forests, for Mishakh's winding passes and the sheltering gloom of her canopy. The easier way of life she provided in absence of the looming shadow of Raukha so close he could almost convince himself its presence pressed against his skin—a cold, bitter touch to remind him that the port was under the cartel's control, its tariffs paid to them.

He would not have been upset to see the city razed, the Raukhas rooted out and disposed of, but his orders did not include them. His targets, two gods and their enablers, agents of other gods who prowled the streets in secret, having been led here in the months precluding this unveiling, a preemptive to ensure certain successes he would rather not contemplate.

God Uldal had sensed the change come over his friend. Had known something was off, that Shakh was not playing the same game he had for so long. His forces were in the city now, had been for some time it seemed, for they had arrived in force, using the Raukhas, unassuming traders, caravans come along the roads and sea lanes, to bed down among his people, hide away in secret.

They had known, somehow, that this would be the site of Ao Nii's landing. Shakh may well have orchestrated this endeavor with Gorgus. It seemed that way.

As his forces streamed into the city, along a road opened from God Uldal's sanctuary, he barked orders. Divided the troop to move into deeper reaches along the appropriate channels.

"Evacuate the city!" he demanded. "Open the lanes for those who wish to flee! Stand in no one's way!"

He needed the streets cleared of the rabble, the Magura and traders from countless other races, expats of foreign nations who had settled here, the Raukha's interests themselves. Jaunz may see fit to use his connections to those peoples for his purposes, may see a benefit in working with them, may even have friends among the Eight Hands. Jaunz was misguided in thinking he could trust any of them, and though the shadow of his palm reached far, he was not strong enough to shift them away from their games of murder and deceit. They were worse than the

Wrath for the Sun God

gods, those bastards, for they knew humanity, knew its weakness, and exploited them at every turn.

He would have trapped them here if he could have parsed out who was Raukha and who were their victims. Would have left them to the fires and the rage those gods burned into each other, but the pressing matter, the matter which concerned him most in the first plays of this conflict, was seeing the civilians to safety.

Rahad healers poured over the city, pursuing the injured and the dying, intent on saving lives, on standing as a bulwark against those raging currents, putting out fires where they started.

He split off three Shards, each an exact likeness to him, bald and tall and dark complected, all clad in the light, leather armor he favored, all carrying replicas of his catch pole, one end weighted with an iron ball and the other bearing a looped, leather cord.

His Shards took helm, leading pathfinder contingents into deeper reaches of the city, each barking orders of their own as they marched their compliments away, toward the docks, onto higher passes, into the belly of the beast.

He wondered where God Uldal would be. What business he was attending to now, where he was in the world and what ends he sought. He had chosen a side, a rare showing of moral fiber as the gods, his kin, took their positions, move and counter move, played the first round of hands in this grand unfolding of their Greatest Game.

There was a man here he must find. His lovers, his spouses, were here, too, and looking for him. Their capture was of the utmost importance. He could see them set into the hands of the Rahad once found, set on a course away from this place, away from homebound shores and onto the sea itself, to find their destiny in darker times. He needed to find them before the enemy did, and his enemy had the advantage.

The hunters defied pathfinder tracking. They moved unseen, their presences unfelt, immersed themselves in shadow and camouflaged themselves against the dusty, cluttered terrain. And if they had the scents of those people, if they had their trail, there was advantage in that, too.

He opened a path along the road, called three squads forward from his remaining forces.

"Go now and find the lovers." He said to their sergeants. "They will be lighter complected than the Magura, bearing some resemblance to the people of the mountains. The woman of medium height, the man about my height and built wide. When you find them, bring them dockside, to the Rahad ship."

"Sir!" they said in unison, clapping blade-straight hands to their brows.

They surged forth, leading their squads through the doorway he'd opened, onto the path he set in front of them, through which the docks were just visible from the height of a sloping, hill road.

The path shifted when the last of them were through, opened onto a scene of brutal violence. Moonkin ran amok through the streets, descended on defenseless victims, gouged out chunks of flesh with whipping tendrils of crimson light, flayed them alive. Magura women and children scattered, pelted down alleys and main roads, fighting to get past tangled crowds, building the barrier bigger, making the going more difficult.

Beyond them, fires raged across the roofs of their homes. A mother lost her grip

Tears for the Moon God

on the infant she carried. It fell into the chaos of stamping feet. He flinched away from the sight, the gore spattered across the road as she stooped down to retrieve her child and was trampled into the dirt herself.

He stepped through, and his troop followed.

The gods will pay for this one day. Soon, I hope.

Gorgus shoved Ao Nii away. Ao Nii soared across the gap and crashed against a nearby building. The building shuddered, collapsed under the force of impact. Three children ran away screaming from behind it. Their parents were dead, their bodies crushed under Ao Nii, mangled ruins of who they had been.

He climbed to his feet, watched as the children pelted away and hoped they won free as a deep melancholy stole over him, dampening his rage for precious moments while Gorgus closed the distance at a slow, methodical walk.

"What do you want from me, Ao Nii?" the Sun God demanded. "What is it we have not settled after all this time."

Ao Nii stepped over the wreckage, flicked gore from his sleeve.

"Where is he?" he demanded. "Where is God Lanfin!"

"He is not yours." Gorgus said coldly. The words came in one voice, but from three open maws. "What you want, you cannot have. We are all better for having those monsters contained. Those would be usurpers."

"Step away from him, Gorgus!" Ao Nii bellowed. "Leave him to his death."

The falcon's head shook back and forth. The human head sighed. "I cannot. I will not. Your demand would seal the fate of a god, earn death for one of us for the first time."

"Yet you would kill me rather than see him exposed."

"If you force my hand."

Ao Nii surged forward. Gorgus met his charge, plasma glow radiating from him. Flash fire blasted across the nearest dwellings. Waves of searing hot air rolled down the passes. Bodies burned and carbonized in moments, and crumbled into ash to be wicked away by the breezes.

He surged forth, wearing crimson light as a mantle. Granular, creeping clouds floated away from his feet, mists to match the depths of his grief crawling over all that surrounded him. He thrashed with fist and claw, and was blocked, his arms cast wide, his blows making contact with nothing, damaging nothing, as Gorgus met him.

Granular mists crawled down the passage Xirakura followed. He stopped to watch as the mists flowed outward, boiled across the road with alarming speed, like rushing waves crashing against buildings, leaking into windows and under doors, climbing to displace clean air, a flood of dense, unnatural fog.

It swept around the ankles of fleeing peoples, and in pairs and alone they stopped short. A man reached for his own face. He dug shaking fingers into the corners of his eyes, wriggled them under the orbits. Blood and black fluid cascaded over his cheeks as he crushed flesh and dragged it from the sockets. A woman drew a hooked knife from a leather sheath at her hip, stabbed and raked a line across her belly. Her guts tumbled out of the seam as she crashed onto her knees.. Another woman gripped her throat, pulled and crushed. Mangled tissues contorted her neck as she rasped through the wreckage, a hollow whistle thrust through impending

Wrath for the Sun God

quiet as still others mutilated themselves.

Caught in those mists, the people so intent on fleeing mere seconds ago turned their fear inward, and ended their own lives.

He spun and ran away from the scene. Helpless to do anything for them, he ran. Anger built in his guts, mingled with dread and guilt as he left them to their fate, to save himself, to put distance between himself and those coruscating, cloying waves.

He needed the docks, what peace he might find there. He needed to drive a spirit down into him, to see these monsters removed from the city by whatever means he could, and their catastrophic influence abated, so that these people could heal. In whatever way they could. Heal from this conflagration and all it bared into them.

Timin saw the waves of granular mist rolling toward him. He set his feet, steeled himself against the impact as his pathfinders took up positions, built up their guards and moved forward.

Absence stole over him, an absence of self, and he walked into the mists, opened paths along adjoining channels and shoved those who still had a chance into them, away from the taint of grief held in those mists, the demand for self destruction.

Around him, his pathfinders performed the same ritual, throwing bloodied bodies aside, knocking blades free of weeping peoples before they could take them to themselves. He pressed onward, intent on finding his quarry, the Spirit Caller, knowing he could not tarry here long, that the hunters were already in pursuit, that they sought what he sought, and would not stand aside to let him have it.

He turned corner, down a thoroughfare and toward the sea. Somewhere down there, he would find that man of the Katuwiti. The docks provided a measure of safety the rest of the city no longer possessed. It was the only place that made sense as a route of escape without the pathfinders to facilitate an exit into the plains.

He felt the weight of a net closing around them. The predatory gaze of the hunters settling on the most obvious, most expedient means of escape for the Katuwiti, the Magura, all of those others who had come to this city to settle for a time.

They would make their move there, hem off what exits remained. Blood would follow. Blood for the Spirit Caller and his kin. Blood for Timin's people. Blood for all those who stood in their way.

He needed haste. Needed them in his hands now. Before it was too late.

Spirit Caller

A woman in red and a man in gray emerged within the deeps at Empress Shao Luin's flanks. She halted her ascent, invited them to her, and they came as obediently as dogs, both wearing queer expressions at the sight of her.

"What is the meaning of this?" the woman asked, her voice a siren song, deep and melodious, warm and inviting and soft.

"Stay close to the shore, you two. But do not draw those mortals to their deaths. It is not their time." Shao Luin said.

"There is violence on our border." The man in gray said, and his voice was rough and high.

"Leave their ships alone." She commanded.

"Then you will allow them to bring their blood feud to us?" he asked, furrowing bushy eyebrows.

"It is not them who are the source of this violence." She said.

"Is it any business of ours what the gods entangle these people in?" the woman asked. "We should abstain. There is nothing for us to gain here."

"I have made my decision. Now leave me. I have work to do."

They drifted away, both intent on the shores, to watch from the shallows as their empress drove into the heart of the conflict on the surface. As, for the first time in generations, she involved herself in the games the gods played, took a side in their conflicts.

For so long, the enemy had been singular and distant, the wars waged between them long ended and the cycle of death cleaved in two. Threats had been exchanged, certainly, but there had been no battle between them. Yet now, she entered into a fight which did not concern her, which even now lent more souls to her domain, to be watched over by her until the time came to defend them.

In is time of freedom, Gora Soft Touch had never been the worst of his kind, but he had been no friend to the seas. She remembered what his lover had done to Sal Fier, her cousin. What he had done in giving rise to the Witch Empress, Sal Seid, and she did not trust him.

An entire ocean suffused with poison, the spirit murdered for the crime of defying the Great King, seeking to block him in his pursuit of Harkahn, who had been far crueler than him, whose power he had coveted.

He would use this mortal, but to what end? All that bore fruit for the great kings was anathema to the oceans. And if his move saw him made greater, saw him into more power than he commanded now...

Will she wake?

There was that woman who slumbered at the crossroads of three oceans, whose domain none would dare touch for her dreams benefited all. The Spirit of Salt must remain sleeping, or they would all fall under her reign, be compelled to serve her in a way they had not since the Era of Unity ended, and the lay of the land was fixed.

She did not covet that prospect, but knew she could not abstain in this conflict. Though his aims were no benefit to her, he was right in his beliefs. If the Lesser Gods saw fit to stand for their divine and terrible purpose, if they had joined hands in pursuit of the one true victory in their game, their Elders would be in the Waxing World soon. They would come, the worst of them, the most destructive seeking to crush their children before their rebellion could take hold, before it could see the greatest damage done and the castes reshuffled.

She did not value that end, either. In their conflicts lay certainty Shah Jagat would come for her, and she would need allies when he did. Mortal death was her domain, always and forever it must be.

She felt Gora's touch near the shore, imbuing his chosen regent with ancient power, power born of his blood. She felt his touch where her waters broke against the shore of the port at Faed City, the first stones of that port set by the hand of her chosen king. Power swelled within her, and her body spread apart, a dark stain in the waters, dissipating into them and fading as the essence of her was drawn into the body of a mortal, to settle there, ride him for as long as his fragile body could withstand her.

If your power is not enough, Gora. If the trickle to remember the torrent you once possessed is not enough, it will be more than just this lone man who dies.

She followed the currents to the surface, and all the spirits of her oceans watched on. Singing rose from the depths, and the surface of her seas was whipped into chaos. Storm clouds gathered to shadow her approach, and the Goddess of Storms made her fury known, for the sea was not her friend, and she would abide no interference from her.

But the goddess held no power to stop her. Not in this. Not in any of her efforts. The goddess raged and spit forth gales, and somewhere in the sky Shol Barak pressed against her, forced her back as high pressure bared down on Faed City and the shore, and she was given, by his grace, a way forward.

The scars across Xirakura's torso burned. The pain choked off his breath, and he stumbled, slammed onto his knee, his teeth clamping together around a snarl. Raw power surged within him. Waves tore through his flesh, ran hot across his limbs, drawn up through his feet and into his body to spread across him, imbue him with a power like he had never felt before.

His hand acted of its own will, snatched the gourd belted at his hip and pressed it to his navel, and his soul whispered out of him, a thin tendril left behind, deep in his guts, to hold his life, to keep him away from death. A second thread wove around the first, was braided into it, lending a stabilizing hand as it spun and knotted itself into place, and the heat settled into his body, a warm, gentle touch,

Tears for the Moon God

almost the caress of a lover.

Thought left him, and his eyes flared with depthless blue light. Another, alien force settled into his body, and he was taken by a spirit, forced into submission as the essence of her settled into him, took up residence in his body, and acted through him.

On the horizon, storm clouds gathered. Lightning thrashed from the sky to stab into deep waters behind a line of ships all looming black in the shadows cast by the black moon where it blocked the sun.

He heard a war chant in many voices, a dirge to match the wrath of the spirit taking occupancy in his body, and the tides rose. And they flooded the beaches, ran white and raging to his feet.

The electric thrill of life bled into Empress Shao Luin. The live wire sensation of riding a torrent in the body of a man. She looked out through his eyes at a city razed by fire. Pathfinders stood at the mouths of open portals through which plains and the post and plank barriers of cattle pens were visible, as city residents and foreigners marched through those portals, an evacuation underway.

She marched with bare, mortal feet up the street, toward the source of the conflagration, a warring of crimson light and burning flame, toward a battle between gods.

Rapids boiled around her feet, swept up and around her host. His spirit held against her might, Gora's touch welded to it, the cord containing his essence familiar in a way that sickened. In a way that should bare into her rage for the affliction he had granted this man.

But elation stole over her. Raw ecstasy to drive away ill thought, to embolden her in the task she must see to.

She climbed the low grade hill, walked in the body of a naked man, the gourd pressed firm against his belly without need of his hands to hold it, a strange sight to behold for those who set eyes on him.

Rahad tended the wounded in streets unaffected by the gray haze of Ao Nii's grief. She knew the moon, had enjoyed a friendship with him in the early days, which had long soured with the arrival of his madness.

She set her feet, drunk with life and fraught anxiety. If Gora's touch slipped away, if he lost control of this vessel, he would die. It would be mere moments, and in those moments, she would have need to divorce herself from him. Too long spent in those last moments within and she would die along with him, and the bounty her domain held would die with her, and the light would go out in her city, and those people who had for so long known her embrace would fall away into the waters, to witness a second death and the denial of their character, as they became one with the currents, and lost all.

The currents carried her, appallingly fast, up the slopes and down adjoining channels, swift as any river, as brutal as any whirlpool.

In their wake, dead things took life. The bodies of Magura and others rose and followed in her wake, marched into the city in pursuit of those who would do harm to their people. The souls of the recent dead who grieved over their own bodies turned their gazes on her vessel, watched as the empress passed, and were consumed by her waters, driven into them and down, to float along her currents, to rush with whitecaps, to lend the power of their souls to her.

Spirit Caller

She emerged on the narrow road where Gorgus and Ao Nii railed against each other, and their attentions snapped to her. Fear stole over both gods as she came for them. Fear and anger at the presence of this newcomer, this spirit in the guise of a mortal. They felt her press against them, knew her strength and knew they could not stand long against it.

But she was not here for their deaths. She was here to save the mortals they had not yet killed. She was here to lend her hand in the unfolding chaos, to see the city returned to peace, to see the mortals returned to safety.

She stood between them, pressed her hands against their chests, feeling the waters shielding flesh boiling as gouts of steam hissed around her touch. Her wrists stiffened, fingers pressed against flesh and cloth, and both were blasted away.

"Stay out of this, empress!" Gorgus roared.

He was climbing to his feet.

She was on him in the space of a breath. There. Waiting for him to take his knees.

She took him around the throat and cast him aside, into Ao Nii where he stood, and they crashed together through one squat home, the next, another after that, and another, until they were near her shores. Until they had reached the docks.

She surged after them.

The spirit caller's soul recoiled away from her, the thread sought to free itself from the body, to fly away into death, and was seized, dragged back into the body as thin cracks broke over her host's flesh, and blood ran over his forearms and chest.

I must do this quickly.

The dead watched from her waters, their bodies engaged in conflicts elsewhere. Hidden figures were touched by her, dragged into the tides as mortal souls and bodies descended on them, dragged them down to drown, to join them.

The hunters could not deny her. Absolute was her power. They may cloak themselves in shadow, render their flesh the colors of their surroundings, but they could not become ghosts. They could not divorce their flesh from itself, slide through walls, become ephemeral beings.

She found them for they were solid and corporeal. Announced their presence to those who would meet them, made useless their camouflage and exposed them. And they fled from her, from the recent dead, fled for safe purchase in a city plagued by fire and water, by dead things and curses and monsters out of legend.

She found Ao Nii and Gorgus at the shores, detangling themselves from each other, struggling to take their feet and seeking to destroy each other at the same time.

She took them both by their heads, one hand wrapped around a jackal's muzzle, the other clamped around a feminine face, and pushed.

Two gods soared away, ocean currents cutting into them like razors as they took up the effort of casting them on.

She turned her gaze to the sky.

"Take them." She said, her voice echoing, rising on unnatural currents to meet the ears of a spirit. "Take them away."

The currents thrashed upward, and the winds caught hold of those warring gods. They were cast high in the air, waves of wind slamming into their bodies. Concussive blasts rippled over the harbor as they were thrown, twin stars, warring

Tears for the Moon God

flame and light, to take their fight to another place.

She collapsed in the shallows, raging waters ebbing, drifting back, carrying bodies out to sea, carrying souls to join their ancestors, their families—brothers and sisters, mothers and fathers, children taken too soon. To drift along the currents, until they found her city in the deeps, and peace.

In slow turns, she drew away from the body of the Spirit Caller, savored the last tastes of life and all of its uncertainty as her essence bled into the waters retreating around his feet, and his soul was guided into the void she left behind, guided by Gora's hand as the rope of influence spun around the thread of the man's soul, releasing him.

Xirakura came to in the shallows. He watched the waters retreat, felt the lacerations against his arms and chest where his flesh had broken, wondered at what had stolen over him.

He looked to the seas, to the land behind him, saw that the raging fires, the light and the clouds of granular energy were gone. The gods had been forced away, leaving a lesser chaos in their wake, a quavering breath as the city knew a taste of relief.

Fury for the Wolf Lord

The North Wind howled across the steppe, driving winds whipped into a frenzy as the uelfin struggled to hear their songs and were met instead with his voice, booming as the spirit descended among them.

From the winds came the howling of wolves, the brooding growl of the bear, the high groan of the deer, countless other sounds in the voices of beasts. Countless voices that belonged to the world before man and had grown with him.

The winds scattered, entwined themselves with dead grasses and bitter snows and gave rise to the forms and figures of creatures of the forest and the plains. The wild hunt charged into the uelfin ranks. Antlers tore into their bodies, thrashing heads gored them and cast them into open air where birds drove skewer beaks into them, knocked them back to ground. Giant bears gnashed teeth around tender throats, swiped grizzly claws across their paths and bounded into the chaos to meet those entities in God Lanfin's keeping, those who knew loyalty to the God of Music, the Keeper of Time.

Corporeal winds rumbled past Chakta, and Tamlin, and Shaki, lending their strength to the children of chiefs, to declare for his side in the conflict unfolding across the world.

And Chakta saw. Saw him in the distance. Behind his wild beasts all of wind, and grass, and snow. Saw the dark cast of his features, thunderheads raging behind sleepy eyes, the smile seen in every depiction of him replaced by a brutish scowl. Leathers and furs crossed his wide, muscular body, flapped in the high, driving winds. Gales of ice laden wind burned across her cheeks as she stood frozen, watching the chaos unfold around her. The uelfin stabbing at what they could not touch, ducking under a bounding stag, railing against a pack of wolves, seeking a pathway through to her, to Tamlin and Skaki, as Ho'o brought his wrath against them.

She saw in his hands a toy horse, which was carved by a crude hand, a child's hand. The dimensions were off, the legs wide and straight, the back too deeply arched and the muzzle too narrow. She saw it there, twined in his fingers, held in a careful caress, his touch delicate. He stepped forward, intent on something she could not see. The snows were driven into opaque walls and she was left without

Tears for the Moon God

sight as he surged forth, into the masses of uelfin, to meet the source of his anger.

Twin blasts rocked the ground. A ball of white hot flame blasted across the steppe and she spun round to face it.

The chief's pavilion was a ruin. Horse parts carved in wood soared away from the wreckage and were buffeted away by Ho'o, who stood before them now, between them and the figures even now climbing out of the wreckage, their hands around each other's throats.

The one, a delicate, emaciated man. Long, dark hair swam around his head, riding wild currents as crimson light thrashed from him. Clad all in white, billowing sleeves were pushed up around wrists like thin porcelain, and his eyes, terrible eyes black with rage.

The other, a lithe man from the neck down, naked save for a strip of undyed linen wreathed around his hips. His head like that of a falcon, but the feathers gold, a crown like a sunburst, tines thin and sharp, worn over the crest. A second head and a third riding his shoulders, one the head of a black dog, the snout long and elegantly tapered and similarly crowned. The last was the head of a man, the hair golden and arranged in neat, loose curls beneath its own crown, the eyes white all the way through and the skin sun kissed to match the god's body.

Motes of energy ripped away from the two gods as Ho'o stood resolute against them, maintaining a safe distance as they railed against each other, protecting those mortals from their touch even as he sought to drive the uelfin back.

And still he held that toy horse in his hands, that crude carving that looked so like a bored child's craft.

He turned to the three Gil Garo youths, and Chakta looked first to Shaki and then to Tamlin as he did. The normally flighty spirit, so intent on avoiding mortal eyes, knelt down to them, but his eyes were not on them. He looked past Shaki's shoulder, in the direction of the cave entrance.

She cast over her shoulder, following his gaze. The Swans had emerged to join the fray, to protect their home and their lover, and the student they had claimed. They streamed through the uelfin, broke through snarling ranks, raked taloned fingers across their paths, waged combat against them.

Ho'o pinched her chin and brought her around to him.

"Focus." He said. "Take refuge in the cave. Duijus Kanh will arrive soon, but this is too dangerous for you three." He snatched pointed glimpses at Shaki and Tamlin. "When this is over, take this with you to Nixir City. There will be others awaiting you there. It is imperative you go there as soon as this is done. You understand."

He shoved the toy into Chakta's hands. She scrambled to take it from him, almost dropped it before she found her grip.

"Well, off with you." He said, shooing them away. "And tell Duijus Kanh to get off his lazy ass, please. He is needed here."

He spun on his heels, and marched forward, toward the fighting gods as gouts of flame and something with a physical heft that resembled flame flew away from those monstrous creatures, as wounds opened against their flesh and black blood leaked from them, as they exchanged blows, sought to destroy each other.

She backed away. Tamlin caught her around the shoulder. "You heard the man. Run!"

He spun her around and pushed, and she sprinted toward the cave, into a

Fury for the Wolf Lord

channel opened by the wild hunt and the Swans insidious movements among the uelfin, who themselves were seeking the cave and what shelter it provided, and what great victory it offered.

"Where is he!" Ao Nii demanded.

He spread his arms and a sword of pure moonlight filled the space between them. He seized the elegant, single bladed weapon and slashed.

Gorgus retreated a step, a brutal maul suffused with golden light materializing in his fist. He swung for Ao Nii, who dug in his heels, spun out of its path and brought a back swing across to slice open the Sun God's flank.

"Where is he damn you!"

"Your lover is dead, Ao Nii." Gorgus snarled. "Let go!"

A second mace appeared in his other hand and he brought them both down savagely against Moon God's shoulders.

Fire thrashed away from the points of impact. Smoldering flesh and cooked muscle tore away from him as he backed out from under those grizzly weapons.

The earth melted under their feet. A glass sheet crawled over it, blackened and shattered.

Already, the wounds in his shoulders were healing. Already, he was mounting for a counterstrike, his blade held before him, thin point angled for the sun god's heart.

Gorgus stepped wide of the thrust and swung his maces for the Moon God's side.

Ho'o rushed into the gap, brought one arm up to block Gorgus's attack, and diverted the other with his knee.

He pushed, and Gorgus was sent flying, flailing. A bonfire surged forth from the place of his impact among the snows. Steam gouted forth, blasted away in boiling waves as he climbed to his feet.

"Stay out of this, Ho'o!" he snarled.

Ao Nii rushed to make contact, to renew their fighting.

Ho'o took him around the middle and spun him away, disrupting his charge and sending him flying into the snows.

Ao Nii climbed to his feet, the sword still gripped firm in his dominant hand. He launched himself at Gorgus, and Gorgus at him.

"Where is God Lanfin, you insolent bastard!" Ao Nii raved as he charged, the sword bared down before him, threatening an upward slash when he made contact again.

Ho'o was on him before he could close the distance. He wrapped his fingers around the god's sword arm, shoved him back and away.

"Stop this, now, cousin!" he growled. "You cannot win this fight!"

"I am not interested in winning." Ao Nii seethed.

"Then go away to your house."

Ao Nii seized Ho'o around the neck and cast him aside. Pain welled in The North Wind's throat where the god's press had come close to crushing bones and cartilage. He might have died.

Where are you, Duijus Kanh! Come forth, damn you!

He rushed for them.

Ao Nii's sword carved an arc across Gorgus's torso, a thin line breaking tanned

Tears for the Moon God

flesh, breaking across compact abs, carving an arc over one, well defined pectoral muscle and breaking past that shoulder.

"Blood for the Moon God." Ao Nii intoned. "The price you must pay."

Malevolent glee twisted his features into something ugly and maligned as he brought the sword around for another slash.

Gorgus thrust his maces into Ao Nii's torso. Ribs shattered, punched through skin and burned cloth.

Ao Nii faltered.

Where is Uldal? Where is Shakh? What madness keeps them back?

Ho'o caught him around the midriff, dragged him back and back, away from the sun god, away from certain death.

And still no one came. No god nor any spirit.

Duijus Kanh stirred awake. He felt the touch of deep shadow on the mouth of his cave, and knew the gods were at war with each other, that even now the unfolding conflict encompassed much more than the petty skirmishes the moon and sun waged against each other. The proof was here in his cave, seated on the floor of his chamber, watching him through eyes shining gold to match his, cold and unemotive.

He remembered that gaze from the time of his pupil's first life, his first descent into this cave, his first emergence.

He climbed to his feet, his gaze steady on the acolyte who had killed a spirit, who had challenged the claim of a god to his house, who had done none of those things. Had not risen to such hubris, such brutal abandon, the reckless pursuit of more power. Who had risen not high enough to fill the mantle he had left behind.

Yet.

Three humans had entered his gullet, and behind them the throngs of uelfin his Swans could not contain. And they had help. He heard the howling, the braying, the groans of the wild hunt at the cave mouth, the rumble of stamping hooves over the lands beyond. Ho'o was with them, and he had taken his side. Soon, all of the spirits and the gods would be compelled into this conflict.

A cataclysm was forthcoming. God Lanfin's attempts to avoid it, the pressure placed on his shoulders to see a new path unfold, had done nothing to abate the anger of the Elder Gods, his betters. They were in the world now. Not just Katcya, but others intent on seeing their ends met, on seeing their designs brought to bear. At the crux of all of these elaborate schemes was a game for possession.

Those uelfin were not here to destroy him. The notion would have been laughable if it was not so obviously designed to hobble him. The tribes moved away from this place in keeping with a grander design, to crush the force that had won Dupec ground in the earliest days, that had helped him oust a god from his home. They had been too blunt with their efforts, had believed the spirits and the gods who favored mortals would not see through their designs, would not see past them to what lay at their heart.

They had not come to destroy Dupec Safar, either. They had come to claim him, for themselves.

And he could not allow it.

"Are you ready, master." Dupec asked.

"I am." He closed on his young pupil, a man who had been past his fiftieth year

Fury for the Wolf Lord

last he saw him before the great reclamation of his lover.

In him was the making of a power to eclipse that he had possessed in his former life, for the echoes of a pulse lived within him, echoes of the strength he had commanded in those days. The mind forgot many things, but the soul remembered.

"It is time." Duijus Kanh said.

"Time?"

"To announce your return to the world, cub." He said. "You will have your peace, but do not squander this chance. I do not like your strategy, but I will grant you this boon, if you can convince him."

He helped Dupec to his feet, and together they walked from this chamber, to speak to the gods of their hubris, to answer their call.

Oe

Rushing waters washed over docks, slid across shins and ankles, cold and unyielding. The river swelled and flooded the lowest streets, and Goths and uelfin alike ran for shelter, clung to beams amid rising tides, clambered onto low roofs and dangled from water wheels as the waters climbed higher, higher still, mounting the hills on her southern bank.

In the distance, amid myriad rivercraft choking her band, a wide fin broke the surface, a vitreous, crystalline sail imbued with the full spectrum of colors, luminous and beautiful to Haffa's dying eyes.

He watched as the mother of all uelfin slid over land, into Cratom itself, listened to her voice as she slid past him, assuring him that his loss would not be in vain, that she would answer God Lanfin's insult, shelter what children remained to her, that she found in him her pride, for he had shaped this song of defiance against her once lover turned enemy.

"There will be an end to this slaughter." She promised.

The long length of her opal-hewed body trailed past him, and he was dragged into her waters, the last breaths leaving him as she laid her claim against him. In dying, he felt her love, and he was at peace.

Oe raised her head, and in the distance she saw God Lanfin coming. A stony snout reeled back over sharp fangs, a lolling, warty tongue bearing barbed hooks for all to see as he sang his song of death. Great, yellow-green eyes bore into her as he twisted his head. A ridged, crimson, leather mane flared around his meaty head. His sinuous body contracted into dense coils behind him.

The people snared between them fled, the waters ebbing, drawing away the innocent among them and leaving behind those uelfin who had found purchase enough to avoid her touch.

He reeled back and hissed, and she opened her mouth, gusted hot, steaming breath across the backs of their fighting children.

"Love me." She breathed in that contralto voice. *"Yearn for my touch, feel my desire."*

"You will not take them so easily." He growled.

Oe

The uelfin song rose in volume, drowning her calls for their infatuation, their desire to do as she commanded, to fall into the warm, inviting waters of her embrace and be hers, irrevocably hers.

Blades lashed out and made contact, uelfin song from both sides warred for control.

She surged forth, and God Lanfin sprang across open air to meet her, fangs bared and sinking into her body as she clamped down on his neck and twisted her body into his, seeking to choke the breath from him, to destroy him once and for all, and end this long argument between them.

He seized against her, his body snared and yet finding purchase, forcing her coils to loosen as battle raged around them and Goths and tourists fled for higher ground, as Raukhas gave up their arguments and fled from the scene of slaughter among them, intent on fighting another day.

Saijin saw as if he was in their presence the serpent god and spirit entwined, the embrace of old lovers twisted into something grizzly as they sought to kill each other. Floodwaters quaked beneath them. Blood ran with the current as uelfin fell to each others blades.

He cowered away from the vision, his back hard against the wall, eyes wide with terror.

"When will this madness end." He whimpered. "What have I done."

"The right thing, I assume." Rhul said.

Fire was taking the slums now. The violence there was swiftly reaching its conclusion. It had not been a long lived fight.

The Raukhas would be coming for them, soon. He hoped Wu managed to win his contest with the woman who had burned him soon, that he would come back in one piece, ready to whisk them away to some place safer.

"You understand what will befall us if she dies." Saijin said.

"The river will dry up. We will have no water then." Samil said inflectionlessly. "All of us will be forced to leave, and it will not just be us affected. Oe runs all the way from the mountains to the sea. Every people across Byrne plain will be affected by her death."

"She will win this contest." Rhul said, though he felt no certainty in that outcome. "And we will leave here. You will have to find ties among the uelfin, Samil. Take up where your mother left off, and win their loyalty through better means. Fear is no weapon of permanence."

"Does my brother possess such wisdom?" Samil asked.

"Sometimes." Rhul said.

Lanfin recoiled from Oe, his fangs withdrew from her flesh, neck extending for a second attack. A few notes thrashed out of his lungs, driving the song in a new direction, seeking to shape the future in his favor.

He rolled under her weight, thrust his fangs into her again, and wrenched her to the side, drawing her fangs free.

Uelfin fell in scores. The warring songs were evenly matched without his contributions, and the waters made treacherous footing for both sides as the currents whipped up rapids and whirlpools for them to contend with.

She screamed, a gout of steam issuing from her throat, and he held his breath.

Tears for the Moon God

He had fallen for that trick once before, had not escaped her embrace until she had drawn the seed from him, dragged it into her band to give rise to those fool creatures who shared with him their blood, the god given gift he had never wanted mortals to possess.

He clamped down harder, hunting for her vitals, pursuing her death and the end to their long struggle.

"You will not succeed!" she intoned savagely. *"You will fail in this and all of your designs. I know what you seek, Lanfin! I know what you have involved yourself in!*

Then die, and make way for this era. It is past time your kind knew their place!

He bound her in coils of rigid flesh. Scales sloughed away from their bodies, showered the band, stabbed through uelfin bodies like great Shards of flint.

"You will not have them!"

She met his challenge, rolled and cast him under her, injecting venom from hollowed fangs into his flesh, a venom imbued with her power.

A haze crawled across his eyes, and he shook her off, threw her across the expanse.

"YOU WILL NOT TAKE THEM FROM ME!" she roared.

An answering roar ripped from his throat. He lunged at her.

She slithered out of his path, wrapped him in a strangling embrace and bit down behind the meaty sale, crushing jaws finding purchase in his mandible, lashing down, shattering bone.

"Sing now, my jaded lover. Sing through broken jaws!"

He recoiled, shook himself in a frenzy to release his jaws from hers. Pain lanced through his skull. Blood weltered from those puncture wounds and slid down his throat, his own blood mingled with noxious, intoxicating poison.

She released her hold on him, and he slithered away down an adjoining street, to a safe distance, hissing and spitting through his mangled jaw as she watched from where she lay, coiled around herself and ready to strike.

"If you did not have a use, I would kill you." She hissed. *"Go back to your rat. Bother me not longer."*

He hissed, and blood sprayed the nearest buildings.

He retreated.

The uelfin of Cratom surged forth, riding the high of their matron's victory, and the lines of God Lanfin's loyalists broke. They retreated after their lord, those who could still stand, and the song died away, leaving behind screams and the growl of distant fire as she retreated from the conflict, into her band, to tend to her wounds.

Wu's mother watched him. An awkward smile alighted on her lips, and she fidgeted with a lace hand towel as she looked him over, taking in all that he had become.

"Why are you here?"

"She was not interested in your father, Wu." His stepmother said.

"I didn't love him. It was not in my interest to remain when I knew no true love could be had between us. We might have gone to Oe and asked for her blessing, but the love we would have known for each other would be false."

"Where *is* father?" he asked, looking from one to the other of them.

"Away." His stepmother said. "On an errand for the king, and wouldn't that be just fitting. He'll miss you, won't he? But it is better this way. You cannot take

Oe

lordship from my son, lest we introduce confusion to the line of succession.

"I suppose it would pain me little if you took over in your father's stead, but then what would be left for me?"

"I didn't come here to stake my claim." Wu said, his gaze still fixed on his mother.

"Then why are you here?" Mistress Bane asked.

"To see to it that you are dead and your crime against me is rectified." Wu said, but he was not so sure of himself now. His mother was alive. Her life changed things. It might change things.

"If I allowed it, would you choose to walk away from this conflict? If I allowed you to take your mother away from this city, to settle at a place of your choosing, would you leave this errand of yours unfinished. Leave me alive, that is."

"Would you leave us alone, then?" he asked.

"Insofar as you did not seek to supplant your half brother as the apparent heir to your father's fortune, I would." She said.

"I have a question...before I make a decision." He said. "If my mother has been alive all this time, in hiding...why did you try to kill me?"

His mother turned to face the woman, a reassuring look passed from one woman to the other.

"I never wanted you dead." She said. "If you had not so obviously hated me, I would have left you alone. But see things from my point of view. I was a lowly drudgery maid in the employ of an uelfin soothsayer. I toiled away at latrines, washed away putrid sweat from sheets where his whores did business. I did not have the skills or the charms or the looks, for that matter, to do the work they did, and I did not want to be like them. They left those chambers bruised and broken. Some of the Johns beat them into unconsciousness. A few left corpses behind for me to remove.

"I did not want to lead that life any longer. It was horrifying. And I did what was needed to see my life improved. Your mother came to me, told me of her reservations for Liudao, and I saw an opportunity. She could go away and enjoy a life with a man she *did* love, and I could assume the role of an ambassador's wife. I did not care if he loved me, or if I loved him. Those were luxuries for women of means, which I was not.

"She stepped aside, but she could not take you with her or the scandal would have spilled over into Liudao's life. He would have been expected to act against her. She may even have been executed."

"She took you into Guldanh Forest." His mother said, taking up the story where she left off. "For me to find. We agreed upon a place, and she restrained you only to keep you from wandering. Just that. But when I found the place, there were only cut ropes to remember you by, just that. You had been taken away from me, and I did not know how to find you. It was a dark time for both of us. I hope you understand."

"I...I don't...but...you're alive." He turned his gaze on his stepmother. "You won't follow us."

"As long as you allow Samil to retain his claim, I will not."

"Then...then I suppose...I suppose I will leave here." He said.

His mother approached him, and he took her hand. Her touch was warm against his skin, and he turned his back on his father's second wife, mounted the stairs.

Tears for the Moon God

Warm and wet weltered over his back. A white lance of pain stabbed through his shoulder, missing his heart and lungs as a broad blade poked through flesh, and cloth, and leather under his clavicle.

The warm press against his hand dissolved with the contact. He watched through wide eyes as the blade slid inch over inch out of him. The blade was black and shot through with threads of a lighter metal, spider veins running up its length. It was curved along one side, tapered toward a thin edge from a thicker plane at its spine.

He spun, rammed an elbow down on the Mistress's forearm, breaking her grip on the sword, and pushed her away as she swung a matching blade wildly.

He looked from the tip of the blade to her, watched as recognition donned on her, that she had miscalculated, driven the butterfly sword in too high and left herself exposed for a counter attack.

He left it in place, fearing the blood loss would leave him weakened even more if he removed it before this fight was over.

Blinding rage surged within him, and he rushed her, relying on his good arm as the other flapped limply at his side.

"YOU CONNIVING WHORE!" he bellowed.

She backed away, toward the back of the room where his father slept soundly against a cot.

Liudao Bane's eyes fluttered open. They settled on his son and widened. He vaulted upright, stared in dull horror as his wife and lost son fought with long knives and short swords, blood welling around the blade fixed in Wu's shoulder as he carved thin lines across her chest and arms, opened a wound on her cheek as she fought desperately to bat the blows away.

"LIUDAO HELP ME!"

But his father was a statue. He sat there, watching as his second wife fought against a man who looked so similar to the son he had raised, so much like himself, shoved her sword arm wide, booted her kneecap, shattered bone, sent her to sprawl across the floor, the blade skidding across hard, undressed stone and out of her reach.

He wrenched her up by her hair, looked deep into her eyes, into those soulless, desperate eyes. Eyes that promised an end to this if he just let her live. Eyes that lied.

"Wu?" his father whispered. "But...you're dead...you *died*."

"I did no such thing father. This lying *witch* left me for dead in the woods one day because she wanted your money. She went to great lengths to make sure I never came back, but she made a mistake when she left me out there. She failed to account for the deer trail she followed into the woods. Even the paths game frequents are trails a pathfinder can follow.

"One found me, Mistress Bane." He growled, so close to her face that all she would see in her last moments was him. Fury etched into the soft planes of his round face, burning in dark eyes, festering to reflect the foul wounds she had left in his soul. "Samil can have everything you built, but you won't enjoy any of it. Not one second longer."

His long knife bit into her throat. Blood sprayed over his chest and neck. Her eyes searched desperately for anything else to look at, some peace in this basement safe room to possess her as she died. She found none. Just his hot, dark eyes, the

Oe

snarl painted across his lips.

Liudao climbed off the bed. Upstairs, an ongoing commotion came to its conclusion. He looked into his father's face. Saw the confusion in his gaze, the unease, the shock of having watched the woman he had spent these last twenty years with killed before him. Murdered in cold blood to satisfy a long, quiet feud between the woman and his son. The spectre of a child he had lost.

"I...I'm sorry." Wu whispered.

He ran for the stairs, away from that face and all of its accusations, opened a path before the steps, and ran into the room above where the assassins all stood vigil over the bleeding body of Garam the Lamb.

While they watched the man die, he seized him around the shoulders, opening another path ahead of him, where a second door led into a closet at the back of these quarters, and dragged him through, into the quiet of the house Rhul had chosen for keeping Samil and Saijin, where he collapsed in a heap against the carpet.

Rhul descended on him then, took hold of the hilt of the butterfly sword planted in his shoulder, and wrenched it free.

He crawled across the floor wordlessly, lay against his Core, and merged with him. The wound hissed and gouted steam as it knit itself closed. Wu whimpered as it healed. There was nothing he could do for Garam, but he would not leave him here.

Saijin hurried over to them as Samil watched his brother climb to his feet. Horrified at the sight of his mother's blood painted across his brother's torso.

Wu spared him a sympathetic glance, a nod all that was needed to confirm it was done. "Go into the world, Samil. And tell our father I love him."

He opened a door, which let out onto a sprawling cave, the vestiges of civilization rising to either side of a broad, sandy expanse. He held that door open as Saijin helped him with Garam's body.

"I'll come back for you when I am done." He said.

"I will await your return, brother. I want to know you. Absent of your hatred." Samil said.

"Do not grieve the wicked." Wu said.

Together with Saijin, they carried Garam's body through the door; and he hoped, for it was all he could do, that a healer was near enough to save Garam from his fate. From the embrace of Empress Shao Luin.

The Moonkin

The signal flared to life from the Tipik position. Gulang sucked in a deep breath and bellowed. His war cry washed over the Kachin forces, spread as far as his voice carried, to snare the hearts and minds of his men, and drive out their fears, their worries. To replace those sentiments with bravery, with furious pride. He snapped his reigns, and his force surged forward.

The Kachin charge rumbled through the trees. The Tului camp swam into view. Tents arranged in neat rows, pens staked out between them. They met no fortifications, no means of defense, no defiance on the charge inland. Swords swung at tent flaps and met nothing. No soldiers running from their tenements. Explosions descended into ringing silence where Guruhl sought to lay slaughter. Tents burned as energy bombs blasted through them.

He slowed his horse. Amid fire and a storm of mounted warriors, there was no response. No enemy in sight.

He swung his gaze to the nearest pen.

Empty.

Pried back the flap on the nearest tent still standing. A barren void surrounding a lone tent pole looked back at him.

What is this? Where are their forces.

He saw the Tipik surging into the camp from the other side, watched as Coltang emerged at the head of his own spear, as the same realization donned on the Tipik chief as was quickly donning on him.

Coltang approached at a trot. Closed the gap between them as a confused army settled in to await orders.

"There is no one here." He said.

"A trap?"

A stream of light slashed through the trees. A plume of dirt blasted away from the sight of impact.

A second streamer preceded a second crash, a dull echo of the blast rippling through the trees amid the sounds of distant fighting. A third, and then a fourth.

A last pair rocked the ground almost under their horses' hooves. Dirt and chipped stones and pine needles showered Gulang's flank, and a column of raw,

The Moonkin

silver light rose from the sight of impact. A pillar clawed through the canopy, and a wide, snow white plank spread to cover the intervening space. A second emerged a foot or so higher, then a third.

The staircase assembled itself at their feet, climbed into the canopy and away.

Screams in the distance. Thundering feet. Crimson light broke through the canopy, and they were on them. Men and women clad in white robes, enshrouded in crimson light.

Gnashing teeth. Clawing fingers.

Blood weltered along the flank of Gulang's horse. In the next moment he was pulled from his saddle. He grabbed his sword on the way down, wrenched it free and laid into his assailants.

All around him the moonkin laid slaughter. Blood sprayed from open wounds. Gil Garo soldiers were dragged from the saddle. Some of those moonkin were sobbing uncontrollably as they opened throats, gouged out chunks of flesh with wild aural blades. Others collapsed in fits of mad laughter as they yanked eyes out of twitching corpses, carved away tongues, took trophies, stole away with live captives to take back up the staircase, were smacked down and trampled by their own kind.

He fought to gain his feet. Lashed out with Sarkahn's power, imbued his assailants with waves of crippling pain, shook their auras like spirits in a bottle, silencing them long enough to mount a counter attack.

He swung his blade wildly about him, fending off still more attackers as they piled over him and ran for fresh targets, new meat, more deaths, more wounding, more, more, more.

Coltang let loose his hammers. Brutal impacts broke bodies. Gore flew in several directions. White fire ripped through ranks of moonkin as they surged toward him, threatened to hobble his horse with him on it. Clawing hands found him in the saddle. He brought his hammer down on them. White fire flared. His horse broke into a frenzied gallop, tripped over a raised root and sent him flying.

He shielded his head with his arms, crashed into a tree and rolled across ground. The moonkin were on him. He recalled one hammer to him. It punched a vicious hole through the chest of his attacker. He caught it, swung for the dirt. The hammer struck with uncanny force, severed feet and shins from the nearest of those frenzied moonkin. He rolled away, climbed to his feet, recalled the second hammer and cast it into the throngs.

Crow Durin watched from the fringes as the moonkin fell onto the Gil Garo. He could not have predicted this new development. Had acted on the orders of his superior only because he was compelled to. This had not been an act of faith. He had not known, when he was called to post camp in that spot, it would be overrun with monsters in the flesh of men.

The tents were a loss his people would feel, but a worthy sacrifice to see two Gil Garo sects destroyed so utterly, humiliated before his very eyes.

He reached into the minds of his Blood Lords.

Wall them in. Deny them escape.

Ibrim leapt off the staircase, into the fray. Manic glee stole over him as the

Tears for the Moon God

musky smell of blood filled his nostrils, as cold, sharp air made a labor of breathing. He lashed out with his god given power, wielded it instinctually, with abandon.

Bodies toppled before and behind him. Blood spattered his robes. He dodged the first clod of bodies, the first writhing hill, and marched into the heart of the camp, where slaughter awaited. Where he could finally prove himself to his god.

Seun lay chase from behind, the madness lingering at the edges of his mind. He took blood from a dying man, smeared it across his lips as he marched after Ibrim, scarlet eyes fixed on his slender back as he pursued.

These were not his enemy. The Gil Garo but hapless victims of a god's cruelty. They were not supposed to be here, were they? Not here, in this camp. This camp which flew the standard of the Tului Royal Army, the finch with wings spread, prepared to gore its prey, to sustain itself with its blood.

Where were his people? Where were their captives?

The pens were empty. The inroads overrun with cavalry and every one of them of a tribe he did not recognize.

He scrambled after Ibrim, who had turned south, who was joining the assault on a behemoth man wielding two war hammers, who would soon be overwhelmed by sheer numbers.

Coltang struggled to stay on his feet against the greater weight of his assailants. He heard Gulang's war cry, felt the bravado building in him again, but this was no time for heroism. His hammers could only do so much. The blasts from their impacts, the washes of white fire drowning out those ghoulish, crimson auras was no deterrent against this force. Rationality would force a fighter away from an unwinnable contest, but these were not rational foes.

He clamped his jaws together, stepped around the tree behind him, tried to open the distance between him and his foes, and they swarmed.

What gaps he opened closed instantly. Acolytes climbed over each other, crushed each other underfoot, all coming for him, all intent on ending his life.

Horses streamed past behind him. Swinging swords sang as they cut through the air above his head.

A moonkin's skull parted company with the rest of him above the eyes. Blood sloshed and brain matter tumbled across frozen ground.

The body fell and was replaced just as swiftly with another.

Ibrim saw his target. Saw the man he wanted to kill. Those hammers provided just the right challenge, just the right lever by which he could propel himself into some greater position. Some place of honor among the moonkin.

He surged forth, was stopped short by clawing hands, hands that found purchase against his robes. Hands that dragged him back and away from his would be victim.

A rage-filled snarl issued from his throat, and he spun on his assailant. The assailant clapped him on the sides of his neck. A pause in blood flow to his brain. He fell to the ground, was dragged out of the camp amid writhing shadows.

Seun hauled Ibrim across the vacant war camp, into the woods where darkness loomed heavy as the moon blocked out the light of the sun, and the trees amplified

The Moonkin

its shadow. There was fighting there, too, but the adversaries were retreating. He looked up to see that those retreating soldiers were Tului, all of them with shadows writhing at their feet.

They were being pursued by another force, a greater force. Soldiers piled in from the south and the east, warriors on foot who ran as if unused to being out of the saddle. Ropes of green light slashed at their backs. Dead rose anew with scarlet eyes and surged after him, but he was too quick.

The Gil Garo warrior pulled back, caught the nearest of them with those whips and brought them down again, incapacitated his kin and moved on.

The Tului fanned out along the southern border of the war camp. Arrows hissed overhead and buried themselves into the flanks of retreating horses. Flashes of light blinded him as he dragged Ibrim on, along the line of contest, seeking a sheltered place to put him until this was over.

Sarri bellowed the command to charge. He kicked his horse into a gallop. Sea spray trailed away from the beast as the Cuu entered the fray. The charge took the retreating and regrouping Tului, a broadside sweep.

Mounted cavalry dug into their ranks and forced them away from each other. Heads came off shoulders, arms off torsos. Tului dropped and were trampled under pounding hooves.

Thunder rolled through the earth as harsh lights blasted across the canopy. Ice swept across his path and was subsumed into his steed's body, ejected as needles from its flanks as cover fire for the oncoming others.

Seun pulled back and away from the flanking charge. He pitched out of the way of an incoming horse and ducked under a scimitar seeking his head. The ground rumbled under his feet as a blast rocked through the earth.

He stumbled, narrowly avoided falling, being trampled by those horses and warriors.

Shadows danced around his feet as he traveled. They clawed at forgotten swords, latched onto their shadows.

Weapons made a dance of their own around him, his shadows seizing on others, driving points into silhouettes as those swinging swords caught still others and laid open their flesh.

Crow Durin marched into view. Gulang saw him there, at the edge of the camp. He shoved the remaining moonkin off him and marched to meet the enemy general. A blade carved an arc across his path. He leapt out of its reach and was impaled from behind, the sword that found him digging through organ meat and slicing out through his belly, letting intestines fall, blood seep past.

The blade retracted.

He fell to his knees. Clutched his belly, tried with shaking fingers to push the organs back in. Blood ejected from his mouth, painted his beard. He keeled forward, and died.

Coltang saw Gulang go down. His hammers thrashed through the moonkin ranks. Moonkin who were spilling out of the war camp, into the forest to reek more havoc on the ranks out there. Ranks of vulnerable Gil Garo unaware of the upset to

Tears for the Moon God

their people, unaware of the costs the Kachin and the Tipik had witnessed.

He marched out of the camp, threw his hammers, caught the Tului who killed Gulang in a blast of white fire.

Moonkin surged past and met the Tului lines. The Tului closed ranks, bared weapons. Ice flowered at their feet, found homes in moonkin flesh, but the Tului were too close. Those auras melted into them, and blood flew from cuts all over their bodies.

Horses screamed. Men bellowed curses as the Chikata and Cuu slammed into the back ranks of the Tului fighters.

A dull roar from the north. Reinforcements had arrived. Ungol met the Tului on the far bank of the creek, pushed hard into their ranks. His familiar leapt from its place on the horse and brought down a soldier in a flurry of gnashing mandibles. Infantile sobs emanated from its spiracles, distorting a newborn's face as he dropped from his horse to join it.

Shaelein found her husband. A mass of fangs and spear-like forelegs fell onto the Tului line. She surged forth with flailing whips of compressed water, drove off the attackers as a crimson glow built in the distance. She was almost there, almost.

Sircha materialized from behind her, wielding whips of her own. Shaelein tried to force her back, but she was too fast, too brazen. The young woman fell to the Tului assault, and was trampled under the Cuu cavalry charge.

Waves crashed through the forest. Arrak guided the white caps with his arms. Bodies fell as those treacherous waters washed over their ankles, stole the energy from them and returned it, cutting their connection to their spirit, denying the moonkin purchase.

An arrow sailed past his shoulder. Answering fire came from the trees his side of the field and took the sniper from his seat. He rushed forth, his waters mingling with cackling newborn spirits, providing Sauman's host with greater sustenance as the power robbed from those Tului bastards was fed into them, sustaining them, allowing them to grow into adulthood, to explore their full potential.

Suen saw him there. A familiar face among so many others. Clad in black leathers and fine chain, his boots iron shod, his features aquiline, so much like his father's. He dropped Ibrim where he lay, marched forth to meet him. To meet Crow Durin. His son.

Death's Defender

A deep shadow took over the sky. The sun's corona was all that was visible behind the black ball of the moon, a searing, thin ring crossed with ethereal waves like drifting smoke cast in shades of gold and gray. Crimson light painted the cliffs. An answering shadow pooled under the feet of the uelfin forces. Tall grasses wavered unnaturally in the distance. The first lines of trees on the horizon in the south thrashed their canopies together in a building wind as Astair made her presence, her anxieties, known.

In villages across Sanguhr, across Tulakh and Saodein, the Fingers, madness drove all rational thought from the minds of those expats come down from the crystal city in the sky, and God Ao Nii brought his wrath to bear against his enemy, protector of God Lanfin, the keeper of the sun.

The shadows crawled across the plains, danced against the lowest reaches of the wall. They deepened to an inky shade and fused together, locked in an inorganic tangle. And the uelfin were frozen in their steps, swords and knives thrust forward, the song their singers sung coming out in rasps as they fought to keep their autonomy, to press their influence into the world and drive their foot soldiers onward against this maligned, doom struck aura.

Cold seeped into Lisandra Almaine, as she held her sword in sweaty palms, her arms threatening to give out under its weight. As she watched in awe these uelfin frozen against time, stalled in their steps, eyes shifting this way and that, hunting for the source of their sudden plight, this curse of stillness laid against them.

And at the foot of the wall, darkness rose. Shadows split apart, moved like clock hands around still bodies. Darkness rose in corporeal form, and settled into a humanoid shape. A tall figure, stag antlers thrust from the sides of a narrow head, the cheeks drawn down toward a pointed chin, his flesh pallid as death and pressed into preternaturally youthful features which seemed molded from soft, white clay. The figure was clothed in rippling shadows, tendrils like silk ribbons fanned out around him, flapping on an unfelt breeze.

He raised his hand, and his shadow surged forth, a broad spear thrusting straight toward her.

She was struck by that shadow, the cold settling deep into flesh, pulling on

Tears for the Moon God

ancient bones, drawing her forward against her will, toward the god. Beside her, Jinga and Kiresh sheathed their weapons, marched in lock step with her toward that creature as uelfin stepped obediently aside, and she wondered if they moved with autonomy or if this god's pull was on them too, feared for what might become of them when they reached him.

"I am the one who waits." His whisper drifted on currents of power, crooned in the ears of all present in this place of battle. This ill gotten place in sight of Gonsai's wall. "He who was born with the world, who brought with him darkness. Obey, for God Mu demands it. Obey, and return to your master."

Figures cloaked in shadow, their faces obscured behind masks of obsidian, emerged from the darkness, took hold of the uelfin and dragged them down, dragged them into darkness. And as they fell away—into those obscure places, to be taken to an uncertain fate—her sword found a home in its sheath, and she knelt before the god, and Jinga and Kiresh knelt before him.

"Father believes you serve a purpose." God Mu intoned, but his gaze was on the dark orb in the sky. "It seems the enemy concurs. They would seek to destroy you, lest you arrive at your fate. They will try again."

His black eyed gaze drifted from his observation of the sky, down to meet her, to hold her in place as her heart pounded in her chest, as frayed nerves drove the hairs along her arms and neck to stand on end.

His gaze flicked to Kiresh. "Your presence is needed in the city. To heal the hunter, the seer's guard against death."

He flicked his wrist, and Kiresh vanished.

"And you." His gaze flicked to Jinga. "I know what you have stolen, what hides in your trunk in the mines, the one no one else has ever seen, embraced in darkness as it is. Find it, for you will need it on the road."

He flicked his wrist a second time, and Jinga vanished from her sight.

"I have chosen my side, and it is elder." He said, his gaze shifting back to her. He stepped forward, cradled the hilt of her sword in long, slender fingers, and drew it gently from its sheath. "This sword is not intended for you, so The North Wind claims. But he has entrusted you to hold it for a time, until it may pass into the hands of the one who must wield it. The one who needs its protection.

"You will be his shield in all things, when you have arrived at such power. Do not flinch away from your duty, for he alone can protect your people, and he must not be driven into madness. Not again.

"Go forth from this place, and pass this gift unto him. Him who is lord of wolves. The great snake is weakened. This play of hands lands in our favor. Do not squander the blessing I give you, for I have saved you, Shield Maiden. The sword is called Spite. Tell him that. And tell him, for it is imperative he understand this above all else, never to raise it against me, but to point it to his enemies among my order, and shackle them to his will."

He returned the length of blackened steel to its sheath, placed his hand on her head, and darkness swallowed her.

And the Wolves Howled

And the wolves howled. All across the steppe they howled. For they knew their master was awakened. That their king was reborn anew into the world.

Amid all the chaos in the world, echoes of the wolf song were heard. From Tao Shein to The Fingers, from Ul Sadh to Gora, the song tore from feral throats, sonorous and haunting and deep. The moon stood strong in the face of the sun, and across all the lands of the Waxing World, wolf song filled a day drunk with shadows, for the Wolf of the West was risen.

Again he was risen.

And the gods cowered away in terror, for the Snake could not stand against him.

Ung Kanh Dui Arisen

The wolves howled. All over the steppe they howled. For they knew the coming of their lord. The man who would lead them, who would rule over them as their alpha. The chief among chiefs.

They knew Dupec Safar had returned. That he had risen. And they were elated.

Coltang froze. Cold ran in his veins at the sound of the wolves. The howls came from everywhere at once. Packs raised their voices to the gods, calling for death and ruin, for the end of the old way and a return to glory.

Tursa heard the wolves howling in the distance. He pitched forward onto hands and knees, bowed his head and prayed.

Kuuda watched him, wondered what had driven his father to such reverence. What could a few wolves howling at the moon mean for them. What could be so significant about them?

"He succeeded." Tursa whispered.

And Kuuda watched him with renewed interest. "Who did?"

"The Cloud Man. Ungol's son. He has risen, Kuuda. He is among us."

Durin saw the man who had fathered him, the stain on his legacy he had, for so many blissful months, believed to be dead. He was there, a man with whom he shared a fate, lord of a dynasty he had extended, in exchange for a similar measure of power.

The breeding pens were for the weak, for those whose great betrayal lay in that they wished to remain just human. His father was one such as them, a liberated beast in the guise of a man, with bloodstained lips and fingers to remind him that the hold of Tuluis Fel on his soul was eternal.

He adjusted his grip on the sword in his hand. Leather bit into his palm as he swept it across in a low arc. Ice bristled, sailed for his father.

Seun stepped out of its path. An answering trail clawed across a tangle of roots and dead foliage, split around bodies as twin ribbons sailed toward him.

He launched forward, sword held in shaking hands, his shadows writhing

Ung Kanh Dui Arisen

against the promise of blood.

Seun met his ill conceived son in a flurry of blows. Metal rang against metal. Shadows seized each other, a tangle of snapping jaws and flailing swords. Blades whirred around them, changed hands, changed angles, met and ricocheted away from each other.

A streamer of ice disrupted Durin's footing. His shadows filled the gap, pooled against Seun's, pushed him away.

He spun around the rat king tangle. Ice coalesced around his fist. He thrust the new grown lance at Durin's chest, grazed him along the ribs.

Chain links broke. An armor curtain parted and hit the earth. His shadows clawed at the exposed flank and were rebuffed.

Durin's sword passed under his arm, arced upward. He bounded out of the way as his son sought to sever the arm.

A savage swing pursued him. The lance took the impact and shattered. Ice Shards surged up from underfoot, ripped through boiled leather, made a ruin of his cheek.

The sounds of battle were lost to their exchange. Cuts riddled Seun's arms and legs, blood weltered over his side.

Ice flowered where the blood ran through, sealing the wounds, making weapons out of the iron laden waters of his life which punched through Durin's armor, found homes in flesh, raked through open gashes and splintered, sending shrapnel to infest his insides.

Durin hissed. He brought his sword up for a defense too late, and Seun knocked it away. He seized his son around the throat and squeezed, his shadows fixing the Crow's in place, denying him a chance at real fighting.

Coltang saw the dagger leave the Crow's sleeve. He threw his hammer, imbued with raw power, at the enemy leader as reinforcements rushed around him.

Wolves ripped through the forest, seized on throats and limbs with vice like jaws, took Tului and moonkin down under meaty, gray cloaked bodies.

The hammer struck home. It tore the Crow's arm away from his shoulder, knocked the knife away as the other one, his attacker, snapped his throat.

He rushed to that defender, shoved when the youth turned to free him, his teeth gnashed together in a vicious snarl.

He raised his arms in a gesture of peace, took a step back amid writhing, fast aging corpses.

A Tului horse warrior galloped straight for them, and a mass of moonkin surged forth to meet him.

He recalled his hammer, ran after the Tului, yanked him back with all of his strength.

The horse warrior met the moonkin, was pulled from the saddle into violently clawing hands as the horse collapsed and died a few paces off.

The other acolyte rose, brushed himself off and moved on.

"Get off me!" the youth growled. "Let me go!"

But he held him to his chest, his arm laced tight around his neck, stealing blood flow from his brain.

He lost consciousness, and Coltang retreated around the dying legion as the

Tears for the Moon God

Dumas rushed past to join the Cuu, to drive those reinforcements back and force the retreat as his Tipik and the Kachin drove outward from the center, broke their ranks and surrounded pockets of fresh fighters.

Dupec emerged. Into the lands he emerged. The sky bore witness to his coming, the gods of those heavenly bodies watched on as he returned. What madness afflicted him in his former life was recalled, together with memory of every glorious conquest he had won in that ill conceived life. Yet the man remained, to witness a clash between two gods amid the wreckage of his tribe's lone, stable pillar, the center of their way of life.

He looked over to his new master, recalled that God Uldal had warned him away from the Wolf Lord. The God of Ways may not approve, but this second coming had not been his choice, and yet he found he could not conceive of any greater choice he might have made.

He turned his gaze from Duijus Kanh to the wrathful gods, invaders in his homeland, the place within which his rule would be sanctified. He was Ung Kanh Dui, first of his name in generations, and he intended to wield that power. To protect his people. To defend his friends. And to see this senseless violence ended.

"Go, my cub." Duijus Kanh growled. "Declare yourself to them."

He stepped forward.

Ho'o's menagerie seized on uelfin all around him. Their song suffused the air, climbed to match the howling winds, sought to drown those growls and cries and rumbles away. The uelfin swarmed on the cave's entrance, and the Swans fell in behind him.

Black eyes filled with malice peered out from within twisted faces, snarls set against pallid flesh as the demented old crones walked in his wake, struck down any who got too close.

Duijus Kanh watched. As the black ball of the moon slid away from the sun, and the first true rays of daylight touched the snows, Dupec Safar reeled back and howled.

A pall of silence descended over the uelfin. The singing ceased. The Wild Hunt marched onward, and the winds calmed as they moved on. Ho'o shunted first Gorgus and then Ao Nii away, and as they righted themselves, one spirit and two gods set their gazes on a legend walking in the flesh. On the myth the gods had fought so valiantly to destroy. That God Lanfin had refused to reclaim when time came that one of those fel katcyakin must cease.

Wolves flooded the lands this side of Shan Lao's ice choked band, stormed into the fray. They seized on uelfin bodies, dragged them into the snows, raked at them with sharp claws, crushed throats and disemboweled them.

Duijus Kanh surged forth, riding on the high of wolf song and the sour odor of blood. He charged God Gorgus, clawed fingers stretching, hands reaching as he vaulted upward.

The Sun God's weapons were forgotten as he was flung upward and carried away.

And Dupec came to God Ao Nii. As Duijus Kanh did away with the sun, he came to stand before the moon, and offered him his hand.

A mad god's gaze traveled up his arm, to settle on the face of a man who had forgotten all that he was. Settled on amber eyes, a wolf's eyes, as what remained of

Ung Kanh Dui Arisen

his anger ebbed away, and a deep confusion settled into him.

"You have quarreled with your foes long enough." Dupec said.

The god reached for Ung Kanh Dui's hand, set trembling fingers against his palm.

From within the gullet of the cave, three chief's children watched as a god took a young stranger's offered hand. As the man they had known so briefly stood over the seated god, helped him to his feet amid the blasted ruin of their winter home. They watched as the god and Ungol's son exchanged quiet words, and the god turned away.

Dupec watched God Ao Nii go away from Gil Garo, and wondered what new shaping this tenuous peace would bring. The god's madness would continue to be an affront to his master, and his master's way would never cease to turn his stomach; but perhaps, in this new shaping, in marrying the interests of the moon with the wolves, a truce could be achieved.

God Ao Nii paused amid what remained of the snow dunes.

The uelfin were retreating across the steppe, away to return to whatever post they'd seized, whatever base they claimed. The wolves lay chase and picked off the weak and the lame among them.

"A last question for you, God Ao Nii?" Dupec said. "Where does my god stand?"

"I know only that he will not stand against me." He answered. "But beware the Hunters. It is God Shakh's betrayal that has drawn your master away this night. If they have not killed each other by morning, the Hunter's Triad will have dissolved, leaving Just Mu and Uldal in which to place our trust."

He turned away then, and a staircase of raw light climbed away from his feet, into the heavens. He mounted it, and left what remained of the Gil Garo at home, and their spirit defenders, to themselves.

Ungol held Arrak in his arms. He had lost Shaelein in the fray. She was somewhere far afield, ranging over dead, delivering final blows, hunting for wounded Gil Garo among the corpses. Arrak stared into the sky through a patch of trees. Arrows sprouted from his chest in pairs and trios and quartets. He had not gone down easily.

He wept over his friend's body, as blood leaked out of him. Ran his hand through his hair.

"Do not be afraid." He whispered. "She comes for us all in the end."

"I...will...see...her...again...but Tamlin...he needs...he needs...."

"Shh." Ungol said. "Save your strength."

Arrak's fingers played restlessly in the dirt. "My son...take care...of him."

Ungol nodded shakily.

A smile crossed Arrak's lips as the light left his eyes.

"I promise I will." Ungol whispered.

Arrak's chest stopped heaving. Hsi fingers stilled.

And he died.

The Secret Path

Xi sawed the stick back and forth against the crack in the join of two stones. It was an oversight on the part of God Lanfin to leave even one tree standing in this place, though where Ank had found anything so truly alive remained something for him to chew on. The man was more of a mystery than any of them, and he didn't account himself overly forthcoming with the details of his life.

Really, an entire tree in this place, somewhere. Hidden in some far off corner where none of us would think to look.

A pile of stones, most little more than pebbles, lay next to him. Sweat slicked his bare back and pasted his bangs to his forehead. Salt burned at the corners of his eyes where droplets began to drip from his eyebrows, forcing him to squint as he toiled away at the wall.

He had not worked this hard at something since he left the safety of Ur. Hadn't been so fixated on a singular task in who knew how many thousands of years.

He had asked Shulraki after the date of his death once, had been surprised to find the interval between their captures to be such a close thing. He had expected a hundred thousand years, and had been shocked to find it had been less than half that.

Still far too long to be trapped here. Away from all that has gone on in the world.

Hou Rok was no longer a simple armorer, but a self styled god of innovation resting on his laurels while mortal engineers and men of science developed new contrivances to aid in his steady consolidation of power. The gods relationship with Rein must have soured. He could not imagine the mountain lord would take to such wild ideas, nor that titan turned king's lack of work ethic.

Liandal's scribblings had become a thing to be feared, her attention a curse when once it had been seen as the highest of honors.

Then again, even in the early days her stories had tended toward tragedies. The only thing that never seemed to change was the endless duels between the sun god and the moon, and those he would rather see an end to. If the Great Arbiter tipped the Scales, perhaps one day he would.

Dust whispered against the stick, showered the ground with a hail of pea-sized stones, and he set it aside, dug into the gap he had opened with calloused fingers.

The Secret Path

He swept motes of dust and debris from the hole, then followed the contours along the edge of a fist sized stone, seeking purchase.

His grip firmed on an exposed horn. He picked up the stick and shoved it past retreating fingers, wrenched on the makeshift lever.

Careful now.

The stone loosened along its height, bit against the flat head of another underneath it. He jimmied the stick against its height, driving in deeper until at last he met no resistance, shimmied it side to side, pulling against the face with his fingers now, and the stone came free.

He set his tool aside and peered through the hole he had opened.

A hall to match this one in composition and dimensions looked back at him. For a moment, he thought this errand had all been for nothing, that he looked out onto a hall adjoining this one. A hall like any other in this listlessly sprawling hell.

A rumbling sigh drew his gaze down a side channel. He could barely make out the corner of a crossing path. The harsh grating of something heavy dragged across packed earth, which was accompanied by the harsher beat of men on the march.

A red, leather sail blocked his line of sight briefly, and a meaty, stone-gray snout followed. A crescent pupil stabbed into the lid of a ridged shield of leathery flesh as the beast passed, sights unfocused as the snake's body slammed awkwardly against the wall of the corridor he looked down. Uelfin leapt out of its path as it sought new purchase.

"She will pay for this!" he hissed. *"For the insult!"*

Xi strained to hear more as God Lanfin slithered down that hall.

"What of the first dissenter, my lord?" An uelfin asked. There was the touch of fear in his voice. Whatever errand they had come from, the tidings had not gone well. He saw deep puncture wounds still bleeding where the god had been injured, wondered what could have given him those wounds. They looked inflicted by an animal, the patterning consistent with the wounds he had seen on deer after a mountain cat attack.

"He is of little concern. His escape is only temporary. God Shakh is with us now. He has grown tired of the long fight."

He retreated from the wall. He would need to find Hanuman and tell him of what he had found, of what he had heard. He would need to mark his path so he could find this place again. In an unassuming patch of bare earth, he traced out the lines of a kugi board and filled one side in with pebbles, forming an arrow pointing to the patch of wall he had removed. He scooped up the rest and filled his pockets, then gathered his effects.

He took Wrath in hand, the sword Rein had given him, that the mountain had not sought to reclaim, and moved on.

A cataclysm was under way and, he feared, the Wanderers may be at the heart of it. The uelfin song, that wayward voice railing against all others, promising a feud between factions among gods and spirits, and men, had shaped the beginning of something, and his brothers had risen in answer, had joined in his rebellious pursuit even as the first singer among them was silent.

He had heard those distant echoes of song sung in many voices, protests seeking to wrest control as two factions brought their wills against each other in some far off corner of the world. They had begun something, alright. Something unprecedented. He yearned to know what.

Heiman

"It's just down here." Hanuman said.

They had been walking for days. Had taken some hours to rest now and again. There was no need to sleep, and the sun never set on this labyrinth. By design, it was to be a place without change, wherein what little change was possible was negligible, and all else was fashioned to produce ennui without end.

They had been walking for days.

Sao had not known how large, how elaborate, a labyrinth containing five men could be. He had not considered how many lives, how many fates, must be stolen in pursuit of wiping one man from the annals of history. How much energy must be required to push a great river off its path, to erect walls out of ether, lay down sands and silts, broken tiles, desiccated vines...how much effort simply to split off each of those thousands, no, millions of pools into isolated bodies.

It was no wonder he rarely saw Xi Didura or Ank the Sanark. To trek across this expanse would have cost them so much of their time, would have required immense effort and, perhaps, careful planning. No wonder, either, they only sought him out when they needed something, even if it was as simple as sharing pasts.

Even Shulraki would have had to put in some effort to get to him, and the path out of his domain was not marked by easy passages. Hanuman had guided him over a raised land bridge when they had arrived at that place, had informed him it was the only one for miles.

Miles. And here we are several leagues from where we started. From where I *started.*

Just up ahead. But had I known it would take this long to reach it, I would not have come. I'd have demanded to know what he wanted to show me. What was so important that he could not just describe it to me.

It'll take just as long to get back, too. Why did I not turn back?

He had asked probing questions in those intervals when they rested. Had been rebuffed, or led down strange avenues where convoluted remembrances pulled the elder's stories in many directions, robbing some of them of sense, never giving a full picture of any one event the Cloud Man had experienced.

It was like listening to a room full of people each chiming in to defend themselves when the story began to cast them in a light they did not like. He suspected Hanuman was not even aware he was approaching things in this way, that he was not intentionally trying to obfuscate anything. He was simply that far gone.

He had stopped asking questions days ago, had made some delicate attempts at more casual conversation and found himself met with the same array of disjointed answers. Even to ask him what his favorite color was, he was met with several different answers all tumbling out on top of each other. Green, violet, the orange of sunset, yellow, blue and dark blue, like his late wife's eyes.

Without consistency, there was little point in speaking, and therein lay the complication. There were times when Hanuman was coherent enough to hold conversation. Times when he had even gone so far as to invite it. But those periods of clarity were brief, and had a habit of descending into garbled gibberish before tailing off into long silences, as Hanuman lost the thread of what he was saying, or forgot what they were talking about completely.

Sao looked where he had pointed. Up ahead was a wall like any other, except that this wall was overgrown with creeping vines. What was more, they were alive. Forested with glossy, spade-like leaves, with little, red berries poking out among them.

He could have cried.

How long had it been since he last saw food. Something he could eat. Something to remind himself why man sought to live. Why he was allowed to know joy.

At the base of the wall were scrubby bushes, some crawling almost high enough to join with the mosses, leaving mossy stones to break through here and there, so that the entire expanse resembled a natural cliff face in some jungle clearing. And the floor was not all sand and broken tile, but a living carpet of wildflowers and sedges which rolled over a break line just ahead of him.

He stopped where he was, stood there drinking in the greens, vibrant scarlet, powdery lavender and a kaleidoscopic array of other colors all fanning over verdant shoots and inviting bees—live bees and butterflies—to court them.

"What is this?" he breathed.

"Home." Hanuman said. "Close to it, anyway." He pressed forward, holding onto the small of Sao's back, guiding him into motion again. "The first of us to spring forth from the rivers were humans, but their lives were not sanctioned. This was the basis behind the first wars the gods fought amongst themselves. The spirits mostly took our side, but they would, wouldn't they? They had been protecting us for quite some time.

"We lived in their forests, fished from their lakes and streams. I think you are aware of their views of us. They may not always share our way, but they do provide. In their own way. On their own time."

"My mother used to say that."

"She may still. Within her new path. Who can say?" he shrugged. "Nonetheless, we could only come out at night in those early days. To come out of the forests in daylight risked too much. Ji Hara had not yet begun taking on rats and other rodents as her spies. That would come later. But daylight was dangerous to us, then. Gorgus and Shirad were not aware of our kind, and had they been they would have sought to strike us down.

"But God Katcya found us, was fascinated by us, and he protected our people for

Tears for the Moon God

a time. And later, after my brother and I had come of age, God Ao Nii fell in love. With Heiman. His closest allies saw fit to love us, too. In their own way. On their own time. Mu. Uldal. Shakh. They did not all see fit to take on human lovers, but they lent their hands to us anyway, to shield us and keep our secret.

"Come now, Emperor. We are almost there."

"But *why* does this reach look so different from everywhere else?"

"Because time's touch still lingers here." Hanuman said soberly. "There remains a source. This is close to its headwaters. Even the gods are not foolish enough to interfere with a place like that. To introduce their own influence to such a sacred place risks tainting everything downstream with that influence." He chuckled. "Just imagine if Shah Jagat meddled so far upriver. Death would plague everything. Even the stones."

"So they don't—"

"We have arrived." Hanuman said. "Just around this corner."

They turned corner, and Sao drew up short. Another step would have sent him tumbling into the blackened pit scored into the earth just ahead of him. The sides of the bowl resembled obsidian, and petrified fish and reeds were extruded from it. Frozen in place as they had been when the crater was formed.

Hanuman looked into the bowl, and a deep melancholy stole over him.

"It was Heiman." He said.

"What happened to him?"

"He died. But Gorgus wasn't satisfied with his death. He was furious with Ao Nii. Thought falling for a mortal, even if our father was an Elder God, was an act of abomination. He compared it to having sex with a goat.

"When Lanfin conspired with the Elder Gods, those who wanted us gone for good, to erect the labyrinth, he allowed Gorgus into it just once. Lanfin filled a chalice with the water containing my brother's life, and Gorgus burned all that remained out of existence. That little cup is all that remains to remember him by, and in all of my memories of times long after my own, my old friend, my brother-in-law as your people understand these things, is driven to madness because of it."

"So it's grief?" Sao said. "That drives him into a rage every time the moon is full."

Hanuman nodded. "It is the same grief that drove me to wade into the pools of my kin in my days of isolation. Before Xi arrived here. I did not know I'd lost anything until he came."

"Why is it so important to you that I see this?"

"Because you must know why I do the things I do. You will never trust me otherwise."

"And seeing this changes...what?"

"Consider what happened to my brother." He said. "What happened to the people around him. At best, they went about living their lives remembering nothing of his birth. My father lost both of his sons, and could not bring himself to have more children with the woman he loved. A woman he didn't recognize a second time around. I lost myself and picked up pieces of countless others. Ao Nii lost his mind, though in a different way. He lost himself to grief, and rage, and if your time is anything to go by, he never recovered. Even Echo lost something he could never get back. The Gods sought to betray him, you know. After the first war had ended." He looked to Sao out of the corner of his eye. "But they bit off more than they could chew with him. Even now, they tread lightly where it concerns him and his woman. Have you never wondered why?"

"I have, but I doubt you intend to tell me."

Hanuman grimaced. "Something else for you to consider. Ao Nii knows that he would lose something of himself if he drank the waters containing my brother's life. There is not enough left of him to plunge into. He should tip out his cup and move on, but he can't. He's been stuck in this state of perpetual insanity for thousands of years. Since the Era of Unity, my time, ended.

"*You* are the same. You cannot sit at poolside forever and expect to get past your grief. Your remembrance of your lover must come from in here." He touched his chest over his heart. "Your grief will not help you win freedom."

"On the contrary." Sao said more aggressively than he intended. "It has once already."

"Do not mistake a window for a door, Sao Njack." Hanuman said, turning back to his observation of the blackened pit. He stepped around it.

Sao followed in his wake.

They ventured a short way down the hall and hung around a corner. In this new expanse was another pit, but this one was so choked with mud it was impossible to see into its waters. It resembled quicksand, and the tail fin of a fat carp flitted back and fourth languidly just above the surface. Its feeble attempts at submerging deeper were met with too much resistance for it to overcome, and he realized then what those fish must be. If the pools contained the memories of these people, the fish must be akin to their bodies, their psyches...the fundamental core from which they drew notions of their own identities. Those fish must be the most fragile, inalienable pieces of them.

He almost laughed.

"This is me." Hanuman said. "The damage done by invading the memories of others. The last time I laid eyes on it, it was opaque with mud, yes, but still fluid. The damage was evident, but it was not this severe. I barely remember who I was in my time anymore. I suppose it should be fitting that this pond is nearly solid now. It could only be expected to hold so much.

Sao dropped onto his haunches at its side. He reached, ran his fingers over the mud. Light emanated through cracks in the substrate, but the pool refused him. It did not clarify. No visions came forth. But he felt *something*. Something that reminded him of better times.

There was a pulse in that pond, which was unique, and stronger than the other hummingbird patterns surrounding it. He could almost identify it as a pulse within the land, like those from which spirit callers first learned to draw on the powers of the spirits they served.

But this was not the pulse of a spirit. It was a pulse with echoes, a mutagenic thing with the power to infect others, to influence them. It was human.

"This can be mended." He mumbled.

"It cannot." Hanuman said.

"Not by you. Perhaps not by anyone else in this place." He insisted. "But I promise you, it can be healed."

Hanuman's hand found his shoulder, and squeezed lightly. "That time is long past, Sao. It is a nice thought, but I am too far gone to ever come back now. There is nothing you, or anyone, can do."

Tears for the Moon God

"No, Hanuman. You've simply been in confinement so long you've forgotten how diverse the array of spirits within the world is. Or you haven't been around in such a long time you have no concept of how much more diverse their talents are now than they ever were.

"I am beholden to a spirit of memory. Salein's gift to me. And memory is bound to the soul. I can fix this, by purging you of the fragmented memories which are bound to the souls of others. I just need somewhere to put them.

"And I think I know where I can."

Hanuman raised an eyebrow then. "Where do you suggest."

"Heiman may be dead and gone, but would he be so upset by the idea of helping you in this way?"

Hanuman said nothing.

"Then come with me. Sit there next to his remains, and let me heal you of your curse."

"Why? Why do you wish to help me?" Hanuman demanded, but a watery sheen had taken his vision. He was beginning to break down. "You have no trust for me. You have no right."

"Hanuman." Sao said tersely. "I don't know you. I know a man who is so driven by mad desire he'd do anything to see his ends met. I know a man who was a shattered ruin of his former self by the time the first of us set foot in this place. Somewhere underneath all of it is who you were before all of this. I'll decide if you can be trusted when I've found him.

"But, I need you to understand something. In doing this, I will be invading your mind. I will see the arc of your life, and I will know you in the very same way you have spent so long trying to know me. You will have no secrets from me. Everything you experienced in your life, and everything that has transpired since you were immured will live in a place you dare not touch. The difference between us is that I will not be changed by it, because my bond with Salein will keep me still."

"And if you still cannot trust me?"

"Then you will have earned an enemy more formidable than any you have ever faced. Because I will know how to counter you at every turn. I'll know when and what kind of move you intend to make before you do, and I'll have a means of countering it you can't comprehend. And what's more. If you seek out more memories, you won't have a means of purging them again. You'll be left with a broken spirit all over again, and there will be nothing you can do to overcome it."

He saw the fear in Hanuman's face. He saw the vulnerability. Walk this path, and he would be free in a way he had not been since the earliest days of his capture. He would be *himself*. But he would give Sao Njack power over him by the same token. Power enough to keep him locked within a cage of a different kind.

Is he sure I will see things his way? Am I sure I won't?

He nodded, and shakily ambled back up the way they had come, around the corner and to Heiman's blackened pit. He sat at its edge, and Sao stood behind him.

Sao placed his hands on him then, and drank in the pulse of his master and his mentor, drank in the pulse of a lake deep under ground, the pulse of a spirit he had first met when he was barely ten years old.

Ice crept through his veins, up through his legs and into his torso, then down his arms and through his fingertips. Hanuman stiffened as the shock took him, and slumped forward. Sao fell on top of him, and they pitched together into the pit,

Heiman

rolled down its steep slope, into its base. And water began to leak from Hanuman's eyes, his nose, his mouth and ears. Water began to leak from his skin. To fill the basin around them, as Salein's influence, as Sao's power, compelled the essences of countless lives from him, as he drew out the poison, and purged the man's soul of its affliction.

Fate's Hand

The hunter saw him there, on hands and knees amid retreating waters. He saw a vulnerable man too weak to stand, confusion painted in the lines of his face, and sneered.

The trail had been swept away with those waters, but a trace of it held in the air. He approached, knife held backward in his hand, the blade cutting sharp arcs in the air at his side as the blood lust drove deep into his brain, enlivening all of those animal parts of him that lacked empathy, that reveled in violence and death.

He descended on the Spirit Caller, drove his knife down for his back, to cut into the kidney, spread its poison into the meat, bleed it into the bloodstream and push him toward death. He would take him to be healed before the rot pushed him into the Empress's embrace, but he would savor every bit of the agony rolling through him.

The tribesman rolled onto his back, panting. The knife sailed through air, and the hunter cussed. He bared down with the hand length edge. If he could not have the easy victory, he would take the one he could savor. The blade plunged forth in his hand, for the man's guts, to disembowel him.

Katuwan pulled Lura out of the sweeping path of a dagger. A momentary glint of firelight along its edge was all that telegraphed the attack. It was gone as soon as it had come. The attacker melted into shadow. He held her back from falling into raging currents rising to her knees.

Waters stirred into a white rage thrashed at him, threatening his own footing as he widened his legs, sought better purchase, the sodden shoes he wore. He kicked one foot and then the other, releasing his feet from the slides and ground his bare heels into the dirt underneath.

Another flash of steel.

He brought up his buck knife to meet it, was dragged back by the current as he twisted out of its path.

The waters rolled around unseen figures, ran unnaturally around physical forms, passed along as if disrupted by the gnarled roots of great trees.

He brought the blade to bear where the waters parted.

Fate's Hand

A man materialized as he stepped out of the path of his swing, snarling as his cover was exposed.

Others materialized around them, boiling out of shadow with the revelation the waters would not hide them. They surged forward from several directions at once, boxing them in, cutting off their exits.

A portal onto a dry road opened behind a line of attackers on the southern side, and more figures bearing weapons poured out of it to meet the attack, lent to unfolding chaos as they dug blades into flesh, met attacks with parries, drove the hunters back and sought to bring them down.

The contest proved an even match. The hunters turned their backs on Katuwan and Lura, opened a downstream channel.

Lura's pull on Katuwan drew him after her, using the swift currents to their advantage as they ran away from those fighting acolytes of gods.

Lura screamed.

Blood weltered over her thigh.

Hands clapped onto Katuwan and dragged him down. Fire bloomed across the back of his knee, and the tendon there rolled up into his calf as the leg went limp.

Hunters dragged him off as pathfinders turned to lay chase. Everything seemed to be happening in slow motion, all was slowed down by the raging currents, the uncertain footing, mud sliding under boots beneath crashing waves.

A blindfold stole the light from him. He wrenched it free before it could be tied into place and found a cord snaked across his wrist, dragging his hand away, revealing figures bursting from shadow, resolving out of open air as these hunters lifted him off his feet and onto their shoulders, as more dragged his limbs back and together, bound them with cords and hauled him away.

He turned his head to see Lura thrashing against her assailants, kicking her legs, flailing her arms, biting at wrists and fingers that came too close to her face. They stuffed her mouth with cloth and bound a strap around her lips, struggled to get her under control as she fought with everything she had to get free.

She rolled out of their hands, a blade clutched in her fist, the very one she used to cut down young jackfruit in early summer. The dull blade made wild arcs around her, the hunters on the defensive as they looked for openings in her fraught guard.

One stepped forward and caught her arm. Another lunged from his knees and laced his arms around her legs, bowled her over into the torrent.

Thrashing. Kicking. Foam spray lashed away from the surface as she was dragged under by five men. As they fought to bring her down, to get those binds on her.

Tears stained his cheeks as she was brought under control, and with her bound, their last hope of escape evaporated.

Blood ran with the current past them. Higher up, the pathfinders who had come for them were cut down, but their bodies rose even as they died, arms lashed out with lengths of steel and took those hunters around them in the throats when their backs were turned. Their bodies joined with the rank and file, waded through waters after the retreating hunters with their prize.

They marched forth to meet their brothers and their allies and their friends, to see them cut down before they could steal away the Katuwiti.

A rearguard turned to meet the animate corpses. They dug their blades into joints, severed tendons, worked systematically to render those corpses useless, to remove the means by which they moved. They did the work soundlessly, unafraid of the dead for they had sent them into the ocean's embrace.

A cannonball sound blasted over the dockyard, across the bay. The force of impact buried itself in his flesh, vibrated against his bones.

His gaze shifted down the way, to see one last time the face of his husband. To see the torrent ebbing as he fell onto his hands and knees in the shallows. As the spirit who rode him left, left him weak, and a hunter materialized over him.

His eyes widened. He shouted a warning his husband would never hear, sought to roll out of the hand of those who held him, to find a path to Xirakura though the distance was vast. Though the hunter was there, even now thrusting his dagger forth for the small of his husband's back.

Lura's gaze was trained on the sky, watching as two embattled gods were thrown from the continent, were picked up by the wind and cast far off and away from the shores of Gora, from Faed City, to conclude their battle elsewhere.

And she wondered what would befall the people where they landed. If the gods would intervene, if they *could.*

She had asked for a hunter. They had them now. And he sensed a goddess's hand behind this, as the hunters hauled them away on yielding currents, picking up speed as the waters retreated into the ocean.

Blunt force rocked through his head, and darkness followed. A dreamless dark as unconsciousness stole over him, and his body went limp against his captors.

Lura watched those monstrous stars retreat to the very edge of the horizon. She watched after them, and wept. So much carnage. So much chaos. So much and all of it a surprise.

Had she known an eclipse was forthcoming. Had she known what would befall them here, she would have sought a different path, would have hastened to find her fool husband, would have spared not a moment for food or finding shelter.

She had been too late. *They* had been too late.

She turned her gaze to the place where the moon held strong in the sun's path, watched as its leading edge slid away into obscurity, as the first burst of true sunlight leaked into the world from its trailing edge, and sunbeams touched the land at the city's height. They drove away the looming shadow of Ao Nii's fury, and the moon god sought new purchase.

Smoke and fire lingered in the city to remember their coming. Smoke and fire and ruin. Corpses drifted with the currents around her, returned to their long slumber as the empress claimed them.

With any luck, we will survive this. If luck holds out, we will see our husband again, and our family will know peace. Finally, peace.

She squeezed her eyes shut against the world. Tears burned hot against raw tracks along her cheeks, and the fight went out of her, a guttering candle finally and totally snuffed.

She would fight another day. She would find her freedom, and then find her husband. She need only find a way to escape these hunters, find someone, *anyone* who could take her to him. She only hoped these bastards did not take Katuwan from her, too. That they would be together through the worst, be where they could work together against this plight, and win free to do what they needed to. To bring Xirakura home.

Fate's Hand

Timin saw it flash forward. He opened a path, set himself between the hunter and his prey and knocked the blade aside with the weighted end of his catch pole. He brought the polearm around and hooked the leather cord around the hunter's neck, thrust down, slamming his face into the road, and held there as the body thrashed, as water filled the man's nose and mouth. Held there, and watched him drown.

Xirakura watched the Magura man with wide eyes as the shock of what had come over him, what might have been, played across his mind. The hunter had materialized in the instant before the blade came down.

The pathfinder, alarmingly close to him, tall and thin and leering at the dying hunter, pressed his boot against his rival's neck, held his head beneath spare inches of water until the thrashing ceased, until he was well and truly dead.

He removed the cord from the hunter's neck, spun his staff around and caught a second assailant in the side of the head with the weighted end.

Within the waters, a pathway opened, an ephemeral doorway onto the deck of a ship.

"Go." The pathfinder commanded. "Go to safety, Xirakura."

"How do you know my—"

"Now, damn you! They have your scent."

Xirakura backpedaled, crawled through the portal.

The pathfinder surged forth as five more figures came for him, and the portal closed, leaving Xirakura with his aching bones and frayed muscles on the deck of that rocking ship, a crew of strong men drawing up anchor, untying ballast ropes, readying for departure.

White robed figures descended on him. White robed figures with red flames impressed against their backs, just below the neckline. They bore gold cuffs in the style of suspended flames around their biceps, and he knew then what they must be.

Rahad.

"He's injured." One man said.

"Lacerations. Nothing serious." Another loomed over him, examined him through bespectacled eyes. He was rubbing a narrow, smooth shaven chin.

"Is this the one who drove the gods away?" a woman somewhere out of his range of sight asked.

"I think...I think so."

"Incredible."

"Help me with him."

Strong arms lifted him from the deck, and Rahad pacifists carried him away. Through a door and into a deeper darkness, down into the hull, past a chamber lined with cots where the crew slept, and into a lantern lit room where a long table rested, and an entire wall had been dedicated to medicinal herbs in glass jars and phials, all arranged neatly along shelves with grates fixed over them, to prevent them falling to ruin when the storms came, when the sea bucked against the ship's deep hull.

He looked into the face of that man with the round lenses magnifying his eyes,

Tears for the Moon God

and wondered.

"Did we manage to find the others?" the healer asked.

"I saw two running for the docks, but I was unable to reach them. The waters blocked me." The other man said.

"The dead, too." The healer's expression gave away the verdict.

"Three Katuwiti this far from home. What drove them out, I wonder."

"Could be something to do with these scars."

Xirakura latched onto the healer's arm, and the healer looked into his eyes, caught and suspended in the moment by a wave of wonder.

"Where did you see them?" he demanded. "Where did you see my husband? My wife?"

The healer turned his gaze away, rubbed the back of his neck.

"They were fine when I last saw them. The pathfinders might deliver them. They were tasked by their god to do so."

"They are still out there." Xirakura tried to sit and was pushed unceremoniously against the table by the other man.

"That is of no concern to you now. You are wounded. Weakened. I sense it in your spirit. What you did took too much out of you."

"I must find them."

"Why are you so far from home." The other man asked.

"If I cannot find them myself, you must do so." Xirakura snapped. "They do not have magic. They are not like me."

"Then we must hope the pathfinders get to them before the hunters." The healer said.

Xirakura looked into his face, but he would not meet his eye.

"They followed me. I never wanted them to, but they did. They cannot die here. They cannot!" he was babbling, trying to appeal to the Rahad sense of empathy, the bedrock foundation of their order's mission. "You must find them!"

"We will do our best." The healer said. "But we cannot tarry here longer, lest the hunters find their way onto this ship."

"God Shakh's betrayal will be felt across the pantheon." The other man lamented.

"There's no sense dwelling on that now." The healer said. "Right now, the important thing is to make sure the people who need it are healed. And we are safe."

"But they are not." Xirakura wept. "They should have stayed away. I never intended for them to endure this. They were meant to be spared. Live their lives in peace until I returned."

"Returned?" the other man said.

"My curse." His hand came to rest across his belly, fingers following the contours of the spirit given brand against his flesh. "It could not be healed. Sufa Salein could not heal it. There is only one who can."

The healer nodded. He looked to his counterpart. "I think I know where he was going. It's good he found us, if my suspicion is correct."

"Tak." The other said knowingly.

"Yes, him." Xirakura confessed. "To take away this curse."

"What is the nature of your curse, spirit caller?" the healer asked.

"I...I do not know. I do not think I am meant to."

Fate's Hand

"We will take him to our lord, then." The healer said to the other. "He will know what to do."

"Wyte Landing will not welcome us."

"We will not stay there long."

Xirakura looked from one of them to the other.

The healer placed warm fingers against his forehead. "Sleep now. Know peace."

His eyes slid shut, and sleep stole over him like a thief, robbing him of his anxieties, his fear. He was forced into a dream, a dream with the taste of a memory. To live in the embrace of his people, his husband and his wife together with him again, if only in this place in his mind's eye. There was no peace to be had in a lie, but he was powerless before the healer's touch, and the lie sprawled out before him, denying him his grief, his worry over the uncertain fate of the two people he loved more than any. Two he may never see again.

Unbinding

Shulraki scooped up a handful of pebbles at lakeside, and cast them into the waters. They struck at several places in rapid succession, and an array of disjointed visions fled from them, disturbing the waters into a frothing, mad frenzy.

He watched, for a time, those broken memories play out, watched them crash into each other. It took courage to confront the unknown, and every man was compelled to do so with each moment they lived. Every man must do so upon the moment they found themselves dying. They must be met with the knowledge that they did not know what would befall them on the other side of the final door, when at last they passed from this domain into the next, and accept their ignorance. Accept their utter lack of control over what came next, what eternity meant for them.

He had met the challenge once before, and knew there was nothing so bad on the other side. Nothing so painful it was worse than what he had endured over the last century or so in these halls.

He stepped forward. Again. His moccasins sank into thick muck at lake's edge. He took another step, and another. He was up to his knees in those waters, broken images spiraling away from his death shroud, his black, linen robes.

Another step. Another. He was up to his waste. Apparitions pulled at him from beneath the surface, and he surrendered to them. He pitched forward, arms spread wide as if to embrace those many strangers, as to accept their embrace in kind.

And plunged.

Beneath the surface.

To be ravaged by the shattered remains of countless individuals. To become a broken thing like them, and to know, finally, the taste of oblivion.

It was all he had wanted for so long. And it was sweet.

But he was not whole.

Thunder boomed overhead, and in its wake came driving rains. Rains from a sky which had never shed its tears, a sky whose listless gray had been known to Ank the Sanark for so long he had believed it incapable of producing anything of the sort. In all of his calculations, his experiments with command and control, his

Unbinding

pursuits of more and more knowledge about how this place worked, what limits it imposed on them, what limits it imposed on itself, he had thought nothing for a change of this magnitude taking hold.

As he wondered after what caused it, a radiant column thrashed away from a nearby hall. It struck at the clouds, lightning rising instead of falling, an anomaly he had seldom seen in life, which he had never seen here before.

He hurried in the direction of that light.

Another column snapped across the air a little distance off from the first. Then another, another. Altogether, he counted six of them flung from earth skyward, and with each lightning strike came an answering *BOOM!*

He broke into a sprint, ran down halls and around sharp corners, ran until he began to smell sulfur, to see smoke rising in tendrils just ahead.

He slowed, and then halted.

Just ahead was a blackened pit where a pool should be. Smoke drifted from its edges, and the smell of sulfur was stronger there. He approached, noted the impression of carp and panfish and eels in stasis at its fringes, how the pool was narrower than most he had seen. All of those impressions of life were frozen under a layer of glossy obsidian, and in the heart of the pit was a man.

He was naked. Waters trickled over his body, taking shape as raiment. A tunic, chain hauberk, leather spaulders, and gauntlets and greaves. The tunic was poppy red, and the slacks under those greaves were black, stove-pipe cut, and well manicured.

He bore resemblance to Shulraki from his hooked nose and pronounced cheekbones, to a sharp jaw and crystalline eyes, and a coin bearing the bust of a woman had been burned into his lips. But his hair was short cropped, and one of his eyes had been replaced with a colorless fake. A series of thin scars around the orbit gave the impression the eye had been gouged out at some point.

The stranger hacked and wheezed. Water issued from his throat began steaming as soon as it struck the bowl. He rolled onto his back, and lay there, stared into the sky, and breathed.

Without thought for what he was doing, Ank climbed into the bowl. He took the stranger in his arms and hauled him out. The stranger did not protest, but pushed him away when they had made it to the edge.

"Let me...hold on." He said.

The stranger cupped his face in his hands, shook his head and gasped.

"I was dead." He whispered. "Wasn't I?"

"It appears that way." Ank said. "Pardon me for asking, but *who* are you? It is not common for people to arrive in this place. And you look...well, you look familiar."

A mirthless chuckle from the stranger.

"I was called Shirad Thufian, but that is a pseudonym. I am the first Shard Shulraki Alran split off on the night before he was executed." He looked around at the cyclopean walls, the nearby pools of murky water, the broken tiles scattered across sandy earth and that listless, unbroken sky still shedding rain in torrents. "This is not hell."

"It is for us." Ank said.

"And who are you, graemein?"

"A Sun Man."

Glossary of Terms

Human Races

Gil Garo: A nomadic tribe who inhabit Tao Shein Steppe. The tribe consists of seven sects: the Dumas, Kirche, Kachin, Tipik, Cuu, Hakka, and Chikata. The Gil Garo spend the warmer months raiding across the kingdoms of Luc, Ao Lein, and the Jahhad Empire, and are not well received by any of those peoples. They have a neutral relationship with the isolationist people of Tuluis Fel.

Goth: The people of the Gotha Kingdom.

Katuwiti: an uncontacted tribe indigenous to Sufa Salein forest. Among the oldest tribes in the world, their histories and folklore are said to be among the most complete records of events from the Wandering Period to the Great Separation.

Magura: A people who inhabit Zanzark Plains. Though their villages hold no formal obligation to engage in governmental affairs with each other, they recognize Faed City as their capitol.

Nixian: A people who inhabit Gonsai's Wall and the Sha Ruhhad desert. They have an amenable relationship with Baduhrak and, as such, are among the most technologically advanced civilizations on Ul Sadh. The Nixians are one of seven guardian tribes who protect shrines to important spirits from outsiders. Their charge is the shrine of Ul Sadh.

Saodeini: the people of the Republic of Saodein, formerly the Kingdom of Saodein. Though most are concentrated within the borders of their nation, a significant population of saodeini expatriates settled in Sarkahn's Fingers during the civil war and have remained there ever since.

Sangar: the people of Sanguhr, south of Gonsai Wall. They are among the most technologically advanced nations on Ul Sadh, having a reasonably close relationship with Baduhrak.

Sarkahni: the indigenous peoples of Sarkahn Plain and the surrounding mountain regions. Sarkahni societies are centered around villages with no formal infrastructure connecting them. They may have friendly relations with other villages which are geographically close to their own, but due to a belief that it will anger the spirit of the plains, they have never established a formal kingdom.

Tulakka: the people of Tulakh.

Tului: The isolationist people of Tuluis Fel.

Uari: a people who inhabit the Sufreit and Ouran mountain ranges surrounding Sufa Salein Forest and the Ba Gora Plains. They trade heavily with the Magura, conducting most of this activity through the Ouran Goul Pass.

Non-Human Races

Graemein: A people who inhabit Sana's Horn and the Graemein River Basin. They possess two souls, each with a unique personality and attributes. Graemeins are a guardian tribe who watch over the shrine of Sana. Their spiritual leaders, Sanarks, are bound by oath to remain present and vigilant against the shrine, never to leave the Horn.

Katcyakin: A people who trace their paternal lineage to Katcya, Elder God of Luck. There are two varieties of Katcyakin with unique attributes. Cloud Men are born with water lines covering their bodies, and possess the ability to alter probability in their vicinities to make negative outcomes more likely. Because they are not born with the ability to control these powers, many cultures consider them too dangerous to be raised among them. Most kill these offspring soon after they are born, but some few grant them mercy, choosing to abandon them on roadsides instead, where a god may stumble across them.

The second variety are Sun Men. Sun Men possess the innate ability to alter probability to make positive outcomes more likely for themselves. Many cultures see the birth of a Sun Man as an omen of good fortune for their people. Because Sun Men are born inherently lucky, their lives are often marked by unlikely successes, and common ailments do not affect them. They are effectively immune to sickness, will not endure broken bones, etc., but have no conscious control over their gifts. When a Sun Man and a Cloud Man come in close proximity to each other, their gifts negate each other, rendering them entirely human as long as they remain within range.

Tak moran: A people who worship Tak the Fire. They are born with a measure of resistance to fire and heat. They maintain a stronghold at Wyte Landing in Moran Laschanh, and are most densely concentrated in the region of Moran Laschanh and Gan Forest. They retain a close kinship with both the Apostates of Flame and the Rahad, as each order centers its theology around the spirit.

Uelfin: A people who trace their lineage back to the Crystal River Spirit, Oe, and the God of Music, Lanfin. They are capable of glimpsing the future and influencing it to an extent. Most inhabit the God House of Music, however, there a large population of them settled in the Gotha Kingdom at Cratom, near Oe's headwaters. The Uelfin maintain that there is one rule among them they must never break. They must never sing in counter-tune to their ancient father, Lanfin. The punishment for doing so is being recalled.

Important Terms

Apostates of the Flame: A group of religious zealots who worship Tak the Fire. According to their legends, the spirit was once a violent and bloodthirsty warrior who waged war, together with the Triad spirits, against the gods. They believe he will one day arise to violence again, and that they will be his chosen warriors when that day comes, taken on as acolytes, and granted the gift of command over fire.

Cadrewaller: a variety of self-propelled vehicle which takes the place of a beast of burden in conducting certain labors. Some models are designed to help carry raw ore away from mine sites or harvest crops more efficiently. Cadrewallers are a technology of Baduhrak.

Chain: an indirect, spiritual bond shared by a spirit and a mortal acolyte which utilizes a surrogate for the spirit's power as a go between. The surrogate usually takes on the form of a familiar, such as a monkey or a toad, who possesses a window into the mind of the acolyte and, in some cases, the unilateral ability to petition the spirit either for access to its power or to suppress access to that power. The Chain is both a medium for that power and an arbitrator with petitioning power. If the Chain does not feel the desires of the spirit are adequately represented by the actions of the acolyte, it may remove access to those powers, and vice versa.

Darkling: an acolyte of the God of Darkness.

Eight Hands: The governing body of the Rauhka Cartel, consisting of eight of the most prominent and dangerous members of the organization at any given time. Seats among the eight hands are taken in one of three ways. A vote is taken among the hands to elevate an existing member of the cartel to a vacant seat. An invitation is extended to a person of interest outside of the organization by unanimous consent. Or, the seat of an existing member is taken by force.

Elder God: a member of the order of gods who inhabit the Heart Realm and occasionally intervene in affairs int he Waxing World.

Great King: the spirit of a continent.

Hand of Raukha: A member of the Eight Hands.

Hunter: an acolyte of the God of Hunters.

Lamb: A Raukha assassin.

Lesser God: a member of the order of gods who inhabit the Waxing World. They cannot leave without the permission of the Elder Gods.

Moonkin: an acolyte of the Moon God.

Pathfinder: an acolyte of the God of Ways.

Rahad: A group of pacifist healers and exorcists who travel the world providing their services to the peoples of its various lands. Most are acolytes of spirits or gods, but all are required to take a vow of nonviolence, not to raise arms against anyone except in the greatest defense of their own lives, never to enter a nation's army or any force which rises to violence, nor to remove from anyone the ability to live peacefully and in freedom, if they so choose.

Raukha Cartel: An organized crime syndicate whose activities span five continents. They are widely regarded as the most successful organization of their kind in history.

Rein Mountain Sword: swords crafted by the spirit Rein, the tallest mountain in the world. Many warriors take pilgrimages to the summit of the mountain in search of one of these swords, but Rein does not part with them easily.

Rein Mountain Steel: a variety of sword whose origin is considered paradoxical. The swords, though extremely rare, can be found throughout the world, and are of exquisite craft, but there is no record in the histories of their making, nor of who made them.

Shepherd: A Lamb's handler.

Soulbinding: a form of magic in which the soul of an individual is conditioned to accept and express certain abilities learned by mortals from gods.

Spirit Calling: (a) a form of magic in which mortals draw on the power of a spirit through a tether or chain, allowing them to manifest the abilities of that spirit. The mortal is bound to one spirit, and most people are only capable of such binding with one spirit at a time. Two exceptions to this rule are the Graemeins, who possess two souls and may hold two such bonds at once, and Katcyakin, who sometimes find themselves having successfully courted two spirits. (b) The practice by Katuwiti shamans of displacing a portion of their soul into an vessel—usually a gourd—and then calling on a spirit to occupy their body. The spirit acts through the Katuwiti shaman in order to convene with mortals or express its powers through the shaman. The spirit remains vulnerable as long as it is housed inside the shaman's body, and if the shaman dies while the spirit remains within him, the spirit will also die.

Spirit: the corporeal embodiment of a specific land feature or land area. Spirits range widely in power and influence, with some being the embodiment of a simple creek and others embodying the sum total of entire continents or oceans.

Steward of Raukha: The highest authority on the island of Liu Saed, which is the base of operations for the Raukha Cartel. The Steward is granted tie breaking power in deadlocked meetings of the Eight Hands. He is also granted absolute authority over the domestic affairs on the island.

Tether: a direct, spiritual bond shared by a spirit and its mortal acolyte. Through this bond, the acolyte is able to manifest the powers of the spirit, but the spirit may sever or suppress this bond at will.

Tetract: a group of four of the most powerful spirits in the Waxing World, consisting of: The Spirit of Breath, The Spirit of Salt, The Iron Spirit, and Tak the Fire.

Triad: a less common term referring to the spirits of the Tetract, excluding Tak the Fire.

Wanderer: one of those people who offended the gods and was recalled to live within Lanfin's Labyrinth outside of Time.

If you enjoyed this novel and would like to help support the author, please consider leaving a review at Amazon or wherever you prefer to talk about books. Every little bit helps.

Thank you for reading, and I hope you enjoyed this trip into the Waxing World.